The Light

By

Charles B. Shanks, Jr.

PRESS

Table of Contents

Preface

*T*he years immediately following the American Revolutionary War saw the fledgling nation struggling under the government of The Articles of Confederation. The states sought very little support from the Confederation nor were they much inclined to render support to it when it was not particular to their own interests. Sectionalism had roots dating all the way back to Puritanical New England, and it was not incorrect to say that one state did not necessarily trust another, especially considering that some states laid claim to identical tracts of frontier land that lay west of the Appalachian mountains.

Pioneer migration westward was spurred on by the promise of free land or land at a minimal cost. Vast untamed wilderness and its abundance of natural resources were chief among the assets of the new nation. Immigration from Europe helped to swell the frontier population.

Citizenry from Ireland, who for generations had labored under the landed gentry, got word of the offers of lands in the new nation. If they could but get there, they could have their own acreage and could be free from the bonds of the serf system that had held them enslaved for generations. It was from these people that my humble beginnings grew.

These immigrant people came west of the mountains and established themselves in the wilderness areas, arriving with not much more than the clothes on their back and possibly an animal or two. They made a living off the land and established themselves on ground that they possessed with the deepest of sentiment and pride in their labors. This itself carried over into their will to survive all encumbrances to their prosperity. And there were many.

They developed a sense of pride in their accomplishment and deservedly so, because they depended on no one for their existence. They took what they needed from nature and wrested a living from their soil. They became free and independent and fiercely resisted any governmental regulation without representation.

These people had little formal education, and few were literate by today's standards. Yet, they developed a culture that is unique to itself and is found in no other concentration anywhere in this nation. They grew into a unique people, having practices, rites and customs all their own. They even developed their own vernaculars, which few from the outside world can comprehend without a keen ear and an open mind.

It is this very heritage that remains so prevalent to this day in the deep mountain valleys and the high ridge peaks in the area where my great grandparents weathered the ills of the War Between the States and handed down their spirit of freedom and independence to their children and their children's children.

It is this deep kinship and love of God and country that I try to represent here in my story. At the same time I endeavor to expose the manner by which they gained so much from life while having so little materialistically. Yet they possessed a peace that was so prevalent in the simple life.

Spelling and grammar are inconsistent in the dialogue and that is intentional. Dialogue among the individuals could be as varied as the peoples themselves, often times with noticeable differences between families separated only by the spine of a ridge or the run of a small valley. Their independence dictated that they remain true to their raising, and this included the values that each family maintained. There was little to be offered in the way of formal education until the generation of my parents. Then at that time, it was the much personified one-room country schoolhouse tended by a single schoolmaster, who just happened to be a little more literate than his pupils.

Yet these children grew into adulthood with a sense of worth, nourished by honesty and hard work. Hard work was not a burden for them, because they had grown up knowing field labor since early childhood. They were poor, but they knew it not. They were loved, and they did know it. They were respectful of their elders and resultantly had a sense of worth and purpose for themselves. They adapted as needed to overcome the hardships that life might have in store for them. They were always on hand for each other in times of need or crisis. They were caring and compassionate, yet they were reluctant to public display of emotion. Their spoken word or handshake served as a contract between them and that was all that was needed or expected in their dealings. They had little need for outsiders.

They passed their cultural values, their appreciation of family, their honesty, their deep-seated love and affection, and yes, their vernacular, on to their children. I am glad that they did.

The story is actually a parallel. One is an account of Jubal at home in his native Cane Valley, while the other follows him through his service as a Union trooper in the Civil War. There is a twist of history ever now and then especially as it related to the East Tennessee area and the political subtleties arising from its strong-willed people. There is no historical basis for any events involving real and actual persons in this story. Inclusion of actual caricature is intended only as part of the saga. Historical accuracy is not the intent nor the claim. The intent is in the message, "I am the Light of the World. Whoever follows me will never walk in darkness but will have the light of life." John 8:12.

Chapter 1

Wounded

*M*oon glow on the face of the dead is ghastly. Jubal had not beheld such apparent anguish in the face of the living, let alone a dead man. He would never have seen this poor wretch had he not tripped in the shadows cast from the lone big white oak that stood sentry to the past few hours of fighting. What had happened was lost in the mist of fade-in and fade-out for Jubal. His right forehead stung smartly, and the blood stained his palm each time he swiped across his face.

"Must have been here long time," half talking, half thinking aloud to himself.

No other voices heard. No movement noticed. Nothing. Just the stillness. The quiet and the solitude. Somewhere was the faint sound of cannon and musket, the clink of bit and bridle, the cries of anguish and the terror in the voices of the fallen. Then again, the quiet.

The glimmer of early morning light was just beginning to come up through the undergrowth on the steep slopes of Pine Mountain. That light was barely enough for Jubal to see out to the edge of the woods where the scale-barked hickories stood in the fence row that marked the edge of the Miller farm. Those two trees always had a good crop of nuts, and already the squirrels made it sound like it was raining under their branches. Nearly a hundred feet to the top, but no trouble for a good shooter to bring down a bushy with every shot. The boy was a good and experienced shooter. There would be dumplings and fresh meat for dinner today.

Jackson had given the boy seven homemade lead balls, seven patches and enough powder for seven loads. It was expected that he come home with seven kills. There were seven plates to be set at the long plank table; one for Ma, Pa, Jubal (the oldest boy), Sarry, Julie, Gracie and Granny Iverson. The log house had only one small window in the dining room, but there would be enough light to see well enough to eat. They had to eat supper before night fall though. Lamp oil cost too much to use so foolishly to eat by. If you ate late, you ate at the fireplace; or you ate in the dark.

Jubal eased up close to the fence line, taking ever so much care not to step on a twig or brush past a limb and create unwanted movement. Taking care in moving in order to make no sound took time. When Jubal got to a point to be able to see the tops of the old hickory, the sun had nearly cleared the crest of the high point of the mountain. In a fleeting moment he thought of the midday heat that would soon beat upon his back and brow as he worked alongside his Pa putting up hay enough to winter the oxen, the milk cows and old Kate (the broken-down old mule).

He walked up to the fence where he could lay the old rifle barrel on top of a post and take rest to secure an accurate aim. It would be easy enough to hit the critter in the body, but then all the meat would be blown away. One had to aim at the eye and get a good head shot. That was how his Pa had taught him, and he sure didn't want to rile Pa. He knew how it needed to be done, and he had learned to be patient and wait for a clean shot, had to see the eyes.

Eyes, the blank stare of dead eyes. The first such eyes would never be erased from his mind. Looking, transfixed, motionless, open, but yet closed to perception; open and pleading to be closed. Relieved of their function, but still focused on their horror. Cold and yet as piercing as a white hot shard bursting out of a mortar bombardment. Alive in their proclamation of the death they had just witnessed.

The first exposure to war casualty evoked the first doubt about the reasoning for fighting in the first place. Life had been simple back in Cane Valley, even mundane. Jubal had grown tired of the laborious life of a dirt farmer and wanted a more exciting and glamorous life. The war offered opportunity and excitement. That glamour and excitement had pinnacled on the road to Haws Crossing. The first sounds of cannonade and musket fire rapidly transformed excitement to unknown anticipation, to heightened awareness, to nervousness, to fear and ended only in the horror of bloodshed.

The sun was just now cresting over the high spur of Pine Mountain. Looking into the hickory and oaks along the fence row would soon be like looking into a steady flash of lightening. Jubal had to get right under the tree to get the easiest shot at his quarry. The brilliance of the morning sun already bathed the topmost branches, and he could see two squirrels busy feeding on the bounty of the old scale bark. Hull shavings rained down all about the base of the tree.

"Crack," the old Hawken spoke in a cloud of acrid black smoke. A hasty reload and another cloud of black smoke, stinging to the eyes, foul to the nostrils. Another kill. Soon more would return to the feast, thinking they faced no peril.

Peril. How can anything be more perilous than this? Jubal wiped his brow with his sleeved-forearm. No red blood, just the dark crimson crust of the dried blood, his blood. The sun was hot on his back and every heartbeat brought a pounding throb to his head. Any movement brought silent screams of anguish. The silence was interrupted only by the occasional flutter of the birds or the faint jingle of a bridle on some yet unseen mount. Reality? Was this not some sort of curse that had been cast down by some evil that he had not seen?

No other voices around him. No one to call out to. Not even sure how he had come to this place. Where was this place? Raising his head, grimacing in pain, then back into oblivion.

Jubal turned sixteen at the last of June. Early manhood had bestowed him with broad shoulders and strong arms, probably a by-product of all the hard work that was needed to be able to coax a living out of the steep and rocky hills at the foot of Pine Mountain. Life was not easy, and the work was hard. It was really the only life he had ever known and had been the life of a generation before him.

There was a wanderlust growing in him that he did not really recognize as such or at least admit to. He found himself alone in the fields lots of times, and this loneliness pulled at his imaginations as to what lay outside the little valley of his rapidly outgrown childhood.

He could read a bit and had seen a newspaper ever now and then. The Review spoke of things going on in places somewhere up north. He had heard the names of cities and towns that rang in no familiar sounds in his world. Places unseen could not be known. The call of those places haunted him more and more each day. He had also become somewhat distasteful of the hunt. He was more than adept at hunting and was willing to do it to put meat on the table for his Ma and Pa, but the thrill and the challenge were gone.

The sun had to be high. Jubal lifted his head and swiped his brow yet again. The back of his hand came away wet and with deep dark crimson stain. His head still throbbed and his heartbeat pealed loud in his ears. He saw only what lay at arm's length, a boot with the toe pointing skyward, a darkened buckskin hat with a side burned away. The earth at his side bore the acrid odor of smoke and fire. Hot, very hot. Thirst. His tongue tasted of dust and ash. His throat burned as does the parched desert earth. Water, just one dipper! Raising to his hands and knees, trying to focus on ghastly forms before him. Arms aching as if trying to support an impossible burden, then collapse; and the silent bliss of the unknowing, who lay about in the sweltering heat.

The springhouse was no more than twenty paces from the back porch, and there could always be found a cool and refreshing drink. Ma kept the gourd dippers neatly hung on the rock ledges above the spring pool and insisted that care be employed in filling them and not muddying the pool. Jubal had muddied the waters more than once and never really gave it much thought, because the spring ran a good stream and would clear the spring pool in an hour or so.

Besides that the spring was always a good place to catch a couple of crawdads.

Today was different. Ma's buckets had all been filled and carried to the old log house. The hot summer sun could not pierce the thick umbrella of the massive old beech tree growing above the spring-house. Many long repeated hot, dry days had diminished the spring flow to a trickle. It took hours for the spring pool to clear itself now if it became muddied. A measure of impatience crept across his demeanor as he prepared to muddy the spring pool even more. It needed to be cleaned out and deepened. That way, a day's water or more could be stored up in the pool and that deeper pool might just get them by until the rains came again.

He would dig out the pool to bedrock in just a few hours, but days might pass before it cleared again. The flow through the spring-house would stop in the meanwhile. That meant no water to chill the milk and butter, which was kept cool by the spring pool runoff. The daily milking would be given to the hogs at day's end. It would be warm milk, or no milk. He would always choose to do without. No spring pool runoff probably would mean no livestock water either. It would be his task to tote water to the stock or lead them across to Cane Creek for water every other day. Why is it always me, was the demon that plagued his innermost being. It seemed to never leave him any peace. Never had to be concerned about his washing or the garden cause there was plenty of woman help around. Seemed like he was always the one who shouldered the heavy work.

Took two days to dig out the spring pool, and looked like it would take longer to fill and clear again. Jubal had dug it as deep and as wide as the spring shed would allow. Pa said he just might nigh undermined the foundation stones anyhow, but sure did have a pool that would hold lots of water. He just hoped the rains would soon come. Tomorrow they would water the stock from the spring pool as they had just about drunk all the branch pools bone dry. If only it would rain. Even the hogs would be glad. Their wallowing hole had dried up some time ago. It wasn't too awfully bad hot yet, but the chickens and the ducks stayed in the shade of the barn and crib shed much as possible.

Jubal walked across the north hill and down through the old Rogerson place to the store. Ma would soon need sugar and salt to make relish and pickles. She would get them all jarred up and hold them up to the light and take pride in how well they shined. She always said that if they shined in the sunlight that they would stay crisp and taste good all year. Ma was always telling how her Ma had taught her things about how to look over them and that ye always needed a good light to get clear signs to go by and to make an accurate prediction and have a clear understanding.

None of the small spring branches all across the old Rogerson place had much water flow to them. The old place was so rough and hilly that there were but few places that water could run still and deep, and all those places had done gone dry. Nobody pastured much there any more since old man Rogerson was getting way on in years now, and he had nothing to pasture but the old milk cows. Bushes and brambles covered most of the hillsides. Blackberry briars were most everywhere, but the berries were small and knotty this year. It would take more picking this year to get the berries needed for winter jams and jellies. That was why Ma had sent him to the store today, and she told him to ask if there was a letter a waitin' too. He reckoned that he could take leisure in getting there cause it was past high noon now, and the sun would be getting low down in the flats by time he come back by here.

The flats. I'll just sidle off up the ridge and see if there be any berries there, since most of it stays in shade most all day. Won't slow me down but a mite. He easily ascended the ridge and hardly broke a sweat doing so. Some folks just hit right straight out for the top and soon is all spent out, but Jubal knew better than that. He angled himself out the ridge and rose a bit with each step. He reassured his footing by placing each step against the upper side of a grass clump, a sapling or a weed hilt. Never missed a step nor broke stride and was on top in the flats in no time at all. Sure enough there were berries there, big and juicy, as big as the end of yer thumb. Weren't all good and ripe yet, but would be in about three days if no rain came. He could tell that the birds had been in them. He saw the droppings all over the briars and on the ground. Must be the turkeys. No sign now, cause it was the heat of the day. Stick weeds all had heads bowed over trying to shield the bloom pods from the heat. Ma says they prayin' for rain and to be able to see the light of another day.

A voice in the distance, a calling, a hoof beat. He heard the sound, but did not react immediately. He tried to reason out the sounds, but it just seemed to all be so far away. Then silence. Then the voice again, more than one voice. The back of his neck burned, and a trickle of sweat coursed from his cheek to his chin. His tongue, though parched, could taste his own salt. Any try at a look around rewarded him with wrenching pain in the temple and a sickness in the stomach. Thirsty, but not wanting to drink. Hungry, but not wanting to eat. Bright light. Must be midday or close by it. A swipe across the forehead again. No blood or crimson clot, just salt and grime. A dry tongue across dry lips brought the taste of the earth, dry and powdered earth. Earth that had seen and felt the thunder of a thousand hoof beats, the pounding of ten thousand uniformed boots. Earth that had been ripped apart by untold musket ball and cannon shot and then wet down with the crimson life blood of who knew how many brave young souls. Young souls, but none to hear his plight.

Could not know for sure but seemed to be fire near somewhere. Smoke lay low all around the open field and seemed in no wise anxious to move away. Perchance the smoke held at bay the sight of the carnage and the death that lay all about. The heat would soon make the dead known to all the vermin that were waiting their turn. The smoke would only delay the inevitable. The voices again, closer now and clearer. No, can't make out no words, but I hear ye now more than ever. Eyes burn, but got to see. Head feels like it a big old punkin, what been busted open for the hogs. How long have I been here? Why do I pain in my head like this? My eyes going bad on me or what, cause I see the sunlight, but I don't see nothing else nowhere. Hear, but I don't see?

No rain came, and tomorrow the stock would have to be watered. No choice yet, but Jubal reckoned he would soon tote water to em as he would drive em plumb across to the creek and then have to wrangle them all back home. That would be a full, long day. That would be tomorrow, but this afternoon he would return to the flats with a bucket and see if he could get it filled with big flats grown blackberries before the turkeys got em all.

He reached the flats in no time, and sure 'nuff the berries were still there, and more too since the sun had been so hot and the clouds missing all the time. Soon had the bottom of the old oak bucket covered, and the sun was still high. He began to pay more attention to the ground about him. Dry and dusty out from the base of the briar stands where the grass ran up tall and hung over in the heat. Tracks in the dust like spider webs, almost. Three little slim prongs spaced out close and one prong pointing away to the back. Had to be the turkeys. If he could just find their run, they could have a turkey feast in the middle of choppin' time.

He set the bucket down and moseyed along the old logging path down to the timberline. Harder to see any tracks here. Then he spied it running right off down in front of a big cedar tree. A few steps on into the timber told the whole thing. He had found one of the slickest runs that he had ever known. Must be plenty of old gobblers using this run cause they had near swept the whole run clean of even a few leaves. He found it, and by jinx them turkeys was just as good as his right then and there. At least that was how he reasoned it to be. Just need to find a close-by stump rot and dig a pit. Could do that in a day. Tomorrow. No, gotta water the stock tomorrow. Dig it now; right now. Well no, got nothing to bait it with. Could bait with blackberries, that be all I got.

Back out on the flats and more picking. "Pick till the bucket is half full then go dig on the pit some. No; ain't found no stump hole yet." More picking, briars stinging his hands ever now and then. "Need to think about picking and not on digging." That way he would concentrate on the job at hand and not be thinking about things that may not even come to be. Took longer to fill the oak bucket cause of not keeping mind to the task, but got it full now. Down off the flats and the length of the old Rogerson place to the crest of the ridge, out of the thicket, jumping the four-strand barbed-wire fence and onto the north pasture. Gonna need bladed off soon, cause brambles grow in spite of the dry.

The hill crested right above the old log house, and the sounds easily carried up to where he stood. The air was still, not a leaf nor a twig made a move anywhere he could spy. He sat down on the dry grass with the bucket at his side, took a few berries and began to eat. They tasted a mite strong and were plenty warm to the tongue. Better get on along and get them to the spring so as to cool down some. Soured berries don't make no good jelly or cobbler.

He had the berries in the spring pool runoff and had all the water buckets filled by the time Ma came out of the garden patch. He told her about the bucket of berries, and then headed on to the garden patch where Pa was chopping in the dry dust twixt the corn rows. He would see about digging a turkey run and maybe get Pa to help dig some too. He knew there was copperheads on Chestnut Ridge, but reckoned that they would be off of the flats looking for water since it was gettin' off so dry now. He had not seen one since two years back when the ridge was fresh logged. Old man Rogerson had sold timber on the stump to the Lawson's to build a stock barn, and he had made near ten dollars helping build that barn. Still had most of that sum too.

Light, red light began to fade in the west. No rain tomorrow, lest it come out of the east. Red sky at night is usual sign of fair day tomorrow. The sun had gone down with the maple leaves a saggin' and bowin' their heads. Everything is feeling the heat and the dryness now. Stock sticking their nose in every hoof pocket all along the branch, trying to find whatever water they could. Not too long now. You get water in the morning. One of you at a time. Two buckets apiece cause that be all I can carry at a time.

Jubal bedded down on the front porch. Drug his straw tick plumb out on the porch and laid himself down on the hard boards. Was cooler there than in the house loft. The big sugar trees shaded the old log home pretty good, but the dry, hot sun heated the loft. It took well into the morning for it to cool down to comfortable sleep. Quiet was most nigh same as peace lots of times. Give a body time to think and reason things out a bit. Nobody talkin' cept for a long off whip-or-will and old screech. Tired, but still able to travel miles and miles in his mind. Things told to him that were in the Review stirred his mind and made him wonder about all them faraway places that now was just a name or a dot on a map. Would that be all he would know about them?

Sleep dulled his senses, but the wanderlust seeds had been sown and the feeling would return. After all, he was not quite yet a full grown man. Sleep, blissful sleep. Maybe he could find a stump rot tomorrow. Maybe he would go see old man Rogerson tomorrow and maybe he would have this month's Review. The reddened sky faded to crimson, then to violet. The crest of the mountains blackened against what light remained in the west. Then all was lost in the darkness. Sleep, blissful sleep.

Seemed like morning came in just an hour or so. The boy awakened with near the same stiffness in his back as the porch floor had in its own self. He sat up and stretched his lanky arms and rubbed a hand over his brushy hair. Faint light in the east, but already Ma was in the kitchen cause the acrid smell of the cook stove fire hung heavy in the still morning air. Hunger also spoke of the time of day. Ma always said a good day needs to start out on a full belly so as ye can go all day and work hard at whatever needs be done that day. Biscuits and hog meat. Maybe tomorrow there would be fresh blackberry jam too. A bucket of berries ought make a crock of jam.

All the stock watered by mid-morning. Already able to feel the coming heat of the day. Pa said he wanted the beans plowed out with the four-footer and then chopped. After that Jubal reckoned he'd go see old Rogerson, who could read him the Review. Might just be war news this week. Since he'd be so nigh the flats, might just as well go look for a stump rot that he could use as a trap pit.

The four-foot was in the crib shed behind the disk. Jubal easily lifted it out clear to the front of the shed, hoisted it up on his shoulders and set off to the bean patch. The four-foot weren't near as heavy as the old turning plow, but yet a body knew he was heftin' a load by it. He put the plow down on the end of the patch and started back to the barn lot to harness up old Kate, the plow mule. Well, Kate didn't want to be harnessed today and weren't gonna stand still for no man's boy either. No brayin' nor such, but just no standin' still so as to get the bits in place. Not without a couple nubbins, no sir. Not this old mule. A trip back to the crib. "Dang you. You sorry cuss. Two nubbins is all, and they gonna be little. Iffin I had a say in it, you'd eat them bits iffin I hadda whup you clean in past next week. Ye ain't no mule, ye just an overgrowed ass what need be learnt a thing or two," half mumbling and talking to himself.

The beans were plowed out, and Kate was as wet with sweat as Jubal. He left her hitched to the four-foot and right at the end of the last row in the hot morning sun. Old tail switching continuous and stomps on every hand. Horse flies biting into sweaty mule flesh. Shaking the old stubborn head and rattling the tracers and the collar shackles like a chain ganger. Made quite a stir.

A good job of plowin' the balks makes for quick choppin' the rows. Soon had it all done and was about to head back to the barn with old cobweb brains when he heard Ma calling for dinner. He would tote the plow back to the crib shed, but Kate could just wait it out till he got done with dinner 'fore she had a drink. "Hateful old cuss anyhow. Maybe I just leave ye right out there till the sun has sweated it right outta ye and then ye want the harness off ye bad. I be just as slow getting it off ye as ye be getting it on ye. One these here days ye gonna smart up and see the light," he fussed.

Light. But gray and cold. Not sure of anything about. The throbbing pain in his head was not so bad now. Seemed that all his stout, young body had been beaten. Ached near all over and did not know why. Able to raise his head and try to see about. Eyes not sure of what they were seeing, still yet clouded and undiscerning. A hand to the face brought the cool morning dew to his cheek, though it could just as easily been sweat or blood. But no; it felt cool and refreshing, awakening. A hand to the forehead, hair seems stiff and matted. Thirst. Throat sore and dry. Tired, so very tired. Cold. Hungry.

More daylight when he realized what he beheld was the red dawn sky. Sometime he had rolled to his back and could see better now. Clouds aglow in the eastern light spurred on his senses. Seemed to take near an eternity just to set up so as to see about him. Hurt just to move, but set up he did. No longer the harsh and foul smell of smoke and fire. No cries for help or screams of pain. No moaning penance of the dying. Just the gentle whisper of a soft morning stir coming out of the sun. A burning in the mind, not knowing why he ached so bad. Unable to get hold of himself. Confused and alone. Got to get on my feet.

Jubal managed to draw up a knee and pulled himself into a half sitting position. He looked about in the cool of the early morning. Coming in from somewhere close was the sweet smell of fresh cut hay. Still no sound of another living soul, save for some soft serenade from some distant whip-or-will. A sound that brought a flash of home; the old log home at the head of the hollow where he first saw the light of day. Both knees drawn up and sitting, ankles locked about each other, leaning with one palm to the ground. He could see well enough now to realize that he was at one end of a clearing and that the tree line was a good piece away in front of him with the sun on only the upper branches. No rustle in the tops and telling marks to give way their kind. Grass still wet with dew. Wet with dew, that be water. Water be a drink. He swiped his upturned palm through the grass and tasted the cool morning dew. He wiped his face with the cooling dampness. He was coming around a bit.

Lighter now and he could see more distant. Struggling to his feet in order to get a better sight. Falling, his face hit the dew-covered grass hard, and pain again took control of his thought. Not really able to cry out in pain, but awake enough to know that his mouth hurt a bunch and that there was an unwelcome taste on his lips.

Jubal ate quick as a fox and had Kate out of harness and to pasture before she got too many horsefly bites. They could turn to a bad sore, and Pa would be sure to spot every one of them. He would be most sure how they come to be, but the boy had not seen any this time. He had most of the chores dealt out to him this time of year. Seems like Pa was always off somewhere scouting out a bee tree or huntin' a tan oak for bark or just anything to be gone during chores.

There was some resentment there, and it was growing more. It was festering, and none of his Ma's poultices would draw it either. He reckoned that Pa had a want for his kids to have things and one way was to find honey and sell it. Might fetch a quarter or so. Tan bark was two dollars a wagon load, if you had it to town for trade. White oak cross ties brought twenty cents apiece, if you had them to the depot when the buyer was there. Hard work all around, but it could pay a little cash money. He had the cash earned building Lawson's barn, and Pa knew he had it too. Jubal just hoped he could keep it all for himself. Didn't know what he might get with it but still wanted to keep it for his own. Ma might need his help sometime, and he reckoned that would be on the up and up if she really needed it. He and his Pa had cut a big tan oak off old Rogerson in the spring and sold the bark. Course they only got a third, since it weren't on their land. Pa had needed all the cash from that to buy seed and such. Jubal reckoned he had done his part in helping just by his sweat and by bendin' his back.

Ma seemed to just have a way of makin' things go along and never seemed to get very riled up at nothing. She worked all the time and always had something to feed her family. Most times there was ample vittles, but he had set down to corn pone and fatback gravy more than once durin' the long winters. Them times was when he lit out a huntin' and a trappin'. Rabbit made a right good pot of stew. Mix in a few saved over taters, and a body could fare right well. Ma had taught him how to well up taters in a pit lined with golden ripe broom sage, then covered with ashes from the wood cook stove, and then set a big old fodder shock atop it all. Taters would keep through the coldest of winter and would still be good when the new ones were ready for gravelin'. That was iffin you raised and stored up enough in the fall to begin with.

Three big hogs killed and butchered in the first cold snap around Thanksgiving provided a winter's need of fatback and shoulder meat, salt-cured and hung in the smokehouse. Pa always tried to sell off the hams once they took salt. That brought a dollar or two and Christmas came outta that too. Ma made sausage out of most ever thing else, save the ribs. Made souse meat from the head and the middlin'. Jubal could eat it, but weren't real keen on it none at all.

Ma always made big old cathead biscuits and always had fresh churned butter to go on em too. Blackberry and dewberry jelly shore made them good too. She was sparin' with the eggs but would always fix for him iffin he wanted some. He most times wanted them and everything else she might be inclined to fix, cause he could put it away and hide most all she set front of him. He weren't none fat, cause workin' daylight to dark took care of that. Lean, tanned and stout. That purty much summed him up.

Ma seemed broke down for being no older than she was. She come from down on Cloudy Creek in the river bottom parts. Pa had courted her when he was working for the county on the Cumberland Road. Jubal knew that much, but Ma had never much spoke of them days. Seemed like she had druther not recollect nothing all about it. Pa had brought her here right after his Pa had took sick. Ma cared for and cooked for them both from the start. It sure must been a heap of a chore, but he never had heard of her complaining about it. But that and four kids right in a row had to take its toll on her. Her hands were calloused much as any man. She chopped out the garden, pitched hay in the summer, gathered corn in the fall, and did all the other things needed done all year long. And now she had took in her Ma on top of all that. Her Pa passed of perishin' of the brain about three years back. Granny Iverson had stayed down on Cloudy Creek in a sharecropper shack long as she could do for herself but had sent word that she was ailing some now days. Back in the spring before the redbuds had come to life, he and Ma and the three girls had took the wagon and yoke and gone to fetch her. Took a whole day to go and the next day to come back. Granny said she missed the bottoms and the river, but seemed to be fair content here in the holler. She had some of her color back now.

Granny would sit by the fire at sundown and talk about things that went on years ago. She could recall some of the Indian skirmishes off to the south and the settlements around the old Alum Springs. Said people use to come there to get the alum water for medicines. Said it was good for the scares and the consumption amongst other things. She would talk long as a body would listen. Most times Jubal would hear, but not really listen to her. Soon she would tire and be off to her straw-tick bed. Granny weren't no ball of fire, but she did do little chores to help where she could. Since the weather had moderated and warmed a mite, she liked to sit on the back porch and enjoy the birds a sangin' and watch the hatchlin's get fed. Ma nailed up old wore out shoes along the garden paling posts and most ever one housed a wren or a bluebird. Ma always wanted birds around the garden to keep down the bugs and beetles much as they could.

The day that they fetched Granny home, the Johnson's came to help unload her bedstead and what few other things she had that she could claim as her own. They was at the old log house a waitin' when Ma and all the young'uns got home. It had been a long tiring wagon ride. Mrs. Johnson knew before that this was the day that Granny would be fetched home. Granny had sent word of her need by the circuit rider preacher, and he had told it in the Cove church where C.C. and his family went to meeting. That was how Ma learned about Granny to begin with. Mrs. Johnson had toted along a basket filled with chicken and the fixing's fer all to eat, cause she knew Ma nor Granny would not have cooked that day.

The Johnson's had a good living, at least till the war commenced. He owned the mill at the mouth of the holler and ground most ever day when in season. Jubal took grain to mill a couple times here in the last year. Pa used to take it, but that fell to Jubal now. If looks were to mean much, Jubal would a run from C.C. the first time he had laid eye on him. Johnson was tall and lanky with a high cheek and a sharp chin. Jubal did not know his real given name, but he had heard him called Chisel Chin Johnson. Course nobody called him that to his face.

The millrace was not a long one because the creek fell away smartly just a piece above the mill. Used to have a old board race, but had been there so long it spilled more water than it raced. C.C. had torn away the old race and replaced it with pipe and had set them on stone rests. Guess he planned on grindin' corn fer a long time, since all his crop land mostly just laid by all the time. Had three milk cows and a buggy team, but never raised any stock beyond that. He didn't even raise hogs no more. Reckon he was worth so much he need not fool with hogs and killin' and renderin' and puttin' salt to the meat, he just bought all he needed. Killin' hogs was hard work anyhow.

Jubal weren't sure just how he felt about old C.C., but he did know how he felt about Lida, his youngest daughter. She had that same high set cheek bone, but the chin features and eyes had to have come from her mother. The family all came to the Cove church, and

Jubal had lately been more inclined to attend meetings on a regular pattern. He hadn't much more than had a word or two with any of the family and that were just a howdy or so, but he reckoned that he had caught Lida lookin' his way a time or two. He knew for sure that he had been a lookin' her way.

Ever since Granny Iverson had come and Lida had come to help settle her in, somethin' had been a stir in the lad. Sometimes he had a mite bit trouble gettin' anything done rightly cause of thinkin' about her in ways he knew were not proper, at least accordin' to his Ma. Ma had told him them kind was high and rich and that they most always wanted the poor folks round about to be beholdin' to them. Ma said they had money and fine clothes and such as that and would never have much to do with the common folks unless they was profitin' off em. The boy was not sure how he understood all that because he never had much and just never thought much about how that made a person be other than they self. He just accepted it as a way of life, until here of late since he had got big enough to run chores and such by himself. Sometimes he would ride old Kate to the store and take Sarry along when Ma wanted some woman's thing or such fetched back from the store. Ma usual sent eggs to trade for whatever special it was that she wanted, and Sarry went to tote the egg basket. Besides that, Jubal didn't want to have to ask for no clerkin' help to fill his Ma's orders. Just another reason to double up with his sister. Kate could carry more than them, if they needed.

Sarry was nigh growed into a woman herself now. She weren't all time spilt over with the giggles no more. Julie and she went with him to the Cove most ever Saturday night now, and he thought they was catchin' some eye too. Sarry had asked him a name or two, but he didn't tell her much she wanted to know. He had not asked his sisters anything about any of the Johnsons, especially Lida, but he was not plannin' on missin' not one Cove meetin'. Lida always acted proper as he saw it. Never carryin' on with no foolishment nor no sashayin' around showin' herself. She always sat with her mother and seemed not to be a mind wanderin' when the circuit rider was speakin'. This fall they would have dinner on the grounds, and he planned to speak to her then iffin he could somehow edge in against her mother long enough. Yep, he would do just that and would have all summer long to get ready. He might even mention it to Sarry and see what she thought about goin' with him on that Sunday. They'd both have to get chores done first, but that would be easy. Sarry would have to take a basket of somethin' cause they would not be a goin' empty-handed. Ma might be a hankerin' to go too, but that was a long time off right now; and it would only trouble her to talk of it now. Pa was not about to go and you could bet yer britches on that, but in time he might let Ma go.

Jubal had been around C.C. a bit since he had been doing the mill runs, but he was not yet sure how he felt about the miller man and his wife. Word was that C.C. was educated up north somewhere and was right good at readin' and with ciphers. He could cipher the boards in a log while it was still on the stump and could tell how many bushels a wagon would haul. Jubal didn't really see nothin' to that, just load a wagon to the top and that there is what it'll haul. He could make out a word here and there in the Review, and that outta be about all he would need. C.C. and Lida could read and cipher good, but he never give much credence to that making them uppity and such. Some folks made them out to be scoundrels and cheats cause they was smart and had learnin'. He just weren't seein' it that a way cause they had always been square by him and treated him nigh good as was ever wanted.

On mill runs and rare trips out the mouth of the holler, Jubal had been noticin' Lida more and more. Would take a thick skull not to take notice of them long blonde locks a twistin' out from in under her bonnet. Probably them rosy cheeks never come from choppin' corn neither. She hadn't spoke more than a dozen words to him, but he could recall every one of them. "How you do, Jubal?" "Hot today." "Daddy is to the mill today." "No." "Yes." "Yes." "Bye now." Was there some other reason that he needed to go to mill soon? Pa had plenty of work for him, and time was pretty much took up ever day seemed like.

Aware of a voice in the distance, the boy raised his weary head in attempt to find the speaker. The first returning thought was the overwhelming thirst, followed close by the sting to the back of his neck. Attempts at sitting up resulted only in rolling onto his back, and then the brilliance of the midday sun was enough to cause pain to the eyes that stung akin to the back of his neck. But the voices seemed to be coming closer, though he could not yet make out any words. He managed to get his forearm up over his eyes and the shade of his arm took away most of the sting. The red crusts on his sleeve rubbed off and fell into the corner of the left eye. Soon the trickle down the same cheek began in attempt to clear away the new-found anguish.

Something moved his arm away from his eyes. Not really seeing who or what, he realized that a shadow had come over him. He could see the outline of a wide-brimmed hat and what had to be the shoulders of a man. He tried to speak, but no words passed his lips. Then the rasp on the back of the neck and his head set to spin. Then he felt it! Water! He felt water on his parched and dry lips, soothing as morning dew to his burning throat. Voices, indistinguishable, unfamiliar and unclear, but yet reaching out to him and calling to him just like a light left in the window for a weary nighttime traveler. How welcome a sight is the lamp at night, and how welcome these voices to the weary and wounded warrior.

"Captain, this here one is alive but about outside his self now. Looks like he took one up side the head."

The boy heard a word or two for sure, but understood not. The sip of water lifted him some. The shadow had raised his head gently and was now talking over him. He wanted more of the life-giving water but could not get the words to come. All that came was a weak and pitiful moaning which was heard only by the shadow of a man over him, who put water to his lips again. Water spilled down his chin and ran round to the back of his stinging rasping neck. Never had anything felt so cool as did that spilled nectar. Swallowing came hard and hurt, almost choking, a weakened cough and a gasp resulted.

"He's gone out again, Captain. Got no color to him, but he moved some and took water."

"Did he say anything?"

"Naw, just a moan or two."

Wonder if Lida would take to some big juicy blackberries right now? If he could just get up to the flats before the turkeys got all the best berries, he could soon get a bucket full. Course he would pick for Ma first. There were plenty up there, if he could just have time to go and fetch em. He had all the chores done up and the stock had all been watered today. Maybe he could slip off up there tomorrow past dinner time, pick a bucket full, and come down off the front end of the flats. That way he could come round the end of Stone Mountain and then he would be at the head of the holler and right on the way home he'd pass right by the mill. Maybe Lida would be out in the mill yard or there about. Never mind where she was. If he had a bucket full of big ripe blackberries, he could just march right up to the house and ask fer her to come get em. Yes sir, by grabs, that's just what he was gonna do. But first he needed that bucket and then needed it full of larp-smackin' good berries. If Ma needed anything from the store, he would go the same route; but then C.C. would be on to him and know that he had come up from the mountain road and that it was the long way around. If the miller man was as smart as folks said he was, then he'd know for sure how come that way was took. Nope, gotta have blackberries, no other sane way to get it done.

The first rays of light crept up over the ridge behind the old log house, but Jubal was already up and about his work. Pa did not come in last night, and he had not given any hint as to where he was or what was goin' on with him. Ma seemed worried near to death cause Pa had never not told somebody what he was in to or where he would be. Jubal figured he'd come traipsin' in later on in the day. He never did do a big lot of work when he was home, just piddled around; and likely as not, never hardly broke a sweat. Not the case for Ma and the girls and Jubal.

Ma never said much about her and Pa, special here lately and since the war commenced. Pa had no ideas by neither side, least he led Ma to believe that way. But still he stayed gone a lot and called it politic business.

Ma seemed set to accept the fact that Pa weren't like most men folk in the ways that he done by his kin and his family. Jubal laid it all on the war before, but things seemed like they outta be handled different. He could see most of the responsibility fell on Ma. Ma had the garden to tend and the stores to put up for winter. It always fell to her to make sure seed was saved for the next year. Pa plowed and planted corn, but never stuck a hoe in the ground after that. He got pigs somewhere, somehow in the spring, but Ma or the girls had to slop all the time. Pa drug in firewood, but he never worked it up. That had to be done to make sure the cook stove stayed hot all morning, every morning. Ma was always up before first light and many a morning had toted in chips and wood to get breakfast started by the time ever body else started to stir.

Ma sat at the head of the old plank table and hardly touched a bite. She claimed to be concerned about the need for rain and how if it didn't soon come that there would be no garden and not much stuff to put up this year. That would make for a hard winter, not to mention lack of seed for another year. Granny said that the rains would come soon as dog days was done. She reckoned that would be in about two more weeks.

Ma got up and commenced clearing the dishes right out from under ever body. Seemed plumb troubled.

"Jubal, how full is the spring pool now?" she asked.

"Near full, but they ain't much runoff."

"How long it take to fill up once we dip out stock water?"

"About a half day, I reckon," came his reply.

She said no more about it then, just went on clearing the dishes. Sarry was drawin' hot water out of the cook stove tank and fixin' to start the wash. He could tell that his Ma was troubled and that the bean rows were not the real matter. Nobody said a word about the empty chair at the other end of the table, not Granny, nor Ma. It was just left be.

Jubal grabbed two biscuits on the way out to the kitchen porch. Tossed them out to Jake, the old redbone hound that Pa had had for six or seven years now. Never hunted him anymore and hardly paid him any mind at all. He just laid up in the yard most times. It seemed like his spirit was broke. He would go with Jubal, if called; otherwise he just did not have much spunk about him. Jake took to the biscuits like he hadn't ate a bite in a week. That weren't the case cause old Jake would go groundhog huntin' on his own. That's one thing he had to be give credit for, cause there was never a whistle pig in Ma's garden. No sir, Jake saw to that.

He watched his Ma through the kitchen window. Her head was bowed low. He thought there was a tear runnin' down her face. Saw her brush her cheek with the back of her hand. Hands that worked much too hard and had calluses like to any man. Even Sarry and Julie had hands that showed their labors, in spite of being young hands. Seems it took all they could do workin' together just to keep fed and clothed. Hard work toughened a body, but it left little room for anything else. He was the only one who could pick through the Review and do his ciphers, much at all. He had meetin' times that he could go to, but never felt good there with patched overalls and faded shirts. Oh, they was clean alright. Ma saw to that with her back bent over the old wood tub and hickory-branch scrub board. Lye soap would clean near anything except its own smell. All the girls had long curly hair way down their backs, but there weren't no ribbons to tie in it. Sharecrops was slim when it come to cash money.

Ma called to Jubal, "Come here son. We need to talk."

He returned to the kitchen door where upon Ma began to tell him how she would like to water the bean rows today. They were in bloom and needed rain bad if they were to amount anything near what they needed.

"It may take most all day, but we all can help. If you tote the water, me and your sisters will dip and pour on the rows. I don't spect you to do it all yerself, son."

Jubal could tell the tremor in her voice. He knew that the spring pool would be gone time they watered just a little bit for each hill of beans. It would fill again in the morning, and they could make do till then. He had wanted to go to the flats and go berry pickin' today, but that could wait. He had also wanted to ask Ma about cannin' him a half-gallon jar to take Lida and her mother later on, but that could wait too.

Jubal dipped the buckets into the spring pool, toted them to the garden fence, and reached them to Ma. She carried it out the rows to where the last left off and then handed the empties back across the fence to Jubal. The girls and Granny dipped in the buckets with long-necked gourd dippers and gave each hill a drink. The refreshing water turned the thirsty earth from a dusty tan to a circle of dark umber. A rake over of loose dirt to keep the sun off the little bit of life-giving water and soon no traces of moisture could be seen. But the thirsty bean hills would seek it out in no time.

Ma came back to the house to commence dinner just as the last bucket was passed over the fence to Sarry. Jubal had made sure the kitchen cook stove tank was full and that the buckets on the bench were full. He had carried ever bucketful to the fence, and had sneaked the kitchen water in while Ma hadn't noticed. He hadn't thought a whole lot about the dry till he had to start fetchin' water to the stock. This morning kind of struck home to him, realizing how it was coming to the whole family now.

Ma had dried apples cooked in the last of the molasses and some parched corn that had soaked in salt brine overnight. The salt made a body a mite thirsty doin' a hot day's work, but it give you something you could hang yer ribs to while the sweat rung the salt right out. Jubal ate, but really was not hungry for anything. His mind was about other things right now. He felt sorry for the plight he saw his Ma in and how there weren't much way it could change. Oh there might be rain come, and the crops make in plenty of time before frost. They might even get more on the share if the crop was good. Since the war commenced, you could sell most anything you took to the store. The army bought near about ever thing, but they never paid off in gold; it was all in paper foldin' money. Seemed like Ma just had more on her than any Ma ought have to reckon with.

He thought of his Ma in one breath. In the next he would fly away, down the holler road, past the mill and as far away as any place he had ever heard about. Places with forgotten names and unknown people. Places that stirred the imagination and honed the wanderlust that had taken seed in his soul. Places, strange and exotic places, any place away from the toil and the drudgery that was the only way he had ever known. Places where he had no use for patched-and-faded-bibbed overalls that never fit. Overalls that were worn out by someone before he ever got them. Shoes that did not reek of the red dirt of the barren yard in front of the old log house. Socks to wear with shoes that smelled of new leather and shined like the gold coins that he did not have. He wanted his Ma and his sisters to have better; he wanted it bad, but he wanted it for himself even more. It just seemed to jump up and bite at him when he was ponderin' what he was gonna make out of himself and what he might think to do for makin' his way in this old world. He knew he weren't lazy and work never bothered him none. He was near onto a full-growed man now and stout as any near these parts. It was time to be thinkin' on the things of growed up life. He had notions on other growed up things too. If there was just a body he could talk with that knew somethin' about some of them places, maybe he could get over such notions and wild ideas and get on to makin' a better life for Ma and the girls.

Girls, dang, why'd he hafta think of them just now? Or rather one girl that hardly knew he was alive or hadn't much more than spoke his name. He had never seen her without shoes. She always had a ribbon tied in her hair or wore a bonnet. He had never been close enough to catch scent of her, but Sarry said she smelt like lavender, whatever that was. Lord how mercy, reckon she ever smelled me? I ain't never had no scent but sweat and dirt. Maybe if I purtied up some and had a good shirt she'd maybe look my way. Ma says if you run with the dogs then you smell like one, but all I ever runned with was old Kate. Don't matter no how, I ain't got no new shirt, let lone no lavender.

Jubal went round the end of the old log house to the front porch and sat down on the log bench. Beech log split right through the middle and hued down smooth with a hand axe. Four hickory limb cuts for legs that was augured into the round side of the log. Wore slick from years of bein' sot on by who knowed how many hinder ends. Hard telling how many good blood-letting splinters that old log give out 'fore it got slicked down. He leaned back against the wall and soon closed his eyes. His mind raced in a hundred directions all at the same time. He stood in places to the far corners of the earth and beheld the marvels told him by the travelers that he saw in deepest thoughts. He beheld all the marvels that foreign lands had to offer, and the call of adventure sang a restless song of wandering and awe.

"Jubal Clay, you wake it up now, boy," rang out his Ma in a stern voice. "We need too much done round here fer you be sleepin' midday." Stern, but yet understanding, his Ma had a way that made a body know when she meant her words as spoke. "I got wash to do and Sarry can do the hot iron. We be able to git done long 'fore night. I want you to go to the mill and there abouts and see can you learn about yer Pa. See if he left word with C.C. or at the store. I need you back 'fore sundown too, ye hear?" Those words really sent his mind to whirl. He could maybe see Lida while at the mill and ask her if she knowed anythin' about his Pa. Maybe he could hear there and wouldn't have to go all the way to the store and then come back thru the flats. Maybe he could go to the flats first and pick a bucket of berries and take to the mill.

He lit out across the Rogerson place almost in a run. Don't reckon nobody spied him grab the bucket. He just wished he had a good lookin' shirt and some decent shoes, but what he had was all he had and that would just have to be enough fer now. He cut in above Rogerson's old house so he wouldn't need stop in and see to the old man, no time to spare there today.

Seemed to him it took awfully long to reach the flats, and his breath was comin' hard time he got there. Sweat broke long time back. He had to stop and catch his wind for a minute or two. He reckoned he had made the flats in half what it normal took. He had run up the hills and flew down the holler and then winded himself good climbin' to the flats. Breath soon came easy, and by that time the old oak bucket had the bottom covered with fine big ripe berries. He culled all but the biggest and the best. The varmint turkeys had got a lot of them, but they weren't about to tromp the tops down to be in reach like he could. There was where the best and the biggest of all and the ripest were, and them was the ones he was after. The big berries filled the bucket faster. The sun had moved the shadows some, but not a lot when he finished toppin' off the bucket.

Now to make fer the store fast as legs could tote a body, bucket in tow. Only now did he notice the scratches and prickle sticks on the back of his hands with little whelps of dried blood beaded up at the wrist. A quick stop and a rub or two with a mullein leaf, and he was back makin' tracks to the store with little sign of anythin' gone foul.

The store seemed near about empty as it come in sight. No sign of nobody but Cleve, the storekeep and some stranger sittin' on the bench in the porch shade. One saddle horse, all broke down and likely not shod, was all the mounts in sight. He reckoned that it was the stranger's mount. He came up near the porch, but kept back a bit.

"Mister Cleve, you seen anything of Pa here last day or so."

"Yeh, he wuz here yesterday about sundown. Didn't' say nary a word to nobody, just come in and bought some laudanum. We wondered who been sickly."

"Which way he leave?"

"He wuz on a big bay and rode out the creek road headed west. I never watched to see which a way he went at the forks."

"Wuz he by hisself?"

"Reckon so, but I never ask him."

"Wuz he alright?"

"Seemed like he was, but like said, he never spoke nary word."

Laudanum, for pain. He been hurt somehow? Pa been known to speak his piece and not give nary a hoot what others thought about what he said. He could'a said too much to the wrong one and got whupped up on some fer it. Or could'a got shot even.

The stranger, he had seen him somewhere before. Who wuz he, and what he be doin' here not speakin' a word all the time? Strange eyes, piercing and prying eyes that stared holes into the very heart. Eyes set in a weathered face that had seen many a year of wind and rain. A leathery face that spoke a book yet said little about its owner. A face that had known much and had grown wise in its own right.

Unable to hold back any longer, he had to ask, "Cleve, who's yer friend?"

"Ain't really a friend, just passin' thru here."

"Where from?"

"Andersonville," the stranger began.

"Ander who?"

"Andersonville."

"Where that be?"

Cleve jumped in. "Let it be Jubal. Ye best not know nothing about that place."

Now just how could a body let it be when you knowed just enough to ask a hunnert more questions? But he had to make the mill yet and be home by sundown. He reckoned he knowed just about all they was to ask about his Pa so he'd not bother C.C. with much more than a question or two that he already knowed the answer to.

"Well Cleve, I'm obliged to ye. If ye see or hear about Pa, can ye send us word?"

"I can do that and will do that, if I learn some news."

"I be back in three to four days."

Took better'n two hours to walk to the mill and call on C.C. Course the lad never ever called him nothing but Mister Johnson to his face. C.C. was in the mill house, but the mill wheel was stopped, so it were right still and quiet. Jubal saw from a ways off that the mill weren't runnin', so when he come in earshot, he began to cough a little hack ever few steps and to set his feet down right heavy on the road's loose gravel.

C.C. and Lida appeared in the mill house door, and ask him to come in fer a drink and sit a spell to rest. He felt he would come plumb unraveled when they asked him in, but he was bound to accept. Danged if he was gonna pick a whole raption of berries and not get no use out of em.

"Hello there Jubal," C.C. spoke. Lida remained silent. "What brings you to mill today?"

"Lookin' fer my Pa, sir. He never come home fer the night."

"Well, I say."

"We is getting a mite worrisome, or Ma is."

Lida eased out from behind her dad's arm and stepped down off the door sill as her eyes moved to the berries. "Jubal where in world's wonders did you find such fine berries? They look like a picture painting."

"Oh I run on them up on the Rogerson place up on the flats."

"They sure is nice ones all right."

"I picked em just fer you," and in an instant he felt his face come on fire and his ears stung like frostbite. Just blurted it right out and never thought how it come on so. First time she ever looked him eye-to-eye, and he done stepped in deep. Stammering a bit, "I reckoned, I guess you might like a big old cobbler pie out of em."

"Oh my, yes."

"Now Lida, we can't take all them berries. It must a took half a day pickin' all that many," C.C. said.

"You can have em," as he reached them to Lida, "but I do need to take Ma her bucket back."

Lida took his free hand in hers as she took the bucket from his other tanned-and-calloused hand. She held on tightly for a brief moment, long enough to feel the toughness of working hands, hard-working hands. Hands that were no older than her own, but hands that had seen much harder a life than her own. She left to take the berries across the footbridge to her house and told Jubal that she would be back soon as she washed his bucket out for him.

That gave him a chance to talk to her dad.

"Mister Johnson, what is Andersonville?"

"Well son, you know there be a war on, don't you?"

"Yes sir."

"You know what folks is at war over?"

"Reckon it be about slaves and all."

"Well that be part of it all, but not total. See, there be times when those who be fighting take the others captive. Then the captors need a place to house and confine them, like they was criminals. So they make up prisoner camps and that is what Andersonville is, so I hear. Two fellers come thru here early spring and say they come from there. Course they done shucked off their blue coats long before they got here. They was decent folks and did us no harm nor took nothing from us what we didn't offer them first. They said they just wanted to get back closer home and didn't want no trouble from nobody nowhere."

"They never took no stock nor mounts?"

"No, we just fed em, and they was grateful for that. Never took nothing."

"Was they from fer off?"

"Reckon they come down from Ohio according to what they said."

"Ain't never been there."

"Well me either, son. Don't reckon I ever will be if this war don't force me. I ain't too much beholdin' to way lots folk feel about ownin' another man and ownin' his soul to boot. Course a soul ain't never to be for sale, since it been bought long time back if you accept the payment. I think a man ought be free to make his own way and earn his own keep best as he can. Some in these parts thinks the states has more say in a man's rights than the government does. They say a bought man is property just like land is property. Beatin' up on a man just to make him work harder and longer ain't right, and I'd have to take stand against that too."

"You ever seen anywhere else, been in the war or such?"

"No, Jubal, and I don't hanker to see it neither."

"How come?"

"You read any, son?"

"Some," he replied with some embarrassment.

"Papers full of bad things that the war cause many common folks all south and west of here."

"Like what, sir."

"Bluecoats come thru and burn whole crops, take livestock and butcher it right there and eat a spell then leave the carcass to rot in the sun. Break in a man's house and plunder ever thing he have. Some even take the women folk fer their own pleasure. Course that be mostly where the Yanks is hated the strongest, not so much here abouts."

"Them Yanks must be pure devils."

"Well, I don't hold to that too much either. I think if they get treated good then they treat good in return. I believe they be mostly good people just like most folks round here. We ain't beholdin' to slave work neither."

"I ain't never seen a slave, I don't reckon."

"Boy, they be no different than you. They be a man just like you. You don't recall your Grandpa Morgan, I know, but he was a full Cherokee. He had dark skin, more than you or your Ma; and he were a man just the same, a good man too. See son, what a man is comes from the inside and not what he be outside or what color he be outside. You be a slave to this world and its ways, you know that?"

"Don't reckon nobody owns me."

"No, but you are a slave long as you choose it."

His mind began racing, but quickly came to a point as he spied Lida comin' cross the footbridge with his bucket. Her hair bounced with each step. She had left her bonnet at the house and was prancing round like a new colt first let on pasture. His ears began to sting again.

"Mother said to thank thee very much and that you should have these too." She handed him three slabs of salt-cured ham wrapped in brown paper and a small lard can full of shuck beans. "Mother said you could bring the lard can back sometime later." She sat the wooden bucket at his feet and braced her balance on his forearm.

He would bring that lard can back tomorrow if he could find a way!! He had just as good as been asked to come into dinner. Wonder how she'd like to have a washin' tub full a berries?

"You get on home now, son. It ain't good to be out by yourself after dark now days," C.C. cautioned.

"Bye, bye, Jubal and tell Sarry and Julie hello from me," called Lida. A fresh shot of blood to the ears again, but it felt a mite easier this time. She had actually talked direct to him this time and by jingo had actually touched him; touched him twice. He had seen her full head of hair and it come dang near plum to her waist. Bet it was soft as silk too. Just how could he know? I ain't never felt of no silk before.

Shadows were long by the time he lost sight of the mill. He was nearing the south of the miller place when he thought he heard hoof beat. Stopping to listen more intent, they seemed to fade for a bit, but then they stopped. He listened and could hear nothing. A few more steps and then hoof beat ahead. They were coming from ahead of him, not behind. Off the road, fast, and into the reed patch, across the ditch. Hoof beat, louder, closer.

The sun felt warm to his face. His head throbbed with each heartbeat. He could hear hoof beat regular as clockwork. He saw shadows, and then bright light made his eyes smart. He raised an arm to his head and no longer felt such a sting. There was no red crust on his hand this time. His right arm brushed something hard and rough. His eyes slowly came into focus, and he then knew he was moving. He was laid out in a wagon bed, and it was moving. He looked to his left, and there beside him lay a Bluecoat with a blood-soaked bandage over both eyes. The bandaged-body spoke not and breathed hard. He began to sense each stone crossed by the iron-rimmed wagon wheels, but the Bluecoat next to him made no sign of feelin' nothin'. He lay back and tried to sort out all that was going on around him and what had happened to him. The throb in his head made it hard to reckon things out. He pulled up by holdin' on to the wagon sideboard and tried to look about.

"Son, lay back down. We soon be to the doc, and he can try mendin' you up some."

He had heard that voice before somewhere, sometime, but put no face to it yet. He tried to look back over his head to the wagon driver, but all he could see were the back and shoulders of a blue coat and a dark mop of hair. Seemed like the old wagon hunted every stone on the road and run smack over it. Every jolt hurt somewhere in his body and sent new throbs to his head.

He thought he could recall some of what had happened if he could just get up and look about him. He tried once more to pull himself to a sitting position, but this time lost his grip on the sideboard and went crashing back to the rough hard boards of the wagon bottom. The jolt sent lightning bolts all through his head, and the darkness and the quiet overcame him once more. The wagon and its escorts continued on for another four hours or so. But the boy knew nothing at all about the remaining trek to the rear lines and to healing help, to hands that were gentle, caring and comforting, now in his time of need.

Far from home and kin folk, knowing no one and not knowing really where he was being taken. Lost in his own right and unsecured in tomorrow and all the tomorrows to come. If only there were someone he could call on. Someone who could be trusted. Someone who cared about him. Someone to show him the way and to guide him home to rest and comfort.

Chapter 2

Touched

A pale glimmer as the sun sank low in the brush. Tired, weary eyes, unable to comprehend the shadows and the nameless figures moving all about. Stillness, he no longer bounced about the rough, old wagon bed. It had stopped. Slowly and weak in his grip, he raised his head a bit, then gathered pitiful weak arms about him and raised to one elbow. Body felt racked with fever, and every muscle begged to be let lay and be still.

Voices, unheard except for a stir about him. Flicker, a fire close by. The smell of smoke mixed with the air of brackish water. Water, life-giving water. His voice trembled. He needed water. Looked to his left, and the poor soul with the bloodied eyes remained by his side. He spoke not and moved not.

The reed patch made a good place of concealment and came none too soon. Had the road not curved around the branch where it did, they would'a seen him dive in there before he got hid. The hoof beat came loud and regular and stopped just as quickly. Jubal froze there in the reeds. They sat high in the saddle and looked about as if they were lost or lookin' for somebody. Jubal parted the reeds with his hands, slowly and quietly to try and get a better look at them. Closest had the backside to and his hat set low in the back. Not much to tell from what he could see. The other one was most nigh blocked out by the first. One that was backside to turned in the saddle and pointed on down the holler to where Jubal had just come from. Turned just enough to tell he had a full face beard, grey and mangy lookin'. The second rider placed both hands on the pommel and spit out a big tabakker cud, got a bottle out of a vest pocket and took a big pull, pointing east, across the Miller place.

"Ain't no sense goin' plum at the Cove Road. There ain't but one place twixt here and the mouth of the holler and that be the mill, and they ain't got what we need anyhow."

He knew these parts, had to know to be reckonin' like that. But who was he and where he be comin' from and where he be goin'? The boy strained hard to see if he remembered him from someplace, but he came up blank. Couldn't put nuthin' together fer old whisker face either.

Tabakker Chewer had a broke down lookin' mount that looked a mite familiar. Eyed the horse real good to get a better look. "Danged if that ain't the mount at the store today; I shore think so," under his breath. "Should'a looked closer then." Then he saw it, bridle button with CSA stamped in it and catching the late afternoon sun occasionally as the mount chomped at the bits and swung his head about to mind off the bitin' flies. Both men turned and twisted in the saddles like they was restless and wantin' to git gone, but not knowin' which a way to git. Another pull out from the flask and passed it over to whisker face. He turned it up and appeared to kill it dry. Handed it back to the first. He turned it up again. Swore a few oaths cause it bein' empty. Threw it down and spurred his mount.

Whiskers followed a length behind. Jubal watched till they turned east across the Miller place and topped the first hill. He stayed in the reed patch to make sure they weren't about to double back. Couldn't help but wonder iffin somehow these two no-goods were in cahoots with his Pa somehow. Well, a body always seems to fret with things that leaves him in the dark. Then when it be all settled, it be just like a light showed all the answers just plain as day and made sense all the time. Ma always said that hindsight was the clearest of all. He stepped back on to the road and peered off in the direction they had gone. He stood close by the reed patch so to dive back in like a skeert rabbit if they topped back over the hill.

It was near black dark when he saw a lantern light in the door of the old log house. He realized then that he was tired and hungry. He could count on Ma havin' him eats ready.

"Wash up son and set down. I got hot fried taters and biscuits made fer ye." Just like he knew Ma would do, but he never expected hot taters this time a day, no sir. A quick splash of water on his face and dried his hands on his overall legs and sat down. Everybody gathered round and began in askin' what he learnt about Pa, if anything. He was more interested in the hot biscuits than he was talkin', but he tried to recall all that had happened durin' the course of the day.

He noticed the sparkle in the eyes of his younger sisters, Julie and Gracie. They seemed to be taken by what he told about the conversation at the store and the visit at the mill. He intentionally left out the parts about Lida and the berries, but Sarry had that fox-in-the-chicken-house look about her.

"Is there any berries on the flats Jubal," Sarry broke in with a smile about like a mule eatin' briars.

"Well yeah, there be berries up there, and you know it. You need to go pick em and make us a pie."

"Bet a big old pie be good about tomorrow down the road."

Dang, she must a seen me grab the bucket. He then told his Ma what Mrs. Johnson had sent them, and with that she had it all down purty much like it come off. Ma weren't no fool and Sarry weren't blind.

"That be real neighborly of Mrs. Johnson. I do declare! We gonna have ham and beans tomorrow, and I'll make corn bread too. We eat high on the old hog tomorrow," Ma chuckled.

Jubal reached for another biscuit. He hurriedly finished his meal, wiped his mouth on his forearm and then asked the eye poppin' question. "Was they any riders come by here today? Would a been in the afternoon or so." He went on to relate his episode on the road and how he hid out in the reeds, and all about how they pointed round like they was lost or such. He had to tell most of it again to answer all the questions fired to him over parts of the tellin' of it. He let on like that were all there was to tell, and soon all had drifted off to bed but him and Ma. It was only then that he told her about Cleve sayin' how Pa come in and bought the laudanum, then rode off to the west on that old broke down bay hoss. That part of the day's tale took the wind purty much out a Ma, and it was clear that she was troubled about Pa and was concerned about the riders and what manner of no good that they was up to anyhow.

"If that was the same mount that was at the store, then they shore had a come cross old Rogerson's place. I never heard anythin', and I never saw nuthin'. But that don't mean they was nothin' done nor no harm done," Ma reasoned, half talkin' and half thinkin' out loud.

"Reckon I need go look in on Rogerson?" the boy asked.

"I reckon ye do, but wait till first light. I hate thinkin' what two rank strange riders might a done, but ain't nuthin' we can do till light."

"Guess ye right Ma, usually are."

"Best get bedded down now, son. Ye had a long day. No tellin' what ye be stirrin' in to come tomorrow. Ye sleepin' on the porch again?"

"Reckon so, Ma."

Tired, but sleep were a ways off yet. He wondered about his Pa and where he was now. Wondered if he was all right or maybe he was hurt somehow. Why the laudanum? He reckoned it was fer achin' and sore and all, but had heard Granny Iverson say how some just naturally craved it all the time. He had never knowed Pa to take anything akin to that, but he did cotton to a good run of shine ever now and then. True he got riled up at his Pa sometimes cause of the way he sluffed off on the chores, but still he was his Pa. Pa hadn't never laid a hand to him, but his kind words were few and far between. He had never been rough with Ma nor none of the other kids either, but seemed he always had other things needed tendin' besides his family. He reckoned he could handle the work and all if he had to, but still he had flash thoughts of places he had only heard about. The wanderlust was quelled for the moment, but it were definitely still alive.

The whip-or-wills sang way into the night, and somewhere way up on the ridge he could hear screech owls hollerin' back and forth. He easily put them out of mind and soon fell to sleep thinkin' about his meetin' Lida at the mill again when Ma sent the lard can back. Seemed that a light breeze had come up from the east sometime durin' the last hour or so. Brought a bit of chill in the air. He pulled the patch quilt tight around his shoulders, and the wool pieces seemed rough against his face and neck. No light in the east yet, so he just rolled back to the wall and let the magic of sleep take him over.

Ma didn't have to wake him up. He had heard her hit the floor and come down the old narrow creakin' staircase. He got up, put on his old work shoes, fetched in the wood chips and built the fire in the cook stove. Ma had gone to the springhouse for milk for biscuits. The spring pool was full now, but stock would need water today and that would pull it down low again. The fire kindled and blazed up by the time she come in the kitchen.

"Ye sleep purty good, son?" she asked.

"Yep, Ma, near all night."

"Me too, son."

He knew right off that were not true, cause he could see the red in her eyes. She could hide most of her feelin's, but hardly ever could cover the hurt or worry when it was so strong that it made for cryin'.

"I'll have it all ready in a bit, son. Iffin ye don't mind, fetch me a few taters and carry up all the buckets a water fer me. And holler at Granny and the girls; they need be up real soon too."

Jubal turned and stepped out on the porch to get the water buckets. He glanced back through the little kitchen window and saw his Ma take up her apron and wipe the corners of her eyes. He knew she was troubled bad, and he wanted to make things right for her. He wondered if all her frettin' and worryin' was comin' from Pa and his antics, or if there be things he was not knowin'. It troubled him, but not like it eat into Ma.

His mind raced. Memories of boyhood days with his Pa and good times flashed in waves before him. He recalled the first time his Pa had ever made him a feather dart. Took a corncob outta the crib and then had to look all about the barn yard for three good chicken feathers. He stuck the feathers into the marrow middle of the cob. Then sharpened a hickory twig and put in the other end of the cob and made a sharp point on the outside end of the twig. Pa then flung the dart and made it twist like a dust devil. Then when it came down, it stuck straight up in the dirt. Jubal had made many a dart since then and made em for younger boys at the meetin' house.

He recalled how Pa had showed him how to set rabbit traps, how to dig a turkey trap, many things about trappin' and trackin', how to twist a squirrel out from a holler tree knot, how to track bees from water to their tree. Pa had taught him the ways of the mountain woods and had allowed him to roam the wilds of the local mountains and learn by doin'. It weren't like his Pa was all bad; it just came on this way since the war commenced.

War, fightin' and quarrelin' in all them places that he had just heard about but did not really know about. Things that he had heard that he did not understand. Brothers against brothers, neighbors turned against one another. It all seemed unnatural. Still wonderin' and thinkin' on all them places and people that he never knew 'cept by listenin' in on the politic talk at the store once or twice.

Old man Rogerson probably knowed a bit of all the goin's on. Maybe I just take some time to talk turkey with him today, see what he might say about this here war. He always seemed to kinda take a shine to me and always was a talker anyhow. Other folks says how he is a devil and a scallywag hooligan. They might be a dab judgmental in my thinking. I reckon he just be old and set and don't rightly care who is offended by his ways. He been here a long time, and I spose he got his druthers as to who he takes to and who he don't.

Old Rogerson lived in a frame shack near the middle of his old worn out place and had been there since Heck was a pup, and he be a growed up dog now, as Ma always said. His wife had been gone for as long as anyone could recall; and if there had been children, no one knew for sure. The house lay at the foot of a long spine of a ridge with deep hollows running off to each side. One hollow had a right fair apple orchard, or it had been an apple orchard in its day. Now it was more or less just a tangle of brambles and bushes with an occasional penance of a fruit tree. The apples were nothing more than knots now, and the crows usually got everything that even looked like it would be edible. Still, old Rogerson would shoo you out of his apples, if he saw you there.

The house was weathered and worn. It had seen many a storm-tossed night, and the wind had displaced some of the hand-hewn red oak shingles. The roof sagged in the middle of the two room structure. The one stone and mud flu looked like it would fall away from the house with the push of one hand. The floor was dirt and packed hard as stone from years of use. Most of the old paling garden fence had rotted away and crumpled to the ground. The gooseberry bush in the front corner of the old garden space was now huge and laced with honeysuckle and poison vine.

The spring was near filled in, and the runoff was now just a trickle. A gourd dipper hung by a rusty piece of old wire to a stone point in the retaining wall above the spring. Stones had dislodged and lay scattered about in the branch leading off, eventually to run down past Cleve and his store and then into Cane Creek.

Rogerson still had two old milk cows, but they had been turned off dry since last winter sometime after calvin'. They were near feral now, sometimes could not even be found in all the brambles that had nearly consumed all once clear ground. Even their barn had long since fallen away to ruin and rot. It seemed as if everything around old Rogerson was about to go to naught. Time seemed determined to consume all traces of the old man and all his life before him. Judging from his life and living, it probably would not be too long in coming either.

It was light enough to see well when Jubal set out across the north hill toward old Rogerson's place. He thought of a thousand things that he could ask the old cuss, but reckoned he would just take things as they come once he got there. He was in no particular hurry, because for years it seemed as if old Rogerson had been immune to time. Nothing ever changed about him. He always had a dingy, unkempt long gray beard. His clothes hung on him like he was not more than a skeleton. His face, or what you could see of it, was tanned like leather turned to the wind. His eyes were deep set in his head above high and prominent cheek bones. Eyes pierced to the soul of whoever looked on his face. Old eyes, but clear as snow melt in April.

Jubal could have seen the house a long way off had it not been for all bushes and stick weed thickets. He had picked up a stick and was easing through the weeds by pushing them to one side then the other as he made way down to the orchard area. All the weeds seemed to resist movement with a rasp and rattle as they got pushed on by the stick and by foot. Dry weather had made them toughen up before their normal time. Birds scurried before him, and the quick startle of a rabbit interrupted his stride. "Better be a mite more careful cause they could be a rattler in here sommers," thinking to himself.

Closer to the house and near the end of what once was the orchard, he stopped under an old gnarly early transparent tree, lookin' for a possible taste. He had eaten from this tree before and recalled how tasty the apples could be. He recollected at meetin' sometime about a tree that was in a garden. He thought on how the circuit rider preacher had told how that was the start of all man's troubles long time ago. Rogerson himself may have set out that tree. No decent lookin' apple in sight.

Not more than a hundred yards on down the orchard, there he stopped dead in his tracks. Tracks! Horse tracks! One was shod and the other not. Tracks goin' against his direction, comin' away from Rogerson's house and cuttin' across the east ridge headin' to the Miller place. Tracks were not new, but easy to see and trail in the dry dust. Weeds were still mashed down some from hoof beats.

"Them is the riders I seen last night," startled aloud to himself. "I make sure where they headin' to." He followed the tracks for about half an hour. Sure as rain they headed up east and straight to where he could see the hilltops of the Miller place. "They hadda come by Rogerson's place."

It was then that reality seemed to jump him square in the face. His throat suddenly dried out and his pulse quickened. Down off the ridge and back to the orchard in half the time it took to begin with. He easily found the tracks in the orchard leading straight to the old shack. The weeds were mashed down against the way he was movin' and that proved that the riders had been goin' away from there. He weren't so sure he was likin' the way this might add up. Soon the top of the old stone stick and mud shack came to his view. There was no smoke comin' out a it. He stopped dead in his tracks and listened. He drew breath ever so light as to listen better. He heard nothing but the sounds of nature, the twitter of a sparrow and the distant caw of a crow. No wind. No movement. Nothing astir. His pulse quickened, and his heart was ready to jump clear to the outside of his chest. He made a dash to the house calling for the old man as he rushed up to the rickety old porch.

"Wes, Wes Rogerson," he yelled into the house thru the ajar door. He didn't know if he answered to Wes or not, but he remembered Cleve calling him by that name. "Wes, ye in there?" No reply.

He felt strange. He was about to go into another person's home unasked or uninvited, and he had never done so before. A body just ought not go bargin' in 'fore bein' ask. Folks needs respect and rightly so.

"Wes, it Jubal, are ye woke up yet?"

Jubal felt a strong hand to the back of his neck and in the next breath felt the cool soothing water on his lips. His thirst at once reared up and announced new-found vigor. Reaction took control and his hands engulfed those that held the water to his parched mouth, the life-giving water that he so desperately needed. The first drops fell away and ran down his chin, spilling onto his now heaving chest. With wanton abandon he summoned all the strength left in his ravaged being and gulped at the water being offered him. Never had he wanted more of anything in his life. Pain shot thru his head, and the entire earth set to spin about him. He held to the hand that held the water and tried to pull it closer to him.

"Whoa, thar now feller. There be plenty, but you might just better ease up a bit. Take it slow," the faceless voice cautioned.

He pulled for more water and felt the soothing nectar flow over his lips and onto his parched tongue. He swallowed and it hurt. Hurt so much that it set him to cough and that brought dizzying pain to his head again.

"See you about woke up now?" the voice inquired. "Here take a little bit more, but take it slow, ain't nobody here gonna take it away from ye."

Jubal raised his eyes toward the voice and could make out only a blur of a face and a wide-brimmed hat. Slowly, almost forever it seemed, the strong hand held him waiting for his head to clear. He pulled the water to him again and let it run its own course to his parched mouth. He managed to take a few drops without starting a wrenching cough. He managed a few more sips while the faceless voice talked. He heard this voice, but it seemed not to matter what he said. All in life that mattered right now came from that hand that held the water flask.

He did not know how long he drank or how much. The voice returned and this time, there was a face that went with it. Jubal opened his eyes and beheld a clean-shaven, big broad face of a black man peering back down at him.

"Lay still, son. We gonna git you outta this here wagon and in a bed. We git you all wash up an clean up too. Yasser, or my name ain't Jugg."

With that said, it happened. Jubal found strong arms under his and other hands around his legs as the hard, stony wagon bed fell away. His next conscious thoughts found him in a clean bed with clean blankets. The comfort of it all was overwhelming to him as he tried to recount his fate and put some sort of order to the chaos that engulfed him. His vision was clear now, and he no longer had the grime of the earth covering his hands and arms. His throat seemed parched, and his lips burned from the rough and open cracks. No clear recollection came to him.

Another unknown dark face shadowed his, as he felt the warm dampness brush across his tortured face. He tasted cool refreshing water on his lips and again eagerly reached to gain hold of the source. His eyes rose to the source of the liquid and another face came into focus. A wide-brimmed dark hat with a gold-braided rope about it. Protruding from beneath the brim was graying hair. A beard, neatly trimmed encased most of the face, save for the dark eyes that bore directly into his own. The glint of the gold buttons and the braided epaulets escaped meaning.

He pulled the water to him with all the strength that he could summons to his arms and hands. The water coursed over his lips and into his stinging throat. Swallowing came hard, but the liquid only began to meet basic needs of his tormented body. Another gulp and yet another. Strong hands pulled the water away from his begging lips.

"Good to see you comin' around some, son. Looks like you had it a mite rough yesterday, but you did yourself proud."

"Uhhhhh." was all the sound that the lad could muster.

"I'm Major Dunn, and this here is Jugg. He is one fine old feller. He's gonna be in charge of you and lots of other young strappin' men that need tending. You don't need to do anything right now save rest yourself and try to mend up some. I need you to talk to me soon as you get up to it and can recollect what happened out at the ferry landing. Jugg here gonna look in on you thru the night, and he can come fetch me if you can talk. You just rest a bit now, and we'll set it all straight by you in the morning."

The major turned and left before many of his words had time to take on any meaning.

No thoughts of anything seemed to make any sense. One minute he thought of the old log home and how he missed his Ma and his sisters. The next moment he could gather no thoughts save for the thundering pain in his temple and the blinding flashes of light that danced wildly across his consciousness.

Major who…? Could not recall a name, but still could see those eyes. They were eyes that had seen much and were the window to a mind that knew much. Eyes that could say more in a blink than some could say in written volumes. They conveyed no fear, but rather radiated with confidence, yet flowed with compassion.

The eyes that beheld him now were not those of the Major. They were those of the one who had first given him water and touched him when he needed it most.

Jubal pushed the ajar door, and it moved only a fraction before it hit something. He pushed a bit harder, and the door reluctantly gave way enough for him to look inside. He first scanned around the darkened room. Only one small window, and the early morning sun had made it hard to see inside for a moment. His eyes fell to the floor in front of him.

There lay old Rogerson! Dark crimson stains on the dirt floor, and his face pressed into the stain. Jubal froze! His heart quickened just as if he had run up to the flats again, but this time it were a lot quicker settin' on than he ever known before. Ma had not cautioned him what he might find and what he ought do iffin he did find it. He stooped and placed a hand to the old man's shoulder. That brought a slight shrug and a groan from old man Rogerson, and a jerk-back reaction from Jubal. His heart raced even faster.

Old Rogerson gathered what little strength he had left in his old, withered body and raised his head to Jubal.

"Thank God it be ye, Jubal."

"What's a matter? What happened to ya?"

"Help me to my bed."

Jubal helped the pitiful old soul roll to his back. It was then that he saw the fear in those deep set eyes, and he saw the gash that had been the source of the red stain. No fresh bleeding, but that did not seem important now. The old man had a three-inch gash above his right eye going all the way into the gray and matted hairline. The better part of his shirt front was crimson-stained and torn almost from his body.

Jubal had come by many times in the past to look in on the old cuss, but he had never before been inside. He had no inkling how the old man lived. Dirt floor. Red mud chinking between the weathered logs. No ceiling. Just exposed rafters and hand-hewn red oak shingles with scattered penetrating shafts of early morning light. The stone and mud fireplace and chimney had lost so many stones it could no longer contained the fire and smoke. The inside reeked of wood smoke, and ashes lay all about that end of the shanty. Dust covered every ledge that would support it. Wooden pegs bored and driven into the logs held rags that resembled clothing. Everything seemed to mock the old man. It was old. It was dirty. It was wasting away and about to fall.

Arms locked around his chest, Jubal managed to get old Rogerson to his bed. The bed was nothing more than a man-sized box full of pine straw and covered with burlap for bed sheets. The bed smelled of must and pine tar.

"Fetch me water boy," in a demanding manner and yet in a begging tone.

"Yessir, from the spring?" looking for a gourd dipper as he answered. He spotted a long neck gourd hanging from a nail beside the small window and reached for it.

"Ye leave that be, boy! That be my seed gourd, and I need it left be."

"Is they one to the spring?"

"Course they is. Now git on and use it," more demanding all the time.

Most times in the past the old man would just howdy and not have much more to say. He would give the boy a page or two of the Review ever now and then, just depending on what Ma sent to him. He never had seen him this hateful before. Reckon it must be cause of him bein' hurt.

He returned with the dipper filled with water from the shallow spring. The old man had raised himself to a sittin' angle. He took the water and drank vigorously.

"Fetch more," reaching the dipper to the boy.

"Who hit ye?"

"Git that thar water."

Another trek to the spring and another dipper full.

"Here ye be."

Rogerson took the second dipper and drank just as vigorously as the first. He saved just a bit, poured it into one hand and went through the motions of washing his face. It left no trace on the tanned and withered face.

"Fetch my jug," pointing to the back wall behind the fireplace. Jubal stepped across the dirt floor in the direction indicated.

"Mind yer dang step boy. Ain't no cause be kickin' up sich a dust, still demanding as ever.

Jubal pulled the corncob stopper and handed the jug to the old man. He rested the near empty vessel in the bend of his arm and raised it to his lips. Two big pulls and then handed it back, demanding that it be returned to its rightful place.

"What do I needs do fer ye now?" Jubal questioned. "What happened?"

Didn't take too much to see that the old man was hurt. He could hardly move, was bloodied from head to toe, most nigh and probably not eat nuthin' in two to three days. The dried blood on the dirt floor made sure that it weren't a right now thing too.

"I need ye to go fetch Cleve. He will know what needs done," instructed the old codger. He seemed to be calmin' down a bit since he got a pull or two off the jug. He lay back on his pine-straw bed and began to finger around his head wound.

"Ye tell Cleve that I be needin' some tendin' to this here gash. He knows about them kinda things and knows how to patch a body as good as any soul I know."

"What happened? Who whupped up on ye?"

"Ain't right shore who. Don't recollect seein' them here abouts."

"When they do this to ye?"

"Ye jest go fetch Cleve fer me and tell him what I say. I rest a mite while ye be gone, and I tell ye both more then iffin I recollect more."

The tone of the old man's voice spoke two messages to the boy. One said that fear was at the core of the matter; the other said that there was more to this than he had let on. He never whacked that gash on his own head that be a fact, and he wanted Jubal out of his house now, or at least it seemed so.

Easing out the makeshift door, looking around in the dust, he could plainly see tracks. Hoof tracks. One were shod and one were not. Few footprints in the dust looked like buckskin boot prints. A track the likes of them would be a dead give way to a body with any mind to the mountains and could tell bunches about who might a made em.

A rustle from inside the house redirected attention away from tracks and prints, for the time at present. Jubal turned and started on down the branch to Cleve's store. He quickened his pace and soon came to the Cove road. By the time he had the store in sight, the morning sun was up well above the tree line of the ridge behind him. He thought of Ma and the girls and what they had to do today bein' as how he weren't there. Stock had to be watered today and that called for luggin' a bunch up outta the spring pool and totein' to the stock trough. Then they be choppin' weeds in the garden rows. Dang weeds dryin' up just same as ever thing else. Ain't much sense choppin' none, less it commence a rainin' soon.

Wonder how the old crank keeps hisself fed? He don't grow no garden and don't milk no cows no more. Thoughts, audible thoughts, here and gone in no time at all. Just a flash of light and then it be all done.

Cleve stood alone behind the counter as Jubal walked in. He had not realized it, but he had broke a sweat comin' in from Rogerson's old place.

Jubal, what in tarnation ye doin' here this time a day?" Cleve inquired as he looked up from his books.

"I jest come from Rogerson's and he be hurt. Told me to come fetch ye fer him."

"What happened?"

"He be whacked on the head and cut open sometime or nuther. He weren't telling' me much more. Said he'd tell ye when we come back to his place. Said ye would know what he needed."

"Well, I reckon so," Cleve replied mostly to himself. He then busied himself to roundin' up things he reckoned he might need once they got back to the old man's place. He gathered a few rags, intended as bandages if needed, and liniment just in case of achin' and painin' joints.

"Ye been into doctorin' long time, Cleve?' Jubal inquired as he watched the storekeep gather what he wanted and stash the things in a flour sack.

"Ain't about no doctorin' no such boy; it be just plain common sense. If he be hurt like ye says, then just make good reason that a body outta have stuff to take measures to help him. He may need patchin' up some or he may need a lot. He ain't eat nothin' in who knows when and probably needs drinkin' too."

"I give him water," Jubal reported.

"Git me a bottle outta the chest there, son. That be the kind a drink he likely need. And git a laudanum bottle while ye be at it too."

"Laudanum, that be what Pa got when he rode off west here few days back, weren't it?"

"Yep, that be a fact. Now step out right smart, son. We need git goin'. I ain't gonna even try to be as smart steppin' as ye, but I be not far laggin' ye. Ye tell old Wes that I be on yer tail and be to him 'fore he know what fer."

Cleve soon was a good bit behind. He walked a steady gait, but he weren't no spring pup like his younger lead. The storekeep seemed wise in his own way and knew most all the folks about here and was respected by most all who traded with him. He could read and cipher so that it took real talent to outwit him at the books. Built about like the pot-belly stove in his store, but he never worked at much more than storekeepin'.

Cleve soon fell out of sight as Jubal turned off the road and headed up the branch, retracing his earlier tracks. Tracks! The hoss tracks is here, they come from off the road! He retraced his steps again and sure as shoot, there they were comin' up from Cleve's store or at least it looked like they come that way. He followed the tracks back till he spotted Cleve. Turned around in one step so as not to be seen and returned trackin' back up the road and back up the branch again.

Deep dust left deep tracks and easy signs. One shod mount and the other not. They were the same mounts as he tracked before, just ye bet on that. They made no mind to cover their tracks or else just plum didn't give a hang. They ought have no mind to cover iffin they be upstandin' and such, or just in too big a hurry. He easily spied where they watered. Hoof marks still deep in mud alongside boot prints close upstream. Easy seen. Cleve ought see them too, else he be close to blind.

Tracks lead straight on up the branch and stopped just short of the old shack in a papaw thicket. Mounts had stomped around there till the ground wore down to dust and boot tracks led off to the house. Jubal stopped, listening to the sounds about him. There was nothing more than the sounds of the critters and quickened heartbeat, his own heartbeat, filled with curiosity and at the same time somewhat fearful for all the unknowns. Maybe Wes could shed a light to all these goin's on and make some sense of it all. He made the last few steps to the door and in that short time, his mind flew to a thousand places and a thousand faces flashed by him.

"Wes, it's me. I comin' in again. Cleve be comin' soon."

The door swung open without any resistance this time. The old man barely stirred, lying still on the pine-straw bed just the way Jubal had left him. Breath came slow. Shallow, but regular. Color still a mite pale. A touch to the forehead revealed a cool but dry skin.

A flutter of the deep set eyes and then a soft sigh. Eyes slow to open up good, but they now seemed to be not so fear struck as before.

"Good ye back so quick, boy, I a mite more better now. Had a time gatherin' my wits about me I spose. Is Cleve with ye?"

"He be comin' on soon. He sent me on ahead cause he ain't light a foot as me. He got his stuff with him too."

Wes rolled up on one elbow and made motions of tryin' to set up. "Help me up a bit here, son."

Together, they soon had the old man up and to the rickety old plank table. Wes nearly fell down to the chair instead of sittin' down, as Jubal steadied him till he got his balance.

"Cleve bringin' me anything to drink or not."

"Yessir, he be for sure, but I fetch ye some more water right now iffin ye want."

"That be all right, son. I wait till Cleve get here just the same." He laid his head over on the table, and Jubal could clearly see where he had been whacked across the brow and that the cut was deep too. He spoke not a word for what seemed like near to ever. Jubal tried to think of what to say, but his mind was too busy racin' all around and a lookin' all about the place. He thought he knew about what had happened and had just about all the answers figgered out, but yet they must a been a thousand things needed cleared up for sure.

"Wes, ye want me do anything fer ye?" he asked breaking the silence.

"I reckon I be needin' some boundgilly buds to make a paste fer this here head cut. Ye know where any bushes be this year, son?"

"Nope can't say as I do." Boundgilly buds were near full this time of year, and he recollected as how his Ma always knowed where they grew. He had seen her take the buds and wrap them in mullein leaves and then mash em up real good twixt two pieces of plank. Then she squashed em into a thick paste. A body could smear that on to a cut and heal it right up, wouldn't even get sore nor nuthin'. Good waxy coat of that paste, and it set up in about a day, and then weren't nothin' much could get to any open cut or scrape. Ma even put some on old Jake when he got copperhead bit. Healed him up and drawed the bite right out. Ma always tried to keep a store in a big crock and set in the spring pool runoff to keep fresh as much as could be. After the buds dried out in the fall, a body could boil em and get some paste that way, but fresh smashed was the best.

"How far back ye say Cleve be?"

"He ought be about nigh here now," answered Jubal.

"Hope so, my head pains me right smart. Think I might take a pull outta the dipper after all, if ye be a mind to fetch it here."

Jubal found the old gourd dipper by the bed and started to the spring for a fresh drink.

"Take a bucket and fetch it full. We gonna need it when Cleve comes." No longer so demanding, more like to asking, pleading, for that matter.

Setting the water bucket in front of the old man and filling the old gourd, Jubal asked outright, "Mr. Wes, who done this?"

Taking a long time and taking a good long drink from the dipper, hands trembling and unsteady to the point of spilling the dipper a bit, Wes answered between breaths, "I ain't never seen them before, best I can recollect. They come on me 'fore I knowed it."

"They whup ye up right off, did they?"

"They just busted in and says they be hungry as bears. Told em I ain't got nuthin' much cept side meat and coffee."

There didn't appear to be nowhere near that much eats in the whole place. Jubal looked about right smartly and then noticed the hanger hooks in the rafters and on hook still held a middlin' meat that looked dry as chips and was green on one side. That would a been all that the old man had, lest there be other stuff about some- where that he ain't yet seen. Coffee beans could be most anywhere in most anything. The old black pot on the fireplace hook had thick set up grease in it. A big iron skillet half full of wood ashes sat on the edge of the old sandstone hearth. No coffee pot was to be seen.

"One with whiskers just up and whack me good. Don't recall much after that till ye come to me and get me up some," his voice trailin' off a bit.

"What'd they look like?"

"One have a full beard like me. Big boned cuss. Other cuss shave few days back I guess, but he be tall and slimmer. Homey lookin' old clod. Never spoke nary a word," after a short pause and long sigh.

"Are ye feelin' a mite poorly or weak now?" the boy asked as much in fear as in wonderment to how the old man would weather this whuppin'.

"I spose I be a right bit tuckered fer sure. I be doin' better once Cleve come and see to me. He bringin' me some fixin's, ain't he?"

"I reckon he got what he needs."

"Well thunder, he get lost tween here and the store?" his voice gaining strength and showing obvious growing impatience.

Jubal thought that Cleve should be near or at least coming on up the branch and up to the old barn by now. Sure he was a heavy set man who had not wielded a pitch fork or a hoe in many a day. But Granny Iverson weren't that slow, and she be a whole mess older than storekeep man. He had no serious doubt that Cleve and old Rogerson went a ways back and that all their trades be on the up and up, but there seemed to be a gnaw in the pit of his stomach about this shenanigan.

"Ye want me go see where he be or you want me stay here with ye?"

"Stay here fer a bit. Iffin he ain't here pert nigh soon then I says go fetch him. Ye might step outside and see can ye spot him or hear him a comin'."

The old porch was just a flat rock or two covered over with a make shift shingle lean-to and a single sagging brace holding the whole thing in place. It did offer a fair vantage point from there to the barn lot. Jubal was somewhat taken by what he saw. Cleve was not coming by the barn lot as he normally would, but was standing on the upper side of the papaw thicket looking off up the hill in the direction of the old Miller place. Jubal stood silent and watched.

Cleve turned and started in the direction of the barn. Jubal hesitated until he had disappeared into the thicket, then returned to the old man's side. The deep set eyes were closed now, and he seemed to be in no bad discomfort, at least for the time at hand. His breathing was more regular now and color had perked up just a bit. It was still a fact that the old man had taken a good lick and that he needed care and needed it now. Any fool outta know that when a body got a whack to the head that left a gash near plumb over one eye and bled

59

a whole pool of blood that he be havin' a serious time of it. Take that cut a long time healin' up and scarrin' over.

"Cleve be near here now."

The old man opened his eyes briefly and replied only with an acknowledging grunt. He appeared to understand but not really care, at least for the moment. Maybe Cleve could get more outta him.

Cleve came in and stood in the door, looking around, slowly taking in the situation and surveying the inside of the place. Strange the way he eyed the place like he was looking for something in particular.

"Well, Wes, what in tarnation ye got into now?"

The old man raised up just enough to see who was askin'. "I ain't knowin' how come they whacked me. I ain't knowin' what they was wantin' other than eats. Told em I ain't got nuthin' to eat on," Wes replied kind of beneath his breath. "Must a riled them up a bit, cause they lit in on me right then."

"Say ye not knowed who they wuz?" asked Cleve.

"That what he said to me first off," Jubal added.

"Ye bring me a bottle, Cleve," the old man inquired.

"Yep, I did at that," Cleve replied.

"Well it ain't gonna do me no count less ye give it here, now is it?" A bit of sass recurrent in the impatient voice again.

"Settle yerself down a mite now ye ornery old cuss, and I take a look see to that old hard head bone. See if it been cracked open on not. I got yer medicine, but ye need hold up a bit, I reckon," Cleve chided.

Jubal had never heard these two banter back and forth in such a way and began to wonder just what there was twixt these characters. Cleve had spoke of Wes as far back as he could recall, and Wes had sent him to Cleve's store for this and that and always sent word that Cleve was to bill it up for him. Rumor was that Wes had sold a slave back long time past and had never been knowed to spend no cash money since.

Cleve had been the one to tell it and reckon he might like bein' the one to lay hands on it too. Ma always said that the best way to learn was to look and listen all at the same time. Reckon that there might just be a truth.

The thought of the slave money did flash in his mind a bit, and he stole a glance around the room just in case it were to be layin' out in plain sight. His thoughts began to fly to unlimited places and to see unknown things. Money could sure help in seein' all those drempt of places and havin' all them things that high falutin' folks had. He could dress fit enough to catch any young gal's eye. He could have three or four to the time iffin he was a mind to. Wouldn't never have to fret over eats and never would have to straddle old Kate no more neither. No sir, he could ride a chestnut mare six hands or better and have a silver saddle too, and boots rather than old brogues or deerskins. Some of these days, he aimed to make somethin' for himself and for his family, whoever that turned out to be. He weren't about to forget his Ma either.

Cleve ambled over to the pine-straw box bed and uncorked the jug. "Here Wes, sit up and take a pull on this. Take a good pull.

"Here son, sit up and drink this stuff. It be good fer you." It was Jugg and he placed a strong hand under Jubal's arm and near lifted him clean up. "Reckon you ain't eat nothin' much in about two days now, not since the ruckus commenced. Must be a mite starved, I says."

The boy was well enough and had rested enough to know that he was, indeed, hungry and thirsty to boot. His entire body still ached and every muscle protested at the command of movement. He did not yet realize that he had been stripped of his dust-laden and blood-soaked uniform, bathed, given a shave and sufficient laudanum to insure a measure of rest and sleep. His head had been washed and a clean cloth bandage applied over his wound.

Jugg touched the cup to his mouth and tilted it upward. Warm liquid coursed over cracked and sore lips, and his taste was rewarded by the taste of salt-seasoned cabbage soup, steeped with a mite of black pepper. Not every wounded Bluecoat solider had such luxury and such care, but not every Bluecoat soldier had saved an officer from sure death either. None of this made a matter at all for now; in fact, not much of it even came to mind right now. Things weren't more than a patch of thick fog for the most part.

Right now, he just wanted more in his stomach and water to his taste. The pieces and parts would all come together somewhere on down the way. No thought of that now.

Jugg took away the cup, but not before its entire contents had been taken in. He still held firm with his free hand and reached behind, sitting the empty cup on a nearby table. Gently he returned the boy to a resting position, after propping pillows under his shoulders and head. Broad shoulders and a gleaming white smile would have been hard for anyone to miss. Jubal looked up straight into that smile and felt a wave of comforting reassurance come over him. Sure Jugg had been told to look after him, but no one had ordered that he care about him. A man just can't be ordered to care, that has to come from the heart and be of the heart.

Knowin' that you are in good care was always a feeling that his Ma had given him when he was back home in the old log house at the head of the holler. That is till this here war came along and changed him. It changed a heap of things and a heap of people. It changed their ways and made them do things they never had done before. It stirred bad feelin' and harsh words where they never were before. It set family against family and neighbor against neighbor.

Homes and crops had been burned. Stock killed or run off and took but not paid for. Families had been split outta fears of one another. Many had fled north on the hope of freedom that they bore up under before, cause they had no other way of makin' a life for themselves. But some still kept the faith and tried to do what was right and tried to be a lamplighter. Jugg was a lamplighter.

"Looks like a mite rest got you comin' round some now. Ye seem to have a hanker fer eats now. That be a heap better'n when I done fetched ye in here day 'fore yesterday. Glad to see ye mendin' up some."

"Who you mean?" Jubal muttered.

"I be meanin' you, son, that who," Jugg answered as he looked softly into the boy's eyes, sensing his fear and his doubt. "I know you ain't full up on what come over ye nor how come ye be hurt. Major, he be tellin' it soon as ye be able I know, cause he done tell me he want me see to it you be took care of and that be what I tends to do."

"What? I have somethin' to do with this here Major who?"

"Major Dunn, son. Major Dunn, he be the ramrod of this here place and all us troops. He the one who make things keep in order and runnin' right. He were here bit back, but you wuz mite nigh outta yer mind then. Don't spose ye recollect about that none now."

The headache was still present, but some of the fog seemed to be gone. There were bits and pieces that came to mind, but it was nowhere near a clear picture, not yet. He remembered the clamor and the panic of the fighting and the scuffle. He could recall the heat of the midday blistering sun. His parched and cracked lips reminded him very well of that. He remembered something about a mounted rider and a fireball blast that seemed to obliterate all sound. It seemed like it had all happened long time past, but his sore and aching body told him that it had been only hours ago.

The foul odor of acrid smoke and burning powder no longer stung his nostrils or hung in his throat. Jugg had taken all that away with a shave and a cleanup fit for pay. A fresh shave rounded out the cleansing. The clean, soft bed had done wonders to the tired aching body. Sips of water and the cup of warm soup had helped in restoring the mind, but not all the way, not yet.

"What's yer name?" Jubal inquired.

"Jugg." came the response.

"Jugg! Huh?" Jubal parroted.

"Jugg Henry Carberry Dunn," he retorted with audible pride.

"Are ye a slave man?" the boy blurted out.

"My pappy and mammy still is, but I is a free man. Thanks be to the Lawd Almighty. Major's pappy gimme to him and he gimme my papers and sign me up and dress me out in this here blue coat outfit and gimme these here stripes on my sleeve. See here they is, right here, all time now. Major say I his order boy now, even how I be most as older as he be now."

"Don't reckon I ever knowed a slave. Ain't got none back in the holler where I come from," Jubal innocently replied.

"Well, don't reckon nobody gonna have none 'fore long. Major say Mister Lincoln done say he gonna make ever last one be free. That what this here war all about, son."

The innocence of a young age does not always mask curiosity about new places, strange faces and unknown customs. Such was the case with the boy in his encounter with the black man looking over him. He had not seen bondage nor cruel mastery of one man over another. He had never given a thought to the concept of liberty and freedom. He had known only what he had heard his Pa speak about, and that was the wanton desire that his Pa seemed to have to always be wanton to somehow rid himself of manual work. He spoke of havin' someone else do it for him and spoke like he had a right to it too only if he had money to buy a good workin' stout-bodied slave man. He had no concept that some of the answers to his questions could evoke pain and hardships of years of previous servitude.

"They chain ye up any?" Jubal asked.

"Not no more, they don't."

"I hear tell they has to keep chains on ye cause of ye runnin' off and such. That be what Pa used say."

"Son, you be young, and they be lot you ain't be unnerstandin'. I tell this much then you need a be rest up some more. Some don't need run cause they got a good massa and others got a cruel massa. Some got they spirit broke all down and some full on spirit what count most. You be learnt up on it some these days 'fore too long. Right now, don't make much matter cause you be young and not know better. One these here days you gonna see to the ways of the world and how bad they be and then you see the light maybe. Right now, jest shet them eyeballs, and I fetch more eats in a bit. I wake ye up when time come," he turned to go.

"Thank'e Jugg."

Jugg turned to face the boy. A broad smile crossed his entire face and eyes danced with laughter. He turned and was gone.

There was a foggy recollection about some ferry crossin' and a ruckus on the banks. There were strange faces but familiar voices. It was just mighty hard to sort all out, right now. Besides he was terrible hungry all over again.

Wes took the jug from Cleve and slowly brought himself to sit up enough to take a pull. Cleve just stood over him and watched his every move, saying not a word. Not really any reason to think so;

but seemed like there were more than met the eye goin' on twixt them two, seein' how they always was a mite edgy and such. Wes let the jug fall to his lap and swallowed hard. That brought on a cough fit and gasps for breath.

"That be fine squeezing, shore nuff," Cleve said in a snap. "Take ye some more, Wes. It'll perk ye right up."

More cough and hacks. Another long pull.

"That'll do me fer now," reaching the jug back to Cleve.

Naw, keep it. Ye be needin' more later on, ye old cuss."

Jubal was a mite taken aback by Cleve oathin' to him right to his face. "Why you call him like that Cleve, they be bad times tween you two or what?"

"We go back a ways, son. It ain't nothin' ye needs be all riled up over," replied the storekeep. "Wes just be old and set in his ways and ain't about nowhere near changin' not one bit."

The cough continued. The old man's face reddened and tears streamed down both rusty-wrinkled cheeks as he fought for the next breath. Each wretched cough gave rise to more air hunger and effort to breathe.

"Look at that now. He really be suckin' wind now," Cleve chided.

"Them squeezin' be a mite too much fer him. Ye done him no count by givin' it him in the first place iffin ye ask me."

"Don't recall askin' ye, son. Now do ye recollect as how I did?" There was a mite of anger in Cleve's voice now. "The whiskey kill the pain, and he ain't gonna need this here laudanum. Besides, I don't see nuthin' round here that he got to pay fer it with. I take this here back to the store and sell it where somebody pay me in gold, like yer Pa did."

Pa had bought laudanum and paid in gold! Now where in tarnation could Pa got a holt of gold in the first place, and why did he be needin' laudanum? He ain't been hurt none. Or had he? He had been off the land a lot here last few days and had been gone nigh two full days now. Cleve said he had rode off west on that broke down old bay and not said where he be headed.

Now here Cleve was throwin' out all manner of sayin's and givin' no answers to nuthin' nor nobody. That fact alone raised more thoughts than Jubal had considered before. Pa always spoke fair of

Cleve, but told how a body had better be watchin' in dealin's with him. Said he'd sell out his own soul to the devil iffin the price were good. Somehow that just stuck in the boy's craw, and it was a bit much just to let it pass, at least this time.

"Ye act like Pa be the only one ever buy laudanum from ye. I know ye got a whole case full, cause I seen it long 'fore now. Pa ain't never be one to be drinkin' it up all the time. Jest why ye be downin' him all so much now?"

"I ain't throwin' off on him none, son. It just be that whiskey don't give the kick that come outta laudanum, and I reckon yer Pa just needed a bigger kick this time," came Cleve's reply.

Another slam that raised even more questions.

"What ye mean, this time?" Jubal asked in as firm a manner as he had ever spoke to any growed up man about anything.

"Son, this here ain't no time fer ye be riled up over yer Pa. Ye gonna help me with this here gash on this old head bone or not?" Cleve bounced back.

Jubal held the old man's head cradled in his hands while Cleve poured whiskey stingily over the open wound. Some light wash caused some fresh bright red blood to ooze into the gash and run back into the hoary hair above the leathered cheek and ear. A fold of cloth and a snug wrap soon stopped the ooze. The old man was all about his wits and had near got over the cough, but he seemed to be weakened good measure by it all. He lay with his head in the boy's arms and looked up into his eyes.

Wes had said very little to him in a kind way all the times before when Jubal would stop by and look in on him or when his Ma had sent him a bite or two of vittles. Jubal would just come in and mull over the paper's big print and sketches for a bit. Wes would sit around on the porch in good weather and by the fireplace when cold came and run him indoors.

The boy in him thought that Wes was just an old goat of a man who weren't about to even give ye the time of day. On the other hand, he felt shame for him livin' the way he did. Dirt floor, and all that went with it. He never questioned him though cause he knew it weren't none of his business, and besides that Ma would'a whupped on him good fer not bein' respectful.

But now eyes that before seemed hateful and cutting were softer and seemed to be silently asking for help, for understanding and for mercy. They conveyed a measure of fear. Now, in the moment at present, the old man was completely in the hands of others and at their mercy to tend to his needs.

Cleve stood up and once again began looking all about the rumbled down old shack. Wes watched him with an eagle eye. Jubal continued to hold the old man's head in his arms. He could easily see the change of feeling in those all-telling eyes.

"Well, there ain't nothin' else I can do fer ye now, Wes, so I be getting' on back.

"Boy, com' here outside. I need speak a piece with ye," Cleve ordered, then stepped out into the late morning sunlight.

Wes reached up and laid a withered old hand on Jubal's shoulder. The look in his eyes had already returned to that of a soul in need. There seemed to be just a hint of a tear in the deep set eyes and a furrow across the leathered brow. He spoke in a soft and gentle manner. "I need tell ye a thing or so boy, so ye not be leavin' me here by myself till I says so, ye understand?"

"Yes sir, I reckon I do."

"Go see what storekeep say and then ye come back in here."

Gently he released his hold on the old grey head and eased it down on to the burlap bag of straw that made for a pillow.

"Boy, you comin' out here like I said or not?" came the impatient jab.

"I on the way."

Jubal joined Cleve outside but made no particular haste in doin' so.

Cleve immediately started in on him. "You ain't got no reason talkin' to me like ye be doin' in there. You don't know nuthin' about our deals and such, and it ain't needed ye know. I say he don't need nuthin' more, but what I done fer him. He just been whacked a mite on the head and addled him a mite. He needs rest up a bit and sleep it off now," Cleve continued.

"Whatcha want me do fer him then?" Jubal retorted, half asking half sassing Cleve.

"Makes me no matter what ye do, but I'm headed back to my store and tend business like usual. I done kilt half a day messin' round with ye two. He got some left in his jug and that outta see him through till ye can look back in on him in two, three days. He ain't hurt bad. He just old and cantankerous, that all." With that, storekeep turned and headed in the direction of the old shackled barn. He took a dozen steps or so and turned to face the boy.

"I'll be speakin' more with ye in a few days about this here matter. We be seein' what Wes has in his head. Be best if ye be recallin' all he be tellin' ye too," turning once again and heading out down the branch.

Jubal stood dead in his tracks and watched Cleve all the way out of sight. He stood still and quiet for a bit longer just to see if maybe Cleve would turn back again or what else he might be up to. He scanned the papaw patch intently but saw nothing more of the storekeep. He heard nothing more than the sounds of the hills that he knew so well and had learned to read near about as well as any in these here parts.

The stillness of the breeze combined with the sultry air told him that the weather was about to moderate and not too long off either. There might be some hope yet for rain. He would concern himself with that tomorrow. Right now he had the old man to tend to. He would do for him the best he knew how. Cleve shore seemed too put out to help him.

Back in the shack, it took a minute to adjust to the loss of noonday sun. He went to Wes's bedside and beheld again the fear in the deep set eyes.

"Wes, what do ye need me do fer ye now?" Jubal asked in a gentle, concerned manner.

He felt compassion for the old man. At the same time he did not really understand why. Wes had never really done anything for him or given him much more than the time of day. Yet he sensed the loneliness that he obviously felt. He could almost feel the fear that the eyes silently expressed.

"Ye think yer Ma might be up to sendin' me some taters and some ponebread, nuff to last me a day or so? I be thinkin' I fixin' to be called outta here. I ain't wantin' to go hungry in the wait."

"Is that be what scare ye a mite?"

"Naw son, I ain't 'fraid a passin'. I jest ain't hankerin' to be hurt no more," the eyes saying as much as the voice.

"I ain't gonna let nobody hurt ye long as I be round here," the boy declared.

"Reckon how long ye can stay with me, son?"

"How long ye want me stay?"

"I ain't knowin' fer shore, but I reckon ye got chores an sich to be tended to fer ye Ma. I ain't got no cause askin' ye stay when ye got work needs be done, but they ain't many here abouts that I'd have look in on me," Wes replied.

"How about Cleve?" Jubal responded.

"Pshaw, all Cleve be interested in be what he get off me. Ye seen what he done with the jug and laudanum. Good thing I ain't hurt no worse. Thousand wonders he fix my head up a mite."

"Dang him anyhow," Jubal intoned in defense of the old man.

"Well he be gone fer now. What time a day ye reckon it be now?"

"About high noon, I believe."

"That about what I think too. How long it take ye to git home and yore Ma fix a bite and git back here?" Wes questioned.

"I be back long 'fore sundown. Ain't that far."

"Tell yer Ma what done happen me and why I could use her fixin' me some eats and all. I be thinkin' that she be understandin' my troubles and not be put out none by doin' so fer me. She be a good old soul. I know fer shore."

Ironic that a rusty scoundrel more than old nuff to be her Pa would call her a old soul was the first thought to flash into the boy's mind, but just as quickly he knew that the old timer meant no disrespect by callin' her a good old soul. That, in fact, be a compliment to her. He knew well that his Ma would send whatever she had and would be glad to help any and all that she could.

"Gimme a pull at that there jug 'fore ye set out and then maybe I sleep till nigh time ye come back."

Jubal fetched him the jug and helped him to sit up on the side of the old pine-straw bed.

Wes turned it up and drained the contents.

"See son, what I say 'fore. Cleve never brung even a half jug. He more so must sold this here one already and just brung me the rittlin's. Ain't nuthin' to him when it come to money," anger replaced fear for the moment.

"He must be nigh on to a miser then," Jubal replied questioningly.

"That be what he always accuse me of last time we have any dealin's. He weren't always that a way. But since this here war be on, he just plumb loco. I ain't trustin' him much no more cause of it," Wes replied as the fear seemed to creep back in on him.

"Reckon if ye got all yer chores done up that yer Ma might see fit let ye stay the night here with me? Never know what a lick on the head might set off." Wes went on.

"Reckon she might at that now."

Wes shooed the boy out and on his way back to his own home and reminded him once again what he wanted from him and his Ma. The old man's voice still conveyed fear and a sense of urgency. Wes had never yet come right out and said so much as boo about bein' uneasy about himself, but Jubal just had a way about him that told of trouble on the rise for the old man.

The riders' tracks had not changed one bit since earlier when first spotted in the old orchard. No rain and no or little wind to wipe them out. Some of the stick weeds had stood back up again, but a blind mule could hold this track. Jubal stood in the track at the point it turned off up the ridge to the Miller place. He was tempted to go up the ridge and cross down to the old holler log road and go back home that way. It would only be an extra mile or so. There be plenty daylight left, and he could ask his sis to help him out on the chores and such.

The sun was hot by now and when he reached the ridge top, he had a good sweat. His breath came slow, regular and easy, and he could have gone on without a stop. Pa always said it be a good thing to take stock ever now and again when out and about in the woods and such. He stood still and listened. Nothing, but the birds. A lone crow cawed at him from high above as in defiance of his presence. One lone crow. Nothin' amiss there cause if they were trouble about, they sure be more than one squakin' his fool head off. The old bird soon flew beyond hearing, and the boy started down the side of the ridge with the track headed straight to the east. Brambles and bushes covered most ever thing, and the track skirted the worst of the thickets and honeysuckle mats. Numerous walnut trees stood along the edges of the bigger timber, and they hung heavy with green hulls. He would remember that come fall.

The trail cut the old log road just as he thought and went straight on to the Miller place at the rise of the road bank. The riders had laid down most of the rails and had not taken the time to put them back up. They had appeared to stop in the road and turnabout several times. The tracks in the dust bore that out plain as day. One mount was shod and the second was not. No boot tracks told that they never dismounted here. Still made little difference. A track this clear showed they were in no concern about being trailed. Most likely they be in a haste to scat plumb outta the country cause of how they done buggered up on old Wes.

Jubal turned and headed up the old log road toward home. Not more than ten paces, and there he saw it right smack dab in the road, plain as ever. Single track of the shod mount and boot tracks where its rider had got down. Boot tracks in the deep dust turned about a time or so then most likely remounted and rode back to where they first cut the road. There laid a short piece of rawhide strap, which might be used to tie on a saddlebag or such. Jubal bent down to pick it up and caught a sharp glint of sparkle coming back to him out of the dust. He stooped to retrieve the rawhide, and the glint was gone just as fast as it had come in the first place. He stood. There again was the glint. The reflection of the hot summer sun bounced back off whatever was there in the dust. This time he kept an eye peeled to the shine and followed straight to it. Reaching down to the glint, he did not at once realize what it was. Only a small part of the glint object revealed itself; the rest buried in the dust right in the midst of a hoof print. He picked it out of the dust and blew it off. A silver button with CSA embossed on it, just like the one he spotted the other time and dang near the same place too. There had to be Rebs about somewhere.

He reached home in hardly no time at all and began to tell his Ma all that had happened during the morning, except he purposefully left out everything related to the Rebs and the trackin' that he had done. He never told his Ma how Cleve made Wes seem so upset. He passed on all of the requests that Wes had made and what had befell him. He told her how the old house were about to fall in, and how the old man seemed to just be wallowing in his own filth seeing as how he weren't much able any more to do much for hisself. He also told her how the spring there was near dried up much worse than their own.

"Well, I knowed pine blank that there be somethin' the matter or ye would'a been back long 'fore now," Ma said. "Are ye hungry?"

"I can shore eat, that be a fact."

"We done all eat, but they's plenty left. Git warshed up a mite and I'll set ye a place," Ma commanded.

"What we gonna do about Wes, Ma?" Jubal asked.

"I see to it that ye be fed good and then ye take what be left and feed Wes. I can fix up more fer him tween now and mornin' and fetch it to ye both then." It was obvious that Ma had a concern for the old man, and Jubal recalled how many times before that his Ma had sent by him with a mess of this or that special when garden stuff was in. She never come right out and said so much but that were just the way she were. She shared what she had with them what needed it and never asked nuthin' in return. Always said that givin' was reward enough by itself.

"What about me stayin' the night with him?" Jubal asked.

"I reckon that be what needs be, son. They likely ain't much gonna come of it, but I think he needs seen to right smart," Ma stated as she set a plate for the boy.

"We ain't got no milk fit fer drink, son. The spring branch just ain't nuff to keep it no more. I fed the hogs and old Jake with it soon as I made bread this mornin'. We got three pone a biscuit bread and that be plenty fer us and fer Wes till I makes more. Sarry made it herself today," Ma informed.

"I not be needin' no cow squeezing no how, Ma. Is they any cold coffee left?"

"Hit's a bit stout. Ye want me water it down a mite?"

"Naw, I take a swaller or three now and take the rest with me to Wes," he answered.

"I fix ye a bedroll and ye can sweep off Wes's hearth and spread it there. That keep ye off'n the dirt and all. Ye might not sleep sound, but I be thinkin' ye and Wes be jawin' way in the night anyhow. I be there after first light and have fresh eats fer ye both, then we decide on what do next."

Jubal started to tell Ma more about the riders and all, but reckoned that there not be much cause to fret her over that now. Weren't likely that riders would come this far up the holler special since the road be dang nigh growed over anyhow. Besides that, Ma knowed how to fend fer herself and the gals. Granny Iverson would be the only thing that would slow them any iffin they had to light out somewhere. He had considered takin' the old squirrel rifle with him, but reckoned he'd just leave it this time. Weren't much powder left no how, and it be hard to come by now.

Ma rounded up a thick bedroll and tied it up with rawhide and a carry strap fixed to the tie on either end. She had packed eats in a small hickory-bark egg basket and put that all down in a miller's sack so as to make it a mite easier to tote.

"Why don't ye harness up old Kate and take her and Jake with ye?" Ma instructed in her usual manner. "They may come in right handy to you'ns, ye know."

"Now Ma, ye need not fret about me. I reckon old Jake best stay here and look about you and Granny and all. He sound off right now iffin strangers come through whilst I be gone. 'Sides that, I ain't too keen on you bein' here without no men folks here. Be best tie him so he not likely to be runnin' after me," Jubal stated rather firmly and with no more argument from his Ma.

"Reckon ye be heap more growed up than I give ye credit fer, son. I be knowin' I can trust in ye to be a man and honor yore word," Ma smiled as she bragged on her son. "I think ye best tote a lantern too, son. Wes may not have one or might not have no oil. I'll roll it up in another poke and pack it in a quilt. Ye can manage that way, can't ye?'

"Shore I can, Ma."

"Kate was in above the wheat house bit back. Go fetch and water her; she be good till past first light. Better take a hobble fer her too. She apt to be a bit roughish on strange pasture," Ma instructed again.

"Shucks Ma, ain't no pasture fer her there. She hafta eat brambles and stick weeds. That and papaws be all they is."

"Well I ain't been down that orchard path in many a day, but it weren't always growed up that a way. Wes used to keep his place clean 'fore his woman passed and when he was still stout. I guess loosin' her just plumb broke him, body and soul."

Strange to hear her talk on breakin' a body when she bound be thinkin' fresh on Pa not accounted fer. He wondered if he would ever know all that his Ma had put up with from Pa over the years. He could recall very little of them ever havin' harsh words or the likes, but he had seen enough to know that Pa had really hurt her deep more than once. She kept most all that tucked tight inside her, but sometimes just the look on her face said more than a whole mouth of words. Sometimes he had heard soft sobs when she thought all the young'uns were asleep.

His Pa had never laid a hand to him and most never raised his voice to him. He honest to God never thought that he hated his Pa; but if there was any hate, it was total on account of how he was by Ma. No real hate between father and son, but there was a mite of a wall betwixt them. He weren't knowin' if Granny Iverson knowed any of this or not, but knowing his Ma, he reckoned not. He weren't about to speak to his sisters over it, cause they most likely ain't seen nor heard none of them things in the first place.

"Kate done slicked off good. It ain't gonna hurt her none to eat honeysuckle a bit fer one night. Reckon Wes be needin' more whiskey or some laudanum durin' the night?" the boy asked.

"We see about that in the mornin' first thing after he eat a bite." Go on now, hike out and fetch Kate. Sun soon be gettin' low. Ye need soon be on yer way."

Kate was her usual ornery self when it come to being caught up. Jubal had stopped by the crib just in case she played out normal. He had done this trick many times before now, and it had always worked before too. Surprising what an old cuss of a mule will do for a couple nubbin's. Kate fell for it one more time and was just as soon in tow back to the house, bridle firmly in place. Gracie met him at the yard gate with two buckets fresh from the spring pool. Kate soon did away with them both. Jubal hoisted Gracie on to her back and led them both to the back porch. Gracie slid down right into Jubal's arms and wrapped her arms around his neck.

"Sarry said you was sweet on Lida," she whispered in his ear.

"Oh she did, did she?"

"Yep," followed by a big ear-to-ear grin.

"Well I tell ye little sis, Sarry don't know near as much as she lets on, but ye can bet that I be speakin' with her about her mouthin' off when there be no call fer it." He lifted her down and gently rubbed the top of her head and coal black hair. She seemed to have more injun blood in her than the rest of them did.

"Don't be payin' much mind to them now, son. Ye got other things needs tendin' right now. And besides that, it be fine iffin what they say is true. She be a fine upstandin' Godly young girl, and ye be a growed man most nigh too. Time ye be lookin' round a bit and start thinkin' on settlin' down," Ma intoned and at the same time quelled the snickers from Sarry.

"Ma, I reckon what ye say be the truth, but she don't much more than know my name."

"We see to that later on too," Ma said almost under her voice.

The evening sun bore down hot. Not much air stirred. Kate stomped at the flies till she made a dust pit right at the kitchen door. Jubal led her over to the old rail fence and tied her off there to the top rail. Ornery old cuss that she be, if she bolted then all she be tearin' down be the top rail. He weren't wantin' fix no fence now. Shade there make her a bit more at ease.

A few red clouds began rolling up in the west. No rain tomorrow. No rain tonight. Guess that be good seein' as how they must be more holes in Wes's shingle roof than there be bees in a bee tree. Bee tree. Pa must have knowed where everyone was for a hunnert miles. Pa, dang it, he outta be here now.

Ma soon had the bedrolls and the lantern all tied up and handed them off to her son. Gracie held up the miller sack. Jubal took it and laid it across the bedrolls. Tied it all together with deerskin and laid it across Kate's back. Balanced it side to side and led her back to the edge of the porch.

"Ma, keep Jake tied all night so as he won't track us. He thinks he be kin to old Kate, and he'll trail her most anytime.

"All right, son. I reckon ye be right about that too."

He took the reins and went out the yard gate and turned back to the west, pickin' up a sidling path up the hill to the line fence between them and the old Rogerson place. He could lay down three to four rails and Kate could step over easy. He had pocketed two more scrub nubbin's just in case she set to be ornery again. Then sun was near the crest of Pine Mountain, and there should be at least another hour of good light. He could make it to Wes in plenty time 'fore dark. Dark should bring a let up in the heat. Still no air moving about. Dry grass crunched under foot. Hoof clomps kicked up little clouds of dust.

He laid down three rails of the line fence, and bless Pete, Kate stepped right over just the way she outta. He laid the rails back up and gave Kate the nubbin's just for not actin' up. He led her off down the south hill in the direction of the old orchard. It would be in sight in no time now.

Chapter 3

Guidance

*D*awn seemed to labor at working its way into the barracks tent where Jubal lay on his back with hands folded behind his head. The first gray light defined only the outlines of things near him. Sounds of sleep and rest still wafted on the cool morning breeze. The sidewalls of the tent had been tied up and probably would not come down, but for sake of a blowing thunderstorm. Noonday sun and heat saw to that.

The lad had recovered from his wound enough that he could be up and about in short intervals. Anything of attempted endurance soon brought on the throbbing headaches and a diminished balance. Reason and reckon had returned to the point that there were many more unanswered questions now. Jugg had been an exceptional help in his recovery and had offered reassurance and comforting instruction at every opportunity. But yet, even the seemingly all-knowing stout-hearted and gentle sergeant could not provide all the answers and explain all the reasons why things sometimes worked out to be considerably less than what had been promised.

He had been told that the war was just as good as over and that if he volunteered he could pretty much rest assured of good pay and safe duty just about to his choosing, if he could just stick it out to the end of the fight. Here now he lay physically recovering, but very much dependent on others for his very substance. He did not even know where his meals came from, only that Jugg or someone in his control brought them on a regular schedule. Back home in the hollow, he and Ma and the girls had to work year round just to keep fed. Yet here he seldom felt any hunger.

How long could this go on, and who did all the work to keep ever body fed so well? It had not been like this at all to hear other men tell about what they had seen or had happen to them. Then he recalled some of the clouded recollections of the past few days. He almost gasped at the memory of the pale moon illuminating death's stare. Some could never tell their story. An often unmarked or lonely grave would be the only thing that could ever speak for them. And who would know? Who would care?

He had seen that face a thousand times over and never even knew a name or where he came from. Did he have family back home or was he just a drifter? Ever body needed to have somebody. No matter what they said, none were strong enough to stand all alone for very long.

His mind raced from one clouded memory, across uncounted miles to vivid memories of home and of his family. Hope seemed to be of little reassurance. Hope could not be held in the hand and weighed in the balance. Hope needed to be experienced in the form of a hug, a gentle kiss on the cheek, or a reassuring word from a loved one. Hope had to be felt to be real. He had hoped for a better life and more material prosperity by joining up with the Union. He had thought that getting out of and far away from Cane Valley would be all that he ever needed.

Reality had begun to set in on him just as had the coming dawn of a new day. Seems that home meant more than he had reckoned and in ways that had never thought before. Just being away and among strangers in a strange land had made him think of his family and the old log home more here lately. Wonder if Lida would still smile at the sight of him?

The first red light of the infant morning shone in the east as Jugg came to the bedside and spoke softly, "Up on yer haunches, son. See can ye hold out to set fer yer eats this fine day. Nigh time you wuz back at it and do enough to earn some keep."

"I ain't mindin' no work no time, Jugg. I just can't get all the things in a row what been the matter with me here last few days. I just ain't clear on things."

"Well, I ain't one to be quarlin' at nobody," Jugg replied, sensing he might have just rubbed a raw nerve. "I just wanna see ye up and mendin' up some. Ye took a right smart lick to that head, son; and you be plumb blessed to be here."

"Yeah, I guess I be a dab lucky after all."

"Now that ain't what I said, son. I said ye be blessed and that be just pine blank what I be meanin' too," Jugg answered without hesitation and with a stern look straight to the eyes. "Any old cuss can have a run of luck somewhere in his life and just maybe he never even know it or not even care; but it be a special man who be blessed, and I be knowin' that myself."

"How you mean by that?"

"Lucky be common as a man want it be, and it not be there his next breath when he need it most. There be no solid thing to hold on to with luck. It fade away just like the sun do when it go down."

"Yeah, I reckon that be some true."

"It ain't some true, boy. It all be true, and ye best be pay me some mind when I tells ye such. Luck be a man thing, but blessed be a Lawd thing; and they be a heap different. I knows that for most all my days now."

"Ye a church goin' man Jugg?" Jubal asked.

"I be that much as I can," Jugg softened his voice a bit. "You ever go to meetin's, son?"

"I been a few times back home, but I never give it much thought most times?"

The mere mention of the little church back home just down the cove road from Cleve's store evoked an instant flood of recent memories. Most seemed to center around Lida and the times that he had been near her while going to meetings. He had to admit, all be it to himself, that she was most of the reason that he even went there in the first place. He had considered himself lucky just to get her to take notice. And now here be a man, who had in such short time earned his full respect, yet was coming down on him and calling luck no more than what a man might wish on himself. His

Ma never said a thing about no differences twixt luck and other such as fate would deal out to a man, and she had been a Bible totter ever since he could recall. Besides that, Granny Iverson was the one that always be leafing through the Good Book.

He had always been upright the way Ma had said he ought be and never hurt narry a soul to the best he reckoned. Never took after matters sich as his Pa had been knowed to do and never had handled no bad talk neither. He knowed plenty so called church goers that had done right smart more than them things, and they ain't seemed to be no more lucky than himself. All that seemed to make any sense right now was that he was still drawing breath while others weren't so lucky. This here church going thing just seemed like it really made no big difference in a man's outcome, at least not in this here old war business. Biggest thing seemed to him to be how good a body could hold out in a skirmish or how he held on to an old hog rifle and how fast he could load and get off the next round. He seemed to have not recalled that the Union had given him the latest and the best arms available to use in his own defense.

Jugg stood with hands on hips and stared down directly into the boy's eyes with a look that could pierce all the way to the soul. "Ye best be learnin' about life, boy. How old ye be now anyhow?"

"Best I know, I be near twenty."

"Near twenty huh?"

"Yep."

"Well now that be fine iffin close always be good fer ye. What about when ye be skirmishin' and doin' all ye can to last out the fight? Would a close aim be good then, son?"

"No, cause I be dead on when I shoot," Jubal retorted.

"Then why ye not be dead on about answerin' what I ask ye? Life ain't gonna be nothin' near close. It gonna smack you with cold hard truth most times, and they be no near this or near that in dealin' with it none neither, boy. Ye hear me, son?"

"I hear ye, but what ye be tryin' say to me with all them words?"

Jugg took his right hand off his hip and pointed a finger straight to Jubal, so close that he reeled back a good bit in surprise. "Ye be in a uniform now, and I ain't really be knowin' much about ye 'fore I picked ye up at the ferry. I weren't thinking much about ye comin' around so fast back there, but I glad that ye did. I ain't been pushin' since then, but now ye be heap better; and I be thinkin' it high time ye be actin' like the trooper ye got recognized fer."

"What you mean Jugg?'

"First of all, solider, ye need call me Sergeant or Sergeant Dunn. Now I ain't tryin' to be hard on ye at all, but ye gonna have to learn to respect rank and authority and talk like ye know a thing or two iffin ye ever move up any in this here outfit. If ye call the Major by he first name or not salute him, then he likely be down on ye whole heap more than what I be tellin' ye. What ye done back there at the ferry crossin', I hear was a gooder thing to be doin' fer the Major, but that ain't gonna give ye no reckon to not show no respect to him nor nobody else out rankin' ye".

"I thought I were here just to kill Johnny Reb."

"They be much more to it than that, son. Killin' ain't no purpose and ain't no glory. How come ye join up in the first place, son?"

"I want things, and I thought I could get em here and make me some money all the same time. I never give much thought about shootin' at them Rebs."

"What things ye be speakin' of, son?"

"Well, I thinkin' I like have me a fine mount and a silver studded saddle. I ain't never had no good duds to set me off, and I never had nary a pair of boots till I got these here ones. Wouldn't mind to have a good piece a ground somewhere back home down on some river bottom. Grow me some good grain and have me some good stock and a good house."

"Uh hu, I see," came the reply from the sergeant. "That be what ye be wantin' outta life. That be what ye labor fer all that time till it come to ye?"

"That be what I be wantin' now, least part of it."

"Just what ye gonna do iffin ye get all that stuff, then what?"

More wandering thoughts and mind sets to faraway locations.

"Answer me boy, and not like ye did when I ask ye yer age," came an impatient jab of instruction.

"Jugg, I don't unnerstand."

"What I just be telling ye about respect fer rank? What I tell ye to be callin' me?"

"Sarge."

"No, I said Sergeant or Sergeant Dunn."

"Huh?"

"Son, ye got to listen me. I be tryin' to help ye."

The confusion and the bewilderment seemed to rise to crescendo. Uncertainty and lack of understanding certainly amplified the anxiety that had been sparked by the sudden verbal attack of the big stout man that had been so kind to him in the short time that he had known him. How could he treat him better than he had known from his own Pa and all at once turn on his every word and thought? Never had anybody been nowhere near like this back home. How can he care any about me and come down on me all the same?

"I just ain't understandin' what ye mean or what ye be wantin'. I ain't tryin' be smart nor nothin'," Jubal retorted.

The broad-shouldered man gently kneeled down and looked in the young lad's face and spoke in a soft voice, but yet a tone that commanded attention. Somehow Jubal sensed the intended seriousness.

"Son, ye ever talk back to yore Ma or Pa?"

"My Pa never be around too much last few years, but he drive me hard when he be at home. He work me hard, but he never help out much with crops and such."

Jugg sucked in a long and deep breath and allowed it to slowly escape his massive chest before he spoke again. He leaned in just a bit closer to the face opposite him. "Son, I ask ye a direct question and ye talked all ways around it and still never give me any answer that I accept. Now what I wanna know is iffin ye talked back to yore Ma or Pa?"

"No."

"And why not?"

"Cause my Ma never would stand fer sich. She'd thumped on me good fer that."

"Threat of a thumpin' be the only reason ye not sass them?"

"Well no. They is my Ma and Pa, and I been brung up to know young'uns ain't spose be sassin' no elders of any kind."

"Glory be. Then reckon ye recollect that yer Ma done learnt ye a mite bit of what we talkin' here. Ye never talk back cause ye been learnt to respect her just fer the simple fact she be yer Ma, and she done long ago earned that just by givin' ye birth. One these here days when yore respect be due ye then just maybe ye might learn respect for others too. Yer Ma be authority over ye and rightly so. But she be back home. I be here, and ye be here. They always has to be a boss man, and I be it fer ye and fer most all else in ranks 'round here. I tell ye fer shore that I done earned respect fer all that I done skirmished fer in all my years in this here army. I gonna get that respect from you too, cause I don't wanna see none of my boys abused by nobody that ain't got no call doin' so. Do ye have any inklin' what I be sayin' to ye?"

"I reckon I respect ye iffin that be what ye be meanin'," came the reply.

"Least ye be headed right. I ask ye straight out, do ye know why I want ye to show respect?"

Again confusion slowed a response from the boy. He opened his mouth and moved his lips, but no words came forth. His mind raced back to his Ma as he desperately tried to justify the way that he felt so close to her and at the same time felt so unattached to his Pa.

The sergeant spoke softly again, "Son, I wanna be able to respect ye just same as all these other troopers here. But ye gotta earn that from me and from ever body else. I want ye to have respect cause I care about ye. I care about what gonna happen fer ye."

"How come you be carin' anythin' fer me? I jest been knowin' ye a day or two?" Jubal asked, still confused.

"That be takin' a mite of splainin' and there be not time 'nuff right now. We best be off to that mess tent, else we miss gravy."

Old Kate seemed to be in no particular hurry or bother as the pair rounded the bottom of the hill. The sun had long since ducked down behind Pine Mountain, and the last rays of crimson faded fast in the west. There would still be plenty of light to make the last quarter mile or so to Rogerson's old shack. There were a few scrappy knots of apples here and there as they made their way into the orchard. Kate smelled them and pulled at the bridle to try and steal one on the go. No way to let that come about. She be an old mule and somewhat all broke down, but she weren't gonna be let choke on no scrappy apple knot.

When he reached the house, he tied Kate up close and went in to check on the old man.

Wes was asleep, but roused up at the first creak of the old door. The light inside the old house was just about all used, but Jubal could see right off that the old man seemed to be a bit better than when he left him alone earlier.

"Got me some of yer Ma's cooking, do ye?"

"I brung ye some ponebread and cold coffee, that all Ma had till mornin' come. Hope it do fer now," Jubal answered.

"That be fine. Beggar ought not be fussy about what he be give."

"Ma said she bring us more come mornin'."

Wes seemed to be a bit taken aback by hearing that more good eats be here soon after sunup. After all, it had been some time now since Ma had sent by the boy with most anything. He normally was never a big eater and could go a day or so and not really be too much put out by not having proper food. However, he was not gonna be one to turn down good cooking.

"I be obliged to ye and to her, son. But what in tarnation make her, or yerself fer that matter, take any a care about an old cuss like me?"

"Well you be a man, I reckon. A good man at that. Ain't no fault ye be on in years, I reckon, and ye be needin' help. We be able to give help and that be our job way I see it. I reckon a body is bound to give help to them what deserves it when they be in need, and ye be needin' tended to and helped a mendin' up a mite. I be thinkin' that ye most like done that very same for others in time. Like says, ain't no fault you be on in years, and Ma always tell me it my duty to others to be there when they be in need."

Wes soon had the ponebread put away and turned up the jar of cold coffee. "Ye be some right there, son. But it been plenty days gone by since I done any pore soul a good turn. Most my days is behind me now, and I can look back and see plenty times I outta did more".

Darkness soon hid most everything in the room. Then Jubal remembered that Kate was tied just outside the door. Hard tell where she might traipse off to if she not be hobbled. With instruction from Wes, he soon fashioned a hobble from a short length of old cowhide and some old rags that had been hanging from a peg beside the crumbling old stone fireplace. The cowhide would restrain old Kate's step, and the rags would pad her legs to keep her from fretting over the hobble. He soon had the hobble in place and loosed the reins from her bridle. He thought a minute or so about leaving her bridle in place, but reckoned she might be a bit more at ease without it. He hung it on the porch post and let her loose. She not much more than turned till she was nuzzling at what little dried up grass that she could find.

Back inside, he soon had his bedroll spread in front of the fireplace and stretched out on the roll. It was only then that he begun to feel the day that was fast ending. Not much of a job to recall all that had gone on earlier, most of that clear as a mountain creek. Alert enough to be able to sense any varmints or critters, but tired enough that not apt to have no trouble dropping off to sleep. Besides that old Kate made a right good pair eyes at night, and she shore could let out plenty warning if necessary.

Wes had ears and eyes like an owl on the coldest winter night. Them two on the lookout, and he ought be able sleep plumb through till sunup. He reckoned that long as he got up time Ma got there then ever thing be good. If old Kate just halfway act herself, then she be good too. He thought a minute that he wished he had let Jake come too, but then he reckoned Ma needed him worse. If somehow Jake did show up and it still be dark, then there be another matter back home with Ma and the gals. The old redbone hound would and could easily track him and Kate. All Ma would have to do would be turn him loose and tell him to go. He hoped that he would not see the dog before daybreak.

He heard Wes complain softly to himself about that coffee runnin' right straight through. A few shuffles and grunts, the sound of the old door swung open, and then some effort in returning to the pine-straw box bed left the old man wanting for his breath. A few breaths came really hard and then began to ease up a bit. Jubal listened to him a good while before reckoning that he was okay and at rest. Soon sounds of sleep were coming from the box bed.

The only other sounds were those of the night that were heard most ever hot summer night. High above, somewhere up in the flats, a hoot owl and a screech seemed to be in a race to see who could call the loudest. But they would all soon stop their shenanigans and get down to a night's hunt. Long as they were making a ruckus, then no need to fret over them. The ones that made nary a sound be the ones that gotta be worried over. They be cruel tormenters and killers, both man and critter.

Jubal had been sleeping sound most all night when he heard Wes cough and sputter like he be nigh on choked. He lay silent for a bit to see if the old man would gain his breath back again or just keep a hacking and a barking. The cough soon subsided and he seemed to be a mite more restful, but he had some wheeze to his breath.

"Wes, ye be at yerself and be waked up?"

"I waked up, but I ain't rightly at my whole self. My side be trouble to me. It be a heap sore. Guess it be that whuppin' I taken off them two."

"Ye be needin' me up tendin' ye or such? Ye need me fetch fer ye?"

Wes coughed hard and winced in the resulting pain. Darkness hid the expressions of such, but the lad knew enough to realize that the weathered old face told the truth of the hurt and the inflicted injury. Soon the coughing spasm subsided and the old man spoke softly. "Reckon ye might find me my jug iffin ye can. A pull might ease me some and quell this here bark."

"Where ye reckon it be, Wes, or ye druther I call ye Mr. Rogerson?"

"Ye call me airy ole cuss ye want, boy. It don't make me no matter no more. Funny ye ask me that in time like this here."

"How that be?" Jubal quired.

"Would ye be here seein' to me right now iffin yer Ma ain't tellin' ye so?"

"Well, I guess maybe. I ain't know fer sure cause she be the one knowin' what need be did fer ye. I ain't never took care folks round these parts 'fore the war commenced. Neighbors and families always on hand fer that back then."

"But do ye be put out a mite by havin' be here seein' after me?" Wes inquired.

Jubal almost came out with a mite smart answer, but held his thoughts inside for a bit. He was not sure where the old man was about to lead.

"I know ye be here since yer Ma tell ye that what ye need do; but iffin she not tell ye that, would ye be here on yer own?"

"I reckon iffin I be able be of any help, then I be here."

"I be glad ye say that, son, cause that tell me a lot of what ye be made outta. I know ye be almost a full growed man now, but still got a mite yet ye bein' need knowin'."

"How you mean?"

"Ye be a body who care about others, and I be thinking ye be honest too. Yer Ma see that be so. I been knowin' her and yer Pa long time now. I all time know she be upstandin' and good hearted. She used be church goin' too 'fore yer Pa done been sluffin' off on his work and earnin' keep fer her and her brood. I be thinkin' ye got more her in ye than ye do yer Pa. That not be a bad turn either."

A flood of thought raced through the young boy's mind. He had always been much closer to his Ma, but over time his Pa had learned him a lot about life in the hills and mountains. Pa never had much of a kind word that he ever could recall, least not to him.

He always had more work and chores that needed be done and always trying to get outta doin' them his own self. That made him think about all the hard slubbish work that Ma had to take on and do. That made him not feel much for his Pa. He done run plumb off this time.

"I ain't seen Pa in a few days now, and I really don't much reckon I be put out by it none either," Jubal mused much to himself.

"Yer Pa ain't up to no good, boy. I know that right off. He lookin' fer quick money and a poke full a gold pieces. I know that. He not be far from them two that work me over."

Jubal managed to find the jug and felt his way along the dirt floor with one foot slow stepping till he got to Wes. No starlight came into the darkened room, but the old man reached and accurately took the jug from Jubal's outstretched arm. The smell of the shine came on strong, and the jug sounded empty as it thumped down on the dirt floor. Wes had most sure took it all in one pull.

"What ye be knowin' about my Pa and gold and all that?" came a quick reply.

"Well, son, would ye be thinkin' that a old cuss like me be livin' in a dirt floor shack iffin he had gold money?"

"Don't rightly think so."

"Ye got any gold, son?" Wes asked him point blank.

"Got me one piece."

"Ye keep it on ye?"

"Naw. Ma say I be apt loose it that way, and it soon be slick wore down iffin I tote it all time ever day."

"Yer Ma be dead right. Ye best be puttin' it up someplace good where ye be only soul know where it be hid. It do ye some good someday, but ye need not be reckonin' on what do with it now. Ye be too wet 'hind yore ears be knowin' that now."

"I done been thinkin' I buy me some good lookin' duds with part my gold," Jubal said with more thoughts and ideas racing through his mind. Lida would be impressed by him then and just maybe so would countless other young lasses in just as many faraway places as he cared to travel to. He never gave a thought to the supply of gold ever runnin' out.

"You got any gold, Wes?"

"Ye ought not be askin' me on a thing like that, son."

"But you just now asked me the very same thing," Jubal retorted.

"I know what I be askin' ye, son. I had good reason be askin' ye that."

"What reason?"

"We talk more on it some other time. Best ye get yer sleep now. Be light soon and then ye hafta go fetch Kate."

Sleep soon came, but only to the old man. His breath came slow and regular. No sound of him stirring around in his old pine-straw box bed. He had raised some more thoughts and posed more questions than he had spoke. Why would he talk about Pa in one breath and then switch to gold in the next? Many things drove the sleep from him the rest of the night, but none more powerful than the hints of a bag of gold and all the lustful things that it could buy for him. He reckoned this old wreck of a man had nary a copper cent, let alone a poke filled with gold dollars, real gold and none of this here war money neither. Why else he be living in such filth and trash and have on rags for clothes? Ain't a lone thing in this whole house be worth being toted off, that a fact. He lay back on his bedroll and once again had thoughts of faraway places. He did not think very long before sleep blacked out all thought.

The big burley Union sergeant seated Jubal at a makeshift plank table and walked away without any further word. The lad looked around him. The tent was large by his measure, two center poles near high as a barn. Light canvas cover with sidewalls all rolled up and tied in place. A peripheral ring of iron stakes secured heavy ropes that held the tent in place and erect. The early morning light showed several tables and accompanying wooden plank benches. Hardly anyone else sat at any of the tables.

One end the big tent was occupied by a wooden platform that was surely the mess cook's area. Grey smoke rose slowly from the stacks of three cook stoves just on the outside edges of the wooden platform. A good sized rack of firewood lay near. Several buckboards and a covered wagon, all without their hitches, stood just beyond the cook stoves. Activity around the area was intense. Apron-clad men scurried all about the hot wood fired stoves, and others worked at nearby tables. The chatter of numerous mixed voices and the clamor of all the activity translated into an undecipherable din to all but the strongest and most intent ear.

The boy had not seen such sights in long days now. He could not recall every event or happening of the last few days. His head still pained him considerable when he sat up fast or got in too much of a hurry. Most anything hurt that required more of him than just reasoning about himself.

Looking out the other end of the tent, Jubal could see a good-sized old frame house with a porch that appeared to run all the way around, at least as much as he could see from where he sat. Beyond the house lay a meadow filled with several unsaddled horses, all busy picking at the short, dry grass. Across the meadow could be seen a slow rising hill with scrub bush giving way to full growth timber. The land seemed to be gently rolling and a mite pleasing to behold. No steep ridges or deep shadow laden hollows. The countryside itself gave no hint of the mortal conflict that it had hosted.

Faint sounds drifted into the tent from all sides. No familiar voice could be heard. No clear voice for that matter, but there was no sound of cannon fire or the rat-a-tat rattle of musketry. This place, wherever it was and whatever it was, seemed to be a place of peace and refuge, a welcome refuge. He recalled in an instant how his Ma had often spoke of a haven of rest and a refuge; a place where there was a peace and quiet and labor weren't so hard no more. His mind raced again, back home to the old log house of his boyhood home, still his home.

He turned to face the center of the tent just in time to see the broad shoulders of Jugg. In that same instant the shoulders turned and Jugg pointed a hand straight at Jubal, while continuing to speak to one of the apron-clad cooks. Stare from deep set eyes followed down the outstretched arm and welled over the boy like a surging tide. He did not have all the facts straight, but he recalled enough to remember that this big stout black man had helped him when he was hurt, when he needed help in the weakest moments. He had been befriended by a strange man in a strange place and for reason that he knew not. His chin sagged near his chest, and his eyes fell to his feet. Emotion welled up in him as he realized that he himself was a stranger in a strange land. Loneliness knocked. He felt its presence.

Hardly noticed, one of the mess cooks approached Jubal with a tin plate, a fork and a steaming cup of black coffee.

"Sergeant said give ye this and make dang nab shore ye eat it all too." He sat it down before Jubal rather abruptly, wheeled around and was back at the cook stove in a hurry.

Hot meals were not so easy to come by for all hands at all times. Not much thought had been given to eats these last few days; but the smell of side meat and coffee stirred an appetite. And the sight of big cathead biscuits smothered in gravy could make near any old cuss be starved near to death. Jubal wasted no time making short work of the entire plate. When he did look about him again, the empty tables began to fill with blue uniforms, most all spotted about with blood stain and fresh bandages. No one seemed to really care what went on or who spoke or who didn't. All eyes seemed to be fixed on the apron wielding man that Sergeant Jugg had spoke to earlier.

A loud clang and at its onset all the tent dwellers sprang to action. All moved in a wave to the cooks and the business end of the place. Seems hot food got a way of getting attention of ever single soul there abouts. The men formed a rough line, some leaning on others, who be better able to get about, others hopping on canes and crutches. Jubal sat in silence, trying to reckon it all out and make sense of it all.

"Get up son, get in line iffin ye wanna eat this here fine mornin'," said a familiar voice.

"Yes sir," Jubal replied without even turning his head to the voice. He knew who it was. He just could not understand why the total stranger, up till just a few days past, why would he care about me?

The men moved about the tent in an orderly manner. Jubal soon found himself holding a fresh plate with another slice of side meat and more biscuits. He made no hesitation in taking them and found his way back to the empty plate that he had just finished. He sat down and began to eat. Looking out the side of the tent, he spotted the sergeant with a coffee cup in one hand and biscuit in the other, and all the while talking to someone that Jubal vaguely recognized. No doubt that Sergeant Jugg had somehow seen to it that he got a double portion his first day up and about. Did he do that for all these other poor souls on their first day or what? Unanswered questions made no matter when it came to the biscuits. They were soon gone just like the first ones.

The same mess cooker bellowed out instructions how each man was to wash up his own plate and bring it forward to one of the designated private cooks. As the men finished their meal, they complied with the instruction, all be it too slow to suit the loud-mouthed apron guy. Jubal did as he was told and started back to the rear area of the tent. It all at once dawned on him that he had not noticed in the first lights of the dawn, which way he had come from. Nothing seemed familiar as he scanned his surroundings.

A hand touched his shoulder and a strange voice asked, "Ye be the one what saved the major?"

"Huh," came an unsure reply.

"Sergeant Dunn say that I best make sure ye get back yer tent safe and sound. So ye best let me show ye where yer bunk be. Ye need be shaped up a mite. I think they be comin' talk with ye soon. I'll be right back with ye a clean shirt and some boot black. Be best iffin ye get spruced up best ye can."

"Who comin'? Talk about what?"

"The major and the sergeant, that who! They done told me get ye ready, and I be tellin' ye that ye best get to it. Now get washed up whilst I fetch yer things; be smart about it too."

Jubal had no real reason to know what they might be wanting to discuss, but that did not stop his wonder and his imagination running the gauntlet from praise and adulation all the way to scorn. After all, Jugg had been a mite stern with him; and he could not reason why, at least not to his way things stacked up. Callin' him by his given name stead of by his rank did not seem to be such an issue. Some things in this here Bluecoat business just weren't all clear. After all, armies was most bent on skirmishin' and the like. One army was spose be whuppin' the other. He reckoned that he been doin' a right smart share of that here lately. Even took a rifle ball in the head fer all the troubles they put him to.

At any rate, he pulled the dirty, sweat and blood-stained shirt over his head and began to lather up his arms and face from the iron pots placed on rough-hewn boards that were supported between two stumps. The trooper that had led him here seemed to know more about army stuff than most. He looked right sharp too, with black polished boots and belt. Had a blue Union uniform with nary a smudge and a dinky little cap that sort'a fell off on one side of his brow. Had his hair all cropped off short too.

Jubal stuck his face down into a large pot and began to splash water onto his head and ran wet fingers through his hair. The bandage over his wound easily loosened and quickly fell away. It was coated with dark crimson dried blood. He looked at it for a bit, threw it aside and resumed his grooming. Fingers creased across the wound to his head. No sign of fresh blood or drainage. He could feel a thick scab all along the side of his temple and knew that any agitation from his probing fingers would result in bright red bleeding. Best let well do.

Fancy pants soon returned with clean clothing, boot black, a razor and a pair shears.

"These may be a bit big on ye, but they all we got. They be better'n what ye had when we drug ye in here. Looked like a stuck hog that day, I tell ye. Give ye a clean shirt and fresh bandage then, but ye done dirtied and sweated them up in no time."

"What be yore name?" Jubal asked

"Young, James Young"

"James, what this be all about? I ain't right clear on what all be goin' on or what done been happened."

"Well, all I know is that ye took one up side the head and still made way to the major whilst he were still down, and somehow or 'nuther ye done get him up and outta the ruckus. I reckon ye done save his hide," James answered.

Jubal still had a puzzled look about him as he started to put on the clean shirt.

"No, wait," James commanded. "I gotta cut yore hair a mite first, then ye gotta shave. Ye do shave that peach fuzz, don't ye?"

"Reckon I do at that," Jubal replied sarcastically.

"Sit here," James said. "I best whack off that mop a dab."

"Cut it all off short; it be a mite hot on a body's head anyhow," Jubal stated in some distrust of his new-found companion.

The sprucing up was soon complete, haircut, shave and all; and the lad did take on a bit more likeness to that of a real Union solider. James then led him to another area near the old frame house, quickly schooled him on how to snap to and throw a salute and best he could as to when and where to do so.

James ushered Jubal onto the long porch all the while giving him last second instruction. A lone sentry stood at the front of the structure and glanced longingly out across the immediate surroundings. Soldiers mingled about in all directions involved in what appeared to be a sea of disarray and confusion. No one seemed to really be accomplishing much at all, save for the cook tent. They were already at work with what would be the next meal. A few horses ambled about without bridle or rein. Others were tied to a rope line strung between a slim white oak and a nearby limestone outcropping.

Grey smoke curled up from a lone camp fire. Rows of tents gleamed in the morning sun.

Soon Jubal was called into what at one time had surely been a parlor, but now served as an outer office to the commander. A clerk at the desk asked his name.

"Jubal."

"Full name, son."

"Jubal Clay Stewart."

The clerk scribbled for a bit on the paper in front of him, then stood and told the boy to stay put. He turned, knocked three rapid raps on the door and entered when instructed. In short time he exited the room and spoke to Jubal.

"Knock, as I did, and go on in. Just remember who you be talkin' to and who they are," instructed the clean cut, sharp dressed clerk.

He knocked and entered as instructed. Sitting behind a desk was Major Dunn, and standing to his right side was Sergeant Jugg. Jubal saluted crisply as instructed and reported as instructed. "Private Jubal Stewart reporting as instructed, sir."

The Major responded, "Good Morning."

"Good Mornin' Wes?"

Ma's voice shocked Jubal from a comfortable sleep to a sit-up surprise. A few eye rubs and he was alert and up to his feet. Wes had apparently slept well on the jug pullin's. Ma began to unpack the basket that she and Julie had toted all the way across the north hill, down to the once-was orchard and on to the house. The smell of sausage and biscuit bread began to replace the musty and earthy odor that the boy and the old man had breathed all night. That fresh aroma soon instilled awareness of how long it had been since the last full meal. It caught the attention of the old man too.

Ma and Julie soon had a generous portion handed out and set about to pour fresh warm coffee for them. Both ate as if it were to be a last meal. Wes seemed to be stronger this morning and got out of his pine-straw bed alone and went outside, apparently to relieve himself. Ma watched him closely until he disappeared into the papaw thicket.

Wes soon returned and reported that Kate was nipping at the dry grasses just on the far edge of the papaws, but that the hobble had come off. She could spook fairly easy in unfamiliar places. Jubal set out to fetch and bridle her again.

Ma began to question Wes. "Ye be yore self, Wes. Ye be about over gettin' whacked on yore old gray head?"

"I reckon I be sound 'cept fer sore in my ribs."

"Now Wes, I ain't be meanin' nuthin' by askin' ye, but how long since ye be cleanin' yerself up some?"

"Some time now I reckon since waters be dried nigh up," Wes responded. He looked at his clothing and at his hands as if to find himself more presentable than he actually could lay claim to. "I just seem like it don't make no difference no more since my woman passed. I know that ain't no reason, but I be gettin' well on in years and that be all right by me. I guess I just be bidin' my time."

"Well Wes, I believe that sometimes the people ye care most for in life is took from ye way too soon, and ye not always unnerstand why," Ma said in attempt to soothe the old man. He held his head in his hands and remained silent.

Ma remained silent. She wondered to herself how old the bearded man might be and what kind of life he had lived before he seemed to lose himself in all this loneliness. She wondered what he would be like if cleaned up and proper cared for. His face and arms were weathered mite heavy, but the muscles and sinew in his arms still rippled with his movement.

Wes finally spoke. "Plain fact I let things go fer long time now. But seem like losin' her just took all the sap right outta me. She were all I ever had 'sides this old place here and the acres 'cross the north hill. Ye know them all too well, I thinkin'."

"I recollect when ye be a hard worker, Wes. Ye was at it daylight to dark when crops be in and always got things in 'fore hard frosts come. I know ye ain't a lazy cuss ner nuthin' like it. Ye just had yer spirit broke."

He raised his head and looked into her eyes questioningly.

"Sometimes Wes, we just need take one day at the time and make most of what it offers. We not be the ones who know all the answers, and we not know what the next day be bringin' us. Matter fact we ain't give no promise of the next day, and we be blessed we ain't got yesterday to do over again."

Ma had seemed to capture his attention. "I know I just let myself go most times, but I got trouble seein' much worth outta life now. 'Sides that, I ain't got no kin no more. It just be me."

"Ye got yer friends and neighbors round here, I reckon," Ma injected.

"They ain't givin' me no thought cept fer you and yer boy. Ain't nary a soul ever come 'round here save Cleve, and he only come when he think he get a dollar outta me."

"Ye ever go see any of them, Wes?"

"Ain't nobody want see a old geezer like me."

"Why ye think that be, Wes?"

"Well look at me. Would ye wanna be spotted with me?"

"Looks is on the outside, Wes. A real body be on the inside," Ma responded curtly. "No matter how hard yer heart be broke, the world ain't about to stop fer yer grief. Ye just gotta keep on keepin' on. How old ye be anyhow, Wes, iffin I should ask such of ye?"

"I reckon I be fifty-four come winter."

"Well, now just ye take a good look at yerself. Ye look a hunnert or better." Again Ma let her thoughts run where they really ought not. She pictured, or tried to picture, him with clean pressed clothes, slick shaved and hair cut proper. She wondered what looks may be underneath all them whiskers. Julie's laugh brought her back to reality.

"I speck I do at that," Wes replied rather meekly.

"Iffin we was set on cleanin' ye up a mite, then I thinkin' ye be feelin' a mite younger by it too. Least it make ye feel fresh. I tell ye, Wes, ye could stand a piece of that. Ye be a bit rank, that be a fact," Ma responded as Julie snickered again.

"Hesh that young'un," Ma corrected sternly. Julie immediately became mute, turned her back and found something that needed her attention and efforts. She chose to roll up the bedroll for her brother and tie it up proper.

Kate remained near the upper edge of the papaw thicket and made no effort to run or wander away as Jubal approached her. She had been at liberty all night long to nibble at whatever suited her fancy. From the looks of her sides, she had found plenty to her liking. She accepted her bridle without incident and soon found herself being led back where she was hobbled the night before.

Jubal was in no particular hurry to return to the old man's shanty of a house; he too had had his fill. Fresh biscuits and good sage sausage really could stick to a man's ribs. He stopped as he led Kate out of the thicket and looked around in the dust a bit. If he went to the right, he would be back at the house in no time. He led Kate to the left, down the branch path toward the road that eventually passed Cleve's store. He recalled Cleve stopping somewhere near and looking back for a spell. "It just don't set quite right," he muttered more or less to himself. He continued along the branch path for a bit until he came to tracks that cut the path. Riders' tracks and footprints too.

Some hoof prints were overstepped by footprints, and some of the footprints had been trod on by the mounts. Best he could tell there were three mounts, two shod and one not, mixed in with a set of boot prints. A few yards down the path he could see that the boot prints ran off near the branch and that no riders had gone that way. Retracing the rides was no effort. Three sets of hoof tracks, two shod and one not, made way clear above the thicket. There more boot prints seemed to lead into the thicket. They led to the point where he had just bridled old Kate and were obliterated by her night's trompings.

He was right back where he had started from but armed with just a bit more to stir his pondering now. This time he turned left and was soon reining up old Kate to what had at one time been the garden gate post. Now it was just a lone sentinel, a solitary red cedar post that had witnessed not only the activities of the previous day but untold previous days and nights.

Julie appeared at the door, hands on hips, "I got yer bedroll all tied up fer ye."

"Good, I be thankin' ye, sis."

"Ma say we gonna clean up Mr. Wes and cut he hair and shave he beard too."

"She say that?" he asked.

Ma emerged from the door, hands on her hips too. "She say that fer a fact, and I need ye bring me water and start a fire," Ma instructed.

"Ma, I start fire in no time, but they ain't no water in this branch, nuthin' but mud and Kate done been trompin' all in it. They ain't water there to wet a cat's paw.

Ma stood silent, hands on hips for what seemed long enough to drown a cat. Without a further word, she wheeled and went back inside, closed the door and stared straight into the old man's weathered face.

"Wes, I be takin' ye to our place so's ye can clean up some, and I can cut that mop ye be wearin'. I guess we gonna need scrape them beards like scrapin' a fresh scalded hog."

"Naw, now I ain't aimin' ye no trouble."

"Wes, ye need tendin' and I aim to do it. Now ye be havin' anythin' in here ye don't want left here. Ye best be tellin' me so's I can fetch it all up and tote it with ye."

"I ain't gonna put you'ns out none like that. I be good in day or so."

"Now Wes, ye've had a lick up side ye head, and I be tellin' ye that ye need it tended to. Won't do ye no harm be fed some too. We got garden and such and ye not be puttin' us out none. We find some place fer beddin' ye down proper like."

"I can't go."

"Why not?" Ma asked rather stern like.

"All I got is right here, and this be where I outta be."

"Wes, I can hear yer breath rattled clean 'cross to here. I know ye need be tended to. I know ye need come with us so's it be done proper."

"But how come ye be concernin' over me? I ain't nothin' to ye now as I see."

"Wes, they not be no need fretin' so much now. I reckon it be what I ought be doin' fer any soul needin' my help. Good Book say so, and I know ye read that yerself time and time over. It just be the right thing, and I wanna be doin' what be right by most folks. Ain't nuthin' but proper."

Wes stood and started to speak again but was promptly dressed down again by a determined, good-intentioned woman and mother that Ma reckoned to be. She instructed her son to get old Kate up to the edge of the porch so Wes could climb on her broad back and ride her back across the north hill and then down to their place. Jubal could lead the animal slow like so as not to be a threat to Wes from her throwing him.

"Wes, they be anything here that ye need take with ye? Anything ye not be wantin' leave behind fer a few days?" Ma inquired.

"There be at that," Wes replied.

"Well what it be and I fetch it fer ye?"

"Can't say what it be."

A bit of frustration started to show on Ma's face, but just as quickly she reined it in and waited for further explanation from Wes.

"Tell ye this woman, it be private. Iffin you'ns go outside and wait a bit, then I have it all took care of. Only take a bit."

"Fair 'nuff," Ma said as she turned and ushered Julie out in front of her.

"Close my door and I be out in a bit," Wes requested.

Ma closed the door and stepped down off the porch and beckoned Jubal and Julie to join her. All three turned their back to the house and waited. All heard Wes as he scuffled about inside. In no time at all, the old rusty hinges screeched, the door flung open and Wes emerged holding his side and coughing lightly.

Major Dunn remained seated as he began to relate some of the events of the preceding few days and weeks. He spoke of the importance of preservation of the Union and of the injustices that had been done to many souls all across the nation. He talked of equal creation and God-given rights. He spoke of custom and curtsy in relation to the military and service to one's country.

Jubal did not really understand all that the major spoke about and had to make an effort just to keep up and pay attention. He forced himself not to let his mind wander. There were so many things that he did not understand. He had known nothing more than a simple and somewhat isolated life before the war flung him headlong into many new and confusing situations. It had all come at him so fast.

The major continued, "I have it on good authority that you have demonstrated very admirable abilities as a trooper and that you are certainly a better than average rifleman. I know from a personal experience that you do not flinch at adversity. I am very thankful to you for what you did for me back at the ferry. However, and I do not mean to be attacking you in any way, you are just a bit rough around the edges when it comes to military custom. Do you follow me so far?"

"Yes Sir," he replied even though everything was about as clear as a buttermilk glass.

"We do not often see courage that you demonstrated, and I will be among the first to recognize it when shown, especially under fire. I have left instructions that you be well seen to, and it appears that you are healing well. Is there anything that you need?"

"No Sir, I reckon not, but I ain't recallin' just all that you say I done. I know I done took a round up side my head. The sergeant here done told me all about that, but he not say what I done or how I got me shot."

"Sergeant Dunn can fill you in on more detail later. I am interested more in you from this day forward than before. You could possibly have a bright future ahead of you in the service to the Union if you choose to do so. I do not know how much education you have, but any short falls could be addressed in time. You have much to learn, but you are at a stage that would present minimal difficulties. I need to know what you plan to do once this war ends, and I have it on good authority that it will be ending in just a few weeks. Have you thought what you might like to do at such time?"

"Well, when I was back home, I wished I could see places and do like some other folks that I've knowed of. I even thought I might get me some fancy duds and go steppin' out some."

The major stood and looked to Sergeant Dunn. "Jugg, I want you to try to explain best you can a bit about the military, but first I think some explanation about life itself may be in order. I think we have a rough cut stone on our hands that needs to be polished before it can be presented."

"Yes Sir, Major," the sergeant responded.

"That will be all for now trooper. We will address this matter again. You are dismissed."

Jubal saluted, turned and exited the room. The sergeant and Major Dunn both uttered their thoughts concerning the need for a lot of polish.

He headed back to the tent where he was bunked down but was soon overtaken by Private Young.

"Now we gotta take you plumb across camp to see old sawbones. He look at yer head and say if ye be fit and able fer duty again or not," Pvt. Young informed.

"What ye say yore name be?" Jubal asked.

"James Young. Ye best be recollectin' things that ye been told already. Ain't nobody got no time fer fergittin'. Ye just be plain lucky ye weren't kilt last week and that Major Dunn be takin' a favor to ye fer savin' him."

"Just what it be that I done anyhow?" Jubal quizzed.

"I weren't there so all I know is what been told here in camp since they carted you in near most dead. They sayin' that the major got his hoss shot out in under him and were pinned down with Johnny Reb beatin' down a mite hard and fast. Talk is that the shot up hoss had the major pinned and that you and some other trooper pull him out and save his hide. Other trooper was kilt, and ye took a rifle ball to the head. Ye got a gash that prove that. Rebs come on so hard that we weren't back at the ferry till next day."

"I ain't real clear about all that."

"Well, talk is that ye be a crack shot with a long rifle, and not many here be able to lay claim there," James said.

A short, but brisk, walk soon brought the pair to the surgeon's tent. It was off to itself a bit and seemed like a new tent, all white and such. Two wagons, hitched and ready stood close by under a spreading elm tree. The horses stomped in the dust and nuzzled at the dry grass that had been gathered and dropped for them. They seemed to be in no want for feed of any sort. To Jubal, they were some of the finest horse flesh that he had ever seen.

Jubal immediately saw himself as the owner of herds of such and finer animals grazing leisurely on some faraway green and lush river bottom farm, far from home and out of sight of the mountain ridges and hills. Ideas and aspirations of material wealth kept eating away at him. There were so many more things to be had in life besides a plow horse and a hillside of dry dust, never knowing if it would be a good season or not. In the same instant, his Ma and his sisters came to mind, and there was Lida. Some things about that old holler were not so bad after all. He had to admit to himself that he missed his folks, and Lida too. He was sure that she was missing him too, at least he hoped so.

A slap to the shoulder from James brought him abruptly back to reality and the present.

"What it gonna take fer you to listen?" James retorted. "Ye act like that rifle ball be still inside yer brain if ye got one inside that hard head. Ye act just plumb addled sometimes. I reckon that might actual be what be goin' on. Guess the doc be one have that say."

"I reckon so."

"Ye ain't one be have a bunch to say now, I reckon. Ye just stay all balled up and fret all inside yerself seems me like. Ain't ye got no friends here abouts?"

"No."

"Ye got kinfolks off from here abouts?'

"I got kin back home," Jubal answered.

"Well, where be home?"

"Upper end of Cane Valley. Where is this here place anyhow?" Jubal asked.

"We be in West Maryland, best I know. I show it to ye on a map sometime, show ye my home too."

Jubal had no real understanding of his location and after further inquiry came to a vague understanding that he was north of his home back in the hills and valleys of East Tennessee. He had no understanding of distance. He had seen much fighting in a short few months and had been often on the march. Only recently had he been attached to Major Dunn and courier duty. It was this duty assignment that had been the reason for so much movement in such a short time.

Many skirmishes had awakened fears and doubts that he had not known before or had never heeded before. He had come to better appreciate life a bit more because of all the death that he had seen. Yet he took his own life more or less without much thought or concern up until a few days ago. The large dark scab on his brow and into his dark hair bore evidence to his mortality. He now saw himself not nearly as much the invincible young stalwart that he had been back in the mountain country of home.

There was just so much happening to him that he felt more and more confused and bewildered by the war and everything that it brought to bear. He did not like admitting to himself that he was afraid, many times terrified by armed conflict. Fear made him wish for it all to just go away and for some other young trooper to take his place and do war for him.

He remembered something Lida had said to him about having protection from evil ones and being able to live without fear, without dread or without worrying about what the next day would bring. She had talked about it one Sunday morning before the circuit rider got started. He had not really been paying much attention to her because she just seemed to keep on and on with all that church talk. Said she never worried or fretted over things because ever thing just seemed to have a way of working for the best and worry never helped much anyway. He somehow doubted that but knew her to be honest and upstanding too. She wore a smile most all times that he could recall, and she never complained to him, ever. She even spoke of how she enjoyed her life and loved her life. She just seemed to glow all the time.

He recalled Granny Iverson reading him something from the Good Book about faith and trust. Granny always had a certain turn to her that seemed to sort of set her apart somehow, but that was more than likely just her way of making the time pass since she was on in years. Not much else she would have strength to do other than set and read a bunch.

He reckoned that he might go hear that preacher man soon as he got back home to Cane Valley. Lida would be proud to be there beside him with him in his best store bought coat and blacked boots. That would make for some good times. That would cause her to cotton to him real strong. He could take her to some place away from Cane Valley, and they could have most anything they would want. After all, he had all that Union army money coming to him. His mind raced, just like all the fine horses that he knew he would soon own. After all, this cuss blasted war would soon be over and done.

Another slap to the shoulder brought Jubal back to reality. James led him to a shaded tent with sidewalls raised. Inside were random tables, a chair or two and what appeared to be supply trunks. Just beyond the tent stood a row of heavy supply wagons with crates piled high. Men in varying dress milled about in what appeared to be unorganized efforts. A tall man in a dingy rust and crimson-stained long coat pointed and gestured this way and that. Each flailing movement of his arms sent one or more of the men in motion to carry out his directive. He extracted a pair of horn-rimmed spectacles from under his coat and put them on after a quick wipe with the coattail.

Off a ways grazed several draft horses, feeding peacefully in the morning sun. Their flanks dry. They had done no recent labor. Overhead crows cawed in apparent protest to the disruption of their feeding in nearby crops of grain.

Many fields of grain had been burned or trampled, but for some reason the fields around camp seemed to have escaped the war and all its wanton destruction. No homes nearby lay in burned ruins. Livestock and sheep grazed unconcerned in distant pastures. Fowl busied themselves chasing insects and scratching in the droppings of the grazers. God's creatures did not appear to be disturbed by the conflict that had so recently surrounded them. The countryside could be representative of most any farm in Cane Valley, if only there were nearby steep ridges and rocky outcroppings of the grey limestone that made up the backbone of Pine Mountain back home.

Scattered camp fires seemed to intensify the increasing morning heat. The scant morning dew was already gone. Grey smoke dulled the blue sky, and a rare cumulus cloud cast a slow moving shadow across the fields all around the encampment. Dust puffs rose from each stomp of a hoof, and just as soon settled back into the dry earth. The heat of the day was here, and the shadows were short. That was one of the few things that the boy could recall his Pa told him. When a man's shadow is shorter than himself, then he is out in the heat of the day.

The man in the long coat summoned with a flick of the wrist, and the two young men approached. As he beckoned, he pulled a chair close to a low table and sat down facing it.

"Which one be Stewart?" he asked without looking up at them.

"That be me," Jubal responded.

"Sit here," pointing to the table as his eyes met Jubal's. "Take that rag off your head."

Jubal complied with instruction and in so doing relieved himself of some of his dark wavy hair. The man then looked at the wound for only a moment.

"Stand up and touch your toes till I say otherwise," he instructed.

"Do what?"

"Do what? Sir," he parroted in evident displeasure at the lack of respect. "I am Captain Ross, and I expect you to address me as such. I am the surgeon here, and I answer only to Major Dunn. He ordered me to look you over and that I am trying to do now. Do you understand that?"

"Yes sir. I do, sir."

"Well, grab them toes like I said."

Once again he complied and touched his finger tips to the toes of his boots and held them. He felt a bit of a twinge across his forehead but nothing that he had not had before.

"Stand up straight now," the white coat ordered.

Jubal stood erect. He felt a brief surge in his head and wavered just ever so slight.

"Look at me."

Both Jubal and James looked into the surgeon's glaring eyes. Neither could read his expressions or anticipate his instructions. Thumbs raised Jubal's eyelids roughly. A firm grip on his chin turned his head so the scabbed-over wound was easier to be seen.

"I've seen all I need. Get outta here. I'll tell the major you are good to go."

"Go where, sir?"

"That is all. Now go!"

The pair returned to their bunk tent only to find the broad-shouldered black sergeant awaiting their return. He stood at a loose parade rest at the foot of Jubal's cot with a rather stern look about him and a stare that would put a hole sideways in a cannon breech.

His boots were blackened to a shine. Uniform clean and fit like a glove. Yellow chevrons aglow like a lantern on a dark night. Each button polished. He carried no arms or saber.

Another equally well uniformed sergeant stood near him.

After glancing looks at both troopers, Sergeant Dunn spoke in his usual slow but commanding voice, "Stewart, the Major thinks you may have what he is lookin' for in takin' part in some of his upcomin' duties, and he needs me to see if I think that be a wise decision on his part. Can't tell you nuthin' now, no details, but you bein' a crack shot what got you noticed well as riskin' yer own hide savin' his. Thing is that you be just plumb dense when it come to army ways and such. We need see if the good be out weigh the rest. Yer chances be lot better goin' places in this here army if ye just learn yer manners and some respect. They must'a been in a heap hurry trainin' where ye signed up."

"I never signed nuthin' nowhere. I just come along with a bunch that was headin' this way," Jubal informed.

James and the two sergeants looked at each other in apparent disbelief. A uniformed trooper who had just come along and followed over hundreds of miles and uncounted skirmishes.

"That be reason 'nuff, I reckon cause ye be actin' such as ye do. I reckon I best be tellin' all this here to the major," Sergeant Dunn mused as he and the other sergeant spun around and were gone.

James watched as the pair entered the cook's area and talked with the apron-clad men, who labored around the cook stoves, the iron kettles and the supply wagons. Soon they were on the move again and James lost sight of them as they moved closer to the frame and brick house on the far end of the camp. Jubal sat on the end of his cot and held his head in his hands for a brief rest. The heat of the day had made his brow moist, and a trickle of sweat coursed into the edge of his head wound. The salt stung a bit, but there was no dizziness and no throbbing pain in his temple. He was glad for that.

He had time in the last day or so to think about himself and all that he had been through, all the shoot outs, cannon fire, and the continuous rattle of musketry soon faded a bit here and there. The thing that played over and over in his mind was all the dead and dying that he had seen. He had heard the agony of the wounded and the pleas for help that eventually became silent as death overtook them. He thought about his own death. Would it ever reach his folks back home and how would they know where he lay buried and would anybody ever come here, or wherever he would be put. What would the end be like?

"James, ye ever think about gettin' kilt? Ye ever get 'fraid when shootin' starts?"

"Course I do," James snapped. "You think a man be a mite crazed if he not have tarnation scared plumb outta him when lead balls be comin' at him. You be sayin' you not fearful fer life yerself?"

"I think about it some, sure do. Some say there be better later on, but I thinkin' and wonderin' how that can be? Seems me like once ye be shot dead, then that be it."

"There be a better life if you want it be that way," James replied in a gentler tone. Sounds me like you be frettin' too much lookin' fer a way 'round the truth and not seein' the silver cause you be too busy lookin' fer gold."

"Funny ye mention gold. That be what I want now so's I can have all the things outta life while I still be able to live a bit. I want land and sich, hosses and cattle, things like that be worth a bunch."

"That ain't what it be all about, Jubal. Hosses, land and cattle can all be took away and then what you be left with?

"Then what ye think it all about James?" Jubal questioned.

"Better fer a man to be unknown to the world than be unknown to his own self. I don't think you be knowin' what you really want outta life. You ain't never say nuthin' that tell me you be more'n just a kid who be plumb wet 'hind the ears, and you be loosin' plumb out on ever thing that really matter."

"Like what?"

"Well just like here. Who there be here that be willin' help you get all healed up in yer head where you been shot? There be a soul here that call you friend or even know you by yore give name? You think anybody here give a horse biscuit about how you be?"

"You been help to me," Jubal answered.

"I were told I had to."

"Sergeant Jugg help me get better."

"He were told to too," James added.

"Who be the one tell ye?"

"Major Dunn, that who."

Jubal was silent for a bit. There be them who he thought had helped him because they cared about him. Now seemed like they were just doing as told by some other that never knew him before. That made him think about the ones back home who he knew cared about him.

"I been knowin' you fer just a few days now, and I learnt a bit about you here and there. I help you now cause I know it be proper thing what need be done even though I done been told do it. A body ought be helpin' where he can cause that the way it meant be. Gold ain't gonna buy you that kind'a thing. That gotta come from way down deep inside a body."

"Then are ye a friend?"

"Most times you gotta be a friend to have a friend. A sack of gold ain't gonna buy a friend. We be responsible fer what we do fer others, no matter how we feel. That just plain be how I seein' it."

Jubal cradled his forehead in his palms and let his mind race back to the meeting house on no particular Sunday morn. Scattered bits of memory brought back scattered words about some traveler, who put a man up in some place after robbers took his money and whupped up on him. One man seeing after a stranger, and here he was skirmishing and taking a life. Do unto others before they do it to you. Maybe not exact like it said, but he didn't recall it all just now anyhow. Besides who would harm a man what owned land and fine hosses and such?

Someone had told him that the army could give him a good life, but all he had seen so far was a bunch of killing and fighting and most ever body either licking his own wounds or tending to his own self. Seemed to him like friends was few and a mite far betwixt one another.

Must have been near high noon by the time Jubal dropped the rails on the north hill and led Kate across to their old home place side. The pace since leaving the old dirt floored shanty had been slow, but steady. Wes had coughed and hacked most all the way and more so as the sun rose higher in the cloudless sky. No one spoke unless it became necessary.

Kate had raised a good sweat just by the leisure pace. They all stopped at the crest of the hill. A big red elm provided a short shady respite.

Jubal looked at Wes and wondered to himself, how can Ma care what comes of this here old man? Plenty other folks scattered round these parts who could use a hand. He reckoned he would just ask her about that later. And what folks gonna think with her taking in a man when Pa nowhere abouts? She had sent him eats and sich plenty times past, but this here be way beyond that. Maybe she know more about him than she be telling or letting on. Maybe he be old miser man and have a big poke full stashed out in some rock ledge or buried some place. There be a thousand places a body could hide most ever thing he want in these hills and hollers.

They all reached the old log house and were met in the lane by Sarry and Gracie. Both girls stood with hands on hips, staring at Wes. Granny Iverson stood on the porch with one hand to the porch post nearest the open kitchen door. A trickle of grey smoke rose from the kitchen chimney as the cook stove fire died away.

Jubal helped Wes down from old Kate's sweat soaked back and escorted him to a hickory bark bottomed chair on the dogtrot. He sucked in each breath with air hunger that made his lips purse with each breath. He was more wet with sweat than the old mule.

He half fell into the chair and leaned forward to try to breathe easier. He rattled in his chest and throat with each breath. Granny fetched him a gourd dipper from the wooden bucket near the kitchen door. He took small sips between the pants for his breath, spilling big drops in his filthy ragged shirt. His pants smelled of Kate and were just as wet. He wore no shoes. They had been left behind. The toughened bare feet were the same color as the dirt floor they had just left behind.

Ma slowly poured water down his back and asked Granny to fan him with her apron.

Slowly, ever so slowly, the wretched old man began to draw easier breath and to cool down a bit. Most of the bottom of his chair was now wet, and a trickle ran off the edge of the trot boards that had long ago been worn slick by untold numbers of steps.

Ma finally spoke in a gentle and soft voice. "Wes, I thought we most sure lost ye a while there, but ye comin' back now. Ye breath be better now?"

Wes nodded his head to indicate yes, but remained silent.

"Ye be hungry?"

Again he nodded, yes. Ma had brung him good eats and plenty of them earlier, but they only whetted a long dormant appetite. He could eat her fixin's any day.

By early evening, Wes had recovered and rested well enough to talk a mite. He had eaten his fill of corn bread and apple butter. The girls had cooked dinner and had it ready before the others had reached home. Sarry was making near about a good a cook as her Ma.

"Granny, I reckon we got a bit to do here, some barberin' and some washin' and some fresh duds to find fer him," Ma said. She then proceeded to give instructions to all. Julie could fetch the sewing scissors, the razor and the strop. Gracie and Granny could fetch a shirt and a pair britches. Ma and Sarry would cut hair and whiskers and then try a shave. Jubal would have to take the old man to the spring pool runoff and clean him up best he could.

Wes offered no protest to the matter. He appeared to be just plumb tuckered out and not really up to having much say to it. First, Ma took the sewing scissors to his beard. She trimmed and trimmed till she had it all whacked down to a stubble, and all the shaggy grey whiskers lay in a heap on the old man's lap with just as many spilled over at his feet. Sarry then began to snip at his tangled mat of hair. It too, soon lay at his feet. Julie brought lye soap and hot water from the buckets on the cook stove. Ma began to gently wash the weathered old face and the stubble that covered it. Wes still offered no resistance, but seemed intent on his breath. He offered only grunts or nods in response to questions.

Once Ma had soaked the stubble in a warm wrap, she began to work the soap in her hands and make a light lather. She then stropped the razor best she knew how and lathered up the leathery face. She nervously took razor in hand and neared his face with a slight tremble.

"Best let me do it," Granny interrupted as she reached out a wrinkled, but steady hand. "I done this many a time fer yer Pa and his Pa while they was bedfast. I reckon I got it in me to do it a mite more." In no time Wes had a new face on him, and it took years away from his appearance. Ma noticed that right off, but made no comment.

Now it was Granny who issued the orders. "Wes, can ye lay down here with yer head off ended, and I try scrubbin' that mop ye got there."

Wes nodded that he could and with effort proceeded to lay his weary old carcass on the trot floor as had been requested. The oak boards were a mite hard but that did not hold back one bit on the eyes becoming heavy. Even with the scrub down of his head, he found a few precious moments where his old bones seemed to be at peace with the world. His hair was soon cleaner than it had been in years, and he actually could feel the air on his scalp. It felt refreshing. He had to admit, all be it only to himself, that he was a mite shamed for the way he had just give up and let self go so long. He could do better, and he knew it too.

When all else was done and it came time to go to the spring branch runoff, Wes appeared to be weaker. A bit of his color seemed to bleed off now and then. He spoke in between shallow gasps and begged to just lay where he was fer the night.

Ma agreed and set about making him a pallet right where he lay. Jubal said that he would sleep with him there too. Granny swept up the hair and the beard and carried it out to the fence and dropped it across into the lane. Jake just happened along about that time. He stuck his nose to it, then turned, heisted his hind quarter and marked it good. A few scratches and he was off on his way for some shade.

The sun was still high in the west, but the old man slept like it was the dark of the moon. His breath came easier and a mite more regular. He seemed to be rested a bit and for sure was sleeping like a milk fed pup. He stirred, mostly tossing side to side. He spoke no words and made no noticeable sounds. Ma had folded a couple of old quilts and put them down as a pallet with a piece of old sheet over him. A folded remnant stuffed in a mill sack served as a pillow.

Jubal sat leaning to the wall in a chimney corner so as to keep a eye out on the old man and watch him during the night. Ma had seen to that and wanted the boy to make sure there weren't nothing turning bad during the dark. Jubal rested as best he could and gave his mind liberty to wander far and wide again.

Sometime way in the night, Wes sat up and coughed as if to clear away the dust of a thousand days' work. Starlight allowed only the faintest of outlines in his nearest vision. The weathered and deep set eyes had little trouble spotting the form that sat near in the darkness.

"That be ye son," he asked fully knowing who would answer.

"It be me," came the expected reply.

"I shore be obliged iffin ye was to fetch me a dipper of water. My whistle be a mite parched."

Jubal silently got to his feet and brought the oak bucket and gourd dipper from the porch shelf at the kitchen door. He filled the dipper and knelt by the old man's pallet as he handed him the dipper. Wes slowly drank the entire dipper and asked for more. Jubal honored his request.

"Bit cooler now. Water be tastin' fresh now too."

"Ye feelin' better, are ye?"

"That be a fact, son. I thunk I might be a goner there fer a spell."

"I glad ye be better. I weren't wantin' see ye goin' downhill."

"I be thankin' ye fer all ye doin' fer me. I hurt a bit more'n I realized once I got to stirrin' around some. Old Kate dang nigh done me in," Wes intoned as he took another mouth full from the gourd.

"It ain't no trouble ,Wes. Ye been a good neighbor, and Ma ain't fergittin' that neither. Ye never took nuthin' off us what weren't yer due. Ye just look like a hard rock case, but ye ain't so bad like others say. I know fer I reckon I able to see fer my own self."

"There be things ye ain't be knowin' of me. Sometime maybe I tell ye a yarn or three, but not now. It ain't proper time."

"I know. Ye best rest cause Ma be havin' us up early. I reckon we both be due a mite scrubbin' and all, least by her measures. She ain't havin' no trash round here and fer shore no filth. I ain't sayin' ye filth, ye know that don't ye?"

"I reckon I know how ye be meanin', son. Yer Ma be a saintly woman more than ye probably ever know. She done a lot fer me last few years, and I ain't fergittin' it none. No sir, not one bit. I make it right by her some of these here days too. Yer Ma be a good-hearted soul that a fact."

"I reckon that be rightly so."

"And ye be a right bright young'un too. Ye be mite near plumb growed up, I reckon. I been knowin' ye ever since ye was a pup, and I ain't knowed ye ever be in nuthin' no count or wrong. Can't say so much fer myself, tell ye that fer a fact. A man gotta be accountin' fer all he done in his life even iffin he never had a proper raisin' up. We gonna stand up and be held up fer all we done all along through life. That be a fact."

"Well Wes, I reckon ye be a good soul too. I ain't never knowed nobody sayin' nothin' bad by ye."

"Well, they be a time or two I ain't right proud of. Sometimes a man can act a fool fer a minute or two, and it make a change in him fer all rest of his time. Ain't no undoin' what already been done, and ain't no takin' back what done been spoke. How a man is raised up and his people may have bearin' on his life, but he still gonna answer fer who he becomes and what he does with his self."

"How come ye tellin' me all this stuff, Wes?" Jubal questioned.

"I ain't rightly fer sure, but ye seem be still a mite wet 'hind them ears yet. I just don't wanna see no harm come yer way nor nary body comin' down on ye when ye ain't needin' it. That all."

The two talked on into the early morning when the first gray light showed in the low eastern sky. They spoke of many things and replayed the last couple of day's events for more than once. Wes told the boy that he had a few pieces of gold hid out someplace where no one would ever find it and how he had hoarded it up over the last few years to the point that he would not even buy decent clothes for himself and his departed woman.

Lately he had been having Cleve bring him laudanum and that was the only thing he spent money for now. He went on to tell how he had come to distrust the storekeeper because of the way he talked to him about his money, saying that it wasn't a good thing to be keeping all that much around the old run down shack. Even how he looked all about the old place as if trying to spy where it might be hid.

Jubal said nothing about the stranger at the store, nor the three riders he had almost run up against on the road back home from the mill. He made no mention at all of the tracks he had seen in the orchard or above the papaw patch. He told of none of this, but it did add more suspicion to the riders and to Cleve. Sure he wanted a sack full of gold coins too, but weren't no way he would take what weren't his. He could see old Wes out spading up ground under a old stump and burying a fortune there or lifting a big flat rock fer a cover up.

"Wes, what ye holdin' out fer with all that money iffin I outta be askin' sich?"

"Strange how ye ask me that when I be fixin' tell ye how hoardin' up a bunch make fer misery. All time worry where be safe keepin' place fer it, cause robbers take it all in a heartbeat. I tell ye here and now they be much more ye be wantin' outta yer young life than gold. Like lot's folk say, hard seein' the silver linin' when ye be too busy lookin' fer gold all time. Ye be a young pup still. I know they be things ye wantin' what cost plenty. But hear me when I tell ye, ever thing that money buy can be took from ye in a day; and things like friends still be there with ye. Them be the things that counts."

"Well, that may be, but I still be wantin' things outta life that I ain't never had yet. I wanna have a thing or two worth somethin' sides these here old britches and a rag-tag shirt," Jubal said rather harshly.

"I done told ye how I feel about all them things and how they can be took from ye in a second or so. Things like friends is what counts in this here life," Wes countered.

"I ain't much on friends. Ain't nobody livin' in this old holler be a friend with. That just one reason I wanna be seein' other places and other people. Ain't nobody here to be friends with," Jubal argued.

"Reckon ye gotta be a friend 'fore ye can have a friend, true and tried."

"Just how I gonna go about that round here? Tell me that now iffin ye can."

Wes sat up a bit straighter before he spoke. "Listen me now, son. I know ye been raised up right, and ye knows right from wrong. And that just how it outta be, but they is things runnin' deeper than that. Ye gotta treat people from inside, and it gotta come from inside a man. He gotta be good to his friend or neighbor simply cause he want to, not cause' a what a body might get returned him. It ain't favor fer favor. It go deeper than that. And a man gotta show by the way he live his own life. They always be folks a lookin' at ye ready to pounce on anythin' ye do that ain't plumb upstandin'. Yore actions gonna say more than yore words anyhow. Ain't no use in holdin' it again a body fer puttin' ye down neither. It just cause ye more grief than it ever be worth."

"I be knowin' that too," Jubal said in a much meeker tone.

"Ain't no use in runnin' off all over creation tryin' find a way betterin' yer self, iffin ye ain't got no reason movin' out. Tell ye this son, it be best ye 'preciate home. Cause once ye leave, it ain't never gonna be the same no more. I ain't fer shore what it be, but there be a change. A man never get the restlessness outta his bones till he know it firsthand. Then turn it right around other way, when ye folks be all passed and gone, then ye got no home to go back to even iffin ye wanted. That can leave a body feelin' a mite cut off and out there all on his own. Life gonna be right much what ye make outta it, and it be a mite smart easier iffin ye have a friend ever now and then."

"How many friends ye got, Wes?"

"Not many now, son. Had some along, but done some things I ought not done; and it cost me bad. That why I be tellin' ye these things, son. Ain't no use ye havin' learn things the hard way, when I done been there and can tell ye how ye can learn from what I done wrong. If I save ye some grief, I reckon my bad times and fool ways not be total fer nuthin' and be help a bit after all."

The two continued until they heard Ma up and about. Soon light would be showing up the hills and ridges all around them. The eastern sky took on the faintest hint of red, and a gentle breeze came out of the darkened western sky. This was the first indication, even a hint of rain clouds forming. Red at sunup was always a sign of coming rain and thunder storms, special during all this summer heat and drought. Rain would make crops better and critters would have fresh drinking water. The parched earth would take on a new life and be refreshed. The rains, if they came, would be a savior. Rain would break the bonds of the dry spell and restore things new and fresh. There would be new growth and life could go on. Rain would be a blessing.

Rain would also wash out any tracks and would bring a halt to any chance to find out what the riders had been up to or where they went. Jubal kept many of the details to himself and had his own suspicions just from what he had already seen and heard. Hard telling where strangers came from or what they be up to, most likely no good. That be almost a sure bet.

Rain would also mean that the stock could drink for them self, since the spring pool runoff would pick up. One more chore that he would be freed from. The garden would come back a bit, and they just might get by through the coming winter. Rain would grow more hay, and the stock could get through the winter better too.

Rain would help grow more acorns and beech mash. Wild game would stand a better chance making it another winter. There could be meat on the table too. Rain would break the sweltering heat, and a body would rest at night as opposed to tossing and turning all night. Rain now just might break dog days a bit sooner.

The sun came up red in the east as it peeked over the crest of Pine Mountain and set the sky ablaze as it climbed enough to clear the ridges. Breeze picked up just a trifle. Still dark in the west when the first distant thunder came long seconds after the distant flash of lightening. If it held, there would be rain in an hour. Its sweet smell wafted in on the breeze already.

The boy pulled on his buckskin boots and hurried to fill the wood box beside the cook stove and fetch water from the spring pool. He did not mind being rained on. Jake came up on the trot and laid down as if he knew just when it would all start. Wes sat up and rolled up his bedroll. Ma went to the kitchen and started to kindle a fire in the cook stove. Granny and the gals soon joined her.

In no time the grey smoke from fresh kindled fire had disappeared from the old stone chimney, and the warbled waves of clear heat remained all that rose into the morning air.

Thunder continued to rumble, and the western sky sparked with flashes of light. A light rain started as the breeze picked up.

The smell of sausage and side meat soon flooded out of the kitchen and onto the dogtrot. It at once whetted appetites. Wes never let on one word, but Ma had fed him more in the last two days than he had eaten in a week. Who knowed? Just might be that a woman's good cooking might take a year or two off a body iffin he got a daily helping for a while.

Julie came out with two plates of biscuit bread, gravy and sausage with side meat fried real good and handed one to her brother and one to Wes. That got Jake's attention, and he began to move in for his share. Jubal shooed him off, and he seemed to know that his share would soon come. He would get a biscuit soaked in grease and that would taste better to him than flour gravy anyhow. He lay back down and patiently waited.

By the time all had eaten, including Jake, the rain had come on steady. The thunder and lightning seemed to be about passed over. It was light enough to see well all about now. The first small trickles of runoff were forming all around the house, making their way toward the spring branch and into the barnyard. Old Kate stood out in the refreshing rain with head down as if to relish in having nothing more to do this early in the day except be refreshed by the long-awaited rain. The oxen picked leisurely at the short wet blades of orchard grass that dotted the barnyard and the lane. It had been seeded over and over each year by hauling in the first cutting hay. The chickens dabbled in the puddled up hoof prints and scratched in the damp covering on the dust whelps. The night critters had hushed.

All over the surrounding hills and ridges, the rain would bring new and fresh growth and renew what had looked to be dead and dried up. All creatures great and small would benefit from the life-restoring rain. Seeds would mature and fall to the ground insuring a new birth next spring. Rain might even help keep down the usual run of fall fire in the high mountains where the lightning bolts so often came to sting the earth. Mosses and slip grasses would be in good supply for all the burrowing critters to make nests. Sagebrush would be tall and provide cover for grouse and quail and could be meat on the table for folks all about.

More important, garden stuff would have time to make before frost cut it down like a mowing scythe. Beans and squash to dry and hang in the old log smokehouse loft would taste good on a cold winter day. Ma and the gals would can all they could have time to work up and dry what they had left after all the jars were filled. Rains would swell the fall apples, and they would keep better when they got their proper growth. Taters would fill out now and grow as big as a fist. They be mighty tasty after baking in hot ashes of the open fireplace.

Corn would fill out and make long ears with good yield. Took to C.C.'s mill and ground into fine meal would make for mighty tasty corn fritters smeared thick with apple butter. Cold corn bread in a glass of buttermilk would make the hungry growls go away. Red eye gravy poured over crumpled up corn cake would stick to a man's ribs so he could chop a week's wood in a day. Punk'ins outta the corn rows would fatten three big hogs, and they would add to the oncoming winter's larder.

Life in the mountains was a bit hard and needed lot of work and toil, but a body had no call to go hungry no time if he knew how to work the land and how to take what the land had to offer him. Sometimes living came by the sweat of a brow and a bent back, but it most always came with a peace of mind and a love for the land. Ever thing in the mountains seemed to know its place and knew to stay in it too. The bears stay to the high country, and the mink and muskrats stay close to the branches. Deer stay in the thickets where they can hide and raise young and not be found so easy. It just man folks 'round about that seem like they get outta line.

Most folks here were good people to know. They kept to themselves for the most part, mainly out of necessity because it took work ever day most all day long to earn keep. They worked hard and thought nothing more of it. It was a way of life, and it was their way. Bonds of family and friends were strong and lasting, but yet they held all in respect and honored their ties to the land and to their kinfolk. Hardly ever did a body come calling on a neighbor without first getting an invite. Yet in times of need or misfortune, they would be right there soon as they got word about a neighbor's misfortune. They helped build each other's houses and barns. They helped each other with major crops and shared the bounty. They helped birth each other's young'uns. When time came, they buried the dead. They shared from the heart and shared their life, love and happiness, as well as the hard times.

Wes had seen most all facets of mountain life and appreciated it for what it was and what it meant to him, but the young friend of his did not yet understand and appreciate his heritage. He did not have the years behind him like Wes did. Time could be a harsh teacher sometimes.

Chapter 4

Pondering

*T*hunder rolled directly overhead, and lightning lit up the camp and surrounding hills in intense flashes of white light. Rain came in torrents. There seemed to be nothing anywhere that could stay dry. Wind delivered sheets of downpour that swept across everything in its path. The parched earth drank its fill and rejected the rest in muddy swells and runoff. Horses stood in the dashing rain with their heads down and away from the gusting winds. They seemed not to be spooked at all by the flashes of light or the deafening roll of the thunder. The entire camp was awake, and most were soaked through and through. None were pleased with the drenching, even if it had cooled the air.

Jubal stripped to the skin and stepped into the runoff of the cook tent for a long needed soaping scrub. The rain was cool, but felt much refreshing. It brought back memories of similar experiences back home standing in the runoff from the crib shed, but never in the raw. Too many sisters' eyes; and if that were not enough, the silly giggles would be enough to cut short any man's bath. Lye soap stung his eyes, and the healing head wound remained a bit tender to touch. The refreshing rain shower soon washed away all the lye stinging, and clean hair lessened the tenderness in the hairline.

Clean from head to toe, the lad stepped from under the runoff and back into the shelter of the tent where he slept and bunked. He sat on the edge of his cot and let the soothing breezes dry his body and his hair. A saved old flour sack served as his towel and soon had him dry all over, save for the bottom of his feet. Dry soil clung there and that was soon taken care of in haste. By this time the first grey light of dawn began to show in the low eastern horizons, overcast and looming low in the sky. The rain abated and the breeze died away, ominous of the heat that would soon engulf the camp. August heat could be brutal and had been just that for near two weeks now.

Jubal had been assigned to cook tent duty. For now, it would be his task to chop enough firewood to keep the three cook stoves going from first light until long past noon. It took near a face cord per day. No real task for a hale and hearty soul such as he, but it had been hot beyond belief. He knew enough to rise early, just as soon as it was light enough to see where to swing the axe. He would have his firewood all cut and racked up before the heat of the day grew to its intense apex.

Daily chopping was hard work and had rendered Jubal even more lithe and muscular than he had ever been before. Each plummet of the axe flexed sinuous muscle that rippled with strength. His stamina had built to a point that the daily face cord of firewood became a routine task that tired him hardly at all. The heat was the only thing that ever posed a problem. He would be wet with sweat after each morning's chore. It was the job of two other troopers to drag the dead limbs into camp, usually from surrounding thickets and timber lots. Some hapless landowner was having all his under growth and trash cleared from his land.

The camp had steadily seen an influx of more troops. Word was that the Rebs may be massing forces and soon be on the move in their direction. Most, including Jubal, did not care for news such as that. This was how it was in every war time, and fights and skir-mishes were all to be expected. Thinking about that made unpleasant thoughts run through a mind, and sometimes put a knot down in the pit of the stomach.

For the most part there had been limited activity in and around the camp for about a month now. Occasional forays were made by Reb bands into the vicinity, but were of no particular consequence. A few shots fired in haste by both sides, and then it would all be over as the raiders swiftly rode off into the dense timber and all returned to quiet. One trooper had been cut down by a single sniper. He now rested in the churchyard to the north of camp. He was a young lad from somewhere up in New York and had no family that anybody knew about. Jubal had talked with him a time or two but did not even recall a name.

Major Dunn had continued to send couriers out to the east most every day with papers and such for the bigwigs back on the east fronts. He spent most of his time in the farmhouse headquarters building and seemed to be in his own world. He called for volunteers to ride courier, but seemed like only the older and more experienced troopers got that assignment. Jugg was at or near his side most of the time and had not spoken to Jubal since assigning him to the cook's crew.

First light brought on a flurry of activity in and around the cook tent. Fires were lit in the three cook stoves. Side meat was hauled out and slicing begun. Coffee pots were filled and clamored onto the warming stoves. Soon the smell of hot grease and coffee would arouse the few who yet slept. Jubal would have most of his cord chopped before he took his breakfast. He had established his work ethic and dependability with the cook sergeant, and thereby would be assured of a generous portion of whatever was fried up that day, plus all the strong black brew that he might care for.

The pole pile was about all worked up, and the replenishment would be coming in from the woods soon as the mules could be harnessed and put to work. The teams both seemed old and broken down, but they never got loaded down very much. So they got along good and had to work only in the fore part of the day, just like the skinners that worked and tended them. The mules and the mule skinners all had taken to Jubal's way of doing all their work before the sun got so hot and the heat of the day set in. Sure made it easier on all concerned. Just had to make it seem like there be more to it than appeared. No reason to be seen idle and doing nothing in the afternoons so as to prompt more chores and assignments. That was why it always took all afternoon to unharness the teams and take them to the creek for water and make sure they had feed and such. Same reason it took a while to tote the cook stove wood from the wood yard to the cook tent.

The night thunderstorm had definitely cooled the air. Spirits seemed to be raised all through the camp. Relief from the heat was reason enough to be uplifted. The coming day would probably take care of most of that; however, as there would be the usual amount of bitch and moan among the ranks. Most of the rank and file had been tied up in this man's war long enough to have their fill of it and just wanted to quit and go home. They had done enough killing. It seemed unreasonable to be at war with your own kind, and sometimes your own people just because they happened to come from somewhere down south of where you lived. Most had been in harm's way more than once, and many had the scars to prove it. Many more would never get to go back home. They would fight no more. That realization bore heavy on the mind of many and caused a dread and a fear that could not be denied, nor could it be dispelled by those in authority. For some reason, most chose enthusiastically to continue the fight rather than just lay down their arms and go home. Doing so would most surely bring about dire consequences on a personal basis, but that aspect of the conflict was hardly ever discussed in the ranks. No one really wanted to dishonor himself, no matter what his doubt or his fear.

The only ones who seemed to be truly lifted up in spirit were the animals. The rain brought on an almost immediate spurt of fresh green growth in and around the camp. All the draft animals busied themselves with the refreshing feast and nibbled close to the dampened earth in effort to get every new blade of forage that dared to raise a new growth. More and more cavalry mounts grazed in the limited spaces around the camp as more and more troopers massed in the area. More and longer rows of tents stretched out along the creek bottoms and on the lower slopes of the rolling hillsides. More and more campfires dotted the early dawn and more and more grey smoke wafted skyward in the still air of the mornings. Riders mingled in and out of the encampments almost continually. Sentries walked their post day and night. The scouting parties went out early at first light, and usually did not return till near dusk, earlier only if they had spotted activity that needed to be reported.

News from distant engagements came irregularly and often as not in conflict to the previous communications. Word was that the boys down south were really wrecking havoc on Johnny Reb and his countryside. Crops burned and livestock taken. Homes and out buildings burned just to see the fires rage. There had even been talk of undue killing of old farmer men and their families for token resistance and attempt to protect their homes. Seemed some just made it a point to be spiteful and destructive without any consideration. There was just a rare and wide spaced tale of mercy or kindness to the Rebs or their families. When there was talk of such, most frowned on it; and did not even want to hear anything more about it.

Jubal and some of the troopers that he had come to know heard one scouting party tell of coming across a mother and three young girls who had been burned out a few nights past and were living in a corncrib just to keep out of the heat. They had little to eat and only the clothes on their backs. Word was that they had been burned and raided by three men who wore neither the blue nor the gray. Word of it was third- and fourth-handed; the place had become unclear in the telling and retelling, but for sure it had been somewhere south in the mountain country.

Word came from the farmhouse headquarters that the entire camp would be on the move soon. Couriers had come in and had brought word of troop movement and masses forming to the east and to the north at a place in Pennsylvania, but no names had yet been passed on to the ranks. Orders to move out, when they did come, would set off a quick flurry of activity. Everything and everybody would have to pack up and be in shape to make long marches, for God knows how many days or how many miles. Jubal had not really seen much of that sort of movement in some time now, but he was not looking forward to undertaking the likes of it again.

He had regained his strength and stamina, largely from the chopping detail. He liked the idea of having duty part of the day, day in and day out. The cook tent duty had afforded him that since he had been assigned to make the chips fly. That was old hat to him and something that he had done as a chore back home.

Sunday morning broke overcast and grey with a stillness that forebode malice and trials for all the camp. Jubal had finished dressing in a hurry. He did not know why, but restlessness ate at him this morning; and it would not be quenched by tossing about in his cot. He was up and about almost before the cooks and the mess mates. He was at the wood yard by the time it was light enough to begin his ritual with the axe and bow saw.

The axe fell with determination this morning. Dead, dry limbs as big as a man's arm parted in one swift blow. A regular and unrelenting rhythm soon produced a mass of ready fuel for the cooks, and it was deposited where it was soon to be consumed. The restlessness fervor had produced a hunger equal in magnitude to the effort exerted in the excited and agitated job just completed.

Sundays usually held in store a little something extra from the cook tent, and this morning was no different. The cook sergeant handed Jubal three sugar cured ham biscuits and a steaming canteen of black strong coffee and told him to go find some place by himself and enjoy it. Said that he had earned it.

By now the morning was well into the daily routine. Still, the woodcutter's duty had been finished more than an hour before the regular time. Jubal stopped by his bunk tent long enough to wash his sweat dampened face and arms; took his cache and headed off in the general direction of the little white church, not too far from the old farmhouse that had been taken over as headquarters. He found himself for the first time wondering about the folks who surely must have been rousted from their home and had it taken from them in the name of need by the military. That was just one more of the things about this war that bothered him. Who took from whom, who had to give up the most, and what would come of a man's seized property once this war was all said and done? Didn't much matter way up here so far from home, but it could be that way back home too. Sure had been a long time since any word from Cane Valley.

Without really paying any mind to where he went nor how long it took to get there, the boy found himself sitting in the churchyard cemetery beside Clark's grave. It had been only a few short days since Clark had been cut down by sniper fire. He was an only son, whose Pa had been taken by the war almost a year earlier not too far east of here. Jubal wished silently that he could do something for his fallen comrade, but the reality of death seemed to overshadow any conscious thought of anything that could make a difference now.

He sat on the ground, cross legged and began to eat. The biscuits had cooled now but still tasted good. The sugar cured hog meat was a welcome treat. He had no recollection of enjoying that since he had joined up and left his humble log home, his Ma and his three sisters. He ate slowly and thought of many things and many places. It did not seem so important to visit all those dreamed of and distant places that had once stirred his mind. He found himself now thinking more and more about the people he already knew and the places that he had already seen, places that had a meaning fixed to them. He still had a burning desire for the finer things that he had never had before, because he still attached gain through affection that finery could bring to him. He still wanted to be somebody; and if it had to be bought, then he would do it. Besides, he had been told that he had several months' pay due him already and that should be a good start.

Thought had blinded him to the few souls that were gathering inside the little framed church building. He did not know how long the chords from the small pump organ inside wafted through the open windows and on to his ears. He had heard those chords before back home, but could not recall any words or name. Soon the sparse but determined congregation began to softly sing the lines from Amazing Grace. The words commanded a closer attention and a more acute ear.

Instantly his mind was transported back home to the little log church in Cane Valley. They sang this same hymn back there; but they never had an organ, just their own voices which all blended together most times in less than harmony. He saw himself sitting near the back, not really paying much attention to anything that was said by anyone. He never did think too much about anything the circuit rider preacher man had to say. He just went along with his Ma and sisters mostly to see they stayed out of harm's way. It was, after all war time.

He recalled the preacher man saying how grace was the same as unmerited favor or special kind of forgiveness when a body had been foul of the law or something. He reckoned then and there that he needed no favors nor no grace from no man, since he had never as much as crossed the law; not one time.

Other times he went on Sunday mornings just by chance that Lida would be there, and he might catch a glimpse from her. He reckoned that she didn't have big needs for grace either, since she nor none of her kin had any problems with the law. Thoughts about Lida mingled with thoughts of other times and places that he had wanted to be with her.

He listened to the little congregation more intent as the last few notes drifted across the cemetery where he sat. He had finished the biscuits and the now cool coffee. He rose to his feet and slowly began walking past the rows of markers, slowly toward the east side of the little frame church, where the morning light occasionally broke through the cloud cover making the white washed lap siding glisten with purity that only a God-sent light could equal, especially in this time of dirty, gory and revolting war. Surely there would be no grace for all the killing and maiming that had gone on. Couldn't nobody be forgiving that.

By the time he neared the open windows the preacher man had begun to say his piece. He spoke about the war and all the horrors connected with it. You would have thought it was the Lord himself who was spilling all the blood and setting all the fires.

"There be conflict and hatred all over this nation. Brother hates brother and neighbor is again his neighbor, and yet we all claim to be His children. We shore do act as children when we be filled with hate and jealousy. God don't want no discord among us, no sir. He desires that we have peace and harmony among us and that means more than just no more fightin'. He wants peace for the nation. He wants peace among men, and he can give it too. We just have to ask fer it."

Jubal took a few more steps toward the open window and sat down in the grass. He did not know why, but he felt compelled to listen to this man and what he had to say about peace. Peace in time of war. Now that be somethin' else. How could that ever be?

The preacher man continued. "We all be condemned to death all our lives. This war be just a mite near nothin' taste of what death really be like; but we must live each day as it comes. We have only today and there be no guarantee about tomorrow. Life be too short to wake up a single day with regrets and sorrows. Life be too precious not to love them who treat you right. We should forget about them what done us wrong and believe ever thing happens for a reason. We don't know ever reason behind ever thing and sometimes we just gotta accept what happens on faith," the reverend continued.

Jubal continued to sit in the grass, transformed by the words of the preacher man, yet not really hearing or understanding all that he spoke. His voice coming through the open window and into the hollowness of the overcast morning just seemed to be what he needed to appease his feelings and doubts this morning. He had let his mind wander back to the old log home place in Cane Valley and to the people he knew and loved, both family and friends. He just this very morning somehow sensed that he may never return there and may never see those friends and family again. The preacher man saying that we are condemned to death all our lives had not done much to remove that doubt; his soft, but firm, voice conveyed confidence and calmness by the words that he chose and the tone of his delivery.

"This war is worrisome to all and to some just plain fear and terror. None of us in here has ever had to endure the worry of battle like all them troopers camped around about us. We never have been pounced upon like some kind of renegade would do. We have seen peace beyond all means when compared to those who have warred against their own kin and those who will yet see the bloodbath of battle before this war be settled. All are worried I know; but I tell you this my friends: worry looks back to what was, sorrow looks down to what was, but faith looks up to what is gonna be. We know this war is gonna be over, and soon we hope. We know that sorrow is gonna end for us one of these days and because of that we can have hope."

Jubal knew pine blank that he had hope. He sure had hope that he would get back home when it was all said and done. He expected that, but he feared what could happen to him. It troubled him plenty knowing what he could be facing soon if the camp had to pick up and move out to the east. Word had it that east be where all the armies be gathering and making ready for big time fights. Might even be big enough to decide and end this here war. Worried? Danged right. He was worried and that drove off any peace there might be left in him.

The preacher man continued, "There be those here today that got family out on the front lines. Some of them still be right here with us this very day in spirit. I know ye be concerned about the Almighty lookin' after them. It may be the will of God that they go into battle, but I also believe that God will not let them go where His power and His grace will not protect them. There ain't nobody else who can shelter and protect like that. If any man be trustin' on Him, then I thinkin' he be protected right up to the end."

Again the boy's mind flashed back to the little log church in Cane Valley. He remembered one time where Lida had took notice of him long enough to talk to him, and on this day she had asked him if he had ever fessed up to all his worldly ways and to the devil mindset that he had, or at least to not recognizing where he stood in making things right in his life. He recalled her asking him point blank if he had ever seen the light.

He reckoned all this turmoil in his mind this morning must come outta him, coming back to linger where Clark lay at rest. Just seemed a lot unfair that a boy so young and fresh and so full of life and took so soon from all he was and from all he had been or wanted to be. No kin that nobody knew of, but still there had to be somebody somewhere. A sobering fact that it could just as well been him laid out there instead of Clark. Clark never would see the light of day again. Never have a chance to live out his life. Maybe things were right with him. Maybe he had hope.

Jubal had hope too. He just hoped that he could get through this conflict and someday get back home and get on with his life. He still wanted the things that brought pleasure and honor and good times. He wanted the things that made a body be looked up to and respected. It never really entered his way of thinking that respect was a matter not to be bought, but one that had to be earned. To him, at least so far, security came in shiny gold and silver coins. What they couldn't get, he reckoned he didn't need nor were it worth bothering over.

To him, peace was the end of war and hostilities. Contentment and satisfaction both came with money; and if he had enough even right now, he could buy his way out of this war and then that would be peace for him. He understood that, but had no understanding about the peace that passed all understanding that he had heard about but never really paid no mind to.

The words of the preacher man seemed to be just a distant murmur as his thoughts traversed miles from his humble mountain home to life in the big towns and faraway places. Then, as loud as a thunder crack, the words came clear and almost as if spoken to him alone. "It says that there will be wars upon top of wars, and this here one ain't the last we will ever see in our time neither. I tell you right here and now that this war is bad, but it will never hold a light to the war that lives in us from the day we first see the light till the day we be laid out to rest. They ain't but one way we ever gonna be able to win that war inside us. That be the war that old Satan himself try ever way known to man to make us blind to the real Light of the world."

"Our life be a war all along. It be up to us to choose how we fight that war. It be our lives that be a witness to how we fight and who we fought for. I just hope that when my fight be ended that those who stand over me can say that I fought a good fight and that my days here on this old earth stood for something good and right. A man ought not leave this old world without bettering it for somebody somewhere along the way. A man needs to leave a few happy tracks somewhere in life. I think it better for a man to be known for what he was and what he did for others than it is for what he had or what he might not have had. No man should be poor in spirit, never."

A dark, low hanging cloud moved slowly across the churchyard and into the camp area. It seemed to want to blot out all sunlight; and at the same time, cast deepening shadows in the mind as well as on the ground. Jubal admitted to himself that he was poor in every way. That was all he had ever known. Rags for clothes and worn out shoes had a way of breaking the spirit when such was all a body had with not much chance for better. The uniform was the best that he had ever had, but danged if it hadn't most near cost his life to wear it. There just had to be more somewhere, just had to be.

"You look troubled, son."

The voice startled him. He had not seen the old black man with white hair and beard approach. He was dressed in a well-fitting brown suit and a snow white shirt with a black bow tie. Jubal scrambled to his feet as the old man extended his hand in gentlemanly fashion. His handshake was firm and comforting to the boy.

"I be Zack, brother to the man you been listenin' to inside. I been watchin' you fer a bit, and I know they be somethin' eatin' at you. I can tell just from the way you stare off to nowhere."

"I just come to see about Clark."

"He be your friend?"

"I knowed him a few days. We talked a bit. That's all."

The old man had a piercing stare, but his eyes conveyed compassion and kindness that Jubal had seen in no eyes since he left Cane Valley.

"What be yer give name, son?"

"Jubal."

"You come from up nawth?"

"No."

"Then where you be callin' home?"

"I come outta Cane Valley down close Franklin County line."

"I know where Franklin County is. I taught mathematics at a college there."

"Ye don't talk like no uppity schoolmaster man."

"Well, I hope I ain't uppity seemin' cause I ain't aimin' that a way. I be thinkin' that it do ye a heap good to come inside and listen to my brother say his piece. He got some powerful words in him. He be knowed here cause he done showed the way to many a sorrowin' soul."

"I ain't done nothin' that I be sorry over. I just sorry Clark got kilt," Jubal retorted.

"That not the sorry that I be meaning," Zack said softly. Come on in and I sit with ye a spell. Ain't nobody gonna be spectin' nothin' of ye. We is all black, but we just like you inside. We all is God's people."

"Naw, I better not."

"Then come stand near the door where ye can hear better." Zack once again reached for his hand and gently led him toward the open door, the front door of the little white church beneath the grey low hanging clouds.

Jubal did not understand his own feelings and emotions that had been unexpectedly stirred this morning. He felt a longing deep down inside, and it was not a longing for home and family. It was a longing that he had not heeded before. He felt restlessness. It was not a restlessness to get away from home and to see new places or to meet new people. Emptiness begat restlessness and longing, but that emptiness was a bit of a mystery.

He never had much to fret over and few concerns to load him down. He shouldered his assigned responsibilities and accepted them. He had been praised and lauded by his superiors and by his commanding officer. Yet, there was something missing.

Zack gently ushered Jubal in and sat down with him on the wood frame bench at the rear of the church. All eyes turned toward him. The preacher man continued and never missed a beat. Surprisingly, there was no sense of uneasiness or embarrassment; no discomfort about being among strangers. Quite the contrary, he felt a slight sense of relaxation. He just sensed that he was in the presence of people who could be caring and sincere. And then, just like a flash of lightning, feelings of guilt and emptiness returned.

"Things of this old earth gonna pass away, but the Word of the Lord will last forever and will not pass away," preacher man continued as he wiped his brow slowly.

"What we do in this here life each day is all we ever gonna have chance to do. We ain't got no cause be grievin' after what we done yesterday cause it be gone from us and never be no more. We ain't got no promise that we see the sun come up again tomorrow neither. All we got is now. All we got is today. Today, my friends. Today is all we got, and today may be last time you have chance to set things right in life. That be the only way we ever gonna have a promise about tomorrow. Ain't nothin' on face of this here earth ever gonna stand in all of tomorrow, nothin' but the Word."

Some of what the preacher man said fell on deaf ears, but some stirred the heart and troubled the mind. It did not trouble him none to hear all the things about being a good friend, a good neighbor, not stealing, not killing and all the like. But talk about eternity bothered him. He got even more restless and discouraged when he let his mind dwell on it. He recalled other times before going off to war that he had heard about how a man needed to make things right, but he had never paid it much mind. It had never gnawed at him this way before. Why had he let himself be took in so much by being here in the first place?

Zack seemed to sense his anguish and restlessness. He reached over and put his strong firm hand on his shoulder with a reassuring touch. That single touch conveyed feeling, and Jubal could not command his body to bolt out the door and flee this place. He felt Zack's firm and steady hand, while his own hands trembled and could not be still. His eyes fell to the floor. He could see himself laid out somewhere at some unknown graveyard and not one soul there who ever knew him. Which tomorrow would that be?

Few of the preacher man's words made any difference after that. The boy jerked himself to attention, stood and bolted past Zack and out the door. In his next conscious thought, he had topped the little rise beyond the cemetery and heard faint organ sounds coming over his shoulder. Already the restlessness was leaving him, or so he thought.

The remainder of the Sabbath passed uneventful as far as the war went. Sentries kept watch. Couriers came and went. Smoke rose lazily from innumerable camp fires into the gray overcast sky. The smell of wood smoke hung low to the ground and seemed to muffle sounds and make them seem far away; when, in fact, they were near at hand. Each man busied himself caring for his gear, his rifle and his powder. Dusk came with no delay or concern for friend or foe. The day was almost passed, and the morning would surely bring a flurry of new orders and activity. The clouds blocked any light the moon or stars may have shed on the camp as complete darkness engulfed all. Campfires were allowed to die, and all who could were soon at rest.

The chores at the woodpile had been no different from any other morning, but tonight Jubal sensed that he was weary and worn, much more than a normal turn at the axe should inflict. He wasted little time in losing his boots and uniform and rolling into his cot. Sleep did not come. All about him were the sounds of the night, as others slept without apparent care or concern. Somewhere beyond the timberline, he heard familiar sounds that he had heard many a night back home. Screech owls sounded just as eerie here as they did up on Chestnut Ridge near home. They sounded just as sinister here as anywhere else. Their sounds stirred the mind in ways that begat a sense of despair and doom, at least tonight they did.

He felt hungry, but he had eaten his fill at dusk. He felt alone, but there were men all around him. He felt cold, yet his brow was warm. His thoughts raced from months past to the day just done. He kept hearing Ma's voice and that of Granny Iverson, as they sat by the fire and read to him from the Bible. He heard those voices blend with that of Zack's preacher man. One minute he felt anger. Anger for being flung in the midst of this war. The next breath would bring fear. Fear that he would meet the same fate as Clark.

Clark had said that he was not afraid, because he had peace. That peace had to have been true too, because it showed in his voice and in his manner. He just had a peaceful turn about him that was hard to know unless you had seen it. Jubal had seen it and now wished that he had listened better when Clark talked on it. The preacher man had said that worry looked back and hope looked ahead. That looked like it ought be just the other way round. Looking a lead ball in the eye ought be a worry to any man and that be just a plain fact what be coming if orders came to move east. How could any man look forward to getting shot or shot at, even? How in God's name could there be any peace in war? He turned to his side and felt a tear trickle down across his cheek. He wanted to go home and be at peace with the land, at peace with his family, and at peace with those he had learned to love.

The darkness dragged on and sleep continued to elude him. He sat on the side of his cot with head in his hands and fought to keep back the sobs. Would this terrible gnawing ever go away? How much longer before daylight and time to get out and get busy with a new day? Then more words of the preacher man cascaded upon him. There might not be another day. Any day could be the last day we ever draw a breath. War made the last day come early for some. Many had had their last day long before they had been ready, long before they had lived out a lifetime.

Too much to understand. Too much to think about. Too many unanswered questions. There had to be some way to better know what to do and how to have a little peace of mind. There just had to be a way.

The night wore on and the restlessness did not die away. First sitting and then lying down, only to toss side to side, while all about him came the sounds of sleep and rest. He had never had a night like this before. Not here nor anywhere else. He did not understand why he had suddenly grown so restless and so bothersome over a few words spoke by a preacher man that he never heard before. Yet his message and his words would not go away.

At last there was a faint light in the east. No air stirred and sounds echoed from the low lying hills and tree lines as if they were only at arm's length. Screech owls called out in loneliness to a forlorn mate, possibly displaced by this nasty war. Occasional snorts of horses tied to the hitches evoked visions of fire breathing dragons and hot breath steeds foretold in the apocalypses. Sounds that normally came and went without a second thought now brought on strange and unfamiliar suggestions of sinister or evil just waiting to befall the unwary or unlucky soul who might perchance cross their paths. There was no logic in his temperament, and he knew it. It just would not go away, not this night.

Without being told, Jubal was back at the wood yard well before light enough to begin his morning routine. He was a bit startled when an unseen sentry challenged him.

"Halt there."

Jubal froze in his tracks. He did not recognize the voice.

"Who are you and what you up to?" the sentry queried.

"I come here ever mornin' fer wood cuttin' chores," Jubal answered.

"You must be about half loco. It still about another half hour till good light. You should still be sacked in," the sentry chided as he came closer to the woodpile and the boy.

"I know, but I ain't slept hardly any at all," came the reply.

"Why, you worried about us moving and being in a really big fracas?"

"Naw, I just restless as worms on a hot rock and don't reckon I really recall why," Jubal answered in anticipation of not revealing any more than he had already said about himself.

"You afraid of being shot like Clark?"

That took Jubal by surprise, because he had not expected anyone else to be aware that he had befriended Clark or knew anything about their short friendship.

"You knowed him too?"

"No. But I saw you and him talk a time or two, and I saw you at his grave yesterday. That's why I think you two knew each other. I just thought that might be what is eating away at your mind. By the way my name is Garth, William Johnson Garth."

"I know some Johnson's back home."

"Where you call home?" William followed.

"Back in Tennessee in Hawks County, little farmstead in Cane Valley."

"I know where that is. I was through there about six months or so back. We chased a bunch all through there and never did catch who we wanted. Word was three riders who were bad stuff. They started out as three and got bigger and bolder as they went. They plundered any and all they came across from Nashville on east. We had word that they were holed up in uplands and in mountain country there abouts."

That set the boy's mind free from the night's restlessness, at least for now, as his mind raced back to the riders that he had come across and to the tracks around Wes's place and what had happened to him. The time would be about right for when the three were just cranking up their thieving and such. They would'a had plenty time to trek all over the ridges and hollers twixt then and six months ago.

"Will, can ye tell me any names or any places by name where ye was?"

"I'd rather be called William, if you would."

"Okay, sure," Jubal muttered apologetically.

"I don't recall any certain names or places, but I do know that we searched and tracked all up and down the river banks on both sides of a place called Clinch. Don't recall any family names or such."

"That be close my old home place, but not real close," Jubal added. "Where you come from?"

"Ohio."

"What ye be doin' when this here war got crunk up and goin'?" Jubal asked.

"I was a schoolmaster. I intend to go back to it just as soon as I can."

"Ye teach readin' and cipherin'?"

"Reading and arithmetic, yes, and other matters too."

"Ye must be schooled right smart bit."

"Education is valuable. It is something that cannot be taken away as long as one draws breath," William stated somewhat defiantly. "It will not rust or be eaten by the moths as will most all other man-made treasures. However, education passes away when a man passes away; therefore, it is not eternal."

Damn, there was that bit again about drawing breath. The restlessness sprang forth again in an instant. What the boy had taken as a sign of care and concern from William and their short conversation suddenly changed to the same condemnation that he had felt only a few hours ago from the preacher man. He in one instant wanted to pour out his feelings to William and in the next thought better of it. He could handle it and could wrest this uneasiness from his inner being. Who else better to advise him than his own logic? Besides there was sure to soon come movement orders and then all would be too busy for any other matters.

William excused himself and soon melted into the grey light of the new dawn. The rising sun would clear the darkness and reveal the world all around, but could have little effect on the cloudiness of the mind. Jubal seized the double-bitted axe and began to work out his restlessness on the gnarled locust limbs piled before him. The recent rain had not dampened the dead and decaying limbs. Chips flew with each thwack of the honed edge.

The camp came to life as usual. Soon cook stoves bellowed grey smoke out the side of the mess tent. Out riders came in as the change of sentries brought in hungry mouths and thirsty steeds. Couriers saddled up in preparation for dispatch to wherever they would be directed. No word of movement had come during the night. There would be no advance toward danger and doom today. That was almost a guarantee that there would, in fact, be a tomorrow.

More of the woodcutter's chores. More of the afternoon off. More time to amble off in the woods. More time to think about all the folks back home. More time to scheme about all the material things in life that were sure to bring the freedom from enslavement to the dirt farm labor. More time to plan a life of pleasure. More time to enjoy the finer things in life. More time to enjoy the company of fine and upstanding ladies. More time to dream like some fool dirt farmer that hardly can write his own name. Just another day caught up in this man's war and turmoil. More time for the mind to be embroiled in worry and uncertainty.

Woodcutter's duty done and finished for the day. Jubal wandered into the pasture below the little white churchyard and strolled leisurely, and for the most part, aimlessly in the direction to the low lying creek. He sensed being followed. Turning, William approached in stride.

"What you following' me fer?" Jubal asked.

"Wanted to talk with you a bit. You seemed to be depressed and confused earlier when we spoke." William responded.

"Why you care?" Jubal asked with uncertainty.

"Because I am in this war the same as you. I want to make it through the same as you. I have had troubling times and others have helped me. I just want to see as many troopers as possible make it through and get to go back to their homes and families. I just sense that you need a little hope and reassurance and that maybe I could be there for you. I don't know if our lives will ever cross paths again, but they have for now; and now is the only time that we have for sure."

Two mounted couriers approached. Without stopping, one shouted, "better go back to camp soon; word comin' to move out soon." They rode on as quickly as they had rode in.

Jubal turned to William, "Guess that about kills out talking."

"We will just have to wait and see what tomorrow brings. Sometimes we need to have faith for today and let tomorrow take care of itself. Besides we can't do much about tomorrow until it comes."

"Guess not."

"Jubal, we will talk more soon, I promise."

"Yeah."

That said, they each headed back across the pasture and each went his own way inside the camp. It would soon be sunset and the western sky looked to be crimson again. Tomorrow, if it came, would be fair. Some wondered what the night would bring.

Jubal lay in his cot and waited for the old screech owl to awaken and announce his presence by his eerie calls. Some of the sounds of the young night were all too familiar and reminded him of where he was and the situation he now faced. Sounds of night riders coming and going assured him that all were not resting or sleeping, as is the way with any military encampment. All around were alert eyes and listening ears, other than his own. The idea of a stranger watching out while he slept only served to add to his sense of being out of control.

Lying back on his bunk, he realized how tired he was. Without any conscious effort he soon drifted off to sleep. It seemed to him that it had only been a few seconds, but the cool of the evening breeze had given rise to a night chill. He soon was awakened by lack of cover. Pulling a sheet up over him soon solved the chill. He tried to return to the bliss of sleep.

His mind wandered back to the log home in Cane Valley and the hot summer nights when he slept on the dogtrot just to enjoy the cool air. He had listened to the night sounds intently then, but had heard nothing of war or conflict or uneasiness. He had heard only the familiar sounds of the mountains and the hollows, the sound of the breezes and the distant rumbles of the scattered night thunderstorms. He recalled the peacefulness that he felt back then. He had never given much thought about all the days yet to come. He was young and in his prime and was just beginning life. Just beginning, until this war got started and put a new and different light on most ever thing and ever body.

He did not understand why he could not have that peace of mind even now as he tried to rest and sleep. He blamed all his feeling of restlessness on the war. He saw that as the cause of all his worry about the tomorrow business and there being no promise of it. He did not think William, or even old Zack, or even Jugg, that is Sergeant Jugg, lacked that peace of mind or at least they never said anything to make him think otherwise. They all seemed to not be afraid and worried about all the tomorrows. How could it be that ever thing could be so calm and peaceable with them when they were wrapped up in war just the same as he?

They were all older than him but that could not be the sole reason for their quietness and sense of calmness that seemed to hold control over them. There had to be more to it. He would have to get back with William and talk to him more. He even thought he might go see if old Zack would talk with him some more, but since he had bolted from the church so fast and so foolishly that may just have put a stop to that prospect. After all, what could a slave do for him, and why would old Zack even give a hoot about a solider from down in the mountains? Just have to wait and see who said what, but there had to be answers out there some place.

Daylight brought a flurry of activity, but no marching orders. Word from the couriers was that Rebel movements had not been as anticipated the past few days. It had been expected that the Confederate brass would soon march east to Washington City and on past. Now it looked like that plan had been sacked. Troop movement reports from out riders and scouts had them coming back west and south. The major had been told from higher up to just sit tight, but to be ready to move on orders by courier.

All camp equipment and stores were to be packed up and readied. There would be no cook stove fires today. Jubal had no assigned duty save for getting himself and his personal gear ready to march. He had been issued a new uniform and a new long rifle complete with all field gear. Some slick nosed young pup of a lieutenant had even made him sign his name for it.

He wanted to go look for William, but did not know where he had duty today. Reasonable to think that he may be on watch just like before. Thinking such, he headed off in the direction of the wood yard and searched the tree line slowly with his hand shading the first morning light. William seemed so calm and not scared of anything and that made a deep impression on the lad. There were other matters too. Maybe William could show him more about how to read proper and how to cipher and all. Improvement in matters should make for a better place in life. Alas, William was not to be found, at least not now.

The morning wore on into the heat of the day, and the day turned to just another day. Soon a week had passed and seemed like every trooper in camp was on edge. They were bored and restless all at the same time. They swiftly grew tired of jerky and hardtack and let their feelings be known to any who would lend an ear. They slept on the ground each night, completely under the stars. They were allowed to unpack only their bedroll. Marching orders could come at any hour. Most would move out in a heartbeat. Anything would be better than the uneasiness of the unknown and the provoking boredom of waiting.

All week, Jubal had looked for William but had not found him. He had returned to the little white churchyard on Sunday morning and had sat alone near Clark's grave. Wonder if Clark had known William or had ever talked with him? Zack had seen Jubal in the cemetery and had come over to say hello. Zack asked how he was but did not try to get him inside the church this time. Come to think about it, it would have been too early for that because the sun was just breaking up the east cloud cover.

The feeling of loneliness had not engulfed him the way it had the last time he came here. He missed Clark for sure, but he had found William since then. But William was nowhere around the last few days. Then he remembered what the old preacher man had said about being a prisoner of death all our lives. Surely that could not have come to William too.

A sense of gloom fell over the boy. He could hardly stand the thought of not having a single solitary friend. He became increasingly uncomfortable in the cemetery and being near the church. Bolting away seemed the only escape from his overwhelming sense of despair. He almost ran back across the small pasture and into what was left of the camp. Everything packed up and made ready created some unfamiliarity, and it took a moment to orient himself to where he wanted to be.

He asked about William and was told that he had been assigned to an outpost and would be there for the day watch.

"Which one?"

"Yonder, west of camp, on the high ground," from the duty officer.

"Good, I go find him," Jubal replied.

"Best you not. That would be a sure fire way you gettin' yer butt shot off. You know better than go huntin' out a sentry when he not be lookin' for a body come up on his backside. How danged crazy are you anyhow?"

"I need to talk to him, bad."

"Then come back here at sundown when he gets off his post."

"Yessir."

At least he learned that William was well and that nothing had befallen him. That made things a bit easier, and some of the emotional panic subsided.

Jubal retreated to the base of a large sugar tree, just below the tree line of the pasture. He sat down and leaned back against the trunk of the stalwart sentinel that had to have been there in that one spot on watch for near on to a hundred years. He checked over his field gear once again. All seemed in order. His powder was dry. He leaned his head back and gazed out to the south. The distant rolling hills and ridges called to him and reminded him very much of home.

When he was home in the mountains, he had never felt this uneasiness and restlessness. He had heard Granny Iverson speak about a man and his soul, but he had never given it much thought. He didn't rightly know what a soul was, nor what it looked like. He had killed and dressed many a critter, and nobody ever showed him a thing outta them that could pass off as a soul. He would have to ask her more about that when he got back home.

But what if he never made it back home? Besides that, Granny was along in years and she might not be there right now for all that matter. There just be too many things so hard to understand. Seems the more a body learns, then the more he don't really know. The doubt and the uneasiness always finds a way to come in and torment the mind. Most times it jumps up and bites a body when they least be looking for it. But then there be ones like William, and like Clark was, that always be not fretting over a thing at all. Just how can they be that way, specially in smack dab middle of this cussed awful war?

Restlessness and lack of sleep had taken a toll on Jubal. He knew he was tired, but never thought that he would sit alone under an old sugar tree and sleep away the better part of the day. His back and neck felt sore and stiff. The tree trunk made for an uncomfortable bed and pillow, and his body was letting him know about it.

He rose to his feet, stretched his lithe and muscular frame, gathered his field gear, and ambled back in the direction of the mess tent, or where the mess tent had been just the day before. It was another red sunset and looked to be hot again tomorrow. Maybe no movement orders would come until a cooler time. A forced march would be hard in such heat. Rains, if they came, would cool the air but would make a mire of the dusty dirt roads and footpaths.

Couriers still came and went frequently but brought no word of any activity in the area. Headquarters may possibly know more than they let out, but it seemed that nothing was astir. Everyone seemed restless and edgy. Personalities clashed and often resulted in verbose assaults on the closest of friends and fellow troopers. Each argument was rapid in onset and just as rapid to be settled and over. Ranking authority would see to that very smartly.

Additional riflemen came into camp every day or so; not in great numbers, but they came and gathered as the camp swelled. There was bound to be something brewing and soon, but no one knew what or where or when it might all come about. Most of the troops came up from the south or from on further west. Each man that came added to the demands and thereby increased the tension in the camp. Some were ready to move out on their own. Others, few others, just took it all in stride, like William. Nothing ever seemed to really rile him. Jubal wondered how that could be.

He set off to find William. It should be about time to set the first night watch, and he should be ready to come in off day watch. It did not take long to spot William. He looked tired but still had that air of peace about him that told more than a thousand words from his own mouth. He carried his full field pack and gear with ease.

"Hey William," Jubal greeted him as he reached the rail fence and crossed into the open area of the camp.

"Evening friend, what brings you to this neck of the woods?"

"I be wantin' ask a few things."

"Well, let me go report in and then we can see what we might do."

The two walked together toward one of the few remaining tents that had not yet been taken down. It served as the duty tent and was a continual beehive of activity. William made his usual report of no contacts, no sightings and nothing to report. He was then given his assignment for tomorrow's watch and promptly dismissed by the duty officer.

"Now I would like to find something to eat before we get too wound up talking," William informed as he began unshouldering his pack. He soon dug out some jerky and unwrapped a few small corn bread cakes. "Now let's go find a place to eat, and we can talk. Have you had supper yet?"

"Naw. I fell asleep all afternoon up yonder under that big ole sugar tree and ain't even thought on bein' hungry yet."

"Well here, eat one of my corn cakes. They go pretty good with jerky and a good red apple."

"Where you get red apples?" Jubal could not keep from staring at the big red fruit that William magically produced from his pack.

"Got them off a tree just over the crest of the ridge up there. Not too far at all."

"Dang, they look mighty fine."

"Here you can have one of them too."

Neither said a word as they moseyed down near the creek and sat down near the water. They sat in silence as they ate ravenously. The smell of wood smoke and campfires soon filled the air and from somewhere came the smell of fatback and coffee. That would have been enough to make a body mighty hungry had it not been for the corn cake and the apples. They had quieted the appetite for now.

William broke the silence. "What's on your mind, Jubal?"

"I ain't certain what it be. I ain't' never been 'fraid nor nothin' like that, but last few days I just dang nigh about be tremblin' some-times. I ain't never been in no such shape. I don't understand why."

"Are you scared right now?"

"No. No, I ain't. I don't understand that neither."

"Anything hurt you, like maybe in the head where you took a shot? Are you off balance or wobbly or anything like that?"

"Naw, not one bit."

"Are you homesick?"

"What ye mean by that?" Jubal looked quizzing.

"Do you miss home and your family? Do you want to leave here and go home?"

"I think about home and my kin, but it don't weigh heavy on me most times."

In that same breath the young boy had visions of home, of his Ma and his sisters. But the most vivid image was that of Granny Iverson sitting by the fire at night and reading by its light. Some nights she would read way on toward midnight; and other nights she would read just a few words and then go on to bed, but she read every night.

"Well, yeah. I guess I miss em some, but I ain't sick none over it."

"What do you think it is that scares you so much?" William asked.

"I reckon I don't wanna be shot no more. I ain't wantin' end up like Clark. I ain't ready to turn my toes up yet," Jubal answered. "I just wanna get through this here war business and go back home and have a good life and a few of the good things outta life that I ain't seen no part of so far."

"What kind of things do you expect from life, Jubal?"

"Them things what bring pleasure and respect to a man. I ain't never been nothin' cept a dirt farmer's kid, and here late I don't even know where my Pa is or nuthin' about his carryin' on nor nuthin' whatsoever about him. He done lit out and never said boo to nobody. Ever body 'round home knows him by what he is and how he run off, and I reckon they be thinkin' nigh on to the same about me. I ain't him, and I ain't like him. But folks back home still looks down on me, and I don't like it none neither. I want people to respect me and not be doggin' me all the time cause of how I come up."

"You want to have things that other people look up to and want then, is that right?"

"That and not have to dig in dirt scratchin' out a livin' all the rest of my days," Jubal responded with just a hint of resentment in his manner.

"What about friends and family? Are they going to stand by you even if it does turn out that you continue to be a dirt farmer? Will they be there if you were to have a run of sickness or something that would lay you up for a while?"

"I reckon they be there fer me iffin I needed them."

"They may be there for you now, but would they be there twenty years or thirty years from now?"

"Well iffin they was alive and lived close I reckon they be there fer me."

"But what if there were none but yourself, Jubal. Who would be there for you then?"

William touched a nerve that the boy had not given much consideration. He had not thought that far into the future. He was having enough trouble getting past the tomorrows. The thing of no assurance for tomorrow kept eating at him without him even realizing it. He had not yet connected that with all his restlessness and uneasiness. He had not even admitted his fears, not to anyone else or to himself. He just attributed it to the chaos and calamity of the war.

There was nothing wrong with him. He was plenty strong and healthy and had no real reason to think he weren't going to outlast this scrape he found himself thrown into all so unexpected. Sure he was green when he first rode off from home. But that had been months past, and he had weathered it all so far. Besides that, he had even took a round to the head and out smarted that. Did that not prove he could care for himself?

"Who would be there for you then, Jubal? Who?"

"Right now, can't say who."

"If you had all the things you want, would they be there for you then?"

"Well course they be there then, cause I be respected by them if I had all them things that I want. Who there be that don't wanna be 'round fine horses, land and money?"

"Jubal, you will not like what I am going to tell you, but please listen to me and at least think about it."

Jubal had a blank look on his face, but said nothing, just waited for William to continue with whatever he thought.

"I can well understand how you feel about wanting to be respected, and I don't blame you for wanting that, not a bit. Having all those material things will get you some respect, but that will fade when all the wealth is gone. Things of this earth that are man-made will never stand the test of time and in the end will be worthless. If that kind of wealth is what you are working for, then you are working for the wrong things. Things that can and will be taken from you at some point and time."

"I won't let nobody take from me, no sir."

"It could be out of your hands, Jubal. What if all your stock got the blackleg or the scares really bad and all died? Could you be in control of that? What if somehow you lost all your money or a flood or storm tore away all your houses and barns? Could you be in control of all that? Don't you see what I mean by material things fading away and then the friends fade away with them?"

"All that ain't likely come to be," Jubal said while brewing doubts about what William was saying.

"Hard to tell what will come to be as a result of all this war and fighting and hatred and such. I don't look for blue and grey to be friends any time soon. It could easily be the onset of troubled times both north and south. But back to the matter of respect, this is what I think and what I believe."

"What?"

"Respect has to be earned. It's not a thing that you can run out and buy at any price. It is not a commodity to be bought or traded, but it can be lost for sure. A man has to live a life that deserves respect and has to show by example that he is deserving of the respect of others. He has to treat others with the respect that he wants for himself. Money and horses will not buy you that. Oh, sure money may give you a certain amount of power and command, but that is not a guarantee that you will be respected. You have to do unto others. You know what it says about that don't you?"

"I reckon, I do."

"If you do that then, I believe respect will follow close behind all the way. I don't know a man anywhere who can buy that with his gold and silver," William stated. "That's what it means about things not made by man."

"Then how come you never seem riled up? Nuthin' never seems wrong with you. Nuthin' frets you none!"

"I guess that's because I got peace in my life. I just do not see much need to worry and fret all the time. It is all under control anyhow."

"Then I reckon you got respect, huh?" Jubal asked.

"I reckon I do, but it took some work on my part," William said as he drew a long breath and looked back to the camp area.

"How's that?"

"Long story, Jubal. I will tell you sometime, but for now just know that respect, or lack of it, is part of why I am now school-master back home. I intend to go back to it if I make it to the end of this mess."

"Then yer schoolin' be what got you respect, huh?"

"No. Not really. The school work just made it possible for me to have a way to earn respect from others that I would not have been able to do otherwise. It gave me a way to be of help to other people, and they respected me for that, not for the education."

"You think all yer schoolin' makes you a better man than most?"

"No. I honestly do not think like that, but it does open up ways for me to do and see things that others may not see or understand."

Jubal was silent for a bit, wondering about what William had just said. "Think you could school me a dab or two?"

"I could read you a lesson or two, but schooling as you put it, is a lifetime thing. You can't just up and latch onto it because you see a need for it. It takes work and a lot of dedication. You have to want it enough to keep at it, and really it goes on all your life. You grow all along the way and learn to see things in a different light. Schooling is one of those things that you cannot assign a dollar value. It is something that once you have it, no one can steal away from you. Your knowledge will be with you and be yours alone until you pass on out of this life. You can share it with others all you want and should share it, but you will never lose it."

"I ain't arguin' that."

"I know," William said softly. "Jubal, you and I are from two different places. We are different. But that is no reason why we cannot be friends. We should treat each other with the love and kindness that would be shared by brothers and other family members."

"Huh?"

"We should treat others just like they were our kin. We should be good to all mankind and be willing to help any man anytime we can. Good Book says that we should do it out of love and service to others," William responded somewhat emphatically.

"I reckon them be words to live by, at least that be what Ma and Granny Iverson always be sayin'. They be right keen on Good Book readin' and all that. Always did think Ma had heart made outta gold. She'd give away her last biscuit iffin she thunk a body be hungry."

"How you feel about that, Jubal?"

"I ain't really give it a whole heap thoughts. I spect it be honorable thing to do by helpin' a body, but I thinkin' ye gotta look out fer self first. Least that be how I seein' it," Jubal responded. "If I don't look after my own self, then who gonna do it fer me?"

"That is why a man needs a friend, Jubal. I sense that you need a friend and have sensed it since we first met. You just seem to have a need in your life, and I want to help fill it for you in whatever measure that I can."

"Reckon I ain't needin' nobody look after me. Just need outta this here war. That all."

"Is that your aim? Is that all you want now?"

"What else be matterin' now cept not takin' a bullet no more?"

"Do you not have any plans for after the war? What about all the days yet to come? What do you want out of life for yourself and for those in your life?"

Jubal gave no response. There was that thing about tomorrow and all the days after that. Why in hell can't today be worrisome enough, he thought. When he got a few things that made life good, then maybe tomorrow would look a heap better. Be a big relief not to be occupied fretting over where next eats come from or where to bed down for a night, then have to move on come daylight. That put things in a whole new light and ever thing be easier then. At least that was how it be after the skirmishin' be over. But it would not be that way for Clark.

That be what the trouble all stem from. There was just too much thinking about Clark. He took a sniper ball and that were just a perchance thing that not be likely to come up no more. Just gotta put that behind and move on. Just need to quit fretting so much over things that be over and done. Just need William to keep on being my friend. Who else is there to be a friend anyhow?

Chapter 5

Suspicious

*J*ubal helped Wes get all washed up and dressed in clean clothes that Ma had hunted up for him. She had come up with a cotton pullover shirt, old worn buckskin pants, and a pair of deerskin shoes that she had made in the past.

It was decided that Wes could bed down in the springhouse loft whenever he could not sleep on the dogtrot. It should be a long time before the nights chilled enough to need to be in out of the night.

Wes seemed to be in good spirits and enjoyed getting spruced up some. Jubal noted that the bruises on his rib cage had turned from red to a deep crimson and that his cough had nearly gone away. He didn't rattle when he breathed either.

Jubal and the old man bedded down on the dogtrot just after dusk and began to talk about any number of things. The only one really showing any interest in actual sleep was old Jake, and he set in to snore like an over-worked mule. The night creatures began their calls and the world took on a more peaceful attitude.

"Jubal, you still got yer gold piece?"

"Yeah, Wes, I do," came the response. "I worked hard gettin' that."

"I know ye did, just same as me back few years past. I ain't sayin' so to be a braggin', but I made a right smart wage back when I first come up outta Alabammy. Don't think I ever told ye about them times I guess."

"Naw, ye never done that fer sure," Jubal responded as much in wondering as in answering.

"Ye know that old gourd I fetched here with us?"

"Yup, Wes, I been ponderin' that," Jubal said.

"There be quite a story behind that cussed thing. I tell ye more about it in a few days." Wes waited for Jubal to question him more about the gourd, but no questions came.

Jubal yawned and rolled to his back and waited a bit before responding. "Wes, I be thinkin' that I know what be in that gourd, but I reckon I just wait till ye be ready to talk on it."

"There be more to it than ye might ever reckon. It soon be time that ye be let in on it."

"Well ye shore got me wonderin' on it. But I not be askin' a bunch about it, cause I reckon that not be plumb right. Can't say as that not keepin' me wonderin' what all in tarnation ye be meanin' by it."

"I say this fer now and then we let it sleep. It be about gold, and more than one ten dollar piece too," Wes answered.

At once Jubal visualized a sack full of gold coins somehow hoarded up by the old man lying at his side. All sorts of wonderful material things that he could buy with a bag of gold coins raced through his mind. Frilly dresses and ribbons for all the young gals that would flock to his side. Faraway places and things that so far in his young life had only been spoken of by someone who may have read about it somewhere.

Random and rambling thoughts soon brought on drowsiness, and Jubal drifted off into a restful sleep. Wes rested at intervals and spoke no more in order not to rouse the sleeping lad. He knew that his young companion would be awake and alert on short notice should he have need to waken him. His ribs were sore and tender, but his breathing was much improved. Rarely did he cough. He had to admit that being cleaned up and shaved had contributed much to his improvement. The night quickly wore on and soon Ma cold be heard astir.

Breakfast was the usual. Biscuits and blackberry jelly with streaked meat fried crisp and crunchy. Black strong coffee with some grounds that had made it through the cloth strainer.

Ma spoke as Jubal rose to leave the table. "Son, I want ye go see C.C. at his mill today and see iffin we might get the use of his buckboard and team. I wanna have a mite things fetched in from Yeary store up in the cove country. Cleve don't have much in his store like he did, and I ain't real keen on tradin' with him."

"Ye want me ask C.C. that? When?"

"Today. This mornin' iffin ye git a move on."

"He take me fer a beggar fool, I reckon," Jubal protested.

"I reckon not. He done told me that he be able to 'commodate me iffin need be, and I thinkin' it be needed."

"Why don't ye ask him yerself then?"

"Jubal, ye don't know much fer doin' business with a body, I reckon, but it be time ye learnt a lick or three and now be just good a time as any. It give ye a chance see Lida, I reckon."

That put a different slant on things in a heartbeat. Jubal didn't say much more, because his mind had been put in a whirl at the mere mention of her name. Emotion and desire welled up inside him in ways that he had never felt toward any other. Part of him wanted more than anything to seize her and have her for his own wants and desires. Yet at the same time he felt a deep respect for her and would want to treat her only with kindness and affection. She was the prettiest thing that he had ever liked, and yet he felt that she was a cut above himself and his kinfolk. For that reason he thought she would never pay him serious mind. But, someday she would be paying mind to some man. It just as well be him as any other, no matter who he were or who he weren't.

"I reckon ye ain't takin' no fer answer, so I reckon I just up and go. But reckon I ought fresh up and put on a clean shirt first?"

"Ye git commenced cleanin' up yerself, and I'll fetch ye a clean shirt. I be thinkin' yer Pa had a white store bought shirt once. It ought fill the bill right sharp," Ma answered with just a hint of a smile on her face.

With that, Jubal made a beeline to the springhouse runoff, stripped and bathed himself from head to toe fast as possible. He soaped up his black mop of hair and stuck his head under the spring pipe till all the lye lather was gone. Did not bother to dry his hair. The morning sun would do that.

Ma surprised him by standing in the springhouse doorway with a towel.

"Here, son. Dry off good, hair and all, then ye can put these here duds on." She had found Pa's white linen shirt and a pair of deerskins.

Glancing over his shoulder again, Ma had already left the doorway and had laid his duds on the nearby bench. He dried himself, his hair too, and dressed in his newfound shirt and britches.

He emerged from the springhouse, boots in hand and walked to the dogtrot where Wes had taken in the whole of the activities. Wes eyed him up and down a couple of times before either spoke.

"Need me some boot black fer these here old clod busters. They be a mite frayed," Jubal said as he sat down on the top step and placed the boots betwixt his bare feet.

"Well, iffin I had any ye could use it, but them kind'a things is hard come by here lately. 'Sides that, blacken be one of them things ye gets to put on that tries makin' a man look like somethin' that he ain't and most likely won't never be."

"I know Wes, but they need spruced up a mite," Jubal countered. "I git a dab' a axel grease and rub em down a mite."

"Wouldn't advise that nary bit," Wes said.

"How come not?"

Make em look slick and shiny fer sure, but time ye walk ten steps they be covered plumb over with dust and grime. Ye be better off just wet em down and wash em off best ye can, then leave it be."

"I guess ye be right. Ye be right on most things ye tell me. How come that be Wes?"

"I just be older and wiser than ye. Some 'a these days, ye be growed up and be a full topped out man, and then ye know more how life be then. Ye be wiser then too."

"I guess there be a truth in that, but seem like I ought be about there now as I be seein' it. Ma say I be all growed up quicker than she ever thought about."

"Don't rush life so much my boy; it run past ye before ye have time to think on it. Bein' growed up and havin' a wife and kids to feed make a heavy yoke fer ye iffin ye ain't growed up to it first."

"I ain't wantin' no kids. I just wanna be growed up and have a chance to make a way fer myself, that all," Jubal answered.

"Well them kids will come that be a fact," Wes said as a smirk came over his face.

"Huh? What ye mean? I just said, I ain't wantin' no young'uns."

"Well they gonna come," Wes said half chuckling under his breath. "Just look at ye right now, and ye ain't even laid eyes on her in weeks. Ye about as moon struck as any old hound I ever seen."

"Aw Wes, all I want is to look decent when I go see old C.C. about the use of his team and wagon."

"I hear ye."

Imagination once again ran wild. Wes had jokingly hinted of passion and desire. Jubal had to admit, but only to himself, that those desires and wants were becoming stronger each and every time he thought of Lida. He had never really considered settling down and the likelihood of rearing a house full of kids, but that idea had in fact crossed his mind a time or two here of late.

Wes seemed to sense that he had struck a nerve with the boy and, therefore, said nothing else of a teasing nature. Enough was enough. If things became serious for her and the boy, then there might be more opportunity for teasing him, but not now. He did not want to encourage the boy to do wrong by her nor no other girl. "Ye keep yer wits about ye, son. Act like a man 'stead of a young pup and ye be fine. I just givin' ye the devil, that all."

"I know that Wes, and I ain't holdin' it again' ye nary bit. I reckon I can take a ribbin' just same as most any and not be riled up by it neither."

"Ye got a good turn to ye boy, and it take a danged fool not be able see it. That why I know that ye be more a man than lots give ye credit fer. Ye just need grow a mite more in good ever day hoss sense, and ye be growed up sooner than ye need be."

"Iffin ye two be about through jawin', it be time ye go, son. I be thinkin' C.C. be lookin' fer ye by mid-mornin' at latest, so ye best hike out now. I would'a thunk a team a wild hosses wouldn't held ye back," Ma said assertively.

"I be gone right soon, Ma. I just need fetch the rifle."

"I done spoke with the Johnson's at meetin' last Sunday a week ago, and C.C. knows what I have in mind fer ye and him be settlin' on. Ye mind yore manners by the women folk to, special Lida."

"Shucks Ma, ye know I will."

"I know, but it don't do no harm to drive the point home. After all, she is right smart a looker fer shore."

Jubal fetched the long rifle from the corner of the kitchen and slung the powder horn across his left shoulder. He sat down on the top step of the dogtrot and pulled on his boots, stood and combed his dark hair with his fingers.

"How many rifle balls ye got?" Wes inquired.

"Four."

"Fresh deer meat taste good, I reckon, iffin ye happen on a doe.

"I keep my eye out fer ye one, Wes. Keep Jake home, cause I know I not see nuthin' with him traipsin' along.

Jubal started off in high spirits as he swung open the yard gate and stepped into the barn lot and started his three-hour trek to C.C's mill.

Wes sat on the dogtrot without a word for a good bit. He thought about his life and how he had wasted the last several years wallowing in his own orneriness and self-pity. Sure he had lost his mate and most ever thing else. He still had his old place. Time was when it was a nice little place, but now most of it was all growed over in brambles and bushes. But now he had seen a taste of how life could be even if one was poor as a church mouse.

Gold! Glory be! He had plumb let that slip his mind. There be gold, and it be his too. He had hinted it to the boy but never brought him up to place on it. Just never seemed like the time was right nor the need was big. Most likely times be worse in the next few years than they ever been so far. Things be hard to come by if there be no gold to buy it with. Paper money be no good then.

Wes raced through the later years of his time spent down south in the forties and early fifties and how he had made his stash of gold coins. Folks in these parts were not on to his past, and it probably best it stay that way. There were mixed minds over the slavery trade in these mountains and hollers and best just let sleeping dogs lie.

"Ye gone back sleepin' Wes, or is yer mind plumb gone outta the holler?" Ma asked surprising him a bit.

"I just be thinkin' on things, that be all."

"Well, I ain't one what be askin' tomfool questions, but I just thinkin' I could make ye a pair a deerskins iffin ye want. They be a mite hot fer August but be better than barefoots all the time. Gravels and brambles be a mite hard on yer feet."

"I would be beholdin' to ye," Wes said appreciatively.

"I made a pair for Jackson, and he wore em outta here the night he told me he reckoned he had better light out a while. I beginnin' wonder what has come to him by now. I got another pair, but I was savin' them fer Jubal fer this comin' winter."

"Then that who needs them most."

"I got one more skin all tanned and dry that I can make fer ye. Never meant that I weren't gonna make some fer ye," Ma critiqued rather sharply.

"I can pay ye fer them," Wes said softly.

"That ain't necessary," Ma barked back at him.

By that time Granny Iverson had walked out onto the trot from the kitchen and seemed to perk up an ear when the pay thing came about.

"Just how ye pay fer ary thang what I'd like to know seein' as how ye don't even own clothes fit 'nuff fer coverin' yer behind?" Granny chimed in.

"That be 'nuff of that Granny," Ma cut in sharply. "I knowed Wes lot longer and lot better than ye. I be more able judgin' what he can or can't pay. Now let it go at that."

Granny got up and dang nigh fell over her own chair trying to get back to the kitchen so fast. Giggles could be faintly heard coming from the washstand by the old cook stove.

"Don't pay her no mind much, Wes. She just old and set to her ways and don't think much of nobody but herself no more," Ma said as she turned toward the kitchen.

If she only knew how well he could actually pay, she would be gape-jawed for sure.

Jubal made regular but attentive steps as he journeyed down the rutted road to the mill. The recent rains had seemed to refresh even the road itself. No fresh tracks were to be seen. No one had traveled here at least since the rains came. He stepped carefully around any lingering mud holes and tried diligently to keep his boots as clean. It would be unthinkable to be in any disarrays that Lida would notice.

As he neared the sand hill grade, where he had hid himself in the reed patch from the three riders, he remembered them and all that he had seen and pondered over about them. He had not seen the whiskered man before. The other two, he had not seen their face very well, but he was sure that he knew who was astride that big roan. Then he thought of Cleve again and how he had acted toward Wes. He wondered if this had any bearing on Ma sending him to C.C. to see about going to the Yeary's store.

He had not gone more than a quarter mile, still not quite passed all the reed patches. There they were. Tracks, fresh tracks! The soft damp earth had made for a print big as life that told all he needed to know about the riders. Three sets of tracks. Two shod and one not. They crossed the road in no waste of time or step. No tracks up or down the road, just across, headed west. Immediately whisker face and the big roan loomed in his mind. That big roan was so plain that he could dang near smell him. Jubal almost without thought turned off the road and started to follow the trail. It would be easy to track. A fresh track was always easy, and this one surely had been laid down some time since daybreak this very morning.

Three steps off the road and into soft reed mud reminded him that he had other obligations, not to mention his own personal callings. He stepped back into the road and stood very still and listened for the sounds all around. There were no sounds. No sounds of hoof beat or rattle of the reins. No sounds at all. Strange that even the birds were quiet. Looking again at the tracks, he noticed one particular print in the soft earth. It was a deep print with mud splatters on all sides, not more than a quarter hour or so old. That was why there were no sounds. All the creatures had scurried for cover and were not yet sure the way was clear again.

It was clear that he could not follow the tracks this morning. There were more pressing issues at hand. Besides that if he had any extra time he could track them on the way home this afternoon. Looked like they might be headed across the ridge and maybe back in the direction of the old Wes place. Couldn't tell right now. Time to be on down the holler to the mill and Lida.

Morning sun was up high by the time that Jubal reached the upstream mill dam and the race that led to the mill wheel. Recent rains had gone a ways to help refill the upstream mill pond, but not enough to run the wheel. It was the wrong time of year for much mill work. Crops would be good in another six weeks or so, if it would keep up with a rain shower or two. No rain would also mean the wheel would stand still, and C.C. would come up short on his fall profits. It wouldn't hurt him as bad as others here abouts if it stayed dry. He could hold out longer than most.

Jubal topped the last little rise in the road and turned into the mill lot.

"Hello Jubal. Come on in and sit here with me a bit." It was C.C. calling from the porch of the mill building. Jubal stepped onto the mill porch and the miller reached out his hand in genuine friendship. "How ye doin', son?"

"I reckon I be good, Mr. Johnson. How about you and all the family?"

"We be good, I reckon. None of us missed no meals yet."

"Say same thing about us too."

"Well, what be new up your end of this old holler?" C.C. inquired.

The boy rubbed his fuzz covered chin as if he were in deep thought. "Me and Ma had go fetch old man Wes outta his run down dumps and put him up in our springhouse loft. Some riders come by his place and whupped him right smart few days back. Think they dang nigh kicked in his sides. One side looks like it been rubbed down in ripe polk berries. Had a bad hackin' cough couple nights after."

"Hold on now, ye say he got thrashed by riders?"

"Yup."

"He know who they be?"

"He ain't had much to say about it so far. I thinkin' they be more to it than he wants be knowed right now."

"How you know what happened iffin he ain't sayin' much over it all?" C.C. asked as he leaned forward in his old hickory-bottomed chair. It was a permanent fixture on the mill porch and had long ago taken on the same weathered shades as the mill siding and shingled roof.

"I tracked them fer a bit. They rode in from someplace on the old Miller farm, crossed the ridge and come down on Wes that direction. Tracks was all over in front of the house and led off down the branch towards Cleve's old store," Jubal informed.

"Ye able to tell how many they was?"

"They was three of em and three mounts."

Jubal went on to relate more details about how he had spent one night in the old digs with Wes. He bragged about how Ma had took him in, cleaned him up and how much improved that he was. He said that he weren't the same man in looks, nor in spirits. Seemed like he had a mite of spunk in him now.

The boy said nothing about seeing the big old roan and rider at Cleve's store nor anything about his Pa riding off to the west and not being heard from since. It might cast a shadow on his Ma if that be known right now. Best let that be for the time present.

The tracks this morning would have perked up the miller's ear a bit for sure, but Jubal thought it best not to tell that right now. It needed seen to more first. It just might be another piece that could be fit in the puzzle. Lord knows there were enough missing pieces right now.

"Wes ever tell ye where he come here from, son?"

"He told me once that he come up here outta Alabammy, I thinkin' it was."

"I recall that be what folks here abouts say to, but do ye know what he done fer a livin' when he was down there?"

"He said somethin' or 'nuther about runnin' boundary lines, I recollect."

"That a fact?" C.C. quired.

"Don't rightly know fer a fact, no sir."

"Well, boy, I don't reckon I know much more neither, but I hear that they was some bad stuff goin' on down in them parts over freed men. Seems like there was some tomfoolery, and he was run off or skedaddled so's to save his own hide. I hear he come up here in these hills and ridges so he could hide out some."

"Really, that don't sound much like Wes that I be knowin'," Jubal added questioningly.

"Guess I got no right talkin' stuff I don't know fer facts and besides that it might all be just a big lie. I ain't gonna be accused of bein' a gossip, so I guess I just clam up on that fer now. Sorry I brung it up, but I just be curious what you might know."

"He tell me once that he had gold. Think he say he got it down in there somewhere. Don't know how much though."

C.C. rubbed his chin and seemed to be pondering over what to say next. "That what I hear too."

"I think I ask him more about it when I get back up the holler this evenin'. He might tell me all of it. Said a day or so back that he would tell me more when the times was right."

"Jubal, I ain't much on tellin' one man how to go about dealin' with another, but I don't think I'd be pushin' him none over it. Most sure make him just clam up over it and not tell ye nothin'. That be how I would do iffin I was in his shoes. He tell ye when he be good and ready."

"Guess ye ain't wrong none there."

"I think best just be patient and let him come to you with it."

Jubal came close telling C.C. about the fresh signs this morning, but he decided to look into them more. Just depending on where them tracks led might give a better insight to what Wes had been up to, or what them three riders was up to if they were the same three that he had seen. The tracks and all the signs matched up. They might be together somehow and maybe even that big roan rider. Pa might be one of them riders. Weren't no way to tell right now and weren't no sense in spreading stuff just to stir folks. Best just see what they be up to and try finding some answers. The more folks knew about it, then the more suspicions would be stirred up and the more edgy ever body would be.

He would hurry up here and get his askings done just as Ma had drilled into him, and then he would hike out and follow the tracks as far as he could or till they told him a tale or two. But then there was Lida. He had not talked to her yet. Matter of fact, he had not even seen her. Didn't know if she was on the place or not.

"Yer Ma tells me that she aims to go to Yeary store out in the cove soon."

"Yeah. She wants me ask if we can use yer team and buckboard fer a day or so."

"I don't reckon that would be no problem. Martha and Lida been wantin' me take them fer some time now. Iffin ye was able do that, it save me a whole day's work time."

"Yessir," Jubal replied as he attempted to keep the excitement off his tongue. Not only would he get a team to drive on a day's trip, he would get to spend a whole day with Lida.

"What yer Ma be fetchin' back from Yeary's?"

"Don't rightly know fer sure, but she say we need several things in order see us through the comin' winter. We need salt fer hog killin' time, I know. The gals always need new cloth. You know how that be, I bet," Jubal answered best he knew how.

"I do know about that," C.C. parroted. "When do ye reckon she be ready?"

"I think her plannin' me and Sarry with a whole parcel of things she will want fetched back. That probably be why she not send me to pack it all home myself. She say it ain't safe goin' that fer and fetchin' dry goods back. Be good chance I git jumped and git ever thing took away by bunch a hooligans or sich."

"Well, I reckon ye both be right there. Tell ye the truth, I be glad ye be goin' with Lida and her mother. I let ye take a side arm with ye iffin ye want."

"I ain't had much use fer a side arm and don't recollect I ever pulled off narry a shot. I think I be better at usin' this here old thunder buster."

"I reckon ye might tote one along anyhow. Lida can hit a June bug square in his eye. I learnt her how myself commencin' in long about the time war started. Reckon she can fend off most any man," C.C. stated rather proud.

"I never knowed she be a shooter."

"That young lady got a heap a things fer makin' somebody a good woman someday even iffin I do say so. Her aim be just a samplin' what she can do."

Jubal was a bit surprised by what her Pa had just said. He kinda took it as a mite hint of encouragement. He would just have to bide his time and see what come next. But it was dang near certain that there was coming a whole day right soon when he could side right up to her and look her right in the eye. Sarry would more'n likely see ever move he made and try best she could to hear ever word that either one of them spoke. He just knew that he would drive the team and that Lida would sit up with him. It never occurred to him that maybe her mother would drive and that Lida would sit up there with her. After all, it was their team and their wagon.

"Tell yer Ma that we be ready early three days out from today. I guess you ride old Kate here, and then you all can pile up in the buckboard if the load don't be big 'nuff fer breakin' down the team. Might have to take the wagon but that slow ye down two hours or better."

"Yessir, that a fact," Jubal responded while silently hoping that the wagon and team would be needed because that way he could be with Lida even a mite longer. He'd have to see that Ma needed plenty so as the load be big and heavy.

"Ye can do what ye like about quizzin' old Wes, but just think on what I say. Just might be best not stir things too much right now," C.C. cautioned. "I keep my ears open too at meetin's and sich. I let ye know iffin I hear it spoke of."

"Yessir. What time ye reckon we best git started fer Yeary's?" Jubal asked.

"It take close four hours one way, so best start right after good light."

"Reckon that be good with me and Sarry too."

"Papa, you and Jubal come on and wash up. Time we eat now."

Jubal looked across the lane to the front porch of the big two story frame house and saw Lida with apron drawn up in her arms wiping away the heat of the kitchen and the old cook stove fire. Face a bit reddened from her chores but still just as pretty as he remembered. Seemed like it took her Papa a long time to stand up and make his way across the lane and up the porch steps.

"Hello Jubal," Lida greeted him as the two stepped on to the porch.

"Hello yourself," came his parroted reply. He wanted to say that he was wondering where she had been all this time but caught himself before blurting out such tomfoolery.

"Get washed up a bit. Dinner is on the table," Lida instructed.

"Better watch her, son. She takes a likin' to tellin' men folks what to do," C.C. laughed as he stepped up to the shelf attached to a wash basin and a fresh bucket of spring water.

Jubal made no reply to that but felt his face grow flush, and his ears began to sting. He knew that they must be beet red by now.

"Pay him no mind, Jubal. He just likes to try and get me all flabbergasted and riled up. I am for sure not a bossy woman," Lida countered. With that she turned and wheeled back into the kitchen.

"Woman," Jubal said to himself. Not girl, but woman. She had called herself a woman. He heard it from her own lips. That put his mind to a whirl. If she's calling herself a woman then that likely mean she be looking for a man for herself. He thought about places and situations that he had only dreamed about and wondered in somewhat bewilderment what it would be like.

Jubal ate his fill and returned to the porch with C.C. Her Papa smoked a pipe and grew and cured his own smoking materials. Jubal had not yet taken up the custom. He had tried a chew or two but had never acquired a taste for it. Soon the pipe smoke spiraled lazily up and around the silvery strands of her Papa's head, and he seemed to be in some sort of mystical trance as he held the pipe and looked intently into the smoldering bowl of embers. For the life of himself, Jubal could hardly recall what had been set before him. All he knew was that he was hungry, not for vittles; but for her and all the overflowing charm that she seemed to possess in abundance.

The flush had subsided from his face and his ears no longer stung, but he still felt uneasy. Not that he feared he would be harmed but that he would say the wrong thing. He did not know just how to handle himself and how to say the things he wanted to tell her. In a lot of ways he knew that he was a man. In other ways he had to admit that he was still right smart green.

"What ye think about the war we be in now days, son?" C.C. inquired.

"Ain't give it much thought so far. Reckon the black man got rights too," Jubal responded without really any serious thought on the matter.

"Reckon that be a fact. You know there be folks here abouts that don't be nowhere near turnin' loose any slaves they hold; and there be them what don't even own none. All right here in the mountain parts. All round here."

C.C. pulled on his pipe until he had a fresh cloud of tobacco smoke whirling around him. He lowered the pipe and continued. "I never held with slavin' myself. I don't think the slave states is gonna win out in the long run, but that ain't really the things that gonna make the troubles later on. I be thinkin' that the hard times be after the fightin' be all done. Things gonna be hard come by then."

"How ye mean by that?"

"Well, store bought goods be as scarce as a hens tooth and iron goods be even worse. They be land grabbers and debt holders just waitin' to pounce on anything and ever thing they can take from folks here and south of the line. Further south ye go the worse it be, I reckon. This war done stirred up a big hate up north for all us down this way. I think we just a mite lucky that we be in a little border place round here."

"They been some riders through here already, but I don't reckon they bothered anything yet that I know of," Jubal responded.

"That true for the most part but there been some goings on in the past that folks ain't got over yet and they ain't forgot who done it either," C.C. stated as he took another long pull on his pipe.

Lida came out on the porch carrying water buckets and set them down at the head of the steps. She looked a bit tired and some of the smile had gone. It was about as hot now as it would be any time today, and it showed on her face.

"Come with me to the spring and carry a bucket for me."

"Sure will."

The pair made their way up the lane, past the mill to the spring pool. Both sat on the rock wall leading into the pool runoff. The air was hot and the heat of the day bore down on them. A dipper of the cool fresh water was sure to be refreshing.

"Here, I'll get ye a cool drink," Lida said as she dipped one of the oak buckets into the spring pool. Then she turned and offered the boy the dipper. He took it and dipped it full. The cool water was a welcome measure even though he was not really thirsty. Lida sat the bucket down on the wall and then turned so that she faced him, eye to eye.

"What Papa says about the war and times gettin' to be hard scares me some, Jubal. I don't quite know how it's gonna be for us."

"Reckon I don't know that myself either."

"Lida said her mother always says we will just have to have faith and trust that all will be taken care of for us. She says she ain't big worried over it." She turned again and leaned into the wall. Her hip pressed into the side of his thigh, and she made no obvious effort to move away from him.

"Ye don't seem afraid," he softly responded in an effort to control himself. He wanted nothing more than to grab her and hold her tight next to him. He thought maybe that she would not resist too much, but her Papa might just be on the lookout too.

"I have no call to be scared right now, here with you, but who knows who or what be through here in time to come?"

"Can't say as I know that either."

Water buckets were eventually filled and the young pair managed to return them to their place on the porch shelf. Jubal did not know the hour nor did he really care. He was in rapt of his company, and she had captured his full attention. He was not about to go anywhere else as long as he could be with Lida. He had not even thought about the tracks he had seen near the sand hill this morning and how they had raised his curiosity and set his mind to thinking all sorts of thoughts about the riders. He was thinking of other things right now, things much more dear to him.

Lida's mother soon called Lida to return to chores. C.C. had returned to the board shelf on the main floor of the mill that served as a desk and a counting table. He seemed to be deep in the books and had not noticed when the pair passed on the way back from the spring.

"I guess we will see you and Sarry early in a few days from now," Lida spoke softly after answering her mother.

"We be here bright and early so we get a good early start."

"I look forward to it," Lida smiled.

"Me too." That was about all he could say without risking some boyish remark that could undo all he had tried to do so far.

"Me and mother can fix a basket so we can have a bite to eat on the way. What would you like?"

"Oh, ye don't need fix nuthin' special fer us. We eat most anything, I reckon."

"Well, how's about I fix you a polecat and some snakeweed?" Lida said laughingly.

"Iffin ye fix it, then I try eatin' it."

They both had the giggles after that but soon said their so longs and parted company. Jubal stood in the doorway of the mill long enough to pay his regards to the miller daughter's Papa. C.C. stopped his bookwork long enough to stoke up his pipe again and proffered his advice about being careful and keeping a look out for all the riff-raff and drifters that they had talked about earlier.

That served to remind the boy about the earlier sighting of the fresh tracks. He made his way out of the mill, back up the lane and started a steady walk back up the holler road. The mystery of the tracks and what they may have to tell quickened his pace and in hardly no time he was coming down the sand hill and had the reed patches in sight. He had raised a right fair sweat but slowed not a step.

He reached the tracks. No one else had come this way since morning. No new tracks. He could see his own tracks made earlier; dried out a bit now, but plain. Soon out of the reeds and headed up the ridge. They seemed to make no effort to hide because they avoided thickets and brambles as much as they could. They had been riding hard, because the tracks were dug in and deep in the soft earth. Even though it was on upland, there had been enough rain to make the ground soft and it gave way easy under hoof.

The track to the top of the ridge brought on a good sweat and the boy was sucking wind a mite hard when he stopped at the crest in the shade of a big red elm tree. He remembered this exact same spot from the early spring when old Jake had treed here. That coon hide was still on the board and should be just about all dried out by now.

Seemed like there was a lot more undergrowth here now, and it was harder to see off down in the direction of Wes's old orchard. Course ever thing was green now and a lot thicker.

Jubal looked toward the sun and at the shadow lengths; the sun was low. He had made it to the upper side of the orchard and had followed the tracks easily. It looked like they headed straight for the ramshackle place that Wes called home until just a few days ago. He followed the trail straight on through the orchard and right up to the front of the old shambles, but the trail went right on past there. They hadn't even slowed down as they passed.

Now what to do? If he trailed any longer, it would be way past time for him to be home, and Ma would fret like a wet hen hovering over her brood. There was nothing betwixt here and Cleve's store and that likely where they had gone. But why such a rush? More unanswered questions.

Jubal followed the trail until he cleared sight of Wes's old place, and it led just as he had figgered it would. Quickest way home now would be back up to the flats and out the north hill. Would be a right smart climb up on the flats, but setting sun would make it cooler too.

Pa had not taught him a lot of things about the world and how to reckon with people, but he had made him work and trap and hunt. So the boy knew his way through the hills and hollers for several miles around. He wished he knew his Pa better.

He knew his Pa had a favor for the laudanum bottle and that seemed to capture most of his time and attention. Jubal did in no way understand, but his Ma had played it down. He could tell that she didn't take too kindly toward that nor pulling on a jug neither. There were lots that he didn't understand, but was dead sure about one thing: He would get outta this old holler and make a way for himself if it took all he had in him to do it. There had to be more than just hard work and digging in the dirt all the time. He had to find a way off the dirt farm and outta the holler.

Then he thought of Lida. He'd just up and take her with him. Bet she wanted all them frilly dresses and ribbons and such just like he wanted leather boots and silk shirts. And oh yes, fine horses and land and a big house with a thousand acres and slaves enough to work it. Ma called it building air castles and she weren't far from wrong in her sayings. Would be kind 'a hard to run out on Ma and the gals anyhow.

The sun had dipped below the mountain by the time he reached the north hill. He would have light to make it home, but it would be dark in a hurry after that. He felt a bit hungry. Maybe Ma would save him a biscuit from dinner.

Within less than a hundred yards from the yard gate, a rustle behind him made him stop dead in his tracks and his heart raced at the unexpected speed. He wheeled around just in time to see the big buck leap across the rail fence that divided the pasture field from the meadow, now dry, but showing signs of late growth that would make a penance of a second cutting hay crop. Maybe it would make enough to feed old Kate or the milk cow for a few days once the snow fell.

He swung the old squirrel rifle around best he could and pulled off a quick shot. The deer never missed a stride and cleared the fence and just as quickly disappeared. Wes would have no deer meat tonight, but maybe he could track that old buck tomorrow. That would make way for following some other tracks too. That way, he could follow the trail and not have to tell what he would be up to.

The lone shot had very adequately announced his arrival to all at the old log home. Since it had come from the opposite direction as everyone had expected, it made for a bit of confusion and concern for the home folks. Julie was the first to see him as he came into the yard.

"Hi brudder. Whatcha shootin' at? Some ole big bugger, I bet."

"No, I seen a deer."

"Where he at?"

"Hard tellin' by now. Reckon I plumb missed him."

He went on to the dogtrot and began to unload his horn and the remaining rifle balls into their respective places. He took the ramrod and a loose fitting patch and swabbed out the long barrel, wiped down the entire surface of the metal parts, and hung the piece on the wall by the main cabin door. He just at that moment began to realize that it had been a long day and that he was a bit tired, not to mention ready for a biscuit. Ma came out of the kitchen, biscuit in hand just like he knew she would.

"What C.C. say about goin' all the way out to Yeary's?" Ma asked.

He say that his wife and Lida been waitin' fer him take them and since we needs go that he send me in his place and that way save his self a whole day's time. We all set fer the last of the week. Wants me be there by good light."

"You tell him I ain't gonna be able make the trek?"

"Yep, he know all about that."

"You and Julie gonna need take old Kate and let her pack ever thing back from the mill fer ye. I be thinkin' it be a mite bit too much fer ye have to tote that far," Ma instructed.

"It might be best. Just how much ye thinkin' we be buyin' from Yeary's?"

"Just what we need, cause they not money fer much else," Ma informed everyone within earshot.

Money. Jubal thought of his ten dollar gold piece. Wonder what he could buy himself with ten dollars. He really had no good thoughts on what ten dollars might buy. He had been to Yeary's before, but it had been a long time past. He had no call to think on dollars then, because at that time he had no dollars. But this time he did, and he might just get some stuff for himself. Oh, of course, he would let Julie get herself a ribbon or some little trinket. Lida! What would be something that he could give her?

Wes asked him about the shot and if he had seen any other deer signs. Jubal related the incident with the big buck and said that he had not seen any other signs. He made no mention of the fact that he really had not been watching for deer tracks, nor did he make any mention of any other tracks. That would come later.

He ate his biscuit, the most of it anyhow. Jake begged him out of a bite or two. He had made many a step today and would likely retrace many of those same steps tomorrow. At least that was what he planned on right now. Just maybe he could fit one more puzzle piece in place that would answer a question or two.

The late August nights were still warm. It would be plenty warm sleeping on the trot, but somehow that seemed not to be the best place for tonight's rest. He told Ma that he would sleep indoors. He told her that he wanted to be up and out early to go to Cleve's store and see about getting a side arm for the trip to Yeary's. This of course, raised more questions from Ma.

Jubal told her all that C.C. had said about the scallywags and the raiders that had been around these parts and that a good side arm might be in order. He knew that Cleve more than likely had no such thing in his store; and even if he did, there would be nothing to pay for it. Ma probably knew that too, but that gave him excuse enough to be gone most of the day. Course he said not a word about C.C. sending side arms with his daughter nor the fact that she could probably out shoot most men. Ma always knew more and understood more than she let on and so it was this time. She asked no more questions and told her son that she would see to it that he was up way before the sun showed its face.

Wes overheard all that the boy had said. "Well, I guess I be puttin' up in the springhouse loft tonight. Ma and the girls done made me a fine straw-and-feather-pallet bed, and I reckon I be thankin' them fer it. Be the finest bed I slept in fer many a day."

"Guess we have to find ye a place indoors 'fore frost comes. Be a mite cold up there then, Wes."

"I reckon we cross that bridge when we get there," Wes said as he rose to his bare feet and faced toward the springhouse. "We talk more on things by time ye go to Yeary's. Might have ye fetch a parcel or two fer myself. Maybe more'n that. Who knows? We just have to see how it all works out."

That took the boy by surprise. He weren't exactly clear what the old man had in mind, but it made no sense him talking on buying a bunch of stuff when he had lived like a varmint and been known as a tightwad all along. Shucks, how could he have much anyhow? Unless, unless there really was something to that Alabammy thing.

"Hard tell how long it be 'fore we get a trip back there. So I reckon, we make ever effort fer makin' it count best we can this go 'round. I try fetch what ye want iffin ye let me know and iffin we got enough fer buyin' it," Jubal said as he silently considered asking the old man how he intended to pay the price of things he wanted.

"I be givin' it some thought twixt now and trip day. There be a heap things we need and plenty more fer seein' us through winter snows. Who know how long this here skirmishin' be apt make fer bad times. We best gear up best we can whilst we can."

Jubal wondered in silence. What's all this we stuff? How come the sudden onset of givin' a hoot or a holler about anybody save himself? How he be gonna pay all that much? Then there be that gourd. He never told me no more about it like he say he would.

"I don't reckon I be freeloadin' off you all rest of my days," Wes continued. "No sir. I aim to help all I can, and iffin it take a bunch then I reckon I can do that too."

"Wes, just how ye plan on buyin' out Yeary's whole store? Sounds me like that what ye thinkin' on?"

"I know what I can do, I reckon," Wes snorted in rebuttal.

"How so?" Jubal countered.

"Dang it sonny boy smarty pants, I know what I am doin' and zackly how I gonna do it. Ye be fergittin' all about me tellin' ye earlier that there be gold involved."

"I remember, but ye never did let on no more," Jubal answered.

"There be a day or so 'fore store time and 'fore ye set out ye will know what I mean. I show ye tomorry when there be good light."

"I gonna try findin' that big old buck early come mornin'. Might be gone best part of the day, and it be close on dark time I get back here." The old man had stirred his mind a bit with mention of the gourd and possible gold, but he still had his mind on tracks and where they might be heading. He could trail them and think on what Wes had said all the while. He could cover a good piece in half a day and still get back home by dusk. That was his aim.

"Then it still be time fer me make a believer outta you the next day or so," Wes said with a surprising air of patience in his voice. The lad had not stirred him as much as he had thought.

"We see how it all comes off, I reckon. Fer now, I be ready to turn me in. I plan on bein' up and out 'fore first light," Jubal said.

Wes responded in kind stating that it had been a long day for him too and that he and Jake would bed down in the springhouse loft. Jake would have to sleep on the loft floor. Weren't no dog sleepin' on his new bed.

The old man made his way to the loft without a lantern and sat on the edge of his pallet. Using both arms outstretched in the darkness, he felt his way to the low gable end of the loft and retrieved the gourd from a ledge over the top plate where he had wedged it in tight. He had made sure that no one had seen him hide it.

He took it down, returned to his pallet and laid down with the gourd in one hand while the other hand slowly and gently stroked the head of the now relaxed and lazy old hound. The sounds of the night soon faded in to meaninglessness, and both were soon in restful sleep.

Jubal had just as readily found his bed, but sleep escaped him. Wes had stirred his mind. Not so much about the money, but how he had come by it and how much there might be. Furthermore, how free with it would the old crank really be? Then there were the riders. How did they tie in? Or did they tie in at all?

Seemed like the night sounds were all faint and distant. Most time that would mean there was astir somewhere nearby. He listened for the faintest of sounds but was soon overtaken by sleep.

Morning came quicker than a jackrabbit could run. Jubal slept hard. It was near full light when he sat up and rubbed his tired eyes. Must be all that stuff stirring his mind so bad that cause him not sleep sound. A quick biscuit and a slab of cured ham, and he was ready to set out.

"Old buck be beddin' down fer the day by now, I reckon," Wes said sarcastically.

"Might be, might not," Jubal countered.

"Best be good light anyhow when ye scoutin' out prey. Darkness make a man stumble more'n one way."

"Where ye reckon that old rutter be beddin' down anyhow, Wes?"

"I thinkin' he be up the flat thickets. Hide in them laurel patches. They so thick that he reckon nothing be able root him out. Should be able pick up a track or three. That tell ye pine blank which a way he run."

The boy gathered his old hog rifle, powder horn and a small hand of balls, stuffed the balls in his shirt pocket, slung the horn and the musket over a shoulder and swung open the yard gate. In no time at all he was climbing the north hill and looking for any signs. Soon spotted the first track, which had to be laid down before the buck saw him. Tracks were close together and even spaced. They were easy to follow. A few yards brought a flurry of deep tracks, and a leap across the old fence had left a sure sign on the meadow side of the chestnut rails. The trail in the meadow grass could be followed by anyone who could open his eyes and see.

Jubal followed the wide-spaced depressions on the slender grass where old buck had made long leaping strides. He could see the trail fifty yards ahead of his own feet. He followed the track till the meadow grass petered out against the timberline. Tracks in the undergrowth were not quite so plain; but to a mountain boy who knew where to look, it was no task. Soon the trail was picked up and just as Wes had guessed, it turned west and headed out to the flats.

Most like the deer to skirt the edge of the woods all the way to the flats and then take to the laurels for cover. That meant running in a circular path near a two-mile jaunt. Jubal knew the flats well and reckoned he would just make a beeline there and try crossing the trail before he hit the first of the laurels.

Most laurels never grew well down low as the flats were. Most lived higher up in the high angled rocks and bluffs. But this one big thicket chose to make its place lower down and had done well. It was noted as a good place to hide in a hurry, and he reckoned that critters knew that as well as did most folks here in the ridges. Most folks had no reason to hide, but they knew it was there just the same.

Always took a strong willed dog to root out a critter from a laurel thicket, just like old Jake was before he had seen so many years pile up on him. He still had the spirit but just could not muster the spunk the way he once did.

He cut the track almost to the tree where he had thought and for sure there was the tracks running straight off into the laurels. He stood watching and listening for a few minutes. He heard nothing unusual. He had no intention of looking for any old buck deer. He had more on his mind than deer meat.

Mid-morning sun began to exert its warmth on the boy's broad shoulders and back as he stepped from the shadows of the woods into the morning light. He felt a bit hungry. Glad that he had taken the last of the morning biscuits and a thick slab of side meat and pocketed them. He sat down under a lone walnut tree and began to eat the now cold bread and meat.

Looking skyward, he noticed that this tree had a thick crop of nuts. Must remember this place come late fall since there be such abundance. Big ones too. No clouds coursed across the immense blue above the trees and hilltops. Even the high points of Pine Mountain and the ridges on to the north could not touch the sky today. There was a hint of color in the scattered tall poplar trees: a sure sign that fall was not be far behind.

Having eaten his fill, the warm sun brought a yawn and a slight heaviness of the eyes. He closed them tight to block out the light and at once saw images of Lida dressed in all the finery that money could buy. Beauty equaled only by lustful desire. Yet there was a feeling of shame for thinking about her in that manner. But what the big deal, it was only a thought. Maybe she had some thoughts too.

The trek down off the flats took only a few minutes, but the boy had broken a mild sweat by the time he walked back up the path to the edge of the papaw patch near the old shanty that Wes called home. So far there were no tracks. He continued the remaining short distance to the house and just as he had thought, picked up a track that led straight off into the rough brambles. Just far enough off the path so as not to be easily crossed by anybody who might just happen by these parts.

That seemed reason enough to suspect that the track would lead to Cleve's store. Brisk pace brought on a right fair sweat but not enough to slow the pace nor diminish the anticipation. He could be in sight of the store in an hour or so if he stuck to the high ground. One steep climb by sideling up the south ridge would put him on course to come out overlooking the store. The leaves from last winter were settled and still some damp from the last rains. Jubal could make good time through the big timber and still be quiet enough not to be noticed if there happened to be others this high up on the ridge. He had not cut the tracks again so he knew for sure that they would be below him, probably staying just under cover of the timber.

Breaking out of the timber and looking down on Cleve's place revealed nothing unusual except for the one horse tied up in front. Brown, looked like an old nag that had been rode hard most all its life. Head hung down and back swayed too.

Trying his best to stay behind the cedars and saplings, Jubal carefully made his way down off the ridge, through the sparse pasture to where he could get a better view of Cleve's store and his nearby barn. He still had lots of unanswered questions and felt sure that Cleve knew some of the answers. Not like he would just out with anything, however. Probably would be hush-mouthed about the whole thing.

A keen eye soon spotted activity in the shadows of the barn haul way. Two men! Yes! It looked like the ones he had seen before when he hid in the reed patch that day on the mill road. At least they had the same build and size.

He watched a bit. Then from deeper in the haul way shadows was the third man. The trio came out and caught up the mule team grazing in the barn lot, harnessed them and hitched them to a wagon waiting in front of the store. All disappeared in to the store. No sign of Cleve so far. Jubal eased a bit more down the ridge but still not in earshot.

"Eeeeei," a high pitched scream so piercing that it startled the keen eyed observer. The whiskered man slammed open the side door of the old store building with a slave girl in tow. She wrestled as best she could but could not lose his grip on her. Seemingly without effort, he dragged her into the barn and with one strong motion, ripped her ragged and dirty sweat-stained dress from her, threw her to the dirt and had his way with her. It all seemed to happen before the boy had time to sort out what was going on. He could hear sobs and crying as she lay in the dust of the barn floor. Whiskers adjusted his clothing and threw the tattered dress in the face of the ravaged girl.

"Shut up bitch and git up."

More sobs.

"I said, shut up." He thrust her rags at her again. Git yer ass dressed and now."

Louder sobs and screams.

"Damn you."

A heavy boot heel caught her a glancing blow across the mouth and landed square to her nose. She was silenced immediately as the bones in her nose invaded the base of her brain. She was now free forever.

Her assailant rose and returned to the store. No sooner in than right back out with Cleve and the other two men in tow. Cleve stooped and touched her neck on both sides repeatedly.

"Damn fool, you kilt her."

"Well what the hell? She just a bitch ain't she?"

"Dead bitch ain't worth a damn," Cleve responded angrily. You fools done let one git away and now you done killed one. You just cost us three hunnert dollars."

"Hell Cleve, we just git more where she come from," Whiskers said as if nothing had ever happened.

"You'ns git yer stuff and git the hell outta here and right now," Cleve commanded.

"What about her?"

"You kilt her. You take her," Cleve shouted as he stomped off back toward his store. "And make damn shore ye ain't found out neither."

The trio looked at each other, then almost in unison picked up the limp body, carried her outside to an empty rain barrel and stuffed her jack-knifed body into it. Then they carried the makeshift coffin to the waiting wagon. Cleve emerged from the store with a lid and a mallet. With a few strong thumps, the coffin was sealed. Whiskers then went back in the store and came out half dragging a shackled, grey haired darkie who looked like he had been near beat and worked down to just bones and hide. He was mercilessly thrown in the wagon alongside the barrel. Cleve turned away. The three men climbed into the wagon, whipped the mules and headed west.

Jubal could hardly believe what he had seen. Many a time he himself had taken the life of an animal, but he had never seen a living breathing person die before this day.

He made his way slowly back up to the flats and over the north hill toward home. He made no effort to get home in any particular hurry. What he had seen weighed heavily on his young and inexperienced mind. Ma had always said that a body ought to treat other people the same way that they would want to be treated. Something about a golden rule or something like that, he really wasn't sure.

All that he knew for sure right now was that he did not want to treat anyone like he had just seen. The vile act played over and over in his mind and was already burned into his memory.

The sun was nearly down and the western sky was ablaze with color when he swung open the yard gate and came around to the dogtrot. Wes was sitting there, but the young boy passed by him as if he did not even exist. He had a suspicion that Wes had somehow been involved with slaves long before now and had made a right good amount in whatever he had done. If it had ever involved something like what he had seen today, then he wouldn't have to think about having Wes as a friend from here on. He reckoned it best that he'd just keep his thoughts to himself for now.

After he put away the old muzzleloader and the powder horn, he made his way back to the kitchen door, drew a bit of water from the wash bucket and washed away the day's grime and sweat from his face, still not saying anything to anyone. Everyone else had already eaten, but Ma had seen to it that there was plenty left for him. She stood in the kitchen door, full plate in hand, and without uttering a sound, beckoned him to come in and sit down and eat.

Salt bacon and beans did not sound like much of a meal compared to what some folks had, but to the boy it was a filling and tasty plate. He ate slowly, still not speaking. Ma made herself busy while he ate. Outside, evening shadows darkened.

Ma lit a lamp and came to the kitchen and sat down opposite Jubal. She always could tell when something troubled him. He knew that he could talk to her and that she would understand and have some sound words for him. He just needed to talk to her where no one would overhear.

"What be troublin' ye, son? I reckon I know there be somethin' eatin' at ye."

"Ain't no bother, Ma. I just be wore slap out and gonna turn in soon."

"I see."

Jubal got up from the table and said no more to his Ma nor to anyone else that night. Still what he had seen that day played over and over in his mind. Sleep had a long wait, and the pallet on the dogtrot was no comfort to him. He could not reason why it had to happen that way. What had they done to wind up like that. And who was that man who always seemed to be in on the sides? That troubled him too because he had reason to think things about it. He ought not be placing blame without knowing for sure.

It was first light when he heard Wes clamoring down out of the springhouse loft. Seems like he tried special to make racket enough so that he would not slip up on nobody this particular morning.

"You a sleepin', boy?"

"Naw, not now."

Wes spoke in a soft voice so as not to be heard by any of the women folk. "Did ye see Cleve yesterday, son?"

"No. I never went to his place, just up the hill to look see what might be goin' on."

Wes came up on the trot and sat down by the boy. Soon Jubal had confided to him all that he had witnessed in the barn and all around the store including the men and the wagon headed off west. Jubal questioned Wes about the three men, and at first Wes denied any knowledge of them.

"Wes, don't ye try puttin' me off none now cause I know about them bein' at yer place. I know how they been comin' and goin' cause I trailed them. I know what I done seen."

The boy could not be put off any longer and that was evident to Wes. They talked at some length as to why the men had come to these parts in the first place. Wes was honest when he said that he did not know them. It was true that he did not know them by name, but he did know them by their aim and their activity. They were rascals who would help a black to run away and then turn on him by taking him back to his owner and collecting the return for him. Wes explained all this to Jubal and finally owned up to his past involvement in the same kind of doings.

Jubal was not really surprised to learn of this and did not think much one way or the other about Wes being involved in it. It did raise questions about his Pa, which for now remained unspoken and unasked. He thought he now had a good idea what Pa had been up to all the times he had been gone and left Ma and the girls to make do the best that they could.

Kitchen sounds soon ended the dogtrot conversation with Jubal telling Wes that he intended to talk more about the business when time seemed better. The smell of sausage in a hot, blackened old iron skillet made it difficult to concentrate on affairs and happenings when there was hunger to be sated. Jubal and the girls were fortunate to have hog meat and other food stuffs, because Reb raiding parties frequently made forays into folk's private homes and took what they wanted. It was not so bad here in the mountain area as it was on further west. Folks in these parts did not cotton as much to the Rebs as other places.

The family ate and were filled again. Jubal was thankful that he had a home and a Ma to look to when he needed a hand up. He had never given much thought to the conflict over the slaves until he had seen the terrible event at Cleve's barn. He just could not get that off his mind, and it continued to eat at him. He sat at the table after eating and just stared into his half empty coffee mug. Ma had cleared the table save for his mug and made herself busy in the kitchen.

Jubal rose from the table and took the few steps into the kitchen and reached his mug out to Ma. Their eyes met.

"What be yer trouble, son? I know there be a stone in yer craw somehow."

"Nothin', Ma."

"Well, iffin' that be how ye want it be, then I reckon I be here whenever ye git ready to spit it all out. Ye recollect that I done told ye many times that the longer ye keep it canned inside ye then the longer it be eatin' at ye. It gotta come out sometime."

"I know, Ma. But I ain't so clear about what I done seen."

"Wanna tell me about it?"

"Not so's nobody else hear me."

Without much more than a few words, Ma had the girls in the kitchen and tending to the chores. Granny Iverson was handed socks to darn, and Wes was told that the wood box needed filling. Ma got a bucket and informed all that she and the boy were going to look for the guinea's nest. They had moved sometime in the last couple of days. If left alone, would soon set and hatch. More could be raised and traded at the store for needed items, but right now they wanted the eggs more than the chicks. Besides it was an excuse for the two of them to be alone and to be able to talk.

Ma hit the cow path below the barn and soon crested the rise and had the house hidden from view. Jubal followed at her heels.

Ma stopped and turned to face him. "I reckon nary a soul be in earshot now and ain't nobody lookin' neither. You wanna sit down and say yer piece or what?" Ma asked rather curtly.

The boy stammered and was hesitant a bit. He had never spoken a word to his Ma about a man and a woman nor nothing of the kind let alone any sort of goings on such as he had witnessed. He had not spoken to her in any detail about the three strangers and the activity that he had observed in them. He had not raised the issue of his Pa nor the suspicions that he had about him.

He had a bit of trouble looking her eye to eye when he spoke about the stranger taking the slave woman. He considered that to be something that a boy should not even discuss with any woman, let alone his Ma. However, Ma seemed to be able to come up with all the right things to say at exactly the right time, and he had soon told her all about the incident and about the three strangers and all that they had been involved with. Ma seemed to be more concerned with detail about the three men than she did about any other facts. She never let on so, but Jubal could see a change in her expressions and her eyes seemed to be more piercing when he spoke of the strangers.

"Ma, I just don't see how a man can take a life and act like nothin' never gone on in the first place. Why'd they cram her in a barrel and cart her off like she weren't nothin' more'n a feed sack? I know she were just a slave bitch at that, but she were a person too."

"Don't reckon ye need be callin' nobody by such name, Jubal. I thought I done learnt ye more respect than that."

Ye have Ma. I reckon I just spittin' back what I been hearin' over to Cleve's."

"Well don't be doin' it no more. Ye ain't been brung up like that."

"Yess'm. I reckon ye be right again, Ma."

"We best get back to the house. Tomorrow is meetin' day, and our circuit rider be one of Andy Johnson's men."

"Reckon he be sided up with the Rebs, Ma?" the boy asked with a perked interest.

"I reckon not. I think ye need hear what be goin' on all over and not just here in these hills. 'Sides that C.C. and Lida be there, I bet. I be thinkin' that be near 'nuff make ye wanna go with me," Ma said with a slight smile on her face. "Ye get all warshed up tonight and be on yer best at meetin', and I bet Lida take notice too."

Jubal had not really given much attention to anything other than the local area. He had heard of skirmishes and raids in other parts of the state but had not really cared much about it until he had seen the killing at Cleve's store. He had no idea of politics or any of the issues of the day which confronted the country and just took it for face value that life would be much as he had already known it.

The issue of slavery had not concerned him before although he was aware of it and had actually heard of some people in the area that owned a darkie or two. He had never thought of them as a person before, but the killing that he had seen had awakened him to that fact. He could not dismiss the inhumane way that had claimed the life of that soul and the cruelty of the man who had ravaged her. Maybe there might be a way he could know more what had happened to cause a man to act in such a way and why he seemed to be so full of hate and scorn. He had tried to reason out what he should have done and then he reckoned that if he had come out for her that he probably would have wound up just as dead. He did not want to let on to anyone else, but he had to admit to himself that he had more or less been frozen in fear at what he saw.

He might get a chance to ask C.C. about all these trappings and then get a better hold on the whole thing. Besides that most times wherever C.C. happened to be, Lida would be close by too.

That evening brought a long and thorough scrubbing in the spring pool runoff. Clean shaved and fresh clothes in the morning, and he would be at his best. Just thinking about the coming day whetted his interest and served to bolster his confidence in himself as a man come of age. Many thoughts and places ran through his mind as he lay in a clean bed. Many questions raced through his mind and many fantasies about Lida excited him. Sleep was a long time coming; but when it did come, it was deep and restful.

Chapter 6

Enlightened

*J*ubal finished his eggs and side meat in no short measure and excused himself from the table. He said nothing to Ma or Wes as he made his way to the barn. He was determined to find some answers to some of the thoughts that had beset him the last two days. He walked the rutted dirt road leading out down the way to the mill. Mr. Johnson was just near the smartest person he could think of to ask. He would know some answers for sure. He had pondered all the things that he wanted to ask the mill master about and seemed like the more he dwelled on it the more questions reared up in his mind.

He had read a bit here and there about the war and all, but still was nowhere near to understanding what was going on. He had only recently been in direct touch with the war and had seen firsthand of its evil doings. He had not raised the issue with C.C. before, but he reassured himself that he could find straight talk and solid answers there. The miller man and all his family for that matter were known to be upstanding and honest in all their dealings, and none spoke of them in any despair at all.

The late August sun was coming up in the east and was near the tree line already, and it was plain that the day would turn hot. He began to break a slight sweat as he strode up sand hill and thus slowed a bit so as not to be wet a sweat when he got to the mill. He would be lying to himself if he thought that going to C.C. for answers was the only reason to make the hike, but he wanted to believe that

Lida had not been the only reason to come. Sure she would be there, but he had not called on her this way before; and he had to use her father and his knowledge as reason to come this morning.

Squirrels were cutting hickory nuts in the tops of the two big scale-barked hickory trees that towered above the crest of the sand hill. Jubal stopped for a moment and observed their foraging. He counted eight of them in the two massive canopies and could have easily taken several of them for the stew pot. He had not brought his long rifle and had wondered if that would turn out to be a mistake. He quickly regained his wind and journeyed on down the far side of the hill and along the branch that soon would be the mill pond.

The final bend in the road, before the mill came into sight, was close enough to tell that the mill wheel was silent. He had not considered that the Johnsons might not be at home or that the mill would not be running. As he neared the turn, he heard the wheel come to life and felt a sense of relief to know that at least the miller man would be there. He continued to tell himself that he was the purpose for coming in the first place, but then the picture in his mind's eye of Lida quickened his pace and stirred feelings in him that he had only recently begun to understand.

He was sixteen now and as much of a man as he would most likely ever be. He began to think more as a man than in the ways of a boy. He knew that Lida was his age by at most a year or so difference one way or the other, and he reasoned that she too had begun to think as a woman instead of girl. She sure was a woman from all appearances so far as he could tell. He would make it a point to call on her after he had talked to the miller man and understood some of the ponderable that were eating at him. Possible that Lida could help with some of the things that he wanted to know, but it would not be proper to go asking her such things, not now anyhow.

The mill came abreast before Jubal realized where he had progressed. He could see that the door was open and that probably would assure that C.C. was inside at his desk or at the wheel. He seemed to keep busy in spite of the war. But then again the conflict had created increased need for food and granary products, so it made sense that the mill would run regularly.

The old wheel creaked in protest as it turned slowly. Lack of rain had near drained the mill pond, and the millrace ran only what the natural flow could provide and that was just enough to turn the tired aging wheel. It would take the fall rains in early November to get the pond filled again, then the wheel could sing its normal hum and whirr.

Jubal turned off the rutted road, stomped a bit to rid his feet of excess dust, and headed straight for the mill door. Just as he mounted the steps, C.C. came out and they near collided.

"Whoa there, son. What be yer hurry?"

"I reckon I not be payin' no mind where I be goin' fer a bit."

"Ye must have a terrible lot on yer mind. Wanna come in and sot a spell?" C.C. intoned as if he could sense something must be astir.

The old man and the boy made their way back into the mill and each found a cane back chair and pulled up to the small table just inside the door. A slight air drifted into the mill, and Jubal soon sensed that his forehead no longer glistened from the sweat he had broken on the trek down this far. The mill master slowly took to filling his pipe and soon grey corkscrews of smoke wound their way upward into the rafters of the mill house and disappeared into the unknown.

"Want a dipper full?" C.C. asked as he handed a heavy oak bucket and a gourd dipper to the boy. "Lida just now fetched it."

Jubal felt a twinge in his chest. Maybe that would be the only chance to see her. He might not be able to study up a way of seeing her now. He could come up with all kinds of pondering to hold the miller, but real interest was in the miller's daughter. He just hoped that she might pay him some mind, if he did get a chance talking with her.

The two made small talk about the weather and how it had been a no good crop season and how scarce things would become cold weather and all. Jubal reckoned he could hunt and trap to put meat on the table for Ma and the girls if need be. C.C. agreed with him in part. Talk soon turned to the war.

Jubal had heard that all the skirmishes were on account of the slaves and such, but C.C. soon began to enlighten him a bit.

"Don't reckon ye know about states' rights and secession and all that politic stuff. By rights I reckon ye ought not be 'spected to. But all that come on direct outta old Calhoun and all his rantin' and ravin'. He sayin' that each state be more powerful than the Union and by sich states don't need be part of Union if they not want to. Him and old Clay been preachin' such since way back."

"Reckon I don't know none 'a them fellers."

"Well son, iffin ye ask me, they be the very ones responsible fer this here old war; and they try packin' it off on the slave trade and all. They thought they would scoot by with their ideas of nullification till Old Andy threatened to hang their arses, and I be thinkin' that he would'a done it too."

"Huh."

""You mark my word son, they gonna run plumb into old Mexico 'fore it be done with. Folks in these parts is Union folks, and it don't take no fool to see what be comin' in short time."

"Ye think war gonna come to here?"

"I hope it don't, but they be some scoundrels here abouts that is bent on takin' whatever they can lay holt on from whoever got anything they be wantin." The miller took time to relight his pipe.

"I...I done seen some stuff goin' on here already," Jubal blurted out.

"What you seen?"

"How much you know about Cleve and stuff goin' on at his store?"

C.C. looked straight at the boy before replying. "I reckon I hear 'nuff about him over time that make me not trade with him much these days. Lots folk say he ain't square in his dealin', and there be some strangers hang out with him now days."

"I seen some riders other day," Jubal replied sheepishly. He wanted to tell the miller man what he had seen and at the same time hoped that he would not ask about it.

"I ain't gonna be surprised by most anything these days. This danged war has made scoundrels and scallywags outta folks that were good folk 'fore the fightin' commenced." Folks gotta live somehow, but I ain't one bit beholdin' thievin' and robbin' let alone all the killin'," C.C. retorted as he packed fresh tobacco in his pipe and lit up. A cloud of smoke near the same color as his hair circled around him before he spoke again.

"You know boy, it be a thousand wonders that some Reb squad ain't already come here a thievin' and sich and made all the boys like yerself go off and fight fer them and the Confederate regulars. I reckon we just been a mite lucky so far."

"I ain't wantin' join no Reb outfit," Jubal barked.

"Way I see it now they not the ones who need be whupped. Most folks here lay blame on states' rights politickin' and all they done stirred up. They got folks all riled up over them layin' claim to keepin' slaves and makin' them do all their work and then them bein' the one that gets rich. I think it ain't right take a man's work away from him no matter what be his color," C.C. said in a louder tone as he stood to retrieve his tobacco pouch from a hip pocket, slowly but deliberately repacked his pipe and put fire to the bowl. Blue gray smoke rose around his head before he spoke again. Jubal knew that the miller man had a yen for politicking and just about knew that he was winding up for some opinion sharing and mind swaying. He had heard other people, including his Ma, comment that it was not always a good thing to get him stirred up since he would be apt to lay it on anybody whose ear he could bend.

Jubal thought to cut him off. "I know one thing, I ain't upholdin' to no man ownin' another. It ain't right."

"Plenty things ain't right in this old world, son. Man best try doin' right all his days. A man ain't gonna get by mistreatin' his brother and never pay. He might pass it here, but he not be able to pass it by on the other side."

"Other side?"

"Yup."

"What other side?"

"Jubal, hear me well now. Ever man whatever set foot on this old earth gonna have to stand his judgment someday. Iffin he ain't never seen the light when he pass on, then he be in the dark rest of time. You know that, I know." Another long draw on the pipe and another swirl of gray smoke. "Ye burn worser'n this carnsarned old pipe without ye see the light."

"I reckon ye be right, but I got time a plenty way I see it."

"How much time ye reckon ye have iffin war come and fetch ye? Good chance a musket ball mess up yer clock, son."

Thoughts of Granny Iverson reading by firelight on winter nights flashed through his mind. Words spoken by his Ma rang in his ears. He had done no wrong. He held no slaves. He worked hard and never took a thing he did not deserve, and he was upholding to the truth. There was something that made him uneasy when he got cornered by talk like this, and he always shied away. But right now it was just him and the miller man, and he did not reckon it would set well for him to just up and skedaddle. That would not be proper respect for the man, and besides that he could miss out a chance on seeing Lida.

The miller man went on talking. Jubal realized that he was hearing him but not really listening. The boy was occupied in his own thoughts. In a day or so he would spend most of the day with Lida going to Yeary's store way out in the Cove country. It would take most from sunup to dusk to go and get back in the buckboard. He would be with her, but her Mother and Sarry would be coming too. So they could not get very much closer than just sitting beside each other on the buckboard seat, but that would do for now.

"Dang it, son. Have ye gone plumb deaf?"

"No sir, I ain't. I were just a thinkin' on how this here old skirmishin' gonna turn out."

"Ye mean the war and all?"

"Yep. That be it." There was no way that he could tell C.C. that his daughter was on his mind so strong. The old man likely pitch a hissy fit on a body what come here with Lida on the mind. "I reckon I fight fer the Bluecoats iffin I fight fer anybody."

"What make ye come 'round on the blue side now? I recall last time we talk any that ye not be rarin' to fight fer nobody. What make ye change up yer mind so sharp?"

"I saw some bad stuff in Cleve's barn, and…" He had said it before he realized what had come out of his mouth. He had spoken too fast and now had to find a way out, "and I ain't never gonna fergit neither."

"I ain't surprised at nothin' what be goin' on with Cleve and his bunch," C.C. said in no short terms as he took his pipe from between clinched teeth and laid it down beside his chair, wiped his mouth with the back of his hand, stood up and took a long pull from the gourd dipper. "I know pine blank that he and his bunch be up to no count things that most folks here abouts don't cotton to. I ain't aimin' to do much trade with him no more iffin it be up to me, no sir."

"I ain't too keen on it myself," Jubal parroted.

"Ye want tell me what ye seen there? I know by yer looks that it be in yer mind's eye right smart."

"There be plenty that I ain't knowin' answers to and plenty things I ain't understandin' but I reckon I ain't got no right troublin' ye with sich. Shucks, I ain't even asked my kin nothin' on some things. I reckon I be just nigh growed up some now, and I reckon I just figger it out fer myself."

"Yer folks be in line fer helpin' ye get growed, I reckon; but others might help take up slack where yer Pa be gone so much since the war come along and all."

"We ain't laid eye on Pa in some time now. Don't reckon we even know where he be."

"He ain't be gone far, I know that."

Jubal was startled to hear that anybody close by would know about his Pa, let alone throw it up to him how he had run out on his family. Yet his mind raced over all that had come about in the last few months and how Ma had dropped hints that she just as soon that Pa not come back.

Ma had really perked an ear up when he had told her about the three riders and had tried to find out more about them than he been willing to tell her right then.

It was a few days after that when Ma told her son how Pa was dressed when he left home. Jubal had not given it that much thought at the time, and he had not since told his Ma that one of the riders matched up to those same clothes, boots and all.

He had not seen a face and had never been close enough to hear a voice except the one time that he had hid in the reeds. Even then the shortest one dressed in the buckskin shirt and gray britches had said not one word and kept his sweat stained old hat pulled low over his eyes.

Jubal knew that there were raiders around these parts now, but really they were out just for themselves. Not above just plain robbing and thieving to lay hands on ever piece of gold or silver that could be found and took from whoever might have it.

Suddenly it dawned on the boy that Wes had once told him that he had some gold, and the three riders had been around Wes's old place more than once. They had to be the ones who had whupped up on him.

"What ye hear about my Pa?"

"He gone, ain't he?" C.C. asked.

"I reckon he have his reason fer bein' gone, but I can't help wonder what he been up to and what he be into."

C.C. picked up his pipe and stoked it up again and lit up before speaking. "I think it be proper to be plum level with ye, son. I mean no harm in sayin' so, but yer Pa is up to no good from what I hear and what I know."

"What ye mean, Mister Johnson?"

"Word is that he done took up with them what be doin' misdeeds all over these parts. Some say a few want his hide fer what he been into."

"Like what?"

"I ain't gonna say nothin' that I don't know firsthand. All else be hearsay and that be all I say about them deeds. I just tellin' ye what I know to be the truth."

"That what I want. I ain't upholdin' to lies and sich from nary a soul, and I don't do it none myself."

"I reckon that be a fact, son. I ain't never knowed ye to lie, least not to me; but ye may not like what I tell ye."

"I reckon I can handle truth okay."

"I reckon ye can. Any man worth his salt should. Ought be good as his word, and word ought be truth just as well."

That hit home to the boy like a crack of thunder in a July storm. Jubal realized that his companion had just called him a man. A full tilt man. Any man ought be wanting a wife mate and thinking on family and such. Immediately he found himself thinking about Lida and desire for her welled up in him. It somewhat scared him to have the thoughts about her the way he did, but he could not make those thoughts go away. He did not really try.

"Yes sir," Jubal stammered, somewhat surprised that he could get himself together enough to make a sensible answer. If the old man knew his thoughts right now, he would put lead in him sure as sun follows moon.

"Yer Pa brung a mare here some time back and tried sellin' her. Said he had her from a filly and that she were a good saddle mare. Now strange thing that I recollected her brand, and it were one of Wider Bray's brand. I never let on that I knowed about a brand ner nothin' else. I just told him that I had no need fer her." He paused long enough to relight his pipe. "Come find out night 'fore, some cuss done cleaned out her smokehouse too and that be when she missed her hoss. They even took her sidesaddle too."

"What Pa do then?" Jubal asked as his thoughts turned away from Lida. Thinking that his Pa might be on the wrong side of the law did not sit well with him. Horse stealing could be a very serious matter and could lead to some serious judging and sentencing. But this was war time, and the law was few and far between. There was such a thing as right and wrong, and Ma had always drummed that into him. She also kept after him about coming of age and accountability, but he just let that pass mostly. Ever now and then something or somebody would bring it back to him, and it always left him a bit troubled. He could not really put a finger to exactly what it meant, but it just left him in a strange sort of mood. But he reckoned it not to be a problem because it always seemed to pass.

"Well I reckon I ain't so sure, but talk is that he laid up in town with some old wider and then lit out to the west, mare and all."

"Then reckon Pa be off in them parts now?"

"Ain't likely cause he been knowed to hang out with old Cleve since then. I ain't seen him myself, but that be the talk."

"Ma don't say much about him no more. I reckon she don't know much more'n I do either."

"That ain't just so, son. Me and her spoke on it a week or so back. I weren't aimin' to be nosy nor nothin' to the kind, but I thought she needed to know what I knowed."

Jubal let his mind race again and thought about all he had seen with the three riders and all that he had not told his Ma concerning them. No doubt that C.C. had told him the truth of the matter. No doubt what his Ma had told him was the truth too. What seemed to weigh down on him were all the truths that nobody had ever bothered to tell him. Likely Ma knew some things that she was holding back, because she probably did not want him knowing all the rumors. But why would Ma try to hide stuff from him? After all, he was past sixteen now, and C.C. had already recognized him as a man.

"Iffin my Pa has done all that folks say, why do ye reckon he done it?" Jubal quizzed the miller man.

"Lord only knows what makes a man do what he does sometimes, son. I think he just fell in with the wrong bunch cause he be lookin' fer the easy way out, and there just ain't no easy way this here day and time with the war and all. Things is tough, and they still be some in these parts that ain't right set on a honest day's work. I reckon it just be in some folk's blood to be that way."

"But Pa always say he knowed hard work since he be a boy."

"Just ye stop and reflect on it a bit now. Ain't he always made ye work hard as a slave whilst he be out who knows where here lately? And who been seein' where things git done? Who been diggin' in and doin' all that needed done up on yer place?

"Well…me and Ma, I reckon."

"So where ye reckon that leave yer Pa? Ye thinkin' that he be much of a man on account of it, or ye thinkin' he just shuckin' off what any man try his best do fer his family and kin? Is that how ye wanna be yerself?"

"Not nary one bit."

"I reckon not too, and I be glad that ye say it right off. I know we done talked 'fore now how ye wants all them finer things and such where rich folks has. I reckon I ain't findin' a heap of fault with ye fer that, but I know ye don't aim takin' from other folks just to fill yer own sacks. Iffin ye was aim to act that way, then I best sent ye on yer way long time ago cause I ain't havin' such around me and mine."

"I never did feel close to my Pa the way I do Ma."

"I reckon I can see that too."

The miller man laid his pipe up on a ledge near him and rose from his chair. The sun was up high now, and the cool of the morning had gone. Afternoon would be a mite warm and would be here well before the boy returned home.

"Son, trot up to the dam and open the sluice about half, then come back here. I show ye how to grind good smooth cornmeal. I may need ye help me a bunch 'round here 'fore this old war be done and over. Good help be scarce as ice in August. I know ye be plenty stout, and ye can do it once ye learn how."

Jubal set out up the millrace and covered the short run in no time at all. The miller man had told him to wait for his signal before he opened the race. C.C. wanted to oil up the pulleys and all. He sat down on top of the double-boarded sluice and listened for the signal from the mill.

The signal from C.C. brought him to the task at hand. He pulled up on the sluice gate and latched it in the first notch. More water entered the sluice box and began to make its way along the millrace. Water seemed to leak all over the ground below. Soon the board would swell and plug the leaks, and all the water would then be directed to the wheel itself.

Not more than a quarter of the overshot pockets had filled until the old white oak wheel began to turn. Jubal glanced up the hill again and just as quickly turned and started down the race back to the mill. When he stepped in the door, the miller man was already pouring shelled yellow corn into the feed hopper. The catch box was still completely empty but would soon be loaded with succulent yellow cornmeal.

"Iffin ye be a mind, ye can help me with this batch, and there might just be water to grind a sack fer ye to take to yer Ma."

C.C. had fired up his pipe again and held it with one hand while he drug sacks of yellow corn out from the storeroom and piled them beside the sheller. Jubal knew all too well how to use a sheller. The miller man did not let on to Jubal that he knew they were smack out of meal and that his Ma had asked if she might get a sack and pay for it later on when she could gather walnuts or hickory nuts and sell them.

Jubal lit right into the sheller and had corn kernels dropping in the catch box like raindrops on a flat rock in early spring. This would be no task for him. Little did he know that the miller man did not intend it to be much of a task. He was smart enough to know how to help a body and still let them keep their head up and not feel obliged over it so much. No doubt he had learned a lot over the years in his dealings with those that came to the mill.

C.C. busied himself feeding the grind wheels and sacking up the meal. Meal sacks had been hard to come by since the outbreak of the war and each one had to be checked close for rips or weakened threads. There were several sacks on hand, and it was necessary to double up on them to insure that they would not spill out being handled. Some folks brought wooden casks and barrels, but they were hard to come by too.

Jubal was well into the corn shelling when he noticed he had broken a sweat. That must mean the morning be almost done. It was at that same moment that Lida appeared in the mill doorway and announced that her mother had sent her to tell them to come to the table in about thirty minutes. She just as quickly said that she had to get back to the kitchen, because she was making a blackberry pie. She had a broad grin on her face as Jubal turned to see her retreating to the kitchen. He could not ever recall her smiling at him that way before.

"Dang fool women. I done told em that once I commence, I ain't quittin' till I git done grindin' or the water runs out, whichever comes first. They know that too."

"I be done shellin' in no time. I be fixin' to take on yer last bag in a whip."

"That be good, cause I know there ain't much water left by now. How much did ye open the sluice anyhow?"

"First notch just like ye say."

"Good. Pitch what ye got shelled in that holdin' bin. We'll try finishin' up right away. Maybe the water hold out too. I done got some ground fer yer Ma iffin need be so we ain't gonna come up short."

Jubal rushed up to complete shelling what corn remained and in no time had it all in a waiting bin. He had broken a right fair sweat by now, and his face and back were salty wet. He followed the miller's instruction, and the last of the shelled corn was in the in-feed when the second call from the kitchen came.

"When are they comin' to the table Momma? Ever thing be ready right away."

"Don't fret it none, gal. I will go and fetch yer daddy and make him come eat."

"What about Jubal?"

"I was thinkin' that ye might want take him a plate over at the mill porch, and ye can brag to him about how good a cook ye have come to be," her mother said with a chuckle and a twinkle in her eye. She knew that her daughter was no longer a child and that she needed a little push in the right direction. Besides that, she had known Jubal for most of his life, and she knew his Ma and all that she stood for and believed in.

Lida wanted her mother to believe that she was not surprised to hear those thoughts and ideas. But inside her heart quickened, and she too began to let her mind race. She imagined the times yet to come when she might be able to sit by his side and talk to him. She could hardly envision ever having a chance to be alone with him.

She had said very little to her mother about her future and what she might want from life, and she had never spoken in such terms to her father. He still acted like she was a child. He had even bought her a porcelain doll for Christmas a couple of years ago. She still had it, of course, and would keep it as long as she lived; but porcelain children were not the ones she lay awake at night and dreamed about.

"Oh Momma!" she taunted.

"Takin' him a plate ain't gonna make ye promised to him ner nothin' of the like. He needs be fed just like yer daddy, and I be thinkin' that he be a mite bashful to sit the table with us all. I be thinkin' savin' him face too, that all." Her mother turned away and if Lida had looked closely she could have seen her mother's skirts dancing from her silenced laughter.

"I guess maybe he would like to taste my pie."

"Take him some biscuit bread too. Ye make a right fair pan if I do say so myself."

"I could'a cooked the whole dinner myself iffin I had a little more time."

"Ye be cookin' full time soon enough child. Now go, wash yer face and brush up yer hair a bit whilst I fix him a plate."

Mrs. Johnson had quickly gone to the mill door and conversed with her husband in a voice, which to Jubal was subdued by the rhythmic drone of the grinding wheel. C.C. therefore dutifully instructed Jubal that he was going to the house and eat and that he should grind what little corn was left in the in-feed and then go up and close the sluice.

He almost ran to the sluice gate, pulled the latch, slammed down on the double-boarded gate and locked it in place. He hit the ground only on the high spots going back down to the mill. Once inside he busied himself with tying up the last three sacks of meal as C.C. told him that Lida would bring his plate in a bit while he waited for the wheel to settle down and begin to dry out.

"Hey, Jubal, I got yer vittles here. C'mon and eat. I fixed a cobbler and made hot biscuits too."

"Ah I ain't much hungry. I eat a heap this mornin'."

"I made it myself. Come see."

He felt a blush come over his face. His ears burned like they were twig switched on a cold snowy day. Lida put the plate down on the miller's table and pulled the chair out and motioned for him to sit down.

He did as beckoned.

Before him were three big cathead biscuits and apple butter, a big slab of sugar cured ham in red-eye gravy and a pile of fried taters with onions. A small dish sat to the side with a saucer covering it and a soft petite hand making sure that no one took a peek. Hungry or not, which he surely was, this could not be passed up. Ma served plenty fatback and souse meat all fried up good, but he had not had a slice of ham in a long time. They needed to sell their hams and shoulders in order to be able to buy the things that had to come from the store.

Lida set a checked napkin by his plate. He picked it up and stuffed a corner in his shirt collar just as he had seen others do on occasion. He saw no point in it; but since she had provided it, he reckoned he best use it. The move gained him a surprised look, and Lida just as quickly removed it and gently placed it in his lap.

"That be the proper place," she softly said.

"I forgot, I reckon."

"Makes no matter. Sometimes they just be another piece to wash and iron, and it be much too hot standin' over a hot iron on a day akin to this one." She wanted him to know that she knew many things about housekeeping and cooking, but she was not yet ready to be bragging on herself.

She had not thought much about the lad up until the last two or three months and for some reason, unknown to her at that time, she found herself pondering over him and letting her imagination take wing. If anyone, let alone him, knew some of the thoughts that had run through her mind, she would blush red as a beet. She had told no one, and she was not about to breathe a word of it.

He did not realize how hungry he had become. The ham literally made his mouth water. It was soon out of sight. He devoured the heap of fried potatoes and buttered up the last biscuit and smeared on a thick layer of apple butter.

"I thought ye weren't hungry," she laughed.

"Well I reckon grub that good make a man turn hungry in a hurry," he had purposely omitted any reference to a boy.

"It always be a pleasure cookin' when it gets eat up so."

"I thinkin' I could go another round shellin' corn now, but your Pa say that there be no more water fer that till couple days off now."

"I don't think he got much more no how. Dry weather hurt ever body this year, and they got no corn to grind comin' on fer winter. I don't know how folks make out, but Momma say that the Lord provides fer His people, and I reckon that be so."

"I hear Granny Iverson and Ma say the same thing too."

"Ye think it so, Jubal?"

"Huh?"

"What I just been sayin'. Ye think it be true?"

"I reckon it be true. Ma say that the Good Book say that."

"You ever read the Good Book, Jubal?"

"It be a mite hard fer me. Big long names and all."

"I could read it to ye some time."

"That be right nice." His mind raced again thinking of sitting alone with her under a big old shady beech tree and her reading to him. Hard to say right now if he would hear a word she read or not. But one thing sure, he sure would be eyeing more than the printed word.

"Ye ever seen that light, Jubal?"

"What light?"

That was answer enough to tell her that he had not seen the light. He had been exposed to the Word and had sat through enough of the circuit riders' sermons to know what it should mean to be in the light. She knew, but she wondered if he had given it any thought.

Yes, he recalled the black-suited preacher man blasting out about the evils of this old world and how we live in darkness. But he reckoned that darkness was just part of ever day living seeing as how he was up and about before first light most ever day.

The sounds of C.C. climbing the mill house steps snapped both of them back to reality. A flick of the flint and the tinder box came alive and just as quickly the pipe produced a swirl of grey blue smoke, and the miller man purposefully blew a cloud in the direction of his daughter's face.

"She give ye anything worth eatin' son?"

"I say."

"But ye ain't had the best yet," she chided as she took away his plate and removed the cobbler lid. "I think it still be warm. I know the berries be good, cause I know where they growed."

The cobbler lasted just about as long as did the ham biscuit.

"That be mighty good, Miss Lida Johnson," he said and then immediately felt his ears burn and knew that his face had reddened. She smiled and took the red-and-white-checkered napkin from his outstretched hand, making sure that her hand gently touched his. Just as quickly she was out the mill house door and was gone. His heart raced.

"She do be a mite sassy sometimes even iffin she is mine, ain't she?"

Jubal made no attempt to answer that one.

200

C.C. pulled up a chair and leaned back against the wall while pulling on the pipe till he had gray and blue clouds of smoke encircling him and his companion. "Use tabakker fer yourself, son?"

"No sir. Never have. Never wanted none."

"Well, be certain and keep it that a way, and then ye won't ever be bothered with havin' to give it up. Won't never burn the house down neither."

"You done that?"

"Almost, once long time back."

"Ye knowed that Wes's house be burnt, don't ye?"

"Reckon I do. How he be a doin' now days?"

"Seem like he be mended up right smart now."

"He talk to ye much?"

"Some."

"I reckon he plumb give up on livin' when his woman passed on. Reckon she been ailin' some time 'fore that." He took time out to restock his pipe. "Wes be a smart man when he wanna be. I been knowing him some time now. We jawed a time or two in bad weather. He used bring corn and have it ground but been long time since he last set foot in here."

"He told me he teached somewhere long time back."

"Think he told me that were down in Bammy some place."

Jubal had not caught on to the fact that C.C. was looking to know how much Wes may have let on to him about what he had done and why he had come to such a remote little valley. The pipe wielding man did not know all the details of the sudden relocation to these parts, but he was sure that he knew more than most. That was if Wes had not broken over and let on to Jubal or his Ma what it was all about and how he had made his way here with what was rumored to be a sack of gold eagles.

"He told me that he come up here so as to get rid of all the summer heat. Said he got so it smothered him when it got so hot down there."

"I hear tell it got real hot fer him right 'fore he come here," C.C. replied as he lit his pipe again.

"He ain't never say much on it to me, but he said that he got money, good money fer bringin' back runaways."

"Ye need come right out and ask him some day, cause he ain't been plumb on the level with ye about that." C.C. stood and walked over to the mill wheel axle and inspected the gears. "I reckon I owe it ye to be up front and tell ye all I know what yer Pa been into round here lately too."

That statement took the boy somewhat by surprise, and he thought he detected some resentment coming from the miller. But all the same he knew that his Pa had been into no good, and he really did want to know for sure what it was.

"You likely already know how folks has had stuff stole right out from in under their noses and had things took that they ain't had no inklin' how it got gone. Son, I know that yer Pa and some of his likes have been the ones what been thievin' off people here lately. I know that fer sure. And I tell ye right now iffin he comes around my place tryin' such, I will shoot his arse sure as sun comes up day after day. I don't hold to such by him nor nobody else. I ain't tryin' to come down on yer Pa any more'n anybody else actin' such. All I be sayin' is that I don't aim to tolerate such from nobody. Ye can see that, I reckon."

"Yes sir. I can, and I ain't beholdin' to what my Pa be doin' neither."

"I know ye ain't."

"Do ye know where my Pa is now?"

"Last count I heared he was headin' west."

"How long it be since ye hear that?"

"Two, three days past, I reckon."

"Then that likely be him that I spied in Cleve's barn." Suddenly the boy realized that he had said too much too quick again. Curiosity over his Pa had caused him not to think on all he blurted out all too soon. He was surprised to hear the miller man's answer.

"I know what happened in Cleve's barn, but I can't say fer certain who it were." He took what seemed forever packing his pipe before he spoke again.

"I saw it too. I ain't none pleased by what I done saw neither. But what's a body gonna do so it don't happen no more?"

"Son, that be a part what this war be all about. All this killin' and theivin' and such, but none of that don't give a man right to take any and ever thing he wants even iffin it be from a darkie. Furthermore, it ain't how we is supposed to treat one 'nother. I don't hold up no such theivin', let 'lone takin' a life fer no reason. That be why I refuse to go off and do any fightin'. I reckon I can justify it on account of my old age too."

"Ye ain't so old."

"No, I guess not so much. I been 'round here long enough to know what be right and what ain't. I knowed that long before I let light shine in on my life too."

"Won't that man what took that slave gal then kilt her have to pay somehow?"

"He gotta be caught first off."

"I reckon that be some chore seein' as how he done run off with them other two."

C.C. had not heard about the three riders heading west with the barrel and its bizarre contents. The boy voluntarily filled him in on the details of how the three had stuffed the body in the barrel, loaded it on the buckboard, and headed off west while the man on the big old roan went on out ahead as if to be their scout.

"Ye say ye done seen these three afore that?"

Jubal extracted the silver button and showed it to the miller and explained how he had come by it and where. He described the two that he had seen well enough to recall some of their features and told of the one who was a bit standoffish and had his hat pulled down so low so as not to show his face.

Lida's dad rubbed his chin with one hand while he turned the button over and over in the other hand. "This looks me like it be the real thing what come off some rebel saddle that most likely be some uppity so an' so. Don't think no big time Reb brass be loose around these parts, so I be thinkin' that it been took and brought here by some scallywag from some Reb outfit somewhere."

Jubal then told him what he had spotted when he went up to open the sluice gate, taking care to explain that it had only been a glimpse and that he could not say for certain what it was.

"I reckon we outta go ourselves up top there and see iffin they be any tracks. We'll take my path up top. It ain't as much grade that way." C.C. knocked the fire from his pipe, ground the ashes into the dirt just outside the mill door and laid the old pipe on a porch rail to cool down. "Come on, son. Let's see what we find."

The path to the top of the hill that directly overlooked the mill, their house, and all the out buildings, was on a good grade. The pair soon reached the top, and the older man stopped and waited for breath to catch up with him. Jubal had hardly broken a sweat. A short walk out the crest brought them to a small clearing in the bushes. In the center there stood a rough log bench hewed from a split hickory and shaved smooth. There were still old weathered shavings from the draw knife lying off to one end of the little circular clearing. Sunlight poured down on the bench through the small canopy window in the saplings and brush. It was evident that it had been designed to be that way. Both sat on the crude bench when they reached it.

C.C. related to the boy that this was his place and how he came here when he was troubled. He told him that ever one in the family used this place for the same causes. He explained how this was where he could find solace and rest for the mind. He wanted to know if the boy had a special place like this. Jubal responded by telling him how he just got out away from his house and family. Seemed like the hills and the woods offered him the peace and solace that he had needed before. But lately there was not much peace to be found.

"I may never get no closer than this old hill top, but up here I can feel close to the Maker," C.C. stated as his breath seemed to have climbed the path and caught up to him. "I reckon we all need a place where we can be close. If the hills and hollers be yer place, then I reckon that serve ye as well as this here place serves me and mine."

Jubal wanted to ask if Lida ever came up here but thought that not right proper to be asking her daddy. Seemed like that he had taken some liking to him, and he did not want to give any cause for that to be taken away. Almost in the same breath he could see himself and Lida perched here on the old crude bench.

"We all come up here in springtime and clean this here place off and then we keep it clean till cold weather sets in. Ever body in the family makes it up here one time or 'nother fer whatever reason."

That had answered his question about Lida, and he had not even had to ask it aloud. He wondered what sort of thing could ever trouble her that she need come plumb up here to think it out. She never had said a word to him as to her troubles even if she had any, and he doubted that she did. He did admit to himself though that this was a nice little hideaway and how it could easy put a mind at ease.

"You ever let huntin' go on up here?" he asked thinking of how that might be a way to meet up here with Lida. He allowed his mind to soar, as he thought of her in an appreciative manner. He liked what he envisioned about her and himself and what the future might hold for them together.

"I won't let most people up here. It be too close in on the house and mill. I ain't right keen on lettin' ever eye that come along see what all be here, special since the dang nabbed war and all them scallywags what trails after the skirmishin' and all."

"Don't blame ye none fer that. This here is a right smart place," Jubal said.

"I cleared it off years ago and been keepin' it so ever since. We needs be lookin' around a bit and then get down off here soon. Ye be wantin' head back up home soon, I reckon."

Mid-afternoon seemed a mite early to be headed back home, but the boy knew better than to overstay his time and ruin whatever welcome he may have for now. C.C. stood, and the lad did the same.

"Show me where that rider appeared to be, and we'll see iffin he left a track or two. They be some softer ground leads off to the east. Iffin he went that a way, then we maybe can see and tell which a way he went."

Stepping off to the crest of the hill and overlooking the millrace, there plain as day were unshod tracks of a single rider. They had come up from the east and headed right back in the same direction. Jubal could tell that they were fresh tracks. He pointed them out to C.C. and then told him about other tracks that he had seen both around Wes's house and in the dust on the road home.

The pair followed the track for a short time till they came to an old log road that led down the valley and past a place called Horne's cave. The place had a reputation for lots of seedy activity and ruffian characters. Local talk had it that there had been several killings there and that the cave itself was full of haunts and boogers. The tracks made no hesitation in their turn in that direction. The horse had never broken his stride according to his tracks.

"Plain as day where he be headed," C.C. said as he drew to a halt as soon as he saw where the trail headed. "Ain't much need goin' anymore seein' as how he done left a clear mark."

"Reckon who he be?" Jubal wondered.

"I reckon I got my suspicions, but I ain't knowin' nothin' fer pine blank sure."

"Do ye wanna go see iffin we can find him?"

"No. I reckon that we ain't got no cause doin' that. Best we stay clear and try lookin' after what be our own and try to keep them from comin' back here theivin' ever thing they can carry off. We best be gettin' our arses back down at the mill."

"I reckon ye be right."

They soon returned to the little clearing and made their way back down to the mill porch where the older man retrieved his pipe and began to pack it slowly and patiently.

"Lida is glad that ye plan on goin' with her and her mother to the store out in the Cove in a day or so," C.C. stated as he pulled steadily on the fresh packed pipe. Yer Ma goin' too, I 'speck."

"Yeah. Before she was not goin', but now she say she be goin' iffin that be alright with ever body."

"I reckon she be welcome."

The afternoon sun was beginning to dip into the western sky. Jubal still had the walk back up the old road to his home. His Ma would be uneasy if he was later than usual coming home. She knew that he was able to fend for himself in most situations, but she also knew that there were no-gooders around now days. She had long suspicioned what certain ones had been up to, but she had for the most part kept her thoughts and concerns to herself. Jubal had picked up on her concerns a bit. After talking with C.C., he knew for sure that his Pa was up to no good too.

Ma had endured hardship in rearing her kids. The years had not been kind to her. All her labor showed in her face now, and her shoulders had become a bit stooped. She seldom looked like she was rested. Besides that, she had her own mother to see to now, and she had taken in Wes on top of that. She had not told him what she wanted from the Cove store but whatever it was, she deserved it.

That made him think about the rumor that old Wes had money put back somewhere and that he had never spent much since he came here from down south. Seemed only right that he owed Ma for what pity she had took on him and for all the help that she had rendered him. It didn't take much to know that he most likely not be around right now, save for Ma and her help.

Jubal and C.C. agreed that the afternoon before the trip to the store that he would ride old Kate to the mill and hitch her to the buggy and then go back home and fetch his Ma and whoever else was gonna go the next morning early. Then they could hitch up C.C's team to the wagon and leave Kate to pasture till they got back from the Cove and got ready to go back home. Jubal could take them back home in the buggy and then bring it back to the mill the next day. That sounded real good to him because he could already see two extra chances to see Lida. Besides that she aimed to make the jaunt to the store too.

"I know there be ruffians about so I be thinkin' that ye best be totin' yer old hog rifle and powder horn. Ye be gone most all day, and no tellin' who be on the loose twixt here and there. Lida been showed real good how to use my navy pistols, and she can tote them along too."

Jubal felt a surge run through him, "Yes sir, I thinkin' that too. Reckon I ought let old Jake go too cause he can get riled up right smart when a body be ruckusin'?"

"Be a right smart ways fer him be walkin'."

"Oh he ride just fine iffin ye thinkin' they be room 'nuff fer him?" Jubal added.

"Might be a good idee. Go ahead and plan on fetchin' him along."

"He won't be no trouble fer sure," the boy said as he saw Lida coming from the house toward the mill.

"You headed home now, Jubal?"

"Reckon so, Lida. It be late soon, and I need help Ma some, I reckon."

"Well, it ain't so long till store day. I reckon I will see you then."

"Yer daddy say I best come and fetch yer buggy afternoon 'fore we set out. So I reckon I be seein' ye that day too."

"We seein' each other a lot here of late," she cooed with a smile and what he thought to be a slight blush.

Instantly thoughts and emotion flooded him, and his mind raced to absorb all that thought would allow. Today his thoughts seemed to be a lot closer to reality and not so much a fantasy. She sure was easy to look on. Those long curls tasseled out under her bonnet and seemed to add honey to the already potent elixir that he hoped she would someday be for him.

"I be a whole heap pleased that we be on seein' terms like we are," he stammer in reply. "Maybe they might have some real nice things at the Cove. I maybe can fetch ye a ribbon or so."

"That would be nice, but I don't have to have ribbon to make me glad. I got a good home and a good mother and a good daddy who cares fer me. I got blessing's too in spite of this here old war and skirmishin'. I ain't yet had to go hungry, not one bit and that be a whole blessin' in itself.

"I reckon."

"That reminds me. This next Sunday be meetin' Sunday. If ye was to come, well, maybe daddy let ye ride back to our house and then ye could soon walk on up to yer place after that."

"Ma probably wanna go too. I reckon she count on me fetchin' her there and back safe and sound. I reckon we all be goin' cept Wes and Granny Iverson. That be iffin any of us be goin'. I never know what Ma be up to till she tell me."

"Oh, I see and I 'pologize. I outta be more considerate of yer family. I guess I weren't thinkin' too good," another blush, this time more pronounced coming over her face.

"I be thinkin' that I will be there somehow, but I already know what Ma will be wantin' outta me iffin she comes. Ye know I hafta see that she be safe and all that."

"Yes, I weren't thinkin' good." As she turned to go back to the house, Jubal reached and touched her arm.

Turning again to face him, their eyes met. There must have been some sort of understanding conveyed between them in that instant. Neither spoke for what felt like an eternity.

"There not be nuthin' that I would like more than to be there with just me and you, but I reckon it ain't that way fer now." The words seem to come easy as he spoke what he felt inside. He knew that he never wanted to do or say anything that would ever cause her hurt or pain.

"I would like it that way too. Mother and daddy both are good to me, and I love them dearly. But I don't think they realize that I am a growed woman now and not a child no more. I was just talkin' like a silly little giggly faced girl I guess. I reckon sometimes I don't act as growed up as I think I am."

"You be growed up as much as any folks I know that be same age as you."

"How you know how old I be?" she asked with a coy smile on her lips.

"Yer daddy tell me that some time back when I brung corn fer millin'. He also say how much he be proud how you act lady like too."

"My daddy be a good man."

"I reckon that be a fact."

"Well, I guess I be seein' you when it be time fer fetchin' the buggy."

"I be lookin fer it too."

The old holler road to home never seemed so easy traveling as it did this particular late afternoon. It was the only home that he and his sisters had ever known. In spite of all the hard work that was necessary for him and his Ma, he loved that old place. He secretly hoped that he could someday have a place of his own that would be just as filled with love as was this old log home. Sure he wanted all the fine horses and the fancy clothes. But at times there was a longing in him that could be filled only by Ma's smile or by the laughter of his little sisters.

Jubal felt responsible to his Ma and his sisters. He felt the same to a lesser degree for Granny Iverson and for old Wes. He had hardly known Granny Iverson before she came to live with them. Wes had been a hermit old man, who lived across the little pine ridge and seemed to want to be left alone. Ma had looked in on him best she could, and he always seemed grateful. Now that she had took him in and cleaned him up, he seemed bent on teaching the boy all he ever knew that would be a benefit to him. Wes had talked with him till way in the night more than a few times as they had bedded down on the porch on hot summer nights. The old codger had asked a lot of mind stirring questions and had not always given an answer. Jubal had begun to realize that he had been questioned that way on purpose so he would mull things over in his own mind. He had come to realize that Wes was wiser than most would credit him and that he had something to offer more than the gold that he was rumored to own and have stashed somewhere. There would be a time someday that he would tell more about it and maybe even share some of it.

Jubal was approaching the reed patch before he took notice of how far he had walked in a short time. He thought of the afternoon he hid there and watched the three riders and how they seemed to be in a quandary about which way they should go. He could only catch a word or so from them but heard enough to know that they did not want to be seen. He recalled their looks and their actions, now thinking more and more all the time that his Pa was somehow messed up with them and that they all were up to no good. C.C. had shed some light what they were about. Sure the war made hard times for most ever person around these parts but that was never reason for thieving and such. He wanted to confront his Pa over it in one instant and then in the next was glad that he was gone.

He also wondered what it would have been like to have had a Pa like C.C. or some other man who could hold his head up and do proud by his family and his business. He subconsciously became determined right then and there that he would be a good Pa to his kids and that he would work hard to make a good life for them too.

Thinking about having kids of his own turned his thoughts quickly to Lida. Much more pleasing to think about her than to wrestle with the mixed feelings about his Pa. Lida was a responsible young woman. He knew that C.C. and her mother had taught her the things in life that were the real values and worth of a person. He never thought much about the fact that he was fast acquiring those same values and attitudes for himself.

Lida was kind to him and never had put him down because he came up a bit short on material things. She never made fun of him when he had trouble reading the Bible and pronouncing all those strange names and places. She helped him to read and explained things to him. She was patient with him and seemed to be genuinely interested in him and his kinfolk. He interpreted this as affection for him. He had to admit that he felt the same for her.

The sun was getting low on the ridge as he pulled the sand hill, and he quickened his pace. C.C. had cautioned him about being out by hisself and suggested that he always be on the lookout for rascals and rapscallions that they had talked about. The miller man had even suggested that it might be a good idea to stick to the woods and fields as much as possible. That way a body could hide a lot easier if it became necessary, and besides that he knew every hill and hollow in the whole countryside around these parts. It would be easy to shake off a chaser by knowing all the thickets and bramble patches so well. He did not feel fearful for himself, but he did check over his shoulder ever now and then and frequently scanned the ridge lines for the shadow of a rider.

He had not thought much about what he would do if he met up with one of those rouges; but if they hurt or stole from anybody close to him, he knew that he would be sore at them and would want to get back at them. He knew for sure that he wanted no part of not being kind or square to any man. His mind immediately flashed to Cleve's barn and what he had witnessed there. That man needed to be shot if there ever was one needed such. He reckoned that he could do it too, if he ever met up with him.

He was tempted to get off the old dusty road and look for tracks leading in the direction of the divide. He knew that there would be no time today to track any distance. He decided that getting on home to Ma and his sisters would be the best thing. If he did find tracks now, all he could do would be try to find a direction and not much of that because dark would soon be here. Besides dark would be a more vulnerable time for Ma and the girls. There would be no one to take up for them save old Wes and Jake, if he was not there. Ma expected him home in time for late chores, and he decided that was what best be done. If there was a track to follow, it would be there tomorrow and a few days after that unless it rained. Clear skies at sunset did not foretell of that as he turned again toward home.

Jake met him at the barnyard gate with a wag to his tail and a deep guttural rumble that said he was glad to see the boy home again. Jubal knelt and cradled the old hound's head in his hands and praised him for the true companion that he was and had been for several years now. Just beyond the gate, Kate nibbled at scattered clumps of short tough orchard grass stools and seemed to ignore everything else around her.

Jubal crossed the barnyard with Jake at his side and came up to the yard gate before Jake bellowed out his arrival to the rest of the family. Unchaining the gate and swinging it open, Jake bounded through first as if to announce his position and prominence to the whole household. He went straight to the dogtrot and sat down as if he owned the place. Jubal crossed the yard and sat down beside his dog as he draped his arm over Jake's back and neck and began scratching behind an ear. The old dog at once began to groan in pleasure and soon had a hind leg in motion as if scratching an itch that was only near his side. When the ear rubs stopped, so did the scratching.

He could hear Ma and the girls in the kitchen and guessed that they had not heard the hound's announcement of his arrival. Walking to the front porch he caught the sounds of Granny Iverson and Wes in some sort of banter. Most times they beat it back and forth about one thing or another in the Bible and for that reason he never bent an ear to them. He decided that he did not want to hear such right now and turned back toward the dogtrot.

Ma was on the porch just outside the kitchen door. "I knowed ye was here. Jake told on ye."

"Jake be a right smart dog, I reckon."

"Get yerself washed up now. We be ready fer eats soon."

"Yes, Ma. I will."

He noticed that the water bucket was almost empty and lifted it off the shelf and headed to the spring pool for a refill. It was a known fact that any time a bucket got low that whoever found it would refill it. It was just understood and expected.

The family sat around the old plank table and ate a generous portion of hoecakes with apple butter and fried side meat. The conversation centered around the upcoming trip to the Cove store. The anticipation of the girls was at an all-time high. Ma did not have the heart right now to tell them that she had not planned to take them since they would be guests of the Johnsons and that to crowd in on that invitation would not be very proper or neighborly. If all went well, she would see that each of her girls got a new dress for the coming winter and that Jubal and Wes would have a new and warm linsey-woolsey shirt.

It seemed hard to think of the winter chill when most of the leaves had only begun to turn. Midday sun was still hot enough to raise a sweat while working at most anything.

There was still plenty that needed to be done in preparation for winter. Two big hogs would provide meat for the winter, if some thieving low-down scallywag did not come through and make off with it once it was hung in the smokehouse. The boy did not directly voice his thoughts along those lines to any of the family, but he knew that he would do all in his power to shelter his Ma and the girls from any such riffraff. Old Jake had some miles and some age on him; but he would still sick em whenever told to get after a critter, and a thieving man was just another critter to him. Besides that, the old hog rifle was never very far away. He did not realize the depth of his passion against some of the things that were happening to the surrounding people and families. He just knew that some things were not right, plain and simple, and that a man ought to stand up against such, not only for himself and his family, but for the good of all the decent folks around him.

Wes ate without saying hardly a word and was the first to leave the table. He assumed his usual resting place on the dogtrot and was shortly joined by the lad and his dog. Dusk was fast approaching, and Jubal began to feel a bit tired from all the day's deeds. He had thought for several days that he would try to make Wes tell him more of what he wanted to find out about his Pa and any of his carrying on that had caused his Ma so much grief. He thought that he had pretty much figured out what his Pa was up to, but wanted any proof that he could get before being completely ready to write him off as gone.

He went to the edge of the trot and sat down beside Wes. He did that purposefully so that they could talk and not be so easily overheard. He thought about asking Wes to go down to the barn lot but then reckoned that would be too obvious to the others.

"Wes, I need ask ye somethin', and I need a honest answer too."

"Well, ain't I always been honest with ye?"

"I got no reasons to be thinkin' otherwise, Wes. But we ain't never spoke on some things, and them things be what I want ye to tell me now."

"Ask away, son."

Jubal hesitated as he rubbed the old hound behind his ears. "Wes, I hear tell that ye was runnin' from somebody and that be the reason ye settled in these parts, so as how they weren't never gonna find ye. I wanna know iffin they be any fact in that."

"Since ye brung it up, I be flat out with ye. I ain't real proud of what I did or how I did it, Wes replied in a lowered voice as if to not let any others in on his past. "Cleve thinks he knows all about me and my past capers, but he don't know as much as he thinks he does."

"He ain't never told me no detail stuff on ye, Wes. He just spoke of ye one time to me, and then he said that ye had a stash somewhere here abouts and that be all he ever say to me."

"Well, see there, he ain't so all-farred smart less he know a lot more than he told you."

"Well, do ye have a stash?" Jubal asked with heightened curiosity.

"You recollect that gourd full a beeswax that I had ye fetch the day Ma brung me here and took me in? Ye recall that?"

"I reckon I do."

"They be six gold pieces in that wax, but I reckon that not be a heap lot to be callin' a stash."

"But what about the runnin' and hidin' out?"

"That be the part that I ain't so proud of, son."

"Spit it out. I wanna know."

"Long story, son."

"I got all night."

"Do ye know how the darkies is brought in on slaver vessels and sold at auctions like in Charleston or in Mobile?"

"I heard of it, I reckon."

"Young stout bucks would fetch a high price. Iffin a man bought hisself one, he danged sure aimed to keep him too, cause he have a heap tied up in him. This be sometime back, of course; but then when he be all broke in and fit fer field workin' then, he be worth even more. But longer he be a field hand, the more he wanna run off and be a free man. But only way that ever come about be by runnin' off north and hope never get catched up to."

"Reckon they less apt slavin' up north from what I hear," Jubal retorted so as not to seem such a greenhorn. "But how ye figger in that?"

"Like I tell ye, I ain't real proud on what I done."

"I wanna know, but I want ye to know that I ain't one to be blabbin' ever thing I hear either."

"I know that, son. I 'preciate that too. Ain't but one other person here abouts that knows the whole truth, and I done buried her some time back. That dang nigh done me in and would have iffin it weren't fer yer Ma."

Wes made small talk about how good Ma had been to him and all that she had done for him and how grateful that he was to her. He also made talk about how he needed to get his strength back so he could do his part with the chores and help Ma get ready for winter. He talked about how he hoped she would let him stay the winter cause all the signs had pointed to a cold and rough time. He hinted that he might be needed as an extra pair of hands when and if it became necessary to fend off the rouges and scallywags that might come through. He never mentioned Pa by name, but it was evident that he knew more about him than he had told so far. Jubal picked up on that enough to ask more questions when the right time came. It was also obvious to the boy that the appreciation for Ma was sincere and genuine. It did make sense that he would strengthen any efforts that would become needed in defending Ma and the girls.

"Tell me how come ye hadda come up here so's to hide out."

Wes hesitated then asked the boy how much he knew about the slave trade and how it worked and how they were bought and sold just like they were no more than a piece of personal property or a head of livestock. Jubal admitted that he had no first-hand recollection of such and could recall only one or two times when he had actually seen one anywhere.

"Son, like I says, I ain't proud what I done. I wish now that I ain't never been involved in sich; but I was, and I can't change nothin' now. So I reckon that I have to live with all I done and that be part why I come to these hills and hollers. True, I was on the run, but that been some time back, and I don't run no more now."

"What put ye on a run anyhow?"

"I tell ye plain, son. I were close on bein' strung up fer what I done."

"How come that?"

"Ye recollect how I told ye how them darkies evermore be tryin' runnin' off and gettin' they self free? Well, at one time I was helpin' them get started out then I would wait till a reward was offered fer them, and then I'd turn on em and chain em up and haul em back to wherever they run off from and collect rewards for my efforts. I tease them into runnin' then run them back. They got to thinkin' that I were they friend and aimed to help, and then 'fore they knowed what was astir I had them back where they started. I was a bit better off moneywise, and they was worser off fer runnin' in first place."

"You mean that you were a double-crosser then," Jubal half questioned and half stated.

"Told ye I weren't proud of myself."

"How come ye quit it and turned to run?"

"Early on, big strappin' buck by name of John Black run off down in Bammy. He was first one that I crossed up and collected on. Well in two-to-three years his old Massa passed on, and with that he freed ever single darkie he owned. Word got out that big John were on the lookout fer me and never had forgot what I done to him. Since he was free, he could come fer me and he done just that. He come up on me one day and I hadda shoot him. Didn't aim on killin' him, but I did right then and there. I drug him off in the river with my old mule, and he went floatin' off. Reckon some others seen what I done, and they went tellin' his family and other freed ones and they aimed to string me up too, I reckon. I didn't have no other course but to light outta there. Barely had time to throw a few duds and sich in a sack and mount up and ride. Two days and nights brung me up near Knox County, and I sorta just drifted off to the east and settled here. That be more or less the whole story about me. Ye know most all else about me since then, I reckon."

"Not really, Wes. Ma nor Pa neither ever say much to me 'fore the war set on."

"What they tell ye then?"

"Not much, just how yer wife passed on and that ye lived like a old hermit man now. They never told me nuthin' else," Jubal stated calmly but secretly stunned by what the old man had revealed to him.

"Folk 'round here don't know near as much as I just been tellin' ye, and I just soon it stay that way. It be in the past and that be where I'd druther it stay. Ye unnerstand that, I reckon."

"I reckon I do. I reckon it made ye be a bit down on yer pride at some time. I unnerstand that too, but what I really wonder is how ye come about sich in the first place."

"It be greed, son, plain and simple. It were fer money and ever thing else that be bad about greed. That be what I done tried tellin' ye so strong about sayin' ye wants fine hosses and clothes and houses and all that. They not mean nuthin' when stood up alongside a good name and honest work. I ain't one cussed lick proud about what I done, but I shore can't go back and undo it neither. I the one who gotta live with it and live with self all the same too. Ye unnerstand that, I reckon?"

Jubal honestly made no judgment about what Wes had told him, but he could not help but wonder about all the talk how Wes had a stash some place.

"Wes, you know of my Pa ever doin' anything the likes of that? I know how he be always runnin' off and sich fer some time now. C.C. been tellin' me bits here and there, but nothin' solid. I wanna know what ye know."

"Son, I ain't never knowed yer Pa do any such other than whiskey drinkin' and theivin' a bit ever now and then. But I be thinkin' that he done fell in with the wrong sorts here lately. I ain't seen nothin' personal on him ceptin' him bein' high as a old pine tree few times. He ain't never done me no personal harm, but I speak only fer myself."

"Who he done fell in with?"

"I ain't got no names, but I hear they be outta Nashville or off west of here."

"Ye ever see Pa with them?"

"I ain't positive, but I thinkin' I spotted him a time or two with em."

"How come ye can't say sure, one way or 'nother?"

"Well, yer Pa, iffin in fact that were him, always have that old sweat hat pulled down so low that his face be most hid, and he always be the one standin' off a piece a holdin' the hosses or such. Seem like he not never want be seen by nobody nowhere. That was how it were when they come and whupped up on me. He ain't done no whuppin' but he held the reins. In my mind there ain't no difference in none of them."

"What the others look like?" Jubal questioned.

"One be a big burley cuss with leather fer a face and big raw jawbone lookin'. He a huge man; look like he could whup a wildcat iffin he needed to. Other one were shorter and have a face full a grey whiskers, look like they never been combed. Smelled like he been hold up with goats. Look like it too."

"Ye see what they ridin'?"

"Big man be on a big old roan. Reckon it take a big hoss fer carryin' a big man."

"What about whiskers?"

"He be on a chestnut mare, and the one look like yer Pa be on a mule."

Jubal thought back to the afternoon that he had hid in the reed patch and observed the three riders. The picture that Wes had painted was the same one that he had seen that afternoon, not that long back. His suspicions seemed to have some truth in them and some of his questions at least had a partial answer now. He did not like the picture that was forming as more and more of the pieces came into the light. He reached into his pocket and rubbed his fingertips across the CSA saddle button. It seemed hot to his touch.

Answers sometimes seemed only to arouse more questions and that was exactly the situation now. The boy now had reason to question the character of his Pa. Furthermore, he had some of his previous suspicions confirmed. He had never talked about it with his Ma, but he had thought for a long time that things were never the way they really should be with him and her. He could recall a time or two when Ma had a bruised face or jaw and never knew a thing about how it might have happened. The way he saw things right now, there was not much way he could have any feelings about his Pa other than bad ones. Plain as could be that he was interested in himself and never gave a hoot about his family. Most time and for most folks here about, their word was good as gold, but he knew that he would never be able to trust his Pa in anything he ever said or did and neither would anybody else that knew anything at all about him.

"Pa ever hurt ye, Wes?" Jubal questioned. "He ever steal from ye?"

Wes hesitated.

"No need try cover any of it up on my account, Wes. Cause far as I be concerned, he ain't no Pa no how."

"I be right smart sure he took things off'n me. I can't put a finger to it positive, but after he been gone a spell things turn up missin' once he come and go."

"Then I reckon ye don't think much of him neither and with reason I might add."

"I just soon he never come 'round me no more iffin that be what ye mean, son."

"That be pine blank what I mean, old man."

"What ye thinkin' ye would do or say iffin ye was to meet up with him right now?" Wes asked with a slight smirk on his face.

Jubal reached in his pocket and took out the silver saddle button and handed it to Wes. "The way I feel right now, I thinkin' I would take a big pleasure shovin' this plum down his carnsarned throat and hope he choke on it."

"How ye come by this, son?"

Jubal explained where and how he had picked up the silver button. He thought about telling all that he knew but pulled up short before spilling all. He had thoughts that Wes had not told all that he knew, and he saw no reason that he needed to do anything but likewise.

The conversation went on till way after dark. Old Jake had long since given it up and was dreaming whatever old dogs dream about. Fall of the year chill began to make itself felt once the sun had gone. The sounds of the night began to rise and far up on the ridge, a lone screech owl made his presence known all around. Wes began to show signs of a long day, and Jubal felt the day's work and travels in his feet and legs as well.

"Wes, it be bedtime, but there be one thing I wanna know first."

"Ask away, son."

"Do ye really have a stash somewhere?"

"I told ye about the beeswax gourd and that be the God's truth."

"But is that all there be to it?"

"Why ye be askin' that, son. Ye be wantin' it fer yerself just like yer Pa?"

Jubal stood and reached for the saddle button and returned it to his pocket. "Don't ye never go relatin' me to my Pa like that. I ain't him, and I ain't gonna be like him."

"We talk more on that later but that be all fer tonight."

Wes lay back on the trot and rolled himself in a wool blanket using his forearm for a pillow. The blanket soon killed the chill of the night, but sleep was slow in coming. He sensed that he had riled the boy and that was far from what he aimed to do. There were just some things that he did not need to know right now.

Jubal went upstairs and climbed in his bed without even taking off his dust-laden britches and lay on top of the covers. He thought about all that Wes had told him and slowly began to realize that his Pa was the source of his anger much more so than what Wes had said to him. He reached into his pocket and fingered the saddle button again. It seemed to be hotter than it had ever felt before.

Sleep eventually overcame him as he tried to think of ways to get even with his Pa for all the injustices that he had done to Ma and to the girls. He thought about all that C.C. had told him about his Pa laying up in town. The flames of spite welled up even higher as he inwardly cursed his Pa, not so much because of what he had done but because of the way he hurt and shamed his Ma. No wonder she never had much to say over him.

Morning had a calming effect coupled with renewed hunger. Big cathead biscuits would be coming out of the oven in no time now, and a certain young man was sure to be to the table on time. Some of his bitterness had quieted, but there were answers that he still needed. He had decided during the sleepless hours that he would ask Ma about Pa. He had never been so up front with her, and he was a bit edgy about it now.

Jubal ate his fill for breakfast and lingered in the kitchen over more coffee. Ironic that everyone else seemed to be rushed to get gone from the kitchen before time to clear the table and do up the dishes. Ma already had a big kettle of leather britches soaking on the kitchen table. Jubal knew what they would have for supper tonight, shuck beans and fried corn bread.

"Ma," Jubal said as he drained the last of the coffee from the old dinged up blue-speckled pot, "How come ye put up with all Pa's shenanigans fer so long now?"

Somewhat taken aback, she did not turn to look at her son, but sort of just dropped her face as if staring into the dishpan. They had a long discussion with Ma not much more than ever looking him eye to eye.

She told him how they had married much too quick, before they really knew each other very well. She told him how she was scared that her Pa would cause trouble if they were not married. She further explained to him how that she had laid with his Pa beforehand and that he blamed her for tricking him into marriage when it was not really needed. She did not ask him if he understood that part, but she knew he was of age now and that he would just naturally have learned about such things.

She went on to explain how that she had tried to be a good wife and that she was forever sorry for things that had happened in her life that she could not change now. Said that she had vowed that she would not make those same blunders again and that was why she put up with some of the things. Besides that, not long after they did get hitched, the kids just seemed to keep on coming about ever year. That was the cross that God had give her to bear and she would accept it.

She also explained how she had learned to turn ever thing over to the Good Lord and trust Him to take care of her and her family. So far she had been able to keep ever body fed and clothed, but she had to admit that the war shed a different light on things and that some things were almost impossible to come by now.

Jubal hugged his Ma and told her that he was sorry that she had seen rough times. He also promised her that if he had anything to do with it that Pa would never hurt her no more.

"Vengeance ain't yours or mine, son. Don't ye even go near him. He ain't around here now, and I just soon keep it so."

"I be thinkin' ye be wrong Ma; he is 'round here too."

Chapter 7

Angry

*T*wo days seemed a long time in some ways. In others it was nothing but a fleeting moment. It had been two days since he had seen Lida and that seemed an eternity. Yet it was only a moment or two that Ma had part way opened her heart to him and told him about things that he had really already come to know. He had done the chores around home as was his normal task and had done them without really thinking on them. What he had thought about was partly what Ma had talked about and partly what Wes had asked him.

Wes had questioned him about what he wanted out of life and what he expected to do with himself now that he was on the very edge of manhood. The miserly old man had the gall to offer him advice on being neighborly and upstanding in all that he did and in his business dealings with others. The old man had even proffered direction on how to make his way in the world and how to provide food and shelter for a wife and a house full of kids. Jubal could not take much stock in the part about provision for a big family seeing as how the old man seemed to be advising on something that he had never been able to do for himself. But he had raised a matter or two that stirred some study and thought.

Wes had talked long about the ill effects that the war was having on folks all around, especially to those down south in cotton country where the slaves were thick and the Reb spirit was higher than a

Georgia pine on a red bank hill. He had speculated that things would be a whole heap different if the North won the war and all the darkies were set free. He went on and on about how bad it would be on folks with no way to get their crops in and such and how ever thing would be hard to come by, even more so than now.

It was only after one of their long talks about such that Wes explained to the boy about the gourd filled with beeswax and told him in no uncertain terms that there was more to the gourd business than he could imagine.

Jubal had questioned him about it as to what he meant and how much and where he got it, but Wes would not reveal more. He had already told the boy there would come a time soon when it might be necessary for him to know more, but not right now. This only served to stir curiosity and opened up more questions. It bothered him a bit that the old man would not take him into his confidence especially considering what he and Ma had done for him. Dang, they had saved his life most certainly and that should be worth something.

He had even found time to sit and listen to Granny Iverson during the last two days. It was some of the things that she said and some of the questions that she asked that seemed to burn the deepest into his recurring thoughts. Granny had come right out direct and asked him what he thought about asking help and guidance from the Lord and if he ever thought about getting down on his knees and talking to the Lord. He really had some trouble with the thought of an ever where, know-all, see-all and hear-all God who could be powerful enough to control wars and nations and be such influence on men ever where and all the while keep track of the rains and droughts. It just appeared to be too much to expect that God could love ever soul on the face of the whole earth, be they good or bad.

Sure he had been told about this Bible business all his life. He was inclined to think that there was something on the other side, but that was apt to be some time off yet. He had just seen sixteen, and all life lay ahead of him. There was time to learn and time to know more later on. But yet, these thoughts and questions continued to pick at him, and sometimes haunting uncertainty would rear up and show its face where it was least expected.

It was not yet a harvest moon, too early for that; but the September night was akin to that of the gathering time. Everything was bathed in a silvery glow, and no light was needed to see all the way to the timberline at the top of the ridge. Even the old split rail fence was easy to spot, especially the fresh hewn chestnut rails where he had mended the fence only a few weeks past. He could see old Kate grazing contentedly on the low side of the big poplar tree, and the haystacks under it looked to be only shocks by comparison.

He did not know what the hour was nor did he really care. It had to be the wee hours of the morning because he had slept for a bit, awakened, and had not been able to lie in bed any longer. The body could have used the rest, but the mind would not be still. He had gone to the trot and then to the kitchen porch for a drink from the old gourd dipper. The dipper had reminded him of Wes and his dipper and that led to more and more thought to the point where he now found himself with his arms draped across the gate to the upper meadow and looking up to the moon high above his head. If this were the dead of winter and it were this clear, the night would have brought a frost that could pass for a young snow. Tonight, there was nothing but moon glow. It was so bright that many of the familiar stars had hidden their face and only those of the most brilliance could be seen. He had to look before he could spot the North Star, and the morning star had just cleared the crest of the ridges. There was silence save for the scratching sounds made by old Jake as he sat beside the boy as if to wonder what could be astir at this hour of the morning.

The silence was a bit eerie and discomforting to the lad, because it seemed to amplify the uncertainty that he felt overshadowing him at the moment.

There was no way to be sure how this infernal war was going to turn out. His thoughts sprang to the thievery and unsavory things that had recently been reported in the hills and hollows. Then he thought of things that C.C. had told him about the questionable characters and activities of certain sightings in his own hollow. It made him cringe with anger to think that harm could come to Lida or her family, or his own family. He thought about his Pa and felt even more disdain for him. He had no good feelings left for Pa; he was sure to be up to no good. Pa always wanted a free ride or the easy way out. The boy knew that there was no easy way. Everything worth having had a price, and most times that price was fair enough if a man was willing to bend his back and work.

His thinking even led him to ask what he should do if he were ever to come face to face with his Pa, knowing what he knew now. He envisioned a number of things, and none of them included a relationship of love and fellowship. A fleeting thought, quicker than a shooting star, reminded him of what Granny Iverson had said just a day or so past about the boundless love of The Almighty and how he loved everyone so much that he made provision for the light of the world out of that love.

In almost the same instant, he swore to himself that he would not be upholding to his Pa if he ever did face him. He could not respect him, and he would make no lies about it. There was just no cause for such.

He thought again of Lida and how sweet it would be this very night, this very minute, to hold her in his arms. The moonlight would make her face as silk, and the softness of morning dew would be as a harlot's scorn compared to her tenderness and caress. Her innermost being would melt into his passion, and she would be his forever. He could ask for no other and would need no other.

An immeasurable span of fantasy and dream had caused time to slip by. When he again raised his eyes to the ridge, he was surprised to see the first faint rays of light in the east. Still he remained fixed upon the support of the old sagging gate. Dang, just something else that needs to be fixed around here. I don't want to do it. Ma should not have to do it. Pa, cuss his hide, should be here and do it himself. Another coal of fire was heaped upon the flame that had just begun to burn a deep crimson; a fire that burned hot, but gave no light for guidance. A fire that would sear and leave a forever scar.

Jake roused up from his sleepiness and perked an ear for a moment. Another effort at soothing whatever itched so much and then a more acute alertness to something unseen by the boy. Jubal noticed the dog's nose held high to catch any unusual scent that could drift in on the stillness of the coming morning. Jake stiffened and dropped his tail, staring intently into the faint light. He lowered himself to crawl under the gate, and Jubal called to him to stop. He did stop his movement, but his senses only heightened. Both were silent. Jubal momentarily held his breath to see if there was a faint sound that he might catch. There was nothing, not even the sound of a bird on wing or a wisp of wind. Jake stiffened again.

Jubal shaded his eyes as if it were high noon in attempt to pry open the twilight just a bit better. He scanned the ridge line above the hay racks and the tall poplar tree and could see nothing against the blackness of the thick timber. Jake raised his hackles and began a low rumble of a growl. The boy reached down and rubbed his head and in effect called for silence. Jake obeyed, but never wavered in his stare or in his concentration. Without doubt, he was onto something and sensed what the boy could not detect.

Jake wanted to ease forward, and Jubal knelt to place an arm around his neck and a hand on his foreleg. It was then that he saw what Jake had seen for several moments. A tiny reflection of moon-light focused his vision; and there, not more than a hundred yards into the meadow, was a lone rider. The swish of the horse's hoofs in the new mown grass was but a whisper to him. He kept his arm around Jake best he could while rising back to his stance in effort to get a slight better look at this unexpected, unwanted and intrusive visitor. Moon glow once again briefly bounced off the rider and his steed. Could this be the same silver-studded saddle that he had run across before? His free hand found its way into a pocket and explored the saddle button that he carried since the day he had kicked it out of the dust. He watched intently as the mounted figure moved slowly in the direction of the faint first light of morning.

He unknowingly wished for more light. He wanted to see more and maybe understand who this could be and what might be their intent. He felt pretty sure that the intent would not be honorable. He had suspicion of who it might be, but it was too dark to tell. Oh, for revealing light!

He followed the moving shadow as it eased up the meadow to the crest of the near hill. The rider was a darkened figure against the graying light, and his movement could be seen clearer now. The figure rode to the old rail fence and dismounted. Jubal could see that he was laying down the top rails. He then led his mount across the lower rails. He then turned and replaced the top rails.

The lone rider held his position and was in no apparent hurry to avoid being spotted against the coming morning sun. The first faint pastels of purple and red began to peek up above the east ridge. That was when the boy and the dog spotted the others coming out of the deep woods and headed out apparently to join up with the lone rider. The light was still too faint to make out any detail, but it was plain that there were four of them and that one was a head taller than the rest. He saw no shadows that would tell of mounted soldiers carrying long rifles. There were none to be seen unless they were Cavalry and carrying Spencer carbines. Not likely. Only the Bluecoats had Spencers for the most part, and no Bluecoats had been seen around here in months.

They all met at the crest of the hill and apparently discussed their movement for a bit. Jubal could see arms pointing first this way and then that. The group then moved on down the far side of the ridge and soon vanished. Jubal knew that they would leave a track that would be hard to miss unless they split up somewhere.

A hurried breakfast, a word or two with Ma and her ensuing caution. Then he was out of the house and fast following the rail fence to the crest of the hill. The trail was like walking down a fenced lane. Easy to follow. Five sets of tracks, all shod but one. The orange and yellow leaves that had already come down were bright, so much so that the forest floor seemed to be ablaze in places. Poplar leaves splayed out as big as an outstretched hand, and the reddish orange sugar tree leaves had spread their points to the four winds. Every step that the horses made had cut across the veins of one or more of these brilliant decorations. All that was needed to read the signs was a little patience and a close look at how they were broken and how they lay on the ground. The boy was young in years, but he was mature in his ability to read a track.

He could see that all five were together and that they were in no hurry, at least not right now. The leaves were cut and broken; but there was no deep imprint beneath them, nor no soil kicked up behind them. All were in single file and none had dismounted, so far. The trail continued to the east into the rising morning, and Jubal had already made speculation about where it would lead. Soon, about another hour or so on due east, would put them at the divide on the old Wick's place. There they would head south down a small valley that ran parallel to his native Cane Valley, or they would cut the crest of short ridge and wind up near Horne's cave. If they turned south and stuck to the valley, they would come out just above Johnson's mill.

Jubal made near silent progress in his quest. This area had never been logged that he knew about, and the size of the timber told it too. Massive red oaks and poplars scraped the clouds. Hickory with boughs bent under the load of nuts. Beech spread a canopy so thick that no light reached the ground below them until the cold winter winds had whipped away their brown and withered leaves. But today was no winter day, and the sun began to make its presence known even in the deep shade of the woods.

There were no sounds that gave hint of anything what did not belong there. Frequent stops to listen for faint or strange sounds drifting in on soft wing would foretell if there was another creature nearby.

He had broken a fairly good sweat by the time he reached the divide. The trail was still plain as a nose on a face, and it told him all that he needed to know. There were five sets of tracks, and they had stopped on the crest of the divide. They had milled around for a bit and one rider had dismounted. It appeared to be the unshod horse that he was riding because the man tracks and the horse tracks were the only ones near enough each other to be anything else. The dismounted rider had emptied his pipe and refilled it as he stood there in the loose soil. There were ashes and sprinklings of spilled tobacco that painted the picture in the mind's eye. It stirred uneasiness in the boy, because Pa smoked a pipe ever now and then. The tracks then led off to the east, across the ridge. It was time to turn back to home. Lida would be in no danger from this brood. They were headed elsewhere.

Ma made a late change in plans. She decided that she and Julie would go to Yeary's. Sarry would stay and help with Gracie, Granny Iverson would do mending, and Wes could tend his chores and that all be fine. Ma had really wanted to go, so that settled the issue.

The trek to Yeary's store had been uneventful and had taken about an hour less than everyone had thought. There was no one else on the road, and there were no patrons at the store when they arrived. Mr. Yeary stood in the open doorway and greeted them with a hearty smile as they pulled up in the buckboard. He was a stooped little man with balding grey hair, presently in disarray as if whipped about and arranged by an uneasy wind. A few quick strokes of an open hand to his head soon improved that. A once white apron gave evidence to many hours of clerking and stocking shelves.

Now many of those shelves stood empty and barren. The war had made it lots harder to have a store full of goods. Many things were not available here or in any other store save possibly in the bigger townships on up north. In some ways the war had mostly bypassed the Cane Creek area and only a limited skirmish or two had even given hint of the conflict. But the widespread indolence of war had made itself quite well known in other ways, and one big way could be seen right here in the little community store.

Mr. Yeary recognized Lida and her mother right off and asked as to their welfare and made the customary courtesy inquiries. Lida and her mother went inside as Jubal and Ma made their way inside and out of the bright morning sun. Ma stood patiently in the background, eyes taking store of the tables and the shelving, some full and others only holding up the dust of their emptiness.

Wes had given Jubal some money and told him to get some shirts and maybe some linsey-woolsey britches for both of them. He also instructed the lad to look for a good pair of boots. Told him to fit himself and that would be a good fit for him too. Jubal made his initial visual search of the entire store stock and at once knew that the choices would be slim. Lots of things were not to be had, and it appeared that folks had either decided to do without or had just gone off somewhere else to find what they needed. It then struck home how serious the threat was that people who needed or wanted what could not be had would just take whatever they could lay hands on. Wes and Ma both had cautioned him about that and warned him not to take any foolish risks when he was out and about. That thought had just that very moment been driven home.

Without being conscious of his action, Jubal found three shirts to his liking and a pair of blackened boots that fit fairly well. Further searching unveiled a similar pair and wool socks to go along with them. The boy had brought along his own gold piece and intended to buy his own side arm if one could be had. So far he had not seen one of any caliber. There was one near empty cask of nails, but that was about all that could be seen that would even hint of manufactured goods.

Lida had found a bolt of yellow colored cloth that looked as if it was once white but had been turned dull by age. She ran her hand over it, folded and unfolded the ends and then replaced it. She nor her mother would settle for any such lack of quality in choosing material for a new dress and matching bonnet. They both had better than that at home.

Everyone, including Jubal, seemed to be a bit let down over what the storekeeper had to offer. It was only after a time that it became apparent to the storekeeper that these people were not out to rob him or to harm him.

"I have other wares that I don't keep out in the open. If you can tell me more what it is that you be in need of, then maybe I can fetch it. I keep most goods hid till I know I can trust whoever comes in here. Hate it has to be like that, but I been took too many times here lately."

"I understand that," Mrs. Johnson replied as if relieved that she may yet find what she wanted.

"What might you be in need of?" asked the storekeeper.

"We need wool or linsey-woolsey. We want to make us new winter coats."

Mr. Yeary excused himself for a moment and came back in with three small bolts of woolen material. He described them as being made up north and shipped in on pack horses not long after the skirmish up near Rotherwood. Again he told of the difficulties in being able to lay hands on dry goods and again offered apologies for not having a store full of choices. He made it plain that he did not support the secessionist movement and the conflict that it had caused. He said that the war would go much deeper than just the killing and fighting because it had already created hardships on folks. Just the whole idea of fighting among brothers seemed to him to be a work of the old devil himself. He spoke of the troubles that had beset his wife's kinfolk down near Andersonville who were in worse shape than people here in Cane Valley.

"I am truly sorry ladies. I will climb down off my soap box now. I am at your service, if you please."

"You seem to be educated well, Mr. Yeary. Whereabouts did you come from before settlin' here?" Mrs. Johnson inquired.

"Well, that's kind of a long story. I once was a circuit judge down in old Bammy, but things got so corrupt and dishonest down there that I just wanted to leave it all behind and get away from it all. Besides that I am no spring chicken anymore, and we just wanted to settle in some place where we could just fade into the local hills and kind 'a take it easy."

"I knew that you weren't from here, but we are glad that you be here now. I know how the war must be other places, but we actually ain't had too much of it here so far. Just hope it stays like that," Lida's mother replied.

After more politeness from the storekeeper, the women folk had concluded their transactions. While that was in process, Jubal had piled his choices on a corner of a small table near the rear door. At that point the former judge was ready to help him with any other requests that he might have.

"How much all this come to?"

"Looks like nine dollars would cover it. I know that is a plenty, but things cost me more now too."

"That be true, I reckon. Will this here cover it," Jubal asked as he produced a ten-dollar gold piece?

"I think it will, plus a bit."

That settled. Jubal asked if he might have a pistol for sale and some caps and balls to go along with it. A wave of the wrist indicated that the boy should come along, and they were both soon out to the rear of the store in a nearby old barn. Mr. Yeary dug down in the loose hay up to arm's reach and extracted a wad of oilcloth wrapped around burlap and tied up with a small rope.

Unwrapping it revealed a navy revolver that obviously had seen its share of action. No rust, but plenty of scuffs and scratches. The sales pitch included the fact that it had been tested and that it fired just fine and considering how hard these things were to come by that he would have to have good money for it.

"I got more just like I done give ye," Jubal responded.

"Then I think we can do business if you never tell where you got it. I think I can trust you and your folks, but I do not want ever creature here in the valley to know that I had it. They would burn me out to get hold on another if they thought I had more, which I don't."

The trade was completed, payments made, and all the goods loaded in the buckboard. It was late morning and Jubal's stomach began to tell him that it would soon be time to eat, or was it just the excitement of now owning his own pistol and thereby being one step closer to manhood?

Cane Creek ran through the small valley pretty much alongside the dirt road that eventually intersected with a main artery that connected the area of the northeastern. Not very far from Yeary's store, the road climbed a small ridge and then down a long slope back to the valley floor while the meandering creek made a long horseshoe trek to reach the same destination. The crest of the little ridge was noted for its brief isolation from the surrounding area. The road there was narrow, rough and strewn with larger dislodged stones and dirt slides coming out of the cut road bank. It was less than a quarter mile of unfavorable road, but required a bit of time and effort to traverse. Too much haste in a wagon would surely destroy the best built of the lot. Many round head rocks and rough limestone veins made the roadbed rough and not very sure of foot for any draft animal. It was a place that demanded respect of any traveler, near or far. Mrs. Johnson was well aware of the place and the situation that it created, and she was the one who tendered the notion that the little party would do well to start for home soon. She and Lida had packed a small basket to stave off any midday thirst or hunger, and she let it be known that she had a place in mind that would be suitable for a short stop, a quick bite, and then resume the day's journey without wasting any time. Jubal knew of the roughness of the road; but he had not considered the isolation, however brief, of that area. Mrs. Johnson had made note of the inhospitable aura of the crest and the road, but had said nothing to anyone else. She saw no need to stir any anxiety for anyone, but she was prepared if need be.

Jubal reined the team off the road under a large sugar tree that was ablaze with crimson and orange flame. The drought of the late summer had not caused any lack of radiance for this aged monarch of the valley. It provided abundant shade from the noon time sun and did it with characteristic autumn glory.

The small basket of biscuits and bacon were soon made short, and the party set out for home. Mrs. Johnson had asked Jubal to drive and somewhat to his displeasure had seated herself beside him. This left Ma, Julie and Lida in the back with all the things from the store, save for the pistol that now was jammed into the waistband of the boy's britches. Never mind that he had not taken time to load it. Ma had bought a big cocker sack of salt, some chicory and some sort of woven goods that were all wrapped up in a canvas pouch. Jubal had his new stuff all packed in a huge bedroll and tied up with rawhide strings. Lida had shoved all of her and her mother's goods under the buckboard seat. Julie soon managed to use this as her pillow and was shortly unaware that she was even in the world. Mrs. Johnson hardly spoke once they had resumed their trek and often glanced back in the direction they had come. She seemed to be a bit edgy.

It seemed that Jubal and William had marched for a thousand miles and almost as many days. It had been near two weeks since their journey's onset from the low hills of western Maryland. Headed east for the most part, they had now turned south. They had received newer orders, but Major Dunn had opted not to let them be privy to that detail, at least not so far. No real matter. No shots had been fired in anger over the entire trek. Game seemed to be plenty, and they had eaten their fill of venison steaks and fresh fowl most every night. Only routine occasional sentry duty had kept them from restful sleep on most nights. Evenings cooled a bit and early morning chills called for appreciation of a good bedroll.

Jubal had been summoned to the commander's tent last evening and had long last received proper paperwork to insure he had all coming his way that would be due him. Records in order and pay accounted for since the day he had been given the blue coat and a weapon with field gear. He was in Mr. Lincoln's army now for sure.

He and William were almost inseparable now, and they had formed a bond that went beyond the limits of military duty. William had come to appreciate the wilderness and woodsy talents that Jubal displayed. He had a way of knowing just where to find game and knew instinctively where to look for the best berries, nuts and fruits. He learned much from the lad.

The closing days of September had been somewhat relaxed for the reconnaissance squad, and they were under standby orders as clouds darkened and rains began. Bivouac in the field never was known for comfort, and the cold rain made for even more pronounced complaint. Cooking fires burned continually, and no one lacked for hot food and drink. The long march of the past few days had worn down the hardiest of the whole lot of them. The rest was welcomed by all, including the brass.

The cold could be dealt with on its own terms and rest would revive the spirits and restore the strengths. According to what was being reported from higher up, this damnable war could not go on much longer. Common knowledge in most of the rank and file was that the Rebs were about whipped. They were on the run all over, and many were to the place where they had nothing else to fight with save for a club or a bayonet.

The politicians were still all in a quandary as to how the conquered states would be dealt with once they were beaten. Jubal had wondered about home and how it would be once he made it back there. It had been quite some time since he had heard any fresh news from Cane Valley. Not too many men in this man's army from that neck of the woods.

Jubal and William sat Indian style in their tent during a gentle but steady rain. No wind at the present so they could open the tent flaps and get fresh air, but this seemed to admit more dampness. William flung a dry blanket over his shoulders and soon felt its warming comfort. Much more of that and he would become sleepy.

"Jubal, my friend, what will you do when you get back home?"

"Not been dwellin' on that. Just takin' this here war a day at a time, I reckon."

"You must have some thought about your future," William replied as if asking a question.

"I guess I just be like most all other folk 'round there. I reckon I can make a fair 'nuff livin' farmin' and raisin' cattle and hosses."

"Is that what you want?"

"No."

"Then what?"

"I'd like settlin' down and havin' me a son or two and just bein' happy. I once thought money and all was what I wanted, but it ain't that simple no more."

"How you mean, Jubal?"

"Iffin I had a thousand dollars right here and now, I reckon I'd fork it all over to just see my Ma and my kinfolk. That make any sense to ye?"

"Sure it does. I miss my folks too."

Jubal buried his face in his hands and rubbed his eyes to hide his emotion. He hated these times when he missed home so bad. There had been other times when he was alone on sentry when he had not been able to contain himself and had wept openly. He did not know it at the present moment; but home, if he ever did get back, would never be the same. The day that he rode away and donned the blue coat was the beginning of a new chapter in his life, and all the things that had happened yesterday were now gone. He was now far away from all those things dear to him in all of his yesterdays. All of the tomorrows were unknown and stretched before him like an eternity.

Eternity, there was that word again that William had talked to him about several times before. Everything seemed like it was a mystery and an unknown. All a body could do was believe it or just pass it off like most folks seemed to do. William had told him of how he had come to see the light and how that now there was a sense of worth and of satisfaction in his life and that he really had no doubts or fears since he had seen the way. He even acted like he was never troubled or worried.

Seen what way and what light? Sunlight? Moonlight? What other light could a man see with his own two eyes? Which way? Which road in which point of the compass? How can a man be peaceful and content in a danged war?

"You on sentry tonight, Jubal?"

"Yeah, I reckon so."

"First watch?"

"Yep."

"We got some time yet. You want me to write a letter home for you?"

"Naw."

"You want me to read you some?"

"Naw."

William had an uncanny ability to read his friend, and he knew that something was eating at the lad. He had known for some time what a fix he was in and what he really needed to do with it, but he was very patient. No sense in rushing up the workings of one who was far above and beyond his meager witness.

"You got all your papers now and pay will be coming to you soon as we get to division. That should lift you up some."

"What in tarnation I gonna do with money out here? Guess I could rent me a dolly mop fer a night or three and make her earn a wage."

"Never meant to rile you."

"You never."

"Saw two deer brought into the mess tent earlier. You think we might get a slab of it for supper if we go soon?"

"Go ahead. I ain't hungry."

"I will try and bring something back for you to eat later, if you want."

"Thanks."

The rain let up a bit and Jubal was glad of that. Sentry time was bad enough without being wet and cold. He was both and had already eaten the deer meat that William had fetched him back from the mess tent. Thankfully he was not hungry and owed his friend for that.

His watch would be over in another three hours and the sooner the better. He could get back to his tent and in his bedroll. Maybe he could sleep and get warm before the first light. He was a bit restless tonight, realizing that winter would soon be coming on and that there would be more cold and more rain, even some snow.

He thought of his Ma and his sisters and Granny Iverson. Who would be there to cut their firewood? Would there be enough to eat all winter long? He thought of the cold wind and how it always whistled in the tops of the big old beech tree that stood above the springhouse, and how lonesome it always sounded. He recalled how eerie its bare branches looked in the light of the winter moon. He thought how the chill caused his ears and his cheeks to chafe and to burn. This war had distanced him from everything that meant anything to him, and he had never felt so alone as he did on this one damp and dismal night. There was no moon to cast a shadow and not a single sliver of silvery light to show the way. There was only darkness and the separation from all that was good. There had to be more, somehow there just had to be a better time and lighter days. This war was evil, and he knew for sure that evil was no good in any way. But where was all the good? Thoughts of home always seemed to evoke feelings about Lida and her family. Most times it evoked feelings of desire and wishing that he could have her near. Tonight he wondered if she was warm. He could see her soft rosy cheeks and her gentle smile. He could hear her voice. But no! Here he was in this danged rain and darkness. May as well be halfway around the world. It was so dark that a hand in front of one's own eyes could scarce be seen.

Lida had talked about the darkness once when it was broad daylight. Granny Iverson had mentioned how she had seen the light and how it had changed her life. There must be something that was a mystery, but he just never could get hold on what the meaning of it was all about.

Jubal walked his post, back and forth, without really being aware of what was around him or what was happening near him. Good thing there was no one around to do him harm, because they could have come up on his blindside; he would have never known they were there until they struck. He was there in body, but the mind roamed far and wide. He just could not understand the way that things were and why they had to be that way. He had known no peace for some time now, and it was beginning to take a toll on him. He knew it and hated himself for it, but did not know what to do about it.

Mrs. Johnson continued to fret and was obviously on edge and becoming more so as they drew nearer to the crest of the ridge and the deep cut of the road. Jubal drove the team with care and took time and patience with them as C.C. had told him. They had not even broken a good sweat, and they seemed in high spirits. The buckboard was stout and could take what the road had to dish out, but there was no need to rush.

Jubal looked down at the road and dust that had piled up between the old limestone balds, and at once picked up the random tracks of an unshod horse. It was headed in the same direction as they; headed back to the mouth of the mill hollow. His mind flashed back to the riders he had seen several times before and the one unshod horse that was ridden by the scoundrel that always had his old filthy looking hat pulled down low over his eyes. There was no way of telling if this track was the same as those tracks, but he already equated the two, and his sense of alertness and observation peaked almost immediately.

Mrs. Johnson began to fumble under her apron, and Lida turned to face forward. It was as if both had sensed something in the same breath. Jubal could not see what Lida was doing without turning and looking at her, but he could hear the rustling of her skirt and apron too. He kept one eye on the road and another on the team. Now, even they seemed a bit edgy. Ma had said nothing. She had not moved. The last glance Jubal had of Julie, she was asleep with her head in Ma's lap. No one spoke as the team came to the crest of the hill where the travel would be the slowest.

A big burley man with a deerskin shirt and an unruly full face beard stepped out from behind a scrub cedar and reached for the horses bridle. Jubal cracked the reins, but it came too late, and the ruffian would not lose his grip on the reins. The buckboard stopped.

"Turn loose," demanded Mrs. Johnson.

"You hear that?" come a voice from behind the buckboard.

"Yep, I reckon I did, but we done hit us a jackpot today. We got hosses and wemmen too."

Lida turned at the sound of the second voice and stood upright.

Bam!! Such a loud clamor right in the ear of the buckboard driver that it startled him so much that he almost jumped from the seat. Mrs. Johnson had in an instant pulled a pistol from beneath her apron and had fired at the bearded assailant. She had struck home. The reins were immediately loosed, and the hand that had held them now oozed bright red blood from between fingers that clinched a left shoulder.

Bam!! Bam!! This time from behind him. Lida had opened up on her target. Hard to tell if her shot had found its mark. He wasted no time in retreat but did manage to return one shot in his haste to escape any further hail of bullets.

Jubal had the team moving again. They had gone several yards before the ringing in his ears subsided enough to realize that someone was speaking to him and that there was crying. Ma was bent over Julie and clutching her bleeding knee.

Lida screamed out to Jubal to hurry. He whipped the team into a gallop and in an instant was clear of the balds. The road sped by underneath the buckboard. All held on as dust kicked up behind them in a swirling cloud. Ma and Lida soon had Julie's knee wrapped in some of the just purchased fabric and seemed to have things in hand as best could be at the moment.

By the time that the buckboard drew up in front of the mill, the horses were wet with sweat and breathing like they had been on a run for life. In fact they had, but not so much for their sake as for others. Before Jubal could get down, Ma had Judie in arms, and she and Mrs. Johnson were halfway into the house. Lida handed C.C. her pistol as he came from the mill porch in apprehension as to what had beset them. Lida told him briefly what had happened and then ran into the house. Jubal started that way too.

"Wait, son. There be nothin' ye can do in there. Let the women-folk tend what needs be tended. These hosses needs cooled down and put away fer the night."

"They shot Julie," the boy said in desperation. "They shot my little sis."

C.C. eventually talked him down enough to get more details of what had happened and what rogues had been involved. They each walked a horse as they talked; and when they had cooled enough, took them to water and let them have their due. Back in the confines of the barn, the light had already begun to fade. Brushing down the mare and the gelding did not take long, but it was enough time for Jubal to compose himself and begin to put pieces of the day back together. He had not known that Mrs. Johnson and her daughter were armed, but he did recall Lida saying that her Pa had taught her to shoot. At the present, he was thankful for her talents.

C.C. told him that he had seen riders along the ridge line more than once here in the last few days. He had not told Jubal about this before because he saw no need in it. But now it was a bit different. The miller man was pretty sure that he knew at least one of them, and he felt that Jubal and his Ma had a right to know everything that he knew. C.C. proceeded to tell the boy that he had learned for sure that his Pa was in thick with the scallywags and rogues who were at work in this end of the county. They knew that it was more or less a Union stronghold, and they took it upon themselves to do as they pleased, since there was no local law. The county was under martial jurisdiction, but the Union troops were few and far between. There was really no one to enforce what law there was or had been before secession. The miller had talked with a Yankee captain and had learned that efforts were at hand to throttle all such activity, but most no-gooders managed to always stay one step ahead of the Bluecoat law.

The patrol had a good idea who they were chasing, but had been reluctant to drop any names, just a description which was not at all hard to interpret. They made a point to let it be known that one of them liked his laudanum and had been to every source around to maintain a generous flask. There was some doubt about one of the sources, and Jubal rightly surmised who that was too.

He thought all along that Cleve was a little less than honest, and this just proved him out. He was the one who had sold the comfort-in-a-bottle to his Pa and had not hesitated in charging a hefty sum for it either. The lad did not really know where to direct his strongest hatred, Cleve for his role in the whole deal or his Pa for just plain running out on Ma and his kids.

"Ye thinkin' he were in on this here fracas today?" Jubal asked.

"Don't know, son. We best talk with yer Ma and Lida. Seems me like they be the ones have the best look at what might been his bunch."

"I never seen the others nowhere ceptin' fer a split hair's worth when Lida shot at him. Reckon she must 'a missed him."

"We'll hafta ask her more on that, I reckon."

The next couple of hours were hectic to say the least. First thing and the most important was caring for Julie's knee and making sure that she was in no peril. Ma and Mrs. Johnson had washed her up real good, and Lida had covered her wound with hog lard. She was as gentle and easy as could be, but even so it was painful for Julie. She was strong and did not waver in her patience. Her facial expressions revealed her pain in spite of all her bravery and strength. She never cried out, but her tears betrayed her.

"Her kneecap is busted," Lida discretely informed.

"I know," said Ma. "I done felt that too."

The wound was soon bandaged in strips of a torn bed sheet, and the patient was soon sleeping in a half bed that the Johnsons kept in a small room just off the main sitting room. There would be heat from the big open fireplace if it should be needed. If the young lass could be kept quiet and still for a spell, then maybe it would not be so bad a hurt after all. If still, maybe there would be no more bleeding.

C.C. and Jubal spent most of the time outside the house on the big long porch. Lida was in and out with updates on Julie, requests for buckets of fresh water and anything else that was needed in the house. The afternoon sun had dropped low, and no one had given a thought to anything to eat until smoke began to rise from the kitchen chimney. Mrs. Johnson had started to fry fatback and make biscuits. She allowed as to how it could turn out to be a long night and that some hot vittles would not hurt at all.

Soon Lida came out with biscuits and bacon. Jubal and C.C. made short work of what she had put before them.

Midnight was near before all the rough spots had been ironed out as to how to best care for Julie and to take care of the rest of the family at the same time. Ma was some embarrassed by the situation to say the least, because she felt it her place to see to Julie's every need and that was going to be an issue if she did not have her home and close at hand. Granted that she needed rest and not to be jostled about in the back of a wagon, but her staying with the

Johnsons would be an imposition. Ma had the other girls and her own mother to see after, not to mention all the chores necessary to keep the home fires burning. Then there was old Wes, who needed his share of caring too.

C.C. and the Johnson ladies prevailed on Ma that it would be best for Julie to stay where she was, at least for a few days. She would be well seen to, and there was never a doubt to that fact. Ma could come every day, any time, and stay as long as she wanted or needed; she honestly was made to feel welcome. She knew in her heart that the miller family was compassionate and that there were no better neighbors than them.

She reluctantly accepted their aid and was most grateful for their concerns. But the needs of the present moment dictated that she think of her own household, the other daughters, Granny Iverson and Wes too for that matter. It was settled that Ma and Jubal would take the buckboard and go on up the hollow to home tonight and let Julie rest as best she could. Ma would do whatever needed done at home and come back tomorrow. Jubal could bring the buckboard and the team back home in the morning.

C.C. insisted that they need not be brought back right away soon as daybreak, but to wait and bring Ma when she was ready. He also insisted that he and his Ma carry a pistol apiece tonight, since it was already way past sundown. No telling who or what they could run up on before they got home.

The more he thought on it, the more riled up he became. Just what made them scoundrels think they could just waltz up and take whatever they had a mind for? Whatever whuppin' they got, they sure deserved. If he could have his way right now, he would lay some more whuppin' on the whole lot of em. Damn their hides anyhow!

There was not much light on the road. The thick brush and brambles hid what moon glow there was, but the horses had no trouble seeing the road. Jubal more or less let them rein themselves. He and Ma said very little to each other, but he knew that his Ma was worried over Julie. A couple of times he had seen enough moonlight on her face to see the pale reflection from the tears that had welled up in her eyes. She never said very much when she was deeply troubled, and he knew that this was one of those times.

He had not recognized the gravity of the afternoon's activity until Ma told him that his sister had a very tough time ahead of her and that it would take months for her to heal, if in fact she did heal. He had not considered before that she might even wind up a cripple or even worse. That realization kindled the fire of anger inside him.

Ma had told him that Julie would be all right. Said that she had just this past summer seen the light and had made things right. Said that Granny Iverson had read to her and talked to her at times way into the night. Granny had read to him too whenever he would sit long enough to listen. Lida, he recalled, had more than once talked on seeing the light. There was some mystery here that he was just not in tune with or maybe just had not paid heed to in the first place.

"Ma, will you tell me about that?"

"Not now, son. I be too tuckered and got too much other to fret on to be any good fer ye learnin' much outta me tonight. Ye needs ask Granny Iverson on that anyhow. She knows better'n me."

Jubal was restless all that night. Sleep was short and interrupted often by his wandering mind. He had not actually seen Julie get shot, but he had relived it and recreated it in his mind a thousand times already. He had sought ways that he might seek vengeance for her. He even thought the very thing that he feared could happen. He did not like thinking about such finality and tried to think about other things. Ma had stirred uneasiness in him by telling him that he needed to talk with Granny Iverson. How could she be of more help to him than his own Ma? What made Granny Iverson so special?

He knew that there was something about her that made her always have a smile or a kind word. He had not really noticed that about her till they had brought Wes here to be cared for. He was as well now as he would ever be, but Granny had said that there would be no need for him to go back to his old digs, and Ma had agreed with her. She never had a harsh word come across her lips.

Granny Iverson had little. She owned no land nor no slaves. She had no stock save for a single old milk cow that had to be as old as the boy himself. Yet, she spoke sometimes of riches the likes of which no man had ever known. Jubal had definite recollections of her saying that she had shown the light to Julie just like her mother had done for her way back when she was a young girl. There was a lot about Granny that he did not really understand. There were some things that he wanted her to tell him more about, but not this night, not even tomorrow. There would be plenty time for that later on.

Daybreak found Ma ready to set off to check on Julie. Jubal had received his orders from her and had the team and the buckboard at the yard gate and ready for the trek to the mill. Ma had told Sarry and Granny what she wanted done while she was gone, and they were already clearing the breakfast table in preparation for the tasks at hand. Ma had told Wes that she expected him to be the eyes and ears while she was gone. She had quickly told him all about the holdup and the shootings and that had really perked up his attention. Jubal thought that he detected a measure of fear in the old codger's face. He would ask about that later. Ma had slipped Wes the old hog rifle and told him not to let it out of sight. She had made Jubal tie up old Jake so he would not follow. She hinted to Wes that he should put the hound on a lead if he moved away from the house and yard any at all. Wes agreed without hesitation.

Convinced that all was in order as best could be, Ma climbed into the buckboard and reached down for Gracie and seated her between herself and her only son. She did not want to leave her youngest alone with all the fear and doubt that had been created in the last few hours.

The run to the mill went by in a drag it seemed. Just a mere three miles or so, but it seemed a world away. There was cause to get there as soon as could be. Ma was primarily concerned over Julie. How had she done through the night? Had she rested? Had she bled more? Did she hurt? Had she been any bother to the Johnsons? All these were ponderable to Ma and nothing short of a first-hand answer would put her mind at ease. Jubal had driven the team the way that C.C. had told him. He had made a safe trip.

The miller man had some questions for him once Ma and Gracie were shown into the house. Had he seen any tracks or signs on the way here? Had he thought out any more about who the scallywags could be and what else they could be up to? No, he had seen no signs on the road. He had looked close as they had come down the sand hill and past the reed patch. There were no tracks, and the new fallen leaves did not look disturbed. He had stopped and got down to look closer at one point, and there were no breaks in any of the veins of the big broad maple leaves. No fresh dirt turned anywhere. Yes, he had thought long and hard about their encounter, and he had no reason to believe other than he had thought before. Pa most sure was one of them and whatever they were up to was bound to be no good.

All the questions and pondering just fed the fire of hate for what had befallen Julie and all that Ma would be put through as she somehow would find the grit to care for her and at the same time see that the rest of her family did not suffer. These were hard times, sure since the war and all, but most did not have the determination that Ma had. She had built up that determination out of necessity.

C.C. told the boy how he had spotted the riders up on the ridge line more than one time in the past few days. "I think they be holdin' up in the doubles," C.C. remarked. Plenty places in there a body could hide. Iffin he kept fires out, then he not likely be found. You know about the doubles don't ye?"

"I hear tell of em, I reckon."

The doubles were ridges running down off the high knobs that interlaced like the fingers of a double fist. They were noted locally for their wilderness nature, steep ravines and spine back ridges. Jubal had never ventured into their isolation and never had cause to go into that area. It had not been known to harbor misfits and scally-wags before the war started. It was rumored to be home to she bears and big bobcats, and not too many folks cared to tangle with either one of them. There was a lone trail that cut the south end of the last ridge, but it was not wise to use it unless time was a big issue. It could save a half day's hike if you came up the Wilderness Road and wanted to go up to the head of Cane Valley or on up river.

"Iffin they be hold up in them parts, why then I reckon they must come out only fer thiefin' and such. I ain't sayin' nothin' sure, but if yer Pa be runnin' with that bunch, then I be thinkin' that he be comin' out sooner than the rest on account of him havin' to have his cussed drugs and whiskey. Hell, I don't know, they all may be on it with him."

"Reckon I could slip in and have me a look see," Jubal proposed.

"I reckon not, son. Iffin any man goes in them parts, it will be Union troopers. I done sent word to them that we're fixin' to need help down here. I reckon they can look into it firsthand. Don't reckon we can do much right yet, but sooner or later they be serious acts done and then there be a heap price be paid for their hides. You just wait."

Ma spent a short time at the bedside with Julie and emerged onto the front porch looking for Jubal. Not a spoken word, but a quick twitch of an upturned pointer finger set him to a trot in her direction. He had seen that twitch before, and he knew that it meant nothing but serious business and right now.

"Julie needs a doctor, but they ain't one near here. I reckon I need you to go fetch old Nanny Bray. Ye recollect her, I know. She got her own buggy so she can fetch herself here after ye go after her. I want ye to light out right now, and git yerself back here on the trot. Ye needs go back home and fetch Kate."

"Hold on a bit," C.C. interrupted. "Are ye fergittin' what just come about yesterday?"

"I reckon not," Ma retorted.

"The boy don't need be trapsin' off like that by his lonesome. It ain't safe. Besides that it take up too much time to fetch Kate and then go. I reckon ye can set a horse can't ye, son? I would hope so anyhow." The miller man got to his feet as he spoke.

"I can ride just fine," Jubal responded.

"Then that be settled, I reckon. Me and you will fetch old lady Bray on my mounts. I got two saddles and the gelding might be a bit testy, but he be broke long time back. I can ride him, and ye can have the mare. We can be back here 'fore sundown."

Ma must have been beyond words, cause she just turned and went back in the house in a seemingly hustle. She had no more gone through the door till she reappeared on the porch and this time directed her words to C.C.

"Will ye be carryin' a side arm?"

"We both will. I'll see to that."

"That be good, I reckon. I hate have ye come back here all shot up or worser."

"Ye ought not fret so much, Ma. We can manage, I reckon," Jubal said as he offered what reassurance he could muster.

"I be here till ye get yerself back and then I need ye take me back home and see that ever thing be quiet and that Sarry be holdin' up on her end." Mrs. Johnson and Lida assured her that they would do ever thing possible for Julie and that she did not need to be at her bedside all the time. That was inwardly what Ma wanted to hear. She knew that they meant it from within, but she was not raised to be obliged to a single soul and much of that raising still prevailed.

It did not take C.C. and Jubal very long to unharness the team and saddle them up. They were soon tied in front of the porch while C.C. went inside. He soon emerged with saddlebags and a scabbard holding a Spencer carbine. Jubal had heard of this new thing that the Union troops were now carrying but had no idea that there was one anywhere near to be had. He knew that C.C. had some clout around here, but this was more than he had ever thought about. C.C. saw that it had caught his eye.

"I tell ye about this here piece someday, but not right now. We best get ridin' and make good time at it too."

Jubal was just about to put a foot to the stirrup when he felt a hand on his shoulder. He turned, and Lida's lips met his in a brief moment of affection. She said nothing and turned and disappeared into the house. He did not know if anyone had observed the moment or not, but right now it did not matter. His heart was pounding, and he did not know if it was from the anticipation of the ride or if his unknown but uncontrolled passionate urges had triggered it. He felt like his face was afire.

The ride to the Bray place was without incident. C.C. and Jubal both concentrated on their horses and on keeping a sharp eye all about them. Both continually scanned the ridge lines and hillsides for any sign of rogue riders or misfits of any description. None were seen anywhere. It seemed to be a day that no one was astir. The horses were pretty much winded and had worked up a good lather by the time the Bray house came into view.

The old place was a bit run down because Mr. Bray had passed on some years back, and there was no one left to do all the hard manual work that needed done around the shop and the house to keep things repaired and running well. The blacksmith shop was to this day just like it was the day old man Bray had killed over at the forge. His widow would not allow anything done with his shop nor with his tools. Mr. Bray had never been a slaveholder and had never had any children. So it was now just his aged widow, and she was a mite particular who she even let come on her place, let alone in her house.

She had always been called on for help by folks in the valley and all around. She had helped many a squalling young'un into this world and had set a bone or two in her time. She was all the help that was available unless the Union army had a doctor or a surgeon somewhere near. It would take time to get him here even if he could be persuaded to come.

"You stay here with the hosses, and I'll see iffin I can roust her," C.C. directed as he dismounted and handed his reins to Jubal. He turned and swung open the yard gate. It creaked in resistance to his advances.

"That'll be about far 'nuff right there," a gruff and scratchy voice called out as the business end of an old blunder bust poked out of a curtained window.

"Wider Bray, is that you in there? I be C.C. Johnson, and I be thinkin' ye know me since some time back. I got the mill back a ways on Cane Creek."

"I know ye all right."

"We need yer help."

"I ain't got no help left in me no more. I done quit doin' most ever thing."

"We got a children what been shot in the kneecap, and we need her tended to bad."

"Who shot her?"

"Don't reckon we know that fer sure, but we thinkin' it be some riders that been hangin' out betwixt our neck of the woods and on into the doubles."

"How many?"

"We seen three most times, but they could be more."

The blunder bust drew back into the darkened window. In what seemed like an eternity the sound of steps could be heard inside, and eventually the front door opened enough to reveal a wrinkled weatherworn looking face. She carried a hickory sapling for a walking stick, which she held firm as a second measure of defense. She went on to tell that she had missed some side meat from her smokehouse, but had not pursued it and only had suspicions that some rogue may have taken it.

"I keeps most to self now days, and I take it kindly iffin ye not spread that too much. Ye know how it is now days and what all be runnin' loose out there. Bluecoats was here three days past lookin' fer somebody. Ain't said who. Say they be back in week or so," Mrs. Bray stated in a rather proud tone as if to indicate they would come back especially for her needs.

It quickly became clear that she was not about to go off treating anyone. After all she was old and had reason for staying close in. Her place was showing signs of neglect. There were weeds and brambles right in her front door. She claimed that she needed nothing or no one. Her body was old and becoming feeble, but her mind was still quite sharp. Her deep set gray eyes missed nothing.

After some urging, she offered the benefit of her experience as to the way to treat Julie. She wanted to know exactly where and how she had been shot. She even asked about how she was sitting when the bullet struck her. Had there been a lot of bleeding and what color it was and how much did it run? Had she tried to walk on it? Did it pain her a bunch? Could she bend her knee now?

C.C. and Jubal answered her questions as best they could, and she then proceeded to tell them what she would do for the girl. Needed to keep her knee washed and dressed ever day. Ought to keep her still for a few days and not let her up to walk for some time yet. When some of the soreness and pain went out, then she could be up on it with a crutch. A light hickory branch with a crook in it to fit under her arm and take the weight would be fine. Knee could wind up stiff, just have to wait and see what would come of it.

"That be all I know ye can do. Now best ye be on yer way. Ain't no more I can tell ye. I got work needs done so ye can git now." With that she backed away from the door, closed it, and the old ramshackle of a house regained its forlorn and forsaken appearance.

"A mite cantankerous ain't she," Jubal implied.

"Well, she ain't always been like that. I reckon she be a mite scared with the war and all them rouges on the loose. I knowed her a long time now. At one time she would ride a day's ride when called on and never think nothin' of it. I ain't finding no fault with her seein' as how things have changed so much. She done told us best she could what needs be done. You pick up on all that, son?"

"I did."

"Well, we best do what she say and get a move on," came the miller man's reply as he reined his horse and turned back to the west toward home. Jubal followed a length or two right behind him. They stopped only long enough for the horses to get a quick drink from a side branch, making sure that they did not take in too much and then were back on their way without sayin' a word. It would be mid-afternoon by the time they neared the limestone balds. Hopefully they could crest the ridge in a hurry and be back on good road before another misfortune had time to strike.

The entire ride back to the mill, thankfully, was without any trouble. The horses were lathered up pretty good, and they would need tended before they were turned out. That job would fall to the boy. C.C. would take care to tell the women folk how Julie needed to be cared for and what to do and what not to do.

The young girl had been fairly easy most of the day. Pain came with any attempt at movement. There was no fresh blood so far, and the new cotton dressing made from the store bought remnant was dry so far. Ma still had that worried sick look, and she seemed to be even more stooped than ever. Would be good to get Julie home where she could see to her and look after everything else too. More work. More worry. More stooped without a doubt.

Near a week had passed and Jubal and his Ma had made the run from home to the mill early each day. Ma got up early each morning to make sure that there was a filling breakfast for all. Sarry had really stepped up and pulled her part of the load. She did all the after breakfast chores. With some pointers from Ma, she was able to put something on the table for lunch too. She never complained about the work and always rushed out in the evening to hear any news from her sister. Granny Iverson even managed to pitch in and help too. Gracie was a bit of a child yet, and Granny coddled her and tried to soothe her as she openly missed her Ma during the day.

Julie had remained in bed at the miller's house since that fateful day and could not yet stand any movement of her leg. The entire left knee area was as purple as a ripe plum and a bit poned up. The bandages were changed ever day, and the knee was gently washed and cleaned. Lida had taken it upon herself to do that part early each morning. She was developing a very strong affection for Julie and had begun to talk to her about what she wanted in life and how she felt about herself and her family. Julie had responded openly and honestly as only a tender heart could. Julie confided that she would like to have nicer dresses and ribbons for her hair and pretty bonnets but that she knew those were not the things in life that mattered. She showed maturity beyond her tender age that she valued love and family more that frilly things. She told Lida how Granny would read to her and her sisters late in the evening, especially in wintertime. They would gather by the open firelight and sit around the aging lady and listen to her as she read from the Good Book, and then explain in her own special way the words that she had just read.

Lida could tell that her heart was right. That gave her a peace that brought a sweetness upon them both that no one could know without feeling the presence and the grace of the Lord. Lida almost wept as she held Julie near her. Thoughts of someday holding her own child ran through her mind. She knew that she had love to share. She also knew that she wanted to tell others what she felt in her heart. Words did not always come easy to those so dear, and often words never spoke as well as deeds. She knew that caring for Julie was a deed. Of course it was a deed, but it was one born of love and for that reason it was a blessing as well.

She was not sure that she was willing to admit to herself, but it was true that she had some of those same feelings for Jubal. She had seen him every day since the shooting but had not had a chance to be with him to talk on things. C.C. had kept him busy with chores and looking after the horses and such so that he was away from the house. It had not been that her daddy had done that intentionally, because he had never even hinted that he minded the two of them being together. She had no fault with the miller man. Besides that, best not to rush headlong into anything, patience being a virtue and all that. Much better being a lady. A time for all things, that be what it says.

Jubal had not failed to see the tenderness in Lida as she looked after his sister, and it had made an impression on him as well. He had asked Ma about it.

"Reckon how much we gonna be obliged to them fer lookin' in on Julie?"

"Don't make no matter there son, whatever. We don't try payin' them kind 'a things. They is just bein' good neighbors and helpin' ever where they can. Reckon they not spectin' on pay back."

"They doin' it on account of we was with them when it come about?"

"No, son. They doin' it on account they care what comes of it. They want her well as much as we do. They doin' it cause they have genuine concern."

He wondered how anybody could be that concerned over one who was not their own kin, but he did not ask his Ma any more about it. That, however, did not prevent his mind from racing. He just did not see taking on something like that without having had more of a hand in it to start with.

Most times, Ma never had too much to talk on as they made their way back to the old log house and the rest of the family. By now, Kate knew the way and plodded along at a leisure pace. Thankfully there had been no signs of the riders. Jubal carried his pistol everywhere he went, even on the old home place. He did not think he was in danger, but he just wanted to even things out if need be.

More than ever before, Jubal began to realize how hard life had become for his Ma, even before Julie took a round to the knee. But now with all the running and tending to her and seeing to the rest of her brood, she had no time to rest or regain her strength. It did not take much to see that she could not keep pace for much longer. Something would have to give. He had done all he knew to keep things going around the old home place, but taking his Ma back and forth to the Johnson's every day and doing the chores that C.C. had for him took most of his day. Besides that winter would be coming, and the days were getting shorter all the time now. The snow would fly soon, but there was plenty needing done before winter set in.

Ma had chided Wes into chopping the firewood for the cook stove once Jubal had dragged it down off the ridge. Kate seemed to know that winter was on its way too because she pulled whatever was hooked to her trace chains and made no fuss about it. Sarry had in such a short time come to be a right good cook and housekeeper. Jubal had told her that he was proud of her and all that she was shouldering to try and help Ma.

In almost the same breath he, to himself, cursed his Pa for not being around to pull his load and do his duty to his family. Jubal swore to himself that he would never run out on his mate nor his kids. Thinking like that turned his thought to Lida, just the way family thinking and dreaming always did. But reality brought him swiftly back to the needs at hand. He would speak with C.C. and see if he could hire out to him full time to help at the mill, and in turn, have Mrs. Johnson step in a day or two a week so as how Ma could rest up a bit. He was more and more concerned about how tired and weary she looked. He had noticed that she snored pretty much just about as soon as her head hit the pillow at night. That was some of an improvement, however, because she didn't even go to sleep the first two or three nights after leaving Julie with the Johnsons. He had heard her and Granny Iverson talking way into the night, and he could hear a word ever now and then. Granny had said later that Julie was all right and that she would be taken care of one way or the other, and for that, there was no need to worry. Granny also told him that he needed to be fretting over himself instead of Julie. Said this whole affair ought be a sign to him. That raised his dander just a bit, but he passed it off for just Granny talk. The thing that really bothered him was the festering disdain for his Pa.

Ma and Jubal continued the daily trek to the mill to care for and check on Julie, but it was becoming more apparent that Lida was the one who was to have credit for the patient's welfare. She was at the bedside practically around the clock and was becoming even more devoted to her tasks. She had found a true friend. Julie was showing some signs of improvement, but the leg was still very sore and painful.

None of the bad signs that old Mrs. Bray had talked about had shown up so far. It was looking as if maybe it was near time to see about getting her on home. Sure would be easier on all concerned.

In light of that, Jubal thought it best not to speak to C.C. about working out obligations to him and his family. He did not consider that they were acting simply out of friendship and a desire to help when and where they could. There was never any mention of who owed what or nothing to the like. It was just neighbor-to-neighbor, but the lad had never known anyone other than kin to show him concern, much less free of owing back some kind of favor.

Today was Thursday, and it was agreed by all that Julie could try going home on Saturday so long as she continued to do well and nothing new cropped up. Ma seemed to be much relieved just to know that she could stay home and not have to be running back and forth. Getting Julie back home would be good, but it had one down side that the boy saw right away. He would not be able to see Lida every day. He could come by once a week or so just to tell everyone how Julie was fairing or maybe on some other thought up reason, but it was not going to be like now. He was not willing to admit to himself how close he had let himself get to her. But there was tomorrow and then Saturday before things would change so much. Ma said it was answer to prayer. He was not so sure about that right now.

Saturday morning came and the trek to the mill came off without incident, much as it had on all the preceding mornings. There was one unusual difference upon arrival at the mill. All about were Union soldiers and their mounts. They looked to Jubal as if they had just stood inspection or were ready for parade. He counted fourteen soldiers. He could see the captain and C.C. just inside the mill door, and they waved arms and pointed fingers as they conversed. Jubal could not make out their words.

He could, however, make out the uniforms and the troopers who wore them. All were spit-and-polish with brass buttons catching the glimmer of the morning sun. Boots were blacked and hats all squared away. Each saddle was polished, had brass trim alike and each had a filled scabbard. Some troopers had a side arm too. Jubal was impressed and without awareness, admired and envied them for their appearance. He could see himself all decked out in a blue uniform.

It was about then that C.C. noticed that he had arrived.

"Come up here, son."

Jubal turned and did as the miller had instructed.

"This here is Cap'n Olson. He be in charge of this here bunch. They been on patrol and such best part of a week now, and they be lookin' in on folks in these here parts askin' iffin they be any trouble. I just been tellin' how Julie was hurt. He say he needs talk to you and Ma about the shootin' and all."

The Union officer went on to ask Jubal if he could describe the men that he saw during the attack. He wanted to know what they wore, how tall they were, what did they say, and what mounts did they have. Wanted to know things that Jubal had not given much thought before. He answered the captain best he could and as accurately and truthfully as he could. He did not relate that he was thinking all along that his Pa was in on it. The captain never asked that, and he never volunteered it.

C.C. and the Union officer had talked in detail before Jubal and his Ma arrived, but their conversation would not be made known to the boy just yet. The captain offered his personal thanks for the information and the hospitality offered by the miller and his family. Horses had been watered and canteens filled from the spring. Commands were barked out, and just as quickly the troops were mounted, formed up and underway again. They turned west, in the general direction of Cleve's store.

C.C. repeated some of what he had learned from the troopers and their leader. There had been more trouble back to the east, on past the limestone balds, past the store and even past old wider Bray's. Somebody had beat and robbed a family near town knob and had then burned them out to boot. No way telling what they looted. Others had come up missing stuff too, and one man had his team took right out from under him. They just walked right in the barn and led them off. Cap'n Olson had said that one family had caught sight of two prowlers one morning near daybreak and that one of them had a bound up hand. They had put their dogs on them, and they had near eat them up. But they had managed to get gone by jumping in a creek. Jubal reckoned to himself that if he ever caught up to them that a bound up hand would only be a start to their troubles.

Julie had rested well through the night and had hardly been awake. Her knee was still sore, and it hurt to move it. But she had been able to sit up in bed as long as she kept the leg straight. Getting her from the bed to the buckboard might be a task, but C.C. had already thought of that and had a solution already at hand. He had found a wide yellow poplar board in the mill loft and had cut off a five-foot length. Julie could sit up straight on that. He and Jubal could carry her and the board and gently put her in the back. Then when she got home, the reverse procedure could get her back in her own bed. It seemed like a good way to get her home. Ma could see a little ease for a change. Julie seemed eager to get home as well. She had been well cared for as a guest, but there was no place like her own home and her own kin. She missed her times with Granny and missed her reading. He thought about the few times that he had sat still long enough to let Granny read to him. Always before it was just because she asked if she could read with him and he had agreed just to please her. The words hardly soaked in, so he thought, but she had instilled in his mind more than he admitted.

Restlessness still stirred in his mind, and the sights of the spiffed up troopers had rekindled his fire of wanderlust and desire for the faraway places. The will to make it in this world and the lust for the things in it pulled at him with an urgency that tore him between love and hate. A sense of kinship and loyalty to his sisters pulled him on one side, and a wish to rid himself of daily sharecropping drudgery goaded him to flee it all.

He had told himself that someday he would strike out on his own and make his own way, but there was another matter that needed to be settled first. He had thought long and hard on that and had resolved himself to see it through. He just did not know exactly how or when, but he knew it would happen. Probably would have to be on the move then for sure.

Lida would be left behind, and he was not real keen on that thought. He could come back to her later. He had not breathed even a thought to her about leaving the hollow. He just took it on his own that she would be there whenever he decided to come looking in on her. Never mind her thoughts or her feelings, he just knew it would be the way he had set his mind for it to be.

Then Wes came to mind. He had hinted to the boy more than once about his gold stash. Never had he spoke about how much he had or where he kept it. He still had the gourd filled over with beeswax, and he had refused to let anyone see it or handle it. He managed to keep it hidden in the springhouse loft. It had to be there, because Wes had been nowhere else. Jubal had not given much thought lately to money. He had been consumed by his hatred of his Pa on the one hand and his attachment to Lida and her daddy on the other. Each stirred conflicting emotions in him, and he often found his thoughts torn between good and evil.

Wes and his gold could be dealt with later. Lida would be there when he came to call. Julie would heal with time. But time would not be kind to his Ma, and time would not ease her burdens. Only revenge could ease some of the pain, and he was resolved to get that revenge even if he had to go it alone. Sure, Granny Iverson had talked about kindness and forgiveness and all like that, but some things just plain went beyond forgiving and forgetting. He had no intention of either. He had to force his mind to dwell on other things.

Saturday came and Ma and the boy made their way down the hollow road to the mill. They had left the old log home well before daylight and were at the mill earlier than usual. The Johnsons were up and about and had cleared the breakfast table and set to the day's chores. Ma went straightway to Julie. She had kept it to herself, but she had been uneasy about her child all through the night. She knew that the shot to the knee was a bad injury and that there could be dire consequences. She had slept little, and her face could not mask her concern or her weariness. In spite of all that, Julie was awake and cheerful, without apparent discomfort. She had a small dark red spot on her dressing, but told her Ma that had happened in the night when she was sleeping and moved her knee a bit. It had awakened her, but she was just as soon back to sleep.

"We come to fetch ye home today child," Ma softly spoke as she leaned over and kissed Julie gently on the forehead. "How do that sound?"

"I been just a waitin'. I knowed ye take me home sometime whenever things was ready."

"There be much more said there than ye realize, my child," Ma responded as the tears welled up in her tired eyes. She had to briefly turn away from her daughter to keep her from seeing how deeply she was troubled.

"I gonna be fine, Ma. It just take me some time, but I reckon I fare just fine."

Lida came in and gave Ma a big hug. That eased her anguish a bit and brought a hint of a smile to her face. The back of her hand quickly whisked away the tears. Her heart was patched up a bit, for the time being at least.

Outside, there was the clamor of horses and the jingle of harnesses. C.C. and the boy greeted Captain Olson and his patrol once again. They were headed back east this time and, as before, assumed a leisure pace that would save the horses for a long day's ride.

"Good morning Johnson," the captain said as he dismounted, removed his thick gloves, and extended his hand to C.C.

"And a good mornin' to ye," came the miller's reply. "What brings ye back here this mornin'?"

"We are headed back to the river flats and the ferry. We found out what we came this way for, and I reckon we will move on soon."

"What be yer findings?" C.C. asked.

"We think we know who has been doing all the chicanery in these parts, and we will get warrants and come back for them soon. Colonel Good is about ready to enforce martial law and then we can really do something about them."

"Them who?" Jubal quired.

"We don't really know names save for one that the storekeeper told us right before he passed on. Some big man on a big Roan horse that goes by name of Halverson. Word is that he come up out of Alabama. They, or he, we don't know for sure just how it was done yet, beat up the storekeeper and robbed him of most ever thing they could pack off on horseback. Beat him so bad that he never made it. Took him near ten hours to pass."

"Which storekeeper?" C.C. inquired.

"Think he said his given name was Cleve," the captain answered.

"When did this all come about?" C.C. wanted to know.

"Must have been going on while we were here or on our way to that direction just a few days ago. We found him near beat to a pulp but able enough to talk. He said a bunch of raiders had come through and cleaned out whatever they wanted from what little he had in stock. Threatened to shoot him right there if he resisted."

"Was he shot?" Jubal asked.

"No. Just beat badly. He told us that the raiders had not harmed him but that one of them had doubled back and done him so near death. Storekeeper said that this Halverson feller had accused him of holding out on him. Said Halverson thought he had stole a bunch of gold eagles from some other old man and had hid them in his store some place."

"That would be old Wes, I reckon," Jubal mumbled under his breath. Neither the captain or C.C. made any comment.

The captain went on. "He told us with almost his last breath that he never had any gold and knew nothing about any old codger here abouts who did. Said that he had seen this same man before and that he was rumored to have killed a couple of darkies near here one day, right in broad daylight."

Jubal's mind flashed back to what he had seen happen in the barn not that long back. This had to be one of the riders that he had seen poking around the shack that Wes called home, and just as sure, he was the one who gave the old man such a thrashing. He must have heard somewhere that Wes had a stash. If word was out, then there had to be something to it.

"Did Cleve name any other names?" Jubal asked.

"No. He was at himself only a few minutes after we found him. We did the best we could for him, but he went out and then took hours to die. Never said another word."

"Was he by himself?" C.C. asked.

"We never saw anyone else. We rode on west till we found a churchyard and another old black man said that we could bring him there, and he would put him away for us. Said he had traded with him some but that had been a while back."

"Don't reckon he had no family here abouts," Jubal added.

"No matter to us after he died. Nothing else we could do save see he got put away proper. Ever man deserves a Christian burial, I reckon."

"What about all his store goods and stuff?" Jubal wanted to know.

"Whatever he had left is all gone now. It burned to the ground about noon yesterday, and we could not find a soul who knew anything about it. It was still smoldering when we had to ride out."

Jubal was taken aback by the news. Cleve had not been too much in his favor, but this was more than he would have wished on him. As for Halverson, anything that might happen to him would be deserved. Dang a man that would commit such acts as taking another's life. Then his thoughts flashed to Pa again. If he was running with the likes of Halverson, then he was just as sorry. The hatred boiled inside him again, and he could envision his own revenge. It really was not a pleasing thought.

As it was a few days before, Captain Olson and his troops were spit and polish. They were polite and courteous. They were well-disciplined and followed orders and instructions to the letter. Soon the horses were all watered, and the entire party rode out in an easterly direction. A full day's ride would put them into the doubles and who knew what they would find there. Jubal had an itch to go with them and had almost asked the captain what he would need to do to join up. He had held his thoughts, however, because he knew that Ma needed him now more than ever.

The miller's voice brought him back to the present.

"Reckon runnin' with evil begets evil or so I be thinkin'. A man reaps pine blank what he sows. Good Book say that too."

Jubal did not answer.

Mrs. Johnson came out on the porch and stood with her hands on her hips looking somewhat put out with her husband and the boy. She spoke loudly without saying a word.

"Looks like they be ready fer us do some totin'. You up to carryin' yer sister out without hurtin' her? She be some touchy, I reckon, iffin we be rough on her."

"I can do it right, I reckon," Jubal responded curtly.

"I know that, son. I ain't tryin' to gouge ye none."

"Oh, I ain't gouged out none, special not at you. I just hate them bastards what done all this."

"I reckon I can see how ye feel, son. But hate will eat you alive iffin ye let it grab holt on ye and fester inside ye. Best ye let it go and move on."

"I reckon Julie have more cause fer grudgin' than I do, but she ain't able take even her own part now, so I reckon that be fallin' to me now."

C.C. knew that it would do no good right now to preach any further to the boy, but he also knew what such determined despise could do to a young upstart, who was a long ways away from responsible. All he could see was the harm that had been done and the evil nature of the doers. He would not tolerate any hint of forgiveness, not right now. The miller man knew that there would be more opportunity to talk with the boy later. Besides that, if his daughter was going to become involved with him, he needed some straightening out and some common sense drummed into his head. Thirty years at the mill had taught him a lot, and this here young sprout needed to know some of the things he had learned the hard way. It could just save him untold grief, but he had to let it sink in. Right now there was no way that would happen.

Mrs. Johnson stomped a foot. It was time to move. C.C. and the boy turned and climbed the stairs to the porch.

Lida came through the door and gave Jubal a look that he did not quite understand. She seemed washed out and pale, but smiled as she most always did. Maybe she was just tuckered from all the nights up with Julie. Best that Julie be took home. Then Ma could do for her. He could see Lida later on.

Julie withstood the trek home fairly well. Only a couple of old sand rocks in the road jolted the buckboard enough to shake her. She never once winced or cried out.

Jubal, Ma, Wes and Sarry got Julie to bed without trouble or further hurt. The afternoon sun had already begun its dip in the western sky, and the chill of fall was in the air. It could frost tonight, but there was a cloud or two so maybe it would hold off. It would soon be cold enough to need a fire in the old stone hearth all night. Julie looked chilled now. She was going to need a good warm fire more than old Wes would.

Sarry had fried up some side meat and made corn pone. All had their fill and soon the darkness closed around them and brought much needed rest and sleep. The buckboard would be returned tomorrow, and then Jubal could set to filling the woodshed and be ready when the blue snow began to fly.

Jubal got the buckboard back to the mill near mid-morning. The trek down the old hollow road was uneventful, and he had let Kate just amble along at her own pace. He had seen nothing unusual along the way. He had ample time to sift through many of his thoughts. It had not frosted during the night, but there was a chill in the air nonetheless.

There was also a chill in the lad as well. He had thought back to the day that his Pa had given him powder and shot to go hunting. Pa had sent him off in one direction while he had gone off in the opposite way to chase the infernal laudanum bottle. Jubal had learned this only a day or so back when Wes had let it slip.

If only his Pa could have shown some real interest in him and took to him like most folks would take to their kid. If only his Pa could have shown that he cared even a little bit. The boy did not really know that he longed for the love that a father would show for his son, but he knew that he had come up short somehow. He felt cheated and shortchanged and blamed it all on his Pa. He could feel hatred for him on the one hand and yet crave for his love and affection on the other. There was an empty place inside of him that longed to be filled. There was resentment within him because of the fate that life had handed him. He harbored hatred on the one hand and reached out for love and tenderness on the other. He seemed to never be able to reason anything out any more, and the indecisiveness tried to destroy any peace that he could muster.

Granny Iverson had talked of peace that came from within, but she was old and had lived her life and had made all her choices already. She reckoned how a body had to be content with what they had and make the best of it, but she had never had much and never expected much. At least she had a Pa who raised her and provided for her till she could stand on her own. She never had money, but she never seemed to care that she was not able to have such. She always showed pride in herself, and he could never recall her in dirty or tattered clothes.

Yet he had no real desire to be like her. He wanted those finer things, and he did expect to have them.

It took only a bit to put away the old buckboard and lead Kate to water. Lida came out on the porch carrying an old flour sack and waited for Jubal to return to the mill porch. She waited until he had his back to her and then walked to the edge to be in his ear shot.

"Wanna go hunt some chestnuts with me?"

He turned at the sound of her voice. His first impression was one of spite. How can she be so bright and beaming with all that has come about here lately. He did not really realize it, but he had some resentment to her giggly attitude. "Ain't none 'round here that I know of," he retorted.

"Well, maybe that ye don't know so much as ye think," responding in a smile and with a sassy twist of her skirt.

"I know these parts dang good, and I reckon they ain't a chestnut tree this side of our ridge."

"That so?"

"Yep."

"Well just so happen it ain't so," she countered as some of the smile left her expression.

"Just where might there be one then?"

"Ye wanna go or not?"

"I reckon I can go iffin ye want."

"That be up to you."

"Lead out. I be on yer heels. Still don't think there be a chestnut tree close here any place, but I let ye prove me wrong, I reckon."

Lida turned and headed up the hill behind the mill. She said nothing. Jubal sensed that she was miffed with him, but he could be just as cantankerous and was not about to coddle to her, no matter what. Both were pretty much winded when they reached the top of the hill where C.C. had made the small clearing. They sat on the log bench to catch a breather. Lida unwrapped her shawl and turned to face him. Her dress was lower cut than he had ever seen before. A hint of cleavage erased all ill feelings that he had churning inside him as he climbed the hill behind her.

When she realized that he had seen her, she partially replaced her shawl and gave him just a hint of a smile. He felt his face turn red and the top of his ears began to burn. "Is there really a tree nearby?" he muttered.

"Yes. There is, and it ain't far."

"Can we get a bucket full?"

"I think so."

They both stood and she led off to the north, into deep woods along the spine of the mill ridge and in no time they stood beneath a slim but towering chestnut with burrs nearly covering the ground. He had been down the spine of this same ridge a time or two, but it was when the leaves were thick green, and he had not seen the tree. He had not even noticed the old burrs as they lay under the years' accumulation of decaying leaves and twigs. In no time the sack was full. He would need to tote it back. It would be too heavy for her, or so she said. They found a suitable sandstone rock and sat down together.

The rock seat was a bit confining and sitting there placed their bodies side to side. He wanted to put an arm around her but was hesitant for fear that she might take offense.

"I saw that look ye give me back there," she said softly as she smiled again at him. Again he blushed. She had him right where she wanted and she knew it. He knew right where he wanted to be.

The walk back down to the mill was in silence. He was inwardly embarrassed by his inexperience, and she was inwardly unrelieved of the wanton desire of a young woman.

Anger beset him once more as he and old Kate made their way home. He longed to share himself and had at the same time a fear of the unknown. Granny had called the unknown the darkness of life. Julie, she said, had come out of the dark and now could see bright as day. Lida had asked him if he ever meant to come out of the dark, and he had brushed her off about it. She was not pleased by his answer and had told him about it.

Dark clouds began to roll in from the west. Ill winds would bring bad weather and bad times. It was early, way too early for a big snow, but ominous clouds darkened the ridges and hills. Darkness, light, what was it all about? How could there ever be any peace in time of a war? How could there ever be any rest when there was so much work that needed to be done? Dang it all anyhow!

Chapter 8

Warring

*T*he Shenandoah Valley saw many a skirmish that fall. Jubal and his troop received orders to ride picket in an area around and along Cedar Creek. There the Rebs had frequently been involved in hit-and-run raiding tactics as their main body had tried to advance from the Richmond area into the Washington City area.

In mid-October, the Rebs staged an attack on Sheridan's forces while he was on his way back from Washington City. General Early's Confederate forces gained an initial victory, but the Union forces rapidly regrouped and routed the Rebels. This engagement, known as the battle of Cedar Creek, turned out to be the end of the Shenandoah campaign except for irregular and infrequent forays by splintered rag-tag elements of the now near defeated Army of Virginia. The end of the war could not be very far off, and most of the soldiers knew and welcomed that fact. However, the fighting was far from over.

Early morning saw Jubal, William, and six other mounted picket riders ready to set out on their designated assignment. They were to look ahead of the main company forces for detection of lingering bushwhackers and Rebels. The frequency of these Rebel raids had been on the decline, and some of the pickets had not been diligent in their observations and had paid with their lives. Confederate gunfire was just as deadly as it had ever been, just not as often nor as concentrated.

The patrol rode two abreast and spaced about twenty yards apart. This morning Jubal was in the lead. He had already been recognized for his tracking ability and his knack for reading the signs of the land. His leaders and commanders had acknowledged his ability because he had demonstrated competency. William had commented to his superiors about Jubal's talent, and his words had not fallen on deaf ears.

Each trooper had been issued a new Colt .36 caliber pistol and a new Springfield rifle. Each had been equipped with new blue uniforms and the latest field gear that was coming out of Washington City quartermaster's stores. Their duty was good as far as wartime combat duty could be considered. Every possible measure had been taken for their safety and welfare. Yet many complained of weariness and expressed desire and intent to return home as soon as possible. Some even spoke quietly of desertion. William and Jubal were not in their number, not yet.

Granny Iverson was born and raised near the mouth of Cane Creek. She attended school at Redmond Ridge along with the Moran kids. That was where the connection originated between Jubal and Les Moran. Les had romped with Jubal as a young lad when their families had been in contact with each other. Les had settled with his Ma and Pa in Poor Valley and had done rather well raising tobacco and hogs. Poor Valley Creek ran the length of the small valley and emptied into Cane Creek just a stone's throw below C.C.'s mill and property. The Johnsons were not intimate with the Moran family but did know and recognize who they were and where they lived. They, as did most everyone in the area within a half day's ride, brought grain to be ground or sold to the mill. The Moran dwelling and Jubal's old log home were no more than three miles distance as the crow flies but were on opposite sides of Pine Mountain and Chestnut Ridges that boxed in the north side of Wes's old place. In another sense they may as well have been a world apart.

Les had joined the Confederacy early in the war and had even lied about his age in order to join up. His Pa was a slaveholder and relied on the sweat of their brow to bring in a good tobacco crop. He needed them to make sure that the wagon loads of the brown and golden leaf cash crop made it to the ferry landings and onto flatboats.

So Les really had no choice. His Pa encouraged him to fight for his rights and for his way of life. He had no thoughts of anything other than farming the tobacco fields, because it had afforded a fairly comfortable existence in the foothills and mountain slopes. The land was well adapted to growing big broad leaves and good grades that brought top prices in the delta counties. It was hard work and a year-round job, but he nor his Pa had to do any of that. They just had to make sure that it was done right.

Many campaigns had hardened Les to the killing, and he had become a seasoned veteran in a short span of duty with the Rebs. He had been at Gettysburg and had come through it all without so much as a scratch. He had lost new-found friends there, and that loss had served only to deepen his hatred of the cursed Union Bluecoats and everything they stood for. War to him no longer centered around the issues so hotly contested by the politicians; it was about kill or be killed, and he had no intention to be a Union victim. He had become so hardened that he actually took pleasure in drawing a good bead on a blue uniform.

He had grown up much like Jubal and in the same hills and hollows. They had even crossed paths a couple of times out in the brambles that was common hunting and trapping grounds. Consequently they both learned from the woods and hills. Les was a crack shot with his old squirrel rifle and could cut one out of the top of any scale-barked hickory. He certainly had no trouble ranging in on a man's chest, even while sitting a galloping horse.

These talents had morphed him into a deadly weapon as he now served in hit-and-run forays along the Cedar Creek area of Northern Virginia. His rag-tag unit had suffered significant losses and often had to depend on the land for mere sustenance. Yet they were still a menace to be reckoned with and had caused concern and fear among those who had to stand in defense against them.

The land was much like that of his native Tennessee. The hills gently rolled off the ridges of the valley and created long gentle bends back and forth in the valley floor. Some places the creek bottoms were three hundred yards wide, and in others the flat lands were choked down to a mere roadway that barely could keep itself above the creek bed. The road banks would usually be strewn with brush and brambles. These bramble thickets would most likely hide any interloper that would drop down on any unwary passer-by.

But it was now well into fall, and lots of the leafy cover was gone. Most mornings saw a good covering of mist and fog, but that was soon burned away by the coming of the morning sun. A keen eye could scan the ridge lines and hillsides for any warning of coming into harm's way.

Les knew how to use what the land provided as a cover. He knew what to look for when tracking the same as Jubal. In hit-and-run tactic, speed is usually the decisive factor between escape to fight again another day or being caught.

Things had not gone well up and down the creek over the past few weeks. The gray uniformed troopers had suffered many losses. They had reverted to thievery just to keep themselves fed and supplied with the basic necessities.

Many times the Rebel raiders would be ratted out to the Union forces. A brush fire could be lit, and its smoke seen for miles. It had become a standard signal all up and down the valley that trouble was on the move. Jubal had seen these smokes many times but had not yet been detailed to investigate or chase.

The patrol that Jubal was assigned to was out early. The gray dawn foretold of the impending rain and coming cloudiness. Jubal scanned the grey dawn for smoke but discovered none. They would patrol down the valley in effort to discover any trace of the Rebel parties. By the time they had covered their assigned sectors and made their way back to the command post, reported in and been relieved, the entire day and most of the fore night would be spent. They would eat and rest as best they could and most likely would be ordered to do the same again.

Jubal and his squad drew night watch next. They would not need to make such long treks up and down the valley, but would make many a step around the perimeter of the tent camp. They would sentry as much with their ears as they would by sight.

The night sounds were familiar to the lad. Silence and darkness were friends to a posted sentry, and he would be wise to be in tune with all the sounds around him while making none of his own.

The silence and the stillness afforded time for thought and reflections. There was much that could run through the mind of a restless, searching young man who found himself far from home and family and in a less than peaceful surrounding. He still had longings that seemed to be at war with each other. He still had desires that pulled him in opposing directions. He still had a yearning to feel like he belonged. He had standards set for himself, and he had long since rejected the complacency of others who had less ambition.

Yet, there were others who seemed to enjoy a peace and stability that he had sought. It alluded him, and he knew not why. Lida seemed to have it, and Granny Iverson even talked about it. Old Wes had been on to him about living in the dark. William looked to be at fault with no one. William even talked about peace so good that it was hard to understand.

He had heard talk about such more times than he could recall coupled with how a man ought to be godly and good. But he also reckoned how he had not really done any harm and how he was just as good as the next. That kept gnawing at him. It taunted him more and more as time passed. It ate at him mostly when he was alone. It troubled him deepest when he thought of home.

He always wondered how things were at home. He wondered if Ma was in need of anything. How was Granny Iverson holding up? Wonder if old Wes was still around? He even thought about old Jake and the mule. He never thought that he would miss two critters the way he did. What about his sisters? How were they?

And Lida. What about her? All of the things that they had talked about, did these mean anything any longer? Did they still have the understanding that had been more or less taken on faith and trust? Why had she told him that she could wait for him a lot easier if only he would step out on trust and move away from the dark? How could she be so sure about what was out there any more than he could? There were just so many wants and worries that he saw no way around or over. Maybe sunup would help, but for now he felt like he was about as much alone as he had ever been in his life.

The night passed. Just before first light one of the sentries spooked a deer, and he let go around in fear that it was for sure a Reb about to do him in. True he was a raw trooper and scared at that, but in not being sure of what was going on and acting as he had, he was in for a bit of ribbing and ragging. Little did he know that Les was close enough to have easily silenced him right then and there.

His actions had shown Les more than he could ever realize. This all would not go unnoticed on upcoming dark nights. The Rebs needed almost everything the Union had as far as supply and munitions were concerned. What better place to get it than from a bunch of candy-assed kids who thought they knew how to fight?

The harvest moon began to lose its brilliance in just a few days, and the nights became deeper and more akin to the spirits of the darkness. Just a few more nights and Les and his boys could move about almost at will among the greenhorns.

Les had made his way back into the deep woods and told the others what he had seen and what he thought they could do on a dark night. That darkness would be upon the valley in just a scant three nights; and if it should be cloudy, then it would be all the easier to slip in and out and not cause alarm. He let it be known that he would go back another night to try and get a hand on where things were kept and how well it was guarded.

The dark of the moon saw Jubal once again on nighttime sentry duty. This time he had been posted near the quartermaster's tent and stores. Some of the local families had come into camp desperate for some of the most basic of stores. The commander had issued instructions that these folks be treated with fairness and kindness and given what could be spared. He had also decided that it would be best to place a night watch on these stores because hunger, no matter which color their loyalty, could cause acts of desperation. The commander and his staff had no desire to fend off anyone who might come back for an unauthorized handout during the night.

Small fires burned throughout the camp well into the night. They actually felt good as they took the edge off the night chill. Jubal knew that a fire would feel good, but he also knew that he must keep his back to the fire in order to keep a sharp eye. A mere glance into the dim glow of an ash bank could take several minutes to get over once you turned back away from its light. It would work the same way for any intruder who might try coming in. Jubal knew this also, and he knew that anyone out there would move at their own pace and would make some sound because of a slight misstep or rustle of an unseen twig or briar. This would give him a slight edge, and he would be much obliged for any small favor that he could get.

Les had picked his route well. He had hugged the damp earth behind a hollow beech log since sundown. He had inched forward only a yard or two at a time since then. He would move and fall silent, listening for any sign of anything that might seem closer than before. He had been belly down on the ground so long now that the chill of the earth nipped at his awareness. He was patient and persistent in his approach to the stable area. If he could get there without being heard, then the sounds of the horses would cover his movements. He would need to be careful not to spook them, but he had been around horses enough to know how to prevent that. They would also be help on the way back out with whatever he could pilfer from the unsuspecting Bluecoats. Besides getting much needed foods and grip, it was going to be a pleasure to outwit a bunch of Yankee city boys who were still a mite wet behind their ears. He would show them just how well a mountain bred boy could do whatever he set his mind to. But for now, it was time to draw back and wait till he could and come back for a real strike.

Morning found Jubal lying in his tent trying to sleep from the night's duty. The ground was wet and cold, but his bedroll and the canvas blocked the chilling dampness from his lean body. Sleep would not come. There was just too much on his mind and too many things vying for his conscious thoughts.

William pulled back the tent flap. "You awake Jubal?"

"Yep."

"Had anything to eat yet this morning?"

"Ate some hardtack."

"Want anything else?"

"I ain't really much hungry. I ain't hankerin' trompin' around in this danged rain and sleet," Jubal answered gruffly.

"I understand that. Would you rather that I just let you rest? Can I bring something back for you?"

"That be me puttin' you out a bit, but I be thankin' ye just the same," Jubal said as he rose up on one elbow.

"I would do that for any friend," William replied.

"And I thank ye fer bein' my friend. It's just that I be tuckered out right now, and I got a heap on my mind too."

"I understand that too. I will be here as your friend any time you want to talk it out and get a load off your chest," William said as he began his exit. "I'll let you rest a bit and then I will come back."

With that, William was gone. Jubal felt some weak hunger pangs and sort of wished he had not been so quick to pass up the chance that William offered. Instead, he turned up his canteen, drained it of its contents, rolled over on his stomach and forced his mind to think of other things. Soon light sleep crept into his tent accompanied by the pitter-patter of increasing rainfall. It seemed to drown out all other sounds and many of the sensations that promoted restlessness. It could not, however, wash the thoughts clear of all that clouded the mind. There was just no real relaxation. There seemed to be no letup. It seemed that there would never be any peace for him. Peace was conceivably in sight for the nation, but he wondered if ever he would have the peace about him that he had seen in others.

Les and his squad made their way through the mist as it cloaked the thick timber and underbrush on the high ridge directly above the Union camp. The dampness softened the forest floor and silenced any heavy boots or misplaced steps that would make undue sounds and betray their presence. No sentries would be posted this high up in the timber, so there was not a great concern about being seen. They just needed to keep down any conversation.

One of the Reb troopers noticed some deer scrapes and pointed them out to Les. That proved that there was game in the area and that opened a possibility for fresh meat. A spring pole trap could catch a deer right here in the Blue Belly's own back yard, and they would never be the wiser. Three or four small apples would make a good bait, and Les already knew where they could be had. He would set that trap tomorrow and have venison the next day.

All were in place long before dusk. Les found shelter in a big hollow chestnut and rested a spell. He slept very lightly for a few winks while listening to the sounds of the timber and the misting rain. No unusual or alarming sounds reached his keen ears. It was reassuring to know that they had not been detected thus far. Dark would soon set in and then they could creep down near the camp and wait for most to turn in. Then they would move among the shadows of the dying campfire embers and make their raid and be gone before an owl had time to screech. They would pilfer no more than they could carry and run with. If it went off well this time, they could do it again and again.

Dark found them slinking downhill in a chilling drizzle of rain. It felt like the temperature had dropped out the bottom, and the cold rain stung smartly on an upturned face. In some ways that was good because any posted guards most likely would be concentrating on their own comforts rather than being a sharp eye. Nevertheless they remained cautious. They had inched to within twenty yards of the stable area and could easily hear the stomping and the snorting of the restless horses. Maybe the horses would settle down along with the camp as the young night wore on.

And wear on it did. After what seemed hours, Les signaled to start on in to the quartermaster's tent. Reaching it would be no difficulty, since there was not a sentry in sight. Most likely they would be holed up under a wagon bed or balled up beneath a piece of oil skin sleeping on their post. The entire squad reached the tent in dead silence. Les slipped under the rear wall and raised it just enough for the others to follow. As agreed earlier, they would grab what was at hand and above all as silently as possible and then slip away back to the high ground and wait there for everybody. All that had been worked out beforehand, and each man knew what he had to do and how to go about it.

Les did not watch the others, but he did note that they worked in perfect silence. Things were going well. He felt good about his men and what he was doing. He lay on his back and looked up at a pair of saddlebags lying alongside a small crate. He groped the saddlebags and was surprised to find a boot pistol inside. The discovery quickly found itself a new owner as he stuffed it inside his shirt. Searching fingertips soon played over the edges of the opened crate to find a store of cap and ball ammunition. The new weapon and a crate of munitions was a bigger prize than he had expected.

He sought nothing else but rather made his way back under the tent wall, raised the crate to his shoulder and walked straight and tall back past the stables and into the brush, all untouched, unchallenged and unnoticed.

Jubal was awake before the first light. He sat up and pulled the corners of his bedroll up over his shoulders. He easily sensed that it had become colder during the darkened hours. He leaned forward and pushed the tent flap open with the back of his hand. Not really to his surprise, there was about an inch of snow on the ground, and he understood why there was a new chill in the air.

Today, he would be on patrol down Cedar Valley. He knew that the fresh snow would leave tell-tell signs of any movements. It would be easy to track anyone who had been out and about during the night. He was not very concerned about tracking anyone but would concentrate on keeping a sharp eye and being aware of the possibility of ambush from the higher ground. He realized movement could not be hidden in the fresh snow.

The patrol was ready to move out at first light. Each trooper had a hot breakfast, was warmly uniformed and carried all of the supplies that he would need for the day's activity. Fresh mounts seemed spirited and ready to go. Movement would be slow and concentrated because of the known trouble spots. If there was going to be any activity at all today, it would probably come from one of these areas. Jubal was aware of the trouble places and would be searching for signs of any pending peril.

The eastern sky began to break brighter and brighter. It was obvious that there were some breaks in the clouds. Jubal knew that if the sun came out and the skies cleared, then it would be hard to see any distance because of the brilliance of the sun on the new fallen snow. It would be necessary to be even more vigilant. The road through the valley floor would be in sniper range frequently. The entire patrol was keenly aware of this, and it put everyone on edge.

William and Jubal rode in the front rank, thus far neither had much to say. It was as if they were awakening at the same pace as the day. The others seemed to plod along behind in a mechanical, uninterested mundane march so as to avoid any dereliction of duty implications. Today's patrol assignments had been made by the brass on the assumption that the weather would be a deterrent to any Rebel activity. Therefore, a strong patrol would not be needed. Jubal and William were really the only ones who had enough experience in combat or on patrol. William knew and acknowledged the fact that Jubal was the only one who had real ability in following a track through the deep woods. He was the only one of this particular squad who had knowledge of the South, the mountains, or the Rebel ways. In reality the patrol was in Jubal's hands.

About two hour's ride down the valley road brought the patrol to a critical point. Here, the valley narrowed and formed a choking hold on the road and creek that ran along the side. There was no more than a few yards on each side of the road before the hills began to rise steeply up to the deep timber. If there was going to be trouble, if there was going to be an ambush, if a sniper was out and about, it would be here.

Jubal stopped the patrol, dismounted and signed for everyone else to be silent. He ran his hand's along the horse's reins and held them loosely at their length. He walked on ahead leading his horse slowly behind. After a few paces, he stopped. First listening, then searching all about for any sign that would indicate trouble. He heard nothing. He saw nothing. He motioned for the others, and they proceeded through the choke and patrolled on down the valley road. Mid-morning passed without incident. Noon saw a change in activity; it was time to turn around and head back to camp. Jubal was thankful that there had been no encounters and that no one had been hurt or injured. However, he was well on to the fact that not every day would be this easy and that there would be a heavy price to pay before it was all said and done. Tomorrow would be another day, but for now, the end of this day would bring rest and relief.

Jubal had trouble sleeping that night and early morning found him alert, but far from rested. He and William had drawn patrol again, the same squad and the same assignment. They would head west down the valley floor and look for any signs of Confederate activity or movement.

The night brought a light drizzle and much of the snow skift had turned to slush. Footing for the horses would be unsure and that would be just one more thing to be on the lookout for. Tracks would not be quite as obvious in mud as in snow. That presented no real issue to Jubal, because he could read a trail in most any weather on most any terrain. There was more to it than just following foot or hoof prints. He knew the language of the woods and mountains. The eastern light revealed broken clouds with patches of coral sky showing through. Clearing would make any movements easier to spot. The whole squad knew that it would also increase the probability of contact with the Rebs, because they would not sit idle when they could move about and not leave a snow trail.

Late mid-morning had proven what Jubal suspected. The sky boasted increasing expanses of sultry blue as high winds rousted any remaining cloud cover and sent it west into the mountains. The sun felt warm on his back, and he was glad to have it there too. Any movements against them would come out of the western end of the valley and that would put the sun in the eyes of his foe. He would have a hand up there because any glint of the sun's light would reflect back to him and give a warning that would go unseen or unknown by the opposition.

William had chosen to carry his Enfield this morning. Jubal slung his long rifle across his saddle and carried it with some trepidation. He and William rode in the lead and talked in a low, rambling voice as they rode slowly along the grassy creek bottoms. They had found the footing in the rutted road less than steady and had quickly taken to the soft, but sure footed meadows. The horses nipped at dried seed heads and stems as they made their way west. They were in no particular formation and had been cautioned against bunching up. That only made sense seeing as how a bunch up could be a very enticing target for a gun crew.

"William, I reckon we might hit on trouble today."

"What makes you think that, Jubal?"

"Never slept worth a dang last night. Reckon I just had today on my mind all night and just got me a bad feelin' about today," Jubal replied.

"I feel that way most ever day that we head out like this. I don't see any difference today from other days. What do you see different today?" William asked.

"Can't say as I really know. Things just been eatin' away at me lately. I be just plum tired of this business. Ever day it just the same old rot. We just namby-pamby around and never get nothin' done ceptin' for goin' off half-cocked while all the uppity-ups act like it just be one big shin-dig. Why can't we whip some Reb ass, get this war done, and go on back home and get on with life?"

"Is that what really ails you, Jubal?"

"Hell yes, I got things back home that need tendin' to, and they ain't gonna get done with me traipsin' all over who knows where or fer how long."

"You ever stop and think about all them that will never go back home?"

"I reckon I have," Jubal answered slowly, almost apologetic.

"I will not press the matter, Jubal; but you ought to be very thankful that you have been spared so far."

"I figger that I done paid my part back there at the ferry crossin' and that be about all I wanna pay too." He felt the uneasiness ebbing and the anger rising. He would need to make efforts not to come down too hard on his best friend, but this best friend had a way of crawling right under his skin and eating away at his very soul, not to mention the feelings of insecurity roused in his mind. He was most uncomfortable when William started on the eternity thing and how we all needed the light of the Word and how that there was only one way we could get there. It was bad enough to have a whole danged army gunning for you; but when you had hell-fire and damnation piled on that too, then how could a body ever get a night's rest?

"I know ye mean well, William; but I just ain't up to it today."

"I understand my friend," William said as he fell silent and appeared to have his eyes closed for a few moments.

"We best keep a sharp eye all things considered," Jubal countered as if to hint that he knew what William was up to during that brief moment. "Help me watch for sun glints."

"Don't think we need be concerned with looking for tracks in this stuff. Any one of us could see a trail here, and I have seen nothing so far," William said announcing his return to the present.

The patrol continued on west for about another hour. Off ahead, Jubal noticed crows sitting high in a lone poplar tree. No movement or no noisy caw-cawing. Unusual for them to be that still and that silent unless others were on the ground feeding. None could be spotted. If they felt at all threatened, they would open up and spread a warning for all around to hear. Sitting motionless and quiet could mean only one thing. They were watching something intently.

Jubal dismounted and pointed out what he had seen to William. He instructed everyone to dismount and lead their horses up close and to get on the down side and use them as a shield. Better to have a mini ball in a horse than in a trooper. The pace was slow, but sure. The crows would soon bolt if there was nothing else astir.

As if on signal, every black devil took wing at once and made it well known by their incessant loud ranting. At the same instant there came a split second reflection of the sun's brilliance from a small sassafras grove just below the tall poplar. Jubal made a quick scan of the hillside and the ridge beyond. He saw nothing further to alarm him. It could be nothing, but something had caught a ray of sunshine and spat it back. They would need to bully up on caution if they were to go any more westward.

Jubal led cautiously and alertly as the party came within range of the little grove that surely held danger and hid those that would do them harm. He watched intently never taking his eyes off the spot where he had seen the tell-tell flicker of sunlight. He watched so intently that he took his steps slowly and used his footing to reveal the lay of the ground. They were still in the tall dried grasses, and the occasional briar patches could afford a measure of cover should it become quickly needed. All in his patrol had sensed the urgency and had their Spencers at the ready. They looked all around them, not sure of where peril would strike first. Jubal, therefore, found it necessary to repeatedly signal for silence and to keep looking ahead instead of all around. Not many more steps and they would be within range. Each advancing step increased the danger and the gravity that they faced. The Reb raiders were a formidable enemy and, although out-numbered, could inflict serious injury or losses.

Jubal continued his forward movement. He would have thought that they would have taken fire by now. They were getting close enough to the grove that a man's facial features could be distinguishable at such a short distance. Yet, there was no musket fire.

Was it possible that there was nothing there after all? Had the crows bolted because of something else? Maybe he should go directly to the grove and see what the disturbance had been. No, too far up the sloping hillside and the others would cease moving while he meandered off on his own. He was in charge of this patrol and, therefore, responsible for it.

They moved on ahead until the threat of the present seemed to be behind them. Tension eased accordingly. Jubal even allowed himself to relax a bit as he remounted. One last look back to the little grove and then they could be about their pace and soon cover the assigned ground and get back to the safety of their own camp. Two or three more hours and they could turn around and head back to safety, to a sheltered tent and a night of rest. Maybe someone else would draw the patrol duty tomorrow.

Movement was casual and unhurried. The western end of the valley was near. After a brief stop by a wide ford in the creek and a chance for the stock to drink, it was time to start the return. The sun was getting low, and it would be at their back for this leg as well. That could work in their favor, but any Reb worth his salt would know that too. Jubal had wondered how the enemy would attempt a position that would gain the same advantage or better yet have them facing the sun. He had been extra alert in the morning because the sun would favor him then, and he was at a loss as to reason how Johnny Reb would strike, or where.

The little sapling grove came into view as they rounded a slow bend in the road. They had given up the grasses of the meadow for the ruts and mud holes of the road. None seemed to mind that because it was on the down side of their duty, and soon it would be all done for this day. Jubal eyed the grove and surrounding hillside as they paced by it. He saw nothing to alarm him. He too was anxious to return to camp. He was tired and hungry, but he knew that just a bit more of endurance and patience would end all that and once again he could let go and maybe get some rest and just maybe, a little peace of mind as well.

He had just taken his eye off the grove when he heard it. It all came in an instant. The sharp crack of a long rifle, the thwack of the mini ball as it found its aiming point and the shrieking cry of pain as its victim was felled. Ben Knox passed into eternity before his pierced and bloody chest slid from his saddle.

In that same instant more cracks and more agonizing shrieks of fear, pain and surprised anger. Turning, Jubal now knew what he had allowed to happen. He had let up just enough to give the foe the upper hand. Now the low western sun was in their face and blinding them from the danger. Shadow figures were running at them in randomness with alarming yelling and cursing. They had to stand and fight or make a run best they could.

Without really realizing it, fear and apprehension almost instantly morphed into dogged resistance and determination. Horses were harshly reined about and spurred headlong into the face of the enemy. Shots rang out all about as return fire came to be formidable and accurate. Blood chilling yells and curses were silenced one by one in what seemed only a few heartbeats. Here and there a shadow of a tattered and haggard figure quickly made a hasty retreat into the upland thick brush. It was over just as quick as it had started.

The patrol took stock of themselves. Ben was gone and Andy had taken a ball in his right leg just above the knee. With help he had tied it off and the red ooze soon stemmed its flow. He could still walk on it and that was surely a good sign. Ben's body was soon slung across his mount and the reins taken in by another who would see him back to camp. A rapid survey of the area yielded four dead Confederates and another that lay near death with a wound to his upper right chest.

Jubal dismounted and cautiously approached the wounded young Confederate private. He was almost overcome with both surprise and disgust when he looked closely at the face, now pale and colorless, trying to speak. He wanted to kneel to better understand this soon to depart young man, but caution held him back as he stood over the wounded. He was sickened when he realized that he was about to witness the ending of so young a life.

Les knew he was dying and that was probably what gave him the ability to attempt what he did. In an instant, he sat up and reached into his boot and withdrew the recently pilfered pistol, pointed it at Jubal and pulled the trigger. The closeness of the shot both startled and temporarily deafened Jubal, but it heightened his reaction as he jabbed his bayonette sharply into the already injured chest lying before him. Blood at once began a crimson staining on the gray coat.

Jubal now knelt and asked, "What be yer name and where ye from?"

"Les," he whispered. "Les Moran...Poor...Valley..."

Jubal did not speak but reached down and touched the brow of the dying boy as a tear came to his own eye. He looked up into the blue of the sky and asked. "Why, why does there have to be such killin' and waste and all them other evils? Why did it have to be him?" By the time that he looked into Lester's face again, he had taken his last breath. He would never see his home again. He would never ride up and down Cane Valley again. His Ma would most likely never know what happened to him or where he fell. Damn this war. Would there never be a chance again to make a life for himself? He felt about as low as he could ever recall. There would never be another chance for Les and all those like him.

William rode up behind him. "We best get moving, Jubal. No telling what may be in these woods and around here. We got Ben, and we can move any time."

"What?" The pistol shot was still having effect on Jubal's hearing.

William got down off his horse and knelt beside his friend. "We best be clearing out of here and soon. Everyone is edgy and scared."

"I reckon I ain't even thought on that yet, Will. I just seen a neighbor pass on and I been the one who struck him a death blow. I ain't never kilt a friend 'fore now, and it just plum makin' me sick. I sick of myself and sick of warrin' and skirmishin' and ever thing about it. Anymore I just don't much give a damn about nothin' no more."

"Please, man. We need be moving out, and we can talk it all out later if you want," William insisted.

Jubal seemed to snap back to himself and to the situation at hand. He picked up Les' boot pistol and put in his own boot. "What about his corpse?" he asked as he turned to William.

"Not much we can do for him now, Jubal, nor the other three that we killed. Their own will come back for them once we clear out. You can't go grieving over one body because you knew him, Jubal.

You just can't. You have to realize what this is all about and why we are here. You've seen other men die, and it never hit on you this way even when you knew who they were. You are stronger than this, and I know it. You just need to be glad and thankful that it is not you lying there. It well could be, you know."

"Reckon you be right as most times 'fore now," Jubal said softly as he slowly stood and mounted up once again. William did likewise, and they reined away from Les and made their way back to the rest of the patrol and headed east for camp, but not without one pair of eyes turning to get a last look at the distant figure lying so still and silent. The body was silent. But the incident would live on causing lingering agony, unlike the finality of death.

No words were spoken as the tension of the hurried encounter eased off. The ride back nurtured perhaps a false bit of security and some comfort that the chance of repeated action so close to the rest of the company would be less with each step. The sounds of the sloshing mud and the occasional snorts of somebody's mount were the only sounds as they rode into camp. Jubal quickly made his report, requested help in taking care of Ben, released all mounts to the stables, found what he could to quench his hunger and made his way to his tent.

Jerky, hardtack and dried peaches would normally be attacked with vigor, but tonight they were tasteless and dry as powder. The gnawing in the pit of the troubled soldier's stomach did not come from hunger or thirst. It came from disgust, depression and worry.

Jubal was disgusted with himself for the way that he had not watched behind for what was now all to plain to see. He was depressed because he had a stark reminder of his home life thrust upon him in a most revolting way. It reminded him of many facets of home, both good and bad and that unwillingly evoked loneliness and a longing for affection instead of aggression. He pined for peace instead of discord. He wanted simplicity instead of uncertainty.

William pulled back the tent flap and lowered himself to his bedroll, sitting in silence for a spell while Jubal went through the motions of eating. At last he could not hold out any longer. "Can I talk to you as a friend, Jubal?"

"I reckon so."

"You will not like what I am going to say to you."

"How ye mean by that?"

"We need to talk about today."

"Then talk."

"Jubal, I think it is way past time that you quit wallowing in your own muck and mire and get a hold on yourself and act like the man that you claim that you are."

"I reckon I ain't lately growed none and that I still be just a boy. That what ye think, huh?"

"No. That's not what I mean," William responded, some anger welling inside him but thusly confined for the present. "You don't think it shows on you, but you aren't very good at hiding it when something gnaws away at you."

"Well hell, what do ye be thinkin' be gnawin' on me so all fired bad then?"

"I told you that you would not like what I had to say."

"I reckon I been knowin' ye long enough to know ye says whatever ye want. Go ahead and say whatever be eatin' on yerself. I reckon then we both be just plumb eat up."

"Jubal, I am dead serious, and all I want is to try and help you."

"How ye gonna help me?"

"I don't know if I can or not, but all I can do is tell you what I think."

"Then out with it."

"I don't want to diminish our friendship."

"What ye mean by that, de...de...min... whatever?"

"I don't want to make you mad at me and us wind up being lesser friends than we are now. You understand that?"

"I reckon I do," Jubal retorted.

"Then I will say what is on my mind. I have heard you talk about going back to Cane Valley. You have said that you are sick of this old war and all, and I agree with that too. You saw death today in a way that it had never hit you before. It was someone who had a name and a family and came from a part of your home valley. He was a part of your life whether you like it or not, and he will be that part from now on. No amount of hate for this war that you ever can muster up will change that and you are not soon going to forget what you saw today."

"And you will?"

"No. I will not," William snapped back. "But I will accept it and move on."

"It could'a been me got kilt today and not Les or Ben for that matter," Jubal said.

"You need to be thankful that it was not you."

"I reckon I am, but I feel sorry fer Les."

"If sorry is what you want then why don't you feel sorry for all the others that have been killed, both Blue and Grey? It just so happened that today you knew a name and a face from back home. You knew Ben and recognized his face too. Are you not feeling sorry for him too?"

"Yeah, but he be different."

"No, not so," William answered without hesitation. "Ben stepped out into eternity just like every single casualty in every battle, in every fight on either side."

"But I never knowed him like I did Les."

"My point exactly," William injected sternly. "I think Les just scared hell out of you by showing you that it just as easy could have been you. I think he reminded you of home. I think you are homesick and don't even know it. I think you are scared and not willing to admit it. I think you are fighting something that is dealing with you and not willing to accept it."

Jubal did not speak but turned his eyes to meet William's. Neither spoke but tears soon welled up in Jubal's eyes, and he dropped his stare to his feet folded and crossed under him. Still he did not speak. Many thoughts raced around inside him. His mind transported him back to the small sassafras grove and the very next heartbeat, he was back at the mill with Lida and then instantly back beside William wondering what he should do or say. Then he would race into the future to try and see where his life would lead and what would happen to him. It all seemed to be so confusing, and there seemed to be no answers.

After a bit, William reached over and put a gentle hand on Jubal's shoulder. He remained silent. He wanted Jubal to speak first. That just might tell him the mood of his troubled companion. He thought he could detect a slight tremble, and there was some definite irregularity to the breathing.

Jubal began to respond after what could have passed for hours. His voice was unsteady, and there was no hint of anger in him now. He was as meek as any lamb had ever been. The time was right.

"I think you need to get off to yourself somewhere and get down on your knees and talk this thing out, Jubal. You need to be able to see your way into the light, and you need to do it now."

"Ye mean prayin'? That what ye mean?"

"Yes," William answered softly.

"I ain't never done that. I ain't so sure I even know how."

"That part is easy my friend. All in the world you need to do is talk to God about whatever is on your mind. You talk to Him just the same way you would talk to me."

"I've spoke some bad words with you a time or two," Jubal said.

"I know that but God knows what is on your heart. If you are honest with yourself and believe in your heart, then I know what you say will be heard. It just has to come from inside you and be true, that's all."

Again Jubal turned his eyes away and remained silent. William reasoned that it would be best not to attempt stronger persuasion, but rather to allow what he had already said have a chance to sink in. He knew his friend well enough to know that he would mull over what he had heard and that it would probably be a sleep robber for most of the night. The dying day had delivered a baptism of fire and now William had heaped coals upon it. Darkness would war against the light in yet another of the ageless wars of the mind of mortal man. There was only one peacemaker and possibly He would come this very night and grant that which was so much needed.

Restlessness definitely was the order of the night. Jubal tossed from one side to the other and drew frequent long breaths with such sighs that William was awake most of the night as well. However, he deemed it best to remain quiet and allow Jubal to wrestle with whatever he needed to overcome and conquer. William knew exactly what was eating on him, eating him alive, but alas he also knew that some things, a body just has to do for themselves. Coming out of the darkness was one of those very things. So, his silence prevailed and the tossing and turning never slowed. First morning light was enough. Jubal bolted from the tent, and William did not follow or try to intercede in any way. It was out of his hands now.

Jubal had no taste for anything that the mess tent had to offer that morning. He knew he would become hungry before he had a chance to eat again, but right now that made no difference. This man's army had caused him to be hungry before, and he had lived to tell about it. This time would be no different. He made his way to the edge of camp, past the stable area and into the foothill thickets. Without really being aware of how far he had wandered, he alerted to the fact that he was in big timber and that he was alone. Being alone is what he now wanted. He had thought long and hard on what William had said, not only last night, but on several other times when he had tried to be a true friend to him.

William had said that he was homesick. Well he didn't know so well about that. He had never been away from home before; and if missing his Ma and sisters was homesick, then maybe, just maybe, he was. He missed the familiar ridges and hollows where he knew his way around and felt comfortable most anywhere he wanted to go. He missed Lida but that was a whole different thing. Here there was no miller man to talk things over with, man to man. Here there were just other soldiers, young boys and men who were in the same place as himself. Most all talked of home at some time or another, but mostly they followed orders and bitched about it all the time.

William had said that he was afraid. Well, who wouldn't be with being shot at all the time? He did not feel that he was any more scared than the next in line. True, he had been worked over pretty good a time or two, but he had made it through that too. He had admitted no fear to anyone or to himself for that matter. Admitting fear would make a man appear as a boy and that was just not going to be as long as he had any dealings about it.

The thing that had really been tugging away at him was what his friend had said about being thankful and how he ought to fall down on his knees and thank God for delivering him out of the fight. Then he remembered something Granny Iverson had read to him about coming out of the shadow of death and walking in a valley somewhere. That had puzzled him too, and he could not understand why it had come to him so many times during the night. William had said something about the valley of the shadow of death and coming out of it and into the daylight. He had trouble reasoning why there was so much ado about the dark and the light. It was simple enough for most folks he knew. Just a matter of light and dark, same as day and night, and there weren't any differences in the dangers of life any more at night than there was at daytime. Daytime just made it easier to see, that was all.

He saw a lone bald rock no more than waist high that gleamed beneath a lone ray of early morning sunlight. It beckoned him, and he approached it slowly and silently. He unknowingly began to tremble, slightly at first and then burst out in heart-wrenching sobs. He had never felt this way before, and he had never lost control of himself this way. It never even crossed his mind to look around and make sure that he was alone and that no one would hear his cries.

He fell to his knees and lingered there until he got hold of himself again. Then he felt relieved to have let it all out. He felt as if a load had lifted off his mind at least if not off his tired and aching body. He began to pray in the only way he knew.

"Lord, I ain't never did this before. I reckon I'll just do what my friend told me. This here be what be on my mind. I reckon I might be a bit homesick. I reckon I miss my home. I wish I was back there now. Iffin I knowed it was proper by you, then I reckon I might just up and set out fer home right now."

"I reckon ye know all what be goin' on in them parts right now, and I be thinkin' that I would like ye to keep Lida special fer me. Don't let her get sweet on nobody else. I reckon that ain't much askin' now, so I be thankin' ye fer that right here and now. Ye might cause her to think on me some too ever now and again, but I reckon it ain't necessary ever day. I got a feelin' she be askin' same on my account too."

"I reckon that pert nigh cover things back home. Oh, I ain't forgot all them fine hosses and fancy duds and all them things either. I reckon they come once all this here war and politickin' be past and done with, but I be willin' to thank ye right now fer all that. I just be a mite concerned over bein' disappointed there though. I reckon ye might fergit a spell, but I can remind ye, I reckon. Anyhow that be what I be aimin' to have some of these here days."

"I am plumb grateful fer the daylight. I done come through the dark and I feel a heap better already since I can see about me now. I reckon William was right. It just ain't good to live in dark all the time. A body needs sunshine some of the time, and today be lookin' like there be plenty light on the way. It be a bit early right now, but that old sun soon be high and then all be light.

"I be thinkin' on when I ought start makin' my way back south and gettin' self on home. Even iffin ye do hold Lida fer me, she ain't gonna wait a whole long time. She be a growed woman now, and she be wantin' woman things and all. So I reckon I be kind enough to oblige her. I be thankin' ye fer showin' me which way I need travel and which way crossin' all them ridges and hollers twixt here and home. I be thankin' ye ahead cause when I light out I know that I won't have no spare time fer askin' then. I be busy coverin' my tracks and makin' miles roll off mighty fast."

"I won't say nuthin' about talkin' with ye Lord, cause they might be some who would poke fun at it. I reckon I be man enough to take the ribbin' but would just soon not have to iffin it be all the same to ye. Reckon what others does and says to ye be their business and mine be mine likewise. Iffin William asks me I tell him we talked, but I was the one who had most of the words. I reckon he understand iffin I not tell ever thing down to the hide and hair."

"I know from home that ye wants folks be good neighbors and love one another, and I reckon I ain't never done nobody no harm 'cept what this blasted war make me do. William said it be another matter when stuff done in war time. So I reckon I fits in with good people. I am right proud that I can say that, and I aim on keepin myself in among the good folks too."

"Maybe we can talk some more sometime. It ain't been near as hard as I reckoned it would. I feel a mite better now, and I be thankin' ye fer that too. Maybe I get William to read to me some more from the Good Book, cause I hear tell it be a lot in there what ye done said in past times. So I be goin' on back now, and I reckon I can find this here same place again iffin' I needs be talk with ye again some time."

He stood and looked around to see if anyone could have seen or heard him. He was thinking that it would be best for now if his little tryst would go unknown or unheard by another because he was not confident in talking with the Lord in the simple manner that had been suggested to him. Back home he had always had some other person that talked to God for him and on his behalf. Now, home was far away and anything that was done on his behalf, he had to do it himself. That was much the way he saw things now as far as this praying business was concerned. He could always ask William what he thought about anything in particular or how he would do about this or that. He might even get William to pray like Granny Iverson often did, asking for protection and guidance and knowledge and such.

Come to think about it, he could not ever recall Granny Iverson asking for fine clothes or land or money or anything like that. Not even for salt or store bought goods or such. All she ever asked for was stuff that no store ever sold. Things like peace and quiet, love and mercy, tenderness and grace and all manner of such words. He could understand some of those things like peace and love, but most seemed to be just words used to stir a body and cause him to fret some on stuff that really he had no control over. He still hoped that Granny Iverson spoke a word for him ever now and then. It brought a slight meaning to him to think that she cared enough to remember him even though there were untold miles between them. He felt the same way about Lida except mostly running in the other direction. He thought on her a lot. He knew that he had feelings for her, but he could not be so positive about her thinking on him. He could only be with her in mind for now, but this war would be over one of these days and maybe sooner for him than for others.

He soon made his way back to troop camp. No one seemed to have missed him or knew that he had slipped off on an unauthorized venture. Repercussions would be smart if he were found out. He elected to not tell William what he had done or where he had been. He was beginning to feel the sleeplessness of the past night and made straightway for his tent. He could easily be found there. If he were lucky enough to draw no duty for the morning, sleep could overcome him for a few precious moments and rest would follow in its wake.

William was sitting cross legged on his bedroll cleaning his Spencer and the boot pistol that Jubal had picked up yesterday. To his right lay an open Bible, tattered in places and worn from use. It was somehow the first thing to catch Jubal's eye.

William spoke first as Jubal sprawled himself on his bedroll. "Do you feel any better now? Do you feel like you are any safer now?"

"What ye mean?"

"Well, you tossed and rolled around all night, and I know you went out alone earlier, and I think I pretty much know why," William answered.

"Oh ye do, huh?"

"Not so sure, but I just hope that what I am thinking is what happened."

"And just what ye think happened?" Jubal barked.

"I just had hopes that you would find or already have found your way out of the darkness."

"Well it was already light when I got there."

"Where did you go, if I may ask?" William inquired as if he did not already really know.

"I went fer a thinkin' and walkin' spell."

"Did it help?"

"Help what?"

"Did it bring you any comfort? Did it settle your mind and make you feel any at ease?"

"Well I reckon I be comfortable soon as I get me a little shut eye, and I reckon my mind be at ease too."

"But do you feel different about yourself now? Has there been a change?" William asked softly.

"There might be after I sleep a bit."

William now had all the answers he needed for the present and knew that it was not the time to dig any deeper. It was plain to him that there was still darkness to overcome and that there was only one who could bring victory into the heart of his friend. He would bear forth the only weapon that he had to fight with for his friend. He would intercede on behalf of his misguided friend. He would try to plant a seed in hopes that it would fall on fertile ground.

"Jubal, we drew night duty again for tonight, so you can sleep all day if you wish. I will not bother you till late afternoon. I have things that need attention. You get some rest. I know that you are in need of it, body and soul."

In no short order Jubal was stretched out on his bedroll in anticipation of needed rest and sleep. Eyes closed and sleep overcame him in a few short breaths. However, it did not last. The silence about the tent was haunting instead of relaxing. Far too many memories rose up to stir his thoughts and welled-up emotions flexed to choke off the very breath he now drew. Unrelenting torment from unanswered questions and unknown feelings pulled at his mind so that it became near impossible to think clearly.

He had no concept of the influence or the workings of evil. He reasoned that he knew right from wrong as well as the next, but failed to see his own needs. He equated his turmoil to the perils and hazards of war and tried to satisfy his longings and shortcomings by reasoning that the war could not go on much longer; and even if it did, he had already formulated his way out. It was a matter of time and each day brought that conjuring closer and made it more real. One way or another he would fight off all the evils that had been heaped upon him. To him, the war was all external, and the conflict that it caused on the inside would never have been in the first place had the fighting never begun. It was no fault of his own, and he was not about to accept any of the responsibility. To him, the war was Blue and Grey. It was not light nor dark.

The day wore on much the same each hour. It soon came time to form up for the night watch. All were still a bit uneasy over the loss of Ben, even to the point of not talking about him. Silence would maybe make it less real; and if it could somehow be dismissed from the mind, then possibly it would soon be as if it never happened. Jubal began to realize just how tired and worn out he was. No sleep to speak of for the last two nights and so much rushing around inside his head that there was no wonder that he was spent. Nevertheless he had a duty to do, and he aimed to do it. He had made up his mind that he was more of a man than he had acted in the last couple of days and that he had shook off whatever it was that had riled him up so and that he could whip it now and whip it again and again if need be. Again, he had no concept of the war within.

Night drug on into early morning, and a cold rain began to fall. He had left his tent in such a dither that he had left his oilcloth cover behind. Now it was too far to go fetch it, and besides that leaving his post for even that short a while could be mistaken for dereliction of duty. Dang it all anyway!

First light saw a cessation of the rain, but it really made little difference now. Jubal was wet and chilled near to the bone, and all his strength and energy now centered around getting out of his drenched clothing and into a dry warm bedroll. There was nothing short of that able to fend off sleep and rest. Exhaustion would demand it. His body would savor it, and his emotions would be calmed by it. Even hunger could not diminish its importance nor delay its anticipation.

Sleep did come. But when he awoke, the chill had not subsided and his entire body throbbed in the grip of soreness that he had not known before. There was relief from the perplexities of his thoughts, but now there were physical needs to be met. Another manner of struggle enveloped him. He knew and realized the gnawing pain in the pit of his gut. He was hungry, and the dryness in his mouth begged for water.

As many times before, William was there for him when he needed it most. Jubal made short work of the water crock and immediately wished that he had taken it slower. The gripping cramp near bent him over, and it took some time for it to subside even enough to allow him to sit up in a near normal position. William did not chide him for his childishness or foolhardiness, now was not the time for that. He merely held out a biscuit and fatback to him. It was received graciously and savored with much less haste. When it was finished, another was offered likewise. It too was taken and eaten slowly.

"You got wet all the way through last night," William finally commented.

"And stone cold too."

"You have slept a long time, and I knew you would be hungry when you woke up. I managed to sneak you a couple of biscuits and some meat."

"I be grateful. I hope ye know that."

"I know it, and you would do the same for me, if I needed it."

"Ye got that right, I reckon," Jubal answered as he continued to eat slowly. "What time is it anyhow?"

"Near nightfall."

"Dang."

"Bet you are thinking that we have night watch again," William said inquiringly.

"I hope not."

"Well, we do not. As a matter of fact, we are off the hook until Monday morning."

"Monday, what day is it right now?"

"It is now Saturday; Saturday dusk to be precise. Tomorrow is Sunday, and I want you up and going strong in the morning."

"What fer?"

"I asked for permission to go up the valley to that little church that we saw the day we came here and made camp. It is just about two miles back east of here, and there has been nothing going on in that direction since we got here."

"What's that got to do with me?" Jubal asked as if he had no idea.

"I want you to go with me. You owe me that much."

"Don't seem like much of a smart doin' to me. Ye forget that we be in a Reb state and that we be Yanks? Reckon ye be out to get us shot on a Sunday in a church of all places? I reckon ye must'a got some water logged too."

"I know all that all too well, but there will be about six or seven of us going. We will be armed as usual should there be any trouble. I am thinking that it will be a peaceful morning and that there will be no problems. The captain had to think on it a bit before he would agree to it and even considered going himself. Of course he couldn't because of his position and his duty, but I think he would if not for that."

"I ain't so sure that I will go with ye."

"Jubal, I will not badger you or push the issue, but all in the world that I want to do or am trying to do is to help you."

"Well, we see about it come mornin' once I sleep on it."

"You slept all day. Do you think you can sleep all night too?" William asked.

"I hope to. I need it. I need rid of these chill blanes and aches too, and I be thinkin' night's rest go a long ways in workin' the cussed things outta me."

"I hope you can sleep too and that you can feel some ease."

Sunday morning came and Jubal did not go with William to the little valley church. He had slept so hard that he did not wake at William's rousting. He almost felt as if he were in a daze. His body was not so racked with aching soreness anymore, and the chills felt much better. He was warm for the first time in two or three days. He was weak but retained full control. He sat up and looked around him. William had dried his uniform and blacked his boots. William had folded his bedroll and left a bandanna on it with more biscuits and a big cold slice of shoulder meat tied inside it. The water crock was full, and there was a canteen of cold coffee. He wondered how long he had been asleep. Pulling back the tent flap provided no accurate estimate. It was far too clouded over to get a fix on the sun. It must be somewhere before noon because William was not back yet, and church most times let out near noon.

He began to think about all the things that William had done for him. It dawned on him that William was indeed a real friend. What did puzzle him a bit, however, was why would he care enough to do all those things when it was enough of a trial just to see after one's own self. He had never had anyone do for him like that outside of his own kin folk, and they had known him all his life. William had known him only a little while by comparison. He would have to remember not to be so short with him in times when he felt crossed or mixed up a bit.

"You missed a good sermon on the parable of the bushel today," William intoned as he entered the tent and sat down on his bedroll.

"Bushel of what?" Jubal asked. "Corn or what?"

"Not that kind of a bushel, Jubal my friend. It is a Bible story that I will read you sometime." He could well see that it would take a bit of explanation on the one hand and that his friend was far less acquainted with the Word than he had judged him to be. No wonder he had made no mention of praying or anything even close to it. He had seemed to understand more about the darkness and all that it involved. William made note that he would need to read to his friend much more and much deeper than ever before. This poor boy was deep in the darkness and so far had not even realized it, let alone any need to be led out of that danger. He was not so sure that he knew all the words to say that could make a difference, but he had known some others who he was sure could stir just about any man to see the light. Just this morning he had heard one of them.

"Right now I need to be readin' the top side of a big ham biscuit," Jubal said as he began to pull on some dry clothes. "Have ye had mess yet?"

"No. I thought you might be awake by now so I came to check on you. I think we could find something. I caught a whiff as I came by the cook's tent."

"I be ready."

"I take it that you feel better now that you have had a chance to rest and sleep. Would that be right?"

"Yep, I reckon I be fit now. Reckon I be all fixed and rarin' fer whatever come at me next."

"But what about the dark, Jubal? How do you feel about that?"

"Well shucks, it be light now, they ain't no dark. I reckon I ain't scared none by dark. Ain't never been 'fore now, and I reckon that not changed none."

William felt a bit frustrated in his efforts to convey what he wanted Jubal to understand. He was even a bit irritated with his friend for being so backward and thick headed about it all. He decided to drop the issue for the moment when he was jolted again in surprise by what Jubal said next.

"Granny Iverson read to me about the light of the world and something about what it all means. Think you know what she was speakin' on?"

"I know what she was reading about. I sure do."

"Well, I reckon some time when we got time, I let ye read me that and maybe ye can tell me what all them Bible words means."

"Any words in particular come to your mind now?"

"I recall some mountain where they fed a bunch with bread and fish or somethin'. I recall how Granny read me a tale about some man sowin' wheat and growin' tares, whatever that be."

"We will read those truths together. We will do it soon, my friend."

William was almost overcome by what Jubal had just said. Obviously Granny Iverson had planted a seed somewhere along the way, and now it appeared as if maybe the Lord was about to cause that seed to bear fruit, all in His own time. William saw a door of opportunity opened ever so slightly, and he was excited that he just might have the chance to fling it open wide. He vowed to himself that he must be prepared and arm himself with the right words and the patience to see it through.

The last days of October witnessed unseasonably cold weather in the valleys of Northern Virginia and deep snow blanketed the higher ridges and mountain uplands. Little activity and movement came to pass as a result, and this afforded more idle time for all the company. Jubal and his squad had less duty time and more personal time than they could ever recall. It was a formidable task just to keep warm and dry in such inclement weather.

The renegade Confederate raiders found the snow somewhat a welcome advantage. They did not have a steady supply of essentials. The only supply they had was what they could steal, raid or find in the woods and mountain uplands. There the deep snow would make tracking game a cinch. Deer could not hide, and the white ground blanket would slow them by half or more. They would be easier game, and one doe would feed them all for better than a day. The only drawback would be the revealing necessity of a fire. Not likely that a lazy good fer nuthin' Blue Belly would track down smoke in this kind of stuff. Besides that after the fire got good and hot, there would be no smoke if they could keep it stoked with dead limbs and dry tender. Both could be found even under a snow covered forest floor as long as you knew where to look. That would be no issue, because they were all woods smart.

The slowdown caused by the wintry onslaught made for increased idle time for Jubal, for William, and for every man in camp. This brought the men into closer and more personal contact.

There was time for man-to-man talks and the camaraderie that can only be known by a bunch of young and inexperienced warriors who think they are indestructible, who think they are fully invincible and capable of doing warfare to the hilt. Only the newest of the company had to sit out on the bragging rights and be content to listen to the voices who boasted of their past endeavors.

William and Jubal both had time on their hands that they could pass as they chose. Cold blustering winds made for discomfort and chills outside, while the tent offered some comforts but nothing like a hot roaring fire. Both found themselves searching out the warmth of a nearby camp or cook fire for a short interlude and then darting back to the shelter and trying to pass some time at rest. They did not always go together or on any schedule, but the times together inside their tent offered some privacy where they could be more open and honest with each other. It was during these times that William began careful but purposeful inroads into just how much his friend did, in fact, know about the difference between the darkness of sin and the light that came from escaping sin. He was content for the meantime to try and find out where he really was and what he knew and what he may have been persuaded to believe or accept along the way. There would be time in the coming weeks to bring him around to seeing the error of his ways once he understood more. William was confident that, given time, he would win out over the demon of the dark.

William sensed that Jubal was not at ease with himself the way he pretended to be. Lately he had been less prone to argue and seldom had an unkind word for anyone around him. He even forced a smile now and then. But at night, when the darkness set in, sleep often avoided him and restlessness made for uneasy nights. On more than one occasion, William thought that he had heard Jubal sniffling and was sure that troubling thoughts were tormenting him beyond his control. Hard to hide some things no matter how strong you might claim to be. It is hard sometimes to be truthful with one's self more so than with a rank stranger. Sometimes it is harder to know yourself than it is someone you hold close. Sometimes a body is just plain mixed up with themselves and that sure seemed to be the facts with Jubal. At least that was the way his friend was reading him.

Jubal did not realize the elements of the conflict boiling within him. He did not yet know and acknowledge the perils of the darkness. He did not realize the blessings of walking in the light. He longed for that peacefulness that he sensed and saw in others, namely in Granny Iverson and in William, but he did not yet know the giver of such peace. The conflict between the Prince of the Darkness and the Light of the World was at the base of his unrelenting inner turmoil. William knew that and could see it in his friend and knew what needed to be done, but Jubal himself stood in the way of that effort. He resisted his inner feelings to surrender his claims to his own good deeds and his self-proclaimed attitude of never having done wrong, save for the deeds and actions of the cursed war.

The war, that was it. The war was responsible for all the torment that he had to carry on his shoulders. It was the fighting and perils of war that implanted fear in his mind. The fear was what caused the restlessness at night and that was what awakened him in the wee hours of the morning and made him bolt upright in cold sweats. The war had forced him away from his home and his family. The way he saw it, he had a leg up on most every other man in this company, including William. If they were feeling any of the things inside them that he felt, then they must be near mad by now. But strange, most acted like this old confounded war was just a day-by-day task, more or less a bother rather than a burden to be overcome and thrown off. None of them seemed to be boiling inside; none of them exploded in fits of rage. They had not cowered in fear nor had they cursed in anger because of where they were or what they were required to do in their service to country.

It was so unfair that he would have to carry the load for the whole danged company. No one else, save for William, cared what happened or what was coming next, it seemed. They just moseyed around with heads in the sand most of the time. It was just not, or should not be, all his fault that things were the way they were. But that was the way he saw it. There could be no reason other than all the embattlement that he had been through and the carnage that he had seen, the lives that had passed into eternity. Was he to suffer the same fate? Would he never make it back to look into the kind eyes and the gentle face of his Ma? Would Lida still hold him dear in her heart?

Questions. Unanswered questions. Torment and uncertainty. Restlessness. Unrelenting conflict. Why? Where was the answer, and why could it be so elusive? Where would he turn next? How long could strength and strong will sustain him? Or would this damnable war eventually consume even him?

Chapter 9

Wishing

*T*he last few days of October were miserable. Slow drizzle fell incessantly, and there was no escape from the dank and dampness that engulfed everything except Major Dunn himself. He managed to parlay the effects of the elements by holding up in his personal tent and using the bourbon bottle as insulation and protection from the wrath of Mother Nature. He had issued few orders, and resultantly there was reduced patrol activity and little attention paid to routine duty. The war seemed far removed and unimportant for the moment. There had been no hostilities in several days now. There had been no civilian complaints of raiders or thievery. Some of the troops had voiced stiff complaints about their circumstances, and there had even been a desertion or two.

The major had admitted to sheer boredom, and it had trickled down to the lower ranks. Spirits were low, and there was hardly any morale left in the entire troop. Jubal and William had both made their feelings known to each other. William more or less accepted the situation as mundane routine warfare, laced with infrequent rushing episodes of panic. The inclement weather did nothing to improve the depressed morale.

November dawned with light snow fall and a chill coming in from the northwest. General Early and most of his command had been rousted from the Capital area and were in retreat farther down the Shenandoah. Hostilities were limited. The general tenet that the war would soon come to an end became even more widespread. Many were encouraged that they would be able to return home, rejoin their families, and resume a pre-war lifestyle.

The weather and the combining effect of all other facets created closer contact in the confines of the camp tents. Jubal and William spent long hours in their tent and had ample time for thrashing out many of their feelings, apprehensions, and desires.

William talked freely about his family, their roots, and the things that they valued. He spoke of his childhood and the relationship that he had with his parents, grandparents and his brother and sisters. He had come from a fairly well-to-do background, but had worked hard to accomplish the tasks that had enabled him to grow and progress. It became very obvious, even to Jubal, that he had a good head on his shoulders and that he had drive and ambition to make something out of himself. He had not yet made a definite commitment to a vocation. His grandfather had made his living in a textile mill up in New England and had moved south into Ohio to escape the harsh winters. His son, William's father, had been a schoolmaster and a surveyor. William had entertained the thought of being an educator as well, but the sights that he had seen in the war and on the battlefield had perked his interest too. He had asked and was quite curious what would be required of him to become a surgeon. He had mentioned these thoughts to Jubal, who had promptly brushed him off.

"No way I'd do that. Bad 'nuff just killin' a hog."

"But a surgeon is more than just a butcher, and you should know that," William countered.

"Reckon so, but doctorin' take a heap learnin' and long time doin' it too. Be a mite pricy too, and Lord knows I ain't got no money like that. Reckon I ain't likely to spend it fer that iffin I did have it."

"Do you not want to be a learned person and have a good strong future to draw on?"

"I reckon I be workin' like I always have. That be all I ever knowed about."

"Did your dad or mom never try to build up a desire in you and give you goals and ambitions to reach for?" William asked innocently.

That one question triggered a noticeable change in Jubal. It changed his mood, his expression, and his tone of voice. He had not talked much to William about his Pa, but had related freely about his sisters and his Ma.

The two young warriors talked much about family and friends back home and how they had lived their lives to this point. Jubal had unknowingly expressed many longings that had never been fulfilled in his life. He had revealed much to his companion that he had never expressed to another living soul, not even his Ma.

On this particular day, William was telling his friend of his childhood activities and relationship with his father.

"Dad took me on my first fishing trip. It was just a short walk to the local creek, not a big stream, but one that had a few red eye and suckers in it. Dad cut a reed for a pole and dug some red worms along the creek bank. I remember that I caught a little red eye not much more than a minnow, put it in a quart crock and carried it all the way back home. Course it was belly up by the time we got back home, but I wanted my mom to see what I had caught. I was proud of what I had been able to do, and Dad bragged on me too. I think that is why I remember it so well. I was just a little shaver then, but I remember it just like it was yesterday."

"Pa never done nuthin' like that. All he ever done was work my hinder end off, and I ain't never recollected him braggin' on me not one time. I wish he would have."

"I'm sorry, Jubal. I didn't mean to stir you up by telling you about my dad, that was not my intention at all," William said realizing that he had struck a touchy spot in his friend's feelings.

"I ain't upset none, I swear. I just don't have no feelin' fer my Pa like you do cause my Pa weren't nowhere near the man that your Pa was and that be no fault of yours. I ain't holdin' nuthin' again ye fer that and ye should know that too, I reckon."

"I will not mention it anymore."

"No. I wish ye would tell me more. Cause and how then I might learn how to raise my kids that I be apt to have. That be iffin I ever get by this danged skirmishin' and get a chance on gettin' my butt back home where I belong."

"I thought you wanted to go places and see things and have all those fine things that you used to speak about," William taunted.

"I reckon they ain't what makes much difference. And I reckon I got rights to change up my mind."

"You think it could be that you are growing up and changing your values? Are you beginning to see a little bit of light?"

"I ain't fer sure what ye be meanin' by that, but I reckon I do think things different now and then. Sometimes I just find myself a wishin' that things wuz different all them times. Well it ain't, and that be the way it be, I reckon."

"Now you have me a bit confused I must admit," William said.

"Yer Pa raised you the way he did and you look up to him, I can tell. My Pa more or less left out and left me and Ma to make do best we could. Iffin I had a Pa like yours, then maybe I could'a had schoolin' and had a way to make a life 'sides scratchin' dry hard ground all my live long days. I might'a knowed how to go about readin' a book or writin' a letter and all them other things that you do that just come natural to ye and things I struggle with all the time. I blame my Pa fer them things. It peeves me a lot the way he done me and Ma, but I reckon they ain't no goin' back and redoin' what done been did."

"You are right about that. Yesterday is gone. A loving father is a wonderful gift to any boy, and I too wish you could have had a dad like mine. You would have liked him, because he was always so kind and devoted to his family, yet he required discipline and obedience too. That was one of the things that made him so easy to get along with. You always knew what he wanted and what he expected."

Jubal listened to his friend telling about his father, while mixed feelings rolled around inside his head. On one hand he felt nothing but ill will and resentment for his Pa. On the other hand, there was a void within him that longed to be filled, and this void was only amplified by hearing of all the goodness in another's father. It hurt to listen to his friend talk about all the good in his father, but at the same time he wanted to know more.

"You ain't said, but is yer Pa still livin'?" Jubal asked.

"Yes, he is and is still quite active back home."

"What he do at home?"

"He gave up running lines and making maps, but he still has his hand in the schools. He is very much involved in his church and community," William answered with a slight amount of pride. He had the firm realization that he himself could just as well have a father who was inattentive and uncaring. It was reassuring to him to know that he could call on his father at any time and that he would always be there. He knew that he would always receive sound advice and that it would be tempered with love and genuine concern.

He could see the void in Jubal that his earthly father had created through his acts of omission. That only served to point up the need for Jubal to know and to develop a trust and faith in the Father that he could always call on and who would always be there for him. He knew that it would be necessary to tread lightly in trying to be a witness to his friend, because there were deep wounds and ugly scars that would not be easily overcome. Jubal just needed to open his eyes and see where he was and then realize where he needed to place a trust and seek a help.

Bitterness over the things in the past would only serve as a consuming and destroying blight on one's life. Those unfortunate times were in the past and that was where they needed to be. No amount of brooding would change what had already been. Good to learn from things in the past; but at the same time, life must go on. One must live each day for its own merits. No going back. But if a body tried to drag the past along, then tomorrow would always be filled with toil and hardship. It would become ever increasingly hard to hold your head up and look ahead. Jubal just needed to know the ways of the light. He had not been able to grasp his needs and seemed to have built up a wall around himself.

The November weather remained unchanged over the next few days with heavy low lying clouds of ominous grey. They hung low to the ground and surrounded and coated everything with moisture.

The Major continued to receive much of his warmth and comfort from a bottle. One day he would order a short patrol that really never covered anything. The next he would order all activity canceled and justify it by claiming that his men needed a rest and that the dank and damp should be enough to deter an already weakened Rebel force.

Those next few days found Jubal and William deeper into discussions of themselves and their contrasting life experiences. Jubal appeared to have worked through a bit of the bitterness that he had expressed concerning his Pa. Possibly those feelings still boiled inside him. William knew him well enough to know that he had learned to hide his feelings whenever he wanted.

The innermost part of the young man from Cane Valley had a burning desire for acceptance and for affection that had for the most part been absent in his life. Sure his Ma loved him. But there were other children, and he had been thrust into the position of provider and protector. He had been forced to grow up early. He had not had time nor means for education or social graces and customs.

Jubal did rest better that night. His feelings were not centered around the bitterness for his Pa, but on Lida and all the tenderness and affection that she had shown him. He had not had word from her since leaving the valley, and it had never crossed his mind that he could write her a letter. He could scarce read let alone write a good letter. He would talk to William about that in the morning. Maybe he could help. He could write all that needed be said.

Sunday morning broke cloudy and overcast. Jubal drifted into consciousness to find William sitting cross-legged on his cot and reading from something. He tried to go back to sleep but was unsuccessful. He lay still for a few minutes, watching his friend seemingly deeply occupied with whatever it was that he was reading. Jubal watched him intently for a bit then began to lose himself in his own thoughts.

He was mentally transported back to the mouth of the old hollow that he called home and to the mill and mill house where sweet Lida and the rest of her family dwelt. How he longed to be there again, especially this morning, knowing that Lida would be dressed in her best as she and her family made their way to the meeting house. Lots of things got lost in time with the war going on, but somehow Sunday mornings always seemed to make themselves known.

William had promised to learn him to read whenever he was ready. Maybe now it was close on time for that.

"William," Jubal said in a startling voice.

"Yes."

"Will ye help me write a letter?"

"Be glad to. You know I will."

"You got paper and pen? I ain't."

"I have none with me, but we can get it in the quartermaster's tent."

Jubal threw the covers off and sat up. He had slept in his clothes as did most all troopers here lately. It was easier to keep warm. He soon pulled on his boots and was ready to head out.

"Tell me what ye want, and I'll fetch it."

"Just tell Sarge that you need materials for three or four letters and a pen or quill whichever he has."

"Shucks, I don't aim to write nuthin' but one letter."

"I know but it never hurts to have a little extra," William said, as he sat up and began to reach for his boots.

"I reckon I be able to fetch that myself. Ye can stay here readin' iffin ye want."

"I know. Just thought that we may as well see what we can find for breakfast too. Might be easier to think better what to write on a full stomach."

"Reckon ye be right about that," Jubal agreed.

In no short order, they had eaten their fill and were back in their tent with writing material in hand. Both were glad to be back in the shelter, because a light cold rain had begun to fall. A new chill was in the air.

A new chill was also brought to mind for Jubal. He had not had word from home, and it had not previously crossed his mind that things at home could be far different than when he was last there. He had no way to know about his Ma and her well-being. He had no way to know if Lida was still at home or if she had took up with some Yankee captain or someone to the likes. Those sobering thoughts drove icicles into his heart.

"Who will the letter be addressed to, Jubal?" William asked as he settled onto his cot in preparation for his requested scriber's services.

"It be Lida."

"She have a last name, Jubal?"

"She be a Johnson."

"Do you know how she spells it?"

"Ain't fer sure. How ye reckon it be?"

"Say her name real slow for me Jubal."

"Johhhhnnnnsonnnn."

"Good, I believe I know now." William went on to explain that there were different ways to spell what sounded like the same name. Jubal looked puzzled, so William decided it best to not linger on the issue but more importantly to concentrate on the letter itself.

William touched the paper and wrote a few strokes. "What would you like to say to her?"

"I…I…well, I…I ain't sure just yet."

"Want to wait till later then? That would give you some time to think about it."

"Naw, I reckon we needs be gettin' on with it now."

"Okay then. You want me to tell her what you have been doing and all the places that we have been?"

"That be a good commencin', I reckon."

William concentrated on writing. He briefly wrote about the places that Jubal had been. Unknown to his friend, he wrote in some detail about what he had observed in his friend's behavior. He told of the restless nights, torment and strife. William was good with words, and it did not take long for him to accurately expose the innermost emotions of his companion. True, he had never met Lida and never expected to be so fortunate. However, he did feel that he knew her well enough to be writing things to her that he felt she would appreciate knowing about her absent friend. Jubal had spoken of her often enough to uncover their mutual feelings for each other and a formation of thoughts of the future. But the war had come along and derailed any possibility of that for now. Jubal had not asked for these things to be written in his letter, but William wrote them anyhow.

William went on to amplify the absence of peace and tranquility in his companion. He wrote how he thought that it could be the Spirit tugging at his heart, but that he seemed not to understand or not to even be concerned until a few weeks back and then only in passing. He wrote of how he had encouraged Jubal to seek out a special place and to try to talk things over with the Lord. He went on to explain how that there appeared to be no results showing so far.

"You want me to ask how she and her family are getting along?"

"Yep, and my folks too."

That served mainly as reason to return to more and deeper writing. William then asked that Lida and the rest of her family remember Jubal in their prayers. He made the correct assumptions that they were already in the light and that they had already made the decision that Jubal so badly needed to make. This letter was already longer than first imagined, but it had a purpose.

It might be that the war would soon be over. Then Jubal could return to Cane Valley and Lida and that life for them would have a storybook ending. William reasoned that Jubal had never really expressed himself to Lida. That being the case, he would set the stage for someday. It was no difficulty for him to express all the things that Jubal had related to him, both verbally and indirectly. He wrote the things that he believed Lida would want to hear. He made it plain from the start that he was just trying to be a friend to her friend and that he only wanted to help him and influence him to see how he needed to make that life-changing decision. How he needed to recognize his need and then know what to do to turn that life around and know the peace of God's love.

William did, indeed, ask about Ma and the girls and even about old Jake. Jubal at times seemed to really miss that old red hound. He had surely spent far more time with that old dog than he had with his Pa.

The writer knew that his letter may or may not be delivered. He knew it could be weeks before it arrived at the mill and opened by Lida.

"How must I address this, Jubal?"

"Huh?"

"I need to know where to send it."

"Reckon she get it iffin ye send it to Johnson's Mill?"

"I need a road or a town or a place too."

"Cane Valley Road be all I ever knowed it to be."

"What county is that?"

"Ain't fer sure but thinkin' it be Hawks or Hanks or such."

"Is there a little town close by somewhere?"

"Rock Hill be it, I speck."

"Then that is where we will address it to go."

"How long ye reckon it'll take getting' there, Jubal quired.

"I really have no way to know, since we do not have much contact from that area and don't really know what is happening there. I think your area is of Union sympathy and preservation hopes. So I would expect that your letter would go through without much delay. I guess that they have a functioning post office there close by and that someone would get notice to Lida some way or another."

William went alone to the quartermaster's tent. According to the quartermaster's list, there was a post facility in Cane Valley. So they just added that to all the other things that Jubal had mentioned. Corporal Garrison was reasonably sure it would be delivered.

The next few mornings were no different. Dismal, damp and depressing. The major had laid off the bottle long enough to order an inspection. He had proceeded to find fault with as many troopers as possible. In more than one instance he had berated a trooper over the most minor of infractions. Some caught an out lash for a speck of mud on a boot. Others had a less than perfectly creased and cleaned tunic. Others had justly been raked over the coals for lack of care for their arms or side arms. Those specific shortcomings could be deemed as dereliction of duty. All the others served only to lessen the spirits and morale of the troops and their squad leaders.

It was certainly a good omen that Johnny Reb made no attempt on the camp during these days. No one would have had much spirit to aggressively fight them off. No one really cared, save for his own hide. They had been relegated to menial patrol duty for weeks now and had been left to dry up from excessive routine and boredom. At least that was the way the lowly foot soldiers and cavalrymen saw it. The bickering, belittling sot of a man, who called himself their leader and commander, only added to the demoralization of the troopers, one and all, including William.

"Makes me just wanna go out and shoot somebody," Jubal complained as he sat down on his cot with a heavy sigh. "One speck on my coat and he climbs all over me. What gives him rights fer such when he done been on his bottle a week now?"

"Let it pass, Jubal. He didn't assign you any extra duty or anything else, did he?" William asked in hopes of quelling anger that was about to erupt into rage. He could see it in his friend's eyes and could hear it in his voice as well.

"I ain't about to shoot him and you know that, but I ain't goin' outta my way fer him none neither."

"I know that, but I just don't want to see you so aggravated."

"Tellin' ye about it helps."

"I would very much like to help you about other things also, my friend."

"Like what?"

"Will you hear me out and listen? Just listen to me for a bit? We have hit on this before, but I am thinking that I may not have talked about it in the best way."

"How long it gonna take?"

"I can't say right now. A lot of it depends on how you hear me and how well you understand me. I really wish that you would just be open-minded and listen as best you can to what I want to talk about. Is that asking too much?"

"I reckon not."

"Then why not throw a blanket over your shoulders and try to warm up a bit? You look cold and chilled."

"I am some."

Jubal threw a heavy blanket around his shoulders and drew his feet up under him and sat cross-legged. The blanket soon afforded some comforting warmth, and he began to relax. William intentionally delayed his questions until he saw the first signs of calm.

Understanding Jubal's childhood environment and the manner in which he was raised made William even more thankful for his own parents. His father had always been a strong positive influence on all his children. They were not wealthy, but they always had adequate warm clothing and plenty to eat. There was always provision for quality education, and cultural development was always encouraged. But more important than that, William's parents had raised him and the other kids in a strong Christian environment where love was personified and the Golden Rule was the norm. Discipline was strong, but always fair. Praises were always forthcoming, but they had to be earned. Chores and duties were a part of daily life, but there was no undue toil or task that was beyond expectation or capability.

There was always a time for family devotions and Bible reading. Church attendance was a weekly occurrence that involved the entire family. Individual faith was always nurtured and encouraged. Emphasis was placed on study and, thus, better understanding and stronger faith. Dwelling in the light was viewed as the only way of life. All else was darkness.

It was impossible for William to number his good fortunes and blessings, but he wanted to recall as much as possible. He wanted an answer and an example for each and every question that Jubal might ask. He wanted to be sure this time that he said all the right things at the right time. He wanted as much ammunition as he could muster to fight the prince of darkness. He so very much wished that he could lead his friend out of the darkness, and he certainly was in hopes that this would be the time it would happen.

William began by trying to uplift his friend. "Jubal, I know you have a kind heart and that I could call on you for help, if I needed it."

"I reckon so."

"I know that you would help a man with any need rather than harm him. I know you have done that in the past. I don't know all the things that you have done, and I don't need to know. Every little thought or every little deed that you have done is a part of you and always will be. We cannot change what happened yesterday. Yesterday is gone. It is gone for all of us, and all we have is the breath that we draw right now. All I am trying to say is that, in the eyes of man, you would be considered a good and respectable person."

"Some things I done I ain't right proud of."

"I think that is true for most of us, Jubal. I know of only one perfect person, and he was killed by a mob long, long ago. Do you know who I am talking about?"

"I thinkin' I know, but you tell me anyhow."

William breathed a slight sigh of relief. He was pleased that Jubal had listened to him so far and had not yet shown his usual signs of disinterest. He now felt he needed a moment or two to gather his thoughts and be sure that he did not get too eager. "I'll get there in a minute or so. Please, just be patient with me."

"I ain't got nowhere else to go. Reckon I can do that."

William remained silent for a moment, then spoke boldly as he sat up straight and tall.

"Do you believe in God?"

"Well, yeah, I reckon I do."

"Where did you first learn about Him?"

"I ain't fer sure."

"Think about it for a minute and see if you can recall."

Jubal cupped his chin in one hand and dropped his eyes to the dirt floor. It was plain to William that he was indeed in thought, and he could only imagine the scenarios running through the young man's mind.

"I ain't real sure but earliest I can recall is hearin' about Adam and his apple and a snake. Reckon my Ma must 'a been who told me that story. I spect I weren't but a toe head then."

"You think that story is true?"

"Ma say it were true."

"But what do you say?"

"Ain't no reason why it ain't, I reckon."

Not a definite answer, but not a denial either. Maybe this would be the time. Maybe he could find a way to shine just a glimmer of light and open blinded eyes.

William continued, "Do you believe...do you think that God exists today?"

"Yeah, I guess I do."

Again, not a committed answer, but enough to afford William a small measure of encouragement.

"I reckon most all folks knows there be a God. That be knowed just same as knowin' the sun comes up east and goes down west," Jubal added.

"I am glad that you do not deny God," William smiled as he spoke.

"How come that make you glad?"

William was ready for that one. "Because, if you deny God, then he will one day deny you. He will say that he never knew you. You will be cast into darkness."

"Don't recollect I ever knowed anything about that."

"I will come back to that later."

William just hoped that he could hold Jubal's attention long enough to get back to that thought. Right now he had other issues that he wanted to drive home. So far there was no evident disinterest to his attempted witness.

"Do you believe that Jesus was the Son of God?"

"What do ye believe?"

William had not really seen that coming, and it momentarily beset his concentration. He fumbled with his words for a moment; and then as if by divine inspiration, he had his answer. He would fire a salvo that could not fail to overcome his friend. Then he would continue in a way that he hoped would nurture interest and stir the innermost cords of his companion.

"Jubal, my friend, I believe that Jesus Christ is the one and only Son of God. I believe He was born a virgin birth and that He lived a perfect sinless life. I believe that He was crucified on a cross and laid in a tomb and that He rose again in three days. I believe that through His death and resurrection that I now have assurance of eternal life with Him in Heaven. That is what I believe, and I will not compromise that in any way. That is what I believe and that is what I stand on. There is more to the details and much more in the scriptures that confirms and reassures me. My belief is founded on my faith."

"You preachin' at me again, ain't you?"

"I suppose I am; but you asked me what I believe, and I told you."

"What about all that there hell-fire 'n damnation spoke on from circuit riders what come 'round back home? You ever read or hear anything on that?"

"That is part of what I meant when I told you there is much in the Bible to explain things like that. The Bible speaks the truth, and you must believe it or reject it, part and parcel, cover to cover, word for word."

"Granny Iverson say it be hard readin' and full with funny words and names."

"Names are just names, Jubal. Some people would think our names to be funny and strange. It just depends on family names, where you come from and things like that."

"Like from a ferin country or so?"

"Yes, exactly."

"Never did have much a hankerin' fer my give name, but I reckon that be what Ma wanted me named, and I just stick with it."

"The name does not make the man," William responded as he realized that he was way off track and that he had let it happen in just a heartbeat. He had to regroup and return to the issue at hand. "There are hundreds of names all through the Bible. Some of them are well known and some are mentioned only a time or two. I just want to know one thing right now."

Jubal made no verbal response, but the look on his face betrayed his false sense of confidence. He was sure that William was going to tell him about all those funny named characters, and he knew that he did not want to listen to all that. Granny Iverson had already told him most of those stories. Every time they were with her, she would tell them a story. Since she had come to live with them, he had heard them even more. Lida even tried to tell him stuff from the Bible. Just because he had trouble reading did not mean that he knew nothing about it. He knew more than he realized but apparently understood little of what he knew.

"Don't ye know most of it already anyhow?"

"That is not what I mean," William answered.

"Then what?"

"You asked me what I believe, and I told you. Now, all I want to ask is whether or not you believe what I said."

"I ain't got no reason not to believe it. I ain't never knowed ye to lie to me, Jubal replied in a simple child-like voice.

William sensed that opportunity was slipping away, but he was determined to continue. He drew in a deep breath and spoke, "The things I just said, do you realize what they mean? What they mean for me and what they mean for you?"

"I ain't so pine blank sure, but I wanna ask you a thing or two."

"Okay, I will answer best I know."

"Have ye ever done things ye ain't proud of?"

"Sure. I have, Jubal."

"Have ye ever kilt a man?"

"I do not know for sure. I have fired some shots in self-defense in this war, but I cannot say if they hit the mark or not. I never fired a weapon at any living being before the war."

"Well, I reckon I know fer sure that I can't say that. You seen what I done. But do that make any difference twixt us; me bein' badder than ye, since I know I kilt a man?"

"No, Jubal. It is not a question of good or bad. It is deeper than that. I simply want to know if you believe in God or not?"

"I reckon I believe just same as you or any other man, far as that goes."

"That is what I have been trying to point out to you. Believing or not believing. Acceptance or denial. It is those things that matter, not good or bad. All of us are bad in that we are born into darkness. Darkness is condemnation, but light is good. Light is salvation. I realize that sometimes it is very hard to accept the fact that a man can lead a life where he is ranked by other men as good, and yet dwell totally in darkness."

"I still don't reckon myself bein' bad."

"I don't think of you that way either, Jubal."

"Then why ye always raggin' on me over it all the time?"

"Jubal, it is only because I care about you. I care about your well-being and your life now and for all times to come."

"I know I ain't nowhere near smart as ye, but I just don't see how it makes all that much matter long as I keep my own nose clean and help a body when I can."

"What do you think about Heaven and Hell?"

"Circuit rider say we all bound fer Hell cause we all done somethin' or 'nuther sometime or 'nuther what be the cause fer it."

"Did that circuit rider ever tell you that we have all come up short but that there is still hope for us, a very definite hope for us?"

"Ye mean like hope fer us gettin' in Heaven?"

"Yes, that is exactly what I mean."

"I don't recollect him ever sayin' much on that. Course I never went and heered him much, cause he come around just ever now and then. He was always a spittin' fire when he did come."

"What sort of things did he preach when he was so full of fire, as you say?"

"Ain't real sure, but thinkin' it was most on cussin' and drinkin' and stuff like that."

"And you never have done any of that, have you?"

"I tasted corn squeezers a time or two. Never liked it none neither."

It was becoming apparent to William what was running around inside the biased mind of his friend. Probably the only real scriptural truths that he had ever been exposed to were the ones that his Granny Iverson had shared with him. The old circuit rider probably had no more education than anyone else in the little valley. He probably could read a bit better, but probably stumbled on all but the most familiar of passages. William had no thoughts on being judgmental, but it was indicative of how easily a person can be misled. He decided that actual scripture would be the best way. He would let his friend read it for himself and would help him wherever he needed.

"Can you read a little bit for me?"

"I ain't real good on readin' and I thought I had done told ye that."

"You did."

"What iffin I don't know all the words?"

"I will help you."

"I be getting' plum tuckered out, reckon we could put it off till some other time."

"We can wait as long as you will agree to read for me later on."

The limit had been reached for now. Jubal would not be receptive to any more today. He would hopefully listen more the next time.

"I wish that you could know what it means to me. I wish that I knew some way to tell you how blessed I have been. I wish I could tell you in such a way that you could know the strength that I draw out of my faith and my belief. I wish I could give you a little of what has been given to me. I do not want to hound you, and I will not do that. But I wish the blessings of the Lord for you, my friend."

Jubal offered no reply. Instead, he continued to stare at the ground beneath him. He gave no conscious thought to all that William had said, but there was a slight uneasiness gnawing at him from within. He still did not see himself as evil. Maybe not so good, but definitely not evil.

In a heartbeat, his thoughts flew to the old log cabin and the glowing fire in the stone hearth. There was peace and contentment there. At least, there was peace until the war came along. Now he wondered what his Ma was doing and if she was warm and well. He wondered if all the chores fell to her, or if she had help. Old Wes was about the only hope she had of real help outside the house and kitchen. He had no way of knowing. They were many miles away. How he wished he could know they were well. Right now he wished more than anything on earth that he could wrap his arms around his Ma and tell her how much he loved her. If he could just do that now, surely it would brighten her tired and weary eyes.

Then his heart near jumped out of his chest. What if somehow he should be killed and never see her again? He could never be sure that she would know that he loved her. He could never do anything to prove himself to her. He could never...never even see her again... never!

For Jubal, the night wore on at an agonizing slow pace. The only sounds from outside the tent were the occasional whip of the winter wind or the faint snort of a horse braving the night in a makeshift stable. The moon had to be near full, judging from the pale milky light that seeped into the tent. He thought about dashing out and walking around a bit. It might help clear his mind. No, better not. Some half-drunk sentry could get spooked.

William was at peace with himself. He was warm under his own blankets and could have easily slept the night through. He kept himself awake by choice. He listened intently and all the while kept remembering this verse and then that one. He knew what he needed to say now and would follow the path that he had been shown. That path had been more impressed upon him this very night, more so than it had ever been before. He knew where that path led. He had shown others that same way, and he was confident that he would be able to do so again. Jubal was in the valley now, but soon he would be beside the still waters.

Daybreak witnessed the fall of steady rain. At least it was not freezing cold as it had been on previous mornings. The falling rain masked any sounds of activity in the camp. It was as if no one was prepared to greet the new day. There seemed to be no need to stir. No Confederate forces had been seen in several days now, and not one raiding party had been reported in the entire length of the little valley.

The Major had not ordered any more patrols, nor did he seek enemy engagement. Evidently the war had taken a personal toll on him. Just a few short months past, he was well known for his leadership and his aggressiveness in pursuit of his assigned duties; and he expected no less of those under his command. He seemed to be a fair man. He delegated responsibility where possible, but stood behind those who followed his orders. He kept his uniform immaculate and had been known to brush away dust and grime even in the heat of battle. He shouldered responsibility without hesitation. But now, it seemed all courage came out of a long-necked whisky bottle. Possibly it was the drudgery of winter, or perhaps it could be blamed on the solitude of command. No one would say for sure. No one really knew. It had, however, affected the unity of the entire camp. About the only ones who held up the standards were the cooks and the two blacksmiths. The bugler no longer blew reveille or sounded taps. Desertions occurred almost every day, but none were pursued.

The events of the new day would change everything. The Major had not emerged from his tent before mid-morning. His aide found him lying face down in his tent with his hands clasped around a bottle. He had imbibed too much, and the spirits' devil had taken away his very breath.

The unfortunate news soon touched every ear in the camp. Most were in somewhat of a bewildered state of indecisive apprehension as to what would befall them. No one expressed concern over the Major himself. They were more concerned who would be sent to take his place, and where they might be sent as a result. They had become used to their uneventful routine. All were made aware that this could come to a halt and that they could be flung headlong into mortal conflict. Johnny Reb had suffered some scathing defeats, but he was not beaten yet.

It was precisely those thoughts that snapped Jubal away from the fears that had beset him all the night before. Without really thinking about it, he checked his Enfield, taking care that it was clean and well oiled. He assembled and checked his field pack and bedrolls. No telling how soon the next shots would be fired. All the troopers followed suit in their own manner. The Major and his bottle had unceremoniously provided a catalyst that was to transform the unit to action that it had never seen before.

"Reckon they done telegraphed somebody about all this ain't they, William?"

"I am sure that has already been done."

"I say we be on marchin' orders 'fore ye have time to think on it."

"Well, we could stay right here. You never know. We are not that far from other units and neither are we that far from Washington City. I guess it just depends on who they send and from where."

"I ain't never seen a place big as Washington City. I might wanna go."

"We will have to wait and see, Jubal."

"Bet they got things there make yer eyes bug out."

"I suppose."

"Ye ever been?"

"No."

"Might get yer chance now."

William wished so very much that he could ask his friend about his thoughts during the night but that would not happen now. It was obvious that the thoughts of big city times and pleasures were the focus in his friend's eyes now. The influences of darkness once again came to the forefront, driving away any hope for enlightenment. All he could see to do for his beloved friend now was to ask God to watch over him and to protect him from evil influences. Previous childish expectations and desires for things of the world now leapt up in his face and blinded his judgment. William was not that much more advanced in years, but he was decades ahead of his friend in maturity. He silently prayed that orders to Washington City would not be forthcoming.

Orders did come, but not as expected.

The major's body had not much more than been wrapped and loaded into a buckboard when his long-time friend and confidant, Sergeant Jugg Henry Dunn, came calling for Jubal. He wanted him to go along to take the body back on the first leg of the journey to Washington City.

Jubal was somewhat surprised at the request. He viewed it as just that and never considered it an order. Jugg had never ordered him to do anything. He had always just asked. Now he spoke in a broken voice when before he had dripped with confidence and authority. His eyes were those of a tired and weary old warrior, not those of a leader. It was plain that his spirit was broken and that he grieved deeply for his long-time master. He had long since been a free man, but remained enslaved to the Major out of sheer devotion.

"Ye want me, and William too?"

"I speck I wants both. I know I wants both you boys," came the reply. "Get yer gear ready. We be leavin' fer Nokesville township by mid-afternoon. Now move yer butts and be at his tent on the quarter." He turned and wheeled away in a heartbeat. William thought he saw a massive big arm brush at a dampened eye as he made the first steps of his retreat.

The pine-box-laden buckboard was hitched to two big Belgians. They were led by hand and turned over to the sergeant. He climbed into the driver's seat and took the reins.

Jubal had been told to take the point with three other cavalrymen. William was to ride alongside the sergeant. All had been hastily issued ample ammunition. Each carried a side arm as well. It was not expected that any trouble would arise, but there was just no sense in going off half prepared. The detail set out in good time and was soon alone on a road in what was once an enemy stronghold. All knew and recognized that fact, but none spoke of it.

Sergeant Jugg remained silent as the broad quartered steeds plodded along at a tireless pace. William did not think it proper to attempt conversation. Instead he asked that the grieving soul receive comfort, not as a soldier, but as a man. William truly wished that there were some kind of special words that he might say to bring that comfort. Instead he just left it to the only one he knew who was capable of such comfort.

Jubal seemed to be back to his old self. Every now and then, William could see him studying the road for signs that might betray an enemy. He rode short forays out ahead of all the others to look and listen for any tell-tell signs that might be carried on a wisp of wind. He made short jaunts off to either side of the road to search out parallel tracks or maybe just to cross another track; but so far nothing. Hopefully it would remain that way. At any rate, awareness and alertness were heightened.

William saw it, and the big black man seated beside him saw it too. "That boy be good out on point."

"Yes sir," William responded somewhat surprised.

"He be a good trooper. I most sure he be a goner when I find him all shot."

"He still has some problems," William responded with some trepidation. "I think he needs to be watched."

"What you mean?"

William hesitated a minute thinking that possibly he had said the wrong thing at the wrong time. He sighed then began. "He gets pretty bad confused and down on himself at times. He misses his kinfolk and his home. He has mentioned going back there several times here lately."

"You thinkin' he gonna desert us?"

"I thought so at one time, but not so much now."

"How come ye change up yer mind on him now?"

"He wanted me to write a letter to a girl back home. I believe he just has had a bad case of missing home, and it got to him. That's all."

"He goin' back thar when this here war be over, or he gonna stay in Mr. Lincoln's army?"

"I doubt he will want to stay here a day more than he can help," William said with a good measure of certainty. "I plan to return home myself."

"How ye earn yer keep back home," the sergeant wanted to know.

"I plan to teach in college and to help my father run survey lines whenever I can find the time. I would like to learn that skill too."

"What about him?" the sergeant asked as he pointed to the front toward Jubal.

"I suppose that he would go back to farming. As far as I know, that is all he has ever known."

"He shore know his way around in woods and mountains. He make a good injun scout, I bet."

"I've been helping him read some and trying to give him just a taste of what some proper schooling could do for him. He seems eager enough to learn, but always seems to get sidetracked."

"What ye been readin' him?"

"We read from the Bible. That is the only book I have with me. It stays in my pack all the time."

"Son, are ye one of God's chillren?"

"I have indeed, seen the light. I have been trying to get him to see it too," William replied as he pointed to Jubal.

"What ye been tellin' him?"

"I have been trying to point out to him that just because you are a good person and have done good by other people, helping wherever you can, and upholding the law, that alone will not bring you out of the darkness. I don't think he has ever understood the light from the dark. He always comes back to the issue that he has never really done anything wrong. At least he owns up to no wrong to me and has not said anything to make me think that he has anything to be ashamed of."

"That ain't gonna work, son. It ain't gonna work. Ye need no harpin' on right and wrong. All men is wrong and ye best be showin' him how come they be wrong and what the Lawd done already done makin' it right fer them what wants it right. Don't it say there some place that all is wrong and comes up short?"

"Do you read the Bible?" William responded somewhat in surprise. He had just not bothered to imagine that the son of a slave would be a reader, let alone a believer.

"I don't read much good, but I makes out most words. I do best I can."

The big burley sergeant opened up to William and soon made known the better part of his life's story. He told how that he had been born into slavery way down south on a rice plantation. His mammy could remember tales and stories told her by her mammy, who had come over on the middle passage and sold to a cane grower. Then the whole family was sold to a rice man, who brought them on over here.

He told how the rice man was a cruel taskmaster and how he could still, to this day, see his pappy being flogged. He could see the whelps and scars across his back. He even had one or two scars of his own.

His mother had told him stories that she had heard from the rice man's missus and her house servants. He remembered her as being a kind and gentle woman, and she never raised a hand to anyone in anger. It was she, who had so much influence on him that he later became a regular at the meeting houses.

It was along about this time that his mammy died. Lady Madeline had used her influence on the rice planter to bring about his and his pappy's freedom. He always thought that she had somehow bought and paid it herself. Soon after, the young freedman and his pappy came north in search of work. They had settled near Baltimore where they had been hired as coachmen and drivers by a well-off sea trader who owned several merchant vessels. One of the sons was a young army lieutenant who wanted and could afford a personal valet. Thus, the beginning of a relationship between that same young officer and a boy, who was raw and untrained to the ways of the military. Time would mold them both, but the castings were to be far different from each other.

"Ye needs show him what it say in there about bein' in sin, which ain't no differ'nt than dark as ye put it. Then ye needs show him how that done been took away by Him. Tell him about believin' or not believin'. Ye needs tell him how not believin' will make him wail come that great gittin' up time. Ye needs tell him about fires in Hell. Hell fire, he needs Hell skeert right outta him, and I be one who do it too iffin I ever have chance."

"He might listen to you better than he would me."

"Reckon I could speak at him, but you got no call shuckin' off on me what ye done commenced. He be yer friend, and I be a boss man. Boss man ain't no friend, never no more in this here damned war, no sir."

"What if you just told him to listen to me?"

"Ain't no use. He listen only iffin ye tell him good and true just like it say in yer book. That be only way. I tellin' ye, it best not be harpin' so much on good'n bad all time. He know ye well 'nuff know ye tell him no lies, don't he?"

"I think so."

"Then ye be tellin' him a heap all along just by the ways ye live yer life. He learn as much by watchin' ye as by all ye says to him. Ye gotta live it same as ye talk it. It say that in there somewhere too. My mammy done told me that way back years past, and she ain't never lied to me."

The trek to the railroad station east of Washington City played out long past dusk. It had become considerably cooler upon first spotting the fire breathing, steaming locomotive sitting at the Fair Junction station. It had arrived only a short while ago and had been ordered to await the body. The elder Mr. Dunn had used his influence to secure the train and have it dispatched to the nearest station. As it has always been, money, power and political associations were used in that influence. Mr. Dunn, the merchant and trader, had wielded that same influence to prevent his son from being assigned to regimental duty where he could be exposed to heated combatants and fierce battles. Now he wished that maybe he had not done so. It would have been better had his son died in battle than in a drunken stupor. He had attempted to insulate his sons from the war in spite of the fact that he had made huge profits from that same conflict.

He had managed to procure very envious and profitable contracts from the Union army. He became involved in materials shipment for the supply of large numbers of troops. He moved munitions and all manner of freight inland on any sort of craft that he or the Army could procure. Three of every ten ships that tied up at eastern ports were registered under the name of Dunn.

He was well known in Washington City circles and knew how to lean on the right people to accomplish what he desired. He was easy going and held sway over the politico before they could get onto him. It was in this manner that he procured a train and crew to transport his oldest son all the way back to Baltimore. Newspapers and telegraphs would say that he had died in the line of duty and would offer no other details. His son would be laid to rest with full military rites and would have none but the finest of everything.

The elder Dunn had no intention of outwardly showing emotion. How could he? He was a man of wealth and power, and with power came strength. Strength would not allow any sign of weakness. However, he did not consider his belief to be a weakness. He found himself not knowing for sure if his beloved son had ever made any confessions of his wrongs or if he had ever realized the fate he would face when his death day came. That day was now here.

He wished that he could somehow know the answer to that. He wished that he had taken more time to talk with his children when they were of the young and formidable years. He wished that he had been less focused on material possessions and more in tune to the pursuit of things that really did make a difference in life. He had other children, sure, but this was his firstborn and should have been the one to follow his success. Would not the happiness and the success of the father naturally fall to the son?

He stood on the station platform and stared out into the darkness. A single tear crested down his cheek. He quickly flicked it away with a gloved-hand, and pulled the collar of his greatcoat higher around his neck. The wind had a chill to it, and he passed it off to his companion as that. But inwardly he cried out, "Gracious Lord Almighty, I have failed my son, and I have failed you as well. My heart is heavy, and now my burden is heavy as well. I ask you for strength. I plead for your comfort and peace. I know that I could have been more faithful to you and to your commands. But I ask you, I beg of you, that you receive my son unto you and that you be merciful to him. I cannot know the whereabouts of his soul at this very moment. I can only hope. Hope is all that I have, and now it is weak. Mend up my heart, Lord. Restore my faith. Carry me through this valley, if it be in your blessed will."

Sergeant Jugg and William rode the buckboard right up onto the station platform as the stationmaster took the lines and gently coaxed the Belgian team into place near the train. They were then informed that the entire party, including all animals and the buckboard would board the train as orderly and as soon as possible. Everything had already been seen to. There would be food and dry warm clothing on the train. There would even be oats and hay for the horses.

All were to continue on, all the way to Baltimore. Everything had been approved through the proper authorities, and there would be no repercussions for anyone. They were to consider themselves under orders from Grant himself. Nothing more needed to be said. The train had two stock cars, a flatcar for the buckboard, two coaches for the troops and a private car at the rear. The major would ride there with all the finery that his father's influence and power could buy.

The train rumbled along at a steady but slow pace. Seemed that it had to stop for some reason at nearly every bend or crossing along the route. It was a total new experience for Jubal, and he seemed to be somewhat mesmerized by it. He slept little. To him the behemoth spoke loudly; and the constant clatter of iron wheels on iron rails made sleep and rest a chore. He had found a hard wooden bench, and used his bedroll as a pillow and stretched out as best he could.

Each man had been handed a lunch pail containing bread and blackberry jam. There was a thick slab of baked red ham and cold potatoes. Each had eaten his fill and was grateful to have had such a feast as they had not seen in days. Tired, but filled, most had fallen fast asleep. Not Jubal. True, he was filled. But the noise of the train coupled with the sight of death that lingered with him prevented his sleep.

He did not know why or how, but right now he felt at ease with himself and with the world. He was out of any area where there might be Rebs, and he had just eaten his fill. The coal fired stoves in the coach took away the chills of the darkness. Occasional lantern glow could be seen as beacons in the dark. He did not know how he could feel this way now; when just a short time past, he had been so fearful for his own life and so tormented within that he could force not a moment of peace or quiet. It never occurred to him that there was another person who was willing to intercede for him and that intercession was what had brought peace to him tonight.

He raised his head enough to look around the coach. He could see that most were sound asleep, and the sounds coming from them only served to reaffirm their restfulness. He rested his head on the bedroll and listened to the click-clack of the wheels. It soon became a rhythmic beat, a relaxing monotone. It was not long before he too fell victim to the mesmerizing chatter of iron. He joined in and contributed his part to the choir of unharmonious songs.

Baltimore spread out beyond imagination. Never had anyone described such enormity and so many people. Many paraded up and down the massive station platform to and from carriages and coaches of beauty and elegance beyond imagination. There were teams of horses that could pass for twins. Jubal noticed one particular team, each animal solid black without a single distinguishing mark. He could not imagine their worth. This was what he had dreamed of back home, but he never imagined the finery that could be displayed in coaches such as these. Then he remembered just how poor by comparison he was. He was reminded of his family and how they had scratched a living from the land for generations. If he was ever underprivileged, he never knew it until now.

It seemed that all of the fair city was at the beckoned call of Master Dunn. Everyone spoke well of him and portrayed him as a kind man, who could be trusted and counted on in times of need. He demanded honesty and integrity of all his associates and received it. He rewarded honest labor with fair wages. He supported family unity and encouraged fathers to educate their children at higher institutions of learning so they could become prosperous and carry on in his own tradition. He supported his church and encouraged missions far and wide.

His son was laid to eternal rest expediently. A private service was held with select attendance. Sergeant Jugg stood at the head of the copper-clad casket for the duration of the entire service. He had received the services of Master Dunn's private valet and resultantly gleamed immaculate in his gold-trimmed Union blue uniform. An honor guard and bearers were equally attired. Jubal and the rest of the transport detail stood attentively in single file behind their sergeant. None would remember the words or the eulogy, but all would remember the somberness of the old man. He shed no tears that could be seen, but his face betrayed his heart. He could not cover up his grief.

Late afternoon found Sergeant Jugg and his charges back at the station platform. The train that bore them here would arrive shortly and carry then back to Washington City where they were to report to one Captain Jeremiah Davis. Captain Davis did not know now that they were coming, but he would soon receive instruction in detail as to what his charge would be. He too, would know the influence of Master Dunn.

A civilian courier approached the broad-shouldered black sergeant and inquired his name.

"Sir, are you Sergeant Dunn?"

"Yes."

"I have been sent to inform you that you and your party are to dine at the Romney Hotel at precisely five this evening. It is one block east from here. You will have ample time before your train is ready to depart. There has been an unexpected delay. I will keep you informed of any changes as I myself learn of such. Do you need direction or assistance from me in any fashion?"

"Is this here hotel a place a darkie can go in and eat too?"

"It will not be an issue, not tonight, I assure you."

It had been an issue in other places and in other times, but tonight Sergeant Jugg decided not to dwell on it. He was feeling a bit hungry, and there was no doubt that he was tired. He was quite sure that the rest of his detail fell into that category as well. He wasted no time in forming up the detail and marching them the one block distance to the hotel. They were met at the door and ushered into a private dining room. Here also nothing had been spared by Master Dunn. He appreciated what had been done for his son, and this was his way of saying "Thank you."

Ham steaks so thick and swimming in red-eye gravy. Baked sweet potatoes, piping hot and seeping with yellow butter. Steaming white rice. Golden squash with a sugar topping melted into a butter and crunch crust. Jubal had never seen nor tasted such a feast. Another exposure to the finer things of life. How much better than this could it ever be?

Apple cake was served for dessert, carried in on silver trays by waiters in snow white coats. It all passed so quickly. It was wonderful to behold, but now it was all over and just a memory. How he wished that he could have Lida on his arm and sit her down to something like this. If he could give her things like this, she would be at his side for the rest of his life. Plentiful food quieted his hunger, but materialism stirred his desire.

The waiters cleared the table and then brought in a brandy flask and left the detail to their own choices. Jubal tasted the brandy without knowing or caring what the others did. He deservedly caught the eye of his sergeant, but received no reprimand from him. He had a second taste, and a third. William was the one who eventually intervened to bring an end to the temptations of the flask. He informed Jubal that it was time to go back to the station platform. Jubal agreed and exited the hotel along with all the other troopers and the sergeant. He felt the warm glow of the brandy and vowed that someday he would have more of the golden nectar and that he too would serve it to his guests.

The train was not at the station when they arrived, and the courier informed them that it was just a few miles off. It should arrive within the hour. Jubal found a convenient crate and leaned back against it to rest. Relaxation soon turned to slumber and snoring. Failing light would bring cooled winds across the platform. Jubal would not feel them. He was filled with the warmth and false sense of security that came from the flask. No wonder that the young Major Dunn enjoyed partaking of the libations.

It was dark when they boarded the train. This time it was only a single coach and a lone stock car. There was no fire in the coach heaters, and the only protection from the chill was the blankets that had been placed on the hard backed wooden seats. To some, it made no difference. They were warmed from the inside, and soon cocooned themselves in blankets and resumed their slumber. It would take the best part of the darkened hours for the lumbering beast to make its way into Washington City. Jubal had to be awakened upon arrival. His head throbbed and his stomach readily told him of its uneasiness. It was a significant effort just to dismount the train and retrieve his already saddled mount. Thankfully, someone had stored his gear right alongside his horse, else he would have had no idea where to find it. He was beginning to wish that he had not enjoyed so much of the finery that he thought he wanted so bad. He had no real knowledge of all the things that his experiences were teaching him, nor did he realize that he was being looked after by a power greater than himself. He did not know that he was the subject of the prayers of more than one person.

The telegraph kept Captain Davis informed of a timeframe. He met the detail at the platform. Jubal heard him say that they were to spend the day and the coming night awaiting further instruction. This would mean a day and a night in Washington City itself. He had wanted to come here and see all the sights and the people. Now, right this moment, it did not seem to be such a grand thing. All he really wanted was a good hot breakfast and a place to lay his unrelenting, pounding head. Both were soon provided.

It was well past noon when Jubal awoke. It had been some time since he had slept in a full-sized bed with clean sheets and a full stuffed soft feather pillow. Nature begged his attention, but he was reluctant to come out of his soft warm nest. Necessity won, and he was on his feet. He noted that William was already up and seated at a desk to the side of the room. He was occupied with pen and paper, no doubt writing to some of his folks. The warm breakfast had died and his consciousness was soon captured by the thought of where he might sate himself once more.

"Hey William, I be a mite hungry. Go with me to eat some place."

"You missed lunch already, didn't you?"

"I reckon I did. Needed sleep."

"You got a bit tanked up last evening, if I do say so."

"Never done that back home. Reckon I had a bit much at that."

"You feel okay now?"

"Just be hungry as a big old she wolf with pups."

"Captain Davis has directed us to eat at the tavern across the street from here. He said that last evening was paid for by Master Dunn, but from here on out it is an army expense, and they do not normally pay for such luxury. The tavern has ample food, but not at so much cost."

"I make no fuss about that," Jubal intoned as he pulled on his boots and gathered himself into a presentably dressed trooper.

"I ate lunch there as you slept, and they have good food."

"Good, lead the way."

"They also have spirits flowing all around if you want more," William retorted, half-jokingly and with simultaneous admonition.

"Made me sleep plumb powerful."

"Made you drunk is what it did."

"You drink any?"

"No."

"How come?"

"I did not need that to make me sleep."

"Tasted good though, huh?"

"I could not say about that. I did not partake."

"Why?"

"I did not want any of it. I do not like the taste of it. I believe it leads to other things that I do not need or want. I just have no desire for the taste of alcohol. Besides that, I believe it to be an influence of evil and wrongdoing. I was not brought up around it and have no desire for it."

"You ever been drunk?"

"No, and will not be."

"Well, ain't you just Mr. Goody-Good hisself?"

"No, Jubal. I do not consider myself a goody-good as you put it. It is simply a practice that I want no part of. I simply do not need it, and really neither do you."

Flashes of his Pa and the laudanum bottle coursed through his brain. Never would he stoop so low to cravings for a bottle of anything. There was just no way he could ever be as bad as his Pa.

The tavern was crowded when they entered. Soon, a bar maid greeted them and asked what was their desire. William explained they were here at the directive of one, Captain Davis, and that they wanted only to have some hot food. She pointed to a corner table. There sat Sergeant Jugg and three other troopers. William and Jubal joined them. In no short order a big bowl of steaming stew was brought to them along with a half pone of corn bread. A small tankard of ale was placed before each. William pushed his, untouched, to the center of the table.

William was nowhere near as hungry as his friend and only made minimal progress at the stew. He did like the hot corn bread and soft butter and thereby managed to gain his fill. Jubal ate heartily and noted that his companion had passed on the stew.

"You gonna eat that?"

William eased the bowl to his friend. Its contents soon vanished. Jubal then turned up the tankard and drank it down. The empty vessel thunked down on the heavy oak table as a sleeve served to wipe his mouth. His eyes found the full tankard that was served to his friend.

"Gimme that."

"I wish you would leave it."

"Why?"

"I don't think you can handle it very well. We've already talked about that and you know how I feel about it."

William had not finished speaking until another bar girl appeared at the table, walking up first to William and draping herself all over his back and shoulders. Her dress did not leave much to the imagination. Quite well endowed, deep cleavage was hard not to see. Sliding around to where he could see her full features, she whispered softly in his ear. In an instant, William removed her arms from around him and told her to find herself another John.

"Well damn, my name ain't John, but reckon ye can hug on me some," Jubal crowed. Someone at a nearby table guffawed, but Jubal was hooked. He never heard the laughs or the cat calls. All he saw were big bulging mounds of soft flesh and red lips. He ignored the pleading of his friend to resist her and her teasing.

The young mountain boy could not say with any certainty how the night had passed so quickly. He had awakened alone in a strange bed. Only the faint gray light of dawn penetrated the darkness. There was no heat in the room, and the chill of November air found its way into every nook of the closet-sized room. He was clad only in a ragged and faded night shirt, the likes of which he had never donned before. He found his uniform draped over an old ladder-back chair with a seat made from white oak splits. At least there was one item in the room that he knew and recognized. His boots lay haphazardly behind the chair. He quickly dressed and exited the room. A narrow hallway led to a window at the opposite end of the passage. A quick glance confirmed what he feared. He had no idea where he was, and he was alone.

He spotted the narrow staircase and descended it. He opened the door at the bottom landing and was at once met eye-to-eye by the son of a slave, the Sergeant.

"You ready now?"

"Ready fer what?"

"Ye ought be ready fer me whup yer butt."

Jubal was sure that he had crossed the line and could already feel the thrashing he was about to get.

"I been upstairs all night too. So I spect we best be movin' off," the big broad-shouldered sergeant commanded as he broke a broad smile. "I found me one too. Big mammy with meat on her bones."

Jubal ran his hands into his pockets. They were empty. The five-dollar gold piece and the CSA saddle button were gone. The sergeant had to explain to him why and how his pockets were empty. He had paid and paid well for the tenderness that was now not even a memory. His mouth felt dry as cotton and his head thumped out the dull rhythm of his heartbeat. He began to question how much of this Washington City life that he really wanted.

Early November 1864 saw the election of Abraham Lincoln as president and commander-in-chief of the Union army. He had carefully chosen a candidate for the office of the vice presidency that would garner the Union sympathizer vote in the south. He had chosen none other than Andrew Johnson from East Tennessee, who had a reputation as a Democrat but was also noted for his staunch support of the Constitution and the preservation of the Union.

The infestation of politics in Washington City kept it a constant din of meetings, conventions, party going, influence peddling and bribing. Handshakes served as inking contracts and cross-party dealings. If only for a few short days, it seemed that everyone was too busy with the state of affairs in the Capital city to really pay heed to the fact that there was still a war going on.

Few of the cavalrymen or the infantry knew much about the election nor did they really care. There were exceptions, however, and William was one of them.

"Hey, Jubal, what do you think about your man being Vice President now?"

"Who?"

"Johnson, of course."

"Don't recollect I know him."

William turned the newspaper that he had been reading so that his friend could see the headlines. "It says here that he hails from Greeneville, Tennessee. I think that is not far from your area. Have you been there?"

"Reckon not. Ain't never been nowhere but where this here army done sent me. I never been nowhere, I tellin' ye."

"I suppose it makes no matter. You want me to see if I can find a map and learn exactly where it is?"

"Might be good knowin' where it be," Jubal responded. "I might go there one of these here days."

"I bet he will be making trips between here and his home on a regular basis. Would it not be something if you could travel home with him sometime? Greeneville ought to put you real close to your valley, I would think."

"Which way that be?"

William pointed to what he determined to be a south westerly direction. "That way as far as I can tell."

"How far ye reckon?"

"I would think about four or five hundred miles," again William was guessing.

"Well, I reckon I'll just go tell this here Mr. Johnson that I wanna ride with him next time he goes off to...to...Green...Greenhill."

"I am sure that there is much more to it than that, my friend, but I do hope that it can happen for you sometime real soon."

"Wish we be on our way there now," Jubal said excitedly, with the idea of returning home freshly planted in his mind.

"I will see what I can do to help you go through chain of command with your request. All they could do would be say no. You being from near his home might be a help. You just never know about these political persons. They do business in a strange way sometimes."

"Don't know nuthin' on them kind, and don't reckon I needs be knowin' his ways. I reckon I leave my part to ye or some other educated man."

In due time, William did draft a letter to the newly-elected second in command and sent it via Sergeant Jugg and the courier service, up the chain of command. Neither he nor Jubal really expected any response from it. They had no way of knowing its routing or who would read the words it contained.

William reminded Jubal that he needed to work on reading and writing skills. He reasoned with him that he might not always have someone else at hand who could or would do his writing for him. Jubal did not hesitate in agreeing to that and secretly and inwardly wished that he could read and write on an equal level with his friend. That also reminded him that he had promised William that he would read some from the Bible. That thought brought back waves of remembrances about the good and the bad talks. He was not really sure what it was that William had wanted him to see. There was this thing about coming out of the dark and seeing the light. How could he be so set on the differences between daylight and dark?

"I reckon we could read a spell. I told ye that I would listen real good, and I aim on doin' what I say I would."

"Do you remember what we were talking about?"

"Day time and dark. Good and bad."

"I want to read to you about something else this time. It is related to what we have been talking about, but in a different manner."

"How ye mean?"

"It takes a little time to tell it the way it needs to be told. Why don't we go across the street and have our stew? Then we can come back and kick off our boots and take up right where we are now. Would that be acceptable to you?"

"Yep, don' see why not."

"Can I ask one favor before we go?" William quired.

"What that be?"

"Will you not have the ale tonight?"

"Do it make that much matter to ye?" Jubal asked in a pleasant but inquisitive voice.

"Just for tonight, it does."

"Then I reckon I do it fer ye."

The tavern was once again crowded with hardly a seat. The banter seemed to be louder than usual, and the crowd reveled in a much rowdier manner. The bar girls were almost in a run to answer the calls of the patrons before their patience wore thin and they became unruly. The oak floorboards were slick with spilled ale and other spirits. William and Jubal looked at each other, as if to wonder if they really wanted to be here or not. In that instant, William felt a hand on his shoulder. Turning, he saw that it was his sergeant, pointing them to a side table where he sat alone. He had noted their bewildered look and had come to their aid in finding a table and getting a decent meal.

All three were seated and soon served bread and stew. No tankards of ale were offered. No explanation was offered by the big burley sergeant, and no one asked why. He had not wanted it at his table tonight and had made it known to the bar girls. All three ate with very little conversation. None of the trollops made any passes at any of them, again by the sergeant's instruction.

Finally, Sergeant Jugg spoke as he looked directly at Jubal. "You not be spendin' all night here again and me neither. I wished I could take it back sayin' I never done it, but that ain't so. I ain't proud a what I done, but I done it just same. It ain't gonna happen no more by me, and it ain't gonna happen no more fer you either. Unnerstand that?"

Jubal did not answer.

"I ask if ye unnerstand."

"I reckon I do," Jubal replied sarcastically. "I reckon it be good fer ye but not fer me. That be what it is?"

"It ain't good fer me neither. It be wrong, and it be wronger fer me cause how I knows better. I let up on behavin' proper, like Good Book say. Now, ye done eat, so ye gittin' outta here with yer friend, now. He done told me how he been tryin' talk ye outta such doin's. I thinkin' ye best listen good too."

"I recollect what he say," Jubal rebutted.

"Then you boys get outta this here place and get yer talkin' commenced. I be checkin' on ye by and by."

"You gonna stay here in spite of all ye tellin' me?"

"No, Jubal Stewart. I been asked to speak to a man about a letter what been done writ to a mite high up officer."

With that, the sergeant stood, reached for his hat, squared it away and headed for the door. His dining companions were not far behind. Outside, the chilling rain fell in a fine mist. The broad shoulders of the sergeant soon disappeared as he rounded the corner and headed up the broad and rutted quagmire that served as one of the principal avenues of the city. William wasted no time in crossing to the hotel and seeking its refuge from the dampness. Jubal was only a couple of paces to his rear. He too felt the chill of the rain and thought of the warm glow that the tankards of ale could have produced.

The hotel lobby was a buzz of activity as gentlemen gathered in random groups engaged in muffled conversations. The two troopers made their way to the staircase and were soon in the sanctity of their room. The distant voices in the lobby below made their way into their ears, but words were indiscernible. It made no difference. Chances were good that the banter was all of a political nature, of which William had knowledge but no real interest. Jubal neither knew nor cared.

William recalled what he and Sergeant Jugg had discussed about talking with Jubal and his personal need. The horrid damnation of the evil of darkness had always been taught him. It was only natural that he would see that issue as a key reason to overcoming evil. He well knew that neither goodness nor works could earn safe passage into the light. He knew that it was a gift of the greatest grace that ever was or ever would be. He never considered this was what people would need to hear. He always believed that people needed to see that they were in darkness and realize all its perils before they could ever come to salvation. The sergeant suggested that more could be accomplished out of love than could be gained by intimidation or accusations.

Jubal was soon sprawled out on his bed with hands clasped behind his head. William sat at a small table and leafed through his well-worn Bible. He soon made his way to the book of Romans and found the verse that he wanted Jubal to hear. Just getting him to hear it and possibly read it for himself would be a new beginning for them both. William would set out on a new effort at trying to reveal the real truth to his friend. Jubal would be hearing words that had been read to him before, but whose meaning had never sunk in.

William stood with open Bible in hand and crossed over to his friend's side. He sat on the edge of the bed, and without being asked, Jubal sat up and acknowledged his friend.

"Here, Jubal, let me show you this, and then you read it back to me."

"Where?"

"Right here," as fingers coursed over the words in the third chapter, twenty-third verse.

"All...uh...all have...signed and...come short of...uh...the... glory of God."

"No, not signed, but sinned. Do you know what that is?"

"Well ye done told me all about bein' bad. Ain't that about nigh the same thing?"

"That is not the thing I want you to see right now."

"Then what?"

"What was the first word you read?"

"All," came the haughty reply.

"Does that include me?"

"Reckon it do."

"Does it include you as well."

"I guess."

"Then does that not mean that I have come up short, that you have come up short and that everyone else on the face of this earth has come up short?"

"I ain't fer sure what ye mean."

"Do you agree that all includes you?"

"Yeah, I can understand that."

"Look at the words on the page. Does it not say that all have sinned?"

Jubal ran his finger over the words and seemed to be deep in thought. William could see that he was silently mouthing the words.

He remained silent and allowed his friend to read as much and as long as he wished.

"It do say that in fact."

"Do you know what that means? Do you realize what sin is?"

"Not sure."

"Darkness, Jubal. Sin is evil and comes from living in the darkness." William realized that he had reverted back to life long tenets about salvation and already knew that these methods were not going to work here. He had started off in a new way but had so quickly fallen back to his old ways. "Sin is wrong doing, Jubal; and God hates it. We can be pardoned from it, if we want it."

The confused look on his friend's face told him that he had stirred the waters enough for one time. If the words of that one single passage could sink in, then there would be something to build on. William realized that the teacher needed some help, as well as the pupil.

"Why don't you think on that for the night, Jubal? We can talk about it more tomorrow and read some more too. I just want you to understand as we go along. It is not really that hard. You just need to understand, and I think I can help you do that."

"Good by me."

William blew out the lamp, and both were soon bedded down for the night. Jubal was glad that he had a warm bed and a roof over his head instead of a canvas tent and a bedroll. William lay awake, deep in thought. Just possibly he had cracked the ice and could really make a difference now. It was soon that he could hear the regular rhythmic breathing of his companion. Silently he slipped from his bed and sank to his knees. There he asked, first, for forgiveness for all his shortcomings; and then he pleaded for guidance and wisdom in his efforts to win his friend. There on his knees, the young man felt a wave of chills down his back, and at the same instant became engulfed in a peacefulness like he had not known before.

No one really expected any reply from the Vice President elect, least of all Jubal. Needless to say, both he and William were surprised when Captain Davis came to speak personally and directly to them. As their officer in charge, he had contact enough with Jubal to know that he had not personally penned the letter. He suspected that William had written it, and he had come to verify his suspicions.

"Mr. Johnson has read your letter and desires to speak with you. You are to report to him in the morning precisely at ten. Sergeant Dunn will instruct you and provide the details. Do you have any questions?"

"Naw sir."

"Then you will report to your sergeant immediately. Is that clear?"

"Yes sir."

"Then that will be all," the captain answered as he stood tall and motionless.

It was ironic that the two young troopers would elect this very instant to recall proper military custom and courtesy, but so it was. Both snapped to attention and delivered a crisp hand salute, holding until the captain returned it. With that, he did an about face and was gone.

"I suppose we better find Sergeant Jugg," William said with evident surprise in his voice.

"What ye reckon this be all about, William?"

"Well, you both are from the same general area back down there in Tennessee, and I am thinking that Mr. Johnson just wants to talk with someone from back home."

"Makes me a mite edgy."

"I understand that," William replied. "We best find Sergeant Jugg."

Captain Davis wasted no time in seeing to the requests of the Mr. Johnson. He had already communicated with the big sergeant and informed him of all that would-be happening and all that needed to be done to that end. The boys did not have to go find the sergeant. He found them in no short order.

"Jubal, son, get yerself spiffied up by sunup. I mean it. Ye best look like any good army trooper ought look. Get yer boot black on, and clean ever piece ye got, packs and all. Both of ye. Ye both goin'. Cap'n done tell me I best whup you in shape and right now too. I gonna show ye how to report in proper and all, and ye best pay me yer best heed. I ain't got much time, so's we best get at it. Both ye get over to the quartermaster and draw new britches. Clean up yer coat, cause and how we ain't got time fer fetchin' new ones. Shine up yer brass. Clean yer arses up good and get yer hair trimmed. Ye can't go see the high ups lookin' like a scallywag. Now move it out. I see ye in two hours. Now git."

They did not need to be told again.

A flurry of effort and activity soon accomplished the mission. Two spit-and-polished troopers stood in front of their sergeant, while he moved in a circle about them with a critical eye. He found only minor discrepancies, which were easily corrected. A small speck of lint here or a tiny splatter of mud on a new and blackened boot was seemingly nothing, but the sergeant would not let such escape without correction.

He gave particular instruction on reporting in. He gave his entire self, partly as a dutiful sergeant and partly as a proud solider, to the task of instruction to his charges. He had always carried out his orders and instructions to the best of his ability, and today would be no different. His beloved Major may be no longer his commander, but he had served him faithfully; and he was not about to change now. He gave his instructions to Jubal and William and had each of them repeat back to him. He had them go through a mock reporting as if he were Mr. Johnson himself. William had no trouble at all, and after a couple of repeat practices, Jubal had it down too.

"Be dressed and be here early. Cap'n Davis will be here near first light. Don't know what time he be takin' ye into see the man, but ye best not keep him or me waitin'. Ye unnerstand me?"

"Yes sergeant," William replied.

"Yes sergeant," Jubal parroted.

Neither of the young troopers slept well that night. There was far too much excitement and anticipation. William had no reservations about protocol and procedure. He had been exposed to that before and had managed it satisfactorily. He wondered why he would be summonsed. He had nothing in common with politics or with Tennessee. All he had done was pen a letter for a friend. Jubal gave no thought to the purpose of the summons. He was worried about himself and the way he would handle the formalities. He could hold his own with most anybody as far as talk was concerned, but he had never attended fancy encounters, and he knew nothing of the gentlemanly manners that Washington City would demand.

William beamed with self-confidence. He stood proud and tall. Jubal had not forgotten his rushed instruction and stood likewise. They were ushered into an inner office and stood at attention before the Yankee from Tennessee, as he was sometimes known. Both soldiers had reported exactly as instructed and patiently waited while their host attended to any number of documents requiring his attention.

"Gentlemen, I apologize for the delay. Some things always need a signature right away it seems. Please stand at ease."

Both Jubal and William assumed a parade rest.

"I will not waste my time nor yours. I will come to the point for my calling you here. You undoubtedly have skills that may benefit my cause and my mission. I have been well briefed by your captain and by your sergeant. Which of you is Jubal Stewart?"

"That be me."

"I understand you hail from East Tennessee. Is that correct?"

"Yes…Yes sir."

"I make my home in Greeneville. Are you aware of where that is in relation to your home?"

"No sir, I ain't never been there."

"You have never been there you mean."

"That be what I say, sir."

"My good man, when I crossed the mountains out of North Carolina and came to Greeneville, I could neither read or write. I had only a remnant of a trade. I learned reading and proper diction largely by the efforts of my beloved wife. She was insistent on teaching me, and I am in her debt to this day. I say this only to demonstrate that one can and must learn new tasks and better his knowledge, if he is to advance in the world today.

Do you see where I am leading?"

"No…I don't reckon I do," Jubal answered with a bit of trepidation. He was uncomfortable to begin with and the verbal taunting was not making it any easier for him.

"Let me regress a moment. Sergeant Dunn has informed me that you possess extraordinary tracking ability and woodsmanship. He also informed me that you are quick to catch on to instruction and that you know how to obey orders. Those are all qualities that I am looking to find. However, the good sergeant also tells me that you do not have much ambition for bettering yourself as to academic skills. That is a trait that I am not looking for. I have related my experience to you solely to demonstrate the doors that can be opened to you. However, you are the one who must pass through those doors."

"Do I make myself clear?"

"I…I don't unnerstand, sir."

"Never mind for now. This is what it means to you now. I know that you can improve yourself and shake away some of the stigma that became attached to you because of where you call home. I did it, and by the Eternal, so can you. I did it, because of my desire to rise above my poverty and my ignorance of the world around me. I did it by reading and rereading to the point where I understood to my satisfaction. Then I read some more, and I read more to this day. I am not going to belabor this issue. I feel that I have said enough already. We will discuss it more at a later time if you are assigned to accompany me."

Mr. Johnson then rose from his chair, walked around his desk and stood behind Jubal and William. They began to think that he was checking for any discrepancy or flaw that might be seen from their backside. In actuality he was trying to decide if manners really did matter that much deep in the hollows or along some mountain stream.

"William, am I to assume that you penned the letter for your companion?"

"Yes sir, I did."

"I commend you on your grammar and on your choice of words. Your education is evident. Where did you attend college?"

"I have not attended college, sir. I have apprenticed to an editor for a short time, sir."

"I see." He then returned to his desk but remained standing. "I am curious as to what you now read."

"I read God's Word, sir."

"Excellent. Have you read our Constitution?"

"Yes sir, but I must admit that some parts are difficult to grasp."

"And well that they should be. Much effort was devoted to making it as applicable and pure to individual rights and freedom as man could make it. It was divinely inspired. I am convinced of that. It is near sacred to me so much so that when I am laid to rest, I want a copy of it for my pillow and my body wrapped in our flag."

"Yes sir," William responded.

"I will make use of your penmanship. I am confident of your abilities."

"Thank you, Mr. Vice President. I will make every effort to exceed your expectations."

"Right now I cannot divulge details, but Mr. Lincoln thinks that this war will end in a matter of months. I tend to agree. At any rate, I plan to return home before the year is out and attempt to survey the mood of the people. I will be making the circuits in almost all areas of the state. I will need competent scouts and trackers when on open roads. I will also need competent scribes to complete all phases of surveys that I may conduct and document them accordingly. That gentlemen explains why you have been summonsed here today. Your assignment to me is tentative at present. I will be in touch with Captain Davis as need be. Until then, you are to remain quartered as you are now. I will tolerate no deviances, and I expect conduct that becomes this office. You may defame me, but you will not defame this office or this government. Are we clear on that issue?"

"Yes sir," both answered in unison.

" Good. William, continue reading from the Bible. And make sure that your friend begins to do some of the same."

"Yes sir."

"You are dismissed."

Both snapped to crisp attention, did an about face, marched from the room and gently closed the heavy oak door.

"What do all that mean, William?"

"It means, Jubal, that you are going to start reading the Bible. It means that you are going to learn to read it well. It means that you will be taking one small step toward the saving grace of the Lord."

Chapter 10

Waiting

*I*n mid-November, news of the Union army campaigns in Georgia began to filter into Washington City. There was an uncertainty in the air about the success of those efforts. Discussion made for a tavern keeper's delight. Ale flowed freely from dusk until daybreak. Then breakfast biscuits and sugar cured ham made their appearance. The keepers' coffers filled.

The days grew longer for Jubal and William. Each morning they had to stand early inspection by Captain Davis himself, unless he delegated the task to Sergeant Jugg. It was necessary for them, as well as the rest of the detail, to remain at the ready until released by someone of authority. That person was usually Captain Davis. Seeing him approach in the afternoon or evening was a welcome sight. It usually meant that the duty day was complete, and the lads could then shuck out of uniform and relax. But right back to the same routine the very next day. It was always hurry up and wait.

Word came that the detail had once again been summoned to meet with Mr. Johnson. They reported to him as instructed, and he received them cordially.

"Gentlemen, I have called you here today partially to inform you of some of the happenings in the war efforts and partially to inform you of my upcoming travel itinerary. Do you recall what I had briefed you on before?"

"Yes, Mr. Vice President," all said in loose unison.

"That is one issue that needs clearing immediately. I suppose that I was all enamored of the election results on our last meeting, and I must admit that hearing myself addressed as such has a certain appeal to it. However, I am not yet the sitting Vice President and will not be until inauguration. I respectfully require, until that time, that you address me simply as Mr. Johnson. Are we clear on that?"

"Yes sir," replied Sergeant Jugg, speaking for the entire detail.

"Enough about that. On with the matters. As you may or may not realize, General Sherman has devastated much of the Confederacy's ability to effectually wage war in the Deep South. I somewhat sympathize with these, my fellow southerners. They must realize, however, that the preservation of our precious Union is of utmost concern to me and to Mr. Lincoln. I have conferred with him at length. We are in agreement. He feels that the war cannot continue much longer, and I am inclined to agree with him. He is attentive to the task of reconstruction. It is in this respect that you, as well as myself, will be directly involved. Efforts will soon be forthcoming to assess the local situations in Union sympathetic areas, namely my home area of East Tennessee. As I have already informed you, I intend for my home state to be the first to reaffirm their allegiance and rejoin the Union. The President has assured me that I will have his full cooperation and authority in those efforts. You will, there-fore, be responsible ultimately to me. Do any of you have issue with that?"

"No sir."

"Very well. I plan to spend Christmas at home. That, of course, will mean travel through most of Virginia, which is very much against the policies and principles of the current administration. It would seem reasonable for any Union activity or travel in that area to be ill received. Do you follow what I am implying?"

"Not real sure of that sir," William offered.

"I feel certain that you are well aware of what the consequences could be if I were to make public my intent. This entire endeavor must be carried out with discretion and without any of the usual political fanfare. I do not intend to agitate sentiment that has all too long been above the boil. I have no passion for the excitement of armed conflict. That is why the proposed effort will employ all possible measures to be as inconspicuous as possible. It will be to your distinct advantage to discuss this with no one, except those in authority over you who will be responsible only to me. Right now the chain of command for each of you as individuals will go no higher than Captain Davis. Is that clear gentlemen?"

"Yes sir," from all present.

"Excellent. I am confident that our efforts will be fruitful and that by the Eternal our nation will prevail. Sergeant Dunn, I would like to speak to you alone for a moment, if you please. The rest of you are dismissed. I thank you for your service."

All except the sergeant made a hasty exit and closed the door behind them. Sergeant Dunn stood tall and proud before the Vice President Elect. He had no trepidations about standing in the presence of one of such office or authority.

"Sergeant, I will not mince words with you. I will be direct and to the point."

"Sir, yes sir."

"It is because of the recommendations from Mr. Dunn of Baltimore that you are here. He has informed me as to your long and faithful service to his son. You have every right to have my respect for those efforts."

"Sir."

"The fact remains that your lineage may not be too well accepted in areas where we will be traversing. I am sure that you are knowledgeable of the sentiments and attitudes of which I speak."

"You meanin' that I come from a slave?"

"Something to that effect. Do you have any issues or problems with traveling into former slave states? Would you anticipate any issues should you encounter any of your family or kinfolk?"

"I been gone so long I reckon I ain't got no kin no more, Sir."

"I see. Must leave some deep scars for you having been treated as you were back then. Are you sure that you hold no grudges? Can you truthfully say that you would seek no revenge from, say the owner of a cotton grower in Alabama or Georgia? You know that the blue uniform would be an object of hatred in those areas right now, especially in light of the antics of General Sherman and his army."

"I be honest sir. I once hated all planter men. Major Dunn make me see the wrong about my way, and he helped me understand many times and many things. He be who lead me where I be today. He be a good man."

"At one time I owned slaves. Does that change your opinion of me now?"

"No sir."

"Why do you say that?"

"You say owned. That tell me it all in the past."

"You are correct in that assumption sergeant."

The big burley sergeant hesitated for a moment. He was not sure how to proceed. He still felt at ease with his conversant.

"They free now?"

"Yes."

"You free em?"

"Yes."

"That because you feel bad fer ownin' them?"

"Well partially. But mostly because going back to the principals of our Constitution, I think all have a right to freedom and its blessings. We have strayed from our intent. I apologize for the diversion, but I think I have seen into the positive character that Major Dunn made reference to. I needed to know that you are dependable and know or try to know where your true sentiments would lie. If I had been in your place, I do not know if I could dismiss such bias and inequality. May I offer a bit of advice?"

"Yes, of course, Sir."

"Do you read?"

"Yes sir. I reads a plenty when I got time."

"I would encourage you to read widely. Read the addresses of Jefferson and others like him. Pay close attention to their manner of speaking. I would like to see you honed a bit. More polished if you will. I could use a man like you, and you could make a way for yourself and your kind. Do you follow me?"

"Not so sure sir, but I listens real good."

"We can pursue this more at a later time. You and the rest of your detail will soon receive instruction from Captain Davis. In the meantime, I hold you responsible to keep those young troopers in line and to admonish them of their need for discretion."

"Yes sir, Mr. Johnson."

"That will be all for now. It has been a pleasure talking with you."

"Yes sir."

With that the sergeant turned and started to make his exit only to be asked yet another question as he retreated. He took a liking to the newly-elected official and could sense a real feeling of respect coming from him.

"Do you know a man by the name of Kirkland?"

"Yes, Mr. Johnson, I reckon I do. From some time back, if he be one and same man."

"We will discuss that more in a few days or weeks. I trust that you will keep our personal conversation exactly that way. I have use for your knowledge at a later time. I will explain later. May I trust your confidence?"

"On my word, Sir."

"Excellent, Sergeant. Captain Davis will instruct you soon."

The gray skies of November did not abate. Each overcast day brought a menacing cold drizzle or a malingering blanket of slush snow. The elegant and groomed carriage teams of fair Washington City hung their heads in weary protest of the elements. Men in greatcoats and beaver hats scurried between buildings. The women, who dared the wrath of nature, exposed only enough face to be able to navigate. It was not enough that the conceived threats of a Rebel incursion would keep man and beast behind closed and protected shelter, but now the infernal cold drove all but the strongest to seek refuge from the wrath of the coming winter.

The rain and dampness bore down on Jubal and his acquaintances. It provided William the time that he wanted. It created opportunity to read more to his friend and to inquire what he understood and how he felt about those verses. It was getting late in the month. Soon December would come. If the detail were to be called as anticipated, then personal time could easily be curtailed. It was not too likely that the party would face grave danger, but that possibility did exist. That was something that did not sit too well with William. It troubled him that he had not been effective in his effort to lead his friend to the saving Light. Jubal was yet a child of the darkness and could be snatched away in a single beat of the heart.

Now is the day. Now is the day of salvation. These words echoed back and forth in William's thoughts. He could not drive them from his mind. He knew what he must do, and he knew who was speaking to him.

"Jubal, do you recall the last time that we read from my Bible?"

"Yes," came the meek reply.

Great, thought William. The Spirit has hold on him, and it is softening his heart. He will be receptive to the Word. "Do you recall what we read?"

"Yes, I recollect...Err...I remember. See, I be tellin' all along that I remember good. I even remember what Mr. Johnson tell me about proper speakin' and all."

"That is good my friend. I have known all along that you have a keen mind as well as a sharp eye. You just need to continue to remember those instructions."

"I plan on it."

"I will help you all I can," William answered. "But now, can you tell me what we read about last time in Romans?"

"How all people is bad and there ain't...there are no good people."

"That is close, but it is a bit different than that. It says that all have sinned and come short of God's glory. Do you know what that means?"

"I know, or I reckon I know what sinun' is. Circuit rider back home say once that killin' and stealin' and all such be sin."

"Well, he was right about that. I agree. But there is more to it than that, my friend. Do you know what glory is? No, let me back up a bit more than that. Have you ever heard of righteousness?"

"Seem like Granny Iverson read me that sometime, but I ain't sure what it means."

"I don't know if I can explain it very well or not, but I'll try my best." William stroked his furrowed brow with the back of his right hand. He hesitated and was surprised when Jubal interrupted his thought.

"Rightness is same as goodness, ain't it?"

"Righteousness goes deeper than goodness, Jubal. It is goodness without one bit of imperfection. It is goodness to all and being just to all. Really it is perfection beyond the abilities of any mortal man."

"Then what good it be when a body can't get there?"

"That is a tough question for me to answer, Jubal. Look here," William said as he rose to his feet and crossed the room with his finger on a passage. "What does this say right here?"

"There are none right...righteous. No, not one."

"Do you know who that means, Jubal?"

"Sounds me like it mean nobody."

"In some ways it does, and some ways it does not."

"Huh? I don't unnerstand that. Not one bit."

"It is talking about all of mankind, Jubal. It means that there are no righteous men on the whole face of this earth. But there once was one who was, and He was the only one, ever."

"You say there was one, but it say right here in the Good Book that there weren't none. Now how come ye tell me that there be one?"

"Well, let me see if I can clear myself. I think I started that off wrong."

"Right. Wrong. Good. Bad. What do it all mean William Garth? Ye don't make sense sometimes."

"Sometimes I get mixed up myself, and this is one of those times. I just seem to never get started off the right way. I never seem to be able to say things the way I want. Words just don't come out for me. I do better writing it down but that is a bit impersonal in my opinion. You ever feel that way, Jubal?"

"Well, time or two that I can recollect...er...remember."

"You are trying, aren't you?"

"I think I best be tryin' with you and Sergeant Jugg always on my butt, and now I got the Vice President hisself on my tail too."

"Vice President, himself."

"That be what I said. You mockin' me?"

"No, just correcting you again. It's himself instead of hisself."

"Whatever."

"How did we manage to get so far off track?"

355

"You the one what say we confused."

"You are right there. I just need to regroup and start all over again. Forget all I have said so far about righteousness. I will go back to where we were last reading. That okay with you?"

"I reckon so long as yer head be on straight now. Ye still seem like ye talk in big circles sometimes. Why don't ye just out and say whatever it is and be done with it?"

"Jubal, there is really more to it than that. It is important to me that I tell it to you right, and even more important that you understand what it is all about. I know that sometimes you don't really want to listen to me, and I can respect that. All I ask is that you be up front with me and give me a chance to tell you what I want you to hear. If you don't want to hear it at this time, then tell me. We can have a go at it on another day."

"No, William, it ain't so much that I don't wanna listen to ye. It's just that you get yer tail all tucked twixt yer legs and don't make no sense sometimes. Why can't ye just read me what ye want me to hear and let me think on it a bit? I ain't so thick headed that I can't reason things out fer myself. I know I ain't said all this like you would. But when I got a piece to say, well then, I just come out with it and then there ye be. Ye don't have no trouble undrestandin' me now, do ye? Seems clear to me, and I know certain I said what I think needed sayin' and not needin' no fancy-pants words either."

"I am glad to hear you say that, Jubal, because it shows me how you really feel."

"You thinkin' I'm mad with ye?"

"No. Definitely not. I am thinking that you are honest with me."

"Well, that goes way back to my Ma's learnin' me things from the start. I got no reason but be honest with ye William. Like I done told ye before, they be some things I done did that I ain't proud or pleased over, but I ain't no fibber."

"I know that, Jubal. I know that you want to make a way for yourself, and I intend to help you as much as you want. However, I want your input on that, not only today, as you have just said, but in the future too."

"There be a lot of things that I want."

"I know. There are things that I want too. But I want to ask you here and now, not to be upset with me when I try to show you things and when I try to correct your talk and your mannerisms. I would much rather that you just tell me to shut up for a while. I do not want you mad at me for trying to help you. And I promise you that I will respect your feelings and back off when I need to."

"You be a damn good friend to me, William. I ain't never... I never have had nobody try help me that way other than Lida, and she talk pretty much same as me. Maybe we write her another letter soon. Huh?"

"No, not we. Next time, you will write it. I will help with spelling and such, but you will write the letter. It will mean more to her that way. You need to write your Ma too."

"That be a powerful bunch of..."

Bang! The door to their room slammed open and there stood none other than Sergeant Jugg decked out in gentlemanly finery with a smile across his face that would have lit up a dark room. Hands on hips, dressed in a dark woolen suit with matching greatcoat and hat. His white shirt matched the brilliance of his smile. He carried himself straight and tall. He spoke not a word.

William and Jubal stared at him for what seemed an eternity before they could speak.

"Look at that, William. I bet he be so proud that he can strut sittin' down."

"Sergeant Jugg, would you like to tell us how you struck it rich or would you be so kind as to tell us who you robbed," asked William jokingly.

"I ain't rich, and I ain't robbed nobody," came the reply.

"Then what in tarnation goin' on?"

"You boys ain't gonna believe this."

The Sergeant proceeded to explain to them that Mr. Johnson had chosen him to lead the detail that would accompany him to Tennessee next month. Since much of the distance would be in Rebel territory, it would not be good to be in uniforms. It would be best to look like businessmen and to act like one too.

He went on to explain how that Mr. Johnson had the full backing of the President and consequently of the entire Union army. The quartermaster services had procured appropriate clothing and supplies, and he had just come from picking up the clothes that had been made for him.

"How come ye come here to strut yer stuff to us?" Jubal inquired.

"I never come here just to strut as ye put it. I come here on account of instruction from Captain Davis and from Mr. Johnson too."

"And what be them instructions?" Jubal asked with no hesitation.

"I come to tell ye two to get yer arses over to the quartermaster and get yer clothes ordered, seein' as how ye will be goin' down Tennessee way too. It be me and you two and four more. Quartermaster be up the street from our eatin' tavern about six blocks. It be on same side and be a sign out over the door. Won't be no trouble spottin' it. So I reckon ye best be movin' right now. We got more things need talkin' on when ye get back. Right now I gonna go tell rest of my detail troops."

"Who will they be?" William asked.

"Tell ye that later. Now git. Best ye not tell what this here business be all about neither. Captain Davis done told quartermaster staff what all ye be needin' and that be all he needs know. So keep yer yap shut. Unnerstand me?"

"We understand," William answered for them both. Jubal nodded in agreement.

The trek to the quartermaster took only a few minutes. William took that opportunity to express his thinking.

"I am sorry that I confused you again, my friend. I apologize for that and promise you that I shall try my best to not let that happen again."

"Well, just know that I ain't sore at ye fer it. After all, I reckon it would take some doin' fer me to be sore with ye over just talkin'."

"Jubal, my friend, I fully intend on continuing our discussions. I hate that we got interrupted this time. We will continue."

"I reckon so. Ye got me wonderin' what be next now."

"Good. At least I have been able to stir some interest. That is encouraging to me."

"I honest do wanna learn more, and I wanna learn speakin' as well. I be beholdin' to ye fer tryin' teach me too. Sometimes I get a mite pissed when ye correct me all the time, but then I realize ye just tryin' yer best to help me. Sometimes it take a minute or two to think it through, and I know that. Ye just be patient with me, cause I ain't never knowed no better. Old ways is hard to let go, even if they ain't the most best. Do that make any sense?"

"It does. And yes, I do know what you are saying, and sometimes I can tell that you are really trying to improve yourself. It may take a long time, my friend. I will help you all that I can, and I will be patient too. You should already know that."

"I...I does."

"Just 'do' is the way you want to say it now. I and does do not agree with each other."

"Well tarnation, how is a body gonna know when it does and when it do or when it don't? Seems me like I ain't never gonna get that down pat."

"It's not easy, is it?" said William laughingly.

"No, it ain't."

"There are other things that we can read to help you. I want to continue reading from the Bible, because there are things there that you need to hear and things there that I want you to know. Sometimes the words used in the Good Book can be a bit hard to grasp without studying them. It is something that will teach you many things and give you entirely new meanings in life, but it takes some effort on your part. I know you can do it, and I know you will be able to understand it. You asked me to be patient with you and I surely will, but you must be patient with yourself too. That will not always be easy, because we tend to be more critical of ourselves than others would be. Change does not always come easy, and that itself requires patience. Am I confusing you even more?"

"No, I reckon not. How long ye reckon it take me to unnerstand the Good Book as ye call it?"

"I am fearful that I will be misleading to you by what I am about to say, but I must be honest with you."

"What now?" Jubal asked with a quizzed look about him.

"You can read it all your life and still find new things the day before you die. I certainly don't know all the answers or all the interpretations, and I have been reading for as long as I can remember.

But you have to have faith and trust that you will receive the truth and the wisdom from reading that will guide you through the trials and tests that you face."

"It be a thick book all right."

"But, it is the content that counts."

William silently reflected on his childhood home and what a gracious blessing it had been for his parents to have raised him in a genuine and loving Christian home. He had never had to know the pangs of hatred or prejudice. He had never been made light of when he went to his dad with foolish boyhood questions or dreams. He had never, that he could recall, been told "not now, I don't have time." Sure, there were times when his parents were busy and could not be as attentive as maybe he would have wanted, but they always explained themselves and made sure that there was a time later on for whatever the issue may have been. But more importantly, he knew that he was loved and cherished. He knew that he was cared for and accepted. He was taught right from wrong from a very early age, and it had become a part of his very being. His upbringing had instilled a strong and moral character in him, and he was thankful for that.

Even greater, however, he had been shown the evils of the darkness and had come to realize his needs. He had stepped into the light, and now he enjoyed the fellowship and blessings of all those who had done likewise. He had peace about him in spite of being embroiled in the raging national struggle. He honestly felt no hatred toward his countrymen in the Deep South. He wished no malice to any of them, certainly not his friend from Cane Valley.

Procurement of adequate civilian clothing from the quartermaster took nothing more than a quick sizing. They were given no real choices in color or style. That had been predetermined by others. Each would receive one suit adequate for business dress and boots to go along with it. Each would receive warm traveling clothes and a greatcoat to ward off the chills. They were to receive field packs, but not military issue. They would appear to be fashioned to individual tastes. No other details were revealed as to how or when they would be traveling. All that would be told them only as they needed to know.

They were told that they would need to return in two days and to bring all their uniforms and issued Union army equipment including their weapons and ammunition. Everything they brought must be in a good state of repair because it would most likely be reissued to another trooper.

Captain Davis met them and gave them a stern warning that matters would be discussed with no one and that there would be no talk among themselves about it whatsoever. He also made emphasis of what lay in store for them if his instructions were not followed.

"Do you understand?" the captain asked sternly and directly.

"Yes sir," William said sharply.

"I need to hear that from you as well," Captain Davis said curtly as he directed his eyes to Jubal.

"Yes. Yes sir. I unnerstand."

"You understand?"

"Yes sir. I understand."

"Very well."

The two lads headed out in the muddy streets of fair Washington City. The onslaught of November rain had obliterated any hope of a street being anything more than a pig trough of muck and mire. No amount of boot black and lard could stave off such mess and filth. No self-respecting gentleman would attempt prodding such pathways. The wealthy even kept their coveted buggy teams stalled up and pampered during such times. Any rider soon became mud splattered and caked as well as his mount. It took away all desire to be out and about.

"What say we stop in at the tavern and have our stew early today, and then we need not be out in this mess again?" William suggested, as they neared the hotel.

"Might as well. That way we just be muddied up one time, but we still need be cross over yonder side and then come back. We be ankle deep both ways."

"I know, but it will just be one time. I bet they make us take our boots off outside on the hotel porch. They will not be pleased if we leave a trail all the way up to our room."

Jubal thought about the old dirt road from his log cabin home, down the hollow to the mill and beyond. He had never seen that road in such terrible shape as were these big city streets. It made him think that maybe, just maybe, that big city life was not all that he had envisioned it to be.

In almost the same instant, his thoughts turned to Lida. Lida, at the end of his road, way back home. Seemed so far away and so long since he had been there. He wondered if she had received his letter. He wondered if she would write back. How would she know where to send it? He had not written anything to let her know where he was or how to find him. Maybe William had seen to that. William was on to things like that. No wonder Mr. Johnson had picked him to do his letters and papers and stuff. William was an alright boy. He knew that he needed to pay more attention to his friend to learn from him all that he could. He could already see where some book learning could be a good thing.

"You boys want anything else that I could give ya?" The young trollop made it a point to press her thigh into William's arm as they sat at a rear table eating leftover ham hocks and beans with parched corn.

"No, I shall not be needing anything you have to offer," William said hardly lifting his eyes from his plate.

"Well now, ain't you some kinda smart assed little whip?" she retorted.

"I take a hunk of rye bread back across yonder if ye got it," Jubal said as she began to come around to his side of the table.

"Do I look like I'm a damned baker or somethin' like that?"

"Be quite frank with ye, I never give ye a second look."

That must have really set her off because she stormed off without a further word, and her heavy heels could be heard long after she ascended the narrow and darkened staircase.

"Proud of you, Jubal. You hardly paid her any attention at all. Are you sure you feel okay?"

"I be fine. She just ain't the woman I want. Not her nor none like her. I don't want no bought woman. Not no more."

"I am not going to ask anything more about that, Jubal. That is your business and some things are just not proper to talk about."

"I reckon ye be right on that just like ye be right on most other things too."

"I don't know all there is to know; not by a long shot. I just try to learn as I go and try to remember all that I can."

"Seems me like ye got a strong mind fer recollectin' most anything ye want."

"Well, I hope so. You still want that bread to go back with us? I'll get it if you do, won't be any bother."

"Naw, I reckon I had about as much as I can hold fer now."

"Okay."

"Ye know what I want?"

"No."

"Why can't we get back in our room and read some more after we get ourselves all dried out and shake off some of this here infernal mud? We look like we been on barnyard jobs."

"We can do that." William was encouraged that his friend had expressed a desire again to learn more. He saw it as the workings of a higher power. He welcomed the opportunity. He knew what it meant to be a light in the midst of darkness, and he wanted so much for his friend to know it too. No one else had ever seemed to matter so much. There was a desire that Jubal, his recently constant companion and friend, should know the peace and comfort that he knew himself. He had to tell him all about the light that could be his.

"Jubal, do you know what faith means?"

"Well, I…I ain't so sure I know how to say it iffin that be what you askin' me. It be a bit hard fer me to put in words."

"Just tell me what you think about it."

"Ye mean like hope fer somethin' or expectin' somethin' or wishin' fer it but not knowin' fer sure?"

"That is very close to what I would call it. Would it be the same as saying that you trusted in something that you could not see or had hope for something that you had only heard about? Could it be believing in something you could not hold in your hands or stand on top of? Would it be trust or confidence?"

"I don't dispute none of that, but sometimes ye gets way over my head."

"Think about being back home, Jubal. Think about every morning when your Ma made biscuits for your breakfast."

"So?"

"Were you ever afraid to eat them? Did you ever worry about them making you sick or anything like that?"

"No."

"Why not?"

"She be my Ma, and she ain't about do nothin' that harm me. Besides that she be makin' biscuits lot longer than I be around here."

"Then you have confidence in her and you trust her?"

"You betcha."

"Then that is part of what I think faith is. Trust in her and confidence in her ability. You ever stand over her and watch to make sure she was making those biscuits proper?"

"Shucks no. She would done toss me out the kitchen door iffin I done her that way."

"You didn't do her that way because you knew she would do it right. You trusted her and believed she would do her best. Is that not right?"

"Yeah."

"You ever cross a foot log?"

"Huh?"

"You heard me. Did you ever cross a foot log or a bridge for that matter?"

"Sure, many a time."

"You had trust in that old log that it would hold you up?'

"Yeah."

"Then that is faith right there in a simple way. I see it as trust in things that you cannot see and in hope for things eternal. Just like with your Ma, you know that she can make you a biscuit and that she does it well, but you cannot see her knowledge or talent for biscuits?"

"No, but she can still make em just same."

"That's true. What about that old foot log? Can you see its ability to hold you up?"

"Well sure I can, long as it ain't rotten."

"This is not going the way I wanted it to go. Give me just a minute to think on other words to try and explain myself."

"William, I ain't no child no more. Say whatever it be that ye tryin' to say and be out with it."

"Okay, I will. I will before you get distracted any further. Do you believe that there is a Heaven?"

"Granny Iverson say they is. Lida tell me that too."

"But do you believe it?"

"Reckon I ain't got no reason not to."

"Do you believe it or is it just something that they have told you?"

"Well...Yeah,...I believe it."

"Not just because they told you, but because you really feel it in your heart?"

Jubal nodded his head in an affirmative move as he yawned and lay back on his bed. William sensed that he would soon reach the point of disinterest and would not want to hear any more. He was soon very surprised and pleased as well.

The soldier from Cane Valley locked his fingers behind his head and asked William if he could read him that part about the shepherd and how he took to his flock. It could be no other passage than the Twenty-Third Psalm. Bless old Granny Iverson's heart. It surely must have been her that had read it to a young boy sitting at her feet. He could almost see her as she read from a tattered old-and-treasured Bible with only the light of a roaring winter's fire to illuminate the words.

"You read it to me good and slow, and then I try my best readin' it back to ye."

It was a bit hard for William to read without choking up.

Three days passed before the sun elected to show its brilliance again. It was a welcome tradeoff for the rain despite the plunge in temperature. The quagmire of mud solidified into a surface rough and cumbersome to man and beast. A fall could easily result in an ice spicule penetrating a glove and stabbing a hand or worse, penetrating into a knee joint. Not that the icicle itself would be a lasting problem as much as the street filth that it would inoculate into the wound. For those reasons among others, the streets were near empty and only essential treks were attempted.

Sergeant Jugg and his charges had been summoned to the quartermaster and were making their way in that direction, being cautious of their footing. William and Jubal had made the prescribed preparation and were dressed in well-fitting and well-maintained uniforms. Boots had been blackened and, thankfully, remained mud and mire free in the frozen streets. No need to look out for carriage or coach traffic this morning. There was none.

They had failed to notice the half dozen other spit-and-polished troopers coming along behind them. The cold wind whipped up a tearful eye, and a head bowed down for protection could not adequately observe its surroundings. A greatcoat would have been a comfort, but none was provided as a part of a trooper's issue, at least not these troopers. Such heavy clothing had not really been needed before.

Arrival at the quartermaster's facility revealed a familiar face. Captain Davis was on hand to give instant instruction and directives. The entire detail was ushered into an inner office, and the door closed behind them. There were two gentlemanly-clad individuals present, who bore no familiarity to any others present, including Captain Davis.

"Gentlemen, these two men are superior to me and that is all that you really need to know about them. I will not trouble you with their names. What you do not know, then you cannot be forced to reveal. Do I make that clear?" Captain Davis spoke as he eyed each of the nine men present.

All were in agreement and acknowledged so.

"This is all in regard to the upcoming plans and travels of the Vice President Elect. Each of you undoubtedly know that already. You do not, however, know why you were chosen individually. You will learn that as time passes. You will learn to work together and to depend on each other. I can tell you in advance that Mr. Johnson is a very fair and unwavering gentleman of high and uncompromising standards. You will find him demanding, but exceptionally rewarding. You will find that he shows no favoritism and expects no more or no less from his associations with others. You will no doubt be called to long hours of duty and service, but you will be asked to do nothing that Mr. Johnson would refuse to do himself. I can assure you that once you have been in his employ, you will find working for any other to be less rewarding and less satisfactory. He will instill a pride of accomplishment in you, and yet you will be humbled in his presence." The articulate captain then remained silent in expectation that all he had just said could be taken in and digested by the nine men standing in front of him.

"Sergeant Jugg, as you seem to prefer calling him, has all the details of your assignments. He will go over them with you collectively and individually. I must, right here and now, remind you that you are duty-bound to all your military obligations. You will, however, be acting as non-military businessmen. You must, therefore, dispense with military titles and customs. Sergeant Jugg will be Mr. Jugg or rather Mr. Dunn. Do you understand?"

Each man was expected to and did reply individually.

"Good. You may take charge of your associates Mr. Dunn. You may go."

Two mornings later found the detail secured in another inner office. This time in another hotel near the noted Pennsylvania Avenue residence. Mr. Johnson had met briefly with the entire detail and had informed them that he had decided to bring Captain Davis along as well. He, however, would be acting as liaison for the Union army and would be in uniform most all the time. He perhaps would be in graver peril from Rebel forces than any others of the party, but would rely on the party for his protection. Captain Davis, therefore, was relegated the task of passing on the idiosyncrasies of the mission and the individual responsibilities for each member.

Jubal had been selected largely through the influences of the elder Mr. Dunn of Baltimore, but ultimately because of his innate mountaineering skills and abilities. William had drawn favor by knowledge of his flair for the written word and being by comparison quite well read.

Thomas Allen hailed from Ohio and had labored on the namesake river barges and canals. He was chosen in part because he was adept at water navigation. It also helped that he had gained some prominence as a marksman with the Spencer rifle. He was a long and lanky individual who minced few words. He would speak his mind, but only if prodded to do so.

Elbert hailed from Louisville in old Kentucky and was well known in his home town as the son of one of the Moore brothers, who made their way in exports of fine tobacco products or at least who had done so up to the onset of wartime restrictions on down river shipping. Elbert would be expected to know his way around the middle and western parts of his state.

Harlan Graves had locomotive experience and knowledge. All concerned had agreed that he would be an asset anywhere there would be rail travel. He also knew how to handle his pearl-handled Navy pistol.

Paul, Gale and Oliver all came down from the Adirondack area of upstate New York. They were chosen largely for their strength, stamina and ability to sustain themselves against most any pugilist, who might have the unfortunate desire to provoke any one of them. Jubal considered himself able enough to take his own part, but admittedly had no desire to cross any one of these new-found acquaintances. It took no genius to discern why they would come along on the journey.

All had given up any obvious attachment to the military, save for the captain. Each had been issued adequate business or vocational attire. Each had been armed with a side arm and a new Spencer. They were repeatedly admonished against any unnecessary show or word about their armament. It would be more or less common knowledge where such arms came from and that attention was deemed unfavorable. Their efforts were not covert in the true sense of it all, but Mr. Lincoln thought it best if the episode be unadvertised.

The entire party would depart from Washington City on a special train. It would be manned by regular Union soldiers and crew. It was to run only over Union controlled tracks and would be subject to movement the same as would any other Union troop or supply train. The locomotive was to be a Baldwin four-four-zero which was state-of-the-art for the times. It could speed along at thirty miles an hour over good level and well-maintained tracks. The consist would carry two coaches for the rank and file. There would be a stock car for the horses and a buggy would be lashed on a flatcar. Mr. Johnson would occupy a personal car from an unspecified owner baron. The locomotive would pull an extra wood tender and thus eliminate a portion of the normal stops for fuel. Both tenders had been heaped to capacity with oak and ash wood. Slabs of old pork side meat had been hung over the sides of each tender. These were suspended on loops of wire gathered from downed telegraph lines. They were never intended for food supply, but a hunk of it thrown into the locomotive firebox would boost the flames and make for an increased steam volume.

Mr. Johnson had detailed some of his intended itinerary to Captain Davis; and he, in turn, had told his charges only a smathering of what probably would be in store for them. They would stop along the way at established points and take their meals as best they could. Such stops would be where Mr. Johnson would be most exposed to a non-sympathizer, and also where he would expect his personal enclave to be at their zenith of protection. He expected them to do their assigned duty and not to stand in harm's way for him by acting as a human shield. He had expressed his desire that all would remain safe and return to Washington City, one and all, as planned. All believed him to be sincere in his concern, and they all respected him for that.

The big conical stack of the locomotive belched and spewed a formidable column of thick dark gray smoke as the fireman began to stoke the firebox. Steam hissed from the drive piston valves as pressure began to build. Water levels were topped off and oil added to the headlamp. Little night travel was expected, but it never hurt to be ready if needed. The engineer did his walk around and gave a final squirt of thick black oil to the slides and the drive rods. All was ready.

William seemed happy that they would soon be in his home territory. It just could work out that he would be able to spend a precious few moments with his folks. Surely the train would stop in order to take on fuel and for its riders and crew to dine at one of the established eateries near the train depot. Jubal had thought that he might get to make a quick run into Cane Valley until William had shown him where Nashville lay in relation to the extreme eastern end of the state. Mr. Johnson had made no definite mention of plans to return to his native Greeneville, since leaving Washington City. Jubal knew that Greeneville was a whole lot closer to his home, but still had only slim hopes of getting back to his little corner of the world.

They would travel north across Maryland and then swing west along the southern edge of Pennsylvania where the famous surveyors had run their line not so very long back. Two days should put William and his companions into Ohio.

Gray skies conveyed the mood of the times and trials of a nation torn by its own internal strife. Many, both in the beleaguered Confederacy and in the Union, lifted up their prayers and hopes to the God of all men that this conflict of hatred among brothers could soon end.

Healing was needed on all fronts. Death had claimed the sanctity of many families. Children were now fatherless. Mothers, young and old alike, had no way to feed hungry offspring. Old men grieved for sons. Mothers longed for word from long-lost sons. Fields lay fallow for lack of hands to turn their soil.

The nation was weary. There was a desire to exert punishment to those vanquished. There was at the same time a passion to forgive, to rise up from such devastation and stand tall again. Perhaps none had a more ardent desire for the preservation of the sacred Union than did Mr. Johnson himself, and he continually made known his intentions to do anything within his new-found power and position to effect that end. It was in this measure that he had set out to plant the seeds of healing, first and foremost, in his home state. He was determined that the people whom he knew to be forthright and upstanding could and would be an example for all others. He would use the full abilities and talents of his party to accomplish that end. He would accept nothing short of all their efforts. He himself, would give nothing less.

"How you feel about headin' home, William?" Jubal quired as the train lumbered along in the late morning chill.

"I really have not had too much time to think about it. I will be glad to see my folks, of course."

"I reckon you will at that."

"If we have a chance, I would like for you to meet them too. My mother would love to sit us down to her dining room table and have us eat till we were filled."

That brought a smile to Jubal's face. It also stirred thoughts that he had not known in several days. He could see his Ma and his sisters sitting at the old poplar-boarded table covered with a well-worn oilcloth and having Thanksgiving dinner of only a few wilted potatoes, sprouts and all, boiled in melted snow, perhaps with hoecakes fried in fatback grease. If he were there, at least he could have tried to get a wild turkey or a duck. They would have some kind of game. He was not there, and he could not provide for them. He could not know their plight. It could be that C.C. and his family had seen fit to lend a helping hand. So many unanswered questions.

Overcome with emotion for the moment, Jubal sprang from his seat and bounded to the platform at the end of the coach. He just needed a moment to compose himself. Cold wind whipping around the moving cars smarted his eyes, and salty tears clouded his vision. William had somehow sensed what was pulling at his friend and had given him his needed moment alone. He waited for Jubal to come back inside and take his seat. When he did, William merely patted him on the shoulder and said not a word. Many times an action can speak much louder than a word, and this was one of those times.

"You okay now?" William asked, after a good long silence.

"I think I be good now. I just had me a little spell."

"It's really hard sometimes. I know it is, and I feel for you like you probably will never believe. I wish I could make all things the way you want them to be. If I could, I would do that for you."

"That be a lot what be trouble to me. I ain't so sure that I know how I want things to be. You done showed me some of what a good book learnin' can be and what it can bring a body. I done seen a bit how rich folks lives, and I already decided that that ain't ever thing in this old world. They has problems and hurts just like ever body else. I just wish I could know more how things is at home and how things is gonna work out."

"Well Jubal, you just need to have faith and believe that all will be well. You have to have hope. You have to believe that good will win out over evil. We have talked a bit on that, and I know that I confused you some."

"Not as much as ye might think. Ye just set me to worry sometimes."

"What worries you, if I may ask?"

"This infernal restlessness. No matter where I am or what I be set on bein' done, I ain't never satisfied. Can't sit still sometimes. All time want be movin' on. I feel like I be runnin' from somebody or such all the time, and I don't even know what nor who."

"You have not been back home since you joined, have you?"

"No, I ain't"

"Are you excited about heading that way now?"

"Well, I…I wanna see my kin, and I wanna see Lida. I reckon she still be there. That worry me some cause I seen how she eyed them horse soldiers that come around her Pa's mill a time or two. I wanna go back home, but I ain't wantin' no more chores and hard workin' the whole live-long day. That part I don't want no more. That be why sometimes, I wanna skedaddle plumb out west to flat land. Then I think that ain't what I want neither. It just don't make no sense. I just stay tore up all time. Never no answers."

"You are getting there, Jubal. You are getting there, and you don't even realize what it is that is moving you there."

The train lumbered on into the late afternoon. The entire entourage became partially mesmerized by the clickety-clack of the rails. Heads nodded and rhythmic, regular breathing was all that could discern any life in the coaches. Mr. Johnson had decided that they would continue travel through the night and had taken on bread and cheese for the evening meal. Thomas had been selected to be the "mess cook" since he had bragged about his abilities. He had somewhere confiscated a baked ham and would make sure that his friends had their fair share.

Jubal was the first to smell the succulent aroma of the ham and approached Thomas like a hungry hound drawn to a kitchen chimney corner. He had not had any inklings of hunger until the meat whetted his sedated appetite.

"Ye got any fer me?" he asked anxiously.

"Got some for us all. One big ham and I think it will take care of us all."

"Looks just like my Ma would bake. She bake hers on a wood cook stove in a big blue pot. Makes me think about home now," Jubal said with a smile.

"You ain't been home yet?" Thomas asked.

"No, this be my first time back. Ain't sure I make it there this time. All depend on what the man wants us do," Jubal answered.

"Don't make much difference anyhow," Thomas said as he continued to slice off big slabs of hog meat. "Home never be the same once you been out on yer own. Things change."

The smile vanished. Jubal was not real sure what Thomas was meaning, but it did not sound like something that he needed to hear, not now leastwise. He took the meat, bread and cheese that Thomas handed him, but somehow he had lost any desire for anything to eat. Floods of doubt and unanswered questions beset him once again. There could not possibly be that much change at home. Not in Cane Valley. He wanted to ask Thomas more about what he had meant, but decided that it would be better if he just waited to get back home and see for himself. Back home: whenever that might be.

Chapter 11

Cold

*N*ovember of 1863 dawned cold in Cane Valley. Harvest time was essentially over, and the dry weeks in late summer had made corn yield much lower than needed. Jubal and Ma had gathered what there was, and it had less than one-third filled the old rickety corncrib. It was already plain to see that this was going to be a lean winter. Even old Kate would be missing out on her daily ration; she would have to make do on a few nubbins alone. C.C. would grind what meal he could for them, but it was going to be hard to stretch a little stone ground meal into a winter's bread for a half dozen mouths. If Jubal could kill a deer that would be a real God send. An old tom turkey would feed them for near a week. Even a rabbit would make a pot of stew for a day. It was not too likely that anyone would starve, but it was going to be an effort just to have meat on the table. There were the two hogs to butcher, but the hams would have to be sold just to have a little cash money to see them through the winter.

Winter meant cold, and it was cold already. Fortunate indeed that Jubal and old Kate had made a number of treks up and down the ridge to fetch winter's wood. They had fetched many a pole of wood and stashed it high in the old open woodshed. Kate could not pull as much of a load as once before, and Jubal had not hitched her up to more than she could easily pull.

Sometime during a summer thunderstorm, a lightning bolt had ripped open a slim red oak, and it had split out and crossed into a dead chestnut tree and both had later come crashing to the ground. Jubal had found them earlier one foggy morning while he was out on a turkey hunt. He had remembered them. He and Kate now had most of them down off the ridge and stacked up outside the old rickety woodshed. There would be time to work it up and split it small enough for the fireplace and the cook stove as the colder weather set on in earnest. Young lean arms could split a week's wood in just a few hours. Staying warm this winter should not be too troubling.

Ma had got out of bed sometime in the wee hours of the morning and started a fire in the fireplace. She feared that Julie might chill, and she wanted to guard against that as best she could. Julie still had very little use of her leg in spite of her wound being almost closed and healed over. She had very little drainage from the wound now, and her bandages needed changing less and less. She seemed to be doing fairly well, but she could not yet manage to walk by herself. It was plain as day that Ma was really worried about her. Jubal could see that in her eyes and in the expressions she made when she tended to Julie. His sister did not really have much of an appetite, and her color was pale as a possum's belly. Granny Iverson never said anything encouraging about her and that was a bad sign too. Jubal recalled how often she had remarked that if a body could not say something good, then best to not say anything at all.

Jubal always felt close to Julie. They had no secrets. They had shared many things and thoughts, even if it had been in child-like manner. He told himself that somehow, real soon, that he needed to find a way to have a few minutes to talk with her. He had no particular thoughts in mind. He just felt that he needed to talk with her. Never know what she might have on her mind. Besides that, she and Lida had spent a lot of time together, and maybe she would tell some of the things that they had talked about. He would get up some night and check on the fire. Never know when a back stick might burn up quicker than it should. If she happened to wake up, then he would sit by her bedside and try to be a good listener.

Not only had Ma seen to Julie, making sure that she was warm, she had slipped on Jubal's boots and made her way to the springhouse loft to see about old Wes. She had found him balled up under every piece of cover that he could lay hands on and still near frozen. She had brought him to the house and made him a pallet on the floor near the hearth. She had not returned to her own bed until Julie rested quietly with regular rhythmic breathing and until Wes snored deeply.

Breakfast was over as usual well before the sun ever showed its face over top of the east ridge. Jubal took down the old long rifle, powder horn and some wadding. If he had any kind of luck at all, there would be fresh game on the table tonight. He was not really too particular what it might be, but a big fat rabbit or two would make a fine pot of stew. He could let old Jake go along and run them up. He knew that he could bag them on the run. Jake was getting some age on him, and he would not run a rabbit too hard.

The boy and the dog started the long, slow walk up to the timberline directly above the old log house. Jubal turned after a bit and looked back at his humble home. The air was still and quite. Here in this small corner of the earth, all seemed to be at peace. All seemed well. How could such a tranquil morning tell of a coming storm? Jubal could still see his breath out, but the bitterness of the cold dark night had been at least, partially broken.

Nighttime seemed like a waste. Nights were dark most times and nighttime was when most bad things were apt to happen. Thievery and all other such evil shenanigans went on in the dark. Daylight just made things so much better all the way around. Sure, a body had to sleep some, but just a few hours was enough. Not much sense to hole up from dusk right on till dawn. Waste too much time that way. Moonlit nights be good times for trapping and trailing. Good times to find fresh game trails.

Jubal had gone only a short hike when old Jake opened on a hot trail in the voice so characteristic of his redbone heritage. Deep and long bellowing groans ending with an upbeat tone just for emphasis. Jubal saw the big brown fur ball turn back on his track long before Jake had a chance to spot him. Hitting a running target at a closing range was no new task for the boy. The rabbit stumbled and rolled to a stop at the crack of the rifle. Jake soon reached the carcass and pounced on it with what enthusiasm he could muster. A few thrashing shakes, and the game was all over as far as Jake cared. No fight, no fun. Jubal knew that Jake would not want to do anything other than shake it, and he let the old redbone do just as nature had intended. He retrieved the game, dropped it into a sack, petted the old hound as he talked gently to him and praised him. A quick reload, and the trek to the ridge line continued.

The process was repeated almost in the exact same manner; there now would be three rabbits in the stew pot tonight. Ma might even fix it in the fireplace since they still had a pot hook that swung on a stout and dependable iron pivot well mortared into the stone face of the firebox. She would add a few potatoes and whatever else she could lay a hand on. The dairy was near empty since the garden had not done so well. There were a few scrub carrots buried up in the sand barrel and a fair measure of late apples that Wes had carried in. It would, no doubt, be a cold hard pull; but spring would come in its own time, and the earth would give new life once more.

Jubal continued to climb the ridge line with old Jake in tow. He had reloaded and made ready for the next shot, but had already decided that three rabbits would be enough for today. Reloading was just routine. If there was a need, he would be ready. As he made his way along the well-worn paths laid out over years by the livestock, he was careful to note the signs around him. A now empty, low slung hornets' nest no bigger than a cats head told him that cold weather was in the making. The woolly worms had broad black striping this year. Old folks said that was to help them stay warmer in the winter. But no matter how harsh the conditions that the mountains could deal out, springtime always brought an awakening and a renewal.

The old iron pot swung in over the bed of red and purple coals. Three long ears, carrots, potatoes, a few slices of dried apples, all laced with a time-tested measure of black pepper would soon be simmering and filling the old log home with an aroma that would perk up any appetite. Good hot stew would be good for Julie. Maybe it would put a bit of color back in her washed-out cheeks and fill in those sunken eyes. Jubal wanted to talk with her now, as the stew brewed. But it was not the time yet. He would manage to be by her side sometime tonight. He would be there for her while all the others slept. At least today, hunger would be staved off, and the cold would be held at bay.

Cloud cover came in well before dusk. The night would not be so cold because of the cloud protection. The wind had laid and the evening would be very quiet and still. It would or should be a peaceful night. Cane Valley was peaceful in comparison to many other places throughout the south. Most of the troubles seen up and down Cane Creek were those committed by thieves and rogues, who were out to get whatever they could by any means that they could. They were cowardly enough that they hid by day and caroused about at night. They were not dedicated to the preservation of the Union, as were most Northerners, nor did they place any value or advocacy on the issue of states' rights. They simply were scallywags, who thought only of their own sorry hide. They had no respect for themselves, let alone anyone else. Such vermin would never know the meaning of self-esteem or the responsibility that it carried.

Julie was awake when her brother slipped in by her bedside to add another backlog to the fire. Small orange and red flames licked up at their new-found prey. The bed of red coals gained new strength and energy. Julie rolled part way up on her side facing Jubal and the new flames. She curled an arm up under her pillow. Jubal sat on the floor, placed his forearms on her bedside and cradled his chin in his hands. He could see the flicker of the flames in her eyes, and the orange glow hid the pale cheeks.

He realized in that instant just how much his curly haired, sassy little sister really meant to him; and it pained him to see her hurt and suffering at the hand of some unknown ner-do-well. He also felt a tear well up in his eye. His face was away from the fire. He knew that she could not see more than just a shadow of his features with the fire to his back. Therefore, he made no effort to dry his eyes or to hide his momentary overflow of emotion.

"How ye feel tonight, sis?"

"I ain't hungry. I liked the stew."

"How much ye eat?"

"All I wanted."

"Ye able to rest any?"

"I do okay, but..."

"But what?"

"I been thinkin' if I ever be able to walk again. I…I gettin' mighty filled up of this here old bedstead."

"I reckon so. Ye got rights fer so."

"I try. I really do try bein' patient."

"Well, sis, I know ye be patient and ain't nobody sayin' different."

"I not be feelin' sorry fer myself neither," Julie added with a certain air of determination and grit in her voice.

"I just wish I knowed who it be that shot ye. I thinkin' I would hunt him down and make dang certain he not be shootin' nobody else."

"What would that solve, Jubal? Would that make my knee any better? Would that make me be able to climb outta this here bed? It just get ye in a big trouble heap. That be all it do."

"Well, it pay him back fer what he done did to ye. Sides that, them scallywags could'a drug ye off and…and…well…they was men, weren't they?"

"I done thought on that too; but it never happened, and they never done such."

"I know that sis, but what iffin they done it again to some other poor soul who couldn't shoot so good or whatever?"

"Can't worry about such brother. I got other things frets me more."

"Like what?"

"I know I gonna be all right one way or 'nother. That ain't what bothers me."

"I listenin'."

"I know that I be weaknin' some. I can feel it. I know I ain't stout like I outta be. I can't do no work nor such, and I ain't pullin' my weight."

"Shucks far, sis, you know we do what needs be done. I ain't spectin' ye chop no wood ner nuthin' like it. Nobody else spectin' it either. We want ye all healed up and stout again like ye was fer sure, but we know that ye can't work none."

"It ain't that. That ain't what I mean."

"Then what sis, I reckon I ain't seein' what ye mean."

"Have ye took note of Ma lately? I mean have ye really looked at her close like?"

"How ye mean?"

"Look in her eyes. She be plum tired out all time now. I be killin' her takin' care of me all day and half the night. I be too much on her, Jubal. I can't even get myself up to piss without her. I just be wearin' her out more ever day. And 'sides that, I ain't got not one bit stronger and most likely ain't gonna. I be too hard on her."

"I reckon we be seein' to ye long as it take. Ye got no cause feelin' down on ye self."

"I really ain't down, Jubal. I just thinkin' that I be crippled up rest of my life and that I just be a burden on somebody else always. I been thinkin' on that, and I ain't so sure that I can live like that."

"Wahl now sis, don't ye be sayin' such. Ye just down on self now. It be better. Ye just needs be give yerself more time."

"No, Jubal. It ain't that way at all. I know I'll be healed one place or the other, and reckon it don't make much difference one way or other. I ain't 'fraid of that. I be more 'fraid of bein' lame fer rest of my time. I just be worried plum sick over our Ma. Her spirit done be broke, Jubal. She be so tired not only in body, but in mind too. She tell me few days back that she just be so tired that she not much care no more. I seen the looks in her eyes, and I seen her cryin' when she thought I be not lookin' at her. I don't like seein' her all broke down and such."

"I know she works hard, but she be stout too. Or used to be."

"She needs help, Jubal. She needs more help than ye can do fer her."

"I reckon I could work a bit harder most days."

"That ain't it, Jubal. She needs help in her mind. She needs help in her heart. She needs her spirits lifted up and needs be happy. She needs feel like she is wanted and needed and not just a slave to us all the time. Wes has helped her some, I reckon, but that ain't the heck of it all."

"I don't reckon I see what yer getting' at."

"Ma needs a mate, Jubal, and has needed somebody ever since Pa lit out. Even long time 'fore that too."

"I thunk that a time or two myself. Not so much old Wes, but about Pa bein' so scandalous and runnin' out on us all."

"That good to hear ye say, Jubal. I wondered iffin I was wrong thinkin' like that. Course it don't matter none, long as Pa stays gone. I reckon Ma could do how she pleased iffin Pa never showed his self here no more. I wish I knowed it would be that way. Far as I care, he ain't my Pa no more and fer that matter ain't never been."

"How do Ma feel about that?" Jubal asked his sister. Seemed like her face had pinked up just a bit, but he could not really tell in the firelight. Wes grunted a low moaning sound as he turned over on his pallet on the floor at the far side of the room.

"I ain't never brung it up with her."

"Wes be awful old fer takin' on a wife be my thinkin'."

"I think ye not know much about such. Ye be too green. Ye ain't no man yet, I reckon."

"I be older than ye."

"Ma ain't lookin' fer no breedin' bull. Lord knows that ain't what she needs. She needs a companion and a partner that could share her load. It be wrong to be uneven yoked. Good Book say so. Granny Iverson done showed me that and told me what all it means too. Ain't important fer ye to know right now. All ye needs know is that I be thinkin' that Ma needs Wes, and Wes needs Ma. That outta be good cause fer it to be."

"I reckon I can see that. But what about Pa? He and Ma still married, ain't they?"

"Yes, Jubal. They are in the eyes of the law, I reckon. I ain't no lawyer man, so I don't rightly know. But who knows where Pa is at and when he be back here?"

"No way to tell, I reckon. Never, would be good by me."

"Me too," Julie quickly answered. "But we don't know that."

"I hear things make me think Pa be part cause of ye gettin' shot in first place."

"How ye reckon that?" Julie asked somewhat puzzled.

"Company he been runnin' with," Jubal answered.

"Be best for all concerned iffin he just stay runnin' with them. Reckon water seeks its own level, least that be what Ma say. I don't never want lay eyes on him no more. Like I say, he ain't no Pa to me no more. Never was much one that I can recollect."

Jubal could not really determine if his sister was trying to tell him her wishes or not. He certainly had no cares for his Pa, and the more he learned about him the less he cared. It would sure be a blessing to Ma if he would just drop off the face of the earth and never bother them again. Too bad he never had the guts to join up with his Reb trash and get himself shot some place far off from here. Course he could get shot right here in Cane Valley.

"He showed me how to do his work and made me do it too."

"I know, Jubal. I seen ye be all tuckered out when he be off chasin' after laudanum or such."

"Yeah, I know. But he ain't here now, and I reckon it be best that way."

"But it be better iffin we could know he won't never be back here no more."

"Ye tryin' tell me somethin' there, sis?"

"No, I reckon I done told ye a plenty. Ye have to make up yer own mind."

A thousand things ran through the young boy's mind. One breath he despised his Pa, and the next he longed for someone who could have been a father to him times past. It had always been work, work, and more work, just so there would be less for Pa to do. Pa took credit for teaching him the signs and how to read a track, but it had been on rare occasions with threats of a thrashing lest he should forget it. There was never that closeness the way it should have been. Now the gulf between them could never be spanned, and he really did not care.

It had crossed his mind a time or two that Ma might take a favor to Wes, but he had not thought of him as a father. There was plenty that neither he nor Ma could know about Wes, but he had a reputation of being an honest man. Wes had been good to him and to Ma and that alone stood for something.

"Think ye could sleep some iffin I shut my face and leave ye be fer now?" Jubal asked quietly. "I will put on another back stick first, then ye can turn over and rest."

"Reckon I could." She reached her frail little arms out to him, and he gladly received her hug. Her face seemed ghostly pale in the flicker of the dying embers. He caught the glimmer of flame in a tear that coursed down her cheek. He did not know if it came from his eye or hers.

Morning brought clear skies. It had not frosted during the night. Ma was up and seeing to breakfast by the time it was first light. Jubal dressed hurriedly and went to the kitchen to see what he could do. Sarry already had mixings on the oilcloth covered table and was rolling it out and cutting biscuits from the rounded white dough.

"Make me a big pone this mornin', Sarry."

"I will soon as ye fetch me my milk crock from the springhouse. It be really cold this mornin'."

He made his way to the springhouse and thought about all the nights that Wes had slept in the loft. He thought of a thousand questions that he wanted to ask the old gentleman. Little did he know that Wes was already planning on having a good long talk with him. It would come all in due time.

Breakfast was soon over, and Wes wanted to know what Jubal was going to do for the coming day.

"I reckon I be workin' on firewood and a back stick or two."

"Well, I be a bit stouter than I was when yer Ma first fetched me over here. I reckon it be dang nigh time I earn a bit of my keep 'round here. I help ye what I can."

"I do it. Ain't that hard."

"I know ye can do it finer than me, but won't hurt none fer me tote some in fer ye. I ain't thinkin' I be up to pushin' a saw or wieldin' a axe, but I needs be doin' what I can. Whenever ye wanna start, I come out to the woodshed and lend a hand. How about that?"

"Be good by me. I see yer old bones out there in a bit. We see how much grit ye got," Jubal said with a wide grin on his face.

"Spoke like a sucklin' calf," Wes said with an equal grin on his face.

Both finished their business and showed up in the woodshed at near the same time. The sun was up far enough for good light now, and long stabbing rays made silver ribbons through the morning mist. It appeared that it would be another good day. Jubal made a note to look and listen for signs of any migrating geese. He would listen for old tom turkeys too.

Generous puffs of dust rose up with every pitch of a pole of wood. Jubal tossed several pieces thru the open woodshed window ready for placing across the saw bucks. Wes made his way into the shed from the opposite side. Both seemed to be in good spirits and eager to get some cutting done.

"I heard ye and Julie talk some last night. I weren't listenin' on purpose, but I waked up and heard ye part time."

"Well, I reckon we ain't talked on no secrets nor nothin' like that," Jubal answered.

"We needs be talkin' things out the way I see it. There be lots on my mind, and ye needs know what I mean and how I feel about things."

Jubal laid the first pole across the bucks and began pulling on the bow saw. Wes took a stance at the end of the bucks where he could off bear the wood cuts and toss them to the side where the stove wood supply would be heaped for the winter. The boy had the saw filed to a keen edge and minimal effort was needed to smartly saw off lengths that would fit well into the firebox.

"How much ye think ye really know about me?" Wes asked. "How long ye been knowin' me?"

"Long time, I reckon."

"Yeah, but how much ye know about me say, ten years back?"

"Reckon I don't recall that far back."

"I tell ye somethin' son. I weren't always a tramp or a filth like ye knowed me lately. I once had a life and a good name to go along with it. I had a mate, and she made ever thing seem worthwhile. She made me have call to be a man. She made me feel good. She give me purpose. When I lost her, I lost all that along with her. Now I admit, I could'a done a heap better fer myself over time, but ye know why I never done so?"

"I reckon ye gonna tell me, ain't ye?" Jubal replied as he continued to pull on the saw.

"I reckon I am cause and how it be part what I needs ye to see and understand about things now, here and now."

"How ye mean?"

"I quit livin' when my woman up and died on me. I quit cause I never cared no more. I give up on myself, and I wished a many a time that I was in her grave in place of her. Ye know why all that come on me?"

"No, I ain't so sure I see what ye be talkin' about."

"All that happened me cause my spirit was broke. My spirit was broke, and I never even tried to fix it. When yer spirits is broke, then ever thing else gets broke too, iffin ye allows it to be so. Ye unnerstand any of that?"

"I ain't fer sure, but what that got to do with now?" Jubal asked.

"I thinkin' that Julie be near havin' her spirit broke. I thinkin' yer Ma ain't very far behind her neither. It pains me a heap seein' them that way too."

"Well, Julie be a children yet. I ain't so sure that she know so much about givin' up or quitin' and the like", Jubal replied as he lifted a fresh white oak pole into the saw bucks and made ready for its first cut.

"She knows more than ye might give her credit for. I done heard her and Granny Iverson talk more than one time. That gal is wise beyond her years. I tell ye that fer a fact."

"I guess maybe so. I never really considered it."

"Concerns me that maybe she done knowed how bad she been hurt and thinkin' maybe she never be any better. Hard makin' mends when yer spirits be broke. She know she ain't been nowhere near able walk on that knee. Maybe that be what got her all down and out."

"She done say she be healed one way or 'nother," Jubal said. "She done told me that."

"Well, I reckon that be true seein' as how Granny Iverson done led her out where she be able see what be laid up fer her. Ye unnerstand what I mean and what she mean?"

"Ye be talkin' on good or bad, I reckon."

"Well, that be close," Wes said as he tossed yet another cut of wood onto the growing pile. Seemed like talking things out helped speed the saw and made for faster work for them both.

"Wes, ye be a good man or a bad man?"

"There be plenty things I done years back that I ain't real proud about. Some things that I done, I can't never make amends for cause and how the people I wronged is done died or moved on, and I ain't got no recollections on them. Stuff ye don't know; but iffin ye did know, it still not make much difference in me now. I ain't like I was back then, and I be sorry fer how I wronged people back then. That be part what took my woman away early, far as I know. I thinkin' that she got took on account of me bein' so sorry all that time. Things she tell me long time back just now bein' bore out to me."

"Like what?"

"Ye can't do wrong and scoot by. It catch up to ye sooner or later. It catch me later and break my spirit. And I thinkin' that be what make me be a loner today. Ye see, ain't nothin' on this here earth I can do make that any different than it already be. I the one who have to live with what I done, and I the one who have to answer all that I done. That the way it is, that the way it always has been, and I reckon it will be that way a hunnert years from now."

"Ye talkin' in circles, Wes."

"I reckon so in yer mind, but they be things ye needs unnerstand about me. That why I say what I sayin'."

Jubal continued pulling the saw steady and regular. A dozen rakes of the saw produced another stick for the pile. Wes could match the pace but had to work at it to keep up. A day or two like this would make a winter's wood, even if it turned out to be a mite colder than usual. Both knew that the pole pile outside the shed would produce a lot of cuts and that there would be no need to drag more down off the ridge. Jubal had made sure of that, and he had laid in a good supply down next to the hog scalder too. Thanksgiving was soon to be here and that meant killin' time and fresh hog meat for all.

"Wes, far as I concerned, what ye been in yer past is yer business. I know ye fer what ye been since Ma been sendin' ye grub and such. Ye ain't never done nary a thing what riled me. Like ye said, them things past is past, and that be the way it be. I ain't got no fault on ye fer that."

Wes pondered for a minute or two before he spoke again. The sawdust raked out of the kerfs and began to pile up below the bucks. Each stick of wood that Wes tossed on the pile made a dull thunk as it bounced off the old chestnut boxing walls or a rasping grate as it slid down the growing pile.

"I made good money years back when I was young. I saved a bunch of it and hoarded it up like some old miser man. I still got most of it too. I got it stashed good where it be safe and ain't nobody know where it be 'sides me."

"Ye meanin' like yer danged old gourd stash."

"Naw, son. It be heap better'n that."

Wes now had the undivided attention of the boy. He stopped pulling on the saw and looked Wes directly eye to eye. He was dumbfounded to think that the old man might have a horde that could choke a horse. He was all ears now.

"Only thing botherin' me now is this danged war. I ain't about go handin' out money when carpetbaggin' and thiefin' and such be goin' on ever where. War done took most stuff outta hand, and most stuff be way overpriced now days. Some things ye ain't even able to get. It just be bad times right now."

"I been thinkin' on that quite a bit too," Jubal stated. "I been thinkin' I ought get myself off some place and join up and help with the whuppin' all them scallywags needs. I be old 'nuff, and I ain't scared to go neither."

"I know ye ain't no pup no more, but yer Ma needs you here. I weren't aimed to bring yer Ma in on this right now. But yer Ma needs ye, and she needs me too. And I need her far as that be. She done took me in and cleaned me up and give me my spirit back. Now she be needin' her spirit give back to her cause she just about broke down too, and it ain't hard seein' why."

"Ye tellin' me ye wants lay with her?"

"No, son. No! That ain't it at all. No way. I told ye that I got a stash. I be able to make her life a heap better iffin things was just so and so. I still be thinkin' ye ain't seein' how I mean."

"Then what ye want me think on it?"

"I ain't wantin' yer Ma just to have a lay woman. Hell fire, if that were what I wanted, I reckon I could buy that fer a week or two. That ain't it at all. Besides that, I done outlived myself long time ago, and you will too some of these days."

Jubal hesitated. He thought about making old Wes tell more about his escapades with the women, but his thoughts soon turned to Lida. He thought things about her that stirred him to the core. He was not sure how he felt about those thoughts. Instead he managed to direct his thinking down other paths.

"How come ye got such a stash now anyhow? How you come by it all?"

"I been tellin' ye that I weren't too proud of some things I done."

"I know ye told me that, but I wanna know how. Iffin ye gonna be layin' with my Ma, then I be thinkin' ye best be comin' clean with me. I could give ye a whuppin' nigh on to what ye got when we brung ye over here."

"I know ye got rights bein' sore at me boy, and I aim on tellin' ye anything ye needs know. What matters to me is that ye be able to see what I want now and how I can make good on what I say. That be a heap important to me."

"Seems me like money ain't much good in this old holler right now," Jubal muffed. "Ain't nobody got none; and iffin they did, ain't nobody got nuthin' fer sale. Only way money be any count be go off from here someplace where ain't been tore up so much by all the skirmishes and fights. Go off someplace where ain't been stole blind."

"Ye be thinkin' right there, son. I know where them places and them people is this very day. That be why I know I can get things done right," Wes said with emphasis and certainty.

"How ye know that?"

"Knowed that since way back when I come up outta Alabammy."

"That where ye make yer pile?"

"I made right good there."

"Doin' what?"

"Well, I helped some slaves get on their way up north. Only ones who could pay mind ye. Most never had nothin' to pay with."

"Never got rich that a way, did ye?"

"No. Made most by bringin' em back from up north. Most plantation owners paid a heap fer bringin' field hands back."

"That how ye made it all?"

"That most part of it. I done some slave tradin' fer a bit, but not much."

"That what ye meanin' ye not proud of?"

"Yeah, most part."

Jubal was not too impressed by what Wes had told him. He never caught onto the fact that Wes had taken money, most times all that a black man or woman could muster, set them out on a leg of the underground, then waited a few days to tell other trackers where they were and what route they were taking. Then he would rustle them back to their owners and collect a handsome reward. All that had come to an abrupt end when the war broke out. Wes feared for his safety in the Deep South and had lit out for the hills and mountains, bringing his worth with him. He had been paid in gold dollars, that was all he would accept; and now they would be worth a fortune. He just needed to protect them from thieves and warmongers.

"How come ye never spend it?"

"Had no real need. I knowed we could make do, but I never took account of the war comin' on and all that it done brung on. I never give no thought on how a bunch a riff-raff would be waitin' fer a slip up and then try and make off with ever thing I had. I can't say plumb sure, but I thinkin' that be what got old Cleve done in. I let word get out that he done took it from me and his own kind done turned on him thinkin' they would get it from him. Serve him right. But he never had it, never knowed where it was ner nuthin' to the kind."

"That why they whupped ye up some?"

"Reckon that be part so. That part why I live like I ain't got a cent. People most time believe what they can see and not so much what they may been told somewhere along the way. Ye can unnerstand that, I reckon."

"I reckon I can," Jubal parroted.

"Well then, I reckon ye can see why I needs be so careful over it now. And that also be why ye can't go blabbin' ever single thing ye know to nary a soul. Ever cut-throat in a hunnert miles of here would come a callin', and it won't be no kinfolk call neither. I said I'd tell ye whatever ye wanted to know, but I done tell ye too much ceptin' ye keep hush-hushed about it all. Ye don't even needs be talkin' it with yer Ma, leastwise not right now. I tellin' ye fer a fact iffin ye ever count on seein' any of it, then ye best keep shut-mouthed. Now that just the way it has to be. When this here war be done, and we get some decent law back in the valley, them things gonna be a mite easier. Then we can all get some good from it. Ye unnerstand me?"

"I reckon so, fer now anyhow."

"I just wanna make sure ye know what I mean when I say I ain't proud of all that I done, but I can't do nuthin' about it now. It done been too long and gone."

"Where ye got it all stashed now?" Jubal asked as he continued to pull on the saw.

"It ain't too far off. I could lay hands on it in a week."

"Ye be only one knows where it be?"

"Yeah, I ain't told none whatsoever."

"Ye gonna tell me?"

"Not right now."

"Well, I reckon ye got yer reasons, but what goes with it when some galoot comes along and knocks ye off? How it gonna do Ma any good then? Don't seem right smart by me."

"If I told ye where it was, can ye look me square in my eye and tell me ye wouldn't go grab it right now?"

"Well...I see how ye be thinkin' that way."

"Jubal, boy, I reckon ye think I don't trust ye. Well, bein' plum honest with ye, I don't, leastwise when it pertain to that much money. It be too much temptation fer ye."

"Ye ain't told me how much it be yet."

"No, that be true, and I am a mind that it ain't that important."

"How come ye say that?"

"They be money that be able make a life fer yer Ma and me and you young'uns too fer that matter. But this damned war is messin' up ever single thing now. Ye can see that can't ye?"

"I reckon so."

"I thought so. Glad we in agreement on that at least," Wes said as he tossed another cut against the wall with a thud.

"They be one other thing I see standin' in yer way too," Jubal said.

"What that be son?"

"My Ma."

"How ye mean there?" Wes asked.

"How ye know how she feels about all this? I tell ye one thing sure, Ma ain't fer sellin' herself to no man fer no amount of money."

"I know that and I ain't said one word to her about no money. Reckon she be in the dark as far as that be concerned."

"Well, there still be one other matter," Jubal said

"What?"

"Pa. She still be married to Pa, and he be my Pa even iffin in name only."

"Well, we have talked on that. Reckon she ain't beholdin' to yer Pa no more. It really be best iffin he never show up around here no more."

Jubal stopped his efforts at sawing and placed a hand on each hip. "And what would ye do when he did come 'round here again, Wes?"

"I wouldn't stand fer him doin' no harm to her nor none of you kids, or Granny Iverson."

"How would ye stop him, Wes?"

"I reckon that be up to him. He act up, then I do whatever be needed."

"He best never show his face here no more."

"Hate him that much, do ye?"

"Ain't got a dang thing fer him. Reckon I be missin' nuthin' by not never seein' him, never, no more."

"But what ye do iffin he do come here again?"

"Wes, I reckon I really not know right now. I be apt do somethin' that I might regret someday. It be fine with me never cross his path no more."

"I hope that be the way it all work out. I hope it be so that I can make things be better fer us all, and I will do it that way best I can when things gets settled out some. Just needs be patient, I reckon. I hope ye not go tellin' yer Ma what I done told ye about my money stash and all. I don't never want her thinkin' I be tryin' buy her nor nuthin' to the likes. Can we be square on that?"

"I reckon we can, providin' ye at least tell me some stuff about where ye stash it all. I ain't sayin' ye needs tell me exact where, but I just needs know a clue so as I know ye ain't foolin' me none."

"I reckon I owes ye that much. Ye know where slick rock is?"

"Yeah, I do."

"Well, it be close by. That be all I sayin' right now. That be anything ye can hang yer hat on to fer now?"

"I can rest on that for now."

"We needs be talkin' out some more stuff too, but I thinkin' it can wait fer now. Ye got anything else on yer mind right now?" Wes asked.

"I reckon it keep fer now," Jubal replied.

The wood sawing and piling continued for much more of the morning with the two mostly making small talk about this and that. Jubal let his mind wander and his thoughts included some fantasies about how he would spend old Wes's money and all the finery that it would bring to him. He even thought of those faraway places and their painted up women that he had heard so much about from the tales that he had heard, mostly around old Cleve's store. Wes brought him back to reality with an unexpected proclamation.

"This here is the last pole."

"We done good, I reckon."

"You right as rain there, son. We done good. Just go to show what can be done when folks works together. That be just more reason to get this here dang war over and done."

"I reckon I be old 'nuff so I can join up and help it be over and done. I been thinkin' on that some too."

"You serious?"

"I ain't so sure. All I know is I want Ma and the girls be safe and not need be worried over some hooligan comin' in here and doin' harm and wrong by them. Iffin I was gone, then they be on they own and not have much protection."

"I ain't encouragin' ye to go off and fight, but I plan to be here and do all I can. I done mended up a bunch, and I be much obliged to yer Ma fer that. I be a heap stouter than I was a month past."

"I be glad that ye be better. Ye was always kind to me and that be more than I give Pa credit fer. He never give a dang fer me, save fer what work he could get outta me. Ain't much way I could ever feel much fer him."

Wes made no spoken reply but was all smiles. He knew that he had won the boy over, and he reasoned that it was not just because of the money story. He knew that whatever Ma felt for him definitely was out of care and compassion, because she knew nothing of the money and would probably be offended by it if she did. That would turn things cold all the way around and that was the last thing he would ever want. Ma had added years to his life already, and he wanted to add years to hers as well.

Late November brought chilling rains, and the gray smoke curling from the old stone and mud chimney bore witness to the warmth and coziness that lived inside the log home at the head of Cane Valley. The ash and sugar trees had held on to their brown and withered leaves as long as they could. Now the dampening rain forced them to release their last vestiges of life and fall away. A thick blanket of leaves would insulate the ground, and deer would come to forage in them for fallen acorns and beech mast. Tracking would be easy, and it should be easy enough to find venison or foul for the Thanksgiving table. Thanksgiving would also mean fresh hog meat as long as the weather would be cold enough on killing day.

The boy could have been out in the ridges and hollows searching for game tracks during the rains, but for the most part had been content to stay warm and dry and stick to the chores around the house. That helped to take some of the load off Ma and Sarry. Julie seemed to be a shade better and sat up in bed some. She was still pale and had little strength. She and her brother had talked again; and he had wanted to ask her some things about Lida, but had decided against it, for now anyhow.

That did not prevent him from thinking about her. He could come up with no feasible excuse to go to the mill and call on her. It would be embarrassing to him to just simply go for no other reason. Not too likely that there would be ruffians out in such foul weather. He reasoned he should stay put, warm and safe. The Johnsons had enough to see them through the winter. If they needed anything from him, he had no thinking as to what it might be. C.C. could run the mill; and if he did need help, then he would get word sent or come after the help himself.

But Lida. Her warm and tender touch lingered with him still. Her tenderness and her smile would make the discomfort of the rain melt away as soon as he had her in his arms.

He would find a way to get to the mill and he would find it soon. Winter was coming on, and it would be here fast now. It would be cold, much colder, and there could be deep snow. That would make any trip to the mill, needed or otherwise, much harder. Yes, he would go to the mill. He would go tomorrow. It just might be better tomorrow than it was today. The rain might even let up.

Jubal found C.C. at the mill, just as he thought he would. He had started soon after breakfast and had encountered no one on the road. He had kept a keen eye on the ridge lines and scanned diligently all along the road for any sign of new tracks, both man and beast. He had seen where some deer had crossed the road near the reed patch and made a mental note to look around there more on the way home. The rain had indeed stopped, and the sun broke through scattered cloud cover now and then. The crows flitted about and did not seem so restless today. They showed no signs of a disturbing interloper. Most all timber was bare now and line of sight was good for longer distances. The boy felt reasonably sure that he was the only one on the move anywhere near him.

"Mornin' Mr. Johnson."

"Mornin' to ye, son. What brings ye down here so early today?"

"Not much, I reckon. I come mostly see how ye be doin' and such."

"Ain't much goin' on here, and I be thankful for that. Captain Olson and his troopers stopped in here three or four days back. They say things is quiet in these parts now. Said they might be ordered out soon."

"Where he think they be goin' to?"

"He thinks they be called back up east some place."

"It cross my mind ever now and then...I think sometimes that I join up and go up east too. I ain't beholdin' to way things is here sometimes.

"How ye mean, son?"

"Well, Julie bein' shot and all. War be the cause of it, way I see it. If I went and help fight, then maybe I help it be done sooner."

"That be what got many a young pup like ye killed too. I know ye want the fightin' stopped, and so do I. I be thinkin' that it can't go too much more cause ever thing down south of here be mite nigh wiped out already. Besides that, yer Ma needs ye here lookin' after her and the gals. She be hard pressed makin' it on her lonesome. I know ye never asked me what to do, but I be tellin' ye what I think be best. I don't mean stirrin' ye none, but that be just how I see things. Far as that part goes, I can use ye around here some ever now and then."

That statement struck a chord with Jubal. More time at the mill would mean more time to see Lida. If he was in the mill, she surely could not keep herself in the house all the time. She would surely want to come around some too. She might even want to go back up to that special place up top of the hill where they went to pick up chestnuts. It might be a bit cold up there now, but it would always be a hot spot for him.

Lida did come to the mill that day. She said that she had seen Jubal from the house and wanted to know how Julie was doing. Jubal told her about her talkin' with him and some of the things that she had said about being fearful that she would never be able to walk again. He told her how his sister had no strength and seemed so weak and pale most all the time now. He told her nothing about his Ma or how he was concerned for her. Wes had really put him to thinking when he spoke about her spirits being broken, and he wanted to ask Lida what she thought about that. He did not get that chance. Lida did not feel too well herself. Her face was pale and her eyes seemed clouded. She had a rasp in her voice and coughed with a deep rattle. She told him that she had been ailing for a few days now and that she was going back to the house and go back to bed. She turned and was gone. He felt cold and alone.

Making his way back toward home, Jubal took note of the early afternoon sky. The few clouds left in the sea of blue appeared to make all possible haste in their progress from the west. The entire sky would soon be devoid of anything except the brilliant blue. No cloud cover tonight would mean a fall in the temperature by morning and good chance of frost by daylight. Ought to be plenty cold for hog killin'.

"Ma, reckon it be cold 'nuff fer butcherin' by mornin' time?"

"Might be, son. Might be."

"How long it take be ready and all?"

"I done got ever thing most ready as can be fer now," Ma replied.

She had no sense of urgency in her voice, just stoic determination to do whatever it would take to get the job done. Jubal had not really taken notice of how really tired she looked; but he saw it in her eyes today, and recalled what both Julie and Wes had said about her. He wanted to ask her how she felt and how she was doing. No, what he really wanted to ask her was whether or not her spirit was broken? Had she reached the point where she was about to give up? He was really needing to know how she felt, but he also knew that right now was not the time to ask her.

"Ye want me go get the fire ready to light off at first light?"

"I reckon ye may as well, son. We gotta have both hogs so we have winter's keep. I ain't sure right now if we kill both tomorrow mornin' or not. I guess we decide that come sunup. But it be a good turn gettin' ready this afternoon."

Jubal headed across the barn lot and saw that Wes was already placing poles and sticks under the scalder pan. He had already carried the gambling poles and chains from the gear room and had them standing close behind the scalder. He had not driven them into the soft earth yet but had brought the sledge with him. About all that was left for Jubal to do was fill the pan with water. That was accomplished in no short time.

"How long ye been at this, Wes?"

"Oh, nigh onto a hour, I guess."

"Ye saved me doin' it, I reckon."

"I done told ye I was stouter, and I done told ye that I aim to help make things better 'round here best I can. It be proper thing fer me to be doin' fer all concerned."

Jubal made no comment, but rather just patted the old man on the back and smiled at him. Wes nodded, as if to say thank you.

It was a long and mostly sleepless night for the young man. The image of his tired and tested mother lingered in his mind. The failure of Julie to gain any strength or color raised doubts. Lida had barely spoken to him, and he felt hurt in his heart. He had no reason to doubt that she did not feel well, but she could at least have said that she had missed him or that…well…she could have just said something. About the only thing that he had to feel good about was the fact that the woodshed was full. There was enough wood worked up for the cook stove, and the scalder was ready. Wes had been encouraging to him, much more than his own Pa had ever been. He got out of bed and crept in near Julie's bed. The fire was burning well, and the back stick was less than half consumed by the flickering flames. Small shadows danced around the walls of the old log home, now safe and warmed. He could see that Julie was resting well. Her breathing was regular and quiet. Wes had his back to the fire. It was not easy to tell if he was awake. It did not matter. He peered out the tiny window on the north wall. Stars shone everywhere he looked. It was cold and clear. There would be fresh hog meat hanging in the smokehouse by this time tomorrow.

The next morning did, in fact, dawn clear and cold. Jubal lit the fire under the scalder before breakfast, then hurriedly put away his portion of biscuits and sausage gravy. He and Wes were at the scalder before the water was even warm. It was taking on the appearance of a good and productive day. Ma had made her decision this morning soon after she got out of bed. She told Jubal to go ahead and kill both hogs. They would work up both of them today.

Wes rounded up another set of gambling poles and the needed chains while Jubal did the actual killing. A swift but strong blow well located on the hog's forehead brought death in an instant. The carcasses were dragged to the scalder in preparation for scalding and scraping. Wes had stoked and stirred up the fire and the water soon began to give off a slight vapor. It was time. First hog into the hot water, turned side to side, hair all scraped away and then hung on the gambling poles and allowed to air dry. Same for the second beast.

Ma was not one to save every piece of the hog. She cared nothing for the cracklings and the organ meats. She did not even want the feet. Consequently, the process moved along with an order that made for fast and easy work. What would be hung in the smokehouse would be the shoulders, the hams, the loin meats and the side meats. All other cuts would be ground into sausage and put up properly in quart jars. Ma would render enough fat to seal the jars and save enough to meet all her kitchen needs.

Both hogs had been gutted and were trimmed as needed. They needed to hang a bit longer in order to drain as much blood as possible. It was then that a short time of rest could be appreciated. Jubal had hardly stopped, but now found an end of a nearby log that would make an acceptable seat. He had no more than sat down and wiped his forehead with a sleeve when he caught a glint of sunlight reflected from high off the ridge above the old log house. He strained to see what might have caused it and caught only what he thought was a quick movement at the edge of the timberline. Just as quickly, it was gone and there was no further reflection. In what seemed only a few heartbeats, he noticed the crows scattering and circling in an obvious excited state. They were almost in line with where he had seen the glint of light. He knew the entire ridge like the back of his hand, and there was nothing there that could cause the tell-tell crows to act up so suddenly. It had to be a big beast of some sort. Then it struck him, no sunlight would be reflecting off an animal. Not unless that animal walked upright.

No one else had seen the glint, and Jubal said nothing to anyone about it. He would walk up there later and see what signs he could find. There was no reason for anyone to be up there, and it made him feel uneasy just knowing that eyes might be on him at that very moment. Two or three more hours and all the meat would be in the smokehouse. The buzzards would soon take care of the waste from the killing. Two days in this bright sunshine and every scrap would be gone. That thought gave him reason to look skyward simply as a reaction. Sure enough, there was one pair of black, outstretched wings, silhouetted against the brilliance of the blue, cloudless sky. They soared on silent currents, far above the valley floor. They circled in effort to pinpoint what they already knew awaited them. He did point out the wings to Wes and to Ma.

"It be the natural order of things," Wes said as he shaded his eyes with his outstretched hand. "It just be one more way that we be took care of."

"We best get to it," Ma said as she picked up a knife and went at the first hog. "We still got a bunch to do."

Conversation from that point on was sparse. Efforts were concentrated on the task at hand. Their efforts were not in vain. Mid-afternoon found all the shoulders and hams on the smokehouse shelves, and the sides and ribs had already had their first salt and were hanging from pegs well out of the reach of any vermin. The ham and shoulder meat needed a bit more cooling and then they could have their first application of salt. Ma had brought salt home from Yeary's store on the day Julie had been shot. She had made sure that there would be plenty for killing time.

Jubal and Wes made good on salting the fresh meat. They applied new salt each morning taking care to spread it completely and evenly. One more day and it could be sacked up and hung. It would keep well into the coming spring and summer without any spoilage. If they had nothing else, there would be ham and red-eye gravy this winter.

Thanksgiving morning came and went just the same as any other morning. There was no special meal or any type of holiday festivities. It was just another day for Jubal. Ma and Granny Iverson had made small talk about all the things that they had and how they were thankful to have them. Jubal thought about how they would react if they knew about old Wes and his stash of money. They might really have something to crow over then. He did not give too much thought to the meaning of the day. He was somewhat content just having things done and laid by for the most part. He would go to the mill next week to sell a ham to C.C. and Mrs. Johnson. They always wanted one for Christmas cooking. The mill run would give him another chance to be with Lida, and surely she would be feeling better by then.

Tuesday morning dawned with a skiff of white powdery snow covering the ground in patches where the shadows had prevented a bright blue sky from warming the surfaces. Jubal made his way to the smokehouse, not noticing the faint impression of a boot heel that pointed away from the door. It took only a glance once inside to note that two hams were gone. They had been cut from the overhead poles that had strained a bit to support them.

Bounding out the door in somewhat of a rage, he soon broke the news to Ma and Wes. They in turn had to see for themselves and made their way to the open smokehouse door. It was then that Jubal noticed the boot track and began in earnest, looking for another sign. Some thieving bastard had robbed them of their hard work and toil. They had taken their sustenance and by the Eternal, if he had a hand in it, they would pay.

Chapter 12

Tracking

*L*ittle time was wasted in gathering gear and the old squirrel rifle. The powder horn was near empty, but there would be enough for three or four rounds. The wadding was left from the last outing. Jubal grabbed it and stuffed it into the small leather drawstring pouch tied to his belt. The pouch held only a half dozen or so lead bullets. It would be all that he had, and he hoped that it would be more than enough. He tried hard to control his inner turmoil; because if whoever had done this deed turned out to be who he suspected, then the entire affair would be messy to say the least.

Whoever took the meat from the smokehouse had been quiet in doing so. Old Jake most always slept on the dogtrot and would readily alert to anything out of the ordinary.

Jubal whistled for the old redbone hound, but he did not respond. Jubal began to look for signs near the trot and in front of the smokehouse. The dry powdered snow did not offer much in the way of preserving tracks. The wind had blown it around and partially filled or erased what signs that may have been left during the night.

Jubal headed to the barn. Sometimes the old dog would seek additional shelter from the chilling wind and had been known to bed down in the stall with Kate. Faint tracks in the skip of snow told the tale. Not only were there dog tracks leading to the barn, there were man tracks as well. They were not easily seen, but could be spotted by a discerning eye. The boy noted how they were partially filled by blown snow and how that the depressions in the ground had been frozen during the dark hours. That would confirm the fact that whoever had made these signs had done so in the forepart of the night. No one was awake to take notice of what hour the snow let up. Had that been known, a closer time could be reckoned as to when the thief was about and maybe some idea of how much head start that he had.

Closer looks revealed that the tracks led to the barn, right up to the gear room door. Jubal noticed the latch secured just about the same time that he heard Jake stirring inside.

He called gently to the old warrior and could imagine the swinging of the stalwart, never still tail. Once he opened the gear room door, it was evident why the dog had not sounded during the night. Jake had been lured into the room with a big ham hock which he had managed to half devour.

"Dang ye dog. Ye ain't got sense fer nothin'. Ye be plum foundered by nightfall. I did aim on takin' ye with me, but I see ye ain't fit fer nuthin' right now."

The tail swung to and fro and the eyes looked as long as the ears. There was no hollow in his gut. He had eaten till he could eat no more. "Who done this, Jake? Too bad ye not be a talkin' critter, but I be thinkin' I know already. Ain't much way ye would be still fer nobody else. Ye stay here and best ye rest up. Yer innards is gonna need all ye can muster up, and I ain't so sure that be all it take fer ye. Crazy scoundrel. Ye was fed better. Ye ought know a heap better. I just hope ye make it. I tell Wes keep eye out fer ye." Jubal closed the door and dropped the peg into the hasp. Jake would lie down and go back to sleep as soon as he heard no more sound from outside. He was going to be one more sick critter after eating so much fresh meat and so much salt. Wes would have to see that he got water in small bits only. If he drank all he wanted, he would bloat and most likely not make it through the next two or three days.

There were more man tracks. Tracks that retraced themselves back to the smokehouse. Jake had been lured into the barn because that would make sure that he was quiet and would not alert to the presence of an intruder. Whoever this was knew exactly what they were doing and exactly how to go about it.

Wes and the boy were in agreement about the old redbone hound. Would be some tough sledding for the old boy, and he would be fortunate indeed if he pulled through it. The next several hours would tell. Wes agreed to look after the family dog and to offer him frequent small bits of water. Needed to keep down the chance of any bloating as best they could.

"Ye keep eye on things here, and I go see where he be headed," Jubal said, half telling Wes and half asking for his cooperation.

"What ye be up to?"

"I see iffin I can track where he be turnin', but I got right strong notion where they be headed anyhow."

"Ain't much snow fer tracks."

"I know, but I can make do, I reckon," Jubal added.

He had delayed long enough to talk things over with Ma and Granny Iverson. Ma had almost broken down to tears at the thought of losing half her winter's store of meat. Julie was going to need all the help she could muster to see her into spring and get mended up. She would have to eat well to do that, and the hog meat was supposed to be a big part of that plan. Jubal knew why she was so upset and that fact alone was enough to fan the flames of his anger and hatred for the one who had wronged them.

"Jubal, son, I'd feel a heap better by ye leavin' that old squirrel shooter here. It vexes me fer ye be out traipsin' all over and totin' that thing. What iffin ye was to run on some Bluecoats, and they took ye to be a Reb? And what iffin ye run on some of them scallywags like took our hog meat? Likely we ain't never see them hams no more no matter what ye see or where ye tracks. They be gone and that just be the way it be. I ain't wantin' ye shot over them. Not now, not never."

Jubal could see the hurt in the tired eyes of his Ma and that bothered him more than the loss of the ham and all the work that had gone into them. No one had the right to treat her that way and vengeance was forefront in his thoughts for the moment.

Floods of many moods raced through his mind. He was not yet fully a man, but he had definitely been thrust headlong into the responsibilities of a man. He had never known anything of pleasure or leisure save for what he could glean from the surrounding hills

405

and hollows. He had longed for the assurances and guidance from a father, but had received little. It was work, work and more work. Ma had tended the cuts and the scrapes as best she could, but she could not cure the deep gashes that had been carved into his soul. Now, he had to go and do as best he could to seek justice and part of that judgment just might come at the hands of the old long rifle.

"No, Ma. I need it with me just in case I needs defend myself. I ain't out fer no hide nor hair today, not just yet," he told her. It was an effort to ease her mind and at the same time let her know that he intended to do as he must to see this deed done. "Anyhow, I might run on a doe some place and that would help take place of what we done lost. Ye done said yerself that them hams is gone, and I reckon ye be right about that too. Deer meat ain't hog meat, but it be better than corn mush when everything else be done eat up. Ye frets too much, Ma."

He noticed a tear trickle down her weathered cheek as she turned to go back to the kitchen. He wished that he had not chided her for worrying. After all, he was her son, her child. What mother would not fret over her child when she perceived him to be headed into harm's way? Best just to push aside his feelings for now and get to the task at hand. Time would erase every facet of any trail, and time was passing.

He quickly followed his Ma into the kitchen, embraced her lovingly, wiped away her tear with a pointed finger, turned, saying not a word.

The morning air possessed a chill, but the mid-morning sun should diminish that enough not to need a heavy wrap. Jubal did not want the buckskin shirt that Wes offered him. He just draped it across his shoulder and started up the draw beside the old smokehouse. It led through the yard gate and along the upper meadow fence to the lower reaches of the east ridge. That route would take him up to where he had seen the glint on the day they killed the hogs.

"Hold up there a minute," Wes said as he attempted to catch up to Jubal. "I go a piece with ye."

"Okay, but I know ye got words on yer mind. Best just be out with it," Jubal responded with obvious impatience.

"Ain't no need be in such a huff. Them tracks ain't goin' nowhere no time soon."

"They done got a big head start on me. Never will learn nothin' standin' here gawkin' over it."

Wes caught up to the boy and paused enough to partially catch his breath. "I reckon I want nigh on the same things as ye do. I wants whoever done this found out and caught same as ye do. But ye needs know a trick or two first. Then ye can and best be on yer way, I reckon. I just want to show ye a thing or two. So take it a mite slower so as how I can keep alongside ye."

"What ye thinkin' on showin' me?"

The two walked on along the fence row for a few yards until Wes tugged on Jubal's sleeve stopping him in his tracks. The boy looked at him with a frown of repeated impatience.

"See that?"

"See what?"

"Look at that track," Wes said as he pointed a few feet ahead of them with an outstretched pointer finger. Jubal was a bit taken aback that he had not seen such a blatant sign all by himself. He justified himself by reasoning that Wes had distracted him from the start.

"See there, see that?"

"I see the footprint," Jubal said.

"But do ye read all it be tellin' ye? See how snow powder be heaped up outside the heel print?"

"Yeah, I can see that."

"Well, ye know what that means?"

"Means whoever made it been low steppin' and puttin' he feet down hard," Jubal said in efforts to show how much he knew about reading a track.

"And why ye think that be?" Wes questioned.

"Ain't so sure," Jubal reluctantly admitted.

"Heap harder to walk soft when ye tote two big hams. Reckon that be about all this here feller could be totin' off. Ain't nothin' else gone is they?"

"No, reckon not."

"Turn yer palm up and tuck in yer thumb like this here." Wes demonstrated by cupping his fingers around his right thumb. Jubal followed his example. "Now see iffin yer back hand will fit in his track. Lay yer knuckles across the ball of his print." Once again Jubal did as he was instructed and his hand filled the print from side to side.

"Ye know what that mean?" Wes asked.

"Tell me."

"It mean that whoever made this here track be near same size as ye be. His foot be same across as yer hand. That make him out to be nigh on same size as ye."

The immediate thought that flashed through the young mind was the fact that he and his Pa were about the same size. Pa had to be a bit heavier afoot, but he and his son were the same build and same in strength. Pa might be some down on brute force since he been on the bottle so much. The rage that he felt welling up inside made him more determined to see this deed over and done and the sooner the better.

Wes added more. "Look here at the broom sage where he done tromped it down." The old man pointed to a tuft of sage that had been laid flat by the heavy foot. "See how it all be pushed over in a line? See how all the straws is lined up? Ye see how they is all creased here at the same place? See how they is all broke the same way and how the breaks all line up? Ye see that, son?"

"Yeah, I do."

"Well that right there proves he was low steppin' and pullin' hard. His foot slipped a mite, that be what creased the broom straws all in a line. Ye keep lookin' fer them kind of signs and ye can track him through thick or thin. He be totin' somethin' sure as my name be what it is, and I be willin' bet it be ham."

"How ye know so much on trackin'?" Jubal asked in some surprise.

"I learn it down in Bammy. I tell ye more on it some time. Now not a good time fer such. Move on up a ways, up the fence line."

In less than twenty yards, they spotted more signs, more tracks very much like the first one that Wes had elaborated on. It already appeared that the trail would lead along the fence row until it came to the corner of the gently rising meadow. From there, there were only two ways to go. A body could turn west and head for the high ridge line and over into pine country. There was really no reason to go that way unless you wanted to cross the higher ridges and slip into the far reaches of the Clinch country. That area was all too rugged for farming and was devoted mostly to timbering. The trail would most likely turn east and follow from one short ridge and hollow to the next until they cleared all of the Cane Valley area. Then they would most likely head for the river flats, and beyond that go most anywhere. The only hindrances would be the distances and the time needed to cross the doubles. Not too likely that a thief would try to carry near sixty or so pounds of extra load that much of a distance.

Wes and the boy poured over each footprint they came across, and each one told them the same things. Low stepping and hard pulling with a heavy load. Should be no trouble reading this for as far as it would go. No more than halfway up to the fence corner, they came upon more telling signs. There were widened long scrapes in the snow mixed in with mud smears that had frozen hard. That told them the culprit had been there in the forepart of the night while the ground had not yet frozen. That had to be somewhere about midnight. It also told them more about the person and his activity.

"Look. See them scrapes?" Wes stated with some apparent excitement. It was as if a long silent talent in him had just been awakened. Jubal was impressed by his ability of observation. "Whoever it is done took a fall here. Knees is what made them marks. He done went down here and slid back a mite. See here where he dug his toes in tryin' stop slidin' backward? Here be where he catched his fall with his hand. Ye see that? Ye see where his fingertips went in the mud?"

Jubal agreed to all that Wes had pointed to. It was plain that he knew what he was seeing and knew how to read all the signs as well. Wes continued looking around, back and forth for several minutes, always taking care not to step in any of the tracks that the culprit had left.

"Come. Look here," Wes instructed.

Jubal went to his side.

"Here be another handprint. Ye see that there?" Wes was pointing to a small blotch of red centered in the palm depression in the snow.

"Reckon he took a right smart fall there. Reckon that be he blood. He done got a hand cut way I see it."

"Ain't much blood. Must not be bad cut," Jubal added as if to bolster his ability to read signs as well as the older man.

"We needs go back where he fell. See iffin we missed anything," Wes said as he turned to go back a few steps and take another look. He retraced himself to the place where he had first seen the signs of a fall. He stood over the first print with his hands splayed out on his own knees and looked intently at the handprint before him. He stooped lower and lower to the ground until his hands reached the broom sage around the prints. Carefully he examined each print.

"Here be what cut him."

"What?" Jubal asked

"See this here little stubble?"

"Yeah, I do."

"Look close."

"Where?"

"See that white right there? See how they ain't no snow up against it?"

"Yeah."

"What ye make it to be?"

"Ain't sure."

"Ye know salt melt snow don't ye?" Wes questioned

"Yeah, I knowed that."

"Well," Wes continued, "I be thinkin' that salt done been knocked loose off a ham and melted that bit of snow. See how the ground ain't froze in that little part?"

"Yeah. I do indeed," Jubal answered with renewed interest in the talents of the man with a past that any hermit would be proud to be known by.

Wes got down on his knees and looked even closer. He poked a long skinny finger into the barren little circle in the snow bounded by the hand print. Then he raised that same finger and twisted it between his pursed lips.

"It salt fer sure. Convinces me that this here trail be made by a ham-thiefin' bastard, and he be headed to the east most certain. Ain't no lone man gonna tote two big hams any distance, and ain't no lone man able eat that much salt meat that be fresh and not have it go bad first."

"He most likely bloat up like old Jake likely do," Jubal added.

Wes continued, half thinking aloud and half talking to his companion. "Ain't no place east where he can unload them hams 'cept Yeary's store iffin he be aimed on sellin' fer cash money. Iffin he ain't fixed on that then he must be aimed on meetin' up somewhere with more of his kind."

"Who ye thinkin' it be?" Jubal asked, already expecting what the answer would be.

"Got a mind it might be one we both knows, but ain't so sure. Had to be a body what knowed about old Jake and how to shut down him barkin'. Had to know about the gear room too."

"That be what I be thinkin' too," Jubal said as he stared out along the high ridge lines.

"Well, when we tracks him down, we look at his right hand and then we know," Wes stated with an air of confidence.

"We tracks em?" Jubal replied questioningly.

"Well, ye with my help, I reckon. I go ye step fer step if need be."

"I be thinkin' ye would old man."

"I be some old in years. I be older than ye in learnin' and experience, I reckon. And that there ain't all bad. I been around some, and I know some too. Ye ought respect that and learn from it."

"Never said I ain't beholdin' to ye, have I?" Jubal snapped back.

"No. I... I reckon ye ain't."

"Then I reckon we best be movin' and see just where these tracks leads us," Jubal said as he stepped out and took the lead on up the fence line heading to the corner a couple of hundred yards ahead.

Wes followed him almost stride for stride, but with noticeable difficulty and some shortness of breath. Jubal took notice of his efforts and slowed his pace and appeared to be making a closer inspection of each footprint and reading the signs that it held. He did notice on his own, some of the signs that Wes had pointed out lower down the draw. They were easy to find and easy to read when you knew more what to look for and how to interpret it once you did see it. Wes soon caught up, and they stayed side by side until they reached the corner of the fence. There they found more prints in a new pattern that told what had happened there earlier.

The prints were many and close on each other. Some were partly erased by a foot coming down on top of where it had just impressed the new powder snow. The culprit scallywag had stood here for a bit and shifted his feet all around as he more than likely rested long enough to get his wind back and to rest his arms a bit. Wes found the prints where he had set the load down. The salt had melted the snow and exposed the dead grass which was pressed down some as well. A finger in the grass and dirt and then tasted confirmed the same.

"I don't think I needs go no more, Jubal. I nigh tuckered plum out now."

"I reckon I can follow the track a ways now. I got me a notion where he be headed anyhow."

"Where that be?" Wes asked as he continued to regain his breath.

"I think he be headed out the east ridge and onto old Horne's place. Trail seems like it be headed that way much as I can see from here."

"How far ye reckon ye track him 'fore ye turns back home?" Wes asked.

"I try goin' as far as the ridge above Johnson's mill. That outta tell me most what I needs know, and I should be able make it that far and back home by nightfall."

"Look like the sun gonna warm up some. Reckon ye best light out. Ye keep sharp eye out on the ridge lines and stay in the timbers as much as ye can. I wouldn't get on no roads nowhere iffin I was ye. Just ye be careful now, ye hear?"

"Yeah, I reckon ye be right. I ain't too keen on bein' seen by nobody, nowhere."

"Lookie here," Wes said as he pointed to the top of a near the corner fence post. "There be he handprint, and he be leakin' blood a bit too. That be another sign ye can look fer."

"Must hurt hisself good when he fall down," Jubal responded.

"He be favorin' that hand, I bet."

"I be headin' out now, Wes."

"Okay, ye keep in mind what I done told ye. I be prayin' fer ye."

Jubal made no further reply, but turned and headed off toward the timberline keeping the tracks just to his side. The trail was easy to follow through the open pasture. It headed straight for the little patch of woods that covered the low point of the east ridge. A quarter mile or so and he would be in the thickets and out of sight from any peering eyes that may be lingering around. He made a quick scan of the lines all around him and into the meadows below. There was nothing to be seen. There was no glint or glimmer from the sunlight save for an isolated reflection from the branch pools where the sun bounced off the calm surface of the crystal clear water. It had not frozen over last night. It moved too much for that. It would take a hard freeze to make more than rhyme ice on it.

He turned and looked to the fence corner. Wes still stood there with one arm resting on a top rail. Jubal thought to himself, "He may be old, but he got spirit. Never would thought it when Ma first fetched him home."

It was no effort to follow the tracks and signs. Jubal even managed to discern where the thief had taken a rest again and where he had rested his haul against the trunk of a persimmon tree. There were slight spots where the snow had been melted away and, as Wes had demonstrated, had left a slight salty taste. The sun had climbed higher by then, and the diamond sparkling drops of melt water increased the brilliance bouncing around the naked tree limbs like some enchanted sprinkling of silver dust flung down from heaven above. The snow would soon vanish under the warming sun, but the impressions made beneath its white blanket would remain until erased by the next rainfall or the next being who walked among them.

A strange turn in the tracks caught the boy by surprise. Whoever made these tracks had turned from the top of the ridge and headed back downhill. The footprints led to the edge of the timberline and were made in a different manner than before. These traipsings were left by someone who stepped a whole lot lighter. They led to a point where the old hog lot and the scalder could be seen clearly off in the hollow below. Jubal recalled that he had glimpsed a movement in about this same place on the day that they had killed. He could go back to the scalder and sight back up to where he now stood but that would take too much time. Instead he cut a cedar sprout about a foot long and hung it upside down in hickory sapling where it could be seen easily from below. The tracks went directly back to retrieve the purloined hams. So, whoever it was had for whatever reason, wanted a look back down on the old home place or at least the hog lot.

Headed on east, it became clear once more that the load was heavy. The impressions showed mashing of the blanket of leaves. Close observation of the individual leaves revealed sharp breaks and uniform crushes in the veins. The steps were made with exertion and effort. The load was becoming a burden.

The signs of rest stops became closer the farther the trail led out the ridge top. Soon much of the salt would be leeched out of the ham hide. Unless more was rubbed on soon afterward, the meat would surely spoil. It had not yet had any borax put to it. Jubal could only hope that Wes or Ma would remember to do that for the cuts that were still hanging in the smokehouse.

Another half hour of trailing and the boy was ready for a short rest himself. He stood the butt of the old long rifle on the ground and leaned the barrel against an oak. He looked around in all directions and saw that he was also under the canopy of a giant chestnut. It took only a few steps to find the burrs below the thick accumulation of the brown crackling leaves. The bushy tails had not found them all yet, and he soon had a pocket full of the shiny brown treats. They would be quite tasty roasted in the open fireplace tonight.

Enough rest. Time to move on. Still a long way to the clearing above the mill. Soon he came on a twist of things that he could read from the tracks. Horse tracks. Two sets of them. One was shod and the other not. Familiar tracks, but there had always been three sets of tracks before. Looked like the horses had been there for a time. Lots of shifting around and some stamping as well. They had been reined in pretty tight for however long they had been there. No one had dismounted either, because there were no new man tracks; and the one set that he tracked stopped there as well. Somebody was ridding double now, and most likely the other mount was toting the stash as well as his rider. No trouble at all to see where two horses made their way through the woods. Any fool could follow that. And they appeared to be headed right where expected. They made no effort to hide their signs.

Wes opened the gear room door fully expectin' to see old Jake in a sad state. Instead he was surprised when the old redbone hound bounded out the door in spite of his best efforts to prevent such. Jake bounded to the spring branch and drank like he had just run a coon race on a hot summer night. Wes got to him quick like and pulled him away from the water. "Ye best take it easy, ye cuss. I aim fer ye to weather this in spite of yerself."

The trot back to the gear room was without effort, and the door closed quickly behind both of them. Wes had the ham hock bone away from the dog and was out the door with it in a heartbeat. Jake let out a long low bay, and Wes knew right then that he would be good to go in a day or so.

Jubal soon had followed the horse tracks all the way out the spine of the east ridge to where it butted up to the mill ridge. Sure enough the tracks veered off onto that ridge as he fully expected. He started for the clearing above the mill without noticing the tracks any longer. What he needed and wanted to know now would be told once he reached there.

The clearing seemed cold and unwelcoming with all the leaves gone and nothing to impede the chill air that stirred the scarlet and fire orange leaves and caused them to dance across the dried grasses and brambles. The old log bench that the miller man had built there was the lone sentinel who stood watch over this little sanctuary.

Right now, Jubal learned all he needed to know from there, and he felt even more assured that he knew where the trail would lead and was more convinced that he knew who had made it.

No doubt that it would lead to Horne's cave, but there was no more time today to follow in that direction. The sun had already begun its afternoon descent into the cloudless brilliance of the darkening blue. It would be cold again tonight and that thought alone made him thankful that he had laid up a good measure of stout oak and ash wood for a comforting fire. It would be past sundown by the time he returned home, and the chill would be setting in. There would be an even harder frost tonight.

It would be good to come down off the ridges and follow the road back home. That, plus the fact that he could call at the mill, made for reason enough to head in that direction. Lida had not been quite up to snuff lately, and it would be a proper thing to check on her and pay his calling to her family as well. Besides that, her daddy needed to know that there were undesirables on the loose again and that he should keep an eye peeled for them. He might have seen something of them already. They had to have passed near this way some time or another just to do what they had done.

Going downhill was no task at all for the young man in spite of all the distance that he had already covered. He felt a quickness in his step as he neared the mill. He wanted to see Lida very much, but also felt like he needed to see her Pa and tell him what had happened. He could see that the millrace was on divert and that the wheel was not running. Not the best time of year to run the mill anyhow. Most folks had already had their winter's grinding done a month or so ago. Mill would not be running when deep snows covered the wheel and the race either. Hard freezes would still the race, and no grinding could take place then even if there did happen to be grain on hand.

C.C. was standing in the doorway of the mill as Jubal rounded the corner to the porch. The miller man was preoccupied with packing his pipe and did not catch sight of Jubal at first. The young tracker stopped and set his gear down, leaning the long rifle against the side of the mill. By that time the miller man had seen him, but waited until he had a cloud of blue grey smoke ringing his head and shoulders before he spoke.

"Hello, son. What brings ye down here on such a day as this?"

"I reckon ye might be some interested in what been goin' on up the holler," Jubal answered. He then proceeded to tell C.C. all about the hog killing and all the varied circumstances related to it. The older man listened intently as he pulled rhythmically on his pipe. The two mulled over the ponderable of who and why and all the what ifs and still came up with no more answers than was already known. Both had very strong suspicions and communicated them to each other without ever mentioning a name. It was as if both already knew the truth of the matter but did not want to admit it.

"I reckon ye be aimin' on trackin, them and see where they go from here?" C.C. asked all the while knowing what the answer would be.

"Reckon so, but not till tomorrow. Need to get back home and make ready to be out and about fer three or four days the way I see it, Jubal answered.

"Well, that gonna kill half day or so just to get back to here. Ye done know where tracks leads ever step to here. Seems me best thing ye can do is come here and stay over till first light and then start out fresh iffin ye set on trackin' any longer. C.C. knew that too much time would be wasted in retracing footsteps and that nothing could come from that other than wasted efforts. The trail would get colder with each sunset anyhow, and if the boy was to make any headway, then he needed to get on with it.

They agreed that Jubal would return by sundown tomorrow and stay the night. He could sleep in the mill.

Jubal bashfully gained the courage to ask about Lida. C.C. made no immediate reply but got up from his stool, went out to the mill porch and banged a yard long iron stake three times against a flat iron plate that hung from a rusty chain on one of the porch rafters. In a moment, Lida appeared in the doorway of the dwelling house and her daddy motioned for her to come to the mill.

"Ask her fer yerself, son. She be here in a bit. I got to get back to my books now."

Lida came to the mill and seemed a bit surprised seeing Jubal as she entered the doorway. "Hello," she said surprised at the unexpected visitor. "I thought daddy clanged the iron for me."

"Well, I was askin' him how ye were, and he told me to ask fer myself. That be when he beat on the iron. He be at his books right now, I reckon. Least that be what he say he needed tend to."

"Oh, I...well, yes...I see."

"I been thinkin' and wonderin' iffin ye felt better by now."

"Well, yes I do. I reckon I be all over it by now. Momma done fill me full of herb tea and made me take the bitters as well. Good thing I be better. Don't think I could take more of them bitters. They taste plum awful."

"I reckon they do at that, but they make ye better in the windup," Jubal replied.

"So what brings ye here on such a miserable day as this," she questioned.

He related to her all that he had just told her daddy, leaving out some of the details here and there and the suspicions that he thought he knew who had been behind it all. He made it a point to tell her that he had been up on the clearing where they had been not too long back. Just telling about it stirred his emotion and desire the same as it had on the day they were there together.

"Have ye been up there lately?" he asked.

"No," she answered with an ever so slight blush to her cheeks and an even more pronounced smile.

"Proud that ye be better now. Don't have no say in it, but I ain't easy knowin' ye have ailments."

"I been wonderin' when ye might come around again. Kinda felt like we needed talk some, and I wondered about Julie too."

"Seem like sis ain't mended up none so far. Her color still be milk pale some nights, and she don't eat much no more."

"Yer Ma keepin her knee clean and dressed good?"

"That be a fact. Julie ain't been shortchanged a bit there."

"I wish she could get well quick. She be a sweet girl."

"So are ye," Jubal said spontaneously and immediately felt his cheeks and the tops of his ears begin to burn. She smiled and reached out and laid a soft hand to his cheek. His hand found hers and time seemed to stand still. He did not really know how it all had taken place nor how long they had stood looking into each other's eyes so intently. The magic of the spell was broken by the voice of her father.

"I been thinkin' on ye comin' tomorrow afternoon. Ye best come in time fer vittles and see where we can bed ye down fer the night. It might be cold sleepin' in the mill."

"Yes sir, but I reckon I can sleep most anywhere. I reckon I ought bring buckskins with me." He glanced at Lida and noticed the quizzical look on her face. Her dad explained the plan they had come up with and then she showed a faint hint of a smile.

Jubal noticed her expressions and was thinking that her dad had not noticed. He was a smart man no doubt, but most likely he did not think in the same terms as a young buck full of unfulfilled desire. Maybe such thoughts were not right, but already he had building expectations and could hardly be expected to hold back on pent-up passion. He was thinking it good that she could not read his mind right now. How would she react? Then again, she had done nothing to discourage him.

"I will make sure ye have good covers. We got a heap of quilts," Lida cooed.

"Ye can tend to that come sundown tomorrow, I reckon," C.C. said in a somewhat harsh and demanding tone. Lida got the message and wiped the smiles off her face and stopped twisting in her tracks. Her skirts hung still now and there was no enticing swagger to her stance. "I ain't one to brush off good company, but it be dark by time ye gets home now. Ain't safe bein' out after dark, leastwise when ye be alone. Ye can stay as long as ye feel safe, but I be thinkin' yer Ma be lookin' fer ye be home all in one piece. I know how much she be dependin' on ye. Ye may not be quite a man in years yet, but ye be a man in responsibility whether ye want it or not. Now, there I reckon I done said my piece again but that be the way I see it; I don't think I be far off the mark either."

"I agree with ye daddy," Lida chimed.

"Both ye be right, I reckon. I best be goin' right away. I will get home soon as I can even iffin I needs trot a ways. I aim on takin' the road all the way home, save me some time and ain't much chance anybody be out twixt here and home."

"See ye tomorrow evening then," C.C. said as he turned and headed for the house. "Lida, don't ye hold him up no more. Ye needs be in the house helpin' yer Momma."

"Yes, daddy."

That ended any further rushes of emotion and somewhat quelled the fires of passion, at least for the moment. Lida followed her daddy into the house. Jubal noticed her slight wave as the living room door closed behind her. He turned and started for home.

He reached the lower meadow gate just before the last fading light lost itself in the western sky. No clouds tonight. It would be another heavy frost. There was nothing heavy about his spirits, however. He would see if Julie would be awake any time tonight. She just might tell him a tidbit or two he would want to hear. A sudden rustle in the branch willows just ahead stopped him dead in his tracks, and he brought the old long rifle to bear. In a few more seconds, just before Jubal was ready to fire, old Jake bounded up out of the branch and loped the few steps to be near his keeper.

"Ye ornery cuss. I been thinkin' on ye today. Look like ye be better now. Wes must 'a tooken good care fer ye." He patted the old dog generously across his massive head and neck, and Jake leaned in against his leg to show his own feelings as well.

"That be ye, Jubal?"

The voice belonged to Wes, and Jubal recognized it right off.

"It be me."

"I been waitin' fer ye, wishin' ye be back here soon."

"Anythin' wrong?" Jubal asked with some uneasiness.

"No, ain't nothin' changed. Ma be worried a bunch, but that be all."

The three made their way on to the house in hardly any time. Ma greeted her boy with a big hug and a new sparkle in her eye. Even Julie seemed joyous to see him back home safe and sound. She sat up in bed and outstretched her arms in anticipation of a hug from her brother. Jubal happily obliged her.

The gathering around the fire that night seemed to pull everyone in together and prepare them for what they knew would beset them sooner or later. Once again, no names were mentioned. It was not necessary. Everyone knew who had betrayed them. No one expressed any desire for vengeance, but Granny Iverson had talked openly about Judas Iscariot and his betrayal on that night so many long years past. Ma openly expressed her approval of her son spending the night at the mill in order to save time in further tracking of the evil doer. The coming days would be very much out of the ordinary, but first this night had to pass; it would be quite cold by sunup. The fire would need seen to tonight for sure.

Jubal stepped outside for a look at the star-studded sky. Wes followed him.

"I got some stuff on my mind about ye trackin' down them scum suckers, but it can wait till mornin'. Ye want me sleep in yer bed so ye can talk with Julie tonight?"

"That be good by me."

"I know ye be close with her, and I respect that. I reckon I got no call hearin' what ye two talks on. I don't want to know either."

"I be beholdin' to ye fer that, Wes."

"I think I be turnin' in soon. I hope my floor pallet ain't too hard fer ye."

"It'll be fine," Jubal said softly as he followed Wes back into the old log house. The fire seemed so quiet, so warming, after losing most of its once captive gathering. It would be a cold night for sure; but if Jubal could sleep any at all, he felt sure that his thoughts and dreams would be warm.

There was no talkin' with Julie that night. It was strange, but she slept the whole night through, and her brother deemed it best to let her rest. Winter was just getting started, and there would be plenty of nights for talking later on. Many mixed emotions coursed the back roads of his mind that night. He agonized over the theft. So much hard work represented there and then to have it taken away so undeservingly. His hatred for Pa heightened, being almost certain that he and his criminal minded so-and-so bastards had done it. May as well never had a Pa. All he ever did anyhow was provide a seed.

He thought about Lida. How could he speak to her and tell her all that he felt about her? He wanted her to know that he had a deep burning desire for her. He had hopes that she would feel the same about him, but he had always been told that those flaming fires could not be calmed by simple animal instincts and actions. That was not the way he really wanted it to be anyhow, but certain parts of him said otherwise. He held her and her entire family in respect, and he had no desire to destroy any of that. Besides that, C.C. was a man that he did not care to cross in any way. He wanted her, yes, but how to tell her that and not be offensive? Why must it always be so hard growing up from a boy to becoming a man? How could he ever learn to be a man and earn his own way and have others respect him?

"Wish Julie was awake," he mumbled lowly to himself as he listened to her rhythmic breathing. She seemed to be a bit stronger tonight. There was no cough and no rattle in her chest. Her color looked a bit better, even with the firelight flickering across the purity of her milky face and dancing up into her honey blond hair. How peaceful she looked. How pretty she really was. He realized how much he loved her and how precious that she was to him and to their Ma. Granny Iverson had said many times that she was a special child, and there was no argument to that.

It seemed that the night was two nights long. But finally Jubal heard Ma stir, and he knew that there would soon be a warm fire in the old cook stove and that hot biscuits would not be too far behind that.

Jubal ate headily and began at once to get his things together to make the afternoon trek to the mill. He wanted to make sure that the wood box beside the old cook stove was filled and that there was a good measure of firewood up on the front porch. He went to the barn and made sure that Kate's manger was full. He carried up all the water buckets from the spring and filled the tank on the cook stove as well. He would be gone less than two full days, if all went well. It was important to him to know that all was done for Ma to make that time as easy as possible.

Wes followed Jubal to the barn so they could talk alone. Jubal had gained a lot of confidence in his tracking ability, and he knew that was in large, due to the knowledge of what he had originally thought to be nothing more than a cantankerous old miserly hermit of a man. Respect for this so-called old man had increased immensely in the short time that he had come to the old log home. Almost every new day brought forth some new and unimagined revelations of wisdom that the old man possessed. Some were very surprising to say the least. Jubal had already learned to trust him and was looking up to him more and more every day.

"How far ye aim on followin' these trash heaps?" Wes asked.

"I reckon I could make it far as Horne's cave and on to Yeary's store if the track led there. I ain't thinkin' that I be gone more than two nights at most and I really don't care nothin' about bein' out in the cold tomorrow night."

"I bet ye could hold up in the mill again iffin ye needed to."

"No, I reckon that might not be best thing fer me to do. Don't know iffin I could or not."

"Don't see how come not. C.C. let ye put up there I be most sure," Wes implied.

"He might not be only one with a say so."

Wes could not hold back a slight chuckle. Jubal failed to catch it, and Wes decided it best not to push the matter. Any ribbing could easily lead to hurt feelings and friction. He wanted none of that.

"What ye reckon ye might do iffin ye run up on these here scoundrels?" Wes questioned.

"I ain't real sure just yet, but I don't aim on lettin' them or nobody else run over me or get took in by them. I know I still got heaps to learn, but I can shoot straight and load fast when I need to."

"I know ye can at that, son. But shootin' a rank stranger be one thing. Shootin' yer Pa be somethin' else."

Jubal was a bit surprised that Wes had mentioned Pa so directly and so decisively. It hit him hard enough that he had no answer for the moment.

"I don't mean nuthin' by that, son. All I am sayin' is that ye best not corner anythin' that be bigger or stronger or meaner than ye be yerself. Iffin ye do run on them, it most likely be three on one and ye be the one. Ye best hang back and do a bunch of lookin' and watchin'. And do it from a good piece away. Ye can't just up and put a rifle ball in their back side neither. That be cold blood. We ain't got much law in these parts, but they be on yer hide like stink on a polecat iffin word got out on ye."

"I done thought on that," Jubal reasoned. "I reckon I got a right defendin' myself iffin need be."

"That ye do, son. But ye needs be on yer best. Be careful like ye ain't never been before and keep yer mind on what ye be doin' too."

"I ain't likely run on nuthin' at least till late tomorrow afternoon. It take me that long coverin' tracks after I leave the mill."

"It be what ye find at the mill that worry me about ye keepin' yer mind on what ye be doin' when ye leaves there. I know how you young pups is when it come to a young whelper," Wes cautioned.

"Ye speakin' from experience, huh?"

"Yeah, but it be several long years back."

"Sound me like ye really been a rounder in yer day," Jubal said as he cracked a broad smile. "Maybe ye teach me a thing or two there just like ye did on trackin'."

"Some things ye just gotta learn on yer own," Wes said as he smiled back.

"Keep old Jake tied up. I reckon I don't need him traipsin' after me this time."

"I do that," Wes replied. "Ye just be pine blank sure that ye be careful."

"I will."

"And ye get yerself back here in two days by sundown. I needs go talk business with old C.C. when ye gets back."

"What kind a business?"

"I ain't tryin' be smart ner nothin' to the kind, but right now it don't need no talkin' on. Not right now, but all in time. I just gonna need use of his gelding fer a day or two sometime here soon. Ye find out about it soon enough, I reckon. I tell ye when time comes proper," Wes said as he patted Jubal lightly on the back.

Jubal started the walk to the mill just a bit past high noon. The sun occasionally showed its face through a break in the overcast sky. A slight north wind stirred and had enough sting to it to water the eyes, if facing into it. Should be plenty of time to make it to the mill well before dark and not have to rush it at that. Wes had insisted that he take an old Navy Colt with him as well as the long rifle. Jubal had not told Wes that he also packed a skinning knife and even had his earlier childhood sling as well. He really was not fearful of what or who might confront him, but it never did hurt to have anything that would help even the odds.

The road mostly followed alongside the spring branch and the other small trickling streams that joined together to form a measurable creek flow by the time it reached the mill. Gentle rising hills to steep rocky ridge lines bordered the road all the way to the mouth of the hollow. Jubal would not have the advantage of the higher ground any place on this trek. He knew that and accepted it, but nonetheless made frequent scans of the places above him that had even a hint of danger in their appearance. He also watched the road at his feet for any revelations of what or who may have been there in the last few days.

There were no signs that caught his keen eye until he was just short of the reed patch and the gentle slopes of the divide. Crossing the road right in front of him were the tracks of at least three deer and a fawn. They were fresh too because they were well formed in the now dirty powdered snow, and the ice spicule formations were cleanly broken and lying in and beside the tracks. He stood in the center of the road and looked off in the direction that they led. Looking for surrounding white oaks and chestnut trees, he remembered that there were chinquapin thickets at the crest of the divide. No time to walk up there now but that should be a good place to bring down a doe and have a good stew pot full of deer meat. Maybe by a few days out from now, they could tank up on venison. That should put some color back in Julie. On to the mill.

Mrs. Johnson had gone to no extra trouble fixing anything from her kitchen, knowing that Jubal would be their guest that evening. She had left most of those chores to Lida. It was her opportunity to display her charms and abilities. There was a full jar of fresh made apple butter. Lida had fried up a tall platter of corn pone and had baked white sweet potatoes in the fireplace coals. The teakettle on the stove could not hide the sweet sassafras tea as the vapor coursed out through its bent and crooked spout. There was cold sausage pats left from breakfast that morning.

"What time ye settin' out tomorrow?" C.C. asked as he pushed his empty plate into the center of the table signaling that he was done with his meal.

"Reckon by first good light."

"I agree with ye there, son. Ye know ye can't stay out in cold and wind like this here past sundown, don't ye?"

"Yes sir, reckon that be a fact."

"Then I hope ye be back here by then. I ain't cravin' on fetchin' ye home myself. Ain't that stout no more no how."

Lida cleared away the dishes and made short work of clearing the kitchen and washing up everything. She and her mother soon returned to the table. C.C. had packed his pipe and now had a thick cloud of gray smoke swirling about his head. The lantern light in the center of the table gave enough of an eerie glow to the tobacco smoke so that it appeared ghostly as if some ominous sign of awaiting evil deeds yet unknown. Jubal had seen that same fore-brooding cloud somewhere before, but could not place it despite his best mind searching. Something somewhere reminded him of clouds by day and a pillar of smoke by night, or was it fire, or could it have been light?

"I think ye be warm plenty over in the mill tonight. I was of a mind put ye up on a pallet in front of the fire, but Lida say ye like the mill bed better. She done got the warmin' stones and the blankets on the hearth now. Been a many a day since we used them stones. Knowed we been keepin' them fer a reason. I reckon ye be the reason," C.C. intoned as he took another long draw from his pipe and blew the smoke upward through a pursed lower lip without so much as raising his head. "Come on, Momma. Let these two young'uns talk a bit. It soon be bedtime, and ye can be my warmin' stone."

Had it not been for the orange glow of the lantern light, the blush on Jubal's face would have been easy to spot. He dared not look at Lida and reveal his uneasiness at what her daddy had said. He had never heard any such hints between a man and a woman before.

Sometimes, being a young whippersnapper was not easy, and this was one of those times.

"Ye get all ye wanted to eat," Lida asked softly from across the table.

"Yeah, I had plenty."

"I done it all myself. Momma never help me none."

"Reckon ye done plum good," Jubal said as he felt the rush leaving his cheeks and the tops of his ears. He managed to raise his eyes enough to meet hers. The lantern may as well have been the sun at high noon in the middle of August. Her smile showed like sunshine off honey dew.

"How is yer sister these days?"

At last, something he could talk about with some ease of mind without stammering and stuttering over his words. "She ain't gained no strength much yet and sometimes she don't eat good neither. Leg don't look so good neither."

"She talk with ye about it?"

"Yeah, some, ever now and then."

"She thinks real high about ye. Know that don't ye?"

"We always been close. Don't like seein' her all laid up."

"I know ye don't, and I don't like it either," Lida said softly as she slid her hand across the table and gently toyed her fingertips on the back of his hand.

"Lord, what do I say now? What do I do now?" Jubal asked himself. He felt restless. He felt a bit like a foreigner in a strange land. He knew no one here would harm him, but there was a good chance that he might show himself not to be the grown-up man that he wanted to appear to be. He waited for her to speak again.

"We talked a lot while she stayed here. I got close to her myself. She really be a sweet girl and her heart be right," Lida said as her fingers continued to play across the back of his hands. He wanted to pull his hands away, but dared not do that, not just yet leastwise.

Jubal remained silent and for some unknown reason felt the tears welling up uncontrollably in his eyes. He hoped that his companion would not see them. He wiped the dampness aside by running his cheek across his shoulder and purporting a cough in attempt to cover his actions. It did not go unnoticed, but it did go without comment. Lida merely smiled softly, and thereby conveyed her understanding.

"Julie been hurt a bunch, and sometimes I think she done most give up on herself," Jubal said before he could rein in his thoughts. He paused a moment, then as if the door to his innermost self had been flung wide, continued. "We talked a time or two into the wee hours of the night, and she leads me to think that she don't never expect to be much better. She don't seem to pout over it, and she don't seem a bit scared over it. I reckon I just don't understand it all."

"She ever tell ye about what she wants out of life or what she hopes for?" Lida asked.

"Not too much," Jubal answered. He felt a bit more at ease with himself and with her now. He could barely recall when they had been alone for this much time before, save for the one time up to the clearing back when it was still warm weather.

427

"I reckon she wants pretty much what ever young woman her age wants. Least that what she led me to think when we talked on it," Lida said softly. "What do ye want outta life, Jubal?"

"I reckon mostly to have enough to make my way and meet my needs and my family needs. Would be nice to have a few things in life what make so much work and such be a mite easier. Be good to have a few smart lookin' clothes too, I reckon."

"What about the things that all the money in the world won't buy ye?" Lida asked as she looked him square in the eye.

"Like a good home and feelin' like ye belong or that ye make a difference fer someone else. Feelin' like ye been able to do somethin' good with yer life and that ye stood up fer the right things in life. Ye ever think on things like that?"

"Well, yeah. I reckon I do. Reckon most ever body do that some time along the way. Ain't that part of getting growed up?"

"I guess it is at that," she answered.

"Your daddy thinks ye growed up yet?"

"Reckon so, but he ain't said too much on it."

"Ye a mite older than me ain't ye, Lida?" Soon as he had said it, he wished that he could recall his words. Julie had told him her age, and he just knew for sure that she would ask him how he knew that. He really did not want her to know that he had mentioned her to Julie in hopes that he could learn more how she felt toward him.

"A bit I suppose. I just turned eighteen in August. I think that makes me growed up by now. Momma says I am anyhow."

"I never aimed to pry," Jubal said apologetically.

"Didn't take it that way. I am just sayin' that I am growed up to where I know what I want. I just ain't so sure how things is gonna work out."

"Obliged to ye fer that, but I try not ask no more stuff like that."

Lida got up and slowly made her way around to his side of the table. She let her shawl fall down her back exposing a bit of her milky smooth tenderness. She nudged a chair up close and sat down allowing her knee to rub into Jubal's leg, crossing her own hands across her lap. His cheeks began to burn again.

"If ye knew what ye wanted and knew that it would satisfy all yer wants and hopes, would ye go after it even iffin it seemed wrong to do so at the time?" Lida asked.

"I... I ain't so sure I follow ye. Reckon it be all accordin' to what it be that ye wants so bad."

"Would it matter what other people thought?" she asked.

"Don't know. Ought not be outside any law, nuthin' like that."

"But what iffin there was no way it be bad save fer what some people thought on it?"

"Like who?" he asked in all innocence.

"Like me and like you. That who." She leaned in and slipped her arm around his shoulder. Now the ears burned as well as his cheeks. He had things that he wanted to say to her and had thought about how to say them many times before. But now that the time was right, he felt like he had a throat full of sand. Words were not easily forthcoming. He turned to look her in the face and started to speak. She placed a finger across his lips and then gently kissed him, ever so tenderly. Neither said a word. They just gazed into each other's eyes. Words were not needed right now.

At last she spoke softly. "When ye want somethin' bad enough, sometimes ye needs go after it. She sat back and took her arm from around him. The shawl recovered what it had briefly allowed him to catch a hint of. "I best see about them warmin' stones and make sure they be good and warm. It likely be a cold night." She knew that she had just lit a fire that would stave off a night much colder than this one would be. She had brief thoughts of being a Jezebel or a Delilah, but easily and quickly pushed those thoughts aside. It was only small talk anyway. Knew what she wanted, but thought that it still may be just a bit beyond her reach. It would be a long time till morning, and she would have time to dwell on it.

"I will get them stones ready fer ye, and ye can turn in any time."

"Reckon I best take a look at the north sky and see what the mornin' might bring. I know it be cold out but I think I be good come daybreak," Jubal said. He waited until she got up to get the stones before he moved out of his chair.

The night was indeed a cold one. The warming stones felt snug and cozy. There was no way that cold could creep in, but there was no sleep to be had. Jubal kept running things back and forth and trying to figure out just how he felt. Respect restrained him on the one hand, but passion and desire urged him on at the other. Why could she not just come out and say what she wanted? Sure would make things a whole lot easier. He was not even really understanding of all that she had said. Her actions said one thing and told him lots about all that he had wanted to know from Julie and had not had the ease of asking. Her upbringing and belief was what nurtured his respect added to the fact that he knew she was nothing short of truthful with him and honest in her feelings. But he had feelings too and could only hope that they were the same as hers or at least close to them.

Lida had told him that if she was awake around midnight that she would get up and bring him some fresh warming stones. She knew herself that she would be awake at that hour. The stones were already placed on the hearth, and a big back stick had been laid on the grate just before bedtime. No sleep came for her either. The same desires welled up inside her as did in him, and she had already decided that respect could be laid aside for a few moments.

Eventually, she heard the mantel clock strike out the midnight hour. Silently, she got out of her bed, threw on a robe, collected the warming stones in the carrier and made her way across to the mill porch. Jubal heard her footsteps and the opening of the big oak door. He remained still and spoke not a word. Lida came to the foot of his bed and laid out the warming stones. She then pulled back the covers and lay down beside him.

The morning was just about as cold as the trail. Jubal had no trouble finding enough tracks to follow, but the freeze had distorted them and made it harder to distinguish the uniqueness of the hoof prints. It was easy enough to see that he was still on the track of two animals, one shod and the other not. What was harder to decide was whether or not one of them had been ridden double. There were no tracks to indicate anyone had walked along with the horses, but there were the broken twigs ever now and then, just like before. He still was puzzled a bit by that. It seemed to be too deliberate as if intending to leave an obvious sign or possibly even wanting to be caught.

The tracks led east just as expected, away from the mill area. They ran the top of the ridge and then headed downgrade. Whoever it was surely had to know that they would soon cut the road if they continued this way. It would seem like any thieving scoundrel would try to avoid the road. Didn't make a lot of sense. After all they had left plenty of signs, and maybe they just thought nobody would trail them this far. Could be that they had no thoughts that they could be tracked over such rough and rocky areas and through heavy timber.

Jubal was just uneasy when he saw that the trail was going straight into the limestone balds of the Cove Road. This was the same place where Julie had been hurt so bad, and it gave the young lad a feeling of insecurity to be there again. He did not step off the banks and onto the road hurriedly. He hung back and took stock of everything around him, looking in all directions and listening for any unusual sounds. He could hear nothing but the occasional caw of a crow. They seemed to not be excited or upset, and he took that as a good sign.

He stepped out into the road and began to search for the tracks he had been following. Sure enough they were there, and they headed back to the east. If they stayed on this road, the first thing they would come to would be Yeary's store. Jubal did not feel too keen on walking the road all the way to the store. Better to cut the ridge points and recheck the road ever quarter mile or so. The ridge points would be steeper than the road, but it would be fewer steps and that way would help to keep him away from other eyes as well. Yeary's store was still a good two hours away; and if he followed the track all the way there, it would be some past noon by then. He would have time to get there and ask around a bit. No problem there, but that would make it really late or even dark by the time he would get back to the mill. It would still take a good while to get back home.

He thought about the night just passed. His mind swirled about in a storm of mixed feelings. He was now more than ever, enamored over his experiences with the young woman, and there was no way that he could get her off his mind. He had guilt over his feelings and could not help but wonder how she now perceived him. Was he a full grown man now or was he just a sapling of a boy who was trying so hard to be a man? Some of his thoughts struck doubt in him, and he could find no solace in his humble reasoning. There had been so much said about good and evil. So much talk on the darkness and the need to see the light. Just what was good and who was to say this or that was evil? Who was to be judge of what he did or how he felt?

Whoever had taken the larder from their smokehouse had definitely done evil, and he had already passed judgment on them. Thievery was a definite evil, and it was done in the darkest of the night. He had not done any such deed. No way. He had done only what he was led to do. He had no reason to think it wrong, but then maybe he did not share the same feelings as others. He would think no more on it for now, not unless it became necessary to stay the night at the mill again.

Yeary's store still had almost bare walls and shelves. The war had made goods harder and harder to get. Jubal was beginning to feel a bit hungry and asked what they might have that he could eat. The storekeeper offered him a ham biscuit that had been left from his own breakfast.

That opened the door to ask if there had been anyone in that would fall into the mold of the characters that he had been trailing. Mr. Yeary was quick to relate to him how that the three had brought in two hams almost totally caked in mud and offered them for sale to him for next to nothing. He had taken them in exchange for a couple bottles of cheap whiskey and a jug of local corn squeezing. The three matched the ones he had seen at the reed patch back in hot weather. They also matched the ones who did the shooting back at the limestone balds. The storekeeper depicted them as dirty and unshaven.

Jubal was convinced that he knew who one of them was and asked if there had been any names thrown around that he could recall. The storekeeper had heard no names, but gave Jubal a good detailed account of each of them, their mannerisms and the way they carried themselves. He had noted the horses as well. One was a big old Roan, and the other was a brown mare, unshod. Mr. Yeary said that he did not know for sure, but thought that they were headed south into the doubles. He was just proud to have them not be around his store any longer. They could be nothing but bad news for anyone who crossed them.

There was little use in trying to follow any trail any more. Too much time had passed, and they would be miles out ahead of him now. He would have to dwell on the whole thing now and see what, if anything, he could do to try running them down. Going as far as the doubles would take several days on foot, and he would need a good horse and saddle, if he ever had any hopes of catching up to them. Right now they may as well be on their way to the moon. He had nothing going for him except his own two feet, and they had begun to tell him how far he had walked today. He asked nothing more of the storekeeper, but turned and began the long trek back to the mill.

Chapter 13

Seeking

Wes slept very little the night Jubal was supposed to be resting up at the mill. He had thought long and hard about the things that he wanted and how to go after them. There would be no problem in paying his way or buying what he wanted and needed. That would be no issue. Hardest part would be finding the necessary things and stock. He knew, or at least thought he knew, who to see and who to ask to help him. He was not free to talk to just anyone. He needed to keep certain things to himself and share with no one. Yet, to do what he wanted, he would have to trust some folks. He considered himself to be a fair judge of character, and he would just have to muster up a little faith in the goodness of some people.

He had faith; faith in himself and what he had been able to do when he set his mind to it. He had some experiences that any man would like to lay claim to. He had been around as some folks would put it. He had done some things which by his own standards had not been on the up-and-up. He had done injustices to others, which he now knew were about as low-down as could be. Men had trusted in him, and he had violated that trust for his own sake and profit. Now he lay on another person's floor before their warm fire and told himself that he needed to have a little faith in the merits of another good-doing soul.

How hypocritical could he be? He could not really answer his own riddle about himself other than to realize that he did indeed have faith, a very strong faith, but that it came from no man. It came in his knowledge of who he was and where he had been compared to where he was now. He knew that he could never undo the deeds of all the yesterdays no more than he could cause the winds to give up their chill. He could never alleviate the sufferings that he had caused. He could never beg forgiveness from souls long since laid in the graves of those forgotten by time. He could never look upon the face of a man he had not even known and allow him to see the genuine sorrow in his own eyes. He found no fault in those who despised him, but tried always to avoid those who would do him harm. He felt that he could not beg them for mercy if they ever found him, because he had shown them no mercy.

It had taken time, lots of time for him to realize that he was without the knowledge of the light and that he sought the materialism of the darkness. Even after he came to that realization, it had taken years for him to accept his wretchedness. It had even cost him his happiness and his sense of well-being. It had cost him his mate and all the good things that she had brought to his life. It had nearly cost him his own life as he dwelt in the filth of his own self-imposed darkness.

It had been the goodness and mercy of Ma and her girls that had opened his eyes where he fully realized his fate. Granny Iverson had laid it out to him so pointedly and so directly that there could be no mistaking the need to acknowledge his state and to do something about it and to do it soon. He had told no one thus far, but he had done something about it and had done it alone in the stillness of the night. In an instant, he had stepped out of the darkness and into the light. In that same instant, he had received a peace that he could not yet understand. He just knew that he no longer suffered the agonizing wrenching of his past. No, he had not forgotten those things; he never would, but he now knew that he would not be held accountable for them except maybe in the eyes of man.

Sorry for some of the things he had done, yes, most assuredly. He also knew very well that all the yesterdays were just that. They were gone, and the deeds that they held were gone as well. The hurt and the discord that resulted from those deeds could and in lots of measures did linger for a lifetime. Nonetheless, they were done and could never be called back again. Things said could never be unsaid. Things done could never be undone.

Years had changed perspective, and Wes could see much of his own misguided ideology now being manifested in Jubal. The desire for materialistic things had driven him to act in deceit and malady in his relations with those who had called him friend. He had gained materialistically but had suffered greatly in loss of friendship. He now had to keep eternal vigil for fear of reprisal should his location become known.

It seemed to take eons for daybreak to roll around. Wes listened intently from his pallet bed before the now dying fire. It still threw off a warming glow. There seemed to be no wind astir this morning. That would be good. The task at hand after breakfast would go better with no chilling wind. The day's trek would be easier without bitter chill.

He waited patiently until he heard Ma stirring. He gave her what he thought would be time to get a good fire in the cook stove before he stirred himself. He dressed hurriedly in buckskins and laid three good sticks on the coals in the fireplace. That would insure that Julie would not chill when she began to stir. She had been able to get herself up to the bedside a time or two lately, and it seemed that she might be on the mend just ever so slightly. Her color had not improved very much, but her smile had never waned in the least.

Making his way to the kitchen, Wes found Ma rolling out biscuit dough on the old faded blue oilcloth bearing the equally faded roses.

"Mornin', Ma"

"Mornin', to ye as well."

"Ye rest good last night?" Wes asked knowing that Ma would be concerned about her son being away from home for the first night in his young life.

"I done fair, I reckon," Ma replied in a feeble attempt to conceal her concerns. She had slept no more than had he, but she was worried and concerned over things different than those that robbed him of his sleep.

"Ye look a mite tired."

Ma made no reply, and Wes sensed that he may have struck a tender cord. He would remember to not make that same mistake again. He reasoned that he may as well have told her that she had lost her glow or that she looked unappealing to him. He could appreciate the fact that she would still have a desire to be wanted and take a measure of pride in a compliment ever now and then. It made him even more appreciative of all the sacrifice that she had made for her family, and now she had taken him on when she had no real obligation to do so. She had done it of her own compassion.

"Ye reckon I might be able slip out down the road a piece today?" Wes asked sheepishly.

"What be askin' me fer? Reckon ye ain't bound here just on account I took ye in," Ma replied curtly. Wes thought that he sensed a little bit of a hurt in her answer.

"I never meant nothin' of the kind. I got me some things needs tended to, and I just needed know iffin ye was a mindset that ye could do without me around here for a day or so. That be all there be to it."

"I reckon I can manage," Ma said, again with a hint of sarcasm.

"I got notions that I needs go see into. I need speak with the miller man on it. That be the God's truth."

"God don't speak nuthin' but the truth, and ye best know that too, I reckon. I know Granny Iverson done told ye that too."

"She has, in fact, and I knowed it to begin with."

"Ye could fetch me a bucket full fresh water, iffin ye don't mind."

Wes went to the spring with an empty bucket and dipped it into the chilled spring pool. The water was as clear as it was cold. Pity it was never that clear or cold on a hot summer day when thirst was so strong. It struck him odd that Ma would brush him off so quickly and scurry him out of her kitchen so readily. He could tell by the tone of her voice that she was not in one of her better moods this morning. He did not recall hearing her toss and turn during the night, but it could be that she had not rested very well last night. She sure had been through a lot lately and had a lot to deal with. He decided that he would be right out with it when he returned with the water bucket.

He stepped across the threshold of the kitchen door and Ma reached for the oaken bucket and handed him a hand carved white oak spoon. "Here, I take that. Ye stir the gravy fer me. I need yer help this mornin', and I thank ye in advance fer obligin' me. Ain't never said it outright as I can recall, but I do thank ye fer all that ye do here. It takes work off me when ye help out."

"I glad whatever I be able to help ye," Wes said as he was inwardly surprised at the apparent and sudden turnaround in her. Maybe he had just not read her the right way to begin with this morning. There could easily be enough pent-up anger to cause her to strike like an old she bear. She sure had enough to cause her to fret over her cubs, one of them all shot up and laid up bad; the other too far off for her to keep watch over. He intended to change some of that but was just not too sure how to go about telling her nor just how much to tell her at a time. He had already told the boy far more than he had told her, and there was no way to know what the lad had shared with her. He felt it best not to ask either of them now, nor later.

"I was thinkin' I ought go down and talk with Mr. C.C. I know he knows plenty folks here abouts. He knows who to ask fer some of the things that I think we be better off havin' here."

"Like what?" Ma asked as she pulled a big pan of biscuits from the oven and set them on the stove top to keep them piping hot.

"Old Kate be all we got here to ride. Thinkin' it be good to have a good saddle mare, maybe even two. And some good side arms just in case we ever had any more midnight visitors."

"Stuff like that ain't easy come by."

"Ain't much to it when ye knows the right people."

"Are ye sayin' that ye knows the right people?"

"Reckon that be right. I do know a man or two here and there."

"Here, I take the gravy now," Ma said, "Hosses and guns costs plenty I be thinkin' special since it be war times and all, and we ain't got no money much no more."

"I do," Wes said emphatically.

"Ain't never seen no sign that be the truth," Ma retorted half surprised and half amused at the same time.

"I show ye right after we eat," he retorted.

"Uh hu, we see about that. This ain't no time be joshin' me, and I be a mite put out with ye iffin that be yer aim."

"Well, keep yer stove hot, and I show ye. I ain't foolin', and ye gonna see that too."

"Wes Rogerson, I ain't never knowed ye be nothin' other than a miser man and a dirty filthy one at that. Just cause I done fetched ye here and cleaned ye up ain't made ye rich. I ain't never had much book learnin', but I ain't no fool neither."

"Well sister, iffin I..."

"Don't call me that. I ain't yer sister."

"Well, okay. I can and I will prove ye wrong. When I makes a believer outta ye, will ye help me do what I want done?"

"First off, actions speaks a whole bunch louder than words. Iffin I be wrong, then I won't be so stiff-necked that I can't own up to bein' wrong. Like I said, I ain't no fool."

"Then I reckon ye will just have to see with yer own eyes," Wes boasted as he reached for a hot biscuit. Ma smacked his hand away and reminded him that nobody took a bite of her fixing's before grace was said over them.

"I gonna go feed Julie before I eat, Ma stated as she filled a plate and made her way around the stove to the oilcloth covered table and poured a small amount of fresh milk into a wooden bowl. "Stoke up the stove however much ye think ye need it, and I be back in here soon."

Wes pulled three big splits of ash from the wood box and opened the firebox door. He had to rake down the coals with the first split but managed to get the three cuts into the stove and the door closed behind them. He cracked open the draft just a bit, and soon the old cook stove was about ready to walk across the floor on its own.

Ma returned with the empty bowl and the unwashed dish. Julie had eaten well but still had very little color in her cheeks. She said that she felt a bit weak this morning and that she just wanted to lay back and rest a bit more. Ma was worried about her, and it showed on her face in spite of all she could do to cover her feelings. She stood by the hot stove as she ate her own vittles. It was not long before the kitchen was empty, save for Ma and Wes.

"Get out the biggest pot ye got whilst I fetch up more water," Wes instructed.

Ma did as he requested, and he returned from the spring pool with two big buckets of the icy water and poured both into the pot.

"Gonna need this boilin' hot."

"It ain't gonna take too long with this here blaze," Ma said.

"I be back in a bit. Ye get ready to do some hot cookin' when I get back."

"Where ye be goin' now?"

"Just to the springhouse loft fer a bit, that all."

"Lordy me. I reckon a body don't never see all there is to see or know all there is to know in spite of thinkin' so."

Wes made his way straight to the loft of the old log springhouse and looked back over his shoulder as he had done so many times before, just to make sure that no one had followed him. He made his way to the darkened corners of the loft where the eaves came down near its sides and created the lowest part of the roof line. Here one could see the underside of the old-and-weathered hand-hewn shingles. These had been rived out of a massive tan oak and had seen many rains and snows. It was no wonder that the loft area stayed dark and damp most of the time, but it did provide an air of secrecy and promoted a mystery-like mood to any who entered into its confines. Wes had no trouble finding what he sought. Lifting a single floorboard uncovered his secret. He reached deep into the notched massive poplar log that held up one side of the loft floor. Someone hacked out a resting place for a floor joist and had cut it about two times as deep as had been needed. They never filled the void but went right on with their work. They left an ideal place for hiding a small cache of most anything.

The neck of the dipper gourd made a good form to get a hand around. No trouble retrieving it. He held it carefully. He turned it on all sides and inspected it best he could in the dim light. He could find no cracks or holes anywhere. In spite of his age and the stiffness of his knees and hips, the retrieval made him want to dance around like a drunken reviler at some hooligan shindig. He held the neck in one hand and brought the gourd alongside his ear. Giving a quick but firm shake told him more good news. There was no sound coming from within. That told him the contents were still intact and preserved just as he had intended all along.

He sat on the loft floor for what he thought would be long enough for Ma's pot to come to a good strong boil. He began to ponder just how his scheme would work out and how all that were involved would react to it. He had hopes. He wanted, genuinely wanted, to make things better as best he could for whatever time he had left. He knew that he had many more days behind him than he did in front of him, but he had long since learned not to waste the pleasure and happiness of today by looking back over all those yesterdays.

He made his way out the loft door and slowly began walking back toward the kitchen. He held the gourd in both hands, still turning it over and over as he walked. He looked up just long enough to see Ma peering out the kitchen door at him.

"What ye aimin' to do, Wes. Make gourd tea?"

"Reckon not; but iffin I was, ye would like how it would taste. I know that much right now."

Ma more or less brushed off that comment and busied herself with clearing away the breakfast dishes and covering the few left-over biscuits with a rough cotton towel. There was no sausage gravy to save; it had all been eagerly eaten. Dishes done, she turned to sweeping the confines of the little kitchen floor with the home-fashioned sagebrush broom with a hand-shaved hickory handle. By that time the pot was at a good boil. Wes snapped off the stem of the gourd and immersed the entire body and stem in the steaming pot. It would take a bit to really soften the dried and hardened outer shell enough to make it soft and bendable. Not long after that, the flimsy body and stem would melt away into a white looking paste and float to the top of the boiling water. Then the inner contents would be released and fall away to be cleansed of their captivity.

"What would ye want fetched from Yeary's store iffin ye could have anything he had there?" he inquired of Ma.

"I don't rightly know. There ain't a whole bunch that I be in need of."

"Nuthin' at all?"

"Well, maybe a new apron or such, or maybe a nice dress for Julie and her sisters. New dress might perk Julie up some, and I reckon they be no way that I give her one and not give to Sarry and Gracie too. That be plum unkind on my part iffin I done that and not treat all three the same. Just on account Julie got hurt don't gain her no more from me than the rest other than tryin' my best take good care fer her."

442

"Ye got a good heart Ma even iffin I do say so myself."

"Ain't doin' nuthin no other she bear wouldn't do."

Wes stirred in the steaming pot with a long carved spatula and noted how the gourd had already begun to soften. The odor that it gave off was nowhere near as appetizing as had come from Ma's sausage fry pan. He added another cut of ash wood to the fire just to make sure that there would be plenty of boil and steam to get the task done. He knew that all the beeswax inside the gourd bulb would already be melted as he managed to turn the softened mass side to side. The wax soon began to float to the top. He asked Ma to get a dipper and skim off everything that came to the top. She did as he asked without hesitation. Soon the milky white paste that once was the gourd itself came floating topside as well. It was likewise skimmed away. Now the only thing hiding the secrecy of the contents was the boiling and steaming vessel itself.

"Let it boil down some and make sure we got all the dregs skimmed off. Won't take much more, I reckon. Then we can see how ye likes my soup fixin's," Wes said with an air of sarcasm to his voice.

Ma made no comment. Her interest was peaked, but she did not care to let him know that he had stirred her anticipation. She could only wonder what he had in mind, but his mention of horse flesh and side arms had certainly led her to believe that there might be some money involved somewhere in the works. Little did she know just how far those works could possibly go and what they might mean for her and her kids.

Wes drug the gurgling pot off the fire and over to the opposite end of the stove top. He shut off the draft, and the stove at once began to show signs of cooling. It seemed to express its welcomed relaxation at not having to mimic the fires of hell, so to speak.

The pot hushed its vulgar boiling as well. Wes peered into the bottom of the pot and saw what he had waited to see. He motioned for Ma to look as well.

"Ye see them there? I told ye it be good soup."

Ma peered into the still slightly steaming pot and could hardly comprehend what her eyes were telling her. There, in the bottom of the pot were gold coins, lots of gold coins. Ma had seen only one like them before and that was the one her son had earned helping to build a barn. She was dumbstruck. She made feeble attempts at questioning Wes about them but could cause no words to course over her lips.

Wes broke the silence. "Told ye that ye would like it. Reckon ye might believe me now. Ye needs help me get ready and get set out. I aim on seein' the miller man and havin' him help me with what I want. Reckon ye can pass me a biscuit or two and fix me up with a bite fer dinner? I need get to the mill and get back here by time Jubal be comin' back. Least that be what I plan on."

"Ye takin' all these with ye?" Ma asked when she was again able to speak.

"Not ever one. Count me out twenty-five of them iffin ye will."

Ma dutifully did as she was asked in spite of the lingering shock of the surprise that Wes had sprung upon her. While counting out the coins, she carefully inspected each of them and noted that they all were ten-dollar gold pieces. She had no understanding what they were really worth or the buying power that they commanded. Wes had not told her anything about the worthlessness of Confederate paper or Union certificates either, for that matter. Many merchants and traders were not at all receptive to paper money and consequently greatly inflated their prices in hopes of reaping profit from money in which they could place little or no confidence. Gold, however, was solid and real in any man's eyes and, therefore, had more buying power. True that goods were a lot harder to come by because of the war and all, but if you knew the right people and had enough money, things could be had. It might take a bit of time, but the right amount of money in the right hands could produce almost anything.

Wes headed to the barn and caught old Kate. She never resisted putting on her harness because that usually meant a nubbin or an apple. Wes gave her three nubbins. If an old mule could ever express happiness, then Kate did by gently nudging at his shoulder and following him step for step.

Making his way back to the kitchen, Wes decided that he would let Ma in on only a part of what he planned on doing. She did not need to know more right now. He had surprised her enough for now and that would be enough for her to chew on until he found out more for himself. He could do none of that by laying around and not making any effort on his own.

"I got Kate bridled up for the ride down to the Johnson's. C.C. be able to shed a light on what I needs be knowin' fer sure."

"Ye stayin' the night like Jubal did?" Ma inquired.

Wes sensed that she did not like the thought of not having himself or her son around for the entire night. "No, I ain't aimed to stay. I just needs speak with the miller man and see iffin he can help me out some. I reckon I don't cotton to leavin' ye here the blessed night through by yerself."

"I be proud of that," Ma admitted without a second of delay or even as much as a hint of reservation. "I don't want no ham-stealin' low-life comin' here no more." Ma had said more in that one breath than Wes had ever expected to hear from her. He was not really sure how she felt about him as man to woman, but he took that one statement to be an encouragement. All the more reason to go ahead with his plans. All the more reason to share a little bit here and there while he still was able to do it.

"I be obliged iffin ye keep old Jake put up till I get a hour or so out. I don't reckon on meetin' up with nobody on the road, and he might just slow me down anyhow. I wanna be back here by sundown. I reckon me and the boy be comin' back together iffin he comes back to the mill before dark."

"Lordy how mercy, I hope he ain't set on stayin' there again tonight, Ma said. "He might use up all his welcomes iffin he ain't mindful."

"I reckon he be mindful of that," Wes replied. "I be thinkin' he not track none past Yeary's iffin he go that far. The trail done be too cold by now to go much more than that."

It was near mid-morning by the time Wes mounted old Kate and swung open the barn lot gate and set out for the mill. There was still a good chill in the air, and the buckskins were welcomed against the cold.

Wes kept an eye on the road to read whatever signs it might show him. The road near the reed patch revealed nothing other than a few deer and fawn tracks. There had been someone else looking at these tracks as well. A lone footprint in the dry grasses stood out like a lantern in a window on the darkest of nights. Wes pretty much knew who had made that track, and he reasoned why it had been made there as well. There was one thing that would cause a tracker to loll around such signs and that would be none other than fresh venison.

Kate had her head hanging a bit low by the time they had the mill in sight. She was getting to be an old gal and what Wes had asked her to do was a bit more than she was used to doing, but she seemed to have her heart in it and was doing the best she could. Wes could not help but wonder if somehow she knew what he was up to and that she would benefit from his efforts as well as everyone else.

Wes had no trouble in finding C.C. He was in the mill at his books as usual when the old wheel was not in motion. The race was not frozen, but there was just no grinding to be done this particular day. Pleasantries were exchanged and customary small talk ensued.

"What brings ye here today my good man?" C.C. asked in some bewilderment.

"I need yer help, plain and simple," Wes answered as straight forward and honestly as he could present himself.

"What can I do?"

"Best I recollect, ye knows a lot of folks all about these parts. Ye know who to ask and who has this or that. Could that be right?" Wes asked.

"Well, I do know one or two good souls, I reckon."

"I be in need of two good saddle mares or geldings and saddles and bridles and such. Might not hurt havin' saddlebags and such either."

"Ye figger on travel some?"

"Not far, just up the mountain a ways. No more than day or day and a half at best, then right back here."

"Good stock might be a bit hard come by with war time and all," C.C. said matter of fact as he pulled out his pipe and began to pack it with home-tied and cured long red leaves that he had taken in sometime back as milling charges.

"I reckon ye be right there, but it ain't no problem fer me to pay fer them. I can cover that I reckon." Wes pulled out his small leather pouch all tied up at the neck and shook it lightly before C.C. He did not open the purse, but the miller man got the message loud and clear.

"Ye ought told me right off ye was on business. Reckon we be warmer iffin we went to the house and set in front of the fire. We can talk there all ye want and won't be nobody the wiser. I can have Lida fix up a bite or two, and ye can eat with us."

"I be obliged to ye." Wes had not thought about anything to eat, and he remembered the biscuits that Ma had packed up for him. They were still in his haversack. He would have to remember to eat them on the way home. He did not think it best to come back home with them. He would feed them to Kate if he had to. He had no aim or intent to do anything that might cross or upset Ma. She had enough on her as it was.

Once before the fire, the buckskins were a bit too warm. Wes unbuttoned the deerskins and moved back away from the flame as best he could. He began to relate to C.C. what he wanted and all the things that he planned to get from Yeary's store or whatever merchant could come up with all that he wanted.

"How come ye had so much change here so lately, Wes? I mostly recall ye bein' down right miserly and mostly hermit like."

"That were just a put on. I hated havin' to do that way, but I were sure that I needed to do that to throw people off my track fer a good long time. Now I don't give two hoots iffin they finds me or not. I done made up my mind that I be gonna do some good by some folks while I still got a little time to do it. Folks been good to me when I never done a good turn back fer them; and now I genuine wanna do fer them best I can, not on account I feel obliged to them. I am obliged to them big time, but I wanna do fer them on account I care about them. They things that they needs bad, and I can help get fer them. That be what I mean and how I feel about it all. I know I be gettin' on in years, so I reckon it be time now fer me to leave some happy tracks. Iffin it ain't time now, then I don't see how it ever will be."

"Sounds me like ye done seen the light," C.C. answered as he lit his pipe again and tossed the burning twig into the fireplace.

"I have seen it. I honest wish I had seen it years back. But that ain't the way it is, and I reckon I ain't never be able to make all them bygone days come back so as I can redo them. All I can do is the best I can today and hope to do more tomorrow. All that will last is what I can do fer somebody else and that be pine blank what I aim on doin' best I can. That be why I askin' fer yer help."

C.C. puffed on his pipe until he had a red glow plainly visible in the bowl. The cloud of gray smoke enshrouded his head and blended with his hair and gave him a ghostly like appearance that flickered in the dancing firelight. He must have inhaled a bit more of the cloud than he had expected. A sharp and coarse cough erupted from deep within his chest, and he labored at catching his breath for a moment or two. Tears welled up in his eyes, and he wiped them away with the back of his leathery hand. He spoke softly as if his throat could be afire but said nothing about the pipe or the tobacco itself.

"I will help you all I know how. What do ye need me to do?"

That was exactly what Wes had wanted to hear. The two talked on about the particulars that Wes wanted. There were several items that he wanted from Yeary's or whatever store that could provide them. C.C. sent Lida to the mill desk for a quill and ink well. He also told her to fetch him a few sheets out of the back of his ledger. Said he needed to write a letter for Wes. "Ye may as well make up the bed over there too. We might need put up the boy and Wes fer the night."

"Oh no. I be thankin' ye just the same, but I reckon we not be leavin' Ma and the girls by they selves overnight. We, least I, needs be back there by night fall. I look fer Jubal be back here by mid-afternoon at least," Wes informed his host.

Lida did as her father had instructed. First she brought him the writing materials that he wanted and then went back to the mill and spread up the bed. Part of her wanted Jubal to sleep over there again tonight and another part of her wanted to bolt away from there and pretend that she had never ventured there before. She forced herself to dwell on other things and soon found herself in the kitchen, stoking up the cook stove with the intent of having hot corn bread and apple butter for supper.

It was later in the afternoon than Wes had figured when the list was done and business completed. C.C. assured him that he would do his best to achieve all that he wanted and make all the contacts. He would concentrate first on getting two good mounts and all the rigging. He would bargain for the best deal that he could get and get the best stock that he could find. And yes, he would keep it all under his hat and not let on to even his own family, leastwise not until Wes told him it would be okay to let it out.

It was understood by both that a deal was only as good as the words of the men who had made it. In these parts, a man was known by his word, be it good or bad. Both of these men had given their word and had shook hands on it. It was a done deal. Wes gave C.C. his leather purse, and he did not even bother to look inside it. It was not necessary, because he knew that there would be enough to cover what it was meant for and that if there was a difference that it would be made up when known to be short.

Once again, the two men shook hands, and Wes made his way to old Kate's side and managed to get himself up on her broad back. She seemed anxious to start home and at once headed out to the rutted valley road, turned right and headed up the hollow. She wanted to be at home for the night as well.

The trek from Yeary's back to the mill was tiring. The trail that Jubal sought more or less ended there. Mr. Yeary had related how the threesome had brought the hams to the store and bartered them for whiskey and tobacco and a few Confederate dollars. They had not lingered at the store but had set out in a generally southern path. That almost sure meant that they were headed for the river crossings and to somewhere on farther south.

It would be meaningless to attempt following them any longer. They had two days start and would be going through some rough country before they reached the river area. Mr. Yeary was apologetic for Jubal's loss, but there was nothing he could do for him short of returning the purloined meat and that was not going to happen because what part of it that had not been ruined by mud splatter and grime had already been carved up and sold.

There was time before reaching the mill for thought and reflection. There was not so much ill will over the hog meat as there was over what had happened at their hand to Julie. That could not be forgiven and begged for justice. Yet, Ma had told him that justice would be done in the end and that he should not be consumed by the evil doings of others. If he did not seek revenge, then who would? It struck him like a summer time thunderclap! No amount of revenge or justice, if you could call it that, would ever make Julie be not shot. Nothing would make that go away.

Best if such low-down-cursed so-and-so trash would just leave him alone and never show a face around him or his own, never again. That would be just fine and dandy. But danged if he would just stand around and let something like this ever happen again. He would forever keep a sharp eye out and always be looking at the signs and the things that the woods and the hills could tell him.

And then there was that girl. Woman, whatever! He wanted to be with her more and yet was afraid to let himself go and be at complete ease around her. He had not cowered to her when she chided him about all the things that he had said he wanted and hopefully, someday, would have. She had not understood that he felt like he could never measure up to her because his britches were thread bare and his shirt tattered. He never wanted her to sense his embarrassment over the fact that he was so poor that he could dress no better. He wanted her as much as he wanted all the material things, and yet she was just beyond his reach. She had not held these things over his head. She had never made mention of them. Sure, they had talked about what they wanted out of life. She wanted much the same things as her mother. Good home and a family with enough to live within expectations. Seemingly not too much to ask for. She wanted to be appreciated for who and what she was and for what she had to offer as a woman. He was desirous of those things too, but there surely had to be more than just that.

She had said that there was joy in the light and that no matter what might come that peace and that joy would never go away and that no man could ever take it away. Well, that just might hold up once you got there but what would it take to put a person on to that? Hard to be full of peace when you been so wronged that it cost an innocent child to be laid up in a sick bed for near on to two months now. Hard to be really happy when you can't even look decent when you go calling on somebody. Would be mighty nice to know all those answers, but right now they just were not in sight.

Lida had been watching for Jubal to return to the mill. She tried to hide the fact that she was awaiting his return by making repeated trips between the living room and the kitchen. This gave her a chance to peer out the windows and perchance catch a glimpse before he got all the way into the mill yard. She had made plenty of corn bread cakes and had them on the warmer, just waiting for him to stop in long enough to sit down and eat with her. Her wait was not long. Jubal came into sight coming down the ridge line above the mill just a few minutes after Wes had started for home.

"Come in and eat a bite with me," Lida said as he came down off the hill and neared the front porch. She stood in the open kitchen door with her arms uplifted on the jamb. "Wes just set out a little bit ago. He ate some before he left, and there be plenty left over."

"I am a bit hungered iffin I do say so. I be thankin' ye."

"Bet ye be a mite tuckered out too."

"Well, it has been a long two days I reckon. I made many a track, but I be okay."

"Good, I am proud ye not be plum wore out."

Jubal ate in a bit of a hurry but was glad to have it nonetheless. Lida made small talk about what he had found out at the store and what the trail had shown him. But she seemed very withdrawn when it came to talking about them or their relationship.

"Ye said Wes just left. I weren't aware that he aimed to come down here. Ye know what he wanted or what it was all about?"

"No. He and my daddy talked a long time, and they shushed us away so we couldn't hear what they was talkin' on."

"That be a mite odd I think," Jubal responded between bites. "Reckon I find out tonight once I get home and speak with him on it."

"I thought ye might sleep on the mill again tonight. It ain't quite as cold as last night, but ye probably still need the warmin' stones again. But, I ain't sayin' that I could fetch em to ye again."

Jubal thought that he could see a slight blush to her cheeks. He knew that she had some reservation, possibly some regret about last night. How could she lead him on like that and still have him to believe that she was sorry for their actions all at the same time? Why did things have to be so confusing? He had no one to turn to for asking about such things; no Pa that cared even enough to see he had a shirt on his back, let alone teaching him about life.

"Lida, I be plum honest with ye, best I know how. I be thinkin how good it be to stay the night and ever other night as far as that be, but I feel like a hound pup that don't yet know how to track a rabbit. I ain't never knowed nobody, and I don't know much else either."

"I don't know a bit more than yerself, Jubal. I reckon we both has a lot to learn. I hope ye realize that in me as well."

"I ain't faultin' ye none at all."

Jubal finished eating and made the customary thank you courtesies to C.C. and Mrs. Johnson. He told Lida that he felt he needed to get on home tonight. He assured her that he would find a way to get back to the mill as soon as he could, for whatever reason. C.C. provided that reason.

"Son, since it be so late and ye done tromped over half of creation, why don't ye saddle up the mare and ride her home tonight? Ain't likely be nothin' goin' on twixt here and yer house, and ye can fetch her back in a day or so. Ye know where she be and ye knows where her saddle and bridle be. Lida can cut a apple and catch her up fer ye in no time.

That was all the clue that Lida needed. She made a smart run to the cellar and emerged with an apple and quickly quartered it. Reaching the barn lot fence, she called to the mare and the gelding and both came to collect their treat. In just as short a time, the mare was bridled and saddled. Jubal was ready to ride. He swung open the yard gate and led the mare through. He turned to Lida with the intention of telling her that he would see her tomorrow. Instead, the look on her face prevented words. She had a look about her that he had seen in Julie's face only a few nights ago. There was that look of contentment and peace that he had seen in few others. Granny Iverson had it, and had it not been for so much hard work and toil, Ma would have it most of the time too.

The two walked slowly to the house. Neither said a word. Lida stopped at the front steps and looked into his eyes. Still, she said not a word. He could not speak. Tears welled up in both eyes. She leaned over and kissed him gently on a tear-stained cheek, turned and went into the house. He mounted the mare and turned her up the road toward home. He had a feeling that he would be traveling this road again, real soon even after tomorrow. He just did not know how to handle some of the feelings that were running around inside of him.

C.C.'s mare must have sensed where she was meant to go. Jubal found himself setting low in the saddle with her standing impatiently at the lower barn yard gate as if to attempt to announce to him that they had arrived. Jubal had not paid too much attention to the road or to his surroundings all the way up the hollow. He had just let the mare have her own reins and set her own pace. He was so embroiled in thought that he did not recall any of the road trip, yet here he was a hundred yards from home.

He dismounted, opened the gate and led the mare on up to the barn. It took little time to stable the mare and bed her for the night. Maybe he could rest tonight as well. Ma would want to know all that had happened and what he had learned. He could tell her that in just a few words and then he could bed himself down. He made his way to the house and soon had all his gear stowed. Ma had a fire going and threw on a big back stick for the fore part of the night. He told her all that he wanted her to know about following the track all the way to Yeary's store and all that the storekeeper had related to him. He told her that he was tuckered and that all he wanted now was to lay down by the fire and try to rest. She understood and left it at that for the night.

The dancing firelight had a soothing effect on the boy, and he had hardly touched his head to the straw-filled pillow when sleep consumed his conscious thought. The chill of the day had long since been displaced by the hearth and the fact that he was home, home where he knew the peace that he had not been able to find anywhere else. Yet, restlessness and wanderlust ate at his very being at times. Not tonight, not right now.

Ma had not made any effort to be any quieter than usual, but Jubal had not heard her stir as he did on most mornings. First thing that he knew, Sarry was shaking his shoulder and telling him that breakfast was ready. He raised his head just enough to survey his situation. There was no one around him except his sister calling him out of bed, and she was already making her way back to the kitchen. He had slept the night through, and still the new day found him tired as if he had not slept at all. Maybe some strong coffee would help.

Wes had not told Jubal the full details of his business with C.C. nor had he revealed all the things that the miller man would try to buy for him. He made quick work of his breakfast biscuits and gravy and told the boy to come help him in the woodshed when he finished eating.

"We best lay in a stock of stove wood and get it all corded up. Signs say it be bad days when the moon changes," he remarked not really having paid any particular attention to any sign of any kind except the fact that it was cold. He just needed to get the boy off to himself so they could talk a bit and set things straight. Jubal made no hurry leaving the kitchen. He had nothing particular to talk to his Ma about but just felt that he needed to be near her right at the moment. She did not ask him anything more about the trek that he had made. She knew him well enough to know that he would tell her what she needed to hear all in due time. She knew that he would open up to her when he was ready and that there was not a cause in the world to try and rush him.

"Best ye go help Wes. Look like we fixin' to weather a spell. Ye can rest all ye wants durin' rough weather iffin we got plenty wood ready." Her hint of a smile told him that she knew pretty much what he was feeling and what was eating on him. That alone, gave him some sense of belonging and knowledge that there was someone who he could hold on to.

It was cold in the woodshed, and Wes had hung an old piece of oilcloth over the doorway. That helped to stop some of the chill air that otherwise leapt through every crack and slit in the old weathered structure. It was a sturdy building made from rived out chestnut boards on a framework of white oak poles. There had been so much wood run through it that the dirt floor was covered more than a foot thick with chips, bark and sawdust in spite of goodly portions being scooped up and used for tenders. The outside had long since given in to the years of sunlight and rain, frost and cold, and had assumed a proud aura of weathered silver grey.

Wes had talked to Ma about what he had in mind but just to a point. There were things that he wanted her to know and things that he needed to tell the boy. They were not the same. He felt like the time would come for them both to know more later on and that once they saw and realized what he was trying to do, then they would both understand.

"Reckon ye know that I went to the mill and had me a talk with C.C. about some matters and such?" Wes asked in a matter-of-fact way.

"Ma told me ye went there the day I traipsed off trackin' over to Yeary's."

"She tell ye what it be concernin' and what I want to try?"

"She not tell me no details."

"Reckon I owes ye some thought on that. I done set things movin' and iffin they works out, then I thinkin' that we all be a heap better off," Wes intoned as he tossed yet another cut of wood onto the ever growing rick.

"What business ye have with the miller man iffin I ought ask?" Jubal questioned.

"First off, I ask him to see into gettin' us two good mounts and saddles and all."

"Two?" the boy responded unknowingly.

"Two," Wes repeated.

"Why two?"

"One apiece, I reckon," Wes responded.

"Why we be needin' mounts? Where we fixin' to head off to?"

"I tell ye where all in due time, but right now where ain't so important."

"I ain't followin' ye," Jubal responded quizzing.

Wes turned and faced him directly. "There be things that we needs, things that yer Ma needs and things that ever soul around here needs in some way or 'nother. Reckon ye knows that without me tellin' ye. Them things takes money and most folks wants Yankee greenbacks or gold fer them whenever they can be found. I aims to see that we gets a few of them things, and we gonna need two good hosses to fetch some money. That be why I been dealin' with the miller man. He knows people and he can find things when I ain't got no notion of even where a body outta start lookin'. Peace time be one thing, but we is in war times and that changes up a lot of how trades is done and such. Ye unnerstand that I reckon, don't ye?"

"I reckon I do."

"I done give C.C. money fer the hosses and a bit more for some other stuff that we be needin' sooner or later. Ye just gonna have to trust me on that fer now."

"Where'd that much money come from?"

"Out my gourd stash."

"Dang. Iffin I knowed there be that much...Well...I don't guess I woulda done nothin' any different, but it woulda been temptin'. Guess it be best I never knowed."

"Well, ye knows now and that be fine with me, but ye don't know all the facts and don't needs know right now. All the gourd money ain't plumb gone, but it be close. Guess ye done figgered out that we gonna travel a bit on account we needs fetch the rest of it. Time was I would'a fetched it by myself but reckon my days has mounted up on me, and I ain't stout like once was. That be why I needs yer help."

"Where we hafta go fer fetchin' it?"

"Near about three days ride. Down in big gap country."

"Reckon that be new timber to me," Jubal responded somewhat in wonderment and somewhat in anticipation of it all.

Imagination once again took precedence to logic and the lad began building castles in the sky. The thought of money ignited dreams and hopes in him that he had partially put behind. Still, there was a want for basic needs being met for him and especially for his Ma. Yet there was a glimmer of hope for the good things in life, although he was not so sure exactly what all those things would turn out to be. He had no real thoughts on what kind of money the old man was talking about. If the dreams were allowed to stir within him, then they may as well run to the hilt. Seems he no more than faced up to the reality when along would come a ray of hope, be it ever so fleeting. He did not realize it just then, but he had an inkling of what the good things in life could be all about. He envisioned himself as a man when, in fact, he was not quite there yet, except for the responsibilities that had been thrust upon him.

"When ye reckon C.C. have them hosses ready fer us?" Jubal asked with anticipation. "When ye reckon we can fetch it?"

"I ain't so sure, son. There ain't no hurry. I ain't thinkin' it be much good idea settin' out in cold and snow like it be now. Best we not leave yer Ma and the gals and it be this bad. We might ought wait to near spring."

Jubal never answered but continued stacking wood against the old shed wall. There was a slight break in the wind wisps and both took a breather and went outside and scanned the ridges and the tree lines.

Both seemed to run out of anything else to talk about at near the same time. The wood racks were stacked high and both realized that there would be a sufficient supply to meet most any weather for many days now. Wes had intended to tell Jubal more about his dealings with the miller man and more about some of the other things that were discussed in the deal, but he also realized that the boy's thoughts were somewhere other than in the woodshed. He had a fair idea where those thoughts would be centered and also realized that now was not the time to go asking about such. The cold seemed to bite more as a result of their mutual silence, and they soon found themselves warming by the fire as Julie slept peacefully nearby.

Jubal looked at her and realized just how precious that she was to him and in the same moment realized just how fragile that she had become. His heart went out to her for all that she had endured, and in spite of all that she still had a cheerful spirit about her and an even stronger faith. He noted that her color seemed pale today but made efforts to convince himself that it was because of the cold. He carefully and gently leaned over her bedside and touched her cheek. She was warm. There was no apparent fever. Why could she just never seem to get any stronger? He could accept the idea that she may never be able to walk so well again and that she might even have trouble getting up in a buckboard or such, but he just could not allow any thoughts about anything more grievous than that. He had sworn to himself that he would get revenge for her if he could ever catch up with her assailant.

Wes looked down on her with deep concern. He saw her the same ways as did her brother, but he also believed that he was more realistic about her fate. He was reassured that he had done the right things in his dealings and instructions with C.C. but must, for now, keep those details locked up inside. He had not given much thought to vengeance but knew where he would stand if opportunity ever came along. He felt that he was doing all for her that could be done, all that he knew to do.

Granny Iverson came in from the back room and reached up on the mantle and retrieved her Bible. She sat down in a cane back chair near the fireplace and let the book fall open in her lap. She began reading to herself. In just a few short breaths, tears welled up in her tired old eyes as she gently closed the book. It supported her small hand as she slowly and near silently drummed her first two withered fingers against the aged and worn black leather binding. The only words discernible from her lips were a whispered, "Be gentle. Be gentle. Please, Lord."

"These here ought be a good pair"

"Look a mite lean I think."

"Well, I reckon they might take a fancy to a nubbin or two."

C.C. had to admit, all be it to himself, the two animals looked good enough, all things considered. A quick look in their mouth proved them to be young. He could tell by the bulge of their features that they were strong, and the shaggy winter coat belied their real stamina. Saddles were far from new, and the other rigging seemed to be a match for usage. They would do, but it was just not in him to accept so easily.

"I ain't be askin' nary a word where they come from. It don't make me no matter. I reckon I can scribe a sale bill myself. But I ain't up to a whole hunnert fer the pair. I reckon knockin' five off be best I be willin' to go. Ye can take it here and now, and I pay ye in Federal gold. Don't come no stronger than that, I reckon."

The deal was done. C.C. knew he had crossed paths with the hoss trader somewhere along the line but could not recall his name nor where he had seen him. He did not ask his name nor anything else. Considering the war times and all, some things were just better left alone. The horses had no brands or other peculiar markings. Most likely they were stolen somewhere to the east and run in here with the intent of a quick dollar. Both were dark with obvious crossed lines. Both had been well shod not long past. Not too many out-siders ran these ridges and hills, and it should not be much trouble to lay legitimate claim to them, especially with doctored papers. Wes ought to be a mite pleased with what he had bought, especially in light of what gourd content had been needed to get them.

The miller man could not help but wonder what all the old miser had stashed up. He had let it be known that he could cover whatever it took to get what he wanted. It took knowing the right people for one thing and that would be worth a gold eagle or two.

C.C. took the leads in his left hand, and with his other he dropped the agreed upon gold pieces into the outstretched hand of the yet unrecognized man with a weathered and wrinkled face. The sky blue and bright eyes spoke of their own wisdom and experience in being able to make a way in spite of the times and the deeds of others. Spoils of war were fair game for anyone who had the will to latch onto opportunity as it presented itself. Some cared only for what they could gain. So it was, and it made no real difference to the miller man. He stood to make a few for himself and had to wrestle with himself to decide if he really would bend to such temptation, especially where his neighbor was concerned.

The Yeary family had been able to get hold of the other items that Wes had asked him to look into and had agreed to deliver them to his mill. They needed some grinding done for their own use and a deal was made. C.C. would have the wares stored inside the mill. Wes had told him of his plans, and he knew the details of those plans and was in perfect agreement.

C.C. had no trouble in hiding the newly gained steeds. He had barn room sufficient to stable them out of sight for the entire winter, if needed. Grain was not an issue either. He had the mill floor nearly covered with bulging sacks of corn and oats. Wes would come in a few days and then they could discuss things more. He could board the horses as long as needed, say for one or two more coins from the old gourd.

"Wes, I think we both ought tote a side arm all time we be out and about. No tellin' when them rogues might show up here abouts again, and I be thinkin' they ain't likely be after just ham meat next time neither."

"Ye may be pert nigh right there, I reckon. Ye still got that old Navy Colt pistol that ye got from Yeary's?"

"Yep," replied Jubal.

"Have ye shot it any?"

"Few times."

"Can ye hit anything with it?"

"Reckon I could kill a rouge scallywag iffin I was a mind to."

"Ye still out fer them low lives, ain't ye?"

"Ain't gonna trouble me nary one iota seein' them laid out. Hell, I even be willin' help bury them dung heaps iffin I had a chance."

"Don't be too bitter fer too long, son. It just cause ye grief and eat ye from inside out. I know. I done been down that branch, and it be a muddy and tangled one at that. Time gonna heal some of them wounds, but scars won't never plumb go away."

"I know ye mean well, Wes. But I see it in my mind's eye ever day. It just ain't ready fer fergittin' right now."

"How's about fergivin'? Have ye considered any on that?"

"Don't reckon I have, and ain't goin' to right yet."

"Ye needs time, son. Time and a fair amount of it to boot."

"Reckon that be nigh all I got plenty of."

"Ye think ye and old Kate might have time to fetch me down to the mill here in a few days? Me and C.C. got some doin's needs finished up on."

"Reckon I can," Jubal answered.

The next few days saw crystal clear skies with a brilliance of blue that was rarely seen in the mountain area. Usually shrouded in a haze or mist, it was no great wonder how the Indians came to call them the land of the smoke. Winter chill would drive away the mist and usually cast it down in the form of dry powdered snow. The long dark nights would allow no new condensations, and the air would remain thin and cold. Only a full moon would change the appearance of the hills and hollows when they would seem to glow. The beauty of the mountains was there for beholding. But then as many times before, those who lived therein saw it not as beauty, but as a place of laborious toil from which there was slim chance of escape.

Each night, Wes would venture out a short ways from the old log home to where he could see the stars and the moon and be out from under any tree cover or other limiting view of the heavens. He knew from long back how to read the stars and see the signs in the skies.

The moon would be new in another three or four nights and that would be when he would start his time. In less time than it took the moon to go through its signs things would be a whole lot different around here, and he would be a proud man then.

Jubal had been out one crisp morning just at daybreak when he spotted a doe and her yearling just above the garden plot. They were probably after the few apples that had made it this far along by burying up in the thick orchard grass beneath the trees. It had not been taken for hay all that past growing season and had been left because of the apple trees. The fruit would have a cushion when it ripened and fell from the laden branches. Bruised fruit would never keep as long as non-marked ones. Old Kate could be turned in on that grass late in winter and she would clean it off. Nothing would be wasted.

The next morning found the lad in hiding before the sun began to show its first light. It was cold, and a slight wind occasionally stirred the tall and dried grasses. They danced in such folly that they seemed to be shivering themselves. Jubal was cold, but he knew that the growing light would soon tell all that he needed to know. He remained still as he could and kept an ear cocked all the while. He thought once or twice that he heard something coming from the meadow beyond the orchard.

Then, as he had hoped and expected, he saw it. The yearling was there. He did not see the doe, but it was not yet even half-light. He slowly lowered the old hog rifle and peered down the sights. Curses, too dark to see the bead. He stilled himself and forced his breathing to become regular and even. The sun was at his back and each new minute would reveal more of all that he needed to know. Sometimes, just like growing up, waiting could take forever.

At the crack of the rifle, Jubal had to look around the cloud of muzzle blast to see where his aim had landed. Much to his amazement, the yearling had not been able to make a step. It had fallen in its track and was most likely dead when it hit the ground. He quickly gutted it and easily made his way back to the woodshed with his prize. Wes had heard the shot and soon joined him as they dressed the meat and readied it for the smokehouse. There would be fresh back strap tonight and good hearty stew for several days yet to come.

The stinging cold maintained its icy grip on the valley and seemed to have no cause to let go. Ice formed in the spring pool each night and had to be broken with an axe before the buckets could be filled. Ma had kept fire in the cook stove all the time just to keep the house warmer and to make morning cooking come off faster and easier. Bread would bake a lot sooner in an oven that was already good and warm. She stoked up the kitchen fire right before bedtime and shut off the draft. That way the fire would keep all night. She knew that Jubal had laid in plenty of stove wood. Besides that, a well-banked fire burned a long time and did not eat away at the stash of good dry hardwood.

Jubal and Wes kept the fireplace going in much the same manner. Ma, Granny Iverson and the girls, save for Julie, slept up in the cabin loft and piled on enough handmade quilts to keep them warm through the night. Most nights Julie appeared to be warm and comfortable. Sometimes she would stir a bit and sometimes try to sit up, looking to see if maybe her brother was awake. Jubal would get up and go sit on her bedside and talk with her, both almost at a whisper most times. Both knew that Wes would be awakened by their talking, but he never made any effort to join in. He had to know in his heart that these were special times between a brother and a sister, and he respected that.

Those times came to be very special to Jubal, and he realized just how much his sister meant to him. He still had that burning hatred desire deep within him to seek vengeance on the ones who had hurt her. At the same time he had a passionate desire to see her get better, and he had vowed to himself that he would do anything and everything that he could to help her. If she could be just a little bit stronger, if she could just gain the strength to sit up a little bit, if she could just get to where she could eat more, anything would be an encouragement.

He was not so sure what she had said to Ma or to anyone else in the household either, but he had not heard one unkind word come from her lips about the ones who had wronged her. There just seemed to be a peace about her, even on those days when she hurt so much or when she was racked with fever. She could just lie back, and you could see the peacefulness come over her. It was in those times that her brother could see her true beauty. It was in those times where she was reassured that she would be taken care of and that all would be well.

Jubal could not let go of his desire for revenge, and he remained hesitant to talk about it with anyone. Julie had told him that she harbored no ill will for anyone about what had happened, and he could pretty much tell that she said what she felt. Still, he had some trouble understanding how she could feel that way when she had been so injured and made to give up so much. Ma felt more or less the same way, but she had come right out and said that she had no feeling nor no respect for those kind and especially not for one in particular. Both knew exactly who she meant there. Ma harbored some deep down desire for revenge; she almost had to, but she never spoke about it. She had just said that they would pay some of these days.

In the next days, Julie seemed to perk up. Her appetite picked up, and she ate heartily at the venison stew. Her color picked up a bit, and she began to sit up in bed enough to read a bit. Granny Iverson made it a point to be at her bedside and read to her anytime she wanted. On cloudy days, Granny would make out like the light was too dim for her to see well enough to read and hand the Good Book to Julie. Jubal saw what she was up to by that because anybody who could read by the light of the fireplace in the middle of the night could certainly read by clouded daylight. Julie most likely saw through it too but went along with Granny anyhow.

"I be thinkin' it be time we call on C.C. and see how he done made out fer me," Wes said as he and Jubal came up from feeding old Kate and the milk cow. This was in the early morning just after Ma had filled them up on deer steaks and biscuits and what eggs she had.

"When ye wanna go?"

"Reckon we give Kate a few minutes on her nubbins, then we hike out."

"We need her fer any certain cause?" Jubal asked.

"Well, I reckon we do."

"How that be?" Jubal questioned again.

"May need her tote a pack 'r two fer us. Hope so anyhow."

Wes answered him by saying that he had asked C.C. to try and buy some things for Ma and the girls and even for Granny Iverson, but told him nothing more.

"How come ye go and be doin' all such like that?" Jubal asked in somewhat of a surprise.

"It be comin' up on Christmas time, ain't it?"

"Well yeah, I reckon so."

"Ain't Christmas time a proper time to be givin' out nice things?" Wes responded with a slight smile on his lips and a little bit of a twinkle in his eye.

"I reckon it be that pine blank. But I ain't never give it that much thought."

"How come ye never dwelled none on it before?" Wes asked.

"Never had nothin' what weren't handmade to give out to nobody. Never had nothin' to get nothin' with. Ye know we ain't never had no other way a gettin' anything."

"I reckon I do know that," Wes said. "But this year it be a mite different, and I proud that I can get them all some little something."

Jubal did not say it, but he could not help but wonder if all included him. He was not about to ask. He still had a little bit of pride. He knew not what that might be worth, but he wanted to hang onto it. Quick flashes ran through his mind again. The same ones that befuddled him many times before. Fine clothes, silk hats, far-away places, carriages and coaches.

Another hour found them on the road down the hollow toward the mill. Wes rode old Kate, and Jubal walked. He had convinced Wes that he should lead out by a couple hundred yards or so in hopes of spotting another deer. Julie had mended up some on the yearling, and he reasoned that if it had done her good, then more would do better. Wes did not object and kept Kate back a good piece. He continually scanned the hillsides and tree lines all the while keeping an eye on the boy. There seemed to be no uneasiness in the crows or other critters, so it was reassuring that there was nothing around to fret over. But that was never a reason not to keep a sharp eye. The vigil continued all the way to the mill. No yearling or doe was to be seen.

Lida stood on the front porch near the kitchen door with one arm draped around the porch post. Her thoughts raced from the little corner of the old mill building all the way to places that could exist only in her dreams. She had thought she knew for certain what she wanted but now that certainty seemed to have just vanished. She knew that she had lots within to give, and she certainly knew that she wanted to be loved and cared for in return. Never did she expect to be just the object of fleeting passions. Yet that was the way it had been. There had been no real return of affection. There had been no compassion. There had just been a loss of judgment and not enough restraint. She had given of herself seemingly what she wanted to give. Now there was regret and some sense of worthlessness. There was still a desire and that desire remained stronger than ever. The wanton lust had made a mockery of the purity that she believed in and held onto so tenaciously. The chill of the night had not gone away, and she realized that she was without a shawl or a wrap. A tear eased its way down her cheek, and it left a path as cold as the dawn itself. Her passion was just as cold now, and there was no warm glow in her heart the way there had been. Why did it end so soon? There had to be more. How could it be so fleeting?

"Girl, ye best get yer wrap on if ye intend standin' here all sullied up like a cornered possum," C.C. said as he gently placed his strong hand to her waist and gently pulled her to him. She melted into his embrace as the tears ran freely down and dripped onto his blue flaxen shirt.

"Oh Papa, Papa…

"We can talk on it later, I reckon. Ye best get hold of yerself cause we be havin' neighbors come soon."

She had just turned and gone back into the kitchen when the miller man picked out the faint sounds of hoof beats coming from the road above the mill. Sounded like they weren't shod so that would most certain be Wes atop old Kate. He saw the glint of reflected light off the old Hawken just about the same time. Jubal was now only a scant few yards ahead of Kate. He had no aim on quizzing the boy or Wes either for that matter. Their business was their business and that was that. The thoughts, however, of another gold piece or two did run through his mind.

465

Jubal was taken aback by the horses and the gear once he realized that Wes had for sure been able to get them and that they would be going back up the road with them. He had scarcely paid any attention at all to the sacks sitting on the mill porch. Wes put him onto them and asked him to get them slung across old Kate and tied off so they could soon be on their way. He was curious as to the contents and asked Wes what they were. Wes gave him a bit of a short answer telling him that they were just gal things and a thing or two that he thought Ma might like to have around the house.

C.C. pulled Wes off to the side while Jubal tied off Kate's new load and informed him that he had been able to get the other things and had stored them in the mill loft for now. He could come and fetch them any time. He also told Wes that it had cost just a bit more than they had figured on.

"How much more ye be out"? Wes asked.

"All come to twelve dollars more'n we figgered on. I paid it cause and how I knowed ye be good fer it."

"That be fact. I got it on me, but I ain't wantin' the boy see me pay ye. How about I go fetch me a drink yonder at yore springhouse, and I leave yer money there?"

"That be good with me," C.C. responded as he could not help but wonder why the old coot wanted to be so much a sneak about it all.

"I be much oblige to ye," Wes said as he set out to the springhouse. "Ye done hope me a bunch, and I ain't takin' it light neither."

"Saddle up, son," Wes said as he returned from the springhouse. "We needs be makin' tracks. Be late time we gets back home."

"Hold up just a bit," C.C. said moving up the kitchen steps. He opened the door and said something to whoever was busy inside.

"I reckon ye ain't aim stayin' fer dinner, but I reckon I can see ye got biscuit bread and a meat slab. That ought tide ye over till supper."

Lida came out of the kitchen and down the steps with a small bundle wrapped in a piece of red-checkered cloth. She went first to Wes and handed him up a big biscuit pone with red ham meat sticking out both sides of the bread.

"Thank ye, Lida," Wes said as he eagerly took the treat.

Lida walked over to Jubal and reached up another biscuit to him. She spoke no words to him and made no eye contact. He brushed her hand as he took what she offered. He tried to think of what to say to her, but no words came forth. She turned and was just as quickly back inside the kitchen. Unanswered mysteries would steal sleep again tonight.

The ride back up the old hollow road was silent. Wes lagged behind and held Kate's reins up tight. No cause for her to spook over new horse flesh. He realized there was not too much a chance of her doing that once he looked back at her. Head was down and her feet seemed heavy. The old girl was tired, and she cared not who knew it. All she wanted was her stall and a fork full of hay. Let these new creatures take on some of the load. She had done enough. She had done a lifetime of work.

Jubal and Wes made short work of bedding down the new horses. Each was stalled up and had new hay thrown down to them to fill their mangers to overflow. Jubal saw to it that Kate had an extra portion of nubbin corn and some good bedding. Wes did the same for the saddlers. Darkness would soon settle over the little valley, and all would be at peace. It had been a long day and that should make for a good night's rest.

The fire burned warm in the old stone fireplace. Its comforting flame danced lazily about the room and seemed to cast its spell on all therein. Julie sat propped up in her bed reading aloud with Granny Iverson at her side. Jubal could hear the words himself but paid no real attention to the verses. Wes sat back in one corner with a piece of slate and busied himself with ciphers about something. Jubal had no interest in that endeavor either. Ma sat silently before the fire and darned thick woolen socks. The others stared aimlessly into the fire as if to be mesmerized by it.

There was no anticipation for tomorrow. There were no pressing chores that had to be done; just feed and water as usual. Plenty of warming firewood was already stocked up. The barn loft was filled with good timothy and orchard grass hay. The smokehouse had a good stock, and Ma had dried a goodly measure of beans and fruit. They would see the winter through in spite of the dry summer and in spite of all else that the cursed war had brought down on them.

Granny Iverson had said many times that the Lord had been good to her and to her kin and had provided for all their needs. Jubal could recall her saying that many times before, and he realized in his own way that she was not far off the mark. He never attributed having their needs met and fulfilled by anything other than hard work and perseverance. Granny Iverson just seemed to have a peace about her all the time and always seemed to be happy. He could never recall her saying that she wished she had this or that, or that if she had the money that she would buy such and so. It really made him ponder some of the things that he had wished for not too long past. Sure, he would still like having all the things that riches could bring. Wes had got the horses and all and had got them because he had money ample to buy them, but where was the thrill of it now? Sure the horses were needed and would make life a bit better around the old farmstead, but there was no overwhelming joy in them. It just led to more questions and frustration.

"Jubal, fetch us in a good back stick. I reckon we been night owls near about long enough," Ma instructed as she laid aside her needle and thread.

There was no response.

"Son, have ye gone deaf on me?" Ma barked impatiently as she stood and folded the darned sock into its mate.

"Reckon I weren't listenin' proper, Ma, that all."

"Well, ye can bank up the fire here directly. I be tuckered out and ready to lay me down."

"I will. I ain't ready fer bed yet. I may sleep on my pallet tonight."

He was not ready for sleep yet, because it was elusive and would be for a better part of the night. His mind could not balance what he thought was the needed things and desire of what most folks would call the finer things in life. There was no one really to turn to for help, at least no one he could bring to mind. Ma never went anywhere when he hinted at such things. She just told him to learn all he could and work hard and everything would work out good for him in the end. Granny Iverson claimed that she had made her own peace, but she was old and never did much anything anymore but set around and mull over who knows what.

Lida claimed that she had seen the light and had her peace too. But after that one night, it just befuddled him what she really felt or wanted. Then she hardly would as much as look at him afterwards. How was a body ever to know what was running around in her mind?

She had acted like she took to him; but last time he laid eyes on her, she acted like he was some kind of evil. He could not see where he had given her any reason to be so peeved at him. He would speak to his sisters about that whenever he could get them alone. Not much chance of that as long as the cold and damp hung on. Might be all way near springtime before that chance cropped up. He felt he could talk with Julie more so than anyone else, but she needed her strength for mending up and all. He liked being close to her, and he loved her for the way that she never talked down to him. She never laughed at him but was all time ready to laugh with him.

She just had a way about her that he liked and wished he could feel the way she did about herself and life. She always had a good word to pass on, and she never had been one to carry on with a bunch of foolishness the way most young gals do. She could be dead serious about things as well and had a clear mind on most book learning things. She could quote the Good Book right along with the circuit riders.

He thought on what she had said about faith. Seemed to him like it ran right much alongside with trust. He had asked Ma what faith was, and she had told him that it was belief that the sun would come up each and ever morning just like it had always done. Granny Iverson had called her hand on that and said that a body could see the sun come ever day and that was not reason enough to call it faith. Knowing that the sun was going to come up would be nothing more than simple trust. Any poor soul could believe in something that they and ever other soul on the face of this old earth had seen many times over. No sir, that was not what she called faith. She claimed that it had to be an expectation in things unseen. It was trust that what was believed but not yet seen would become fact and that it would come about as told. Granny Iverson said that you needed to have trust before you could ever gain and know faith and that was the way that things was meant to be. She said that if you sought faith, then all else would come in time. He was not so sure that he understood all she had said, but it was burned into his mind all the same. She had lived a good long life and she, like Julie, was not one to complain. She and Julie must have come from the same mold.

Wes had spoke about trust a time or two, but he never went much further than that. He was wise in his own way and appeared to have no real worries about himself either, especially since Ma had took him in and got him all cleaned up and such. Jubal felt he could talk to the old man about man things and that he would be truthful with him. He did not know what to expect from him about some of the things that repeatedly ran through his young mind, but he intended to ask when the time was right.

The springhouse loft afforded a shield from any chilling winter winds, but it offered no other comforts on such a cold and dank day as was the present. Jubal and Wes had found their way there shortly after breakfast where Wes was about to open the sacks that he had stashed there.

"What all ye got there, Wes?"

"Not much. Just a thing or two so's I can give it out fer Christmas."

"Like what?"

"Like this here," Wes answered as he pulled a light blue dress frilled with lace and ribbons from one of the sacks. He gently and carefully unfolded it and held it up by the sleeves. "I got this here fer Julie cause I heered her tellin' ye one night that she would like to have a store bought dress. So I fetched it fer her. Got a dress fer her two sisters too, but not all fancy and frilled up like hers."

Jubal could not make any spoken reply. He was overtaken by surprise at what the old man had done.

"Ye think she might like it?" Wes asked with a slight grin on his face.

"Well I... I reckon she will."

"I got fixin's and such so Ma can make one fer herself and fer Granny too, but I ain't gonna give her it 'fore Christmas. Reckon ye can keep shut-mouthed fer them few more days, can't ye?"

"I can."

It was readily apparent that Wes had not taken all the contents out of the sacks, and Jubal could not help but wonder what all might be left in them. He had enough upbringing not to ask. He did respect Wes for who he was and in no way saw him as a step stone for his own use. He could not help but imagine that there would be something inside one of those big old mill sacks that would wind up being for him come Christmas.

"How ye come by all this stuff?"

"I had C.C. and his wife and gal help with the girl things, and he be the one who come on them horses fer me."

"I figgered that much, but where in tarnation ye able to find stuff like this? Ain't the Reb army done nigh cleaned out ever thing they is to be bought most near ever where now days?"

"It can be had iffin ye got the gold and knows who be best fer askin'."

"Ye cleaned out yer old gourd?"

"Partly."

"How come ye doin' this?' I hear tell ye never spent nothin' and now ye done cut loose and gone loco seems me like."

"Things changes sometimes."

"Like what?" Jubal questioned.

"Sometimes a man sees things that changes him. Sees things that other folks does and how it makes things be different. Sees how it makes things be better than they would'a been otherwise."

"Ye ain't makin' much sense way I see it right off," Jubal rebuffed him.

"Well, ye ain't near old as me, and ye ain't seen near all the traipsin' around that I have. Ye ain't seen near the troubles that I done seen in other people's lives. I done seen things that ye won't never see. I done things that ye won't never even think on doin'. Ye can just take my word on that. All I mean is that I done seen why I ought done things different a long time past. I never though and ain't no changin' that."

"Still don't hold much water as I can see it," Jubal rebutted again.

"Reckon ye just ain't understandin', are ye?"

"Reckon not."

"I ain't sure that I know how I can get in yer head then," Wes answered. "Yer Ma done learned ye right from wrong, and I know ye done took to it most ways. I can see that in ye already, and ye ain't whole growed up yet."

Jubal was a bit offended by the idea that he was not yet fully a man in the eyes of another. He kept those thoughts to himself, however. His Ma had indeed raised him to respect his elders and that raising was showing through right now.

"Well Wes, iffin I was yer age, I might know more what ye is talkin' on. But I ain't yer age, and I reckon I might see things with my own eyes instead lookin' through yours. I don't mean that bein' smart-mouthed or nothin' to the kind, but that's how I see it now, whatever it be that ye wantin' me to see."

"Well spoke, son. Sometimes yer words is beyond yer age, but I can see yer Ma in ye durin' such times."

"No. But really, how come ye done spent all this when ye never done such 'fore now?"

"Like I done told ye, son. Things changes a man, not just when he be a whipper snappin' greenhorn but when he be old and bent as well. Anytime a man get where he can't or ain't willin' to change things that make him a better man, then he be dang nigh worthless then and may as well crawl off and die somewhere. Any man who ain't willin' or won't help nobody else once he has opportunity ain't much count fer nothin' else either. That make any better sense to ye?"

"I ain't got no issue with that."

"But do ye know what I mean by speakin' on helpin' somebody when ye gets a chance?"

"I thought I knowed, but now I ain't so sure. Ye done fiddled over my head some."

"What part don't ye see son?"

"Just don't see why, all at once like that ye come by such change in yer mind and turnin' yer ways and all."

"Well son, some things ye just needs grow into, I reckon. Time has a way of changin' a man. Ye be a pup right now, and all ye got on yer mind is gals and stuff what make ye think make them gals like ye. I know. I been there once, but it been many a day now. Ye won't really know how I feel and how I mean till ye gets some miles on yer carcass and some grit in yer craw."

"Sometimes, I reckon ye bein' nigh onto a fool old man."

"In yer eyes, maybe so," Wes quipped. "I reckon I can see how ye feels that way, but I know what I feels now. I know pine blank how I want things done and danged if that ain't the way it gonna be long as I have a say so in it."

"Well, just smack my butt a lick or two. I never aimed on pokin' up yer ashes none."

"Ye never done that," Wes replied in a calmer tone. "I just never give no thought on how ye might really see me. I reckon I just thought ye might see what I was tryin' tell ye all along."

"Why don't ye just out with it and tell me then?" Jubal said.

"Blamed iffin I won't just do that then; no holdin' back. But first, I wanna ask ye a thing er two."

"Ask," Jubal responded with a heightened interest which he actively attempted to conceal from his aged counterpart. At least Jubal considered him aged.

Wes rubbed his chin for a moment as he pondered his words. He wanted to make sure as best he could that the boy just might see some things his way. He recognized that the boy was wise for his age in some ways; yet by other measures, he was far behind.

"Well son, try steppin' in my shoes fer a bit. I be on in years, and I know pine blank that I got more days on my backside than I got up ahead of me. I reckon that don't give me a whole bunch a days fer much doin's no matter what I choose fer them. Reckon on account of that and other reasons as well that I be heap better off by doin' what good I can fer what time I can in place of hoggin' up ever thing I can. I got a mite I can part with I reckon, and fer blame sure I ain't gonna take none of it outta here with me. Ye hear me so far?"

"I do, and I see what ye sayin' so far."

"Then I take it ye know why I done bought all them things to pass out come Christmas time."

"I can see that," Jubal answered.

"Well then I reckon ye be right minded on doin' good fer other folks same as me then. But answer me this then. Reckon ye would do a body a good turn iffin need be same as next man, but I wanna know how ye thinkin' on the hereafter. Do ye think folks live hereafter?"

"Ma say they does, and Granny Iverson tell me that too."

"But I wanna know what ye think."

"I ain't never thought on it all that much," Jubal replied.

"Someday ye gonna needs settle yer own answers concernin' such, and ye best not be on in years like me when ye gets it done either. I see now where I been wrong so many years that weren't necessary."

"I just ain't never bothered about such," Jubal said somewhat impatiently.

"I tellin' ye here and now ye can save grief and woe iffin ye gets yerself all lined out right now. I ain't much on speakin', but I just know what I know myself and that be it. I reckon a man best work it all out fer I ain't knowin' no other way. I know ye be thinkin' I just talk through my head, but it don't matter no how. I just wanna ask ye one other thing straight up."

"What then?"

"Iffin Julie don't get over her knee and all, ye reckon she can live hereafter?"

"Why ye ask me that?" Jubal fired back in a measure of surprise and confusion all at the same time.

"I asked ye on purpose. I wanna know what ye think."

"I don't know that answer. I don't know iffin any person knows that. What ye think old man?"

"I don't think, I know."

"Then how come ye askin' me?"

"We goin' in circles ain't we?" Wes added.

"Ye are, but I ain't."

"I know I done riled ye some but that weren't my aim. I tell ye what I know. I think back to times when I knowed my mammy and my pa. They been gone many a day now, but I still can recall them and lots other folks what been gone a long time too. They all be still livin' in the beyond, and I be tellin' ye how I know it too."

"How ye know that?"

"Cause when a body thinks on another body or has thoughts on a body, they is still alive. They is alive in memories, and there is reason plenty to know that they is alive over yonder on other side. I know that don't mean nary a thing to ye, but I just tellin' ye so ye can study on it. Someday down the road a ways it might come to ye just what I been tryin' say to ye. I got no cause whatsoever to raise yer dander. But I feel it my God-spoke duty fer ye to hear me out on it, and ye can bet yer bottom last dollar that ye gonna have to reckon on it too some of these here days. Ye may just brush me off right now; but it'll come to ye someday, and ye will needs be reckon with it then. I just be tellin' ye what nobody never told me till few years back, and I most had to learn fer myself. I wish I hadda knowed long time back and a whole bunch a things would'a been better fer me a long time back. I could'a had much more meanin' outta life."

"I reckon ever man best live a life what suit him make do best he can. That be most how I sees things," Jubal said curtly.

"There be some truth in what ye be sayin' now, son. But it never hurt nobody learnin' on some other poor soul's bad times. Take a mighty thick head not take lessons from folks like them what done had learn hard things and ways. That be all I really tryin' get ye see. Ye recollect what I done showed ye how to track a man and what signs to read and know what they be tellin' ye? Ye heard me then didn't ye and never give no thought on questionin' me did ye?"

"Had no reason question ye then," Jubal said.

"Well there ain't no reason to question me now neither. I be just same as then. It just be that we talkin' on other matters now. I ain't out to be no less truth now than then. I just ain't made no other ways, and I just wantin' ye to benefit from my bein' young and foolish in my days just nigh on like you be now. I ain't pokin' ye none. I just hopin' to help ye be a better man someday."

"I be mostly man now, I reckon," Jubal bragged.

"Ye be most a man in years, I reckon. But ye ain't seen nor did all it takes to be a man in bein' wise. Only age can teach ye many of them things. I just be aimin' on savin' ye some grief and hard times somewhere on down the road. Ye ain't got no cause fault me fer that."

"I don't fault ye fer nuthin' no how. It just seem like ever single soul I ever knowed in my whole life be bent on tellin' me how, why, and when I need do this or that. No man ner dog done ever tell me do as I please. Reckon iffin I do as I please, then ain't nobody else needs live with it other than me. That be how I see it and seem like I be the only one who do. I just wonder how come it be that way. Is it cause I ain't yet turned twenty, or is it on account I come across like I don't know squat?"

"It ain't neither, Jubal," Wes countered. "It just be that folks wants ye not to have the stumbles that they done made. They not be doggin' ye just fer sake of your ways and such. They just do that way cause they care about you and only wants good things fer ye, same as me."

"I reckon I know that deep down, but sometimes I just druther folks lay off me," Jubal said a bit defensively. "I reckon I just need a little space ever now and then. Ain't much wrong with that are they?"

"I reckon not."

"I ain't aimin' be a hard ass nor nuthin' akin to it, but sometimes I just wish folks would quit tryin' so hard on me and just let me be. I reckon I can learn fer myself just same as next man do and then I reckon I know pine blank what I done and what I needs do later on. That way I done it myself, and I know how and why I done it. Now what ye thinkin' on that?" Jubal shot back.

"I not callin' ye out on account of that, but I need ask ye one more thing."

"Well what then?"

"I be thinkin' that ye be a right good feller, but I just wonderin' what ye would do fer helpin' out wherever ye could to whoever ye could. I still hold yer Ma done raised ye up good and her good done rubbed off on ye."

"I dang tootin' never got none of that from Pa."

"I got no argument there, son. Ye might not know it, but I can read ye like newsprint. I reckon I can tell what ye thinkin' most times when we talks like this."

"How ye know that?'

"Well, ye ain't much count when it comes on hidin' yer thoughts."

"That so now, huh?"

"Yep."

"Why don't ye light in and tell me all I been thinkin' on, Mr. Know-it-all?"

Wes chuckled in his own way as he began. "I know who ye been ponderin' on, and I just bet a corn crop that I know why too."

"Who?"

"Not nary a sole other than that miller man's gal. Ye been all shut-mouthed here last few days, and I reckoned out when ye commenced and how come ye be that way too."

Jubal made no immediate response but could feel the blood rush to his cheeks and the fire stinging his ears. He could not recall saying anything to Wes or to any other person. He had thought long and hard about Lida and what had happened between them, but had not realized that it showed on him.

"Son, I tell ye here and now that what a man does always say a heap more about him than his words do. Action speak much louder than words. Ye been sayin' things just by how ye been actin' these here last few days that make me know most sure that ye be in a quandary over that there miller's gal. I reckon ye be bent on sortin' it all out fer yerself and not lookin' to nobody nowhere fer any help."

"How come ye thinks ye knows so much?" Jubal answered somewhat surprised and somewhat annoyed at the hint that Wes, above all people, might be onto him and what had come about.

"I done seen how neither one of ye can look the other square eye to eye and how ye ain't got nary a word fer each other now. Ain't many other reasons I know of fer you two feelin' such."

"Ain't none of yer business, and ye best be hush-mouthed about it too," Jubal stated flat out.

"Ye got no cause frettin' over what I would say, cause I ain't gonna say nothin' fer I ain't got nothin' in it. It don't matter none to me other than how it shows up on yerself. Yer Ma done noticed how ye be actin' too, I reckon. Ain't said nothin' to her and ain't gonna do so. I just tryin' to show ye how folks can see right through ye when ye go and wear yer feelin's all over yer face. Ye ain't gonna change what come about yesterday. All ye can do is move on with today. Iffin ye reckon ye done messed up, then all ye can do is live up to it and be a man fer it. Ye can do that or ye can just up and try runnin' away from it all, and I can tell ye fer a fact that ain't no answer to no situation."

"I wish it never happened, but I know I can't change that. She just come on to me, and I just never give it no more thought till it were all over and done."

"So ye packin' it all off on her are ye?" Wes asked somewhat sarcastically.

"She were the one what come and laid herself in bed with me. What else could I done otherwise?" Jubal asked.

"I reckon ye done what any boy would'a done. You just needs live with it now, and ye two has to be the ones who works it all out, Wes replied. Ever give a thought to what ye would do iffin she took?"

"No."

"Well, I reckon chances of that ain't so great with just one time and all; lest of course, there be heap more than I be thinkin' about you two young sprouts."

Jubal sat in silence for a bit and then almost as if to the point of tears said, "Wes I just need bad to decide all fer myself what I want and how I can go about fetchin' it. I just need to know that there be more fer me than this here old dirt farm and these damned hills and hollers all the rest of my days. I just needs find my way in this old world, and I don't see much way of finding' nuthin' with war and all that it done brung. I even been ponderin' on goin' off to war myself and see what that might be all about. I just don't know all them things and such. Right now, all I want is some answers and somehow or 'nother find some end to bein' so danged dirt poor and not havin' nuthin' worth more than a wood nickel. I just wanna find my way and be what and who I wanna be."

"Who do ye wanna be, son?"

"I ain't plum sure. I just don't wanna be stuck here all my life, Wes."

"It only natural fer a man wantin' make his own way. Ain't a thing wrong with that. Thing is that ye don't have to make it all in one day or even all in one season. Ye got all yer life ahead of ye, and ye can't do but one day at a time. I ain't even gonna try tell ye what ye needs do, not now nor not then. But I don't want ye messin' up when it could be done by goin' off short sighted. Besides that, we needs get through Christmas time first of all, and yer Ma and the others is gonna need ye around here fer a bit yet. I reckon ye ought be studyin' on that fer a bit first off."

Jubal stood and crossed the few short steps of the springhouse loft. He laid his hand on his friends shoulder and said, "I thank ye fer hearin' me. I reckon ye done give me answers, at least fer now."

"I hope so, son. Just remember them things what yer Ma done been tellin' ye all along, and ye be fine. I know ye been told it plenty times, but it be worth sayin' one more time. Ye know a man be recollected more by what he done all his lifetime than by what he say day in and day out. And as long as he be recalled by them what knowed him, then I reckon he be livin' right on and on. That there might not make no sense to ye now, but it will someday. Ye just hang right in there and do best ye can and make yer word be good, and then folks will look on ye favorable and trust in ye. Now iffin ye got trouble with yerself and that there miller's gal, then ye needs be a man and work things out with her and make it right whatever it takes. Ye needs consider her wants and such just same as yours. I ain't tryin' tell ye pine blank what ye needs do ner nuthin' of the sort, and I don't aim on sayin' nary 'nother word on it lessen ye asks me. That be good by ye?"

"I reckon so. I just wanna find my way and do what be the right thing."

"Well I hope ye see the light soon, son."

Chapter 14

Hope

*T*he cold had let up a bit as the days leading up to Christmas slipped past. Not at all unusual to have a moderation in the winter's grip. Winds coming up out of the south usually brought warm rain but could also bring deep wet snow.

Deep wet snow made movement difficult. Usually in such times, it was easier to travel the south facing slopes. Snow melted quicker on the warmer slopes, and the winds could be a bit calmer there as well. Better by far to stay sheltered somewhere, but getting out and about was never a real issue to a determined soul, especially a young man in his physical prime.

Jubal had stayed by the hearth with Julie and Ma about as long as he could take it. He had made up his mind that he would get some game today even if it took all day. The snow had stopped during the night, and the clouds overshadowed everything. The air was calm, and the snow gave little sign of melting. The morning was yet young, but the bitter chill of winter seemed to be missing. Snow, wet and heavy up to mid-calf, made for slow moving and uncertainty of footing. Jubal had the old long rifle slung over his shoulder, and he secured the trusty old companion with his right hand firmly clasped around the business end of the barrel. He might lose footing some-where, but there was no way that he could let the weapon fall into the snow. Any number of problems could come out of that, not the least of which would be wet powder and flint.

He had left the barnyard without a direction in mind. The trek up the north hill to the timberline was done with hardly a thought before he made his first stop to look around. He was hardly winded at all from the climb, but he reactively held his breath for a few moments just to make sure that he missed no sound, no matter how faint or distant. He heard nothing.

Though the sky was gray and overcast, it still spoke to him. Birds were absent from the thistles, and no movement could be seen on the pokeberry brambles. No crows cawed from the outstretched limbs of sentinel locust trees. There would be no talons soaring on updrafts today, the winds lay quiet. No signs of life on the move. The thoughts of more impending snow did nothing to lighten his mood. The thought of being snowed in bothered him.

Julie seemed to be a measure or two better now, to the point where she wanted to lie awake and talk with him way into the night. Not that he minded talking to her, but she had been saying some things that were beginning to really bother him. The things that she brought up gave him reason to ponder and think in ways that he had never seemed to be able to deal with before. He loved her dearly as his sister, but sometimes he just needed to have some time to himself. This morning was one of those times.

He reshouldered the old long rifle and made his way down onto the north face of the ridge just far enough to be able to cut the track of any deer that might be headed into the high cedars for shelter. Fresh back strap all fried up golden brown would be mighty tasty, and the shoulders would feed them all several good meals. Julie could have her fill of hot stew.

He followed the ridge a good distance without thinking about where he was going. Once he thought on it, he became very conscious of other thoughts. If he followed this ridge far enough, he would find himself above the mill and near the spot where C.C. had made his own little clearing.

That realization prompted thoughts about a certain young lady and those thoughts stirred feelings of desire and passion. He had those same thoughts more than once since the night he slept in the mill. Some of those thoughts troubled him, and the uncertainty of it all gnawed at him like old Jake would handle a ham knuckle. Those thoughts brought on questions that he could not satisfy and caused burnings that he knew not how to quench.

Then all the things that Julie and Granny Iverson had been talking to him about, all the sayings that they had thrown at him, how could they know and recall so much? Maybe if he read like they could, then he might know like they did. But Julie had told him that he didn't have to read; all he had to do was believe. She said it was sure as the sun coming up in the mornings. Well hell, any fool believed that. Julie just seemed to be so all fired sure of herself all the time and never wavered from it. He just failed to understand how she could be that way; and yet it vexed him that he could not catch the gist of all she talked about, always the same and never changing. She had even said that it was not good to add to or to take away from it all. Wes had spoke to him a time or two about the same things.

Ma had talked to him as well, but all he could see in her face was the wearisome exhaustion that spoke of years of troubles and turmoil. That look alone elicited deep-seated feelings of vindictiveness and vileness in him that he did not like. There was a reason for Ma being all broken and aged before her time, and he knew where that responsibility fell. He felt like he had no real malice in mind, but he knew that he would never back down if he ever had to face up to that reason. He had spoke of that to Granny Iverson once, and she had told him that ever body had to pay up some time or another and for that reason he ought not trouble himself over it. That might be true, but it still burned at him each and every time he looked into Ma's face. She tried to cover her broken spirit, but she could not always hide her sorrow.

Soon Jubal had walked far enough down the ridge that he knew he was above the reed patch. He crossed back to the south slope and looked down across the fields to the road below. There was nothing to be seen but the snow.

He remembered the scrapes that he had seen two months ago in the papaw thickets near the crest of sand hill. He had seen nothing on the high ground, but maybe there would be something in those thickets. He headed downhill and soon reached the road. A left turn would lead him eventually to the mill. Heading right back up the road would return him home. He did neither.

He shouldered his weapon again and crossed the snow covered road and went straight into the reed patch. They were now not much more than slender sticks and twigs that wavered in the usually prevailing west wind. Deer foraged on them when other food became scarce or exhausted. The dry summer had cut way back on the beech mast, and acorns had grown not much bigger than a pea. If he could pick up a track here, then he might have back strap for supper tonight after all.

The reed patch yielded no tracks. It was most all eaten clean. There would be no reason to look any more even on the side, uphill from the roadway. There was a moment of anger that welled up in him. Dang, ever body needed meat; and most had been able to raise whatever they needed, but his and Ma's had been stolen right out from under their noses. Sure they could make do without those hams. What would really make it right, at least in his mind, would be…Well now, he had been over that a hundred times, and he still had no good answer.

Ma had said time and again that it was not his place to seek revenge. But she just did not think the way he did, and he was most certain that he was right. She had said that sometimes a body just needed to settle on what he got and not hope so much for all those things that others had. Something in there somewhere about a neighbor's ox or something like that.

Back to the road and a right-hand turn. Another hour or so would get him to the upper end of the millrace. Had no intent on going that far, least not today. Just far enough to see if anything had been near the lick, down the south side of the sand hill. Might just be a track there. Plenty of snow and would be easy to find and easy to follow. He had seen a rabbit track or two, but he had set sight on bigger and better.

The clouds seemed to be breaking just a bit. There was more of a glare on the snow up high on the ridge lines, but there was no blue sky yet to be seen. Most likely be colder tonight, and he knew he best be near home by the time what light there was began to fade. That really would not allow time enough to stop at the mill. He had fretted over that enough in the past few days and going there now, he reasoned, would only throw coals on the fires that already burned within.

The short trek to the lick revealed no tracks. It did relieve some of the torments that pulled in many directions all at the same time. Ma had said something about the salt of the earth and how sometimes it lost its worth. That might be why no critter had been here as of late. Maybe the lick had lost its savor. Strange that the Good Book would be speaking about a salt lick. Just no sense. Maybe he might ask Julie or Granny Iverson how come the Bible spoke about salt.

The lick itself was not much bigger than a table top, and Jubal felt sure that he knew just where it lay. The deep snow made him a bit unsure so he decided to look on a bit farther just to make sure that he did not overlook something. He recalled the lick coming out from under a bank where a slick limestone slab jutted out from above. He soon found the bank and the rock.

There were tracks for sure, but they were not made by any deer or other game critter. These tracks were made by a big booted man, and there was blood-stained snow all around. Not much, but enough to leave no doubt that something had gone wrong here. He looked around even more and soon came on a second set of tracks. These were made by a smaller person, and he reckoned it to be a man's track since it had been made by a boot with a broad heel. He had no recollection of ever seeing such a track as this. Must have been made by somebody from away from these parts. His mind raced back to the three riders that he had seen in the dusty road back in August. He made no connection between the strange tracks and any of them three. He had not seen any such as that on them. He had not noticed any such footwear on any of the Bluecoat soldiers that had been at the mill that day. They all wore black boots like all other troopers. No, whoever had laid down these tracks had come from somewhere else.

A few paces on down the slope and he could see where they had come out of the timberline. Did not make too much sense to him to backtrack them, not too much good in knowing where they had come from. He reckoned that they had come in off the north ridge in the direction of the flats. He followed the track till he came onto where they had hobbled their mounts. Only two horses and two sets of tracks. Now only an occasional red stain in the snow. Evidently they had stayed the bleeding, or it wasn't serious to begin with. Plain as day, they were headed on down the road straight toward the mill.

Now he had to follow the tracks to make sure that all was well with Lida and her family. He had no choice. If he could not make home before dark, well then that would just have to be the way it would be. He could make his way by starlight. Dang, clouds and overcast would hide the stars. Made no matter, he knew his way. This was his old stomping grounds.

A quarter mile or so above the mill, he could not understand what he was seeing. The track left the road and headed up into the trees and brush again. He followed all the way to the top of the hill that overlooked the old Lawson bottoms. He could see that whoever this was had wanted to avoid being seen passing the mill. Once out of sight from the mill, they had cut back west and headed in the direction of Cleve's store. Wondering if they knew what had happened to Cleve, he made his way in that direction. He could stay up in the timber and come down ever quarter mile or so just to see if he could spy anything moving around, and if need be come down even more to cut the tracks again. If he did not see anything, he could head back home up through the flats and still make it home before late.

It was dark when he entered the barn lot, and old Jake was right there to greet him with a deep bass growl and raised hackles. Jubal called to him and instantly the hackles went down and the tail began to sway side to side. There was a lamp glow in the kitchen window, and the smell of burning pine was in the air all around the yard. A pine fire meant a hot fire and that would mean that Ma might be whipping up something special or it could be that she was boiling out bandage dressing for Julie. Ma could not stand any proud flesh about no open sore and would do whatever to keep it down when it did try coming up.

Jake hit the porch first and let out a low and muffled bark as if to say how glad he was to see his master back home again. He had been locked up in the gear room this morning, and he had been put there so many times that he seemed to understand what it meant. Don't try to follow me nor trail me. You be a good old hound and look after things around here, and I will give you a hog knuckle when I

get back. Jake did not know it, but tonight would be leftover venison knuckles. Jake's announcement brought a face to the kitchen
window just as Jubal stepped up onto the porch. He peered in and
saw his Ma, and she had a smile on her face to welcome him home.

He opened the kitchen door eagerly and stretched out his arms
to his Ma. She bolted to him still smiling broadly, but with tears
streaming down her face. She made no effort whatsoever to conceal
them or to make them stop flowing.

"Go see yer sister, son. Go right now."

That startled him a bit and made him think that maybe the worst
thing imaginable was about to transpire. But if that were so, then
why would Ma be smiling so much?

"Git. Go do what I say."

No more prodding was needed. He flung open the kitchen door
without so much as looking about the kitchen to determine what the
late evening roaring fire was all about. Stout, quick steps moved him
to the fireside where he was taken aback to see his sister sitting bold
upright in a cane bottomed chair with her bum knee bent straight
down most like normal. Her cheeks were ruddy, and her color had
returned. She wore a smile as well.

"Here brudder, come gimme a big hug."

He immediately obeyed.

Old Wes and Granny Iverson wore grins like a pair of moon-
struck young flirts out on their first time alone.

"Dang, sis, I be plum shut-mouthed, ye done took me without
no notice. What ye done went and done makin' ye so much better
so quick?"

"Ain't really much to it. I just make up my mind that I ain't
stayin' here in this old bed fer the rest of my days. I got myself up
and that be when it all commenced."

"What commenced?"

"Bent my knee right sharp, and it broke open and spilled all
kinks of corruption outt'n it. Run plum to the floor. Felt better mite
near instant."

"Ye act better too."

"I am better, thank ye. A whole bunch better."

"I be a heap proud fer ye," he said as he bent down to give her a hearty hug. He felt the tears welling up in his own eyes, but they in no way diminished the smile that now spread over his own face. He was happy that she seemed to be a lot better. It would be putting it up some short to say that he had not been worried about her for some time. Now there seemed to be, for the moment at least, a measure of hope, a ray of sunshine.

Ma came in with a big thick slice of salt cured ham between a big cathead biscuit and handed it to her son. "I be thinkin' ye might could use this here. Been a long spell since ye lit out this mornin'. What'd ye find anyhow? I see ye ain't got no game."

"No signs of any deer meat nowhere, Ma. But I ain't done lookin' yet. There be another place or so that needs looked about. There be game here in these old hills; I just needs find it."

"I cut our last ham today, so we gonna need a mite of helpin' fer seein' us through till springtime, I reckon. We still got a chicken or two that we can have, but they just make one day's meat."

"I'll find more, Ma."

"We'll make do with whatever we have and be grateful fer it. We could be like most folks closer in towards town and done had ever thing took by the Rebs and scallywags and thiefin' bastards, but that ain't befell us yet, save fer that one time."

"Ye be right, Ma. We pert nigh know who done it too," Jubal replied.

"How ye figger that?" Jubal asked.

"Ye know that we done spoke some on things akin to that. Ye and me done laid some plans on that. Don't tell me ye done forgot," Wes said as he sat on up to a cross-legged position.

"No, I reckon I ain't forgot nothin' ye done told me. But ye ain't never said when we gonna do it."

That statement raised some puzzled looks from Ma and from Julie. Granny Iverson sat by the fire and continued to pretend reading from the Good Book, but Jubal noticed her eyes darting over to old Wes. Wes had told her casually that she might get a new apron and a new bonnet before too much longer, and she had already decided what they should be like. Jubal looked at Wes in somewhat of a similar inquisitive manner, but he knew far more what was astir than he was willing to talk about right now.

If all that Wes had said worked out the way he had laid it out, then there would be room for much more than a new apron for Granny Iverson.

Jubal thought it best that there be no more talk on it right now. "Julie, gal, I be heaps glad ye be better. I weren't never gonna give up on ye. I hope ye know that."

"I know that. Ye always said ye hoped I be able and better. Well I be headed that way now and I reckon I knowed it all along. I had hope, and I had faith."

"I know ye did, sis."

"And I still do. A body gotta have hope. There ain't much left iffin ye lose hope. May as well just dry up and fall off the tree when ye loses hope cause that be what gonna come on ye anyhow. Ought never lose faith."

Jubal and all the gals experienced a night of hope and happiness. There were many smiles and heartfelt laughter all around. Tears flowed like rain at times, but they were happy tears indeed. There was reason for rejoicing. No one seemed to be tired, and no one had any thoughts on going to bed until way long after the fire began to turn to red hot coals instead of leaping flame. Ma lay on another big beech back stick as she announced that she had work to do come daylight. There would be extra warmth in the old log house tonight, and it would not be because of a second back stick. Those things that warmed the heart so much tonight came from within.

There was much on his mind, but Jubal was in no hurry to turn in. He wanted to spend time with his beloved sister. He never did think that her spirit had been broken, but he was pretty sure that her will had weakened a time or two. She had mentioned passing a time or two, but he had not known what she was really meaning or how she really felt. She had told him that she was ready and all the like, but he just sensed a slight fear in her voice at those times. He just tried to be loving and understanding with her. He held her when she wanted to be held. He listened to her when she wanted and just sat with her in silence when she wanted. Tonight, she wanted to talk and so did he.

Conversation went on well past midnight. Usually Wes would pretend sleep there on his pallet, but tonight neither Jubal nor his sister doubted that such snoring could be a put on. The old codger might have had some funny ways, but no doubt, a kind heart beat in his chest. Jubal looked over at him recalling the pitiful shape that he had let himself fall into right before Ma fetched him here and cared for him. He also thought about all the times that Wes had tried to set things straight and point out the right ways to turn when times got bad. Some things seemed just plain hard to understand.

"Julie, what done made ye perk up so fast and so much?"

"I just come to realize that I had lost faith fer a while but thankful that I done had it give back to me, and I be thinkin' that what done it," she replied.

"But it done come on ye so quick."

"Well, brudder, I ain't got nobody but self to blame fer wollerin' in my own misery. That never cured nobody. I just be so thankful that I done seen the worst of it all, and I plumb sure that I have. I been healed enough to know that I ain't gonna be took outta here, leastwise not no time soon. I reckon I might be a mite lame fer a spell yet, but I ain't gone."

"I be a heap glad too, sis."

"I don't reckon I ever know full how come the Lord done put all this on me and gimme so much a load all these weeks. I reckon it all be fer me to accept and go on best I can. I be thankful fer all that been done fer me, and I have trust enough to believe that I be took care of from here on out too."

"You right there sis. Me and Ma look after ye as long as need be."

"I ain't speakin' about you and Ma lookin' after me. I speakin' on some other body much more stronger than ye and Ma. Ain't that I be ungrateful or not beholdin' to ye fer all ye done and all that ye will do fer me. It be that I just been told again and again who really be in control of me. Ye know what I meanin' don't ye?"

"I reckon I purty much do, but I don't see how it all can mean that much to ye and make change in ye the way you says."

"I don't know how I can make ye see through my eyes nor feel like I do, but I know without doubt what be in my heart. I know that it all be good stuff too. There ain't no blame nor nothin' akin to that, and I can say that without no fibbin' on it neither.

Certainly, I would'a druther not had my knee shot up and been laid up like I was, but I know now pine blank sure that I be on the mend. I ain't got no cause fer nothin' but be thankful fer how ain't nothin' but good comin' on fer me now."

Jubal just looked at her and smiled. Her words came soft and tender, and he had no reply for them, not now.

"I just wishin' that I could get this peace of mine fer ye and poke it down in yer craw, and then ye could be a smilin' all the time too, brudder. But some things has to be did fer self and nobody else. Ye gotta walk that valley fer ye own self. Ye know what that means don't ye?"

"I reckon I do, sis."

He would have been very much reluctant to go into that any deeper, but it did set his mind to wandering. He was not fully understanding of that, but he believed that whatever he made in life for himself would be the results of his own efforts and that he would someday be able to make his own way out of the grip of these old clay and limestone hills and mountains. If he could do that, then happiness would be on his heels.

"Well then, I reckon ye be a mind not have to walk all yer life alone do ye?"

"No sis, I don't. I reckon I take a wife some of these here days."

"That ain't what it be all about."

"Then what?" Jubal asked quietly. He knew most certain where she would be headed with that; but he was happy that she was better, and just because of that he reckoned that he would hear her out if that was what she wanted.

"Ye know what I be talkin' on. We done tried to hash it all out more than one time. I thought ye might be ponderin' on it even now. I don't aim to harp on ye none, not now nor not ever, but I just be wishin' and prayin' that ye somehow open yer eyes and see what all could lay in store fer ye. I ain't wantin' nothin' but good things fer ye and that be what I have hope fer."

"What about yerself? What ye hope fer?"

491

"Don't reckon I need much. I would like be able to walk good again. But iffin it ain't to be, then I reckon it just be that way; and I make it best way I can. I reckon I be blessed purty good just like it be right now."

"What about that bastard what shot ye? What ye hope fer him?"

"Iffin he just stay outta my life, whoever he be, then that be good by me. I don't aim to harbor no spite on him."

"Ye sayin' ye wouldn't shoot him back ner nuthin'?"

"I reckon not."

"How come? That don't seem right to me. He done laid ye up and all. Are ye sayin' that ye ain't holdin' no grudge?"

"That be exact, brother. I don't hold no grudges on him, cause holdin' a grudge is just lettin' somebody live in yer head and not pay no rent. They takes up part of yer mind and keeps ye from usin' it fer yer own good. I want my mind all fer my own use. I be the one who decides how it be used, and it ain't gonna be used up and spent by hate fer some old soul who ain't worth it to begin with. It just ain't the right thing to do by keepin' such in yer mind."

"Ye probably be right, but how do ye fergit it?"

"I never said I forgot it, and I never will. I just be sayin' that I harbor no ill-will or nothin' to the likes. I can forgive all I need to, but some things just ain't never meant to be forgot. That don't mean that they has to eat away at ye all rest of yer days. Besides that, Bible says that we is supposed to forgive them what uses us and does us wrong. Ye recalls that don't ye?"

"I reckon Granny Iverson or Ma read me that some time or other, but I never reflected on it a whole bunch."

"I be thinkin' ye ought reflect on that and on all them other times I done tried openin' them eyes of yours. If boxin' yer jaws right good would help any at all, I would'a done it long ago. I hope to my never iffin I wouldn't do it again right now. I done said that nobody could walk the valley fer ye. It got be yerself what go there. I just be a might flustered that I can't make ye see that. How can I ever make ye see?"

"I got a keen eye sis," Jubal said as he got up to scratch in the coals with the big iron poker. "I needs get out at first light so as how

I can get ye fresh back strap. Ma fix ye up some roast and gravy. How ye like seein' that on yer plate fer supper?"

"Ye be plum hopeless. Ye may as well go on to bed."

"That be where I be headed."

"I be keep on prayin' fer ye, brother."

Sleep came easy that night. Ma was up at her usual time and making a fire to start breakfast. Jubal got up soon after he heard Ma stirring and joined her in the kitchen. Ma was already mixing up the biscuit dough and had thick slices of side meat ready for the iron skillet.

"It be a shore 'nuff blessin' that yer sister be perked up some ain't it?" Ma said as she looked her son square eye to eye.

Jubal returned her look and saw a face that he had not seen in a long time. Ma had that twinkle in her eyes and a happy grin about her that had been missing for far too long. Jubal knew full well that she had been worried sick over Julie, but he just at that moment came to realize how much she had been troubled. The realization that she did in fact, care so much made him realize her love for her child, not only for Julie, but for all her children.

"Ye done took good care fer her Ma. Reckon she be a heap beholdin' to ye. We all be fer that matter, includin' old Wes too."

"I ain't done a thing what any mother worth salt would'a done fer her kid."

"I know that, Ma. I reckon it just say how much we done all tried pullin' together to git by."

"I ain't gonna speak fer nobody but myself, but I done been doin' me a heap time prayin' and askin' that the Good Lord look after us all. I might not always acted like it, but I feel it in my heart all the same and that be what keep me goin' lots a times. I been askin' all along fer ye to have yer eyes opened too, and I still yet want that fer ye. Ye ain't really got no other course to go fer the rest of yer days, lest ye just plum dry up or get blowed away like wheat chaff. Ye may not understand it now, but ye be aged where ye be 'countable now, and I can't answer fer ye when time comes fer settlin' up."

"Ye ain't the only one who done been tellin' me that," Jubal answered softly while still looking at her wrinkled, yet kindly face.

"And I ain't just plumb dismissed it from my mind. I think on it now and again."

"Well, what does yer mind try tellin' ye about it when ye does think on it?" Ma asked as she continued to knead the dough.

"They be some things that I reckon I not be quiet understandin' about. I reckon once I know, then I can move on it."

"How ye planning' on learnin' them things what ye say ye don't know too good?" Ma asked again.

"Reckon I don't rightly know on that," Jubal answered.

"Ye think iffin ye read up on it that ye could know then?" Ma inquired.

"I reckon I might, but ye know I don't read best in the world. Wes done teached me some, but I still stumble now and then."

"Well, I don't reckon I reads that well either, but I never let that be a stopper fer me. I always find me a body what can read good and have them read it fer me till I can know what it say. Yer Granny Iverson be a heap good reader and so be Julie. Ain't no cause ye not bein' able. I reckon ye do wanna know don't ye?"

"Yeah, I do."

"Ye ain't just sayin' that now, are ye?"

"No, Ma. I reckon I meanin' it."

"Then they be hope yet," Ma said smiling as she began to pat out the biscuit dough. "I reckon they be hope yet."

The morning brought a moderation in temperature. Jubal had made the pull to the timber hardly breaking stride. Looking around him and reading the signs, he knew things had a good chance of being better than they were yesterday.

He cut a track not more than a quarter mile from the ridge above the reed patch. Looked like there were two grown deer and a smaller one. Could be a small yearling from the size of the tracks. They were fresh tracks too, because he could find muddy water in some of them. They were not even old enough to let the water seep back down into the ground. Good thing that the old hound did not come along. He would most likely spook a critter into a dead run to the closest thicket. It seemed right that they could be headed for the lick.

He stopped well above the lick and listened intently. The old long rifle got slung into his forearms, and he began to ease on down nearer to the salt lick, listening and looking around all the while.

He saw no tracks of any sort as he made his way downhill. Probably no more than a thousand yards or so to the licks. Time to turn on the silence. He had no intent to miss a chance at a deer because of being in too much of a hurry or by making too much commotion. He felt sure that the lick had users there right now. Best move on down, but do it silently.

A quarter hour of carefully placed steps brought sight of the licks. It was necessary to peer between the tall poplars and scrub walnut trees to get a decent look at whatever may be there. He had to shade his eyes with a down-turned palm or wait for the next cloud to drift overhead. A quick look to the crow perch told him that he was still undetected. Just wait. Wait and see what might be there. Another fifty feet closer might help. Get under that big cedar and won't have to fret over the sun popping in and out. Patience, just be patient.

There had to be something here. All the signs were too fresh to mean anything less. Just need to be patient and wait for them to show. Keep quiet. Be still and wait. The morning was still young, and there was time yet before the critters would head for the thickets and bed down for the day. Just be patient he kept telling himself.

He waited for what seemed to be an eternity. There was that word again. Granny Iverson had asked him where he thought he would be for all eternity, and he had just brushed her off and not tried to answer her. According to what she said, not making a choice doomed you already. She said that unless you see the errors of your ways and come out of the darkness that you had thereby made a choice already and that it was the wrong choice. Seemed kinda like she talked in circles, but her words had become an earworm to him, and he could not keep from hearing her voice over and over to the point where he could not get it out of his head.

He had become so deep in his thoughts that he almost missed the movement below. He detected the slightest flutter in the scrub brush right at the upper edge of the lick. Again he froze and took slow deep breaths to minimize any chance of being sensed. There…there it was again. And then it stepped out into the clear and was as plain as day. There was a yearling in plain sight. Head on and busy savoring the minerals he had just uncovered. Tongue darting in and out of his nostrils repeatedly. A doe stepped out just behind the youngster.

Careful now. He took steady aim at the yearling. It was going to be a fairly long shot, and he had to make it true. He could get a good throat and heart shot if he could get it away when the beast's head was up. That could easily be a kill shot and would be much better than trying a head shot, especially at this distance. The young hunter had charged the old long rifle a bit on the heavy side just in case a situation like this came up. Wes had been the one who had offered that little bit of an edge.

At the crack of the rifle, he had to step aside of the smoke cloud to see if he had hit his mark. The acrid smoke smarted his eyes, and the chill brought a welling up in his eyes. He brushed the dampness away with the back of his hand, and then he could see it. The yearling was down, and the hind legs thrashed about in the snow without any apparent purpose or control. He could hear the fading racket as the two does tore through the nearby underbrush. Ten thousand crows, it seemed, all sounded their protests in unison. He heard it all, but the trump of it all was the yearling. He raced down to secure his kill before there could be any chance that it could elude him.

Reaching the lick revealed what he had anticipated when he first cut the track back on the ridge. It was in fact a doe yearling. It no longer thrashed about. His bullet had found a killing mark and had done it in no short order. A bit small but deer meat nonetheless.

It took only a few strokes with his razor sharp knife and the animal was field dressed, hung on a gambling stick and thrown across his shoulder. He picked up his trusted old rifle, cradled it in his forearms and headed for the road that would take him back to the old log home and his Ma. There was no need for silence now. He made regular and purposeful strides, taking note of his footing, but no longer trying to move in secrecy. He could be home by high noon and have his kill all dressed in no time. There would be good eats on the table tonight and back strap and biscuits for morning. The hide was a bit small, but he and Wes would tan it and put it to good use.

He knew there would be no need in going back to the licks for several days unless it rained. Only the scavengers would be there now. Too much scent for more game animals.

Ma took the quarters and dressed them out lean and clean. She then had Wes carry them into the smokehouse and lay them up for salting. The thick chestnut slabs were white with salt stains. There would be enough to salt two quarters; she would cook the other two and eat as much as they could before it went game. Good thing it was winter time, else the salt nor nothing else would make it last more than a day.

The back straps were cleaned and put in a big heavy crock and covered with water and salted down for the night. They would take a good bit of peppering in the morning but would come out golden brown and piping hot. Jubal and Wes both could all but taste it now.

"I be thinkin' that come mornin', ye ought take one of these here straps down to C.C. and his family," Ma said as she covered the crock with a cotton cloth and started to the kitchen with it. "We could easy eat ever bite of it, but we could just as easy share with them. They has been mighty good by us here late, and I feel like we owe them a heap. Not that they is runnin' a bill on us ner nothin' to the likes, but they is good neighbors; and we ought be the same as they."

"Ye got a good heart woman," Wes added.

"I reckon it be a fact, Ma," Jubal added. He was glad to see his Ma in so much better spirits than she had been a month past. It was good to see her weathered face bring forth a genuine smile. He would do anything he could for her, just because she deserved it and had proved herself time after time.

"Take old Kate and make a day of it," Wes suggested. "I can fetch in what wood be needed fer ye tomorrow, but don't ye be getting no notion that I do it fer ye all the time. I know I gotta earn my keep, but I don't aim on knockin' ye outta yours by it." The smiles on the old man's face said far more than his words, and Jubal knew that he valued what he and his Ma had done for him.

"I thought on takin' one of the mounts ye bought us," Jubal said.

"No. I be thinkin' that not be best," Wes spoke more seriously. "Best I know they ain't many here abouts knows we got them, and best it stay that way fer now. Reckon ye might be seen twixt the mill and here and back again."

"Can't argue that none at all."

"Ye best take a side arm as well as yer hog leg," Wes added. "Ain't been no scallywags seen close on in some time, but ye never know."

"I reckon ye be a bit smarter than I give ye credit fer, Wes."

"I just been around longer than ye, that's all."

"And I respect that too, believe it iffin ye wants to or not, but I do."

"It don't matter me that much, but I just tryin' make ye safe as best I know. Hate sayin' it, but we all need ye around here."

"I reckon they be a way no matter what come of me. Ye get by somehow."

"We don't aim on tryin' it, son," Ma injected. "Ye just chew on that ever time ye gets a wild hair on yer mind."

The next morning broke clear, and the snow continued to melt and fill every little branch and gully near to overflow. Sure would have been nice to have the earth watered with some of this melt way back in August. This would get the water table up a bit and maybe next year's crops would not have to thirst near to death. A good growing season in the coming year would make for an easier winter.

Jubal harnessed Kate and started down the old mudded road to the mill. Ma has sacked up the back strap meats in a cotton pillowcase and tied it up securely. She had given Jubal a piece of oilcloth to lay under it and hang it on the harness hames. That way nothing from old Kate's hide could penetrate into the meat. Jubal hung the sack just as Ma had told him.

He rode the most of the way until he approached the reed patch. He continually scanned the roadway in front of him for any sign or track of any description. He checked the ridge lines with a keen eye for any signs of movement. The bright sun reflecting off the snow melt made for squinted eyes that protested by frequent tearing and running. He would combat this as best he could by wiping the moisture away with the back of his hands and by looking away from the sun as much as possible.

Near the reeds, he dismounted and led Kate along behind him. He wanted the best look he could have at the road from here to the licks and maybe all the way to the millrace. Kate seemed to be relieved of her load, but still kept her head down most of the time. Jubal had not bothered to put her blinders on, and the bright sun may have been troubling her a bit too.

He found tracks cutting the road and going into the reeds, but he knew they were his own and paid them little mind except to note that they were only about half as deep as they were yesterday. No wonder water was running everywhere. Three hundred more yards put him to the top of sand hill, and still there were no new signs of any sort. The same pattern held true all the way to the millrace.

Once he reached the mill itself and turned off the road to get up to the porch, the ground all around was littered with horse tracks, and it was obvious that several men had dismounted and milled around and mingled their tracks so much that it was impossible to read anything from all the confusion.

"Howdy there, son," C.C. said as he flung open a window shutter over the mill desk.

"Same to ye," Jubal echoed.

"Right smart snow we done had, I reckon. I most nigh ready fer openin' the race and let my wheel go a turn fer a while. Ain't had no calls fer no grindin' in several days now. Leastwise not before yesterday."

"That be what all them tracks be about?"

"Partly. Bluecoat patrol came by here yesterday and brung me a few sacks of millet they wants ground fer some special hosses somewhere."

"They tell ye any war news?"

"Not much cept what be goin' on in close parts here abouts," C.C. informed as he stuck a fresh packed pipe between his teeth and and stuck fire to it. Soon clouds of grey smoke swirlled out the open shutter and disappeared into the cold air. "Said the nineteenth bunch was on a rampage north of here in the Powell River area and was strung out all the way up towards Bristol. Said they most time stayed north of Pine and Clinch but was raidin' and takin' most anything they could use fer food 'n gear. Reckon they must be a mite on desperate now days."

"They ain't been 'round here none?" Jubal quired.

"No, not them direct. But they has been some who try tradin' with em what steals whatever they can and then tries sellin' it outright to them. They be just like a bunch a mad hornets. They just keeps peckin' away at folks 'round here till they gets just plum fed up with it. One of them got hisself shot somewhere out close to the doubles, and the Union patrols just wrote him off. Old woman shot him, and they never said nothin' to her nor tried her ner nothin' to the kind."

"They know who it was?"

"Reckon not, but said they was two others what got away."

"They track em any?"

"Didn't say," C.C. quipped as he fired his pipe again and took in a slug of smoke so strong that it set him to coughing.

"I seen some tracks a time or two. I'd wonder iffin them tracks would match up to them that I trailed a piece back when it was still yet good weather. I seen them tracks more'n one time and in more'n one place."

As far as anyone knew, there had been fairly limited incidences of stealing and such in the immediate Cane Valley area. Maybe most outsiders thought it would be slim pickings and not worth traversing all the hills and ridges to find anything of any value. Those who had suffered loss all had the same story to tell. There had been three of them according to all signs. If one got killed, then he most sure got his comeuppance. If all that held true, Jubal could not but wonder if his Pa was the one what got himself shot. Evidently the Union patrol had not volunteered any details or C.C. was being somewhat shut-mouthed about it.

"I brung ye some back strap and a foreleg. Killed me a yearlin' yesterday up above the licks. Ma sent it fer ye."

"That be plumb nice on her part; yer's too fer fetchin' it."

Jubal retrieved the sack from Kate's harness hame and handed it to the miller man as he descended the porch steps.

"I have me a mess a that tonight."

"It be right smart tasty. We had some this very mornin'. Went down good."

The two crossed the yard together, and Jubal reined old Kate to the gate post. The sun was up high enough to be felt some, and he knew that Kate would hardly make a step as she felt the warmth on her back. No pesky flies to mind away nor such. She would be content to be left to herself.

"Reckon them army troops knowed who it was they spoke of? I be a mite curious myself to know who it were."

"Well, they never told me no details, but they said the old hag that done the shootin' was some kin to old woman Bray," C.C. answered.

"No, I mean who it was what got kilt?"

"I never asked."

"Which army bunch was it?"

"Same ones what been here twice before. Why ye be so interested in that?" C.C. asked with somewhat of a questioning look on his face.

"Just wonderin' iffin them scallywags be ones what got in our smokehouse."

"Could be, but ye know them hams be long gone don't ye?" C.C. remarked.

"Yeah, I reckon they be gone soon as they got took outta our smokehouse."

"I be of a mind that they was the same ones who done shot yer sister and tried robbin' ye the day ye all went to Yeary's," C.C. stated.

"I think so too. That be one reason why I keen on knowin' a name or two. I don't reckon Julie be holdin' no grudges like I do, but I would like to meet up with them just the same."

"What would ye do, son?"

"I might just cut down on them the way they did on us."

"Well, I kinda thinkin' that gunplay and all be more for them troopers and the law dogs than fer us folks. But these is bad times. Some folks is desperate just fer a bite to eat now days. That be one reason I done teached Lida how to shoot. None the same ye can't just up and shoot a man just cause ye think he tried robbin' ye or such. That be a lawman job."

"I ain't never seen much law in this here holler. I reckon they think we ain't needin' no lawin'," Jubal returned in defense of his statements.

"It be best iffin ye never cross up with such scoundrels. Ye be far better off just let it be. Ever dog has its day, and they get there soon. I reckon people ain't gonna stand by and let such slip without strikin' back. Ye pester at any old lazy mongrel long enough, and he jump up and bite ye big time. He get tired of bein' pestered, and folks here abouts get tired of it too. We just be blessed that Rebs ain't thick here like they is some places."

The sound of the kitchen door swinging open put an end to that discussion.

"Hello Jubal. How ye be?" asked Mrs. Johnson as she wiped her hands on her apron.

"I be fine, thank ye."

"And how is yer Ma and Julie?"

"They be good. Julie bust open her knee few nights back, and it not be poned up so much anymore. Corruption pored out. Run plumb down her shin. She been up in a chair now, and all her color done come back."

"That sounds wonderful."

"Yes it do. She seem so much stouter now."

"Bless her heart. She be a sweet child."

Jubal easily recalled the joy he had seen in Ma's face because of her daughter's turnaround. He could sense her relief and her comfort in realizing that there was yet hope for her child. He was happy for them both. He felt a sense of thankfulness that he could not fully understand even as he thought on it now. He was thankful for Julie and her lifted spirits and her healing knee. He was greatly pleasured to know that his Ma was not so down and out any more. Thankful, but thankful to who? Who could he go to and express his gratitude? Many words that Granny Iverson had read to him now rang through his ears, not the least of which was words about knowing the truth or seeing the way. There was even something in there somewhere about standing outside your door and knocking.

"That...that be a fact. She be a heap better sorts now," Jubal informed her.

"Look here mother," C.C. said to his wife as he handed her the parcel that he had been given just a few steps ago.

"What's that?" she questioned as she reached over the porch railing to take the sack from her husband.

Jubal answered the question for her. "It be yearlin' back strap and a fore quarter. I got it yesterday up above the licks, and Ma reckoned ye ought have some."

"Maybe it best that Julie eat it all herself. Make her mend up faster."

"We all done had our fill. I be out after more in a few days and be thinkin' I know where they can be got easy and all."

"I hope that hold true fer ye. I be askin' fer a blessin' on ye to get another 'n as well. Ye tell yer Ma that I thankin' her and that we all is thankin' her."

"I do that very thing."

Lida came out of the kitchen door just as her mother had done wiping her hands on her apron. "Hello, Jubal. How ye be today?"

"I reckon I be good."

"Look here what he done fetched us," her mother remarked as she handed the deer meat to her daughter. "Reckon we ought fry up some fer dinner and invite this young man fer eats with us. How's about ye tendin' to that whilst I finish up with all the rest?"

"Yes, Momma." And with that Lida was back in the house and out of sight as quick as could be. Maybe there would be time to talk on things with her later on. At least he could hope so.

"Come on in and we set by the fire till they gets our grub all spread out. Lida been bakin' this mornin', and I think it be nigh done by now. She turnin' out a plumb good cook, iffin I do say so. I be a bit proud fer her, iffin she is my daughter."

Jubal had to try to control himself to keep his thoughts from showing. Lida excited him almost beyond reason. The fact that she was plumb good sight to look on was no help in behaving himself. He just hoped that he could be with her and talk with her and not make a fool of himself. Sometimes she seemed cold and not the least bit interested in him, and other times it seemed like she was pleased just to see him even if they had no chance to be by themselves.

C.C. laid hold of the poker and stirred the red hot coals in the bottom of the grate. Sparks flew all about and were at once sucked up the chimney. The miller man laid on a big hickory stick and soon the flames cracked and danced about with temerity.

C.C. cleaned his pipe and packed it carefully for the next smoke. That would wait for now. "Ye ever try smokin', son?"

"No. Never thought I would want it none."

"Don't never start and that a way ye won't be bothered with it. Wakes me up at night sometimes and me thinks I ought get up and light up. Now ain't that plumb loco fer me lettin' it grab holt on me like such?"

"Most men I know smokes."

"Reckon that be so, but ain't no call fer bein' a slave to a twist nor a pipe neither one."

Lida and her mother soon had a meal on the table and called the men folk to wash up. That directive was followed in short order, and all soon found themselves seated around the poplar board table smoothed by years of use. Lida had fried the back strap and black pepper adorned the golden brown cuts. It was a feast to behold.

Conversation took second to appetite as all ate heartily and insured their fill by repeat portions. In spite of voracious appetites, there was ample food for several more hungry souls.

The dishes were soon cleared, and the leftover food moved to the center of the table and covered with a cloth. This would be supper. This was the way it was in Cane Valley. It was unheard of to waste food, and most considered it wrong to do so. No one made a hot meal for supper unless it was some kind of special time or celebration. About the only routine justification for a hot supper would be in the case of illness.

Lida began to think that she was not going to have any opportunity to speak to Jubal after everyone had eaten. C.C. announced that he needed to get back to the mill to tend the chores and get ready for grinding tomorrow.

"Ain't no cause fer ye leavin' our fireside just yet, son. I best be at my work and books fer a spell. Iffin ye pardon me, I be at it. Make yerself comfortable fer a while," C.C. said to his young guest. "Lida been helpin' me with ciphers and such, and she works my books most times right here where it be warm."

That seemed like a good stout invitation to have her saddle right up next to him and talk a bit. He just hoped he could say what he felt. He just hoped also that she would have patience with him and not get all riled up over things past. He had figured it out that she had desires and wants just the same as he. But he was not so sure that he understood her.

"Mind if I join ye?" Lida asked softly as she pulled a caned-bottom chair up beside him and sat down.

She had taken off her apron and her pale pink dress clung to her torso like a satin glove. There was just enough light from the fireplace to amplify her outlines. He felt those old devilish passions awakening in him yet again. She twisted a long dangling curl between her fingers. He caught a twinkle of firelight bouncing off her eyes. He wanted to touch her rosy cheeks and take her in his arms and hold her close to him. He wanted to tell her how much he thought about her and how she burned in his heart.

"I be plumb pleased iffin ye sets with me a bit. I had hoped we might have a minute or two 'fore I heads back up the holler."

"I never knowed ye was comin' here today or I would'a tied up my hair and wore a ribbon fer ye."

"Ye be fine just like ye be now." Fool, remember what Julie done told ye about how girls like to be told they are pretty and all that. "Matter of fact ye looks way yonder better than fine. Ye looks wonderful to me." He could feel his own cheeks reddening and burning. He chanced a look into her eyes and was a bit surprised to see that she was smiling and seemed to be pleased.

"Glad that ye think so, but I could purty up real good fer ye had I knowed it and had time. I could really make them cheeks red under proper chances."

He just knew that his cheeks would singe his sideburns any second now. How on God's earth could she know what he was thinking about and tease him all the same? Was she glad that he felt that way or was she just making light of him right to his face?

"There be things I feel like I needs say twixt me and thee, but words comes hard fer me. Ye know that, I reckon," he stammered and returned his stare to the floor in front of him.

"Listen to me a bit." she replied as she gently laid her hand to his forearm. "I don't recall ever judgin' no person total on what they say. Them things that comes out a mouth ain't always what be inside a person. Words is only words. But what comes outta a heart is what make a body who he really is and that be the one that counts most. Ye ain't never say nothin' that hurt me none. Ye always been kind to me."

"I ain't never be aimin' hurt ye none."

"I know that already," she replied as she gently squeezed his forearm.

"What…what about that night in…"

"We not need mention that. Not here leastwise. I tell ye what I thinks about it sometime later when they is plenty time fer us bein' more alone and such."

"Do that…that mean ye ain't mad with me over it?"

"I told ye we talk later. Just trust me. I reckon iffin I been mad then I not be here with ye right now."

"I hoped a heap that ye not be mad…or hurt."

Neither could bring forth any words. They sat in silence and stared at the floor as if it would reveal some captivating line that could break the seemingly awkward silence.

"Tell me about Julie. How is she comin' along?"

"She be some better. Got her some color back in her cheeks now." He could feel some of the redness and burning ease off his own cheeks. He had not told Lida the things that he really wanted. He had not said the things that he wanted. He had not been able to express his feelings toward her, and now the spell was broken and the opportunity lost. No telling when such a chance would come again. "Ma say there be good chance she pull through this after all. Might wind up a crip, but that just the way it is, I reckon. I hope she not gotta be that way, but I reckon we just wait and see how it all comes out."

"I do hope she be good too. She be a sweet girl."

"Yeah, just same as ye be." There...He had said what he was thinking. More reaction than thinking, but he had said it just the same. Some of the sting came back to his cheeks, and he could sense it immediately.

"Well, I do declare. That be nice of ye to say that. I never thought ye had noticed me that way."

"I notice all the same. Noticed fer some time now."

"Then why ain't ye never told me?"

"Words don't come easy fer me, never have," he said as his eyes bored into the floor in front of him.

"Look here at me. Look at me now." He felt her hand return to his arm gently pulling him toward her. He turned and looked into her face, the fire dancing in her dark eyes. "Words don't come no easier fer me neither, but I reckon I know one thing about it. Most words is just that. Words! They be empty most times. Words gotta be truth, and they needs come from yer heart to mean anythin'. Ye see what I tryin' tell ye?"

"I ain't quite yet got it, I reckon."

"Well daddy and ye was talkin' earlier weren't ye?"

"Yeah."

"What did he say."

"Not much. This 'n that."

"See. Ye talked, but now there ain't even no recollection what he done say. I bet he can't tell what ye said back to him neither. See there, them was just empty words. Weren't neither one of ye mad ner nothin' to the likes. Ye was just talking, but ye weren't really sayin' much."

"Back strap done went to yer head ain't it?" he said jokingly.

"No, it never."

"I be up front with ye Lida. I ain't understandin' what ye be tellin' me. Just come right out with it and say whatever it is that be botherin' ye."

"What one person say to another don't mean much iffin it ain't from their heart. They gotta be honest and not coverin' up stuff and all like that."

Jubal just looked her in the eye and shook his head in bewilderment. He still could not see where she was leading. He began to be just a bit uneasy with her and searched frantically for his next words. He did not want what he said to be empty or untruthful, whatever that meant.

"Ye still don't understand, do ye?"

"Reckon not."

"Then just open up and say what ye thinkin' right now, this very moment."

"I can't say that girl, not now."

"Why not?"

"I reckon ye might be plumb put out with me iffin I did."

"And what makes ye think like that?"

"Cause it just ain't proper. Sometimes I ain't right proud thinkin' like I do when ye comes traipsin' through my mind."

"So ye do think about me ever now and then?"

"Most nigh ever day." That was not the exact truth, but he thought for the moment that it be best if she did not know just how much he did think about her and that most nights he went off to sleep with her on his mind.

"Well now, did it hurt too much to say that?"

"No...but..."

"What?"

"Makes me a bit uneasy sayin' what be on my mind."

"I don't understand why, Jubal. Ye don't never seem troubled when ye talks to my daddy."

"Yer daddy don't wear dresses neither."

"There might be some chance fer ye yet, I reckon," Lida said with a smile on her face. "Wanna tell me anymore?"

"I thinkin' I best not say no more right now. I done spoke too much now."

"Reckon ye done told me more right here than ye ever done before."

"I ain't said much," Jubal avowed.

"No, not many words, but ye done spoke from yer heart and that be what say so much and speak so much truth." She turned in her chair to face him and brushed her knee into his leg for just a moment. He could feel his cheeks heating up yet again.

"Do I excite you, Jubal?"

What in tarnation? She had never said anything like this before and he knew, or thought he knew, where she was headed with this. Uneasiness boiled up in him like he had never known before, and his excitement came on right along with it.

"I ain't gonna answer that."

"You just did. Don't see why ye can't just open up to me and say whatever ye wants to say. Reckon I don't bite."

"Ye can slap though. I be right on that I know."

"See there, ye done told it all again, Lida bragged. "I reckon I can read yer mind. Ye be thinkin' on me and ye together again, ain't ye? Like it was a bed in the mill that night. I know cause I got feelin's too, but ye don't know what they is, do ye?"

"Ye best be glad we here in yer house right now and not over there after dark. I reckon ye said we ought not talk on it here, but I done been suckered in on that. Ye got me there."

Lida laughed under her breath and heard her mother bang the kitchen door. She would be in before the fire with them in a few more steps. Lida moved her chair away from Jubal and started again to tend the flames and add another stick to the already glowing heap. Both them knew the time alone was over and thus the end of their talk.

Lida got the answers that she wanted. She could remain coy for later encounters and become more certain of his feelings. She reasoned that raw passion also brought along a measure of affection that could be nurtured by patience and persistence.

He had only become more confused and frustrated. He knew that he desired her, but that desire carried a measure of guilt. Was he just seeking self-satisfaction or was this all a new adventure? "Trust in me and I will guide thy paths." Granny Iverson's readings seemed to come over him at the strangest times. How could that be?

He was polite to Lida and her mother as well, but it was time to say his piece and make his way back to his own home and be before his own fire with his own kin.

"Thank you very much again for the deer meat. We will have the rest of it the next couple of days," Mrs. Johnson said as they all made their way to the porch, and Jubal descended the stairs and untied Kate's reins. "I will expect more when ye get the next one," Lida added with a smile. "Ye can bring it any time."

"That be a fact, son," C.C. added as he came from the mill. "I apt to need a bit of yer help iffin the Union soldiers brings all their grain to me like they said they would. "Why don't ye come back in two days or so just makin' a fact they brings it? Ye don't have to have no deer meat to come. I hope ye do get more, but it ain't a requirement fer ye to come."

"I be obliged to ye, and I be glad on helpin' ye grind, iffin need be."

"I see ye in two days then," the miller man added as he headed into the fire to ward off his own chill.

Jubal made his trek back up the road without incident. He did not pay much attention to the signs and sounds around him because his head was swirling with all sorts of unanswered questions. He thought that he understood what Lida had said to him, but the more he thought about it the more unsure he became. Unsure of what she said. More unsure of what she meant and even greater confusion about how he felt himself. Might be that Julie could help him some, but it would not be much different talking to her than it would with Lida.

Wes was at the barn taking care of the other stock when Jubal got there and prepared to unharness Kate and feed her.

"Wes, when we gonna use these here saddlers and go fetchin' like ye done talked on?"

"That be part why I been down here lookin' in on these animals today. We done had them barned up several days now, and they needs out fer a bit. Still yet don't want them runnin' out all daylight times. Don't reckon they been seen yet; I just soon keep it that way. I just hope that nobody don't come nosin' here abouts and try take away what rightly be ours, bought and paid fer. I reckon that not be apt happen iffin they is kept up and outta sight most times. I been thinkin' we ought harness up and lead them around outside some after dark, and I thinkin' we ought do it soon."

"When ye wanna do it?"

"Clouds is high now. Apt be a clear night and not much moon. Might be a good time tonight. Ain't likely be no scallywags out pilferin' around. Be too cold and nasty fer any such low lifers."

"We can do that, I reckon," Jubal said as he pulled Kate's harness off and hung it on its peg in the gear room. He then turned the old mule out to let her water in the spring runoff while he shelled a few nubbins. He could run three or four ears through the sheller like it was nothing. Strong arms made short work. Kate knew the sound of the sheller and was back waiting for her stall door to be opened.

Jubal thought back on some of the talks he and old Wes had in times past. He could recall the old man advising him on some of the things that had vexed him so much today. He thought about asking him things that most any son would ask of a kind and loving father, but it just did not set quite right with him. Wes was good to him and all, but he was not his own father.

It would not make a bit difference if Pa was here. Wes seemed to genuinely care. He also had a way of knowing things without ever being told. He knew how to look into a person's eyes and know what was on their mind. "The eyes are the window to the soul." Had Granny Iverson read that to him sometime?

Julie seemed to get stronger by the hour and delighted everyone in showing off her improvements. She could get herself in and out of bed now. She dressed herself, except for putting a sock on her foot. She lifted the spirits of the entire family. The war and all its atrocities seemed far removed from them now.

"I be thinkin' I needs me a crutch, Jubal," Julie said as she turned to face her brother. The flicker of the open fire radiated from her cheeks. "Reckon ye might be able to find me a fork what make a crutch? There be some young sapling's up on the flats I know fer and how come I seen plenty when we went a berry pickin' this past summer."

"Yeah, I know where they be."

"Ye don't have to fetch it right away. I be of a mind that I can help out in the kitchen and all iffin I had me a crutch, just till I mend up good mind ye."

"Ye been laid up long time, ain't ye sis?"

"I have, and it be time it be over. That be a fact."

511

"I fetch it fer ye in a day or so soon as I can," Jubal said as he came over to his sister and gave her a big but gentle hug. Their eyes met and no other words were spoken. Yet, each knew and felt the love for one another.

"Me and Granny Iverson needs get back to readin' to ye and teachin' ye how to read better. I promise I will commence in on that first time ye can make time fer me. I reckon it would please me a heap to read to ye and hear what all Granny Iverson would say about what I read. She knows a heap about the Bible and she can reason out things a heap better than myself. It pay a body to listen to her."

"Some things what she done read to me, reckon I won't never let go on what she say. Sometimes them sayin's come on me when they ain't no cause fer it. They just keeps runnin' thru my head till sometimes I ain't able to think on nothin' else fer a spell. Kinda vexes me sometimes," Jubal tried to explain to his sister.

"What sayin's?" Julie asked softly.

"Well…Like livin' in dark all the time when it be broad daylight and the like of that. And about bein' able to see the light. Ye and her both done harped on me many a time about that. How could I not recollect on that? I done heered it a hunnert times or more?"

"Thank ye Lord. They be hope fer him yet," Julie delighted as she put her palms together and rocked them back and forth in front of her bowed face and head. "I had them feelin's once, and I know what ye be hearin'. Ye gonna understand it all one day when ye answers your callin'. And that be what it is, Jubal. Ye is bein' called and sooner or later ye is gonna hafta answer or deny, one or the other."

"What callin' ye mean?"

Julie continued to improve over the next few days and seemed to double her strength and energy all the while. She had regained just a slight bit of motion in her knee, but it was still very painful for her to exert much pressure on it. She could walk well by holding on to someone else and using them for support. It was just about as if she had been reborn another whole new person. She had expressed that concept to Jubal and talked to him about how a body needed to die to this life and be reborn to another yet better life and to live in the love and peace known only to those who had answered the call. Jubal had once again pondered her words but really had pushed those thoughts to the back roads of his mind. She had told him that the beckoning call would not always be there, and when it was gone, then it would be too late to answer.

He reasoned that he had the rest of his life to pay heed to such things. After all, he was a young man. He knew that he had a lot to learn. There were things that he wanted to do and see before he took on all the cares and responsibilities of a family. Once he did decide to settle down, then there would be time to ponder on things that would come into play for the rest of his life. Julie had told him how there was no promise of tomorrow, and he realized that. Nevertheless, the seeds that Julie had planted would not lie idle forever.

Jubal headed out for the flats in search of a forked locust or elderberry limb that he could clean up and fashion into a crutch. He was in no real rush to climb the hill. He had made this trek many times over and knew almost every stone and bramble along the way. He had the old long rifle slung across the bend of his arm and kept one eye peeled for any sign of any game.

They still had a quarter of the yearling but that would soon run out. Never hurt to be watchful for any unexpected opportunity. He also watched the timberlines and scanned the ridges for any unusual motion of evidence of someone stirring around where they had no cause.

He stepped out of the thickets and onto the flats and almost immediately saw what he had come for. Not more than a few steps away stood a slim red elm with a perfect fork just over head high. Jubal wielded the hand axe, and in a few powerful strokes the elm bowed down to him and sacrificed to his service. He tied a length of sinew to both ends of the branch and slung it across his back and was off in the direction of the salt lick. Since he was this close, no sense not checking to see what might be there. Could be fresh tracks telling him what game was about. No black squawking devils could be seen in any of the treetops near the licks. Most likely there would be no new droppings either.

There was nothing to see at the licks. Most all the snow had melted away, and the chill wind foretold of freezes in the coming days and nights. Some of the critters would hole up and wait out the coldest of the nights, and others would forage wherever they could. There would soon be fresh signs to read, and those signs would tell where opportunity would allow a successful hunt. Jubal knew he was able; he just hoped that there would be more opportunities for him to provide for Julie and his Ma.

It took only one evening before the fire to fashion a good functional crutch. Jubal whittled off the bark and smoothed the underlying sap wood with a piece from a broken bottle. Surprising how well a sharp edge of raw glass will cut and shave a piece of wood. After shaving, Jubal put a small bit of sand in a piece of buckskin and holding the skin so as not to spill the sand, began to rub the pressure points of the crutch. Soon it was so well polished that it actually had a slight shine to it. Julie tried it and after shortening up the shaft just a bit, had a perfect fit. Julie managed to get around the room quite well with it.

"Ye have made me proud," Ma said to her.

"Me too," echoed her brother. "Was a time not long back that I reckoned ye done nigh give up on bein' well, sis."

"Oh I reckon I let myself sink a mite a time or so. But I knowed in my heart that it always be too soon to quit and that I just needed my faith propped up a bit ever now and then. Reckon it were all on account I needed be made a stronger person and have my faith built up over it."

"I feared ye was a goner there a time or two, Wes added.

"I had thoughts on it myself," Julie answered. "But somehow I had a peace on me that kept tellin' me I had other work needed be done."

"Ye weren't able do no work. Ye was weak so bad ye never even talked none there fer a day or so. Don't see how ye needed be concerned over work," Jubal commented asking a question of her all at the same time.

"I still got that work to do," she echoed.

"I don't think Ma be askin' ye fer help just yet."

"Jubal, it ain't that kind a work she be speakin' on," Granny Iverson added. "It not be works of a man."

"That be a fact," Julie added. "I know pine blank how come I was able to heal up so good, and I be just nigh good as ever real

514

soon. The work I got in front of me be a work of tellin' and spreadin' and helpin', and I aim to get at it with ever chance I get. I got me a chance right now too. Hand me my Book, and I read ye some right now, Jubal."

"We best rest that knee a spell," Ma said. "Ye done bled through yer wrap a bit."

Jubal was pretty sure that he knew what she was about to read to him. How that all live in the darkness until they asks for forgiveness and all that. He had heard it all before, and again he reckoned how that he had not ever done so much wrong or evil that he was so bad as to need all that forgiveness. He was not in too much of a mood to hear it all again tonight. He figured that it was just to his credit that he did not have to hear it again after all, at least not tonight. He knew that Julie would corner him about it again soon, and he knew that he would listen to her like always just so as to not rile her up. He would do that just to show her how much he cared for her and how much he wanted her to be all well again. If it meant so much to her, then he would not deny her.

Sleep was a long time coming again that night. Jubal lay on his pallet near the old stone fireplace until the flames had given up for the night. Not so sure, but numerous times he had thought he heard singing. He had raised up on one elbow to peer at Julie, but it was obvious that she was sound asleep and resting as peacefully as could ever be wished. The harmonious voices did not seem to come from any place in particular, but crazy as it might seem, they just drifted about the room in beautiful melody. The words were unclear, but he was sure that he had heard an amen or two.

Many thoughts ran the back roads of his mind, and there were things and sayings that he could not let go. There was no reasoning why he could not clear his thoughts at times like this. Try as he might, sometimes things just had to run their course. Times like this no longer riled him so much, but they did cause him to question himself in some ways. He felt he had a pretty good life in spite of all the hard work that he had to do in helping out around the old place. He thought himself to be a right upstanding soul, and he reckoned that there were plenty of others far worse than him. He just hoped that someday, somewhere, he could come to understand it all.

The sound of Ma stirring broke the spell again. He lay there and watched the embers without really thinking of anything. Soon he was up and had new wood on the fire, and the flames were not long in discovering a new quarry. The fire quickly grew hot and filled the room with a new warmth. There was something in there somewhere about a lake of fire. How could a lake be on fire? Such thoughts! Would they never let him be?

"Rest good did ye?" Julie asked as she awakened to the rekindled fire.

"Did fair."

"Want me read ye some after Ma gets us all fed?" Julie questioned further.

"I thought I might try fer another deer this mornin'. They ought be out and about since all the snow be most nigh gone now. I be thinkin' ye might like more stew, iffin I got one today."

"I would at that."

"Deer meat and a elderberry crutch done made ye a new girl, I reckon. More ought make ye plumb well again," Jubal said with a wide smile across his face.

Julie started to tell her brother who had really made her whole and who had restored her health, but she decided that it would be better some other time. She knew her brother really well and could tell when he had his defenses up. She just hoped down deep in her heart that he would be troubled so much by his unknowns and unanswered questions that he would come to her on his own and ask her all about what she so desperately wanted to tell him. She hoped even more that he would see his need and that she would be able to take his hand literally and lead him out of his darkness. She wanted so much for him to have the peace and happiness that could be found nowhere else.

Jubal was in no rush to reach the flats and descend to the lick. He had not planned to try doing anything else the entire day. He liked the times he could get out and roam over the hills and hollows and see all the things that signs could tell him. He reasoned that he knew enough to take care of himself in much the same way as the creatures living in his world. Much he had learned from others, but he also credited himself with learning through seeing and doing on his own. Experience had been a good teacher for him.

He had to admit to himself that he was a bit green and unskilled when it came to relating to another person, especially if that person happened to be a miller's daughter. Not a good time to dwell on her right now. Julie had said that she thought a big pot of rabbit stew would taste mighty good. Jubal had made the trek yesterday and had set some spring loops and a couple of dead fall traps. He wanted to check the dead falls first; because if he had been successful with them, they would be the easiest for scavengers to raid and steal. He could check the loop traps any time, because they would not kill unless the old cotton tail happened to die of fright.

The first dead fall was thrown, but there was nothing there. He looked all around for tracks or signs and saw that whatever had thrown the trap had been bloodied by it. The ground all around was scuffed and only one or two readable tracks could be found. Looked like there had been a big bobcat there. No way to tell if he got the rabbit or if he was the trapped one himself. He searched out away from the fall a few paces in all directions and really did not see much. Not worth tracking anyhow, but the pelt would have made a nice warm cap.

The next dead fall had not been thrown. No sense in leaving it set because he would not come back tomorrow just to check on a single trap. He found a length of a dead limb and tripped the fall. The weight of the rock coming down so hard made the pole jump almost out of his hand. The shock stung smartly. He shoved his throbbing hand into his coat in efforts to warm it and ease the throb. It would probably make a right smart bruise. Just as he had hoped, two of the loops had provided what he wanted. Each had a big fat doe rabbit securely hanging by a hind leg. One was stiff and lifeless. It must have met its end late yesterday afternoon and could not last the cold night. The second one was still alive and kicking a bit. It too was soon field dressed and on its way to the stew pot. Julie would eat well at least one more meal.

The stock path leading down off the flats and up past the old Wes house was easy to follow. It was on a fair grade and avoided the steep banks and rough rock outcroppings. It was an easy path to travel.

The path to the light is narrow, but the path to death and destruction is broad. He had heard that before somewhere. He just had to make sure that he did not stray from the narrow path that would lead him back to his old log home and the safety that it afforded. He did not understand the implications of the words that Granny Iverson had read to him about the straight and narrow. He did not understand a lot of things that she and Julie had read to him. Sometimes this bothered him and other times he just brushed it aside.

Took no time at all to dress the rabbits, and Ma soon had them in a pot at a slow boil. This would make them tender and easy to dice up for stewing. Jubal really did not have a taste for them but would indulge Julie nonetheless. He would see to it that she got his share or the most of it anyway.

The year's end came and brought a moderation in the wintry temperatures. There was still plenty a good store of firewood and cook stove wood in the old shed. It was plain that winter was well on now.

"Reckon we ought be readyin' ourselves to make our run," Wes said as he and Jubal tended to the horses and to old Kate. They pitched down fresh clover hay and brushed the animals a bit to remove dead hair and the cold weather accumulation of burrs. Kate seemed like she had mended up a bit, and the two saddle horses were fit as ever.

"When ye thinkin' we needs go?"

"I need tell ye a thing or so first. We talk on that here soon when we be out away from here a spell," Wes stated.

"I need go see iffin C.C. need me help him anymore. Thinkin' I might try do that in a day or so. Would ye wanna go with me? We have plenty time fer talkin' then."

"Don't need that much time. Just need tell ye one or two things fer certain. Rest ye can learn as we go," Wes informed him.

"Iffin that be so, then I might not go see the miller man."

"I be thinkin' ye needs go so ye can hear any war news. It be good to know what be happenin' where we be headed. Anyhow that give ye another chance fer seein' that gal again."

"I ain't so keen on that either. Not right now no how."

"She done got ye all in a stew again, ain't she?" Wes said half laughing.

"Do it show that easy?" Jubal asked, partially embarrassed and partly mad at himself for letting it show so much.

"It been plain to me fer sometime now. Reckon ye must have took a shine to her."

"So what iffin I have?"

"I ain't aimin' on rilin' ye up none. I just ask. That be all," Wes defended himself. "Ye can do whatever ye wants today. I just need talk with Mr. C.C. about them Rebs and what they been up to. We needs know that and needs know recent stuff too, so Wes decided to go after all."

The trek to the mill was uneventful with Jubal and Wes making mostly small talk about the weather, the possibility of getting another deer or maybe even seeing a big cat track. Wes looked for signs for good places for trapping but really did not see anything worth any efforts.

"Good seein' you folks. Git down and come on in," C.C. said as the two came into the mill yard.

"Ain't seen ye in quite a spell," Wes responded to the miller man's greeting.

"And howdy to ye too, Jubal."

"Good mornin' ye self," Jubal echoed.

"Ye look good, Wes. Ye mended up a heap since I last laid eye on ye."

"Reckon that be most on account of how Jubal's Ma done tooken me in and jerked a crook outta me. Be most obliged to her too."

"She be a hard worker all right," C.C. added.

The trio continued their banter for a bit when C.C. set Jubal to work bagging up big burlap sacks of ground millet that had been mixed with oats. These were for the Union cavalry, and they were supposed to come and pick them up in a day or so. Wes took advantage of being left alone with C.C. and talked with him at length about the latest war news and all he could find out about the Tennessee nineteenth regiment. He asked all about their movements and their casualty counts and all he could think about that had any bearing on his plans. C.C. was obviously curious to know why the detailed interest in unfriendly troops, unfriendly to Cane Valley folks anyhow. The miller man contained his curiosity and asked no prying questions.

Jubal worked at the mill tasks and left the older men to their own ends. He had no trouble handling the big bags of feed but could feel his breakfast begin to fade. He felt pretty sure that Lida and Mrs. Johnson would put a spread out soon and that he and Wes would be asked to join. That was just the way neighbors did in and around these parts. Besides that, it could afford another opportunity to catch a few moments with Lida.

Wes and C.C. sat before the Johnson fireplace and talked until the shadows were drawing out in length. Jubal had easily finished all the chores designated to him. C.C. had already taught him how to stop the wheel, divert the millrace and stop the flow over the wheel. He had done it only a few times but had mastered it well. He had even washed down the grist and managed to stay clean. Lida had watched him doing parts of his work, and she told him that she was impressed with all that he had learned in such a short time. She always encouraged him in the things that seemed to matter.

"We needs plan us a little ride here real soon," Wes informed Jubal as they headed away from the mill. Shadows were long now, and the night air let its coming chill be known. It would be good dark by the time they reached home. Ma probably would save them a part of the bread pone, but it really made no matter because both had eaten their fill at their guest's table.

"Where we gonna go?"

"I tell ye more on that in a day or so."

"How long we gonna be gone?"

"Most likely just one night. Ain't that far where we needs be traipsin' off to."

"Are ye up to such?" Jubal asked seriously.

"Gotta be, I reckon. I be a heap better than back in hot weather. I think I be fine, but we still needs be at our best."

"I just wishin' ye ease my mind a bit and tell me what this all be about," Jubal said in a questioning manner.

"Ye recollect me openin' up that old dipper gourd, son?"

"I recollect alright."

"Well, this here business be some the same. Iffin we can do this here trip and keep our wits and all, then we ought be in fair shape no matter how this here old war comes out and all."

"Ye talkin' of more shine stuff what be round and all sparklin' like?"

"I think ye be understandin' what I mean now. Part ways anyhow," Wes answered.

"I be all ears and no mouth," Jubal countered.

"We needs a clear night on a big moon so we can make our way after dark. Ain't no call fer havin' any onlookers."

"Moon be full in about a week, but I ain't makin' no claims on the clouds," Jubal said somewhat boastful. "Might be light 'nuff even iffin it be some cloudy. I reckon I see pert nigh good as old screech owls lookin' fer a rabbit."

"Ye ain't that good now, and I know better," Wes laughed. There was not much he could say against youth and such a strong will. "I reckon iffin a copperhead bit ye then he would be the one got sick," Wes said with a big grin on his face.

"Yeah, I stick him through a hole in a rail and then tie a knot in each end. That fix him, I reckon."

"Ye be full of it, ain't ye?"

"I reckon I can whup yer hinder end mostly nigh any time."

"Well pshaw, son. Iffin I was yer age I would show ye what a whuppin' is. Whuppin' up on a old man don't say much fer ye."

"Reckon I might needs whup ye anyhow iffin ye don't tell me what ye drummin' up, old man."

"I speck I owe ye that much anyhow," Wes added almost apologetically.

"I never aimed it such," Jubal quipped.

"Don't matter none anyhow. Answer me this though. Iffin ye had money, what ye reckon ye might do with it?" Wes asked bluntly.

"How much money?"

"Right smart bit. More than ye ever have before."

"Reckon I might needs dwell on that a spell," Jubal replied.

"Glad ye say that, son. It show ye growin' in yer brain as well as in yer back."

"What ye mean by that?"

"Well boy, ye ain't much a boy no more. Ye near a man, and it be time ye thinkin' like a man. Use was ye talk on fine hosses and traipsin' off fer the big city life and all such tomfoolery. Least now that not the first words outta yer mouth. Tells me ye done smartened up a bit, and that be good."

"Ye reckon, huh?"

"I reckon so," Wes echoed.

They were just about to the crest of sand hill when Wes bent over and peered down at the rutted-and-muddy old road. Jubal stopped and scanned the ground for several yards ahead but saw nothing that would tell him anything.

"What ye done found old man?"

"Lookie here."

"What? I don't see nuthin'."

"Fur. See that fur tag?"

"Yeah."

"Ye know what it be?"

"Polecat?"

"Why ye thinkin' that, son?"

"Black, ain't it?"

"Polecats ain't only thing here abouts what be black. Look how fine it be. Ain't no polecat ever had hair that fine."

"What it be then?" Jubal asked with increased interest.

"I reckon it be a panter. I thunk I heered one screamin' about a week back when snow first come. Ain't seen one in this here holler since way back. Reckon that be why we ain't seen no elk this year. Ain't heard none of em bugle this year either come think on it." That be why they ain't no deers much no more, I bet."

"See a track anywhere?" Jubal questioned as he looked about more diligently.

"Naw. He most likely done jumped clean over one bank to next. They is skiddish and don't leave much of a sign. He pick his steps and not put down a paw where he leave a track. They ain't many in these parts and that be just his nature, I reckon."

"He be black all over?" Jubal questioned.

"Yep, with big yeller eyes what shine on darkest a night. Some say he can charm a man or beast. Reckon I don't say so myself. I ain't believing' such."

Jubal looked off to each side of the road. "Reckon I could find a track uphill a bit."

"Ain't worth yer efforts. Iffin ye did find one, ye ain't apt on findin' more nowhere close. Like say, he be mighty picky where he step. That be part why he still be able make a track. Iffin he don't wanna be seen, then he ain't gonna be. Ye just needs listen out fer him on dark nights. But then again, ye might go a lifetime and never see one."

"I give a dollar fer him bein' in my rifle sights."

"I reckon so, son. He make a fine fur wrap. Kind like ye used talk about."

"Any man be proud wear such, huh?" Jubal said.

"I thinkin' more fer a woman, a young sassy woman at that," Wes trumped in with that all-knowing grin on his face yet again.

"We best get movin' on home," Jubal quipped.

Ma had baked a big pone of fresh corn bread and made a skillet of ham grease gravy. It was a poor man's supper for sure, but it tasted good to all and all had their fill.

The fireplace was especially comforting after a good hot supper. The wind had laid and the world seemed to be at peace in Cane Valley. Worry not for tomorrow, for the evils of today are great. Granny Iverson had read that to him just a few days ago, and it had stuck with him. He could recall many of her readings when he really thought about it. One thought most always led to another. First thing he knew, he was just near overcome with readings and such. He had it in his mind to steal away with the Good Book sometime and see just what he could read for himself.

It must have been the warm supper and the comfort of the warm hearth that gave everyone heavy eyes and a need for rest and sleep. Julie fell fast asleep just about as soon as she leaned back on her bed. Ma and Granny Iverson disappeared upstairs before Jubal had a chance to miss them. Sarry and Gracie were sound asleep at the foot of Julie's bed. No one bothered to wake them and have them move to their own bed. Wes had his usual place on his pallet and had turned his back to the fire. His rest came on quickly and his regular deep breathing assured rest would be complete.

Morning came and brought a restful awakening to the boy and to the old man. Jubal looked over at Wes who had already got the fire built back up and was sitting before it. His face looked a bit vexed, and Jubal could sense that he was deep in thought. He did not make any effort to gain his attention.

Wes was hopeful that he had learned enough from C.C. to make a good judgment about all the goings around the area where he needed to go. It was not that far from the old log home and Cane Valley, but they would be headed right into the lion's den, so to speak.

Some of the intense fighting had been done in and around the Gap area in order to control all movements through it. Whoever owned the Gap controlled the north and south movements. Rebs wanted it to advance into Kentucky, and the Union needed it to gain control of the Knoxville area and places deeper into Dixie. The Rebs had been able to hold most of the Powell River valley and the road on into Bristol where the railroad connected up to the northern Virginia area. Many stories had come out of that area about the ferocity and the hatred of the Rebel troops and how they handled the Union sympathizers. Any Union forces that were overpowered in that area soon found themselves on their way to Andersonville, if they were not killed out of pure spite to begin with.

Wes and Jubal would need to cross Clinch and head west. They would need to lay as low as possible once they turned west. May even need to travel at night and hold up in the thickets and brambles in daylight. There could be no cook fire, and they somehow would need to keep the horses fed and quiet all the while.

There would be some risk for sure, but Wes was wise to the situation, and he knew that Jubal would have a thousand questions about the whole affair. He would start today and tell the boy all that he needed to know. Tell him just a bit at a time so that he could mull it all over and be sure to remember all that he needed to know.

"I reckon we ought get ready and set out late this afternoon. Weather looks to be moderated some, and it ain't too bad cold," Wes announced shortly after Jubal had filled the kitchen wood box.

"Reckon ye done planned it all out ain't ye?" Jubal asked.

"Hope I thunk of ever thing we needs."

"Tell me what ye want me doin', and I be turnin' to it soon as I get this here wood split fer Ma. How many days' wood I need lay in fer her, ye think?"

"Four days at most," Wes answered.

"We must is goin' a fur piece."

"No, not really. We just needs be plumb certain that ain't nobody find us out nor what we be up to. That why we be on the move most times at dark. Harder to move around good in the dark, but that be best for us on this here trip."

"Ye really don't wanna be seen do ye?" Jubal asked.

"No."

"Any reason fer that?"

"Well, fer one thing, ye wouldn't take kindly to a body takin' our hosses right out from in under us would ye?" Wes answered.

"No, I reckon that be a fact. I don't aim on lettin' nobody do me that way," Jubal quipped with an air of vengefulness.

"Ye gotta realize that we is headed to Reb territory, and the war situation has made them a desperate bunch. They take whatever they can lay hands on just to get by, and they don't much care who they tromps on gettin' it. So the fewer times we be seen, then the better off we be. That be how I see it."

"Ye 'fraid of Rebs?" Jubal asked.

"Call it 'fraid or caution either one ye wants. I just be knowin' that I don't want no dealin's with none of them kind. Iffin they learnt that we was from Cane Valley area, then that would be same as Union territory to them. They don't cotton to folks who tolerated the Blue Bellies. C.C. say most of them be up north of the Gap and that be best for us. Just hope they stays up there a few more days."

"Hope so too," Jubal echoed.

"How abouts ye let them hosses out fer water, and I pitch down fresh hay fer em. Ye can shell a few nubbins for each one and may as well give old Kate a few too."

"We gonna take her with us too?" Jubal questioned again.

"Naw, she ain't up to it I reckon, but she need some corn just same. Be good iffin ye could shell about half a sack to pack with us too. Handful or two keep up a spirited hoss a long time. They gotta make this here trip in good time same as we do."

Jubal made no fuss about doing what Wes had laid out for him. The horses went straight to the spring pool runoff and watered themselves. Wes had thrown down the hay as he had said. Jubal soon had shelled corn in their feed boxes. They would be in good shape for another day and night.

Wes got down the bridles and saddles and went over them completely to make sure that there was no torn leather and that all the rivets were tight. He took down the saddlebags and started rubbing them down with beeswax and lard. This would restore the softness of the leather and would also add a measure of resistance to rain. He hunted for some good sacks that had no rips or picked places in them. He found what he wanted and doubled them up and gave them to Jubal. "See iffin ye can shell nubbins 'nuff to half fill these here. Leave em doubled up like they is now. Ye can tie it off real tight and then we hang one on each saddle horn."

They would need an axe and a spade. These would need covered in a sack or a wrap of some sort. One would be tied on each saddle, but they needed wrapped to keep metal off metal and making a telling clink-clank sound. Something like that could be heard for a long way off on a cold windless winter day. Just one more thing that could help them to go unseen in unfriendly territory.

"We best have us a heavy piece outta some old cows hide fer sleepin' on the damp ground. There be a hide in your Ma's smokehouse loft, and I be thinkin' that do fine. It'll sleep one of us at a time, I reckon, whilst the other keeps an ear out," Wes said intending that Jubal would catch onto the seriousness of it all. He was just a bit confused as to why the boy had asked no more questions this morning. "Are ye plumb ready fer this? Are ye up to it?"

"I reckon I am at that."

"I be tellin' ye more as we go. I don't aim on holdin' out on ye. It just be that ye can't tell what ye don't know iffin we runs up on trouble some place."

"We ain't got no troubles, and we ain't gonna have none. We got good horses. We got side arms and these here new long rifles that ye done got from Yeary. We outta be able to whup our way outta most anything comes along," Jubal said assuredly.

"Well, they be some truth in that, but ye best remember that others got guns and mounts just as well as us," Wes replied. "Last thing we wants is to be in a shootout. The less we is seen then the better off we gonna be. We needs be like we ain't even there."

"I reckon ye be right," Jubal answered.

"Neither of us has much time in a saddle here lately. Likely we be sore from sittin' after a bit, special fer me on account me bein' older and stiff. We might wind up on foot quite a bit, if needed. Make it easier fer the hosses that way too."

"I don't reckon I be walkin' no more than most. I can set a horse all right, thank ye."

"Well, I reckon we'll see on that," Wes came back.

"I ain't tryin' be smart assed nor nuthin', Wes. But there be no wrong in ridin' as much as a body can is there?"

"No, but there be some things that ye just gonna have to trust me with, son. I tell it all to ye when time be right."

It took a major part of the afternoon to ready the packs and get all their gear tied up and ready to sling across the saddles. Bedrolls were thick, but rolled tightly and tied up securely. Wes had told Ma all that he wanted her to know. She too could not tell what she did not know if any troopers came around asking about him. He had told her that if she needed to tell anything on him that she was to say that he was on the run from Union forces because he had taken stock from them and that they had accused him of trading with the rebel carpetbaggers over near the ferry area. He had told her where they were going but asked her not to say anything to anybody. Just send them off on a goose chase in another direction. She was not to share anything with anybody until she heard otherwise from himself or from Jubal. She had understood and agreed.

Supper that evening was a quiet time. Everyone sensed that there was danger ahead and that risks were involved. No one talked about all the things that could beset the two as they made their way across the mountains. Granny Iverson sat for a long while with her hands clasped together. There was no doubt what she was up to, and everyone sensed her urgency. Julie had hobbled to the kitchen and sat beside her brother. She held onto his arm as he ate. She had few words to say right now, but he could sense a closeness to her that made him have every desire and hope to return.

Wes had outlined what needed to happen in the first night. They needed to reach a certain point, but must remain unseen at all costs. The old man had been so insistent in his instructions that Jubal began to realize the real dangers involved. The fact that they may encounter real troopers, who would show no mercy, began to weigh in right heavy on his mind.

Ma and Julie packed the hardtack and the side meat and wrapped it securely. It would be far different from biscuits and thick slabs of ham in the morning, but it would stave off the hunger and provide some nourishment. She had already promised herself that her two men would be fed like kings when they returned. She and her daughters would see to that.

Wes saddled the horses and led them up from the barn lot. It took only a short time to tie on the bedrolls and the other essentials. The axe and the spade were wrapped in old sacks and tied on securely. Saddlebags bulged and hung heavy across the horses' backs. Both had donned buckskins. Jubal made sure that he had his horn and shot inside his coat where he could easily reach it.

The sun was low in the west, and dark would come soon. There were only a few scattered mare's tail clouds. There would be no rain tonight, and the moon would be in its first quarter. There would be just enough light to make steps easier and landmarks easier to spot. Most of tonight would be fairly familiar travel, but morning would bring strange trails and unfamiliar pathways.

Good-byes were said and hugs exchanged. The two travelers set out to the west following the sinking sun. Jubal never looked back toward the old log home. He did not want to chance anyone seeing the emotion that was welling up in his eyes. He was going where he had never been before, both physically and in his mind. He had all expectations that he would make it through this. Granny Iverson had read him something about expectation of things unseen and hope for things yet to come. He thought she called it faith.

Chapter 15

Away

*D*arkness did not bring the anticipated chill. Instead the wind calmed, and the clouds broke up and scattered. The pair of riders soon made their way across the old home ridge and headed west down the banks of Poor Valley creek. They appeared to be in a world all their own. The moon came out just enough to see the crest of old Clinch and the outlines of the spurs running down from it. They had made a few intermittent stops just to look around and to listen to the sounds of the night. There was neither man nor beast to be heard or seen. That was just the way they wanted it. Both realized that the more westward they journeyed, the more likely they would encounter the Rebs based near the Gap.

"How far down this here valley we be headed?" Jubal asked.

"Reckon it be time I fill ye in on a thing or so, ain't it?"

"Would be gooder iffin I knowed where I be headed," Jubal quipped.

"Well, we go down along side this here creek till we gets down where it turns south and heads fer the river. That be our mark to head straight up Clinch and head down the north side. Mind ye we best be a mite more careful after that and stay up high in big timber best we can," Wes instructed.

"Rebs be on north side?" Jubal asked.

"That be what C.C. done say."

"Reckon that all be new ground fer me," Jubal added. "I wonder what it look like."

"Be about same as at home, I reckon. Ain't much other than where we done come from. Funny, but most times a man spend a lifetime wonderin' what be over the next mountain or beyond. Most don't even know it when they do see it. Ye crosses one mountain and then there be another, and ye don't know what be past it neither."

"How many we gonna cross?"

"Just one," Wes answered.

"Ye make it sound like a bunch."

"Reckon I do at that, but I ain't speakin' on earth and stone just now. I be speakin' on life mountains. Ye just gotta take stock on things sometimes and take it fer what it be. There be things in life like that."

"Huh?" Jubal answered.

"I just be talkin', son. I just be talkin', but what I say have a lot a grit to it. Ye don't see it right now, and now ain't no good time fer tryin' to cipher it all out. What I be sayin' in short be that life sometimes hands ye a hill to climb, and ye just gotta set yer mind and do it. That make any sense fer ye, son?"

"Reckon so, a bit."

"We needs step it up a bit iffin we is gonna be climbin' up Clinch come daylight. I don't much reckon we be troubled none this side, but I thinkin' we needs be on other side in big timber not too long after first light. We can rest up several hours and spell the hosses too. We be near halfway when we comes down off yon side and hit out along the river. We still needs head west then too."

Jubal began to feel the loss of sleep a good while before daylight and found himself nodding in the saddle. A few hours rest would be welcome. It crossed his mind that this big old wide world he had fantasized so many a time might not be all game and glory. Being tired and in strange lands had a way of waking a body up to reality, and yet he was only a few meager miles from home and family.

The ascent up the mountain took more time and effort than either of the two had thought. It was good light when they got up to the south side bluffs. Usual limestone outcroppings along many of the larger ridges made an effective barrier for crossing, save for particular breaks and gaps.

"We best keep on west and look fer someplace we can cross topside. Then we can find someplace to hold up a while," Wes instructed. "We need someplace outta any wind what may come up."

"Ye lead off. I be right hind ye."

The bluffs were not really all that formidable, but sufficient to where a horse could not climb at just any location. Most were under ten feet, but that was plenty to stop a rider and his mount. These outcroppings were old, and many fractures provided crevices from a few inches up to a few yards. The limestone cracked and fell away with eons of freeze and thaw, and many of the boulders that became dislodged could be found hundreds of feet below.

A cleft was soon found that broke open clear to the north side, and it was easy enough to pass. "Well, that was easy fer us, I reckon," Jubal said.

"Yeah, and look out yonder," Wes said as he pointed on to the west. What he had spotted was a outcropping of size enough to provide a good cover between the two massive rock ledges. There would be good cover and wind shelter for them and for the horses. "Ye see what I see?"

"Yeah. Look ready-made fer us, don't it?"

"We can rest up here. I be thinkin' that ain't gonna be nobody seein' us here. We can stay here till near dark, and I reckon we won't need be so keen on watchin' fer some scallywag come pokin' around where he ain't got no call," Wes said as he reined his horse in that direction.

Little needed be said when they rode into the sheltered spot. It was perfect. There was enough overhang from above to provide a small sheltered area from the rain, if need be. Not too much chance of needing that today, because the sun was coming up bright. Horses were soon unsaddled and reined to low hanging shrubs. Jubal cleaned off a small spot for each and poured a few loose oats in the loose soil.

The bedrolls and saddles were spread and occupied. The early morning sun beating down against the gray stone produced just enough warmth to lull both travelers into a quick and peaceful respite. Jubal heard Wes cough lightly and then the warm glow upon his face pulled him into unawareness and forgetfulness. This time there would be no lying awake and wondering about this or that.

The sun was high when Jubal awoke. He had slept for about three hours and now felt the cold and dampness of the ground. He had laid out the sailcloth just like Wes had shown him, but it did not shield all the cold of the earth. It had kept him dry, and he could be thankful for that. Being chilled was one thing, but being chilled and wet was a whole other predicament.

He looked around him and saw that the horses were just where they had been tied, heads down, evidently feeling the soothing warm sunshine as well. Wes had rolled up his blankets, but the sailcloth was still spread. Jubal listened intently but heard nothing. Suddenly there was a rustling in the leaves off to his right. Looking intently, he soon saw the noise maker. A big red fox squirrel was trying to find a salvageable hickory nut. Jubal looked skyward for a moment and spotted the big scale-barked hickory not thirty yards away. Jubal thought how easy it would be just to cut down on the old bushy tail and roast him over a spit, and just as soon recalled how important Wes had said that it would be to stay unseen and unheard. No telling who or what was below them in the valley, and there was no cause to have them come looking.

Then he thought he heard footsteps. They were getting more distinct now, getting louder. They began to sound like someone deliberately tromping through the leaves and brambles. Then he heard a keen short whistle. Wes? Wes had been out and about for some reason and was announcing his return. He came into view carrying something in a small bundle of deer skin.

"Here, I found us a few walnuts and some big acorns. Ain't much, but it help some. We eat them and a bite of side meat, then we be good. We find good water later when we eases down off here some. I done spotted smoke a place or two, so they be some dwellers down there somewhere. They might have somethin' we could lay hold on come dark."

"We find us a hen house and get us some aigs," Jubal said.

"We might do just that but we not have no fire, so we just suck em down raw."

"Ain't never done that and ain't hankerin' to neither," Jubal responded in a distasteful air.

"They ain't so bad; and iffin ye be hungered, they soon fills ye up good. No taste much."

"Druther have me a big raw tater," Jubal answered.

"We might find us one of them. They give us water, and hosses eat them, iffin they be hungry. We not go without, they be too many things preventin' that."

"I reckon ye be right there. We eat us a big bait when we gets back home," Jubal said as much to himself as to Wes.

"Hunt yerself a hammerin' rock, and we see iffin these here nuts be any 'count or not. I done seen squirrels pilferin' hickories, but these here walnuts be more fer less crackin'. The walnuts were good, but they had grown strong since falling and were now just a bit bitter. Wes cracked one and got out a big eagle. Biting into it, he spit it out almost at once.

"Too strong. Best not eat none of em. They burn ye up and give ye the trots too. Ye don't need that fer sure."

Jubal tossed the nuts in the general direction where he had seen the big red foxtail.

"Here, ye can have the trots and the runs, not me."

The remainder of the first encampment went by rather fast. Preparations were made for the coming night long before the sun dipped below the distant ridges. Jubal felt rested and ready for a new night of adventure. It was something that he needed to do, not just for himself but for others as well.

Shadows were growing long when the two headed down the north slopes of the mountain. They and the horses could use some fresh water. It was not something that had to be right away because both knew that there would be rivers of water in the valley below, but they might need to stay to the high ground to keep out of sight.

The gurgle of rushing water soon came to earshot and a few more yards brought the thirst-quenching water. Both dismounted and had their fill of the cold mountain stream. Wes cautioned against allowing the steeds to have too much all at one time. Cold water could cause them to block up and that could just not be permitted.

There would be plenty of little branches and creeks all along the way.

They continued downhill to the point where they could see out from the edges of the undergrowth. Looking across a long gentle slope running all the way to the line of sycamores at the river, they could see one settlement with blue gray smoke rising slowly. Maybe there could be better food there, but best to have a good look around before traipsing down unannounced or even worse, unwanted. The aim was to go unseen as much as possible and both decided that would be their course.

Jubal noticed Wes looking in all directions and pointing out in his line of sight. "What ye see, Wes?"

"Nothin' fer sure. I just tryin' line out a landmark or two fer iffin we needs stop here on our way back home. They may not be no more places fer many a mile, and we might have to come here by then."

"Ye thinkin' it be safer comin' home?" Jubal asked.

"Maybe so, maybe not. Just don't know."

Darkness found them just below the timberline riding slow and easy to the west. There was no snow on the north slopes to leave betraying tracks, but any mountain inhabitant worth his salt would have no trouble following two horses.

Infrequent stops revealed no sounds of anything astir. The night was still, and the silence was mystifying. It was as if the world was standing still. It was like the world was at perfect peace and that there was no malice and certainly no hatred. Jubal recalled Granny Iverson talking about a peace that no man could understand. Something about peace that passed all understanding.

Travel was good in the upland grasses. Jubal did not try guessing the number of miles they put behind them. He was content just to let Wes lead while he took in all the dusky countryside. He was in strange places and was somewhat in awe of all that he was seeing. It awakened a touch of wanderlust in him.

"We ought be close by mornin', Wes said as he reined in his horse and turned in the saddle to face Jubal.

"Ye ain't told me yet pine blank where we be headed."

"We lookin' fer little church house called Logan's Chapel. We be wantin' in their graveyard after dark. Reckon ye up to it, ain't ye? Not be skeert ner nothin'?"

"Naw, haints and boogers don't rile me none. Don't believe in em no how."

"Me neither," Wes echoed. "We be diggin' in there a bit. That gonna be anything ye can't do?"

"No. Not iffin ye be there with me."

"I be there same as ye."

"Then seems me like all we needs do is get there," Jubal said.

"Well, there be just a dab more to it than that. We needs find the right markers and be able to read them names and such."

"I take it ye knows which ones and where they be."

"It be drilled in my head like in stone. I laid awake many a night ponderin' over it makin' out pine blank that I don't never fergit it. Never knowed just when I might be able get back there and fetch it."

"What ye done did? Ye bury it up some place?" Jubal asked. He had pretty much figured out that part, but there was still a lot of the story he did not know.

"Yep. That be a fact, son. It be buried in a graveyard."

"Ye be one who put it there?" Jubal asked again.

"Yeah, that a fact too," Wes answered.

"When?"

"Way back in fifty-one. It been there years now," Wes said as he seemed to be a bit more open about it all now.

"How many...how much dollars we be talkin' about, Wes?"

"Best I can recollect there be over two hunnert gold pieces. Most of em be eagles too."

"Awh pshaw, Wes. Ain't no man 'round here got money like that."

"No. I reckon not, but it never come from these parts."

"Ye ain't never said much on that."

"Well, it don't matter much now no how, but I tell ye more on that later on. Yer just gonna need trust me on all the rest of it. I ain't real proud what all I done back then, but I reckon it be what it be."

"Ye done told me that when we busted open yer gourd back there in the springhouse loft. I recollect that much," Jubal commented.

"Ye just wait and see iffin we has any luck. I reckon I might tell ye more on it once we is on our way back to Cane Valley."

"Look like I ain't gonna be headed nowhere else any time soon. I reckon I stick with ye till we be back home. Then ye can tell me and Ma whatever ye wants."

"I tell ye," Wes said. "But ain't no need Ma knowin' all about it."

The first shades of crimson began breaking in the east. Wes frequently turned to observe the sky and the coming morning. He did not particularly like the signs that he was seeing. Red sky at dawn held ominous meanings. It could be a sign of changes in the weather for coming day.

"We best hit the higher ground and hole up soon," Wes said as he urged his horse upward and into the timberline. "We been in good speed so far, and I be mighty glad fer that. But I thinkin' we needs us someplace fer shelter today. Maybe we find some out cropper up in the bluffs. I done brung us foul weather stuff, but it never hurt one bit stayin' dry."

"Ye thinkin' it gonna snow?"

"Ain't cold 'nuff yet. Would druther have snow over rain. We just needs be ready fer whatever comes," Wes instructed.

It was almost as if old Wes knew exactly where he wanted to be to hold up for the day. He led them to a low outcropping of limestone that overshadowed a fair-sized opening back into the rock bluff. It afforded shelter from the rain or snow, whichever should come. The overhang was sufficient even to shelter the horses, and the cave opening broke any chilling winds. The sun was up enough to make good light all around. Wes looked about to see if the place had been used lately. He found no fresh tracks. That was good, because it meant that no one had been down this direction in several days.

Inside the cave there was a fire pit lined with good-sized stones. There had been a fire of sufficient strength where the flames had licked these stones and blackened them readily. Someone had kindled a hot fire most likely from dead and dried wood so as to not make much smoke. They could do the same, but any smoke at all would be too risky. Besides that, they had no food with them that needed a fire. Sure it would be good to have a warming fire for the day's rest, but it just might call in unwanted attention. They would be here only a few hours and would just make do with what they had at hand.

Jubal found smooth faces on the rocks and gave the horses another good handful of oats and millet. The beasts ate without abandon and seemed quite content with what they were given.

"I think we ought be able to get there about midnight tonight. That be iffin we be where I think we be right now."

"Seems me like ye knows this country right well old man," Jubal quipped.

"Spent a few days here back a ways."

"Back when?"

"Seven eight years, give er take a bit," Wes answered.

"Then ye do know where we be."

"Course I do. Just not sure to the foot, that's all."

Jubal fetched his bedroll and began to clear off a place to lay down. Wes had not yet made a move in that manner. He seemed to be thinking about other things or even other places in other times.

"I gonna hit the crest and head west about a half mile or so. If we be where I thinkin' we be, then I can see the church from that high spur yonder. I need yer oil slicker so I can cover up anything what might catch a glimmer and give me away. I drape yours and mine over me, and then I be covered good. Ye can crawl back in yer cave bed and rest, but keep yer rifle close by. Don't reckon they be anybody bother ye while I be gone. I be back in about two hours. Ye be okay with all that?"

"I reckon I can fend fer myself that long," Jubal said smartly.

"Good. I knowed ye could. Grab yerself a wink or two iffin ye care to. I get me some when I gets back."

Wes made the short climb to the spine of the mountain and was soon looking out to the west. It was not the easiest thing to spot a tiny white church house through all the leafless sleeping timber. It would have been impossible when timber was thick green, bad enough now. But sure enough, there it was! Right where he had remembered! From up here so far above, it looked as if it had not changed at all in the time that he had been away. There was no way to tell from here if the stones and the markers were still in place. He was just banking on the fact that most in these parts considered a graveyard a place worthy of respect and reverence. There was no law to speak of in these parts, but the laws of nature dictated respect for the dead, and few if any ever challenged that aged law.

Things just had to be unchanged. Yes, it was there! It would be there tonight as well.

Just as he was about to turn and head back to their day camp, Wes spotter riders coming east on the valley road far below. Too far away to make out any distinguishing features, but there were nine mounted figures with about a dozen or so on foot. Studying the spectacle more intently, he could see that it was a Reb patrol with a few apparent Bluecoat prisoners. Just what he did not want to see, military activity of any sort.

He watched their progress until he was satisfied that they were going to continue on up the valley and not veer off to high ground.

Wes made his way back to the little cave and related what he had seen to his companion. He was pleased that he had spotted the church and that all seemed to be as he recalled years before. He also expressed his concern about the patrol movements and what it might mean to their own plans.

They would stay on the mountain until about two hours before dusk and then make their way down and cross the open meadows to the churchyard. They could hide the horses in the underbrush behind the church and still should have enough light to find the markers. If the right headstones could be found and lined up, then this would be the last night they would need to be so secretive.

Jubal listened to all that he had to say with keen interest. The boy did not express any apparent concern over the military movements one side or the other, and Wes was quick to take note of that.

"I hope ye know that it won't be good if we get ourselves all hung up with one of them patrols. They could spell trouble fer us," Wes said.

"I ain't plannin' on no such, and I ain't worried on that none either. But there be one thing I think ye owes me right here and now," Jubal said as he sat up with his bedroll pulled in around him.

"What it be that eatin' on ye?" Wes asked.

"Ye done told me where we be headed and what we be after, and I reckon I ain't got no issues with that. Ye done proved yerself with yer gourd. I think I got cause to know how much we talkin' on, and I think ye ought tell me how ye done come by it all. Ye done let loose just a bit here and there, and right now I ain't got no choice but to conjure up my own stories on it."

"What ye say be true I reckon, but it be a mite long story start to finish. Ye want hear it now, leastwise a start or ye wanna sleep a bit?"

"I reckon we ought nap a bit iffin we is fixed to have a busy night," Jubal answered.

"Wise answer," Wes said as he untied his bedroll and made himself as comfortable as conditions would allow. He had learned some time back to sleep with one ear opened, and this day would be one that would warrant doing so again. He pondered just a bit on what all to tell the boy and where to start the saga. He decided that he would tell him the whole story and leave nothing to doubt. He would try to explain just how things came about as best he could. If the boy turned out to be judgmental of him, then that would just be. He was pretty sure that the boy trusted him. He was just as sure that Ma trusted him. Those trusts had to be honored and respected.

Wes awakened a bit before Jubal. He had his bed all rolled and tied when Jubal woke. Both were soon ready for the ride to the church. The red morning sky had not brought the bad weather that they had expected, and they were both grateful for that. It would be good to have a slither of moonlight tonight. It would make reading the headstones a bit easier.

The churchyard was empty when they rode up. Wes quickly directed Jubal into the nearby thicket with the horses and told him to give them a few more bits of grain so as to keep them quiet. He untied the spade and the axe and brought them back to the graveyard as he had been told. Wes was already busying himself trying to locate the first headstone.

"What name ye seekin' out?" Jubal asked.

"Leroy Stone be first one I need to find. Should be close by this side some place best I recall. It was scratched in deep so it ought not be faded out none."

Both continued to look for the stone as the evening light began to fade markedly. Would be a while before the moon got up enough to cast its silver glow among the headstones and give the entire churchyard a spooky atmosphere, especially since they had it in mind to dig up some poor wretch's bones. Or that was what Jubal had assumed.

"Here it is," Wes announced. "Come stand right here fer me." Wes stood a few feet in front of the stone and pointed exactly where he wanted Jubal to stand. He then walked to the edge of the cemetery and turned back to face Jubal. "Now ye stand right there while I find the second one." He began making an arc back and forth, checking the names on each stone as he moved in nearer the boy with each pass. "Should be close by here. I never thought it be this far inside."

"We soon need us a torch. It gonna be last light soon."

"No, we can't have no light. Might cause too much attraction, and we ain't needin' that. I just needs find that marker and then we don't need no more light," Wes said as he continued his search. He stopped and stood erect for a bit, not moving and not speaking.

"What now?" Jubal asked a bit impatiently.

"Nuthin', I just takin' a listen."

Wes resumed his search. He was down on hands and knees reading faded stones. He had to put his face nearly against the cold gray slabs to make out any figures. There was only a penance of daylight left when he found what he sought.

"Here she is," he said as he noted his position and that of his companion. He quickly walked back to where Jubal stood and handed him the end of a small coil of rope. "Hold this here right on top of Mr. Leroy's marker. Hold tight cause I gonna be runnin' that line straight over the Beal woman and on out yonder to the edge and cross the rail fence. We needs hurry so we can see to mark our spot.

It took only a short bit to run the line and determine a spot. Wes kept the line straight using the two stones as a guide. The end of the line put him slightly into the underbrush at the rear of the church-yard cemetery. That established his distance past the fence. Now all he needed to do was swing back and forth a few feet each way until he could find another marker. He would need to brush away the accumulation of fallen leaves and what dead grasses there were left from the summer's growth. Still on hands and knees, he began to swing his hands to sweep back and forth, using the end of the line as a guide. No way to see much now. He knew he would have to wait for some moonlight if he did not luck out and find the stones by feel. He kept sweeping back and forth with his hands as he crawled along the ground. He was becoming very concerned that he might not be able to find his mark at all, but he was nowhere near ready to give in.

Just a bit more. Then if no luck, I'll go back the other way," he said as much to himself as he did to Jubal. Down on hands and knees, sweeping along with open palms was no way to protect from sharp twigs and roots, but persistence dictated that the discomforts of such be continued.

"Let the line lay and come help me." Wes called to the boy.

Just as soon, Jubal was on hands and knees searching behind his mentor. "Just what it be that I be lookin' fer old man?"

"Iron stake about five er six inches outta the ground and ringed with rocks near about double fist size. Ought not be so hard findin' it."

"How long till daybreak ye reckon?" Jubal asked.

"Ain't gonna be soon. Night still early."

"We got time fer lookin' all around then ain't we?" Jubal said.

"Yeah, that a fact."

"Iffin we ain't found it soon, I thinkin' we ought rest up a bit more then look some more. I be tuckered right smartly now."

"Ain't no fireball myself," Wes answered "Why don't ye go see to the hosses and make sure they tied up good and then come back here where we been scratchin', and we bed down fer a spell. Not all night mind ye, but three or four hours anyhow. Rest a spell might be what we needs to change up our luck."

Jubal needed no further prodding. He made sure that the horses reins were tied securely and that they were tied so that they could not get tangled. He then returned to the edge of the cemetery where Wes had already spread out his oilcloth and was just then pulling his heavy blankets over himself.

Sleep soon would come to both of them despite the chill of the earth and the occasional stir of the winter wind. It was not a harsh night as far as winter nights go, but Jubal found himself thinking about the open fireplace back there in the old log cabin and how warm it could feel.

Wes was vaguely conscious of the sound of rustle in the leaves as he opened his eyes to discover a big red fox squirrel foraging just a few feet from his face. He just as quickly realized that dawn had already broken, and the first sun rays of morning were finding their way under the big timber and creeping into the undergrowth. They had slept much longer than they wanted.

"Wake up, son. We done slept the night through."

"Huh."

"It soon be good daylight, and we ought been done here and on our way back home. We best get movin' and be fast doin' it too. Ye go check on our hosses and give em a few more oats. That keep em quite fer a spell or so."

Jubal jumped up and headed off to see about the horses. Wes immediately turned his thoughts back to the search. He had made no more than a half dozen steps until he found what had eluded him in the darkness.

"Amazin' what bein' able to see can do fer ye," he said mainly to himself. "Thankful for the light this mornin' iffin I ever told it in my whole life."

There! Right before him was the iron stake he had driven in the ground way back years past. It stood out from the green moss and drab leaves. He dropped to his knees and began to brush aside the accumulation of years of rotted leaves and grass. This just had to be it.

He turned and retrieved the spade and stabbed it into the rich black earth. The spade hit something solid. He turned up the first spade full, and his heart raced with anticipation. Yes! Yes indeed! There was supposed to be rocks about six inches down. The next thrust also found a solid mark. More excitement and anticipation. Wes seemed frenzied with each new spade full and soon had dug a two-foot circle all around the iron stake. He grabbed the rusted metal and began to wrest it side to side. It resisted, but he overpowered it and pulled it free. Near onto two feet long, just the way it was supposed to be.

Jubal returned from checking on the horses and saw what was happening. "Have ye found it, old man?"

"I think so. Get yer young arse in here and help me dig."

"Tell me what ye want done, and I do it."

"We needs get this here ring dug outta here first. They just be in our way. Then we digs down a bit more. Iffin this be it, we gonna hit a flat sand rock be near on a hunnert pounds or so. Reckon it take us both tuggin' at it fer movin' it."

"Then what?" Jubal asked as he took the spade from Wes.

"All we needs is roll it up on one side," he responded as he began to pull the ringed stones, one at a time from the loose earth. The ground was cold and his hands hurt from the warmth being sucked right out of them. He took enough time to retrieve a piece of oil skin from his bedroll and wrapped it around his hands. He was just as soon back at the stones.

"Dig a little wider," he instructed.

The chill of the early morning took on less and less significance as the two worked feverishly at their task. Soon Jubal was out of his buckskin shirt and had broken a slight sweat.

"There! That's it! That be it!" Wes said excitedly.

"Be what?" Jubal parroted.

"That be the sand rock I done told ye about. All we needs do now is get it rolled up off there. Get down in here with me and see can we get hold on a edge and move it any. I ain't aimin' to dig plumb to Chiny."

Both plunged into the hole and soon had a ring cleared around the edge of the entire sand rock. Fingers curled around an edge and straining with all they could muster managed to barely loosen the flat covering. They sat in silence on the rim of the hole and sucked in the cold morning air. Jubal was back at the task before Wes had any chance to catch his wind. He was able to raise the unyielding burden another few inches. Several repeated efforts brought the obstruction to a vertical stance sufficient for Wes to investigate.

"Lean it on over against there where it won't fall on me," he instructed Jubal. I need the spade a bit now."

Wes got down in the hole and began to carefully shovel out the bottom of the cavity. "I needs make sure I don't break nothin' after we done come this far."

"What be there fer ye to break?"

"Crock. Two-gallon crock, and it be upside down.

"Upside down?" Jubal seemed confused.

"Yeah. I put it upside down so it make a water tight cover fer what be in it."

"That be yer gourd, I reckon," Jubal said questioningly.

Wes explained how he had first taken a gallon crock and poured the bottom about a third full of wax. Then he had taken the gold coins and put them into a leather purse string pouch and put them in the crock. Then he had filled the little crock complete to the brim with wax, thus sealing in the pouch and its contents. Then he had turned that crock upside down in the larger crock and filled it completely with wax and placed it in the soft earth, bottom side up. Thus the pouch was sealed all around. Hiding it in the ground under all those rocks would keep the critters away from it, and the big sand rock would hold it all in place.

"Dang, Wes. How long it take ye doin' all that?"

"Three days or better, I reckon. Weren't in no hurry like we be now."

Wes readily uncovered the crock bottom and raked away all the loose dirt. He soon had it ringed with careful thrusts of the spade. He ran his fingers into the loosened soil until he felt the rim of the interred vessel. Gentle rocking soon had it loose and out of its earthen vault. Wes seized it and handed it up to the wide-eyed boy.

"Careful now. Don't bust it yet."

"Is this here what we come fer?"

"It is, and now it be time fer us make our way outta here. Don't reckon we been spotted so fer. Grab up yer bedroll, and we be gone in a hurry."

"Ye wanna fill in yer hole?"

"Naw, ain't no need. All I want is outta here and back home."

Wes rolled the crock into his bedroll and tied it up securely. Jubal picked up the axe and the spade. They were just as quickly mounted up and headed back across the valley floor.

The upland pastures and meadows stretched away to the east as far as the young lad could see. Even though they rode high near the timberlines, the openness and abundance of the fertile valley beckoned to anyone who had never seen anything but the confines of the hills and hollows of a place like Cane Valley. There were homesteads all along the road below and many seemed to be abandoned. One ever now and again lofted grey smoke from a stone fireplace.

Some of the grasses had been pastures to herds of stock that had long since been confiscated by the Confederate army and later by the Union cavalry troops. Each side had deemed it a must to have control of the gap in order to command movements in and out of the Nashville area. But now, the land and its inhabitants, having been raped of all they had, feared for their safety and had abandoned the valley in masses.

"We best hit the timber and keep in it all the way back to the low gap. I think iffin we can make it that far we might be able to stop and rest a spell. But fer now we best keep on the move. I want outta this here valley soon as we can. Are ye up fer a hard ride?" Wes asked.

"I reckon ain't much other choice. Don't make no sense how such a peaceful lookin' place could be so mean."

"No peacefulness nowhere in time a war," Wes added as he reined his horse uphill and into the edge of the big timber. He was far enough in that it would be hard to spot them from the road below, but yet he could peer through the standing timber and get glimpses of the world below as they rode easterly. The low gap would be a welcome sight, and the sooner they reached it the better their chances of making it all the way home without any trouble. They would try to find the rock outcropping and rest there.

The sun had begun to fall into the western sky by the time they spotted the low gap. It seemed to take on a more subtle shape and appearance from the north side than it had coming from the southern slopes. Wes had to study it from a distance before he could be sure. They headed higher into the big timber after they had their landmarks, and soon the old man knew for sure that he was on the right path.

They had only enough grain left to give the horses one last little nibble. They had eaten most all of the hardtack, and the side meat reeked of grease now. Both were longing for one of Ma's good hot hog meat breakfasts. The sun would soon sink behind them, and darkness would descend quickly. Wes entertained the thoughts of kindling up a fire and frying what meat they had. Then he remembered that they had brought nothing with them in the order of a skillet or a pan. That really would not stop them because a piece of flat limestone would fry most anything when you got it hot enough. Smoke from the fire would be a dead give-away, but darkness would hide most of that. They would be at the outcropping in only three or four hours, and then they could make for home where they could have all the fires they wanted.

Once they reached the sheltering rocks, Wes dismounted and climbed topside of a huge boulder that afforded a good view to the south side. It was then that he saw what he had tried so hard to avoid. A Rebel patrol was approaching up the very same trail that he and the boy had traversed only a few hours past. The lead trooper had his eye to the ground and looked for sure to be reading all the tracks and signs that they had left.

"We got company comin' and comin' soon," he said as he reported back to Jubal. "We best just keep on a movin' if they don't cause us no trouble. Best ye let me do most of the speakin' fer us. I make up some kind of bear tale to put on em if need be."

"How many they be?"

"I count six, all mounted."

Wes had just remounted and reined his horse to the south when the first trooper crested the mountain. He jerked his reins instantly when he saw Wes and the boy and his right hand immediately went to his side arm. The other troopers were at his side in an instant. One sported sergeant stripes, big yellow chevrons on a grey sleeve that was about two inches too short.

"Who in hell are ye?" he bellowed gruffly.

"Wesley Rogerson," came the reply. "And my boy."

"What business ye got here?" the striped arm roared again.

"We just come from the Gap and be on our way back to Greeneville," Wes responded.

"State yer business."

"Courier service," Wes responded with as much authorities emphasis as he could.

"Who fer?"

"Gave my papers and payroll to Major George Clemons. I ain't fer sure who he serves under. He were who I spoke with."

"What outfit ye be with?"

"I ain't with no outfit. I just doin' what I can fer Tennessee and the nineteenth."

"They be in the Gap?" the sergeant questioned in a much more civil voice.

"They be north about thirty miles or so, Wes answered.

"How much payroll ye took em?"

"I never looked at it other than seein' it all be paper bills."

"Ours or they?" another trooper asked.

"Ye knows anything else about the nineteenth?" stripes asked.

"Not much, I reckon."

"Then how come ye doin' courier runs fer em?"

"Long standin' friend of the Clemons family. That and fact that I ain't beholdin' to no Yanks nowhere, no time," Wes declared hoping to sound emphatic in his remarks.

"I see."

"We be headed back to Greeneville area and see what need be there now," Wes said as he more or less concocted his story as he saw fit.

"Ye best be on yer toes. There be plenty Blue Bellies holdin' on to most all river fords and ferries twixt here and Greene County. Most roads south is cut," the sergeant informed.

"Reckon we stick to the hills like we been doin' all along. Man go a month unseen iffin he wanted to that way," Wes added.

"Know yer way 'round these parts do ye?"

"Mostly south and west of here."

"How far to the Gap?" stripes asked.

"Three days ride unless ye be in a heap hurry. Can be did in two, but be hard fer yer hosses, and ye yerself be whupped out that a way."

"Which way ye come?"

"Rode easy and stayed in the timber most times. Took longer than we thunk, and we be short on grub now. So I reckon we needs keep at it. Ain't no folk down yonder got anything they can give and reckon they wouldn't iffin they did. They been hit mite hard here abouts, and they ain't very fergivin' neither. Most done left out some time back."

"How come that?' another of the grey clad troopers asked.

"Been a hot bed last couple years, I reckon. Union try takin' this whole valley so they can cut the lines all way into Bristol, and our boys been taking raids on em and runnin' straight thru to Bristol with prisoners. Hear tell that they is sent straight to Andersonville from there," Wes added.

"Hell, we just come up outta there. Ain't no place fer no good trooper to be assigned. Any bungled idiot fit the bill fer a guard there. All ye needs do is shoot a Blue Belly ever day er so and nary a sole give a hoot nor a holler what else ye do. It ain't nothin' but a cess pool with pine poles fer walls."

"I heard of it, but I ain't never been there since this here war started," Wes added.

"Ye gonna stop over here fer a spell?" the sergeant asked.

"Reckon not. Like I say, we short a bit and best keep on the go."

"We ain't got much neither. Got a few strings of jerky. That about it."

"We run on a turnip patch this mornin' and had them raw. They was so dang strong they burnt us both all day. They be just this side that white church ye gonna see. Ye might find a few that the hogs ain't rooted out."

"Hogs?"

"Yeah. Hogs done got loose and run wild now. We never seen none but seen where they been," Jubal informed the party.

"Hope I sees one. I be eatin' ham tonight if I get him in my sights," stripes bragged.

"Ye gonna hold up here fer the night?" Wes asked.

"Might."

"Ain't much place else give ye any shelter on west of here. Ye could build a fire here and not be seen after dark," Wes added.

"Ye see any Bluecoats on west?"

"Naw, reckon not. But they be known fer bein' all up and down here, Wes replied as he began to rein his horse away from the inquirers.

"They be but six of us, so I reckon we stay in big timber too. We ain't runnin' from no stinkin' Yanks, but we wanna join up with our outfit too. Then we whup some Bluecoat arses big time."

"They be strength in numbers. That be a fact." Wes added as he urged his horse forward.

Nothing more was said, and Jubal followed close on the heels of his companion. They rode a good hour until darkness hid them from other prying eyes. The night seemed to pull at every ounce of purpose that Jubal could muster. He was cold. He was hungry, and he was so tired that he ached almost in every joint. Yet, Wes plodded on as if they were nearing home.

Jubal thought that it took a long time to come down off old Clinch and turn back east. Daylight would help him to know the lay of the land and to spot his landmarks. He had no reason to suspect that he would need to go it alone. It was just a thought that flashed before him, soon dismissed and forgotten.

The moon danced in and out of the clouds and cast its intermittent light into the valley as if offering a guide.

"Ye tuckered out?" Wes asked as he pulled up his mount.

"Yeah, I am."

"I think there be a barn about a mile on up here. Not likely we be spotted if we was to hold up there a few hours. I could use a rest myself."

"How far out we be now?" Jubal questioned.

"Ten or twelve hours or so, I reckon," Wes answered. "If we start at first light, I think we can pull in home not long after dusk."

"Who gonna wake us up?" Jubal questioned again.

"Won't need no wake up. Won't sleep that much anyhow. Be a bit much cold and damp. I know we both be tired, but we ain't in no soft bed neither. We be awake in plenty time. We half day's ride out, but I don't think I can sit this here horse another hour without some rest.'

"Me neither."

The barn had a center haul way and an overhanging hay loft. The stalls were from rough-hewn poplar logs without any chinking. They offered only minimal shelter from wind and cold. The loft was a different matter. There were no stock of any sort around. There was an abundance of sweet clover hay, theirs for the taking.

"Throw a bit down and feed them a bit," Wes instructed. "Not too much. They get the runs iffin they gets too much."

Jubal did as he was told. He knew how much feed to give a critter. He was just a bit agitated at being told everything to do step by step, but he let it slide for the time being. He was tired and chilled to the bone and hungry to boot. He could deal with the hunger for a while, but the cold was beginning to eat at him.

Wes untied his bedroll and began to climb the ladder into the hay loft. He carried the bedroll up with him but did not untie and unroll it. "Climb on up here and bury yourself up in this loose hay. Ye be warm in no time. I think we might just be safe here for long enough so we can make it on in home come light.

The boy needed no other prodding. He found a deep bank of hay and wormed himself into it up to his neck. He could feel the immediate warming as he was sealed off from the night air. Sleep soon would catch up to him. The curiosity about Wes and his money was now amplified even more. There was just so much that made no sense. He planned on answers and soon, but not now. He would talk it all out soon whether the old man liked it or not.

Nonetheless, they were not home yet, and there was that remaining leg of the trip to get behind them. No guarantees of that, and he well understood why Wes wanted to be unseen as much as he could. Sleep took control. The night chill no longer existed. The implied dangers melted away. There were not even any thoughts of faraway places. Voices ceased to speak to him. There were no more admonitions about the darkness, and there was no one calling his name. Right now, there was no such thing as war, and the whole of the world lay in magnificent peaceful silence. How could there be such stillness and such peace? Was this the peace that Julie had talked to him about?

Wes must have been even more exhausted than he had thought. Jubal was up and tending to the horses when he awoke. He too had burrowed himself deep into the sweetness and comfort of the hay bank and had been refreshed by it just the same as his younger companion.

Jubal heard him stir. "Best be up old man. Soon be light. Best be on our way."

"Right ye are."

550

Wes felt a great deal safer now that they were back into the valley and on the south side of the mountain. The folks here about were not near so bitter and so quick to pass everyone off. There had been far less hostile encounters on this side of the mountains, and the war was more distant among these upland farmers and their families. Still, there was reason for caution.

A few hours rest had made a difference in tolerances to the saddle, but it had done nothing to alleviate the emptiness in the pit of the stomach. It was only a matter of a dozen or so hours out now, but that was a long time especially since it had now been days since either had known the simple joy of a hot meal.

Wes had taken the lead as usual, and Jubal had no problems with that. They had taken to the higher ground and were just inside the timberline, yet able to see into the valley below. The curl of gray chimney smoke rose high into the still morning air, and it could be seen long before the little farmstead house came into view. Another few minutes ride had them looking down on a picturesque farm with a small frame house sporting a stick-and-mud chinked chimney, one small barn and a couple other small out buildings. The early morning fire most likely was a cook stove fire and that would mean hot breakfast.

"How hungry ye be?" Wes asked.

"Reckon I be like a last triplet waitin' my turn."

"I got a few loose coins here. I think we might find us a bite or two down yonder. Ye wanna go see?"

"I do indeed," Jubal responded with awakened interest.

Wes reigned his horse to the left, and they made good time in reaching the shanty. After a short ride toward the house, Wes noted a white-haired old man step out to the side yard looking up in their direction. He had heard them or seen them coming and was not about to be taken unaware. He had a long rifle draped across his forearm, and the left hand rested on the hilt of a huge knife.

"Mornin' to ye sir," Wes said as he pulled to a stop at the yard gate. The house was surrounded by a semblance of a split-paling fence that had long since been in need of repair.

"What ye want?"

Wes eyed the man about as intently as he was being eyed. The man was old with signs of many a day's exposure to wind and weather. Snow white unkempt hair, shabby rags for clothing and a face that could easily be that of a slave girl's child sired by a white landholder. Wes dismissed the appearance as insignificant because he immediately saw an image of himself that was not too far removed from this very day. "We be hungry, bad hungry."

"Ye don't look to me like ye even missed yer supper last night."

"We would be grateful for anything. Just a biscuit if ye can spare it. We can pay ye fer whatever ye can spare."

"Money ain't worth spit here. No place fer it. No place fer trade. No panhandlers ner nuthin' here abouts no more."

"I got real money, not the worthless paper stuff. I got a silver dollar iffin ye can feed us a bit. That be all we wants. Then we be on our way and ye never see us no more," Wes added.

"Pitch it here. I wanna see it first."

Wes dug in his belt and retrieved a silver dollar, leaned down to hand it to the aged character. The old man moved not one muscle but stared intently at Wes.

"I said, pitch it here!"

Wes did as he was told. The coin was seized upon and inspected as if it were a king's ransom. Bony fingers turned it over and over. It was held up to the pale morning light and turned again. Jubal thought that there was just a trace of a grin creeping across the ancient wrinkled face.

"Wait thar. Keep yer arse glued in them saddles." The old cuss turned and disappeared into the shanty. Jubal thought that he could sense a faint smell of fatback or side meat. The smoke continued to rise from the old stick chimney. Someone must have just thrown on a new stick because the smoke blackened just as it rose into the cool morning mist.

"Smell that?" Jubal asked.

"Yeah. Hope he be fetchin' us whatever that is. Makin' my tongue slap my mouth plumb outta shape. Hope he ain't long. We still got us a fer piece to go yet. Time be valuable iffin we ain't wantin' spend another night out in this here weather."

"I be thinkin' I can ride a long way iffin I gets myself fed good," Jubal said.

The oldster soon reappeared on the porch followed by a black slave gal who eyed them as intently as had the old man. He carried a small sack held tightly around the top. He still had the long rifle cradled across his forearm. He stepped down off the porch and made his way near the gate.

"Ye got any more them dollars on ye?"

"No dollars, just a few smaller coins," Wes answered

"Pitch em here," he said pointing to the ground in front of him.

Wes dug into his belt and retrieved three more coins without even looking to see what they were. He knew them to be of little value by comparison to the silver dollar. "There, they be it. That all I got."

The man looked down at them quickly and then his eyes bored into Wes like a hot poker. "Ye see that there step stone yonder?" He pointed to the large squared off stone about fifty yards or so to the east.

"Yeah, I see it."

"Ye two ride past it till I says stop."

"Then what?" Wes questioned.

"They be six biscuits and meat in this here poke. I put it thar. Ye can fetch it, and then ye best be gone."

"That what we aim on doin' fast as we can."

"Then ride."

Wes and the boy rode east a few yards past the step stone and reined up their horses. The hoary headed old man put the sack on the stone then backed away slowly to his yard gate.

"Go get it," Wes instructed.

Jubal did as he was told and snatched the parcel from its rest without missing a stride. Just as quickly, he was back by his mentor's side. They both spurred their beasts into a gallop easterly down the valley. Soon they slowed enough to investigate the sack.

Wes reached into the sack as Jubal held it out to him and withdrew a biscuit so thin and hard that it more resembled a wafer. Jubal drew one much the same except that it held some shreds of dark meat that had no lacking of grease and fat. He spent no time in looking at it, but rather sank his teeth into it with abandon. The bread was hard; but it was bread after all, and he was hungry.

"Reckon this here be the bread of life that Granny Iverson speak on sometimes. Never knowed it taste so salty," Jubal said.

"I think not, son."

"What this meat be? Ain't seen none this black but what ain't been burnt."

"Taste it," Wes replied while he chewed on his so-called biscuit.

"It be a mite stout. What ye reckon it be?"

"It ain't hog, Wes said.

The horses were slowed to a walk. Few words were spoken as the two consumed their new-found sustenance. Wes knew what it was all about. The bread had been made with stone ground flour and little or no lard, probably just grease drippings and obviously plenty of salt. There was sure to be nothing other than that in the entire stores of the skiddish old man and his woman. They had nothing any better for themselves and were doing best they could.

Hard to realize how just being on one side of a mountain or the other could make such a difference. Here the war was evil and real to the valley. On the south slopes, the conflict seemed to be more of a horrible apparition than a reality. The steep ridges and the deep hollows did afford some protection. That isolation was very important to Wes and to his now thickened bedroll.

The sun was making its climb into the morning sky, and the chill of the night was falling away. Jubal had eaten his share of the salty grub and now began to think about water. There was a stream all along the valley floor, and he could drink about any time he wished. He would wait until Wes began to thirst. He was not so hungry anymore, and the few hours' sleep had helped. He had never set a horse this much in his entire life, and he was now feeling it in every bone and joint in his young body. In a way, he felt sorry for old Wes, because he must feel even worse being so old and such. No credit was given him for being toughened by years.

Poor Valley seemed to be at peace with the world in spite of the war. Martial law had been declared over much of the area by first one side and then the other, both claiming jurisdiction. Local officials were token positions at best, and they attempted to exert little to no influence on their constituents. Most law enforcement was primarily for the protection of the locals. For the most part, there were no issues to contend with. Some local thievery was about all that had ever been reported around here and that had been even less on the south side of the last lone ridge that Wes and Jubal had in front of them.

The sun had been out a good while during the morning and had warmed the air. It did nothing, however, to relieve the saddle weariness that beset both of the travelers. The afternoon was far enough along that the sun, what there was left of it, was now to their back. Wind had picked up a bit and the clouds were coming in from the east. Not a good omen.

"Fear it turn nasty on us here in a bit. See all them low hangers and how dark they be?" Wes asked as he pointed off into the eastern sky.

"Yeah, I see em. Reckon we be in a bad spell here soon. I been watchin' them clouds past hour, and they looks mad to me."

"Ain't cold 'nuff fer snow. Might be easier on us iffin it was," Wes commented.

"I ain't hankerin' one single bit fer bein' wet and cold no more. I wanna be home and put down roots in front of the fireplace." Jubal barked. "How fer ye reckon we be from home now?"

"Six hours be my guess. Weather be on us long time 'fore then."

"Reckon we ought look fer another old barn or such? We could hold up till the rain passed over."

"Might come down all night," Wes added.

"Don't think so. Look how fast them clouds is. It blow itself out in no time."

"Ye hope that anyhow, ain't ye?"

"Yes indeed, I am," Jubal added.

"Well, me too. We try holdin' up some place, but we ought keep movin' till we either finds a good place or it commences comin' down on us. We still got a half hour or so, I reckon."

"Ye got any biscuit bread left or ye done eat it all," Jubal asked.

"I got a piece or two left."

"Still ain't decided what that meat were. A mite strong iffin ye ask me."

"Might be best ye don't know," Wes informed him.

"Ye know, don't ye?"

"Thinkin' I do."

"What it be?"

"Most likely it be a night critter."

"Thought so."

They continued to ride, and the clouds continued to roll and boil as if mad at the entire universe. An Easterner was in the makings and that could spell nothing but bad times for any man or beast caught out in its full fury. Both spotted the ramshackle old barn just about the same time. It appeared that it had weathered numerous storms so much so that it showed signs of age and decay. The red oak shingles on its roof could do no more than filter the rainfall. The ones still in place were covered with greenish moss and probably struggled under the accumulation of all the ash leaf fall. Naked and leafless poison vine crawled all over the west end and only one door hung to its post. It was all there was in sight, and it was for the present a welcome sight.

"Look like we done found us a place fer a bit," Jubal said as he pointed to the run-down structure.

"Yeah, I reckon so."

The first few drops of cold rain were falling when they rode into the haul way and dismounted. It was noticeably colder than it was when the sun was poking through.

"This could turn out bein' one of them old deep wet snows. I hope it ain't, but it won't much matter cause iffin it commences in a snowin' we can make it on in home without it bein' so deep. We just got a few more hours yet. We gonna be okay after all, I do believe, "Wes said.

"I don't see no hay ner nuthin' fer them," Jubal said as he looked around the inside of the structure.

"Don't look like they been much a nuthin' in here in a good while. Ye got any feed left fer them?" Wes asked.

"Maybe a handful fer each. That be all."

"Gimme half here in my hand. Ye take rest of it in yer hand and hand feed it to yours. No tellin' what been on the ground and such here, and ain't no need takin' a chance on no black mouth bugs ner worms. We water them later," Wes instructed.

"Reckon I ain't never seen a critter with black mouth."

"Ye don't want to neither. May as well shoot em and end their sufferin' early on," Wes said as he ran his hand back and forth across his bedroll. Yes, all was in order and the stone crock was still very much secure and all snuggled up in the blankets and oilcloth.

"Rain pickin' up a mite," Jubal said as much to himself as to his companion. At least it wasn't running down his back right now, and he was grateful for that. The thoughts of being this close to home seemed good, and he was encouraged by that. It was a good thing to be out of the saddle for a bit though. He just knew that Ma could help get over being so sore with her biscuits and side meat.

"Old man, how long ye reckon we needs be hold up here?"

"Can't say now. Rain and such tells us that by dark, I reckon, iffin we stays here that long. Just can't say right now."

"I don't see much use in spendin' another whole night out here bein' we this close in. I think we ought hit out by dusk at least."

"That about what I be thinkin' too. Most likely no moon tonight, so it be pitch dark. We will needs be a bit slower, but I reckon we ain't got no other choice. If we beds down here we might wake up and be knee deep in white stuff. If it gonna come a big snow tonight, I reckon we be out in parts of it but ever step will get us closer in home."

"We can make it. Hosses can see good at night," Jubal said.

"Yeah, but we still needs one more landmark."

"What that be?"

"We needs the gap in old Pine. Don't wanna go east too far," Wes explained.

"Riders comin' yonder," Jubal said as he pointed out the end of the open haul way.

"Where?" Wes questioned as he wheeled around to face the indicated direction.

Sure enough, a couple hundred yards down the road were eight or more riders, and they were coming straight on. All had on rain gear and looked all alike. Could be nothing but a Union patrol. But why would they be here where they had not been known to patrol for some time now?

"What we do now, Wes?"

"Reckon we stay put. We ain't got no time fer runnin' right now. Most like they done spotted us anyhow. They might ride on by. We just wait, see what happens."

It became obvious that the troopers were indeed Union. The blue and the gold trim stood out even with the overcast sky and the drizzling rain. They did not ride on by, but pulled up directly to the east end of the barn. Two of them dismounted and strode directly up to Wes and Jubal. Both had a hand on a side arm, but did not appear to be edgy about it.

"I am Lieutenant Long and this is my sergeant. I need to know who you are and where you are headed, please."

"I be Wesley Rogerson, and this is my boy."

"State your business here please," the young officer replied.

"We been out near the gap checkin' on kin. We headed back home now."

"And where is that please, sir?"

"Up near head of Cane Valley, up a spur holler."

"How long have you been away from there?"

"Four days I reckon, ain't it, son?" Wes answered as he glanced around at Jubal.

"I assume that you plan to return there tomorrow."

"Actual, we plan bein' on in home around midnight tonight. Ain't about to get caught out in no big snow."

"It is only rain at present, sir."

"I know that, but I done seen too many a big dumpin' come outta clouds like these here ones. Won't be no good iffin it happens neither."

"Yes, well, have you seen any other riders today?"

"Yeah, we seen a Reb patrol topside the mountain. They was six of em, and they said they had come from Andersonville, where ever that be."

"Did you learn where they were heading?"

"Said they aimed to join up with the nineteenth Tennessee."

The officer turned to his sergeant. Have the men dismount and come in out of the weather. Detail one to secure the horses and see if we can get a small fire going. There is no need of pursuing them any more since they are headed into a confederate stronghold. We are only a dozen, and I do not intend to be foolish in my chase."

He turned to Wes. "Excuse me for a moment. We will soon have a fire, and I can offer you hot coffee and perhaps a bit more. I will then tell you why we are here. I must see that my men are afforded all that I can provide. I will not be long." With that, the two of them exited the haul way and were about their business. It was only a short time until a fire was ablaze and coffee aroma drifted into the barn.

The Union lieutenant was good on his word and soon offered Wes and Jubal a steaming cup of brew. Both received it thankfully and began to savor it with enthusiasm. Jubal was not really that keen on coffee, although he had enjoyed it on occasion with C.C. back at the mill. This cup, however, was a treat. It was warm, and it offered him a measure of revitalization. Wes commented about the brew to the lieutenant and thanked him repeatedly for his consideration. Soon the entire patrol sought shelter in the haul way and each found his own place for rest. The cold rain had taken its toll on them all, but the barn shelter and the warm brew improved the lot of them.

Wes, as well as Jubal, was quite anxious to hear any news from home but did not push the matter. The officer had said that he would tell them what he knew; and he must have questions for them as well, but he seemed to be in no rush. Wes had learned long ago the merits of patience.

"We have ridden all the way from the ferry on the Holston and have not seen what we wanted at any time. Possibly you can enlighten us a bit," the officer said as he sipped at the coffee. "Tell me more about what you saw atop the mountain."

"I will do best I can," Wes responded. "What might ye want?"

"Martial law is in place all up and down the valley now, because Rebs and their associations have been rampaging the ferry area. They have spread into more remote areas and have been taking just whatever they want. They have no respect for individuals or property whatsoever. We have been on the trail of a party of at least six Confederate soldiers and three or four of their companions."

"Was one of them a striper?" Wes asked.

"If you mean a sergeant, then yes," the lieutenant answered.

"Thinkin' we seen them back yonder when we crossed top of Clinch. They was just the six of em and weren't no others with them."

"I doubt that they really had come up from Andersonville since they were seeking the nineteenth. The nineteenth has never had anything to do with Andersonville or much of anything else as far as that is concerned."

"What they done then?"

"They came down from southwest Virginia somewhere and raised a ruckus all down the river and then north into the Clinch area; and as they related to you, they are obviously headed to the Gap area. They pilfered and took whatever they could lay hands on most all the way down. That is until they tried holding up a miller man and his family."

That perked up Jubal to the point that he could not hold back any longer. "Where that mill be, and what was it they done there?" he asked point blank.

The lieutenant took a long pull on his tin ration mug and swallowed hard. "They tried to take something away from the miller, and he and his girl shot them up pretty bad the way they told it to me. Said the girl never missed a shot. Winged two of the troopers and shot two of the others as well. Defended themselves right well."

"Was they hurt any?"

"One of the other men whacked the miller man right smartly. He took a gash to the head and was laid up a day or so, but I think he might be good as new in a few days. The girl had her dress near torn off her, but I doubt she was hurt. She never said anything about any injury although she was sporting a big bruise on her cheek."

"Did they tell ye what them men looked like?" Jubal questioned.

"Well, yes. They did. Seems one was a bigger man with a full-face beard and buckskin for a coat. The other was short and had a hat pulled down low so as to hide his face. Said the third man stayed back a distance and hung onto the horses and kept a lookout down the road. The miller man said that he thought they had been around that area before and that he might know who one of them was."

Wes knew what the boy was thinking and made no effort to restrain him. "Tell all ye know, son." Wes encouraged.

"I know who one of them men is, and I bet I know where ye can find him."

"Oh, well...tell me please," the lieutenant remarked, somewhat surprised.

"That sorry so and so be my Pa, and I bet I could find him in a week's time. I know where he hides out, and I know where he goes when he runs outta laudanum. He be no good fer me ner no one else way I see it."

"Do you really think you could find him?"

"Damn right, I could and would be proud doin' it too."

"Can I ask ye one question, sir?" Wes inquired.

"Yes, by all means," came the officer's reply.

"Where be this here mill that ye speak of?"

"It is on Cane Creek very close to the road that heads east to the river or west on into French Broad country."

"Then we be speakin' on the same mill," Wes replied.

"Miller man name be Johnson," Jubal interjected as he finished his cup and stood to stretch his legs a bit. "He be a friend to me. Any bastard what hurt him be answerin' to me, iffin I find him."

"Would you actually turn in your own father?"

"He be my Pa only cause I come outta his seed and that not be somethin' I be proud of. He ain't my Pa nary bit, and I ain't proud sayin' that. I don't claim him in no way. I done seen too much first-hand what he done. And his thiefin' bastard buddies ain't no better."

"Ye said they was shot," Wes added.

"Yes, but not too bad, I suppose. They were able to get away after they put down the miller man. Gave him a good blow to the head and may have broken his leg in doing so. I do not really know exact details," the lieutenant offered. "Where do you think your father and his friends might be now. Would they try to see a doctor somewhere?"

"Not likely," Jubal said. "They just hold up somewhere and stay low till they have a chance to heal up a bit. They ain't gonna look fer no doctorin' only if they was gut shot or such. Serve em right iffin they bled out."

"Where would they hold up as you say?"

"They be plenty caves and thickets they can use fer cover iffin they stays in the valley, but I reckon they most likely head to the doubles and hide out there a while. That be what I would do," Jubal added.

"You might be of value in searching them out once we start back to the ferry. Would you two be agreeable to guide us for a day or so when we come back that way?"

"Could be, I reckon," Jubal answered. Yes, he could do it if he had the chance. And yes, he would like to get that chance. Otherwise, he tried to imagine what exactly had befallen C.C. and the rest of his family, especially Lida. Thinking about her and her daddy stirred other emotions in him, but also kindled the hatred and embitterment that boiled inside him.

The boy walked over to Wes and laid a hand on his shoulder, "I think we ought get started and get on home. It ain't puttin' down no snow right now, and it may not after all. Iffin it do, then we be most way home by time it deeps up any."

"Ye might be right there, son. How saddle sore are ye right now?"

"I be okay. It ain't good, but I can make it on home. I can walk from here iffin I needs to, I reckon," Jubal answered as he looked Wes square eye to eye.

Wes could read the determination on his face and could see beyond that to the concern for Lida and her daddy. It would not be any benefit to delay his passions any longer.

"We can start out about any time ye wants," Wes said. "When will ye be back that way Lieutenant?"

"Probably in three days. We have orders to ride on west to reconnoiter a bit. Then we will return to the ferry."

"Ye can find us by askin' at the mill, iffin ye want," Wes said. "One of us most likely be there next few days."

"I be there," Jubal said emphatically.

"I will report in by courier in a day or so and will act according to any new orders that I am given, but I anticipate that I will be expected to report back to the ferry as soon as our present assignment is completed. We may be granted a day to look for the culprits since it is obvious now that we cannot chase and catch the Confederate detail. I will not enter the Gap area unless ordered to do so or engaged by the enemy. I will make it a point to stop in at the mill as we return. I am thinking that would be a good place to have my courier meet us upon return. Do you think that would be an issue for the miller and his family? I do not want to cause any issues there."

"I thinkin' that there would be no cause fer trouble by that," Wes said. "Ye agree, son?"

"Reckon so," Jubal answered.

"Then that is how it will be. I will stop there, and then we will determine what, if anything, needs to be done."

Wes stood and offered his hand to the Union officer. "I thank ye fer the coffee and yer hospitality. Most folks around here never seen a real gentleman, but I been around enough to know one when I see one, and I think ye fit the bill very well."

"Then I assume that you and your boy are about to start for home."

"You are correct, sir," Wes answered.

"Are there any concerns that you have at present?" the lieutenant asked.

"Which way did you take gettin' here?" Wes wanted to know.

"Tell him if you will, sergeant."

"Yes sir," he replied as he stood and turned to face Wes and Jubal. "I studied the maps best that we have, and we left the mill and headed west until we came to the first road north. We took that until we crossed over into the valley and then headed west again. We stayed in this valley all the time till we met you two."

They had come basically the same route that he and Jubal would take the rest of the way home except they would head east across the flats before reaching the main east-west road. That would be taking a long way home and would add another two or three hours to the trek.

"Did ye see any other riders between here and the mill?" Wes wanted to know.

"No sir. It was just forsook all the way. Reckon the weather be a bit too nasty to be out in unless it be absolutely necessary."

"Can't argue that," Wes added. "I reckon we will head on out now. Reckon you stay here until mornin' comes? I would in yer place, but we needs get home even more so now, and we ain't stuck out here so far away from home like ye is. Where ye from anyhow, lieutenant?"

"I and my men are all from New York."

"Well, there must be a bunch a gentlemen up there. I wish I had time to talk with ye a bunch more, but I don't. So I reckon we will be leavin' out. I look forward to seein' ye at the mill in a few days. Remember that my name is Wes, and this here is Jubal. Ask fer us by name when ye gets there."

"I will, sir."

The last remnants of gray light were sinking deep into the western sky when the two mounted up and rode out of the haul way into the elements. The cold rain continued at about the same rate. If it did turn cold enough to make snow later, it would take many hours to build up any accumulation. Wes was somewhat relieved to note that the rain had not increased and that the last leg of the trek might not be as tiresome as once thought. He swung his right arm behind his back to feel his bedroll. Yes, it was still there. He still had the future of those now near and dear to him secure. He would not allow himself to chase dreams or build hope for now. The matter at hand was now to get home and get there safe and sound.

Wes pulled up and stopped after about half an hour's ride. He put a finger to his lips as if to signal to Jubal to listen. There were no sounds to be heard save for the regular and rhythmic breath of the horses, the occasional shifting of a hoof in the rain softened earth. It would be good if the snow would hold off a bit more. Tracking would be no task at all in new fallen snow, but in soden ground, the rain would hide their tracks in just a few hours.

Wes plodded on without much to say. Jubal could tell that he was tired. Both were pushing the limits of their endurance, but it made no sense to spend any more time out in the weather when home was so near. They had only to follow the creek upstream and that would lead them to the place where they would turn south for the last time and ride across one more ridge into familiar territory. The inky darkness parented by the low-hanging, moisture-laden clouds made the landscape hard to distinguish. Nonetheless, once they crossed Pine, they could find their way even if there was no moon. The rain had all but ceased, and the wind was picking up. They could still be caught out in a chiller, but every step that the horses made put them just a bit nearer to home.

The creek diminished in volume as they followed it upstream. Wes knew by the lack of volume that they had to be close to the road that would lead them to the junction. They would take that road and cut off up to the flats and on across the north hill to home. They just had to be sure they did not head too far east and miss their road.

Luck would have it that they did see well enough to sense the low point and could tell the creek had headed off in that direction as well. It was just about two hours from home. Rain had stopped altogether now, and the night chill was taking a sharper bite. Nostrils flared with each breath that the horses drew, and the exhaled moisture took on the semblance of a maddened and raging beast who could breathe fire at will. They were showing the strain of the night as well as their riders.

"We be on the flats now ain't we, boy?"

"Yeah, I know pine blank where we be now."

"Then ye take the lead. Ye knows this here ground better 'n me."

The old north hill looked mighty good even in the darkness. Jubal thought he could catch just a whiff of wood smoke. The wind was coming right. They would soon know. Down off the hill and into the lane leading up to the woodshed, they saw it. Ma must have sensed where they were. There was a light in the window. They were home.

Chapter 16

Revealing

*B*reakfast was special. Ma had fried up a plate of back strap and made a big bowl of thick hot gravy. Julie had made a pan of big cathead biscuits and even Granny Iverson had added to the feast with a fresh morning-made round of apple dumplings. Sure did a body a lot more pleasure than cold jerky and hardtack.

Jubal was anxious to get going. He had seethed ever since the lieutenant had reported the mill being pilfered, and the miller man being injured. He had wanted to ride straight on to the mill last night, but Wes had convinced him that it might be a good way to get shot. None of the Johnsons would be expecting a visit at that hour of the night and would certainly have their guard up. But it was light now, much later than he had intended. He was reconciled to the fact that Wes had been right about waiting until this morning.

Wes had filled Ma and all the others in on what they had learned back there in the old barn. Ma and Granny Iverson were somewhat surprised to learn of the misfortune at the mill, because they had seen no one or heard nothing about it.

"I be headed down to the mill, Ma. There be somethin' ye wants me say or do fer ye or take somethin' fer ye?"

"No, I reckon not now. Ye just gets yerself back here and let us know what be needed there iffin we can be of any help. They done help us plenty, and I be obliged to them all. I be pleased doin' like-wise fer them."

"Ye want me go too?" Wes asked.

"Might be good iffin ye did," Jubal answered. He did not really know what to expect when he got there, and he had learned that the old man was pretty wise in things when it came to dealing with people. He always seemed to know what he was doing and how to talk to others.

"Well, we best get saddled up again and git on our way. We ought be there in little better than an hour."

"What about yer bedroll? Jubal asked.

"We deal on that later on," Wes answered. "It be safe fer now."

"When will ye come back here?" Julie wanted to know.

"Can't speak fer him, but I wanna be back here by dusk at latest," Wes said. "Jubal might need stay a night or so. We just need see what be goin' on once we gets there. See how C.C. and Mrs. Johnson be and all."

"Ye up fer more saddle time old man?" Jubal asked sarcastically.

"I reckon I can ride yer arse off any day," Wes stabbed back.

"Do whatever ye needs do, and I go saddle and bring up both. Best ye be ready in three shakes cause that all it take me," Jubal said as he made for the kitchen door slowing long enough to pocket two more biscuits and another cut of back strap. He had some more catching up to do on Ma's cooking.

He tried to imagine what might greet him as he approached the mill. Would it be ravaged and torn to bits, or would the damage and the hurt be mostly unseen? Could they recover, or would this mark the end of a chapter in all their lives? How would he react to what he did find when he got there? So many uncertainties. Sure, he was going to be upset over whatever had been done to any of them and would want a pay back. No telling what they needed or would want in such a time as this. He would do whatever he could to see that this wrong was paid in full.

The sun was up fair and much of the frost had been driven away, save for the shadows and the north ground. Gray smoke from both the main house and the kitchen chimneys clawed its way up through the cold winter air and disappeared into the clear blue above. The smell of split red oak fire was all that lingered outside and that carried all the way to the end of the lane. There Jubal and his mentor dismounted and tied their horses to the top rail. They could not know that this was the exact location where the six Rebel soldiers had stood and watched the encounter. They would learn more details later.

It was less than fifty yards to the mill, and the house was just beyond that. They would need to announce themselves before approaching much more.

"Hello in the house," Wes called out. They continued although a bit slower and even more cautious.

Lida cracked the front door just a bit and then realized who it was. She stepped on out in full view and immediately invited the guests inside. Jubal could not help noticing the seemingly extra-large side arm griped so tightly by the small and delicate milk white hand. The reasons for such caution were obvious, and she was wise to be alert.

"Come in; it be too cold out here. Come in to the fire." She held the door ajar and motioned them in with the business end of the hand gun.

Jubal stepped up on the porch and looked directly into her eyes and said with genuine concern and compassion that he was sorry that this had happened and that he would do whatever he could to help them. He could see the worry and the hurt in her eyes. He saw the bruise under her right eye and the swelling in her cheek. He reached out his hand and as gentle as a feather on a summer breeze, touched her cheek with the tips of his fingers.

"Who hurt ye, Lida?"

"We talk on it later. Just get ye inside right now, please. There be plenty that I want ye to know about, and we will have our time sometime later on. Just be patient right now. That be all I ask fer now."

"I do whatever ye needs," he replied compassionately.

Mrs. Johnson stood before the open fire in the living room and unconsciously wrung her hands back and forth. She was very concerned about her husband and did not attempt to cover up her worries. "They hit him really hard a couple a times, and he fell hard. Lida saved us all. I know she did. But she near fell apart once it were all over."

"It were awful," Lida added.

"Did ye see faces 'nuff to tell em again iffin need be?" Jubal asked.

"Daddy did. He said he thought he knowed one of them and maybe another as well. He told ye that too didn't' he, Momma?"

"Yes. Yes, he did indeed, and I be wishin' he never told me."

"How come that?" Jubal asked thinking that he already knew the answer.

"I hate to be the one tellin' ye Jubal, but reckon the truth best be told no matter what. C.C. done told me that one of them three was your Pa most sure, and the big bearded one was the one up yonder on the balds the day Julie got hurt. I don't know iffin they come back here this time fer revenge on us or iffin they was just aimin' on pilferin' whatever they could carry off. They was a tryin' to rob C.C., and he fit em off best he could. He was hollerin' fer Lida when they knocked him in his head. That were when she commenced to shoot. That put em on the run, but she knocked one of em down. I seen him go down and seen the others hoss him up and run with him. The chicken arse Rebs run then too, but they was all mounted. I know ye ain't got much use fer your Pa, and I must say that I ain't neither, least not now."

"He ain't no Pa of mine far as I be concerned. He sorry as they come now, I reckon. I just sorry all this done fell in yer faces. How is Mr. Johnson anyhow?"

Lida slipped her hand inside Jubal's arm and drew him near to her side. "Come and see him yerself." She guided him into an adjoining room that had a narrow bed and a table beside it. A large oil lamp burned brightly and cast a golden glow over the face of the man lying there. A large blood-stained bandage covered a good portion of his forehead and temple. His eyes were closed, but his respirations were regular and unlabored. The dark bruises under his eyes bore evidence to the severity of the licks that he had been dealt. His hands lay still across his chest. The right hand was bandaged. He had tried to shield himself from the blows as best he could.

"How bad is he hurt?" Jubal asked.

"We don't really know yet. Think his right wrist be busted up some, and he be talkin' one time and then be passed out some like he be now. Says he hurts bad when he be awake. Worries me. Worries Momma too."

"Concerns me too," Jubal said as he slipped his arm around her waist. "What can I do to help ye?"

"I don't know right now, Jubal. I just wish we could be someplace alone fer just a bit. I think it would help me a bunch just to get it all cried outta me, but I can't do that right now. I gotta hold up fer Momma and fer Daddy too. They both needs me now, and I aim to be there best I know how."

"That be what ye should do and that be just how ye should feel too." He pulled her a bit tighter to his side. She did not resist.

C.C. opened his eyes and asked for a sip of water. Lida gave him water by dipping the corner of a linen towel in the pitcher and touching it to his lips. The miller man pulled on the towel until the dryness of his mouth had been chased away. He lightly stroked his parched lips with the back of his left hand and was just as quickly back to sleep.

Lida nor Jubal had noticed that Wes and Mrs. Johnson had come into the little room, until Wes spoke.

"Looks like he took a right smart lick. He be bruised up some."

"He's been hurt bad, I fear. I be much concerned over him," Mrs. Johnson said as she began once more to wring her hands in despair.

"How has he been takin' it so far. Can he speak good or do he make any sense? I would think a whack like that would addled him a bunch, Wes said.

"Reckon ye ought know," Jubal said. "Ye done took a whack or two yerself, best I recall."

"Yeah, but I never had my head split plum open like he must' a had."

"They hit him with a rifle butt. Reckon they never had it loaded or he could a been shot instead. Lida said that they never got off nary round, but I thinkin' maybe they did. She lit in on them like a duck on a June bug. All so quick and all they must a been took really off guard. I was in the kitchen. By time I come out, it was done nigh done. They was runnin' heap fast. I saw them mostly draggin' the one what Lida said whacked her Daddy. That riled her and she took it to them. Emptied that there pistol," Mrs. Johnson explained. She had hardly slept since her husband was hurt, and the absence of rest only amplified itself in her eyes. Eyes that were tired for reason, and eyes dried out from the tears.

Jubal said nothing. His eyes said all that needed to be spoken. Intense hatred fueled a fire inside him, and he knew that there was only one way in which that fire could be quenched. He just secretly hoped that fate would not deny him opportunity for vengeance.

Lida took his arm and began to pull him aside. "Come outside with me a bit. It be too hot in here right now. A few quick steps put them on the front porch. The morning chill had eased just a bit, but still had a bite to it. Snow crusts still covered the sheltered patches of the yard and the lane. The sky was brilliant blue, but it was winter time. It was January cold.

"Scares me some the way ye looked in there, Jubal. I could tell that ye was upset some over yer Pa and all.

"I ain't as upset as ye might think. I just hate he done picked you and yer Daddy to prove what I already knowed all along. This just be what done put me over the edge with him. I was in hope that it were him got shot and kilt back there back in the doubles, but it weren't. Now he done showed up here causin' more ruckus on good folks who ain't never done him cross."

"I'm sorry I shot him," Lida repeated.

"I ain't," Jubal echoed back. Iffin he be hurt bad then he needs be laid up somewhere and that ought make him a heap easier huntin' down."

"Ye ain't aim to do that are ye?"

"Not today."

"Please don't carry on talk like that, please."

"Well, what ye have me do then, not say nothin' more on it?"

"That be it, and not do nothin' on it neither."

"I ain't gonna make no promises," Jubal said.

"What would yer Ma think, Jubal? How would she feel?"

A bolt of lightning could not have had more pronounced effect on the young lad than did Lida's searing question. He had never considered that his Pa, evil as he may be, was her man and that in spite of all that he had done and all the heartache that he had caused, she might just possibly hold some feeling for him. But how could she now after all he had put her through?

Lida had stolen some of his fire and thunder, and it showed in his face immediately. "I never give her nary a thought in it all. Reckon she feel nigh same as me and rightly so."

"But ye don't know that fer a fact," she insisted. "She ever say anything make ye know how she feel?"

"No...not as I recollect, but I done seen her broke down a time or two."

"Did ye ask her what it were all about?"

"No."

"Did she tell ye what it were?"

"No."

"Then ye can't know plum pine blank how she feels. Just ain't no way."

She paused a few moments to try and let it soak in for him. She could see the torment all over his face. Could there be no justice in his way? The care and compassion for his Ma was the salve that cooled the fiery ache in his heart. Granny Iverson had once read him about an eye for an eye. Vengeance is mine. He had heard that read before.

"But woman, I know where he be hold up iffin ye done winged him, and I thinkin' it be my place go lookin' fer him. Mind ye I ain't said nary time that I lookin' to shoot his sorry arse. Just ye bear that in mind on account I ain't ready fer ye to preach me down over such. Not right now anyhow."

She knew that she had touched to the quick because he had never called her woman. She hardly knew how to take it and was just a bit fearful of his welled up anger.

"Jubal realized at once that what he said was upsetting to her, and he wished that he had not said it, at least not so harshly. "I sorry I said that, and I reckon I owe ye fer it. I wish I could take them words back and chew em up, but reckon I can't do that." Lida wanted him to take her in his strong arms and hold her. Hold her and protect her, even if just for the moment.

She reached under his buckskin coat with both arms and pulled him close to herself. She lay her head on his chest and began to sob softly. He returned her hug and did exactly as she had wanted. He held her tight and said nothing. Time seemed to stand still for both of them.

"I be chilled, Jubal. We best go back to the fire."

"Yeah, I reckon so," he replied but drew her to himself even tighter before letting her go. She lingered long enough to touch her lips to his ever so tenderly. He burned with an entirely different passion.

Mrs. Johnson had told Wes all she knew about the incident. How it had all come about so quickly. The way that C.C. had reacted. How he had been injured. All about his wounds, and what she had done to care for him. He had been abed since being hurt and complained about such awful pain in his head when he was awake. She said that he would wake up when she would talk to him. Said he seemed to know what was going on around him, but she was concerned that he appeared to be harder to arouse at times. No, there was no irregular pattern to his breathing nor nothing like that.

Wes assured her that he thought everything was just about as well as it could be and that she was doing all for him that could be done.

"Just needs keep up the faith and keep them prayers goin' up," Wes assured her.

"I been doin' that since the outset, Lida too."

"Well, they ain't no stronger medicine than that, I reckon," Wes added. "What can me and the boy do fer you all?"

"Don't know that we needs much right now. Biggest thing worry me is iffin they comes back again. Doubt them Reb soldiers be back no more. But I can't say that fer them three scallywag scoundrels, iffin I should say such about yer Pa, Jubal."

"That don't fret me none by ye sayin' so."

"I just hope all this ends up on a good note fer us all and that there ain't no more hurt nor no more bad blood nowhere. They done been plenty with this old war and all. I just wish it could all be over and folks could get on with livin'."

"Ye could do well by keepin' that in mind, son," Wes added as he turned his attention to Jubal. He had no way of knowing the words or sentiments that Lida and the boy had shared, but he was fairly sure that he knew the thoughts that coursed through his keen and sometimes judgmental mind.

Wes redirected his attention to Mrs. Johnson. "Would it help any iffin one of us stay with ye tonight or the next few nights?"

"Well, me and Lida been spellin' each other at C.C's bedside at night. I reckon we can make do on that for a while yet. We be a mite frazzled and wore, but we is okay so far."

"Reckon it not be quite fittin' fer Ma or Julie come set with him at night, but me or Jubal could spell ye a night so ye could get rested up some and get catched up on sleep. That might boost ye up a bit. We could always call ye iffin we needed ye fer him. I done some sick bed tendin' in my days, and I be proud help ye out iffin ye would like me to. Be plum proud to do it," Wes said.

Mrs. Johnson's first thoughts were to decline, but something told her that a good night of rest might be a good thing for her and Lida. "Well...Let me dwell on that a bit while I get us up some dinner. I got a pot of leather britches cookin'. I can make a corn pone in a snap, and then we can all eat, includin' you two. Then maybe we can talk more about what ye say."

"Good by me," Wes added.

No one had much to say over the beans and the bread. All ate heartily and were soon filled. At least the war had not brought on any serious issues with keeping fed. Oh sure, there were some things that were a bit hard to come by, such as coffee and cane sugar. Mountain folks were known for their self sufficiency, and the Johnson household was no exception. C.C. was not much on farming himself, but he made enough at his mill to buy or barter for the farm produce that he and his family needed. As long as there were crops raised in the little valley, there would be food on their table, that is, as long as the mill could run.

Lida cleared the table while Wes and Mrs. Johnson went back to the miller man's bedside. Jubal stayed in the kitchen while the dishes were being done. They shared no words for the time being, but both let their thoughts run free.

Jubal partially wanted to stay the night and on the other hand sort of feared what might possibly happen if he did. Old feelings of wanton desire reared up and brought some guilt for thinking the way he did, and at the same time those same passions begged to be sated.

Lida wondered just how far she would need to venture out to get to him and show him her desires without being too aggressive. She just did not understand why that he seemed to hold back sometimes. She knew how she felt and thought she knew what she wanted, but there was just a sliver of consciousness in her that would dictate that she act the lady that she really wanted to be.

It was agreed that Wes would stay tonight and give Mrs. Johnson and Lida a chance to get a full night of rest. He would station himself in a chair just outside the door to C.C's bedroom and listen to his breathing and wait on his call should he need any help. He would also tend the fire to make sure that his charge kept warm and comfortable. Jubal would return home with both horses and come back again in the morning and bring whatever Ma deemed appropriate. They would then tend to the situation one day at a time. The Union patrols should be through here again most any day now, and they might have some news that would be of use. It would never hurt for troops, friendly troops, be in the area.

"I don't like havin' ask ye Mrs. Johnson, but do ye reckon we might take a bit of feed fer the horses, since they been rode heavy over the last few days," Jubal asked as his face reddened just by asking.

"I don't really know what C.C. has over there, but ye are welcome to go look and take whatever ye find that ye needs."

"I know where it is, Jubal. I can show ye to it," Lida announced seizing upon yet another opportunity to be alone with him. "Just let me fetch my wrap." She turned and was off up the stairs to her room.

Mrs. Johnson must have sensed some of what her daughter was feeling and what could possibly be astir between the two of them. She positioned herself at the foot of the stairs and waited for Lida's return.

"I reckon ye best not be no Jezebel whilst ye be huntin' fer hoss feed," she quietly and insistently instructed her starry-eyed daughter.

Another bolt of summer thunderstorm lightning struck home. Lida was unable to make any comment in response to her mother's cutting remark, but did not miss a stride in her path to the door. How could her mother know her thoughts and her feelings? Did she have no shame? Why did there need to be such difficult and confusing questions in life? It would be hard to turn her feelings inward and hide them deep within, but she could and would do it if that was what it would take. She knew that she could influence him any time she wished but that was not the way she wanted it to be. She wanted him to treasure and respect her for what she really was and who she was. It would not be by the way of Jezebel.

Jubal and Lida made their way to the mill. Lida was near tears over the stinging that her mother's words had brought on, and she knew that she could not hold it back if she tried to say much at all. Jubal, likewise, was fearful that he could not conceal his passion and deemed it best to say nothing that would betray him. Lida pointed out the millet barrel and the cracked corn bin. Jubal found a bucket and soon had ample feed mixed and sacked up. He tied the sack and hefted it across his shoulder.

"I thank ye fer the help," he said.

"Welcome," she replied curtly as she turned and made for the door. "Latch up fer me, please."

He wondered why such a change so quick. He had no way of knowing that the uncertainty invoked by mother's words had made the difference.

The winter sky remained clear, and the evening sun would sink fast since the days were so short now. The solstice was only a couple of weeks past, and the change was not noticeable yet. It was time to head up the road to the old log home.

"Ma, tell me how ye feels about Pa."

"Ain't worth talkin' on fer as I see it."

"That ain't what I mean, Ma. I wanna know what ye would do iffin he ever come here again on the likes of what he done been up to at the mill?"

"Reckon it be best he not do that," she replied.

"He might a kilt C.C. He could pass yet."

"I won't be toleratin' no such in or around my house, so he best keep his distance."

"That still don't tell me what I needs to know, Ma."

577

"Then out with it, son. Spit it out and be heard."

"What iffin I hunted his arse down and got in a tussle with him and his keeps? What iffin it come to where they needed be handed their dues?"

"Him gettin' his comeuppance wouldn't bother me none, but I don't want ye involved in it none whatsoever. Ye hear me on that?"

"Yeah, I reckon, I do."

"Some things is just best left be and let lie, and this here be one I know pine blank ye don't want no meddlin' in," Ma added with emphasis. "I don't aim on sayin' no more on it, and I reckon ye best let it be as well."

Jubal agreed with his Ma to her face, but he knew that he just could never drop it. He felt sure that the scoundrels would hold up in Horne's cave or head for the doubles. Either way he could find them, and he did not really care where they were. He knew what needed to be done, and he was just the one to do it.

He did not really care that Pa may or may not have been shot and that it could be a fatal wound before things were said and done. If it turned out that way, then would Lida be held responsible for it all? He rationalized that she was only defending herself and her family and that she could not be held accountable for any wrong doings. But if he could get to Pa and his cranks, then he would be seen as the one who caught them and made them pay up. No need whatsoever having her be blamed for anything at all. He could take care of it, and he would take care of it somehow. He would just keep things to himself for now.

Ma wanted to ask Mrs. Johnson what she needed and what she could do for her. She would not go to the mill herself this particular day, but would come any time that she was needed. Julie was up and about pretty much on her own now and could fix up a bite or two for the rest of the family whenever needed.

"Ye best go back this mornin' and check on them folks fer me. Wes most likely be itchin' get back here and tend his doin's whatever they be. He done told me that you'ns was able to do what ye set out fer and that now he had stuff needed took care of. He ain't told me no details, but I reckon he heap glad to be back here and all."

The entire recent episode flashed through the young boy's mind. Wes had told him enough to make it really intriguing but had not revealed his exact intentions from here on out. If it had any similarity to what he did with the gourd contents, then things ought be a mite smoother on down the road. "He said he would talk with me on that sometime soon. Reckon we just been in such a hurry that he ain't had time so far."

"Don't see why he can't let me in on it too," Ma said. "After all, I reckon he aims on stayin' here now."

"I don't think he aims on havin' no secrets," Jubal replied.

"Well, ye best get on down there and see what be goin' on. Ye stay the night iffin they needs ye and Wes too as fer as that be. I reckon they might need ye and him more than me right now and that be okay too. I be here when ye decides it be time to come home."

There were chores that needed attention. The wood box was just about depleted, and there was none that had been split. The remainder of the morning was spent stocking up wood for both the hearth and the cook stove. Jubal spelled himself swinging the maul or the axe, depending on how many knots were in each cut of wood, and then carried it into the house. He soon had a good rick stacked against the outside kitchen wall and knew that it would be enough to last five or six days.

C.C. had been at himself enough to want to get up and go to the mill, because there was a turn of millet and corn that needed to be ground by the week's end. It was a job for the Union army, and they paid off in hard cash. Jubal and Wes had readily stepped up and were going to do it for him. He just needed to tell them what to do and how to handle the work. The miller man made it a point to tell them just how much his daughter knew about all the things that needed to happen to get a grinding job completed. He said that all she needed to be a good miller was more muscle, and then she could do it same as himself.

It was, therefore, decided that the two visitors would stay the night and do the milling job in the morning and that way they would have all day, if needed. Lida had readily agreed to help or at least show them how and what to do. She seemed to have resolved whatever issue was troubling her yesterday and was much more jovial today. Hard to understand sometimes.

"We might ought walk the race this afternoon and make sure it ain't fouled ner such. Then we be ready fer settin' it in the mornin'. Won't take long," Lida informed Jubal as she fetched them in for more leather britches and corn pone.

"We do what ye say. Ye the boss on that there task," Jubal agreed.

"Me and ye can do that easy. No need Wes climbin' all over the race and maybe takin' a fall. It be slick, special this time a year and even more so iffin it be iced up. That one reason we needs check it this afternoon while it be a mite warmer. Then all we needs do tomorrow early on is set the gate, and we be ready fer millin' then. Get yerself all washed up. Momma and me have it on the table in two shakes." She turned and headed back to the porch.

"Well now, ain't that a change from yesterday?" Jubal quipped.

"What ye mean, son?"

"Yesterday when we went in the mill fer hoss food, seemed like she couldn't get away from me fast enough, and then today she done told ye to let us be and be by ourselves, just plain as can be. Ain't that a turnabout fer sure? How ye figger that?"

"Ain't no way, son. Just take it fer what it be at the moment cause it may be apt fer change any breath. That just be the way it be. That's all I know, and I been tryin' to cypher it out lot longer than ye have."

"Hog wash," Jubal smarted as he got up and made his way to the house. Maybe a belly full of beans and bread would be better anyhow. The air outside was not biting or quite so chilling, but the heat from the old cook stove did feel good. Jubal felt just a twinge of heaviness in his eyelids. His lying awake last night trying to answer all the unanswerable was showing on him.

The race was clear all the way from the dam and the intake to the wheel trough. There was no ice, and the water coursed freely. The wheel would turn at the filling of the first few troughs, and the milling could begin.

Darkness soon found Jubal and Wes before the warm open living room fire with their ear bent to listen for any call that C.C. might make. He had apparently improved a small measure but was still having considerable shoulder and arm pain. He would have benefited from a good stiff pull of spirits or a hit of laudanum. There was neither available. He would make do without. Sleep sometimes was the best medicine.

"Are ye tuckered, son."

"No. I feel right smart even iffin I do say so," Jubal answered.

"I don't aim on blabbin' all night, but this be a good time fer us talk on some things."

"I can listen real good, I reckon."

"Reckon ye know by now what was in them crocks we dug up. I reckon ye thinkin' that ye got me all reasoned out by now and that ye know me well. Am I about right?"

"I know what ye was when Ma took ye in, iffin that be what ye mean."

"Don't know much about me before that though, do ye?"

"Recollect ye said ye come from down in Bama someplace"

"But what about me before that?" Wes prodded.

"Don't recall ever hearin' that," Jubal said. Wes had already captured his interest.

"I'm gonna tell ye things that no one around here knows. I have been here long enough so that people once connected with me and my past have given me up for dead, best I can find out and that was and is the way I wanted it."

"How come that?" Jubal questioned.

"I'll get to that."

"I listenin' fer it"

"Where do you reckon I come from when I was younger?

"Dunno."

"I am not what you think I am, son. There is much more to me than you think. I am an educated man, believe it or not. I went to schools in Pennsylvania and took up tutoring for my trade when I finished my university schooling."

"That why ye tryin' talk so fancy and all now?"

"No. I just want to show you what it all involves and why I have done as I did. I am here in these mountains by choice, and I learned to talk the mountain talk on purpose. It has been a long time since

I made proper use of good conversation, and I must now make a conscious effort to use it. I left it behind on purpose when I left Alabama.

"What did ye work at down there?" Jubal wanted to know.

"I was head master at a military school near Mobile, but that was just a sideline on the last.

"I don't unnerstand. Iffin ye had such high falutin' jobs as that, why did ye up and leave it all behind?"

"I had to. There were people down there would have shot me on sight if they had ever had the chance. That is why I came here. I came here to hide. After my woman passed, I just about let myself go completely under. I was wallowing in my own sorry self, and it just about got me down. But you know that part. That's really the only part you ever knew about me that was the truth.

"What got ye in trouble so much?"

"It happened over a good while. I did some evil things, and that was what caused me so much grief. You see, son, I was close associated with lots of folks down there who had a lot of money and influence as well. They most times had their way whatever they wanted. I was just the schoolmaster for their kids. Some of those kids had slave nannies and guardians that would bring the kids to school and stay with them all the time. I got to know some of those people real well. Some of them picked up on the kids' school lessons themselves just by being there. The plantation owners never wanted their slaves to be educated in any fashion, because they thought that would give them cause to riot and such. I never did feel that way. I taught the kids; and if the slaves learned in the meantime, then so be it. Lots of them began to teach others in their family to read and write a bit here and there, and it was no time hardly until those coloreds treated me with the utmost respect. I think they trusted me more than they did any of their masters or owners."

"Well, what be so bad about that?" Jubal quired.

"They put trust in me, and I took advantage of them for it. They learned to read and write, and I began to encourage them to try and do better for themselves. I urged them to try and make their way north and look for better work there. Most became excited about making it to freedom. Mind you these weren't the field hands and the likes. These were the household servants and the upper crust of their kind, the best of them who had some desire and some get up to them. They were more than just darkies under a whip all the time. They got to trusting me, and I began to honestly try helping them. One time, several times, I even planted the idea in their mind that they should run away north. Then I found them safe places to hide when they might need to lay up a day or so. This went on over some time, mind you. Things got to going right well there for a while, then Greeley Sams came along."

"Who was he? What he do?"

"Greeley was a riverboat gambler if there ever was one. He came through Mobile one spring, and we got acquainted quite by accident. He was the one who told me about these mountain hideouts around here and how a man could come here and get himself lost for as long as he wanted to be lost. Said he had hold up here more than once while a jealous man cooled down or a gambler had given up on finding him. He was some character, but I did what I did. I can't lay all the blame on him for all the things I did."

"He must a been a real rounder," Jubal remarked as visions of life aboard a riverboat flashed through his mind.

"He was. He was the one who showed me how we could work together and make a lot of money and do it easy and quick too."

"How was that?"

"He saw that the darkies trusted me so much that he allowed how I could start them out headed north and then tell him where they would try to hold up or such and then he would go with whatever law was needed and bring them back to their owners and collect the rewards. Me and him did that together several times over a year or so, and he always gave me my part of the rewards. I soon had a right good sum. He always demanded payment in gold so that was what I was getting too. Ye see now where my gourd money came into the picture don't you?" Wes questioned.

"Ye got it all that way?"

"Well, not exactly. We carried on this little caper for about a year, and then Greeley went and got himself killed in a poker match over in Labatra. That really threw me for a loop. I had already been bitten by the greed and had a good touch of gold fever."

"What you do then and how come ye talkin' so much different to me now than before? Ye don't make no sense in doin' that."

"I got a reason for it and I will get around to that later. Just you be patient if you want to hear the rest of my storied past."

"I wanna hear it, that be a fact. I ain't tryin' be smart ner nuthin' like that. I just don't unnerstand," Jubal replied. "Go on with it."

"I had already seen how much reward money could be offered and how quick the cotton plantations would pay. I just had to do it all a bit different now. I could have all the gold and not be sharing with anyone. I just started going after the runaways by myself. It worked well that way too, for almost three years or better. I was fetching a runaway back home about ever month or so."

"Must a had a pile by then."

"I did. I had a tidy sum all in gold just like this here." Wes dug into his pocket and retrieved a gold piece and passed it over to Jubal. "Look it over. Read what is has inscribed on it."

Jubal took the piece and stared down at it. The orange flames from the open fire danced all around the eagle. He rubbed it between his fingers and would have swore that he could feel its warmth. He had one like this once, but that was back some time past. Now he was holding another in his hand, and it was captivating to him.

"Ye got more of these?"

"Some are like that. Others are not. Read it. See what it says on it."

Eyes were fixed on the lettering as the boy strained to decipher the letters and images on the coin. He turned it over and over in his hand, struck almost speechless by what he was seeing.

"It say ten dollars, and it say 1847 whatever that be."

"That is the year it was minted."

"Huh?"

"The year that the piece was made by the Union mint. A mint is a place where they make money."

"Oh! Well, I see now," Jubal responded, still awe struck. "Is that what be in the crock too?"

"Partly."

"And ye tellin' me that ye got it all catchin' darkies?"

"That is the most of how I came by it," Wes answered. "I told you before that I was not proud of all that I have done, and I must say that it almost cost me far more than I got from it."

"How ye mean?"

"All them planters and shippers began to wonder how it was that I was always the one who knew just where and when to find their runaways. Never realized that they were getting onto what I was doing until it was almost too late, and then it was a freed slave who broke it all open."

"How the devil that happen?"

"One of the first that I ever helped in an honest way actually made it up north, and made enough to buy himself freedom from old Cyrus LeBeau. He was an indigo cropper and owned old Raymond, who was a young whipper snapper by comparison. I taught ole Raymond how to read and taught him ciphers and all and actually helped him get work back in Ohio in a printers firm. He saved his money and had a young abolitionist lawyer procure his freedom and papers from old LeBeau. Raymond stayed up in Ohio and worked to save enough to buy his sister and mammy as well. He eventually made enough money and came back to Mobile looking for them. Just so happened long about that same time I was fixing to send them out and then catch them and collect the return fee on both at the same time. Raymond found out somehow what I had been up to and came looking for me. Word got out that he would kill me on sight for what I was trying to do to his folks. Anyway he tried to catch up to me, but I always managed to stay a step or two ahead of him."

"How ye do that? Did ye hide out all the time?"

"No. It was not that hard avoiding him, because he was a darkie and had to contend with all that went with being assumed to be owned by somebody else. That was an advantage for me, but he began talking and telling what he knew. Soon the growers and shippers and the plantation owners and ever body else began to see what I had been up to and then was when it really got hot for me. Then was when I really had to run, and I remembered what Greeley Sams had told me about the mountains. That was when I made my way up to these hills and hollows. I had to or they would have strung me up for sure."

"Ye come up here from old Bama and tried to be one of us. That how it was?" Jubal asked.

"Not at first, but that was the way it worked out after a while. I thought I could just disappear here and no one would ever know the better, but my talk and my speech stopped that dead in its tracks. That is why I took up your tongue so to speak. I learned all your talk until it became part of me."

"Sounds me like ye pokin' fun at us all."

"That may seem so to you, but it is just not true, Jubal. I did it for my own good, and it just became a part of me in everyday life."

"Then why ain't ye talkin' like that now? They ain't no other ears here now," Jubal said with some detectable annoyance.

"Do you recall the three scallywags that beat up on me just before you and your Ma rescued me?"

"Yeah, I recollect them."

"You remember the big one, the one who did all the thumping on my old hard head?"

"Yeah."

"He somehow got wind of what I had hoarded up and how I had done it. He was after that for himself. I don't know how he learned that I had come this far from Mobile, but he knew somehow. He fell in with the buckskin guy somewhere west of here and probably told him about my capers as well."

"And what of that third man," Jubal questioned.

"I believe you already know who that one is," Wes added softly.

"Dang his sorry arse. Ye be right on that," Jubal countered.

"I don't know where he fell in with the other two, but it makes no matter now. Seems to me that all he has an eye for is the laudanum bottle. But, of course, having a pocket full of money might just make it a lot easier to find that bottle. I reckon I am not telling you anything that you and your Ma don't already know, and I hope I am not offending you by saying what I have told you so far."

"I got no axe grindin' to do on yer account, old man," Jubal said.

"The way I see it now, the only one I need be concerned about is the big fellow. He could still be after me and my gourds. I don't think any of them know about our little journey across Clinch and that is in our favor. I am not concerned about your Pa, and the buckskin guy won't do anything without the big one telling him all the details. I hear tell he is just a bit touched."

"Then why'd they come here and run around here?"

"Most likely they needed a dollar or two for whatever. The big guy probably thought he might get to me through the Johnsons, but I bet he never thought that Lida would be slinging lead balls at them either."

"She done good by that way I see it," Jubal added. "Proud of her for it too."

"Well, me too. But would have been better for me, and for you too, if she had nailed old big boy instead. He might have been completely out of it by now. But he is still around, and I still need to contend with him."

"What ye aim do about him?"

"Well, I won't be chasing after him, because I don't think that will be necessary. I don't think they will be shooting anybody, because I don't think they got any powder or shot. They would have used it here if they had any on hand. They did all they could do and that was run."

"Ye know any names?"

"Not really, but I suspicion who the big one might be."

"Who ye reckonin' they be then?"

"Big one is some blood kin to Raymond, best I know. That goes back a good while to Alabama days."

"He don't look no colored."

"Well son, that is just the way it is anyhow," Wes added. Best I know, he and Raymond had a common grandpa who owned a sternwheeler out of Mobile; that's how they hooked up together, best I know.

"Ye thinkin' him and Raymond is in cahoots now?"

"No, that is no concern now," Wes added as he got up and put a big white oak split on the fire, dusted off his hands and looked in on C.C. The miller man was resting well, and his breathing was full and regular. At least he was resting tonight. "You remember what you told me you saw happen in Cleve's barn?"

"Yeah, I do. What that got to do with this here business?"

"That darkie that he killed, you remember that?"

"Yeah." Jubal did not need to dwell on that scene. It had been seared into his mind so that he would always remember that day and the evil that he had witnessed.

"That old slave woman that he killed was Raymond's ma, and the man in the loft was her brother. I think that if Raymond ever catches up to old big boy that there will be trouble between them plenty. I am willing to just set back and let them two settle things and then maybe I won't need to do a thing more about trying to hide. Maybe then I can go back to being myself."

"What ye mean by that?"

"I can't go back down to Alabama and take up where I left off, because there would be too much bad feelings there even if the war was not an issue. The life and pleasures that I had there are all gone now. I realize that I did it myself, all for the want of the gold and all that it could bring me. Now I am an old man and don't even want all those things any more. The things that I would like to have now will never be, can't be."

"What would them be?"

"First off, I wish I could have my woman back and spend these last days with her. But that can't happen because of me, and the path that I chose to travel. She warned me from the start what it would all lead to, but I never listened to her till it was far too late. I was happy with her and the rather simple life that we had with me as headmaster. We had enough to keep us fed and sheltered and could afford some of the pleasures of life ever now and then. Now those things are not to be had at all. I try to blame it all on the war and all its corruption, but that is not entirely true. I guess that I just have a hard time owning up to it."

"Old war be bad. I know that a fact," Jubal said.

"Oh that be true, but I have to take some of the blame myself for the shape I am in now; and I do, hard as it pains me. I hope that I can be some use to somebody someplace before I pass. I still have something to offer, and I would love to share with as many as I can."

"Ye mean share yer gold?"

"No. Not necessarily. Gold is up here," Wes said as he pointed to his head. "I still got my learning, and I wish there was some way that I could share that with kids all around here. I could teach them a lot of things that would make a better life for them in the long run. I could help them have an easier life, and they might not have to toil and labor so hard all their days. Like your Ma, for example. If she had a chance time past, I just bet she would have wanted a better way for her family."

"She done the best she could, I reckon," Jubal said in her defense.

"I am sure that she did, but what I am saying is that she never had a choice. She never even knew of any other way and that is just what I am speaking about. I want folks to know that there is a better way and a way to be at peace with one's own self and with the world around him."

"I thinkin' Ma be a peaceful one already," Jubal said again in her defense.

"I am not saying that at all, son. You just don't see what I am trying to open your eyes to do you? Not the real truth of it, do you?"

"Ye still got my ear."

"Life is just what you make out of it, son. I made a mess out of mine. The only thing I can say good about it is that I now know a lot about what not to do and what not to want. I guess some of that comes with going through some hard times. Some of it you can't ever know until you cross fool's hill. But it be a proven fact to me at least what I have heard all my life about riches and the want for money and such. It cannot and will not buy the things that really matter."

"And just what they be?"

"What do you think I mean?" Wes shot back.

"Granny Iverson once tell me iffin she had money she would buy back her young days and do them different. I reckon she just be makin' fun of me then, but I recollect her tellin' me that it not buy peace of mind and the likes."

"Well, Granny be wiser than you give her credit for. I know that she has found her peace of mind now especially in her older years, and I am glad that she has. She has that inner peace that comes only out of living in the light. I am so very thankful that I finally saw where I was headed and got myself turned around."

"Granny Iverson all time talkin' on dark and light. Julie too fer that matter. Puts my mind at trouble sometimes when they does that," Jubal said as much to himself as to Wes.

"Eats at you some then?" Wes inquired.

"Yeah, I reckon it do."

"It ought eat at you all the time, and I hope it does until the day comes that you can't stand it any longer. I can tell you what a difference it can make for you, but you will never really know until you know it for yourself. It really is the difference between dark and the light of day. I just want good things for you, son. You have to accept it for yourself. Now, I know I am supposed to be an educated man and all that, but it is still somewhat hard for me to really say all that I feel. Granny Iverson says things a lot better than me. You would do well to talk to her and above that to really listen to what she has to say. Julie too, for that matter. But Granny Iverson is older and wiser and has had time to learn a lot more out of life than your sister. So listen to her and learn from her."

"Lida been known fer raggin' on me," Jubal added. "Reckon she and Julie be about same there."

"Well…you reckon they are serious about what they try getting you to see and accept?" Wes asked.

"Never give it that much thought," Jubal answered curtly.

C.C. roused up and started coughing like he was choking. Both were at his bedside in a heartbeat. He sat bold upright in bed grasping his chest with his left arm and hand. The coughing subsided just as smartly as it had begun. He soon settled down and resumed his rest.

"How long till it be light?" he asked.

Jubal and Wes exchanged surprised looks. How did the old miller man know what they had been talking about? Not likely that he had heard any of their conversations. He was only a few moments in getting back to sleep and the peaceful and restful look on his face was quite evident to Jubal. Wes saw it too, but the spell was broken now. He would chastise the young lad no more tonight. Wes felt like the knock was there, but Jubal had not opened the door. Maybe, hopefully, next time.

They both returned to their place before the fire. It would be daybreak in a couple of hours, and Mrs. Johnson would be stirring before that.

"We ought try to sleep an hour or so. It will be a long day milling if we be all tuckered out to start," Wes instructed as he slumped down in his chair and rested his head on the back of it. Sleep soon came to both.

Jubal climbed the race to the wheel inlet and opened the sluice about two inches just as Lida told him. The old wheel creaked and groaned as if to protest its rude awakening and reluctantly began to move, very slowly, gaining in momentum as the water coursed the sluice, filling the first trough, overflowing to the next and so on until the massive wooden structure succumbed to the pull that the icy water placed upon it. Below, in the mill itself, the grist wheel began to rotate rythmicaly. Wes began to fill the in feed with shelled corn to the point where gravity would provide a steady flow to the slight space between the grist wheel and the slot stone. From this, the course ground corn would be allowed to free fall into a meal bin and there be ready for sacking.

The water wheel did most of the work. There was little hard labor involved, save for lifting the laden sacks of grain. Man's work that was too heavy for any young woman or her mother.

Once all was in order and runnin' well, there was not really any need for Lida to stay in the mill and be exposed to the chilly winter air. Her cheeks were already rosy red and her every breath was betrayed by a whisk of white fog. The men could call for her if they had any issues. She thusly wasted no time or effort in making her way back to the comforts of the hearth. Besides that, Momma would need her to help tend to her Daddy, and they soon would get started making something warm and filling for the new found work hands. The grinding continued without any troubles.

"Old man, ye ain't told me why ye commenced in on all yer smart talk and such," Jubal said as he tied up another sack of ground millet and stacked against the wall.

"I have done it because that is who I really am, and I don't want to pretend any more to be something or somebody that I am not. You understand that?"

"Reckon it don't matter that much anyhow, but ain't ye still 'fraid somebody find ye out?"

"No. Not really. Not now, because Raymond seems to be busy looking for the big man, and he is looking in the wrong places. He is busy west of here, if he is still looking at all. I can't say for sure. Leastwise, I am through being something I am not."

"What ye gonna do with the gold?" Jubal asked in earnest.

"That will come later," Wes quipped. "I do not want to be remembered for all that I have done in the later parts of my life, and I sure don't want to be remembered as a gold hoarder. I can't give the money back and make things right, because I don't even recall their names or where they came from, let alone where they might be now. I would much more be remembered for all the minds that I influenced, and those whose life I may have improved by teaching them something that they could use all their days. That is the kind of thing that counts in life, and the only kind of things that will stand the tests of time. I changed for that reason, and by chance to show you that there is something more to life than you might ever think. You can do most anything you want, if you know what it is that you want and if you go after the things in life that really matter. I know you don't see it now, but if I could just teach you to read and write well, much of it would come to you easier and clearer. That is just a small part of coming out of the darkness and into the blessings of knowledge. No matter how much I harp on you about that, you are the one and the only one who can change yourself. I cannot do it for you nor can Julie or Granny Iverson or any other person on the face of this old earth. It is going to be up to you and to you alone."

"I reckon it not hurt me none iffin I could read a mite better."

"Well, that's at least something. I will teach you as best I can."

"We'll see when we gets back home. I reckon we be headed back by dusk or so. Ain't nobody say nuthin' fer the comin' night, leastwise not to me."

"Not to me either."

"We open up them crocks when we gets home?" Jubal said in anticipation.

"Dang it. I wish I could just open up the top of your head and pour it in."

"Huh?"

"Never mind, I guess I am just talking to the wind."

"Well, what of the gold? What ye aim on doin' with it all?" Jubal asked just as anxious as ever.

"I'll tell you that when the time comes, but some of it may be needed right here before it is all said and done."

"How that?"

"Well just look at C.C. No tell how long it will be until he can run his mill again, and they may need a thing or two just to get by. You never know. Besides that, he is far from well right now. Things could take a really bad turn and then what would become of them?"

"Mrs. Johnson speak on that to ye any?" Jubal asked.

"No, and I did not ask her. But she did say that she had a sister and her family that lives up on Big Creek somewhere. I just took it for granted that she might have thought on that for a bit."

"We could run this here mill fer her."

"We would need to be asked first, and Mrs. Johnson might not even want to stay here any longer if something were to happen to her man."

"Reckon ye be right on that. I never thought them thoughts. Reckon it not be proper go askin' things like that either," Jubal said as much to himself as to Wes.

"We agree on that at least."

"Dinner be ready," Lida announced form the door of the mill house. She spoke with authority, since it was necessary to make herself heard over the creaking and groaning of the milling. She stood in the doorway silhouetted against the outside sunlight like some malingering statue in a faraway place of fantasy or dreamland. She seemed to be looking around to assure herself that her instructions were adhered to and that the work was being done properly. Her expressions were not really discernible by either of her student laborers. Her voice was upbeat, and both took this as a sign of a mood change from before. "Get washed up smart now because it be on the table in no time flat," she continued as she turned and headed back to the kitchen door. Jubal thought that he detected just a bit of a smile as an instant of sunlight caught her face.

"Guess we best do what she say," Jubal said as he tied up yet another sack of millet and added it to the growing stock piled against the rear wall.

"I'm ready. This is just about as hard as being in a saddle all day, and I am hungry too. Lead the way. I am right behind you," Wes added.

The table was not lavish by any standards, but there was plenty. Mrs. Johnson had streaked meat and hominy and corn bread. Lida had made dried apple dumplings, and there was cold buttermilk for whoever wanted it. Jubal declined that because he just could not get past the sight of the glass once it was tipped a bit. Never had liked it and was not going to try it today.

Lida was not at the table right now. C.C. had seemed to perk up and had said that he was powerful hungry. Lida took pleasure in being by his bedside and making sure that he got the choice part of her dumplings. Jubal did not know it, but she had saved out an equal portion for him.

"Send them boys in here. I needs talk with they a minute or two," C.C. commanded of his daughter.

"I will Daddy, but eat this here last spoonful fer me since I made it special fer ye."

The miller man made no protest as he willingly obeyed her orders. With the exception of his broken, or apparently broken arm, and the bloody scabbed over gash on his head, he seemed to be doing well.

"I be much obliged to ye fer grindin' fer me. Lord knows I ain't fit fer it right now, and can't say when I might be again. I know my arm must be busted on account how it pains me with least little movement. Ain't never had a busted bone and don't want nary 'nother either. But that be 'nuff about me. Reckon ye got no troubles millin' and all?"

"No. reckon not," Wes answered. "Your girl told us plain what and how to do."

"She knows plenty alright, and she can show ye how to shut down later on when ye gets done. Some lets a mill wheel run days on end, but I don't like mine done that way. Burn up yer wheel too quick, and they ain't easy replaced. She come over later and help ye shut down. Reckon ye be done by dusk, won't ye?"

"If not, we finish by lantern light," Jubal quipped. Visions of him and Lida alone in the mill after dark flashed through his mind. Just as quickly he snapped himself back to reality.

"It might be a bit riskier climbin' the wheel and shuttin' off the sluice after dark. That be why ye always quits long 'fore dark, so's ye can do that in light times. Don't want ye takin' a fall off a slick wheel or sluice. That the most of what I needed tell ye, so now ye can go back to it and know what needs be and when. I got my paunch full now, and I think I might rest up a bit more." C.C. grinned as he eased back down in his bed.

The sky in the west was growing ever deeper shades of crimson and purple. In spite of best efforts of both, the milling was yet a ways from being finished. It was agreed that it would be best to get up at first light tomorrow and then complete the task. Pallets would be spread for the guests, and they could keep an ear open for the miller man all the while. Since he was resting better, they could rest as well.

Jubal climbed the race and pushed down the sluice gate. The groaning old wooden wheel willingly gave up its task and fell silent. Darkness would soon blanket the entire mill. The moon was already rising and there were only scattered mares tail clouds high overhead. Probably would frost heavy tonight.

Jubal lay on his pallet and looked into the open fire. Flames danced about lazily and cast eerie shadows on the far walls. He could feel sleep coming over him. He then realized that he was tired. The mill work had been more strenuous than he had imagined. He had helped the miller man a time or two, but never on a job this involved. No wonder the old codger was tough as shoe leather. He had to be to run his business as well as he had done for so many years.

A strange sensation took hold of him, and he struggled to recognize what it was that beset him. Voices, but not discernible. A familiar voice, but not understandable.

"Jubal." And again his shoulder argued for his attention. "Wake up," Lida prodded as she shook his shoulder even more vigorously. "Wake up, now."

"What's wrong, Miss Lida?" Wes spoke as Jubal gathered himself into consciousness and responded as Wes had done.

"Listen, Listen outside."

The rhythmic splash of the water spilling over the mill wheel could mean nothing other than the wheel in motion. Something was amiss and needed to be looked into, darkness or no darkness.

"What ye want me do?" Jubal asked.

"I'll fetch a lantern, and we can go see," Lida answered.

Moonlight would have been enough to light the way to the mill, but not to climb up and see the sluice. It had not frosted yet, but that would not be long in coming. No winds stirred the naked branches or the dry leaves anywhere around the mill or the house. Had it not been for the sounds of the wheel, the night would have been as the silence of a tomb.

Lida carried the lantern as they made their way to the rear of the mill and approached the race. The shadow of the mill darkened the better part of the race and the wheel. The lantern gave only a feeble illumination of what they needed to see.

"I think ye best not climb up there in this here dark. It be wet and slick to boot. We best go on up the race and open it up at the head end. That stop it and be easier to set back after it get day."

That task was soon accomplished and they soon found themselves back inside the mill. Their arms eagerly entwined with a glimmer of moon glow coming through the small window above the table where C.C. sat to keep his books. Along the opposite wall were the millet and corn sacks that Jubal had tied and neatly stacked. It was not much of a bed, but they made do.

Somehow the dying embers in the old stone fireplace burned hotter than ever known before. Jubal slept no more that night.

Chapter 17

Determined

*M*rs. Johnson told Wes there was no more grinding to be done for a while. The Union army was to send a wagon to pick up the sacks in just a few days. Would it be too much to ask if he and the boy would come back in about a week to see what might be needing done then? Wes had agreed that they would be glad to do that and if they should need anything at all before then, well just get word on up the road somehow, and they would be right there. C.C. seemed to be no worse, and she thought that he would be up and about in just a few more days.

Wes had kindled a fire just outside the old smokehouse and had the three-legged kettle holder in place over the growing flames. Jubal had carried six oaken buckets of spring water to fill the big iron pot. He and Wes lifted the heavy blackened pot with a locust post threaded under the big iron handle and nestled the load onto the stand. Jubal then began to pour the water into the waiting vessel. It would take some time for a full pot to come to a boil.

Wes had carried the stone crocks out from the springhouse loft, still secured in his bedroll and laid the cache on the ground and untied the rawhide straps. The bedroll had held its contents safe and secure for well over a week now, and it was time to get into it and seek out its real worth. Jubal was a bit anxious to see just what and how much it contained. Wes had still not answered all his questions, but right now it made little difference. He knew enough to know that Wes had come by it all in a devious way and that it had all been at some risk. But that was all in the past, and now was all that seemed important.

Once the water was near the top rim of the pot, Jubal carried a big arm load of split hickory firewood from the woodshed and deposited it near the cauldron. It would take this and maybe more to get the water to a boil. Once boiling, it ought not take long to learn about the contents of the crock within a crock. Wes had said that he would boil away all the wax from the larger crock first, and then he could get at the smaller one much easier.

"Why don't ye just bust off the big one, and then there not be so much wax to bother with?" Jubal asked.

"Ain't no call bustin' up a plum good crock. Ye ain't gonna do it iffin I have any say so on it," Ma said as she stood by the fire and warmed her backside. "We can always use them."

"I reckon so," Julie said as she looked on with anticipation as well as the rest. Wes had told the entire family what was in the crocks, but he had only hinted at how much there might be. He had told Ma almost as much as he had told her son, but had held back a lot about his wife and how she had suffered so much as a result of all his chicanery and evil doings.

"Fire be goin' right good now," Jubal said. "Ye want me start throwin' on some big sticks now?"

"Go ahead," Wes answered. "Water ought boil sooner that way." Jubal complied with the old man's request.

A hot fire had the markings of a soon-to-be-boiling cauldron.

"Ain't never done no such cookin' as this here," Granny Iverson said with a big grin across her face.

"Me neither," Ma echoed.

"Not be too long now," Wes said as he stood over the pot looking down into the clear spring water with the old stone crock showing plain as day through the onset of the slowly rising steam.

"What ye gonna do with it all?" asked the boy.

"Not really sure just yet. What would ye do with it, should it be yours?" asked Wes.

"Reckon iffin they be 'nuff of it, then I could live the good life. I could soar with them eagles. Have a high time."

"Gratitude be the only attitude what make fer any altitude in life boy. Ye ought know better. Ye been told time and time over how I reckons on that," Granny Iverson stood as she spoke in apparent preparation to really light into her grandson if he persisted in such foolery.

"That be a fact, son," Wes said sensing that Granny Iverson was full cocked and ready to lambaste away at him. He just did not want to hear it right now. "We talked on that several times now, and I thought that ye had begun to see a little bit of light. I still think some of what ye say about the high life is just you building all them air castles. I know ye know better, and I know ye want more from life than just a pot full of gold and all the worldly things ye think it might buy ye. I got me a good notion what ye really wants, and it ain't too far off neither."

Jubal could feel the burning in his cheeks, and he knew that the redness would soon follow. "Ye knows too much already, old man. I ought never talked so much with ye."

"I never asked ye any questions. Ye was the one who done all the talking," Wes said in his defense. "I just want ye to see the right way to live and be able to live life the way it was intended. That is possible, ye know."

The fire soon had the pot to a full boil and would soon have the wax oozing out of the crocks as well.

"How ye gonna get them crocks outta that boil, Wes," Julie asked.

"Won't be no problem. Reckon if ye could talk yer brother into fetching the big poker from the fireplace and a dipper, other than a gourd, then I will show you how here in just a few minutes," Wes answered as he turned to look at Jubal who still had a slight glow to his cheeks.

"I fetch it old man, just like I fetch plenty fer ye."

"I hear," Wes responded in a whip.

By the time Jubal fetched the poker and dipper, Wes had pulled some of the larger sticks of wood away from the underside of the pot. It was boiling vigorously now and some of the wax had made its way to the surface. Wes carefully dipped it out of the boil and was careful not to fling the hot wax on anybody. He then poured it away from the gathering in such a way that it would not be stepped on and tracked all over the yard or into the house.

The fire would have to be stoked up and then pulled back several times over before success could be noticed. The wind had a slight chill to it, but no one seemed to notice. Every eye was on the pot and remained there except for brief turns to warm the backsides. The wood was dry and made little smoke, but an occasional drift did sting an eye or two.

Wes continued to dip off the wax as it came to the top.

"How much longer ye think?" Jubal asked.

"Not much," Wes responded.

"Then will we know how much ye got."

"I think it might needs be polished up a bit so a body can tell what it be. Might be a ten piece or might be one of them eagles. I reckon we will just have to add it up once all that gets done."

"Well…whatever ye say, I reckon. I thought ye knew how much already," Jubal answered seemingly a bit confused.

After a time, Wes dipped out what little water remained in the pot and poured it on the remnants of the fire. All but Jubal had given up their vigil and returned to the warmth of the fire that warmed the old log house.

"Go ask Ma if she can spare me a pillowcase or a cocker sack," Wes instructed.

The boy did as requested and soon was back by the fire. Wes tapped lightly and quickly on the sides of the kettle to test how much it had cooled.

"Still hot?" Jubal questioned.

"Yeah, but not much longer. Ye can fetch a bucket from the spring branch if ye don't want to wait for it to air cool."

"I reckon I can wait."

"Good. Glad to see ye got a measure of patience in ye."

Wes took the pillowcase. As soon as the kettle had cooled enough, he scooped out the crocks, tossed them aside with the old fireplace poker and then dipped out some of the wax that spilled from the upturned crockery. He could see the naked coins in the bottom of the pot. They did not look anything like gold. They were dull and discolored like some old useless and abandoned harness ornament, like tarnished brass.

Wes delayed only enough for the water to become a few degrees cooler. He plunged a hand in and retrieved a fist full and then held them to the wind for a moment. He then dropped them into the pillowcase. He repeated the move until all the coins were in the sack. He made no attempt at counting what he had.

"When we gonna clean em up?" Jubal asked with anticipation.

"Soon as we can find us some real fine sand. Might need to have old C.C. grind us up some. He might be talked into that, but sand would soon eat up his grist stone. Doubt he would like that."

"We could grind it, and he might not even know it," Jubal replied.

"Could be. But I think we ought not do him like that. We would not need but about a bucket full or so and that ought not be too hard on his mill. I intend on paying him well for it too," Wes answered as he tied up the sack and set it between his feet. It would get cleaned and counted later.

Grady Rowe, the bearded ruffian, stood just outside the mouth of Horne's cave and stared off into the cold of the night. Had he not moved out from behind the cedar thicket, any hapless passerby that was unfamiliar with the area would never know that he or his pair of ruffian cohorts were holed up down in the deeps of the limestone cavern. It offered some protection from the elements and was a heap site warmer deep inside than the chill of winter's night. The sun never had any influence below the surface, nor were the howling winds of winter ever able to blanket the depths.

The lanky man stroked his unkempt beard and scratched freely wherever he pleased. A growl deep within reminded him that it had been days since he had eaten anything other than turnips and a couple of Hubbard squash that had been scrounged from a cornfield. These had been collected more than a week past, and they had been a bounty at that. He had dragged his accomplice there and had tried to tend to his gunshot leg and get him mended up enough to head out to the west, but mending was slow if it were to come at all.

He thought about setting out on his own, but he was a bit edgy over making his way where he was unfamiliar with things. Hated to own up to it, but he needed the pitiful piece of work, at least until he could get well on down close to the big river country. Besides that, who could tell who or when troops would find that the cave was in use and who was using it? It was time to move on; and if things did not change a bit in a day or so, then he would set out by himself. The other two could just rot for all he cared.

New moon tonight so there would be scant light. He could have a fire down inside the cave, and the smoke most likely never be spotted. The thoughts of another night sleeping on a cold and wet earthen bed disgusted him. He walked out a few more yards and hacked down a half dozen young cedars and carried them back to the mouth of the cave and tossed them down the entrance. Very little scavenging was needed to produce a big armload of fallen limbs from the banks above. These too were carried into the cave like some pack rat stowing away his larder.

The fire warmed the cave in no short order. Shadows from the flames danced back and forth across the cold, gray limestone walls and gave the appearance of any number of evil beings lurking just out of reach, a mere arm's length away. The dried dead limbs burned hot and made little smoke. There was none to sting the eyes nor to give any outside sign that the cold damp earth held life within. The fire would burn itself out before first light, and nothing would be left to betray them when the sun rose. The cedar bushes shielded away the cold of the damp earth, and soon the body chill wandered off. He could sleep warm tonight and rest should be a welcome companion. His company had already succumbed to their weariness, and the warmed air only added to the depths of their slumber. The hunger had not gone away. He would deal with that some way tomorrow, for himself, if not for the three of them. Tomorrow would be a new day, and it just might be a day that could bring a new turn for him. He would check the dead falls that he had set. There could be a rabbit or maybe at least a squirrel, anything, anything at all except another damned turnip. Consciousness soon deserted him as well. He would awaken only when the fire had consumed itself.

Renewed hunger pangs and daylight came at almost the same breath. Grady got to his feet and realized just how hard he had slept. He felt a bit of a stupor about himself much the same as he had seen a love for the laudanum bottle. He shook it off just as quickly as he had many times over and made his way to the surface of the earth. There was a fair frost. He realized that if he got out and about before the sun had a chance to chase off the nights sprinkling of white that he might pick up a rabbit track. He pulled his coat collar in tighter around his neck and set out for the nearby branch. A splash of cold water to the face should heighten his senses, and a couple of good hands full would quell the dryness in his mouth and throat. He would not venture out too far, because it would be best if he could keep unseen. He was well aware of his doings and knew what could be his fate if certain folks nearby knew of his presence.

No more than three or four days he told himself. No more sleeping in a hole in the ground after that. He had decided. He would head out back toward the ferry and on west in spite of the danged Blue Bellies and all their law and such. Anything would be better than this place.

Lieutenant Long was stepping lively when he came off the front porch of the Johnson's house and made his way to the picket fence gate. "Soldier," he said as he addressed young Illinois volunteer, "pick three men and ride on up this road to the end. You should find an older man there called Wes Rogerson and a young man who goes by Jubal."

"Tell them that Mrs. Johnson would like for them to come here now. Do not tell them anything more. If they ask, you can tell them that you do not know any details, only that you were sent to fetch them. Do you understand?"

"Yes sir. I do."

"I do not expect that you will encounter any Rebel forces or any locals for that matter. You are to engage no one unless it is in pure self-defense, and there is no other way out. I do not want any private little wars going on for any reason. Take two extra mounts with you for them to ride back. We may be here several days before we get further instruction, but we need those gentlemen here today. I repeat that you are to give no details. Mrs. Johnson and myself will take care of that when you return. Mrs. Johnson's daughter tells me that it is just about two hours on foot so you should be able to get there and back in good time. Do you have any questions?"

"No sir," the young trooper replied.

"Then choose your men and be at it."

"Yes sir," with the accompaniment of a sharp salute.

"The rest of you men dismount and tend to your horses. We will stay in that small field beside the creek. Go ahead and prepare for the night if you wish, but keep alert and post one sentry a bit down the road. Call me immediately for any issue whatsoever." With that the smartly uniformed young lieutenant turned back to the house, ascended the steps and rapped smartly at the front door. Lida had been watching him all the while through closed lace curtains, but she purposefully delayed opening the door for a moment or two. She needed just a bit to compose herself.

The quartet of Union cavalry reached the barnyard in just a few minutes over an hour, and the corporal immediately made his way to the old log cabin. Wes had heard them approach and walked out into the yard.

"Are you Mr. Rogerson?" he asked.

"Just who need know that, son?" Wes quipped.

"Mr. Long has dispatched me here to fetch Mr. Rogerson and a younger man by the name of Jubal."

"Fetch us? Where to?"

"Down the road about an hour to a miller's place. I have brought two extra horses for you to return with us."

"What be the matter there?"

"I do not know, sir. Mr. Long has not told me. He just sent me to fetch you. He said Mrs. Johnson had requested you."

That got Wes's attention in a hurry. "Well then, I reckon we best go with ye. Jubal is up yonder in the timber after a coon old Jake treed last night. I reckon he can hear me if I beat for him. Be back in just a minute."

"Yes sir. Please be smart. Mr. Long will be waiting I am sure, and he will not think kindly of delay."

Wes started for the old horn and intended to blow it as hard as he could. It was nothing more than an old bull's horn with a slight bit of the tip filed away and a rawhide strap tied onto each end for strap, but it was very effective in calling the hounds back from the fields. He walked out to the woodshed where there would be no obstruction between him and where Jubal should be. He raised the horn to his lips and started to blow when he saw Jubal coming out of the timber and heading directly in his direction. Evidently he had seen the quartet approaching the barn about the same time he had heard them.

It took only a few short moments before Wes and the boy were ready to mount up and head down the hollow. All that either of them knew was that Mrs. Johnson had sent for them and that was plenty reason to go. They rode two abreast with Jubal and Wes in the middle rank.

"Reckon we be needed fer more mill work?" Jubal asked.

"Could be, but I got me some questions about why we would be fetched by the Union army. I just got me a bit of uneasy feelin' about this," Wes answered trying not to sound overly alarmed.

Jubal said no more. They rode at a steady but easy gait. The corporal did not push too much, because he judged his charges not to be accomplished riders. Wes knew that he would be pretty much unfit for anything come morning. The saddle was giving him a right smart thrashing, and it would tell tomorrow.

"Pleased to see you back so soon corporal," Lieutenant Long commented to his underlings. "See to your horses and join the camp yonder," he instructed as he pointed out the little creek bottom that had become a hasty cadre of Union troopers. Three tents had been set up, and a cooking fire was already performing its designated duties. "Mrs. Johnson has been kind enough to share some sugar cured ham with us and some parched corn. See to it that it is used and divided properly."

"Yes sir."

Wes and Jubal made their own way up the steps and to the front door where Mrs. Johnson met them. She looked tired.

"Come in gentlemen. It is good to see you this mornin'. Please come in."

The request was honored at once and Mrs. Johnson politely pointed them to the open fireplace which was banked with a deep bed of coals and one big hickory back stick. Wes looked into the fire with a knowing eye while Jubal stood customarily with his backside to the flame, hands interlocked behind his body. He had not seen Lida and was vexed by her absence.

"I suppose that you wonder why the Union boys are here this mornin' and why they fetched you here," Mrs. Johnson said as she folded one hand around the other and brought them both up under her chin.

Jubal thought that he could see just a slight reflection of the fire-light flicker in her eyes and in that instant realized what it was that he was witnessing. Something was amiss; it had to be. Possibly she now knew about him and Lida. Lida had broke down somehow and told her all about them. A moment of fear swept over him. He felt his heart quicken. Had it not been for the want of a lamp light, the redness of his cheeks would have given way his burning need to take flight.

Wes turned to face her. "We did think it a mite odd that they was in such hurry and all, but the trooper in charge told us that they was just on routine rounds and that ye had asked them to fetch us."

"What he told ye be the truth," she replied.

"Ye needs more mill work done, and they come fer fetchin' the feed?" Jubal asked.

"I wish it was that simple. Lord knows I wish it so," Mrs. Johnson continued as she seated herself in a cane bottom chair near her side.

"Is there trouble with them Rebs again?" Jubal questioned.

"No, there is nothin' with the Confederate army nor no troops in particular. The Union boys seem to have them pretty much under control now. We have had no trouble since the last time when those three men were here and the Rebs stood by and just looked on and then rode off."

"Ye speakin' of when they hit Mr. Johnson?" Wes asked softly.

"Yes, that be the time."

Wes knew what was coming, or at least he thought he knew. Jubal had not thought about anything that could be a consequence except Lida telling on him. He knew nothing else, and therefore said nothing else.

"What can I do fer you?" Wes asked.

"I don't really know what I will need in the days comin'. I thought I would need yer labors soon, but Mr. Long has assured me that he and his boys will see to that."

"What has happened?" Wes questioned.

"C.C. passed away this mornin' long about daylight," she answered as she cradled her face in her open hands and sobbed openly.

No one spoke, and Jubal was dazed by what he had just heard. It took several moments for reality to set in.

Wes broke the silence after a bit, "What happened with him? I thought he was doin' well, leastwise it seemed like that when we was here last."

"He complained last night of his head just a poundin' like, and said he was a bit dizzy too. He drifted off to sleep. I thought he was gonna be good come daylight, but that weren't so." Mrs. Johnson was plainly upset, and she did not really try to hide it. Tears coursed slowly down her cheek as she tried to gain hold of herself, wringing her hands all the while.

"I am truly sorry," Wes said meaning every word of it.

"Me too," Jubal added, still at a loss for his own words.

"I heard him moanin' and such just before daybreak. I come to look in on him, and his bed clothes was all bloody and soiled. He had blood comin' out his right ear and looked like some drained out his nose as well," Mrs. Johnson continued. The Lieutenant told me he had seen that before on men what had took a hard lick to their head. He said the surgeon told it was from blood wellin' up inside his head."

"I've heard that called perishin' of the brain," Wes commented.

"He is gone now no matter what ye may call it and that be the cold hard truth. That is what is so troublin' to me and to poor Lida too. But she don't be troubled one bit more than me. We was together many good years, but now it be over."

"What ye need us to do fer ye?" Wes asked.

"Ye can help Mr. Long and his men I suppose, if ye don't mind."

"How might that be?" Wes questioned again.

"He done told Lida that he and his men could do the buryin' if I could just point out where. I be thinkin' that I want him put away in the churchyard at the Cove. He always liked it there. He always said it was a heap nice place. It would mean a lot to me iffin ye could go and show them where it is."

"We can do that. Any place special ye want when we go there?"

"Put him under one of them big cedar trees. He told me one time that was where he wanted be put."

"Ye want me go fetch Ma and Julie? I know they be glad to come help ye dress him and all," Jubal said, finally composing himself enough to be able to speak in a sensible manner.

"No, that ain't necessary. Lida done near got him all bathed up. Besides it just be proper that we do that fer him, cause it will be the last we can do fer him. I thank ye, and I thank yer Ma just the same. But we just want this last bit of time with him. I thinkin' ye understands that, least I hope ye do."

"Yes. Yes, I do indeed," Jubal answered. He had wondered where Lida was, but there was no way he would ask in the present situation. He had been given an answer and had not even considered what duty and family would demand from her. He felt true compassion for her and would like to take her in his arms and just hold her tight and tell her how sorry he was for her, but that could all come later. Right now there were far more pressing matters. He aimed to do all that he could to help in their time of need. He knew the Cove church and its grounds; he had been there several times. It was not that far, and it would be only a short ride. He had a million questions on his mind right now, but they would just have to hold on for a while. All in its own time he kept reminding himself.

After a bit, it was decided that Jubal would ride with the lieutenant and his party to the Cove Cemetery to point out the place where C.C. would be laid to rest. Jubal had convinced Mrs. Johnson that he knew enough about the place and that he knew where she was talking about when she mentioned the big cedar trees. She had told him that she had confidence in him and, therefore, would not worry about it. He had no problem in doing all he could for her and for Lida as well.

Lieutenant Long had detailed six soldiers to accompany him and Jubal. They were making ready as the boy came down off the big front porch and exited through the gate. The lieutenant had instructed the other troops to maintain their bivouac and to keep a protective eye on everything around until he returned. They would return as soon as they had completed their task.

Jubal rode alongside the lieutenant, and the two of them soon fell into conversation. There were lots of questions that the boy wanted to ask him about the military, and he also wanted to know more about what had taken Lida's father. What was it that had killed him when he had seemed to be improving.

"How long you been in the army," Jubal asked.

"Almost two years now."

"Where ye be from?"

"My home is in upstate New York."

"How old ye be, iffin ye don't mind my askin'?"

"I don't mind your asking, and I am twenty-two last month."

"Then that make you be borned in February. Is that what ye say?"

"Yes," the lieutenant replied.

"That be same as my Granny Iverson."

More conversation, primarily of no particular depth, soon found them at their destination. Jubal found the spot that Mrs. Johnson had described and pointed it out to the work party. They immediately got to the task of opening a grave. While the four enlisted men labored, Jubal had opportunity for some serious questioning.

"What ye reckon caused Mr. Johnson to take a bad turn and up and die on us so sudden like?" Jubal asked not really expecting much of a reason or an explanation.

"The blow that he took to his head would be my guess."

"What about him bleedin' out his ears and all that?"

"I am no doctor, but I would think that he had some blood vessels that were damaged when he was hit, and that they just gave way and caused his brain to perish."

"Then the man what whacked him be a killer. Ain't that right?"

"I believe that would be an accurate statement, but you have to take into consideration the fact the war is being carried on; and although he was not in the army, I suppose you just have to say that he was a civilian casualty. However, that does not give any soldier the right to just arbitrarily do away with whoever might cross his path."

"The man what hit him weren't no solider," Jubal added.

"How do you know this?"

"Lida seen it all happen, and she shot one of them."

"How many were there?"

"They was three, and I know who they was."

"Are you certain?"

"Pine blank. I know who they be, and I bet I know where they be too," Jubal announced somewhat braggingly.

"Then they could be held accountable. At least I see it that way, since this area is under martial law for the present time."

Jubal did not really understand martial law, and the Lieutenant was patient enough to offer him a brief explanation. He himself was a young man, not much older than Jubal, but he was from a different part of the country and was aware of the worth of education and training. He honestly did not look down on Jubal and his kind, but it did make him aware of just how fortunate he had been in being brought up in a positive environment where values and important assets in life were not, out of necessity, so centered on just pure survival and having food and shelter. He realized that Jubal and many like him were slaves just as sure as were the field hands and servants living in bondage under sometimes cruel and unforgiving masters. Jubal was a slave to his environment and to his lack of schooling, even in the most basic matters. A tour in the army might open opportunities for him that he could never be exposed to otherwise. Just a thought he told himself, that could be explored later.

"I need a coffin for him, and I reckon Yeary's is about the only place close by that I can find one," Mrs. Johnson said to Wes, still wringing her hands a bit. "Reckon ye and the boy could fetch one?"

"Won't need do that." Wes replied. "There is one right yonder in the mill house. Been there since last fall."

"I don't understand at all," Mrs. Johnson replied with a bewildered look about her. "Did my C.C. buy it back then? How come it there?"

Wes took time to explain that he had ordered it and that C.C. had agreed to hold it in the mill house until it was needed. He explained how it had appeared that Julie would be the one who would need it and that he had only been trying to be prepared and get Ma and the whole family prepared best he knew for what seemed inevitable. He went on to tell her how that her husband had been agreeable to helping him get all the other purchases he had wanted. Ma and Granny Iverson and the girls knew nothing about his dealings with C.C., and Jubal knew only a bit here and there. He had not even known about the coffin. Wes and C.C. were the only ones who had known about it.

"Where was ye gonna put her, Wes?"

"I had not broached that to Ma nor nobody else, but now it be right sure that she will not need it any time soon. Hate sayin' it, but she most likely be crippled and may even be crutch bound; but she mends up more ever week now."

"C.C. told me that he had helped ye get some things, but he never told me no details, special about no coffin," she remarked.

"Your man was a good man, and he tried hard to help them what needed a little boost. He always treated me good even when I had give up on self and on life. He friended me in spite of myself, and I be always beholdin' to him too."

"Some folks he never had no use for, and he just never did even want them kind around here, not one bit."

"I feel the same as he did. Just got no use of em neither," Wes added.

"I reckon some might think him not much obligin' fer some folks, special them what was down and out a bit, but he helped a lot of people down through all them years. He just saw people's needs and filled em where he could. He was a good man no matter what some might say."

"I think so too," Wes said kindly. "And that be a large measure of a man's character in how he treats them what can't be no benefit to him. That be a measure of a free heart and a kind soul. That be how I see it, and I think that be how he felt too. He took no pride in it neither; he just done it out of pure want to. He done it cause it needed done, and he could see that plain as daylight at high noon."

"Me and Lida is gonna miss him. We may be comin' on hard times, but I reckon the Lord will provide. I just read a few evenings ago how he said he would meet our needs and how he knows what we need and when we need it. I reckon I just needs be seperatin' my wants away from needs and then dwell on that and have faith all the while.

"I reckon me and Jubal can help ye with man's work and all. Ye just needs let us know."

"Wes, ye know I be grateful. I will call when I need help, but right now I ain't thought much on all them tomorrows yet. All I can do now is just take one day at a time and hope I have strength for the day at hand. I just ain't had no thinkin' on what lies ahead no more than that."

"I reckon ye be wise in yer own way, and I uphold ye fer that too. I just wish they was more that I could do fer ye and your girl." Wes thought that she probably would not want to be called a girl no longer. He could look upon her and easy see how she could stir the feelings of any young man. She had matured into quite a young woman that any man could appreciate.

"I will do all I can, any time I can. All ye need do is get me word," Wes said in attempting to assure and comfort Mrs. Johnson.

"I know that, and I thank you very much too."

"I know that too."

"Strange ain't it?" Mrs. Johnson said as much to herself as to anyone.

"What that be?" Wes responded.

"Well…Strange as it may seem right now, just in two or three generations there won't be a soul on this earth what ever heard his voice or looked on his face. He will be forgot and all his memory erased by time. But the things he done for others is the only thing about him that be likely remembered over all the years yet to come. That just be the way things is, and it say so in the Good Book. It plainly say that one generation passes away and that another takes its place. Tell me, Wes, do ye think that means that the next generation is charged with doin' whatever their parents did? Do my children be expected to act and do as I did all my life?"

"I think they be a lot of truth in that. I think a child will act as he been raised to act, and he ain't likely to veer off his mark none if he was raised up right," Wes responded.

"I hope ye be right there. I know fer a fact that C.C. was raised up in the light and that he knowed it from a tender age too, and it done stuck with him all these years. I know that as well as I stand here right now. Ye know, it cuts some of the edge away right this very minute."

It was down late in the afternoon when Jubal and the Union troopers returned form the Cove churchyard, and the sky had turned to a darkening gray. By that time Lida and her mother had C.C. bathed and dressed. He would lay corpse that night and would be laid to his rest the next day. Reverend Bruce, the circuit rider was at the east end of the county this week; therefore, there would be no ordained person to speak over the miller man. Mrs. Johnson had agreed that they would just go and do what needed be done come noon tomorrow and that anyone who wished could say whatever they wanted. If that was nothing but respectful silence, then that would be fine too.

Morning skies broke with dark-and-low-hanging clouds that looked as if the heavens would open up in torrents. Rumbles of early spring thunder raised a voice in apparent protest to the coming daylight, clouded over as it was. The heavens were as dark and as heavy as were the hearts of the miller man's family. It would be a dark day, and a day that would forever be burned into memories of caring souls.

It was again late in the afternoon when everyone made their way back to the mill house. Six of the Union troopers had been detailed as bearers; Mr. Long had seen to that and his instructions had been followed to the last detail. The rain had held off until Lida and Mrs. Johnson had climbed down from the carriage and stepped onto their porch. It was as if that had been the opening of the flood-gates, because the thunder spoke, and the downpour began in earnest. Jubal saw to the horses and the carriage. Lieutenant Long and his troopers made fast for their tents. It was over. All that was left behind now were the memories. It would be sundown early today.

"What do we do now?" Jubal asked.

"Well, I reckon that be largely dependin' on what Mrs. Johnson wants us do," Wes answered unknowingly. "We ought not leave her alone this night of all nights. I know the Union boys is here, but they ain't locals nor such. Would be good if Ma was here, but reckon that can't be just now, and I ain't real keen on ridin' back up the road after dark. Besides that we ain't got our own mounts. We been in Union saddles, if ye think about it. I reckon we could bed down in the mill tonight and that ought not bother none."

"Ye reckon Ma and Julie be all okay since we both been gone?" Jubal questioned as much to himself as to Wes.

"I been thinkin' the same things, and all I reckon we can do is just hope. She knows where we been, but she don't know no details yet. That be the bad part the way I see it. Least one of us needs get back there come first light."

"Reckon I need go now?" Jubal questioned again.

"They ain't much likely be no highway men out in this here soup. It might not be all that much peril iffin ye did go, but I just ain't up to it till I rests up some. Like I said, we ain't got our mounts.

"I could take C.C's team and buckboard. That way I could fetch Ma and Julie back soon after daybreak."

"I still don't think it best ye go by ye self," Wes cautioned. "But ye be right in fretin' over Ma and all, so maybe that is what ye ought do. Why don't ye ask Mr. Long if two of his troopers could ride with ye. They could stay over in the springhouse loft and that ought be better than a tent and a bedroll on the ground. I know Ma would feed good come daylight. They ought like that too."

When Ma learned all that had transpired and what had been done, she could hardly believe the things that her son told her. He and Wes had been away only a few short hours, not really much time at all considering all that had come about. But she had been witness to a thing or two herself.

Sometime during the past night, some low down so and so had come and got in their barn and made off with the horses. Worst part of it was that she had found old Jake in the feed way with the side of his head all bashed in and covered with dried blood. That told her that he had been silenced on purpose and with a vengeance. She had so wanted to spare telling her son the cruelty of it all, but there was no concealing the truth. He was naturally quite beside himself, he felt he knew who was behind it all.

Jubal questioned his Ma for every last detail that she knew or could recall. She did not tell him that she had seen shadowed figures going away from the barn with the stock in tow nor that one of them was a big man who best she could tell had a full beard and another looked like he had a hat that was about three sizes too big for his head. She was almost sure that she knew who the thieving scum were, but she thought it best to keep that to herself, at least for now.

Before good light Jubal was already reading the signs and following the tracks. He had not reached the tree line above the barn until he knew where the tracks would lead. They turned east and made a beeline for the ridge crest that would lead to high ground above the mill and then on to the cave area. He knew the whole route just like the back of his hand and knew that he could get back to the old log home, have a good breakfast, get Ma and Julie all loaded in the buckboard, get them back to the mill and then have plenty of time to cut their track well east from there. As a matter of fact, he could save time by doing just that rather than follow the tracks step for step.

It did not take long at all for the three of them and the two troopers to get ready for their short ride. The troopers were indeed appreciative of the ham, red-eye gravy and biscuits breakfast and were more than expressive of how good they thought it tasted. They had even helped Jubal to lay old Jake to rest and said that they regretted that he had come to such a cruel end.

The ride back to the mill was over and done before the sun was up very far. Jubal immediately brought Wes up on what had happened. Wes knew just as well who had done it, but kept his thought mostly to himself. He thought that best.

"I be thinkin' I can cut their track a bit east. I plan on takin' one of C.C.'s team and makin' certain I know what already be true. I be thinkin' I don't even need no track. I be thinkin' I can just ride straight there and see all I needs see."

"Ye might be right, but don't ye think ye ought speak with the Lieutenant first? He might even have a trooper or three ride with ye just in case ye was to need a hand," Wes suggested. "If they be that desperate, then no tell what might come about once ye stirred them up."

"I will tell Lieutenant Long what done happened and what I be thinkin' on it, but I still aim to ride over at Yeary's and get me a look see, even iffin I goes by myself," Jubal replied. "Ain't no way I can't go."

"I reckon that be so," Wes answered.

Jubal conversed at length with the Union officer about the whole situation concerning the thievery; not only the last evening, but the whole picture. He related how he suspected who was behind it and all the encounters that he had seen and how they all seemed to tie things together. Lieutenant Long listened intently. He did not indicate such to Jubal, but he had reason to gather all the information that he could about certain things, namely the demise of storekeeper Cleve and the torching of his property. There was more involved there than any of the local citizenry had any idea about. There were issues there that had connections all the way from Nashville to Washington City. Lieutenant Long knew that Jubal had no need to know any of those details, and even if he did know, there was little that would have any bearing on him personally.

"I think that you possibly should ride to that cave that you speak about and just observe whatever you can. I do not expect that you would take any civil action. That would fall to me and my men to see to that, but I would be interested in any information that you could get to me as to the whereabouts of those men. I would urge extreme caution and to keep yourself unseen."

"I can be back here by mid-afternoon," Jubal said. "Then ye reckon we can go nab all three?"

"That will need to be looked into. I have standing orders in such situations, but as of this moment I need more to go on."

"Well…just what might ye want me to look about?" Jubal questioned rather smartly.

"If you were to spot the stolen horses that would be evidence enough for me to take appropriate actions," the Lieutenant replied. "I could detail two men to ride with you, if you wish."

"No. I reckon I can make better time by my lonesome," Jubal said in a much more civil tone. "I know the way, and I know when and where I needs be quiet and where I can light out in a run iffin needs be."

"Very well. I only need a rough sketch of a map to include in any report I might need to make. Help me draw it up quickly and then you can get started. Just remember that I need only visual proof. You do not need to take any unnecessary risks. I will possibly need you as a guide later, so just be sure you get yourself back here to report. Can I count on that?"

He wanted to state that as an order, but reasoned that the boy would not be too keen on orders from any source just now.

"I get myself back here and let ye in on everthing what I see. I right smart sure I could tell ye that right now, but I know ye needs me say I seen it with my own eyes. Ye gonna see it with yer eyes too, time it all be said and done."

When Ma and Wes learned of the intended course of action, more cautions and warnings poured forth. "Don't do nothin' foolish now, ye hear me?" Wes intoned.

Ma did not have a lot to add to that. But the hurt in her eyes and the worry in her face was plain. Even Lida and her mother were alarmed at what he was set on doing and urged him to reconsider and leave the whole matter to the justice that could be brought down by the Union army.

"No. I can't sit here and do nary a thing about all the wrongs that they done. I am determined that they pay, and that they pay up full too. I done made promises to myself that they needs be took care of, and I be thinkin' now be proper time fer it too," Jubal rebutted in unbending determination.

Jubal mounted up and reined toward the rise behind the mill. Wes grabbed the reins and stopped him short in just a step or two.

"I see ye be bound to go so ye may as well stick this in under your jacket," Wes said as he handed up a Navy Colt. "Just keep it under wraps. They be lots folks would give a whole heap to have one of them things. I just lendin' it to ye, and I expects it back as well as yerself. I expect ye back before sundown too."

"I plan on it myself," Jubal quipped.

He rode straight up the rise behind the mill and turned east out the crest and made straight for the ridge that would lead him to the small clearing above Yeary's store. He could come down and hit the road if he needed to make slight better time and that would be an option once he cut the track and could tell which way it would lead. He figured he would cut the track about a third way out the top where it met up to the ridge above the sand hill.

He had never really had to face any controversy like this. But then again, he nor his family had ever been wronged like this before. Ma had harped on vengeance belonging to the Lord, and the Lieutenant had said that it would be his decision. Well, he figured the Lord might take kindly to a little help ever now and then, and the Union army looked like they had about all they could see to already. Wes was the only one who made any sense, and he had done his part by giving up his side arm. Jubal had his old long rifle, of course, but the side arm was a good insurance, and he was glad to have it.

Redbuds were trying their best to burst out, but there had apparently not been enough sunshine so far. Most trees except the ash and the oaks already had little mouse ear leaves. The edelweiss was in bloom, wherever the bushy tails had not yet found it and devoured it. Birds flittered around everywhere with grass and twigs in tow. Spring was definitely on its way. Dogwoods were not budded out yet, so there would be at least one more cool spell and maybe a frost yet to come. Raven black eyes watched him from top most limbs overhead but made no sounds. Somehow they must have sensed that it would be best not to communicate his presence to others, man nor beast.

Jubal cut the tracks almost to the step just where he had thought. Now all he had to do was follow enough to see which way they would lead. That was no task at all. Tracks were bold as the sun at noon.

Unfamiliar thoughts raced through the boy's mind. What would he do if the three scallywags stepped out from behind a rock or a tree the way they had done down on the road? He had no real answer, and in a sense of reassurance felt for the Colt beneath his shirt. Thumbing the hammer ever so slightly sent a shiver up his spine, and he quickly jerked his hand away from the weapon. For the first time, he questioned his determination and rationalized it to be momentary fear. Not fear as lesser of a man would know, but fear born from a startle. He could not see himself as being afraid, just not thinking straight, just for a breath or two. His hand returned to the pistol grip, and his courage returned with it. At least he saw it that way.

At the point where he thought the track would lead down in the general direction of the cove and Yeary's store, there was an unexpected turn back to the north. That could mean only one thing. The riders were headed to the cave and whatever seclusion and concealment it could offer. Local folks had long since labeled it as a place where drifters and derelicts would hide or hold up for a spell. It had a reputation as such, and folks in these parts avoided it most times. Jubal knew that there was a cedar thicket nearby that could hide almost anything. It was less than a couple of miles from where he now stood, studying the tracks in the soft earth. He decided it best to walk the rest of the way and lead C.C.'s horse. Should be quieter that way, and he should be able to hear better himself. No sense in unknowingly giving away his presence. A slower pace would dampen the sounds of the horse's gait, and he could for sure control his own.

The approach to the cedar thicket was almost without sound. He tied off his mount just deep enough into the thicket to hide him from open sight. Shade and shelter would keep him quiet and unseen.

The thick stand of cedar growth was unique in its own right. It provided shelter and sanctuary for a number of critters, big and small. The ground beneath the massive old trees had seen many seasons of needles dropped and decayed to form the blackest of earth. Some folks had even come here and carted away wagon loads of the rich humus to use as seed beds for their garden plants. Each footstep was muffled by the thick mat of needles and the sparse grasses that thrived only by the thick canopy of overhead green.

Jubal eased quietly downhill in the general direction of the cave opening. He had been here before, but was not as sure of his direction as he had thought he would be. Accordingly, he began bending and breaking small twigs off the lower branches in order to retrace himself should he need such. Besides that, he had to get back to his horse eventually, no matter what he may or may not see. He stopped frequently to listen. No alarming sounds, just the soft rustle in the branches above and the coo of a dove now and again. He felt through his shirt for the pistol grip. Yes, it was still there and just as reassuring to the touch as it had been before.

A low-sounding thud caught his ear, and he froze in his tracks. He listened intently in all directions looking for any sign of anything that might be astir. Nothing! Not another sound. He moved on a few more yards taking care to mark his path with bent or broken cedar twigs. He looked back on his own tracks thinking that he could retrace his own trail if it became necessary.

There it was again! Thump! Just as before, and this time clearly off to his right. More waiting. More intense listening. Nothing! Just the birds and the wisps of wind in the topmost branches. He made his way slowly in the direction of the sound for another few yards and stopped to listen again.

This time he heard a low rustling sound, faint but definitely a rustle sort of like willow rushes in a springtime rain shower. The thick cedar canopy darkened the sun even at noon, and it was an effort to see very far in the thick growth. That did not diminish his sharp eye.

Thump! And almost immediately again! This time he thought he had seen just a bit of movement down low, just at ground level. Down on hands and knees, he made his way toward the sound taking care to avoid putting weight on a dry twig or such and making any sound that would betray his presence. There it was again! This time a definite movement and a repeated rustle. He felt his heart quicken. More waiting. More listening. Reasoning that he was yet unseen, he made his way another twenty yards or so, stopping to listen and search all around him yet again.

This time he did see movement and heard rustle as well. He had no problem in understanding what was astir now. Less than a stone's throw were two horses hobbled and bridled, busy at what looked to be scraps of last year's fodder. Spring had invaded their temperament as well because they were in search of sprigs of green and nosed the fodder aside in their quest. The hobbles were drawn up tight and thus they were not about to move very far.

He reached the pair in hardly any effort, taking care to remain silent. It was obvious at once where the stock had come from. He knew them as well as he knew his own family. Their markings could not be mistaken. Slowly and gently he unbuckled the hobbles from one and then the other. They made no effort to move away or to bolt. It was as if they knew him and trusted him completely. They had reason. He had cared for them and seen to it that they were well fed from the day Wes had bought them and brought them up the hollow to the barn. The pair made only a few steps until they realized that their binding shackles had been thrown off. Still, they remained gentle and stirred very little.

Jubal made his way back to where he had dismounted and tied his beast. The pair followed him and seemed content to be in the company of another of their own kind. The three murmured to each other and rubbed neck to flank and appeared to make preferred company. Jubal let them have their way for a few moments and then began to lead his animal slowly and as quietly, out of the thick cedar thicket and back the way he had come. He had seen and learned all he needed to know for the time at present. He needed to get back to the mill and to the Lieutenant in good time and report for fact what he had known to be the situation when he first learned about it.

Still, he was determined that the horse thievery would be the lesser of the evils that had been wrought. Nevertheless, the punishment for horse stealing could be no less than the willful taking of a life. Vengeance might belong to the Lord, but disgust and hatred could be his as much as he wanted. He would have vengeance himself if he had his way and had half a chance. He had given his word that he would return before night fall, and he intended to do what he had said. Once he cleared the area above the cedars, he mounted up and began a slow gait along the ridge top.

He soon made his way out the ridge to where he had first cut the tracks. He stopped here just to listen and look around again. The sun was still plenty high for him to make it back to the mill well ahead of dusk. The breeze had laid. There were few sounds even from the birds. It was as if all creation were stilled, anxiously awaiting some foretold prophetic happening. There were no senseless noisy ravens announcing his every move and no ground foragers scurried away in fear of his presence.

He made no attempt at being unseen or unheard as he descended the hill to the mill yard. His unfettered newly recovered friends came right along behind and halted when he did.

"Where'd ye find them?' Wes questioned as he came out of the mill to greet the lad.

"They was hobbled in the cedars over near the cave."

"Horne's cave?"

"Yep. I cut the track just like I knowed I would. They ain't got much smarts when it comes to hidin' they self," Jubal answered rather proud of himself.

"Did ye see anybody?"

"No, but I reckon I don't need see to know who it be. Ain't nobody else around nowhere close other than them."

"I reckon ye be right as rain on that," Wes answered.

"I know without askin' but these here is your hosses, ain't they?" Jubal asked as if to amplify the fact that he had proven beyond all doubt that he had answered all the unknowns thus far.

"They are indeed."

"Well I ain't surprised none. They was right where I thought they would be. Ye know who stole em too, don't ye?" Jubal asked, already knowing what Wes would answer.

"I reckon we best go speak with the Lieutenant and see what he have to say on it. I think that be proof enough to go fetch em and make payday come to them full and furious," Wes responded knowing all along what would be the outcome. "It will take some time before the Union can try them or see to it that they is brought up on any charge. Reckon we have to abide by what they say as well as the next man does. I am not up on how they deal with such."

"I will deal with them iffin needs be," Jubal replied with sternness and determination in his voice. "They is gonna pay, even iffin I have to be the judge and the jury myself. I reckon I can be the hanger man too iffin nobody else will do it."

"We best go talk with the man and see what he says before ye go off on a cocky notion and wind up in trouble yerself. Trouble can find you, ain't no need ye goin' out lookin' it in the face. It find ye easy enough. We want this took care of proper. Then they won't be no trouble or fixes to try and worm out from. It just needs be done right," Wes tried to explain but was almost sure that his words were falling on undiscerning ears.

Lieutenant Long listened intently as Jubal related his findings, and all the circumstances surrounding the entire affair. He was clear as to most everything that had occurred, especially concerning the thievery that the trio had been suspected of committing all along. He had even been briefed on all the incidents concerning Cleve and the losses there. He had even heard about the happenings with the old Bray widow. He had already determined that Jubal was a bit of a hothead as the three men related to him and his family, and there was no need whatsoever to heap coals on that fire. It would be a task to keep him in check as it now stood, let alone further stirring.

He wanted to know if Wes had a bill of sale for the horses and was informed that was indeed the case. "Where is your bill?" he asked of Wes.

"It be back up yonder to the log home in my stuff over the springhouse."

"Then I take it you could produce it for evidence later if we were to need it in court or such," the Lieutenant questioned.

"I can," Wes replied.

Lieutenant Long had a few more things to ask, mostly about the lay out of the cedar thicket and the surrounding area. He wanted to know if Jubal thought he could find his way to and into the cave. He asked about the insides of the cave and how many entrances and exits there might be. Jubal answered all his questions as accurately as he knew.

"I am due back at the ferry camp in three days. I am going to send a courier and three troopers back there tonight and request an extension of my patrol here. Otherwise, I might not be able to take advantage of this opportunity. These three have caused incidents all around here, but this is the first time that loss of a life has been directly attached to them; and it is the first time that definite horse stealing can be attributed to them. As far as I know, it is the first time that they have had any direct evidence or positive proof attached to them. The Union army is near victory and may very well be the only authority that can keep order in the area once hostilities cease and the Confederate survivors begin returning. The area does not need the likes of these men once that becomes reality. There will be enough difficulty without such as them on the loose. I think you can understand that, can you not?"

"I reckon we do," Wes parroted.

"Then I have only one other question," the Lieutenant replied as he turned to face Jubal. "How long would it take for you and myself and six of my best men to reach the cave?"

"From here, no more than three hours and that be with some of it on foot near the last," Jubal responded with rekindled enthusiasm.

"And what if we were riding in the dark of night?"

"I would add about another hour, I reckon," Jubal answered.

"Give me time to instruct my courier and to speak with my men. I suggest that you find yourself a hearty meal and prepare for a long night. I will be back with you in another two hours or so. Then I will tell you what I intend to do. Thank you for your information. I will be depending on you to lead us to where we need to be." With that the officer turned sharply and made quick time to his camp tent.

Jubal and Wes headed to the mill house and had hopes of finding a hot meal. They were not disappointed. Lida and her mother had made a big skillet of cathead biscuits, fried some streaked meat and made gravy. There would be no reasons for hunger tonight.

The plan became quite simple. The Lieutenant and his party, led by Jubal and Wes if he elected to go, would head out about midnight and make way to the cedar thicket and be in place well before daybreak. Hopefully the breaking light would tell them all they wanted to know about the cave and any suspect inhabitants. It was almost a foregone fact who they would find there, but they just needed to know for sure before they went on a blind charge. Darkness would cover them until then.

"Good chance we be able to fetch em back here," Jubal said to Lida and her mother. "Ought be no trouble now."

"I don't want to lay eyes on none of em, and I just as soon they not be nowhere near me again," Lida retorted.

"The army needs ye to finger out the one what hit C.C. so they can have a witness," Wes tried to explain.

"What happens after that?" Lida demanded.

"I reckon they be in irons, and then they be took away by the troopers. They won't be here no longer than need be. Ye can count on that, I reckon," Wes added further.

"Well, I reckon I know which one it be. I reckon I can shoot him again iffin I get a chance. And I would too," Lida quipped.

"Now that won't bring your daddy back, and it won't make ye feel no better either. I know ye ain't had no time to grieve, and neither have I. But we have to move on with life, and all we can do is take one day at a time. I don't want ye to be no more troubled than what ye are already. A bunch of hate will never make it any better. It only makes you bitter, and bitter with everyone else around ye. I don't reckon it makes a heap difference what comes of them three as long as they is outta our life and don't never be back around here."

"But Momma, they took Daddy away from us, forever," Lida answered. "And they needs be made pay."

"I know child, and they will pay some of these days. I hurt just as much as ye do, but I know and accept the fact that bitterness is a hard dose to swallow. But it don't help ye none to dwell on it. Ye can't always have answers to all ye questions. Ye have to have some trust and some faith that ye will someday soon be given comfort and that maybe sometime on out yonder ye will come to understand. Ye just needs recollect the one what be in control, and let go of all that poisonin' hate that be brewin' inside ye."

"That may be so Mrs. Johnson, but I intend to see that they pays," Jubal replied. "Then ye can commence on the bitterness work."

"Ever thing to its own time," Wes added.

"Finish up yer eats. I don't reckon I got any more to say on it right now," Lida said as she picked up her plate and disappeared into the kitchen. Jubal could easily tell that she was upset most near to the point of tears. He wanted to go to her and offer what comfort he could, but correctly reasoned that now was not the time. Just like Wes had said, everything in its own time.

Midnight was fast approaching and it was near time to head out.

"I think it be best that I stay here," Wes said. "My joints ain't what they once was, and I don't see so good at night any more. But I will go iffin ye want me to, son."

"I reckon we can do the job," Jubal responded. We ought be back here by mid-mornin' at the latest, Jubal said. "We might need go see about Ma and Julie by then. They be wantin' know all about everthing, I think."

"All I ask is that ye not do anything what come back to bite ye. Think before ye act. Ye got these here troopers on yer side. They is prepared to do whatever needs done. Let them do their work. All ye needs do is see that they gets there proper," Wes said almost pleading. "Ye still got what I handed ye early today, ain't ye?"

"Yeah, I got it right here," Jubal said as he fingered the handle.

"Watch him fer me, Mr. Long. Ye been solderin' a heap long enough to know what ye be doin', and he can sometimes be a bit hot under his collar. I don't want him in no undue fixes," Wes pleaded, this time to the officer.

"I will do that sir, to the very best of my abilities. If we can apprehend these ruffians, we will have them well away from here by sundown tomorrow, and they will not be coming back here."

"We best get started," Jubal said thus ending any more admonition from Wes.

"I agree," the lieutenant said as he turned to the ones that had volunteered to go with him. "Mount up."

Starlight made visibility just enough to avoid getting slapped in the face by low-hanging twigs and branches, all the more reason to move at a slow pace. A full gallop could cause a serious or blinding eye injury to either man or beast. Besides that, a slow pace was quieter.

Jubal was in the lead and set the pace. He knew where the thickest of the undergrowth posed the greatest hazard and kept his companions informed accordingly. They had been briefed about the trek and what to expect. They moved out the ridge tops in apparent ease.

Jubal had told the lieutenant that he would stop at regular intervals to listen and to read the signs, whatever they might be. The others most likely had no idea what he listened for, and they would not know how to interpret it if they did.

There were few night sounds, but they could be a wealth of information if you knew how to read them. There was no wind, so the smell of smoke from a fire pit would travel only a few paces. There was only a sliver of a new moon, so there would be no discernible shadowy movements. There were intermittent sounds of foraging critters, but there was no wanton or abandoned racing for cover. Thus there were no predators near. Screech owls bantered back and forth from unseen perches. There was little on the wing as a result of their banter. Their eyes were much too keen for any prey to be astir within their range. They were just another sign that all was normal.

They reached the cedar thicket without incident. More listening and more waiting. It was still about two hours before good light, and the stars were out in full. It should break day clear and bright. Sight would be good, long before the sun popped over the doubles off in the east. The horses were secured well back, and a man was detailed to tend them. He was to keep close reins on all of them and make sure none wandered off, not even a step. They had all been grain fed back at the mill that afternoon and should all be well at ease. They could be rubbed down a bit, if needed, and that should quell any restlessness.

Jubal and the troopers made their way to the cave entrance. It took the boy just a bit to make sure that he was headed right, but close attention to his steps soon allayed any doubts. He saw familiar markings and then knew just precisely where they needed to be.

As dawn began to break, Jubal and his companions were no more than a few yards from the low-slung opening that led into massive caverns deep into the limestone bedrock. A body could easily lose themselves from the outside world in the depths, but most would never venture there because of the intense darkness and the stale air. Best anyone around knew, there was no other opening, and consequently, no means of air exchange. Local lore also had it that there were ghosts of many past generations forever trapped within, waiting only to capture the soul and spirit of some uninformed wanderer.

Thin wispy threads of blue grey smoke rose slowly from the lime streaked portals of the cave opening. They could barely be seen in the coming eastern light. The acrid smell of cedar brush came riding on what little morning air was astir. Someone was in the cave, and Jubal was sure he knew just who it was. He and his party eased closer to the gap in the low slung wall of stone.

In a low whisper, Jubal spoke to the officer crouched beside him. "I reckon they be there now. Ye see that smoke, don't ye?"

"I see it. I think we should get a bit closer."

They all began a slow silent, but sure advance. The light was enough to see well now. Individual shrubs and crevices in the rocks were easily seen. The sun had yet to paint its color scheme upon the face of mother earth, but it was enough to see what was before them.

Unexpectedly and to some alarm, there came rustling sounds from inside. Then a low and dull sounding thud, followed immediately by more rustling, only growing louder. Jubal and the lieutenant made simultaneous signs to hit the ground and keep a sharp eye.

Jubal could feel the excitement rushing into every ounce of his being. His heart pounded! He had to restrain himself. He had to maintain control. He could not be a child now. He had to be a man and had to act and react as such.

The continued rustle abruptly produced a silhouette emerging from within the earthern hideaway. He stood erect just below the cave entrance and stretched himself as if trying to awaken and greet the coming day. The patrol remained frozen as he began to walk straight to them. Only a few dozen steps or so and he would be right on top of them. Jubal could now see well enough to make out distinguishing features. He was dressed in buckskins and had an unkempt and messy beard with equally untended hair billowing from beneath what was once a gentleman's fashionable hat. Indeed, he was one of the three.

His advance continued. In no time at all he was on them. He was taken down by strong hands and pinned face down so that his hands could be bound securely behind his body. A strong gloved hand covered is mouth and nose tightly. He would suck in air only when his captor allowed it. He thrashed and kicked in useless attempts to free himself. He even bit down hard on the gloved hand covering his mouth and tried to voice his hatred all at the same time. A firm and well-placed knee kick brought immediate results. Resistance ceased, the gloved hand was replaced by a silencing gag made from a sturdy broad rawhide strip. He would not chew through that for hours. He was dragged back to the hiding shadows of the dense cedars and told that it would be to his best treatment to answer the forth-coming questions. He must have sensed his fate. He indicated that he would cooperate.

Yes, the other two were in the cave. Buckskin man had told all he knew. He was made to sit at the base of a stout burled cedar and shackled to it, arms to his back and legs pulled up to a lower branch and tied securely. The rawhide gag was checked for its security as well. He was left there under single guard while the others made their way back to the cave. They could hear approaching footsteps. It took only seconds for them to take whatever cover was immediate and bring arms to bear.

Just as quickly, another figure emerged from within. He was a big man, just as roudy looking and unkempt as his buckskinned cohort.

He froze when he realized that he was the aim of six Springfield repeaters. His brawny arms were just as quickly secured behind his back. The Union troopers in no short order had him into the cedars and secured to the same tree as his buckskinned companion. The lieutenant was on both in a rapid staccato of questions and demands for answers. His voice quite adequately affirmed his authority, and the big man could sense his wrath.

"Who are you? What is your name?"

"Don't see how I needs tell any blue-bellied sum bitch nary a word."

A sharp swat across the neck with a pistol barrel brought a trickle of blood that drained down onto a filthy gray shirt. It also brought an immediate change of attitude.

"I will ask you only once more. Who are you? What is your name? And I will tell you this, the three of you are going to have to explain your presence and your actions. We have just about all the proof that we need, and I will not hesitate to put a rope around your thieving neck here and now if you choose to not answer me or if you give false answers. I am authorized by the full power of the Union army, and I will not hesitate to use that authority as I see fit. Do you understand that?"

His nod was in the affirmative.

"I believe you have been involved in a long run of wrongful activity, and it is my intention to see that you are charged and arraigned accordingly. As I said, I would not be reluctant to hang you right here and now, but I will not lower myself to such base standards. Thievery is one thing, but the taking of a life is another. I will charge each of you for only what you have done, and you can rest assured that I will find out what you have done collectively and individually. Now, would you care to state your name?"

"He be Rowe; and I be Mays, Oscar Mays," Buckskin blurted out.

"Well now, Mr. Rowe, it might be of interest to you to know that we have already recovered the two horses that you took and that we have a witness to your doing so. We also know about a storekeeper and the obvious arson of his property. And lately there is the issue of the miller man and his family." Lieutenant Long made it a point not to relate that the blow to the miller man had recently turned fatal. He had it in mind to play one against the other to see who would break first.

"Where be yer other scallywag?" Jubal asked.

"He be in yonder," Buckskin replied as he inclined his head toward the cave entrance. "But I don't think he be in no good shape much now."

"Shut yer damn yap," Rowe barked.

The lieutenant knew what he was doing. He instructed his men to get Rowe off a good distance where he could not hear or influence his cohort as he was questioned more intently. Lieutenant Long released Buckskin's hands and instructed one of his troopers to keep his Springfield three inches from the back of his head.

Now, Mr. Mays, Who killed the storekeeper named Cleve, and who torched his building?"

"Jackson done it. I swear he done it. Not me, I swear."

"And just who is Jackson?"

"He be the one still in yonder."

"And why would he have cause to do harm to the store man?"

"Laudanum. Wanted laudanum and store man say no. Jackson flew off in a mad rage and belly stuck him big time. He took a big hit when he found a bottle then pitched a lit lamp and that took the store and the storekeeper out that very night. I swear that be the truth. I ain't kilt nobody."

Two troopers brought out the limp form of the Stewart man. He had a large gash to the side of his head, and the blood had dried in a deep crimson crust. His face was the same color as ashes from an oak fed campfire. There was not one hair on his head that was not tangled or matted. His clothing was filthy and reeked. Stains bore evidence of soiling himself repeatedly. His belly was blown up like a new spring calf with milk scares. There was no discernible pulse.

"That be my Pa," Jubal uttered with a bit of a quiver in his voice. "Who hit him and why?"

Mays made no attempt to reply.

"Would you like a swat to your head as well, Mr. Mays?" the lieutenant asked.

"No, it weren't me."

"Then I suggest that you answer the man's questions," the lieutenant said as he rhythmically tapped his pistol barrel against his own leg.

Jubal repeated his question.

"Grady hit him with a flat rock."

"When?"

"Some time in the dark. Don't know what time, but it was long time till light."

"Why he hit him?"

"Grady had a shot in a jug, and Jackson wanted it."

Jubal was dumbstruck. In spite of all the hatred that he had let boil up inside himself, it was troublesome to know that his own Pa had lost his life over such. No matter how evil Pa had been, he was still blood kin; and there was a flicker of tenderness that still lived in the depths of his young heart. Part of him was hurt and another part of him was ready to explode with rage. The desire for revenge was becoming an inferno that would not soon die down.

Lieutenant Long took out a small leather bound journal and made his desired entries. "Bring Rowe here." Two troopers turned and fetched the ruffian. "Take Mays back where you had held him and keep him there until I send for you." The pair led Mays away as they had been instructed.

"Why did ye kill my Pa?"

"Cause he needed it."

A sharper and more forceful pistol whipping blow struck home, and Grady found himself flat of his back in the dirt.

"Answer his question."

"He weren't no more than a whiskey lapper and a bottle sucker and had done been shot through and through in a thigh anyhow. I knowed he weren't gonna make it outta that damned hole. He done showed us where two good mounts was, and I had no more use of him. I reckon I favored him by haltin' his sufferin' and such. He weren't no count no how."

The rage in Jubal's eyes was no less than the evil in the eyes of this devil that lay before him. Jubal seethed with speechless anger. "What did ye aim on doin' with him? Was ye just gonna leave him fer the varmints?"

"Yep. He weren't no more than dead meat no how."

"You bastard," Jubal said through clinched teeth.

"On your feet, now!" the Union lieutenant ordered.

Grady rolled over on his belly, struggling to get to his feet, hands still bound behind him. No one offered to help him up. Buckskin was already being led back to join the rest of the grouping.

It was determined that Pa's body would be taken back to the mill and that Ma could have a say in where he would be put to rest. The lieutenant had asked Jubal what he wished to do about him, and he had not been able to give a suitable answer to that issue. He asked if he could be taken back, and the officer had readily agreed that would be the best thing to do.

"I should have thought to bring extra animals," Mr. Long stated.

"I reckon I can foot it back, and we can sling Pa over my horse," Jubal said.

"Ought just leave him fer buzzard bait," Grady chided looking directly at Jubal.

"You bastard," Jubal raged as he lunged at the big man and buried his long rifle butt deep into the manacled man's stomach.

The big man barely reacted, but did manage to launch a big wad of spittle that struck Jubal square over his left eye. He wiped that away with his left forearm while the other hand seized the pistol grips. In less time than one could sense, a single shot roared and Grady was dead before his body splayed out on the earth, hands still bound behind him.

"I seen that," Buckskin blurted out, trembling all the while.

Jubal stood motionless. Lieutenant Long eased the side arm from him and gently led him away from the immediate scene. "It would have been best had you not done that."

"I ain't one bit sorry. He needed that. He even owned up to killin' my Pa."

"That is true," the officer said. "But you shot him in front of a civilian witness, and he had his hands bound behind his back when you did it. He could accurately claim it as a murder. Do you realize what trouble you could be facing?"

"No, not really I guess," came the stunned and subdued response. Jubal now felt the knots welling up deep in his gut, and he had almost an uncontrollable urge to throw up violently. He began to tremble and worked hard to control himself. He was unable to think rationally.

"Sit down here and try to calm yourself. I need to speak with each of my men and get some things moving. I will return your side arm in due time."

Jubal held his head down, almost down between his knees and wept silently. He had not thought. He had reacted and that had taken no more control than that of a fool and a young wimp. He thought he was more than that, but doubts and here-to-fore-unknown fears raced through his innermost being. He had extracted some measure of vengeance, but it brought no pleasure and no sense of justice.

The troopers opened a shallow grave and placed Grady Rowe practically where he fell. Someone said "God rest his soul." Jubal resented that, but made no sounds of protest. Pa was wrapped in a bedroll blanket and slung across Jubal's horse. It all seemed to happen so swiftly. It seemed unreal. Jubal still trembled and felt like his legs would buckle under him as he got to his feet. The lieutenant had said that it was time to move out. He would need to take the lead until they got back to the ridge line that ran along above the mill. The boy led his party somewhat of a daze and had no realization of time. Mr. Long followed close behind, but issued him no orders or instruction. He himself was deep in thought.

Chapter 18

Sworn

Wes had agreed to fetch Ma and Julie, if she was a mind to come, and to have them help decide where to put Pa and how to fix him. The boy had already asked Mrs. Johnson if he might put his Pa up above the mill in the clearing that her C.C. had liked so much. She had agreed to that, and he reckoned that Ma would be of like mind. He had already decided that he would tell her anything that she wanted to know about him as long as it was something that he knew to be fact. He was not about to sell her short or to cover up anything at all.

It had not quite reached noon when the lieutenant and his patrol rode back into the mill yard with Jubal and Buckskin. Wes had wasted no time in starting up the old hollow road. He and Jubal had talked briefly and had agreed that Ma had to be there, and Julie too if she felt up to it. Mrs. Johnson had given them free use of the buckboard and the team, so it should not be too much for Ma or Julie to return with Wes. They should be back by sundown or shortly after that.

Lieutenant Long sat at his makeshift field desk and wrote in his log intermittently for some time that afternoon. He paced back and forth at times and would wander off to where Buckskin was confined, then return to his field desk once again. He had lots to think about. He wanted to make sure that he reported accurately and honestly, and at the same time in such a manner that would serve the best interests of all concerned.

He now had no way to prove who had actually done what, save for the words of old Buckskin, and he was quick to implicate his former cronies on all counts while at the same time denying that he himself had been guilty of anything more than by association. All of that had bearing on reporting properly. Besides that, he had been a witness to the execution-style shooting of old Grady. Sorry a man as he was, he had been taken down wrongly in the eyes of the law. However, the Union army was the law at the time and each trooper or officer of that army was in fact an agent of that law.

He did not want any charges to be brought against Jubal, but yet he had to reckon with what he, his troopers, and above all others, what Buckskin had witnessed. He and his troopers would not be an issue. They were under orders and directives and had acted accordingly. The boy's actions were another matter. How could he circumvent such an injustice as having to report a murder? It was going to take some doing, but he would find a way.

Ma and Wes made it back to the mill just about sundown. They had made better time than expected. Julie did not come, because she and Ma both thought it best if she stayed home. She could get about fairly well now, and most of the soreness had left her knee. It was still stiff, but not so sore. She would manage well for a day. Ma had said that she would be back home before sundown the next day, and she had every intention of doing just that. Jubal was more than able to do all that needed to be done, and she would set him straight as to what she thought was best. Wes had not told her how it had all come about. Ma did not know how her son had reacted to the situation that he had been more or less pressured into. He had wanted his own revenge and that had surely been a strong influence on him.

Jubal ran to his mother and threw his arms around her. He wanted to say many things to her all in one breath, but words would not come to him. Wes led the team and buckboard on off to the barn in order to leave Ma and her son.

Jubal wanted to tell her how much he loved her and how much he resented all that she had endured because of Pa. At the same time he wanted to tell her that he now had his vengeance, but those feelings were just not there. The hate and resentment that he had once allowed to boil up inside were now meaningless and for the most part, gone. It made no sense how he had detested his own Pa and now that he was gone, how he could feel sorry for him. He did not realize that a void had been created in himself that would never be filled, no matter how long he should live. Could it be that he just hated the actions of the man and not the man himself?

"Where is yer Pa right now, son?" Ma asked.

"Ain't fer sure. I reckon the troopers has him someplace," Jubal responded in somewhat of a wavering voice.

"Did ye see him or is he covered up somehow?" Ma asked.

"They toted him outta the cave and put him in a bedroll. I never actual seen him."

"I see."

"What all did Wes tell ye?" Jubal questioned.

"Not much, just that Pa had been kilt and that ye wanted me come to the mill with him. That about it," she said as she loosed her arms from around his broadening shoulders.

"I needed know where ye might want him put or how ye might want him fixed and all such."

"I know ye won't understand, son. But I don't want nothin' more doin's with him now than I did before. Far as my part, he ain't the man I once knowed. That man passed on some time back, and I done made my partin' with him by now. I reckon it be up to yerself how he be took care of now. If Wes be willin' to drive me, I aim on goin' back home soon as I can."

"Ye don't wanna see him laid to rest, Ma?"

"I knowed ye wouldn't understand."

"But he was my Pa in spite of all he done," Jubal remarked with a questioning look on his face.

"I know that. I know it well. Some of these here days ye will understand better. I reckon he never did think too much on me; he even said so a few times. He weren't much of a Pa fer you kids and were less of a mate. I ain't fond of tellin' ye all these here things, but that is just the way it were. I can't change none of it even iffin I tried. I just wanna get through this here old war and all and live a few days of peace. I could never do that long as he was around someplace. I hate it fer ye, son. But I reckon ye will see it through different eyes some of these days, and I hope how soon. Ye was his seed, but that be all the Pa that he ever was to ye. They be things come about when ye was little that I be speakin' on that ye don't and can't recollect; but I know them, and they still pain me. I can't feel nothin' fer yer Pa. I ain't gonna make no lies about it. That just how it be, son. I hate it fer ye."

"What ye want me do?" Jubal asked with an overwhelming sense of emptiness beginning to engulf him.

"Put him in high ground. Ain't nobody needs a watery grave."

"Do ye wanna see him?" Jubal asked softly.

"No. And I be thinkin' it best iffin ye don't look neither. Iffin ye do, it be burned in yer mind fer the rest of yer days, and ye don't need that fer lifetime burden."

"But don't he need a good Christian burial?" Jubal asked his Ma.

"He need it. That be a fact. But he never lived that way, and I don't see no need sayin' he did. He just never did see no need fer nothin' worthwhile, I reckon. He be gone now, and I ain't much sorry fer it."

"That sounds a mite cruel to me, Ma. I hate sayin' it to ye, but that be just how I feel on it. He was my Pa after all."

"They be a heap that ye don't know nary a thing about, son. I reckon it just have to be that way now. He weren't no Pa to ye then, and he fer sure ain't now. He never treated ye like a son should'a been loved and all. He seen ye more as a workhand and treated ye the likes in spite of me. I reckon iffin I ever felt much fer him, well, he done managed long past to kill it all plum dead. I don't feel fer him now, and I ain't aim to pretend that I do."

"Will ye tell me more about him some day?" Jubal questioned, more confused now than ever before.

"I tell ye about a Father that ye ought know. That I will do, but not anytime right away. I just ain't fit right now."

"What ye have me do then, fer now?" Jubal asked.

"I think ye need lay him to his rest and move on. Ye needs get on with yer doin's and whatever it be that ye aim make outta yerself."

"How can ye be so cold time like this?" Jubal asked almost demanding an answer.

"Life be cold and hard sometimes, son. It sometimes smacks ye near beat plum down. I hope ye can see that in this here too. I ain't tryin' to be cold on ye, but I want ye to know what real life can be. I don't want yer life cold and hard like mine done been."

"But ain't ye gonna be with me when we puts him in the ground."

"No, son, I ain't. I just ain't got it in me to make over it none at all. I honest just plain don't care on his part."

"I don't understand it, Ma."

"Ye got some growin' up yet to do, son, and that apt take some time. Ye don't understand what a dark world he lived in and how much darker he made it fer me. All them years, the only light I ever had was what Granny Iverson shared with me. She been my rock these few short months since she been with me. She has tooken some of the edge off all the hurt that I been put to fer so long. She led me to understand what be the difference twixt the light and the dark, and it made heaps of difference fer me. I know ye don't understand, but Granny Iverson could make it all plain fer ye, iffin ye would just listen. Julie could too, and she would be proud doin' so too."

"Ma, I just need ye tell me about my Pa, please."

"Not now, son. Ye best go fetch up that soldier man and ask him help ye lay out yer Pa. Ye go do that whilst I pays my respects to Mrs. Johnson and her girl."

"But Ma…"

"No buts. Ye just hike out and do what I say."

In some ways the boy felt that he had just been shoved out of his own home. He felt alone and could feel the weight of the entire ordeal coming down on him. He had never felt the harshness of his Ma so strong. He knew enough to admit that stern as she could be, she was usually right in the end. He knew that she always spoke her mind. She had done just that tonight, but it had cut deeper than ever before. He did not know exactly what he was going to do or how, but he felt that his bond to home and hearth had just been broken. Sure the door to the old log cabin would be open to him, but there was just a change that he had never felt before. His Pa was gone, and he did not know if his Ma had turned her back to him or not.

Jubal prevailed upon the Union lieutenant to detail a party for burial once again. He took it upon himself to put his Pa up above the mill in the small clearing. He had asked Mrs. Johnson about it. She had approved without hesitation.

And so it was. Pa was interred just as he had been removed from the cave. He was still in the bedroll, and Jubal did not remove his body. He had not wanted to look at his Pa after all that Ma had said about it. He just silently stood by while the detail did their task, also in silence. The night would be restless.

Wes met Jubal at the mill steps as the sun began to show over the ridges to the east. "Yer Ma wants me take her back home this mornin', and I reckon it be best iffin I do. Ain't much I can do here."

"That be good by me. I reckon she been here all she want. Ain't nothin' more she can do here neither."

"Ye want me come back fer ye later on?" Wes asked.

"Can ye find me a rock fer a marker and fetch it back? I think Pa ought be marked at least. There be some flats in the spring branch down past the old barn. It don't have to be the biggest one there, but I would like to have a rock. I can tote it up there and stand it up fer him. Then I reckon I can go on home after that."

Wes agreed to the request. He and Ma were soon back in the buckboard and on the road to home. Neither had much to say on the trek, but there was a definite air of sadness and regret about them as they made their way along the old rough-and-rutted road. Maybe the old log house would afford some solace and some comfort. Granny Iverson might even know some words once she learned all that had come to pass.

Wes found an appropriate stone and carried it up to the roadside. He would load it in the buckboard and go back to the mill in the early morning. His bed in the springhouse loft would seem like a palace this night. He would know tranquility that had eluded him for many a day.

Jubal passed the better part of the day milling about in the Union encampment talking little, but listening intently. His mind raced to and fro about all that had happened, about what he had done, but he just could not dismiss the words of his Ma. He could not really pin down what troubled him so deeply, but it just did not seem like her the way she had reacted. There seemed to be a bitterness in her that he had never noticed before. She just did not seem herself; seemed hardened like she had thrown up a wall all around herself. Maybe she did feel some hurt, and this was just her way of working through it all. Maybe she had let on something or another to Lida or Mrs. Johnson. He would have to remember to ask about that sometime. Right now, he had enough thoughts of his own to deal with.

He found himself wondering about Lida. How did she feel having so recently lost her daddy? It must be hard for her and for her mother as well. But yet, he had seen neither of them in any times of wailing or anything of the sort. There could be, no doubt, that they both loved the miller man and surely had to miss him greatly. Yet they seemed to be themselves as always before and not troubled with doubts the way he was. How could there be such a difference? One man was a good and gentle man, a hard worker and a provider, while the other was a drunk, a thief and never gave two hoots about his family or much else that did not come out of a bottle. Yet he, the kin of the sot, was the one who saw the unrest and the anguishes. Why? And how could it be that way? He just did not understand it.

The night seemed forever to him. He had not rested well. He had awakened many times all the night through and had tossed about until sleep would return. The smell of wood smoke and crackling side meat told him that the night had long last ended and that he should be up and about. It was gray light now, and the day was fast approaching. He wondered what it would hold for him. He realized that he had not eaten in some time. His empty stomach reminded him of that.

Glancing across the camp, he noticed that there was a light in the kitchen. Lida and her mother would be up now, and they would have biscuits in the oven soon. He migrated in that direction.

"Jubal," A voice came from the shadows of the porch. "Get yerself washed up. Breakfast soon be ready."

"Ye want me fer breakfast."

"Yes, son. We do," came the answer.

He realized then that it was Mrs. Johnson who had called him and not Lida. He needed to wake himself up proper.

"Wes tell me he be back with the buckboard and the team soon after first light. I reckon ye and him both be near starved, and me and Lida aims on fillin' ye up."

"Yess'm."

Mrs. Johnson had set her table as usual with a place setting at the end where her husband always sat. Jubal did not know if she had done this out of respect for him, or if she had just done it from habit. Either way it did not seem to make a great deal of difference to her or to Lida. Neither made mention of it. The boy could not help but wonder about it, but he asked no questions. There were other things that he wondered about too, but knew enough not to ask. What beset him most was how they both could be so at ease and so apparently untroubled by all that had transpired. They seemed to be so rested and so much at ease with themselves. He could not understand how that could be.

Wes had done as he said he would. He had selected a good-sized flat piece of creek bed limestone and brought it with him. Wes had unharnessed the team and put the buckboard away, but had laid off the stone by the mill yard gate. Jubal had asked if he brought it, and where it was.

After breakfast, Jubal shouldered the stone and began to make his way up to the clearing. Only this time he bore the heaviest load that he had ever had to carry before. This time the burden was pressing down not only upon his shoulders; it loaded down his heart as well. He told Wes that he wanted to do this alone and that he could easily tote the stone. He made no mention of the burden weighing down inside him.

He did not stop until he stood at the head of the fresh grave. The climb had winded him. He laid the stone down and just stood there. His mind raced. He fought to keep himself in control. He soon regained his breath and then set himself to placing the limestone in place as a marker. He found a stout white oak limb and soon had scraped away enough of the dirt to hold the stone. Once again he lifted the cumbersome weight and stood it on end facing east. The stone would know no name. The only inscription it would ever see would be that written upon it by the passing of the ages.

With ungloved hands, he raked the slate and soil back around the stone, taking care to see that it was packed in and as tight as he could manage. He soon finished the task, but made no haste in returning to the mill yard. He had never told his Pa that he missed him or that he loved him. He realized now that he should have.

Lida had purposely lagged behind as she followed Jubal up to the clearing. She had stood well back as he had worked to place the stone properly and to his liking. Now, with him standing in quietness, she approached, taking care to rustle her feet just enough to be heard as she approached. Jubal turned and saw her nearing and then turned his head back to the east. He was no longer in full control of himself and tears began to course down his cheeks. The back of his hands did not wipe them away.

Lida came on up beside him and gently laid her hand on his shoulder. He did not move or say a word. He stopped trying to dry his face and just let it be what it would be. Lida waited. She wanted to give him time to say whatever was in his heart. She knew that he was tender and caring. It just had to find its way out form inside him.

"I don't know how come I feel like this. He weren't really no Pa to me, not hardly none at all, never. All he ever wanted outta me was what work I could do."

"It be okay now," Lida said. "I be thinkin' ye buried a body here, but ye be missin' a Pa that ye wished ye had but never did," Lida said softly.

Jubal turned and looked into her eyes for the first time since she came to his side. He saw in them a tenderness and a compassion that he had not recognized before. He felt that she really cared and that she showed it more by her actions than she did by her words. He wanted to turn to her and pull her to him with all his mite, but like asking for answers to all his questions, he could not muster the strength or the will to do it, not right now.

"I wish ye could'a knowed my daddy like I did," Lida said softly.

"I knowed him better than I knowed my own Pa," Jubal replied just as softly.

"But ye never could know how tender and sweet he was to me and my mother. It pleasured him much to be able to give us things and to do fer us. I think he would a tried give us the whole world had he thought we wanted it.

"Pa never did give me nothin', as best I recollect."

"I really do wish it weren't that way fer ye. I wish ye could a been loved by yer Pa the way I was by mine."

"I ain't got no real reason feelin' this way far as I can see, but it makes me feel like somethin' or nother been tooken outta my life now just knowin' I ain't got no Pa no more. I don't know how come I feels like that. Vexes me a mite."

"I think I know how ye means. I miss my daddy bad, but I try to think on all the good times and the good things that he done fer me, and all the things he give me all these years since I was just a children. That be about only way I can get me by day-to-day without comin' plum to pieces. Besides that, I gotta hold up fer my mother now, and she needs hold up fer me too." Tears began to well up in her eyes, and she buried her face in Jubal's shoulder and clung there until she felt she had better control of her feelings.

"Yer daddy was a good man," Jubal said softly.

"And kind and gentle," she added.

"Reckon what he would a said about me and ye, the way we been doin' and such?"

"He knowed I was of age, and I think he would not been too surprised. I ain't sayin' he would a liked it none, but I think he would understood. He have no cause fer anything else, not yet leastwise."

"What ye be meanin' by that?" he asked.

"Well…Ye ain't harm me none or anythin' to the likes. That would'a set him off right quick, I reckon."

"Don't matter none now. My Pa be gone and yer Daddy too. That just how it be, and we ain't gonna change none of that nary bit."

"I still wish ye could know a Father like mine. And I know that ye can know. All ye needs do is believe and have a hope and faith that ye can see and know what I say. I don't reckon I know how to go about tellin' ye, but there be them what does know iffin ye only listen and learn."

"I ain't so sure I know a thing no more. I just feel all mixed up inside. I been thinkin' I just needs get myself away from here and put it all behind me," Jubal stated as he unknowingly clinched his fists tighter and tighter to the point that his hands were turning pale.

"Just what it is that troubles ye so? Can ye tell me that much?" Lida asked.

"I ain't never seen none of my kin be put in the old cold ground before now. It just bothers me, special since Ma never give a what-fer. Bothers me she been cold about it all."

"I guess I ought count my blessin's, since I ain't never really known what ye and her been through with Pa. I be tryin' understand both what ye say and what yer Ma done. But it be hard knowin' what be inside a body other than yerself. I know that and that be why I ain't sayin' such as I know what ye mean, fer that ain't quite it. I hate ye have all this on ye, but I honest don't understand or know how ye feel."

"It ain't too good. I know that," Jubal answered.

"What can I do fer ye?" Lida replied.

"I don't reckon I can answer ye there either."

"All in time. All in due time," came her reply.

"I don't know how much time that be."

"Then I reckon I will wait till that time comes, whenever it be," she said as she kissed him gently on the cheek.

"Ye don't know about old Buckskin and that man what named Grady do ye?" Jubal asked after a bit of silence.

"They be the ones what hurt my Daddy. I know that much."

"They be more to them two than that," Jubal answered.

Jubal retraced the episode at the mouth of the cave and the happenings in the cedar grove that led to the killings. He had not yet told her what had happened to Grady and how it had come about. All she knew was that his Pa had died in the cave, and that they had brought him back to the mill for his burial.

He began to reveal everything that he had done. She was unnerved a bit when he told her that he had shot Grady point blank while he had his hands manacled behind his body. He also told her that Buckskin, whose real name was Oscar Mays, had seen the whole thing. He further related how the Union lieutenant had tried to explain to him how serious his actions had been and what some of the consequences could be.

"Even though he were a prisoner, I could be charged fer murder, so say the lieutenant," Jubal told her. Ye see why I be so tore up don't ye? Ain't no small matter that I be lookin' at."

Lida made no immediate response. Her mind was in a whirl. She could and did envision the worst for him and that scared her to her very foundations. Surely the martial law people could see through it all and understand how it all happened.

"I were so mad that I never give no thought to what I done. It were all done and over before I really knowed what had happened. Sorry as he were, I still wish I didn't have done it."

"I believe ye, and I think ever body else would too," Lida consoled as best she knew to do. "We just have to have enough trust to see this here thing over and done."

"Lieutenant say it be better iffin Buckskin not seen me do it. That way they be no witness."

"What about them other soldiers?" Lida asked.

"That just it, they is soldiers. They follows orders like they been told to do. Lieutenant done told me that. He say he gonna write it all up in his reports. Say he make it best fer me he can. Say he and me set down and talk it through soon. Maybe later today."

"I ought just shoot him and then he be outta the whole mess too," Lida quipped half-heartedly, not really thinking about what she had said. "Dead man can't be no witness on nary a thing. That be how I see it."

"Reckon that be true, but he ain't dead."

"Well...he could be time he leave here."

"Ye ain't told nobody else that have ye?" Jubal asked somewhat surprised.

"No."

"I reckon I ain't thinkin' clear like I ought, but I don't think I need ye tellin' me such as that. I ain't aimed fer ye have no troubles on my account. Just ain't right ye should have to shoulder such on account of my doin's. Iffin ye be thinkin' such, best it not never go nowhere but twixt us."

Lida made no verbal response, but just buried her face deeper into his chest. It was a moment that would become burned into her memory and, like so many other moments in life, would be part of her for an eternity.

Shadows were growing long and low when the couple came down from the clearing. Scattered clouds were rolling in lazily from the west, and the air carried the faint smell of rain. The mouse-ear-like foliage of early spring fluttered leisurely as the wind enticed them into rhythmic dance. In spite of the death and burial that had been so prevalent for the recent past, the earth brought forth its evidence of rebirth and new life. Darkness would soon end the day, but there remained evidence of resurrection and the coming promise of a new dawn. Spring was in the air. There ought be peace in that assurance, but it eluded the eyes of the troubled lad, at least for now.

The light from the campfires burned dull orange as they were allowed to wither and die. They had served their need in the preparation of evening rations and would not be needed further until the early light of the coming day. Occasional spirits riding on the puffs of the breeze kicked little ash clouds into motion and acrid grey smoke stung the eyes. One ray of brilliance stood out and made its prominence easily recognizable. It came from the lantern that sat on the makeshift field desk of Lieutenant Long.

A courier would arrive from the ferry tomorrow at midday, and a full written report would be needed as a reply to any additional orders or instructions. The seasoned Union officer knew that he must be complete in his report and at the same time be accurate. There were things he must report that were not in line with the way he would prefer. There was an after action report that had to include all aspects of the episodes he and his troopers had conducted. He had put a lot of thought and effort into his report. Nothing he had put to paper had suited his wishes so far, accuracy and fact, yes, but not without unwanted implications. He tossed his report into a nearby fire and began the task yet again. It had to be done tonight.

The lieutenant got to his feet. He himself would find Jubal and sort this thing out once and for all. He did not have to look far. Jubal and Wes were sitting on the porch steps of the mill.

"Stewart," Lieutenant Long said as he approached and announced his presence.

"Right here," Jubal duly responded.

"There are some matters that I need to discuss with you before I make my report in the morning. Would you mind coming to my tent?"

"When?"

"Now would be an excellent time," the lieutenant answered with just a hint of sternness in his voice. He stood tall and did not allow his facial expressions to give way his thoughts or his frame of mind. "My tent will be the larger with lanterns hanging inside. I will expect you there without delay." He then turned and made way to his quarters.

Jubal turned to Wes. "I wonder what he be up to."

"He more or less told ye. Did ye not hear him say that about his mornin' report and all that?"

"I reckon I did, but that don't say much by my way of thinkin' on it," Jubal replied as he got to his feet.

Wes had it fairly well lined out, but he kept his thoughts to himself for now. "Ye best go see what he wants, and now."

The lieutenant's tent flaps were open, and he saw Jubal approach. "Come in and sit there." He pointed to an ammunition crate in front of a small table. Jubal plopped himself down on the crate, and the lieutenant rested his hands on his chair back.

"I do not feel that I need to remind you of anything that has transpired around here over the last few days. You most likely recall some of the details far better than any other. I will ask you for details as needed, and I expect nothing but complete cooperation from you. Is that understood?"

"Yes."

"Is that any problem for you?"

"I reckon not."

"Do you understand the idea and purpose of the martial law that has been recently imposed in this valley?" the lieutenant asked, as he stared continually into the young and inexperienced eyes before him.

Jubal gave his answer as best he knew and understood. He was pretty much on track with a few exceptions. He thought it was only to augment and assist with the local law. He was a bit surprised to learn that it replaced all local law and authority until such time as it would be declared at an end. His pulse quickened, and he could feel tension rising all over himself as he thought of what would be coming next.

Lieutenant Long went on to explain that he and his men had been detailed here for a specific task. That was to find and arrest three men who had been strongly implicated in numerous nefarious episodes up and down the valley, the most serious being the destruction of Cleve's store and his personal unaccountability from that time to the present. It had also been learned that one of them had taken the life of a freed house servant and had beaten her mate near to death as well. That task had been completed with Jubal's able assistance. It was not, however, anticipated that the task would be accomplished in the manner it had transpired. It was that end that had presented the difficulty and that needed to be resolved.

"A few points that we need to touch on just to make sure that we are in agreement," the Union officer stated as he moved around the chair, still resolute in his manner and his tactics. "Do you recall me asking if you would lead us to the cedar grove and cave area?"

"Yes."

"And did you do that of your own choosing?"

"Yes."

"Would you then agree that you were acting as my guide?"

"Yes."

"Would you be willing to answer these questions in a likewise manner if they were put to you by superior officers?"

"What officers?" Jubal asked.

"That really makes no matter one way or another. I suppose a better question would be to ask if your answers were truthful, truthful completely."

"Yes, I have told ye the truth," Jubal stated without complete understanding of the meaning and purpose of what he was facing.

"I just wish to be as accurate in my reporting as possible and yet give you all due considerations. It is obvious to me that you know or understand little of military customs and courtesy. That can be addressed as needed. Right now I am more concerned about your being implicated in something more than you might be able to overcome. Under the most severe of ruling, you could be charged with murder or a lesser charge of manslaughter. Both are serious and carry severe penalty."

Jubal could not speak. He could hardly believe what the lieutenant had just told him. Fear ran rampant through his entire mind and soul for an instant. "That man needed shot, and I ain't real sorry that I done it," he added.

"He was indeed a wanted felon and that will be a factor in your favor should the need arise for it; and you did, in fact, play a deciding role in his apprehension. I myself am pleased that I do not have to contend with him or provide incarceration for him. You effectively saved me much time and trouble. However, you have created issues that require careful reporting and explanation. I believe that I have already stated the seriousness of your attack on the man and that being complicated by the fact that there was an eye witness."

"Ye talkin' about old Buckskin?" Jubal questioned.

"Yes, I am speaking about Mr. Mays. I have no positive indications that he is directly responsible for any of the actions or events that are in question other than the words of two others, and they are both not with us any longer. With that in mind, all the charges that he may be facing would be as an accessory to the others and their actions. If it were not for him being a witness, then your situation would not be so grave."

Jubal suddenly recalled parts of his earlier conversation with Lida. "Then iffin he weren't' here no more then that would take a heap off me. Is that right?"

"From what I am saying, either way, the facts must be dealt with and accurately at that. I will not compromise myself in any manner in that regard," the Lieutenant emphasized.

"But all yer troopers seen me too."

"They will do and say as I direct them, to the man."

"They lie about it fer ye?" Jubal questioned.

"You miss the point of what I am saying about my men. I have earned their respect and loyalty by respecting them as persons and not just merely as pawns for me to use and move around at my leisure. They know that I ask nothing from them that I would not do myself and that I lead them by example and ask only their best in return. They give that freely. They know me and know what I stand for. They know where they stand with me, and they also know that I will defend them to the ends of the earth as long as they are in the right and are loyal to me in return. They will not be an issue as far as you are concerned. I can assure you of that."

"I reckon I ain't got no choice but trust ye on that," Jubal responded somewhat taken aback by the lieutenant's frankness.

"I do not believe there is a board of inquiry anywhere in the Union that would press severe charges against you as a civilian. The character and the charges against Mr. Rowe should and probably would negate any actions of that manner. I anticipate that Mr. Mays will be more than willing to tell all he knows just to serve his own cause as best he can. If that be the case, then the authorities must hear him and take actions as they deem needed. That is a possibility, and I would like to reduce the chances of that ever happening."

"Are ye set to do him in?" Jubal asked with a renewed interest.

"No. Not by any means am I implying any such thing. Possibly I have devised an acceptable solution both for you and for myself, and one that would require no further killing."

"I don't reckon I understand what ye mean."

"You agreed to lead the detail for me. Correct?"

"Yeah, I done said that."

"I know. I am just trying to explain my reasoning. Listen to me please."

"Okay."

"Since you agreed to lead me, then technically you were in my services and responsible to me. As such you were under my directives and instructions, and I distinctly recall instructing you and all the rest of the detail to be cautious and alert to potential dangers from the trio. I judged Mr. Rowe to be resistant, unruly and threatening to all concerned. His actions against you were hostile and offensive. You, in some ways could be considered to be defending yourself and the others in the detail. You could not in an instant have not known whether or not he had slipped his restraints. You acted decisively, even though it was reactionary and without scrutiny. It could in that respect be considered a defensive measure. You could not be charged, if it were determined to be such."

"Reckon it might hang on how it be wrote up and all," Jubal replied.

"The only problem might be the fact that you are and were part of the local populace and not a sworn member of Mr. Lincoln's army.

"What that got to do with it?"

"If you were a regular trooper I could write it up in my report that you were acting under my direct orders and that way you would not be accountable as you now are as a civilian. It makes a tremendous difference as far as martial law is concerned."

Jubal stared at the lieutenant, not sure of what he was saying or what his meaning ought to be. He did not really understand and communicated that to Lieutenant Long.

"What I am saying is this, plain and simple. If you were to enlist in the Union army right now, I could make it appear that you had done so before we made our trek to the cedars. You agreed to lead us, and I could state in my report that you expressed a desire to join our forces and continue as our guide so long as we remain in this valley."

"What about when ye leave here?" Jubal questioned.

"Then you would go with us because you would enlist for a year at a time, and you would be subject to any orders issued to you. You would be an actual part of this army and subject to all its rules and regulations."

"I don't know iffin I would know what to do or not."

"Never fear. You would always be told clearly what to do and when to do it," the officer answered. It is near ten o'clock right now. I will give you until midnight to decide. After that I will compose my final report and either way, I am prepared to submit it to the courier when he arrives around noon tomorrow. It will then go back to the ferry area and cannot be altered in any way after that."

"How long ye reckon ye be here after your report gets read back there?" Jubal quired.

"I would think not more than two or three days since we have already accomplished our main objective. It would take another courier about that long to bring new orders to me and I would then, of course, act accordingly."

"Midnight, huh?"

"Yes, I can wait no longer than that."

"That don't give me a heap time fer thinkin' on it," Jubal responded.

"Let me ask you one other question before I dismiss you."

"What that be?"

"What are your intentions for the future? What do you intend to do with your life?"

"I be thinkin' I want away from this here place and go somewhere I can make somethin' fer myself," Jubal said as he started to stand.

"Sit," the lieutenant said as he placed a hand on the boy's shoulder pushing him back to his seat. "Then you do have ambition, I assume?"

"I reckon so. I want more than this whole valley can give me. I don't aim on bein' stuck here all my live-long days."

"Well, the army can teach you and develop your organizational skills. It can demonstrate many things to you, not the least of which is discipline, and you have already demonstrated some need for that. It can also hone your ambition, but you must be wary there. Because ambition can be a jealous god, and it can narrow you focus so much that you cannot recognize opportunity. I seriously believe the time you would spend in service would be very beneficial to you and that you would grow from it. This war will end, and I think soon. Then military life would be a leisure by comparison. I plan to request assignment out west as soon as I have opportunity. I hear there are still many open ranges there, and life should be adventurous to say the least."

"I ain't heard much about any place 'cept around here. I reckon I could do myself all right by a turn or two strutin' a uniform and all like that."

"I take it that means you are willing to volunteer."

"I reckon so, but I wanna talk with Wes first."

"Just be sure that you are back before me well before midnight. Otherwise, I will out of necessity, have you placed under camp arrest. Do you understand that?"

"Yeah," came Jubal's reply.

"That should be, yes sir. You may as well begin your training right now. Remember that. It will serve you well to practice respect and courtesy."

"I will be here on time," Jubal barked. "I wanna go back home tomorrow and talk with my Ma and my sisters. Will I get to do that?"

"I think that would be permissible. It should take a courier at least two days to make a round trip from here and back from the ferry assembly. I will allow you twenty four hours beginning at midnight tonight. You may leave for home any time you wish after that and you must be back here on schedule; otherwise, you will be deserted. Believe me that would be serious."

"Yes sir."

"Good, you are learning already."

Jubal made his way back to the mill and found Wes still on the porch, but this time talking with Lida and her mother. Lida made small talk about it getting late and that she was quite tired. She and Mrs. Johnson made their departure and were soon out of sight. Jubal told Wes all that Mr. Long had said. He listened intently, although realizing already what Jubal was telling him. What he did not know, however, was how he had been offered immunity for what he had done. He made no comments about the entire situation.

Jubal told him how he would join up come midnight and then be free to go home and tell Ma and Julie and all the rest what he was doing and then be ready to make his goodbyes, at least for a few days or weeks, so he thought.

"I don't want nary a soul knowin' about Grady, special Ma and Julie. It just fret them, and it serve no purpose that I can see fer them to know. Ye know all about it, and it don't need go no more than that. I be dependent on you fer that."

"I don't have no cause to say nothin' more about it, and I don't think they know anything what would cause any questions about it. Seem to me like yer Ma saw and heard about all she cared for, and she made that plain as could be, I think," Wes added.

"I want head home soon as I join up. Lieutenant done said I could, and I only got till midnight tomorrow. That why I need go home tonight, and I want ye go with me too. I ain't afraid to go at night, but I want ye there when I tell Ma that I be leavin' this old holler fer a spell. I know she ain't gonna cotton to that too keen."

"I be ready whenever ye be," Wes assured him. "What about Lida and her mother? Are ye aimed to tell them sometime before tomorrow night?"

"I reckon I owe them that much, but I ain't lookin' forward to it, not none at all," he answered as he first sat on the porch edge then stood, obviously a bit edgy.

It was about ten when the lad returned to the officer's tent and announced himself. "I am ready, sir."

There was little to the entire event. Lieutenant Long administered an oath of allegiance to the Union. Jubal, likewise, swore to defend it to the best of his abilities. He also swore to follow all orders and obey all commands. He did not really pay too much attention to the wording of what he had vowed to uphold. He was not really sure if he understood all of it, but was somewhat amused that he was now official army.

Lieutenant Long made all the necessary and appropriate entries in his journal and in his report. He thought that he had gained an asset in this raw-backwoods boy because of his tracking ability and his marksmanship. He had already decided that grooming him into military life would be a challenge, but he thrived on challenge and considered himself able to meet almost any situation that would confront him. He had seen fierce action at Chickamauga and Lookout Mountain. Compared to that, this duty was nothing.

It was well past bedtime when Jubal and Wes reached the old log home at the head of the hollow. Everyone had already bedded down, and it took a few minutes to unsaddle the horses and turn them out to graze. They would need them again tomorrow, but not so early in the day.

Jubal made his way across the old barn lot and neared the yard gate. He made sure to make enough noise so that he could be heard inside the house. He delayed a bit just to allow Ma or whoever would get up first ample time to light a lantern or grab whatever they needed. Just was not a good idea to be unannounced at such a time of the night.

"Who's there?"

Jubal recognized Ma's voice. "It be me, Ma. Me and Wes."

"Well fer Pete's sake, come on in here. What in tarnation ye be doin' out traipsin' around in the middle of nighttime anyhow?"

"Wes is tendin' to the hosses. He be along shortly. But he done said he be some tired, and he thinkin' he bed down till it get light. It been a long day."

"I reckon it has at that. Now come on in. Ain't no cause fer ye lingerin' out here. It be a mite cool iffin ye ask me."

Jubal did as Ma said and found himself seated on the kitchen bench in front of leftover corn pone and two sausage cakes. He did not wait for them to be offered. He made quick use of them and swiped his mouth on his sweat-stained shirt sleeve. He and his Ma both knew that there would be no sleep this night.

"I might as well get a fire kindled up fer when it be breakfast fixin' time. It be a mite chilly in here tonight anyhow." She turned her attention to the wood box and scratched in it retrieving a bit of tender. She put a few small sticks on top of it and struck a flint stick to the tender and soon had a small flame going in the blackened cook stove. She soon returned her attention to her son.

"Now just what it is that be so all-fired important to roust up the whole place in the middle of the night?" she wanted to know.

Jubal went through the entire epic, almost moment by moment. He purposefully left out the short part about his particular action that caused his dilemma. He did mention Pa and how he had been laid to rest and where. He had little else to say in that matter. Ma had pretty much said it all herself back at the mill.

"I done joined up with the Union, and they say it be good fer me. They say it make me a better man."

"They be a war goin' on. Ye do any thinkin' on that did ye?" Ma asked without any hesitation. "Ye could be a dead man, ye know that?"

Ma surprised him a bit. He had to admit to himself that he had never really thought much about that possibility, and the good lieutenant had not said anything along those lines either. He had said that he thought the war would soon be over. It had been going on for three years almost to the day.

"Reckon I might not even go very far from here. Lieutenant said that we just might be left here. All his men say they done been through worst part of it, and what they been up to here ain't no danger hardly at all."

"I think that just be hogwash myself," Ma said with an air of suspicion of the army and their actions in the valley and the surrounding countryside. She was well aware that there was serious conflict between the Blue and the Gray all around. It just so happened that none was in their valley and in some sense was, therefore, far removed. "Ye ain't heard much about things way off from here have ye, boy?"

"Ma, I ain't no toe-headed little boy no more. I know what I want, and I aim on goin' after it too."

"What do ye think ye want?"

"I want outta this valley and off this old dirt farm. I don't aim on diggin' and scratchin' in dirt and mud fer a livin'. I want more than that."

"It ain't gooder 'nuff fer ye, I reckon?" Ma snapped.

"No, Ma. It ain't that. I just want better fer myself and whatever woman and kids I might have some of these here days. That ain't askin' so much is it?"

"Reckon ye gonna leave me and the gals here to do best we can then. Be a heap more work I be doin' then. Ye thunk any on that?" Ma asked acidly.

Jubal could feel fire rising up inside himself. He did not like what he was thinking and had blurted it out before he realized it. "Reckon ye gonna have me be yer plow horse just like Pa, is that it? Huh?"

"I ought smack yer smart-arse face fer ye, but I reckon ye are a bit more a boy than that. Iffin ye believes that then ye ought well understand why I said what I did and why I told ye what I did about yer Pa and not wantin' nothin' do with his buryin' nor wantin' put nary a eye to him neither. I reckon ye ought chew on that fer a good long while cause it be plain that ye got no notion whatsoever what I felt and how I done reconciled all that matter long time past. Ye ought know what I done put up with. Ye ought know that I reckon I don't owe nary a soul any more than I done give tryin' make a life fer the likes of him. I danged well ain't gonna take no grief over it now. Iffin I done rubbed yer feathers wrong, then I reckon I be sorry fer it, but I am done with him and anythin' what smacks of him. Ye still got some growin' ye needs do, but I reckon what ye learns the hard way ye won't soon fergit. Ye just might be right. Army might do ye some good. I just don't want ye kilt some place far off or such. Ye just hit me with so much so fast ye done put my head in a spin, and I done mouthed off too much already," Ma said as she covered her face with her leathery weathered hands where the veins stood out like ropes, gnarled and toughened over the years from hours of hard labor.

The lamp light seemed to amplify all things that had not been kind to her features. Jubal looked into the partially hidden face and again saw the build-up of endless toil, the heartache of unfulfilled hopes, and the covetous desire for a kind word or a single expression of gratitude. He had no idea that in her lashing out at him, that she was, in her own peculiar way, working through her grief and pondering just how she would make her way and a way for her family. Granny Iverson talked of peace that passed all understanding, but he saw none of it in his Ma and knew little of it for himself.

"I reckon I know that, Ma. I just been a bit mixed up, that all. I reckon ye got right say whatever ye wants. I just gotta do what I gotta do. Plain and simple. I don't think no less of ye nor nothin' of the likes. We just never seen eye-to-eye, I reckon. And now it don't much matter when ye come right down to it. I just wanted things not to be so hard fer ye. It looked like ye was all bitter. Ye seemed like ye just wanted run away from it all."

"I did want away from it, son. I still do."

"I understand, Ma. I reckon ye can understand why I want away from here. Least I hope ye do. It ain't like I don't never want help ye no more. That there ain't true. I just don't want to always be tied to this here place all my days."

"I reckon I thought I could run off from myself, but it ain't so," Ma added.

"I can't neither, but I reckon I ain't got near what ye do to run off from. I see that now. I still wants better things fer ye and ever body else too."

"I hate seein' ye go off, son. Not because ye is a good work hand, but because ye is my blood. I don't want no harm come on ye. Understand that don't ye?"

"I do. I really do."

Ma and Jubal spent the rest of the darkened hours with each other and made peace with each other, to the degree that Ma actually had a smile on her face when first light came. Jubal felt that he had learned more about his Ma and her feelings than he had ever known before. She had poured her heart out to him. She had tried to show him how it was so very important to know early on about thinking things through before just jumping in whatever choices you made in living your life.

She understood that he was now obligated to the army, and there was nothing she could do about that. She knew that she could not shield him any longer and that he had decided on his own that it was his time to venture out on his own. All she could do now was to be beside him in spirit and in love. She vowed to herself that she would ask every day for his protection and that he would somehow be led into the blessings of knowing the way.

Jubal saw no need in lingering around the old log home any longer. It was near mid-morning and Ma had filled him full of biscuits and side meat gravy. He was just a bit restless and wanted to be on the move. Besides that, he wanted to get back to the mill so he could talk to Lida before the lieutenant got new orders, and he and his men had to move out. No way to know exactly when that would be. The big guns at the ferry crossing would decide that.

Jubal asked Wes to go back down the road with him. He could bring the horses back home, and it would give them a chance to talk a few things over. Jubal fetched the pair in from the pasture and had them all saddled up in no time short. He did not bother taking any arms or powder with him except what Wes might need on the return. The Union would provide all that he would need once they got back to the ferry and saw the quartermaster.

Jubal said his goodbyes to his Ma, to Granny Iverson, who teared up so much that she could hardly speak, and to Julie and her sisters. Julie told him that she would be stronger and walking near normal when he got back home; she just knew it in her heart.

Emotion welled up inside him, and it took all that he had to keep it in check. It began to dawn on him that he was beginning a part of his life that he had not really prepared for. He was stepping out into the unknown and that invoked an uneasiness.

Wes and the boy rode side-by-side at an easy and slow gait. Jubal looked over at Wes and saw the years that had piled up on his face. True he had mended up tremendously since they fetched him to their place. He had eaten well and was slicked up good by comparison, but he was still and old man and nothing was going to change that.

"Wes, ye reckon this here war will end soon?"

"I don't have no way knowin' any more than you, son; but I sure do hope so."

"I might get myself in on it yet," Jubal said as much to himself as to his companion.

"I think ye know enough to look out fer yerself."

"How ye reckon Ma and the gals be able to make it without me workin' the old place?"

"I intend to do all I can. I know certain that I don't aim fer nobody to go without eats and proper clothes. I can promise ye that," Wes stated.

"Ye never did really say what ye aimed on doin' with all them gold dollars. I reckon ye won't be wastin' none of it, and I take it ye aim seein' to my kin with it iffin need be."

"I can promise ye that," Wes answered in no short order.

"Good fer ye. That makes me feel a heap better fer bein' gone. Me and Ma might have our differences, but she still be my Ma. I want her took care of and well treated."

"I aim to stay there with her as long as she don't have cause fer runnin' me off. I don't aim on givin' her no cause on my part. She been good to me, and I owe her fer that and always will be obliged to her."

"Well, it might be that I not need be gone fer so long. At least maybe I can come home ever now and again."

"I reckon that be so, but I wouldn't count on it real stout," Wes said. "Ye needs not fret over her and her gals none. I intend to see to them best I can."

"I know ye will, and I be grateful to ye fer it."

"I just hope ye don't get in thick and get yerself all shot up or even worse than that. I think folks back here got more to be concerned about fer ye than ye do yerself. That just how I see it."

"How ye mean?" Jubal asked.

"Well, ye won't like what I got to say concernin' that," Wes answered.

"Out with it. I reckon I can take whatever ye be thinkin' in yer head, so out with it."

"Ye is most nigh a man; I give ye that. But ye ain't had a hand in much happenings and don't know a heap about many other people, special them what ain't from these parts. People is different, and ye gonna have to deal with them when ye ain't in these here old mountains and valleys. Ye gonna find out about them other folks, and ye gonna have to get along with all of them and live with them. Some ye might not like so well. Yer temper could get ye in a tight spot, unless ye can learn that sometimes it best to just clam up and not say nothin' to nobody. Do that make any sense to ye?"

"Can't say right now. Ain't right sure what ye be tryin' to say," Jubal replied, truly not understanding the gravity of what the old man tried to tell him.

"Sometimes, things is best learned through hard knocks, and I reckon that apply to ye too. Ye won't soon fergit what ye learns the hard way. I just tryin' to save ye some grief fer later on, that's all."

The pair continued their slow pace on down the road toward the mill. They continued to talk back and forth about many things, mostly concerning how things would be different without the boy and how Wes would try to fill in his place best he could. Jubal even hinted that Wes should take up with his Ma and make a life for both of them while they still had a few years to enjoy.

Wes did not come right out and say it, but that was exactly what he had in mind from the very minute that he learned about Pa. He did not want to be so brass about it, but Ma's reactions about it all served as a sign to him that she would like it that way too. He had enough money to take care of her and the rest and could think of no better way to use it. He had not told Jubal or anyone else about it, but there was more that he could fetch, and it weren't more than a mile or so from the old log home. He knew where it was and could find it in no time.

Jubal had feelings for Mrs. Johnson, being she was widowed now; and those feelings carried over to her daughter as well, but not in the same manner. Lida had told him that she would wait; he distinctly remembered that. Now she was going to be without her man for a spell too. He had never given any thought to what might come to pass around the old mill should he be away for a good long while. He just thought that things would always be the same and that he could come back to them any time he wished and that they would welcome him with open arms. After all, what young woman would not be swept away by a sharp dresser in a blue and yellow uniform come riding in on a spirited horse with a fine leather saddle and all? His youth ignored reality and played upon fantasy. The wanton desire for material possessions reared its head once again and clouded what should have been clearer judgment. Shades of darkness once again exerted their prevalence over truth.

It was early afternoon when the riders pulled up at the mill yard gate. Jubal looked around to see if he could spot Lida. She was not anywhere in sight. He offered to tend to the horses, but Wes advised him there was no need. He intended to start back up the road to Ma and the old log home, and he was going to take both his horses with him. After all, he owned them, bought and paid with real money. Besides that, the Union army would furnish the boy a horse and everything else he needed.

There was no reason for Wes to linger at the mill, and it only seemed logical for him to get back to Ma. There was not now near as much of a chance of any drifters coming her way and causing trouble. That issue had been pretty much settled, permanently. The whole valley should be able to rest a bit easier now. The main thing to work for now would be to end the war as soon as possible and have an end to the dying.

"Lieutenant wants see you right away," a roving sentry announced as he made straightway for Jubal and Wes.

"Where he be?" Jubal asked.

"In his tent."

"Guess I best go then," Jubal said as he turned to face Wes.

"You as well mister," the sentry reported.

The lieutenant stood just outside his tent with hands on hips as the pair were escorted to him by the sentry who rendered a sharp and proper salute. Once his report was rendered and he was dismissed, he did an about face and resumed his duty. His actions and his mannerisms did not go unheeded or unnoticed by the new volunteer.

"I assume that you have just returned from your home at the end of this road. Is that correct?"

"Yes sir it is," Jubal answered.

"You, as well, I assume sir," the lieutenant said as he addressed himself to Wes. He had heard mention of his last name but could not recall it at present.

"You are correct again, sir," Wes responded. He knew that he was conversing with an educated being and that if this conversation continued at any length, he would be well advised to show evidence of his own real inner self. "May I ask why these questions?"

"Follow me and I will show you why I am concerned. But first let me ask you another question, and I address this to you both. What time did you leave camp last evening?"

"About two hours before midnight best I recall," Wes answered.

"And the two of you remained together through the night?"

"Yes," Wes answered. "We were both in the same house all night but not directly at each other's side."

"Is there anyone who could verify that?" inquired the officer.

"Yes, the entire family could do that."

"Under those conditions, I do not think I need to inquire along those lines any deeper. I will accept your statements as actual facts." The lieutenant then repeated his previous instruction. "Please come with me."

Another sentry was posted in front of another tent in the shade of a large creek bank sycamore that had managed to put out its canopy a bit ahead of the surrounding trees. Inside, Lieutenant Long pointed to a form wrapped in an army issue poncho and blanket.

"This is, or was Mr. Mays. I need to know who had done this and why. Obviously it could not have been either of you, but I must ask if you have any ideas or information that you would pass to me."

"What happened him?" Jubal asked.

"Last night or early morning I should say, there was a single shot that seemed like it came from behind and above the mill. I sent three men to check on it, but they saw nothing or could find nothing. There were no other shots or sounds. I had them go back and search for any visual clues once it got light. Again they found nothing. Then when the mess cook went to feed the prisoner, Mr. Mays, he found him like this." The lieutenant unwrapped the body enough to show that his throat had been slit almost from ear to ear and that he had almost surely bled out in just a few short moments. The dried blood had not been washed away, and the crimson faded into ebony as it was soaked up by the aged brown of the deerskin shirt.

"I do not know who did this, and I frankly am not going to exert a lot of time and effort trying to determine that. The courier will be here soon, and I have other matters to attend to. This man needs to be laid to rest, and I solicit your help in doing that."

"What can we do?" Jubal asked.

"Speak with Mrs. Johnson. Tell her only that Mr. Mays has passed and that I need her permission to bury him on her property. I will comply with her instruction as to where she would have him placed. I will have a detail do the digging and nothing more will be required of her in the entire matter. You have my leave to go and speak with her now as we need to get the body put away as soon as we can. As far as I am concerned, he is ready now, and I will not instruct my troopers to wash or clean him in any measure. If any one wishes to say any words over him, I will not prevent it. Do I make myself clear?"

"Yes sir," Jubal snapped.

"Then go, and do as I have instructed."

"Do you have any further need of me?" Wes asked the lieutenant.

"Thank you, sir. No, unless you wish to speak with Mrs. Johnson. You are at your leisure, and I thank you for your cooperation."

Jubal waited long enough until he was sure that Lida and her mother had finished dinner and had all the dishes done and put away. Shadows were getting long, but there was still plenty of daylight left. He strolled into the mill yard and pretended to be checking something about the spillway and the flume. He knew that Lida could easily spot him from the house and was in hopes that she

664

would come out and talk with him. He was still just a bit shy around her mother and felt she would not take to him as readily as he would want. Nevertheless, she did spot him and made her way to the mill porch and sat down. He pretended not to see her for a bit and continued with his pretend inspection of the wheel works.

"I hear ye be enlisted now," she said as he neared the porch.

"That be a fact."

"Well, I reckon ye be goin' off and be all involved in skirmishes and such. No tellin' what or where ye wind up," she quipped. "And I reckon I be stuck right here all the while."

"Lieutenant Long say we might be here few more days. He don't rightly know exact when we be called on. He say I get my blue uniform and all else I needs fer solderin' soon as we can get me to their quartermaster, wherever he be."

He made no mention of old Oscar and his demise, and she said nothing of it either, at least for the moment. They continued with their make-talk bantering until Lida leaned her head over and rested on Jubal's shoulder.

"I will admit that I will miss ye when ye be gone. I reckon I don't got no right in doin' so. But it be fact, and I ain't denyin' it."

Jubal said nothing but took her hand in his and cradled it to his face. He had no words for the moment but just held her hand tenderly in his own.

"Worse part now is that ye volunteered when it weren't really necessary, not now no how," Lida lamented softly.

"What ye mean by that?" Jubal asked a bit puzzled at her.

"Lieutenant tell me and my mother about Oscar. Now that he be gone there won't be no soul whatsoever speak out on ye shootin' old Grady Rowe. Ye could just stay here now and not join up. I don't see how ye would need do that now. All cause be gone now."

"It just don't work that way," Jubal said as he turned her hand in his to rub his cheek. It was in that instant that he spotted the small dark crimson stain at the base of one fingernail. He made no indication or comment about it and was not sure what it really was. "Ye said that ye would wait fer me. Did ye really mean that?"

"I don't see how I got much choice in the matter now. I can't go nowhere else or nothin' like that."

"Would ye want to go someplace else? he asked.

"I might have to sometime," she answered. "I ain't real proud of everthing I done, and I reckon I will pay whatever price there be to it. I reckon I'll do whatever needs be done one way or another."

He managed to steal another glance at her hand. He could still not be sure of what he saw. She made no efforts to hide anything or to withdraw from him. She just seemed cold and distant from him.

"I don't understand. I really don't," Jubal admitted.

"You never did," she said as she turned her face outward to him. I done it all on account of yerself, and now I reckon I will face up to it by myself." She pulled away from him and ran back to the house, bounded up the steps and into the darkened living room. He could do nothing now but return to the campsite.

The detail had finished their task and had returned to camp. Old Buckskin was laid to rest alongside Pa in a shallow unmarked grave just as Mrs. Johnson and Lieutenant Long had agreed. No words were spoken over him, and no one seemed to care.

No courier came in that evening or during the night. That would give Mr. Long another night to compose another report and attempt to explain yet another death and burial. He could now compose one report that could cover the entire episode and still have no sound reason for all that had transpired. He decided that he would include only the facts that he knew and evoke no speculation from any others. He wanted this matter behind him and the sooner the better. There was nothing about this assignment that he wished to continue. However, the miller man's daughter had not entirely escaped his notice. He had noticed, but that was as far as he was willing to let it go. There were young ladies back home that she could not compare to. He did not know her true character nor her heart, nor did it matter. In a day or so he would be gone from there, and she would be only a fleeting fantasy.

Jubal was assigned quarters in a tent but offered to sleep in the mill. The Lieutenant was quick to deny that privilege. The new enlistee deserved nothing more than what the rest of the troopers had. He was given a bedroll and would sleep on the ground just like everyone else. There would be no special treatment, not here nor anywhere else. He would be treated fairly as long as he followed orders and kept himself out of trouble.

Sleep avoided him most of the night. He lay still and listened to the voices in the darkness. He could hear the hoof stomps of the horses as they whiled away the hours, enjoying their allotted rest. Voices could be heard at times, though too distant to comprehend. Occasional coughs grabbed his attention only to be ignored with the next conscious thought. He could hear the eerie voice of an old screech owl somewhere off in the distance. It sounded lonely and forlorn, like some broken-spirited soul seeking solace in the wails and cries of the betrayed. He could easily let himself slip into that character if he allowed himself to dwell on it. After all, he was soon to leave his valley and his home. He was leaving behind the one who he most wanted to be near, and she had just told him that he would never understand. She was right about that, at least for now, because he was very unsettled by what she had said and what he assumed he had seen on her hands. He could not allow himself believe there was anything less than angelic quality in her character and that anything even evil could have come by her hand. It really did not seem to make much difference now anyhow. The army had closed the issue; therefore, it surely was over.

Sleep, welcomed sleep, came to him in the wee hours of the morning. He would indeed see the light of another day.

That day came abruptly. He was stirred to consciousness by sure, but gentle kicks to the soles of his booted feet. A likewise firm, but gentle voice instructed him. "Best be up and about. Time for formation soon, and you cannot be unaccounted."

"Yes sir," Jubal said smartly as he got to his feet.

"Don't call me, sir. That's reserved for the officers, and besides I am a trooper just the same as you. I just been here a little longer than you."

"What do I need to do?" Jubal questioned.

"Not much, just answer your name when it is called. Just stay close to me, and I will do what I can to get you through your first few days. It's not all that bad, and you will take to it before you know it."

"I be obliged to ye. By the way, what be yer name?"

"My name is Lee, Conner Lee. Understand you are Jubal."

The two made their acquaintances as Conner dressed and brushed off his blue and gold uniform. He showed Jubal how it should be worn and gave him some hints about how to keep looking sharp.

"You will get a good fit once we get back to the ferry. They have a quartermaster wagon there, and it has most anything we need in the field. You may even get one of them new repeaters. Some got them now."

"Wes had one, still got it far as I know," Jubal bragged.

"Best be careful who knows about that. I doubt it is pure legal to own one just yet. Bet he paid a bunch for it if he in fact does have one," Conner advised. "Just don't go bragging about it. Could easy cause your friend some trouble."

Jubal realized that he had let loose things that had best been not said. He recalled Wes cautioning him that some things were just best left to their own and not talk it up to no one, nowhere. He would not make that mistake again.

A courier did come in that day around mid-morning, and he did bring new orders. The entire patrol was to return to the ferry tomorrow at first light. A full report would be expected upon arrival. That meant that Lieutenant Long had only the remainder of today and the coming night to complete his reports and be ready for moving out come daybreak. He had no issues with that because his report was already complete, save for who was responsible for the death of the third and last felon. All had been accounted for, their presence verified. He had decided that he would make no inquires of any of the locals, because they were obviously not capable of any such atrocities.

As far as the actions of his most recent volunteer, there now were no issues to be explained. The lad was under his command and as such was cleared of any doubt or concern. There should be no delay in getting a timely start.

The courier had come in under armed escort as usual. They had brought along an extra mount, again as usual. Therefore, Jubal was assigned a horse, and it became his immediate responsibility. That was no challenge to him. He had been around livestock all his days and could handle them as well as the next.

He made his way nearest the mill that the confines of the camp would allow. He had been told that he was not to be at his leisure and that he might be called on for additional duty or assignment at any time. He had hoped to have a moment or two with Lida, but it seemed that it was not to be. She did not venture outside the house as far as he could see. Evidently, she did not wish to talk things out any more. There was a lot that she left unclear as far as he could tell and in doing so, had raised even more questions. But she had said that she would wait. He could get things all settled then, whenever then would be.

The cool earth made for a better bed that night possibly because the day had been long, and he had not realized there were so many things that needed to be done. Breaking camp involved packing up everything and securing it to an animal's back or into a pack and a bedroll. Fire pits had to be cleared and filled back in. The trenches had to be covered over and filled back level. Grass sods had to be replaced as best could be. All gates had to be secured. The perimeter fence had to be checked and mended where needed. All this had to be done before sundown, because there would be no time for it come morning. First light movement would be swift and purposeful.

It would take the better part of the new day to reach the ferry encampment, and the lieutenant had instructed the point patrol to make good time, but to keep a sharp eye. Caution could never be abandoned without due cost.

The detachment reached the ferry area well before sundown and reported in to the commander. Lieutenant Long made his way to the command tent and requested permission to tender his reports. The Major welcomed him and received him very cordially. The reports were gone over, and it was determined that all was in order and that no further issues were to be settled.

"You have conducted yourself well, lieutenant, I commend you," Major Mack said. "I would not be the least bit concerned to have more young officers under my command such as yourself."

"Thank you, sir."

"I see in your report that you have secured the enlistment of a potential tracker and scout. I would anticipate that he will be of exemplary service to us in the future. Is he experienced in such means?"

"That might merit a bit of explanation sir."

"Go on," the major said.

"He has lived all his young years in the hills and backwoods and never until now, ventured out of his own little valley. He is not even proficient in reading nor in writing. He is, however, about the best that I have encountered in reading natural signs, and he knows the lore of the woods very well. He can follow man-made signs and tracks that neither myself nor any of my guides could even see. It is almost as if he had the eyes, and the mind of a creature itself. There may be some issues with his adapting to military life, and I am quite sure that he will never be polished in customs and courtesy. I would think that he would be much out of place among officer corps."

"I do not foresee that as a potential problem. I would think that he can best serve by doing that which he knows best."

"Yes sir, I agree," Lieutenant Long stated.

"I believe it would be best to assign him to another man who could more or less show him what will be expected of him and at the same time I will charge you to insure that he is used to his potential in the area we spoke of and if that requires that he be isolated from command posts, then so be it. I do not anticipate that anyone of authority will be coming to review us in this remote area but if that were to happen, then I would expect you and your troopers to see to it that he did not create a situation or cause an issue simply because of his lack of formal education. Do you see any problems with that?"

"No sir."

"Very well. Does he have arms and adequate equipment?"

"No sir. Not at present."

"Is he a marksman?"

"He says he is a good shot sir."

"We will find out soon."

"Yes sir."

"Get him the things he needs, get the proper paperwork completed for my signature."

"Yes sir."

"And ask the quartermaster if he has a repeater to issue him. If he can execute as well as I hope, then we may very well be fortunate to have him join us in spite of his shortcomings and rough edges."

"Yes sir," the lieutenant repeated again.

"That will be all. You are dismissed."

"Thank you sir," he said as he rendered a crisp salute, which was promptly returned. He turned about face and was off in search of his new recruit.

Next morning found Jubal in a new blue uniform with polished buttons and spanking new black leather boots. He received regular issue back pack and mess kit complete with canteen and its cork stopper tethered with fresh cut tanned rawhide. He was issued a new Springfield long gun and a portion of ammunition.

Conner had been chosen to play lead to him and had received his instruction straight from the lieutenant himself. Things ought to be easy for them both the next few days according to what the young officer had said.

"You best get used to the feel of that thing. You're gonna be using it some here in a day or so, and it would be best if you did well by it," Conner advised.

"I think I can do it right nigh good already. Ye recollect what it was ye said I ought not said ner say no more don't ye?" Jubal answered.

"Yes, I do. Let's just leave it right there too, and you know why."

"Reckon that be fact. I ain't sayin' no more. I just shoot it."

The balmy days of early spring soon turned to repressive summer heat with humid days and nights. Fortunately, there was little involvement around the ferry encampment.

All the regular troopers and staff fell into an unintended laid back attitude and operation. Sure, the sentries were still posted as usual, but they often found a place to catch a few winks while still at their post. Meals were still prepared on schedule, but most took their good slow time about eating and moving on to their daily assignments. Even the major was known to sometimes sleep in a bit and skip his morning meal. Duty just became too easy and far too undisciplined.

Jubal made some patrol excursions around the area and demon-strated his marksmanship on repeated occasions, shooting targets picked out by the major as they ventured out and about, mostly at the officer's pleasure. There was just no opposition in the area. The Union had solid control on the area, and it appeared that officials higher up were bent on keeping it that way. More supply wagons had rolled in and new barges came up river on a regular schedule, always loaded with supplies and munitions.

Jubal had adapted well enough to military life and routine. He had picked up enough custom and courtesy to get by. No one seemed to be grievously offended when he did not exactly hit the mark or failed in protocol. He had just about decided that soldering was a pretty good thing, at least for him. He had been issued all he needed for his duties. He had a new uniform of which he was overly proud. He had learned the required routines and had proven himself to be adept in reading the signs and following a track. Trouble was, there was just not much going on that needed his talents, at least not then.

July of that year broke with a surprising and unusual chill in the pre-dawn hours. The silence was a bit eerie as well. No night critter calls, and no rustle of the thirsty leaves. No scent of pollen laden mist rising off the cool river pools and ringlets.

Jubal rose and dressed well before first light, and it had to be more than chance that both he and the major had decided that a short trek down to the ferry landing would be in order. They had made their way in that direction only a short distance when the first dim gray light appeared in the east. The stillness persisted, but Jubal did notice the distant lonesome cooing of a dove. It seemed ominous. Little did he know what lay in store.

As if summoned by devastating thunder and lightning, a hail of musket balls and a roar of determined cannon fire broke the silence and awakened the entire encampment. The Rebel forces had pounced with total surprise, and there seemed to be no end to their coming. Their yell and their revelry were nearly as unnerving as the gunfire itself.

Jubal saw the major's horse go down and pin his rider's leg. In just as short a time, he was off his own steed and at the major's side. The two together managed to free the leg and regain their footing.

What seemed to be hundreds of Confederate soldiers ran past them either not realizing that they were running right on past the post commander or that they were more concerned about the encampment area itself. Jubal handed his reins to the major and had intended to ride double with him to somewhere more out of harm's way.

A swift and solid blow of a rifle butt placed between the shoulder blades sent him face down into the dust. The errant aim from the side arm of a mounted grey clad officer stopped the pain from the blow to the shoulders. Fortunate for the lad, the bullet only grazed the side of his head. The concussion from the shot silenced the cacophony of the battle, and the senses no longer broadcast the dangers that engulfed him. He was given up as lost, and the major rode off to leave him to the fortunes of the new day.

The situation in and around the ferry had changed, more or less in the time span of a single morning. The skirmish would endure for several hours, but Jubal would have no more part in it other than to lie deathly still and suck in the hot breath of the day. He had no cares or concerns for anything. He had only one duty now and that was to cheat death.

Chapter 19

Challenged

*T*he train rumbled on at a good rate, but not near fast enough to suit the man in charge. He wanted to get to Nashville and survey the entire situation both civil and militarily. The entire area had been wrested from the Confederacy, and Union sympathy was known to be strong in the city and in the surrounding counties. The only hostile activity that had been reported in some weeks was an occasional raid or a foray into some remote woodlands, and as such seldom amounted to more than an investigation by a patrol or two. No casualties had occurred in some time now. Those were all indications to the Vice President Elect that he could travel into that area more or less at his leisure and that light guard would be all that would be necessary to insure his safety. Besides that, he had nurtured and cultivated strong friendships when he served as the governing authority over the town.

He needed to conduct his business on a tight time schedule, because the March Inauguration Day was fast approaching. Thus the need for speed and punctual meetings and discussions, swift but sure evaluations, and accurate formulations of conclusions; and a likewise swift return to Washington City to render his reports and recommendations.

There had been late reports of major engagements in the Northern Virginia area. According to those, if they were accurate, it would seem that the war could not go on much longer. Besides that, there was a regular stream of former prisoners coming out of the confines along the James River near Richmond, and even some from as far as Andersonville. The freed prisoners all told basically the same story. The Confederacy was broken and had no way to mend itself. Its manufacturing capability had been destroyed, and the railroads of the deep South were in shambles. The Gray army could move only at a march, and the Cavalry had lost so many men and animals that it was very much ineffective now. Lee seemed to be hanging on until the death knell would sound. There was no way to account for all the carnage and now seemingly useless slaughter.

"Mr. Johnson says he thinks the war will end soon, Jubal. What do you plan to do when it does?" William asked.

"Not thought a lot on that so far."

"My year will be up come the last of March, and I sure would like to see things come to an end by that time. Then I might make it back home in time to get a school all lined up for the next term. I would like that very much. Yes indeed, I would."

"I think my time be up about a month or so after ye," Jubal added.

"Are you wanting to get back home too?"

"In some ways I am, and in others I really don't know how I feel about it. I wanna see my folks, of course, but I don't know iffin I would be satisfied there no more or not," Jubal responded. "I still have a hankerin' about me that still needs be quenched."

"Have you thought about it anymore lately? Do you want to tell me about it? I know how to listen if you recall," William said hoping that his friend could be coaxed into revealing his thoughts and feelings. Jubal needed guidance just as much now as ever. William realized that they both may soon take separate paths and that his opportunities to be an example and a witness might soon cease. "I just wish I could make it all happen for you, Jubal, my friend."

William and Jubal continued their conversation when Elbert entered the rear of their coach. He had just been relieved of his post at the rear of the train, more or less as a figurehead lookout rather than a security necessity.

"Jubal, Mr. Johnson said he would like to speak with you if you could make a moment for him. He be in his car, next to last on the string."

"What he want with me?"

"He never said. Just said for me to tell you, that all I know about it," Elbert said as he fixed himself down on a bench near the old potbellied stove and began to warm himself.

"I wonder what I done now," Jubal fretted as he began to gather himself and follow the request.

"Come in," came the answer to the knock at the door to the private compartment in the Vice President Elect's car.

Jubal entered and softly closed the door. "Yes sir. How can I help you tonight?"

"I do not really need anything. I just wanted to talk with you a bit. I have noted that according to the records that both you and William will soon have served your year; William just a bit sooner than yourself, and I think he might be completing his second year. I am not real sure about that."

"I thinkin' it is right close on a year. I do recollect that be fact," Jubal answered.

"If this war ends soon, and I anticipate that it will; then what do you intend to do once your time is up? Have you given that any consideration?"

"It be hard fer me to say what I aim on doin' when that time come. Reckon I gotta last out this here old war first off," Jubal responded with a slight discernible air of arrogance.

"Oh, it will end. You can count on that, and there will be plenty of folks on both sides who will be faced with decisions that will be with them for the remainder of their days. I just think that it will be important to be informed best we can and to make decisions that will be in our own favor not only as individuals, but as a nation. One nation of one accord. It will take time to bind up all our wounds, but that can be done and healing will come in its own time."

"I never thought on that none yet," Jubal answered.

"I would not anticipate that a man of your youth would, not under the present conditions. But I do think you need to consider what you want for yourself. If you want a career in the army, you

need to decide on that before your term is up so that you would not
lose any continuity of service."

"I don't know yet, but I got a few days or weeks yet, I reckon."

"True, but I am just talking and wondering what many young
men like yourself will do and how they will manage when they are
released to return home. I am thinking of the boys in gray as well
as the ones who wear the blue. What would you do if you decide
to go back home? I believe your home is near mine, if I remember
correctly."

"Not much I could do back there. I guess I turn to sharecroppin'.
That be all there be back home fer me. That be unless I could be a
miller man. They is a mill near where I come from, and I have done
some work there," Jubal replied.

"Would you be able to make a living at that?"

"I think I could iffin I could build up a trade and keep folks
comin' back," Jubal responded with just a hint of enthusiasm in his
voice. He had visions of Lida and himself working together running
the mill and living in her house with her mother. He could do worse,
he reckoned.

"Would that be satisfactory for you or would you want more?"
Mr. Johnson asked.

"Well, I reckon I might want best they is to have, but that may
never be fer me. I got no fine schoolin' ner the likes, and all I know
is work."

"There is nothing whatsoever wrong with work. Besides that,
the happiest people in the world are not the ones who have the best
of everything, but rather the people who make the best of everything
they have. Some of the most miserable people that I know are those
who have almost anything they could imagine. I tell you, son, happiness does not have its roots in someone's purse. Some things must
be worked for and not just purchased at some extravagant cost. Life
is not all that structured. It takes effort to be successful, but it takes
trust and hard labor to be happy. Unfortunately, some folks never
see the path they need to take to get there."

"Seem like I done been told that a time or two," Jubal answered.

"I suppose that you have. I just bet that your father may have
told you that."

"No sir. My Pa never told me much about anythin'. He always wanted a laudanum bottle or a pull from a stone crock."

"Sorry to hear that my boy, really sorry. But permit me to tell you something about fathers, one in particular. You need to have a Fatherly influence all your life. It is a continual growth and learning process. If you choose to rebel against father, the Father, he will allow it, but he will grieve over it as long as his sons are in rebellion. If you think fatherly teachings are unwise and unjust and rebel against them and not take to heart what the Father says, then you will eventually gain your rebellion and will at the same time ensure your life long separation from the Father's teaching and instruction. I know, because I have a son who has some of the rebellious traits that your father seems to have. Did you ever know your father's father, your granddad?"

"Never knowed him."

"Well, I just wondered if there was rebellion between them. Just curious, and I do not mean to be prying into your life."

"I never took it that way, not a bit," Jubal answered.

"I am glad you can say that, and I feel that you mean it as well. My father tried to steer me right, and his father before him as well. I am very appreciative of that. I have been blessed."

"Yes sir. I reckon that be so."

"Would you be offended if I offered you a bit of advice?"

"No sir, I would not."

"I hope we can talk some more later. Not very often that I get to converse with someone from near my home or someone who reminds me so much of myself when I was about your age. I was more like you then than you might ever imagine."

"How ye mean sir?" Jubal questioned.

"Would you think that I was grown before I ever learned to read very much? I come from a background much like yourself and not too far removed from your typical area either. I had little formal education as you mentioned and had only the necessities of life for what seemed ever so long."

"How did ye get yerself up so far in life?"

"Determination. I wanted things for myself, not material things mind you. I was willing to spend the time and exert the effort to attain what I wanted. It was not easy, and I had times that I thought I was ready to quit. Then I recalled that someone had told me that winners never quit, and I hold to that until this day. And you know, they were right because it is always too soon to quit. I still learn things most every day, and I realize now more than ever how important that is. You just can never give up on yourself. Life is dynamic, and you must treat it that way. You can do much for yourself if you set your mind to do so."

"Was you poor and all the likes when ye was a kid?"

"Very much so. I had hardly anything when I came to Greeneville. Had it rough for a few months, but I had some kindly folks who boosted me a bit and pointed me a time or two, and I am still grateful to them."

"I'd reckon so," Jubal said.

"I just bet that there is some kind soul somewhere who has tried to set you on the right road, and you may not have even realized it at the time. You may not realize it even yet. But I am inclined to believe that if you thought about it for a while that you would have an eye opener."

"Why ye think that?"

"I know the mind of young boys, when they are at the close of childhood but not yet into manhood. I know that, because I have been there and so have my own sons. That is why I wish to help others avoid the pitfalls that I and my own have had to overcome. I suppose you know that my future requires that I invest in the next generation, and your future will likewise depend on your nurturing your children. Our nation and our progeny are locked together in that manner. What we are able to do today, for someone else, is the only things that will stand the test of time. Nothing man makes or builds will endure. There is only one thing on the face of this earth that will endure and stand the tests of time, and I feel sure that you know what I mean."

"I thinkin' I do," Jubal answered as he searched his mind madly to come up with the right answer.

"Well, you think on that for a bit and then come back with the right answer. I will then be able to know that my confidence in you and your judgment is sound. I am most always a decent judge of character, and I think I have assessed yours fairly accurately. With some polish, you could be refined into a gentleman; and I for one would pleasure in seeing that happen. I have said that the war will end soon, and I will maintain that. There will be new opportunities opening all over the nation. It is just going to take some insight and determination, and those who can muster it will be the winners, big winners. You could go far with the right leadership and influences."

"I'm not sure I understand," Jubal answered.

"I am speculating a bit, and I sometimes let my thinking get ahead of myself. I do not expect you to see and understand things as I do, but we can talk more on that later."

"Yes sir."

"How would you like to make it back home and check on your folks?"

"That would be good, sir."

"Our time in Nashville will be short. Not enough time to get to the eastern area of the state most likely. I would like to make it back to Greeneville myself but am not going to attempt it this time. I plan to return there for a brief visit soon after the inauguration. That is the reason we are rushed now. I must conclude my affairs in time to be back in Washington City for the swearing in ceremony. Were it not for that, we both could possibly make a quick run home on this trip."

"I understand sir."

"That begs another question. Do you think you would be satisfied back at home with the life that you had there or would you see it as a step down from where you are now? I suppose you wonder why I would ask you such a thing, but I am looking out into time possibly even years from now."

"I was kinda wonderin' why ye ask me so much now that ye mention it," Jubal replied, not really knowing what or why he was being asked.

"I will tell you right up front. I have plans for myself once I serve in this upcoming venture back in Washington City, and I am going to need the help of a few men very much like yourself. I want to do what I can to secure a good life and a good living for all my countrymen, but I have specific plans for some deserving souls; and I think that those who have sacrificed for the welfare of the Union are the ones who deserve my primary efforts. There is going to be a need for positions of authority and leadership out in the new territories and in the new western states. I think that I can be instrumental in some of those appointments in due time. I will want men about me of conviction and ethics that will serve in the character that I uphold and desire for all our citizens. I see some of those qualities in you, and with a measure of refinement, I think you could do well."

"That seem a mite over my head right now sir," Jubal said with some doubt about his own desires and direction. "Right now, I just wanna get myself through this here war without bein' kilt or maimed. My Ma always tell me just do one day at a time cause the present day be evil enough."

"Your mother is wise, and she has definitely given you good advice."

"She be a hard worker too."

"I intend to speak to you and some of the other men on this detail at a later time. I am of the opinion that you will be interested in what I have to offer. But for now, let it suffice to say that it will involve a commitment from you and some effort on your part. I feel that you are capable or else I would not waste your time by conversing with you. Do you think you could commit yourself to something that would be life changing?"

"I reckon I would try to handle whatever I could, sir," Jubal responded.

"Well young man, that is all well and good, but sometimes it is not what you are given that counts. It comes down to how you can handle what you have. That may not make much sense to you now, but it will in due time. You will just have to trust me for now; and like you have said, the most important thing now is to get through this war and move on both personally and as a nation. One nation.

"Yes sir."

"I suggest that you attempt to get some rest if you are not assigned to night duty. I want to run a bit faster tomorrow as soon as it is light enough to see well. You know that we can make much better time when the sun is up high, and I wish to exercise that advantage tomorrow. We will need sharp eyes for lookouts and a steady hand on the throttle. I have some matters that need my attention tonight so I am going to my writing table and get started. I want you to think about our conversation, all aspects of it. I will get back with you in due time, and we will evaluate things in more detail then. I intend to keep you on my detail for some time yet, and you will learn more as needed. For now, that will be all."

"Yes sir."

"Thank you for your attention. You are dismissed."

The locomotive huffed and groaned long into the night. The conductor had received his instruction shortly before dusk and consequently would be stopping at the appropriate telegraph station just before dawn. Mr. Johnson kept in touch by wire and was abreast of the latest happenings in and around Washington City and in his home state capital as well.

The time frame would not allow much flexing, and it was imperative that he be back in Washington City a day or so before Mr. Lincoln and he were to be sworn into office. There had been reports of renewed conflict north of Nashville, and sporadic forays were still to be contended with. The purpose of the predawn stop was to learn the latest of those conditions. No one had received any communication about any breech of secrecy concerning the train and who it was carrying, but nonetheless, no precautions could be ignored. Safety of the party was paramount, and if a detour or a delay were needed, then that is how it would be. Time was significant as well. Each mile traversed in a southerly direction would need to be retraced and that would require a given amount of time. It just had to be that way.

Good speed and clear tracks made for distance, but the time came for water and wood. It was timed to coincide with the telegraph stop as well. The stationmaster stood ready as the screech of iron rail against iron wheel brought the behemoth to a silencing halt. He boarded the train and made straightway for the private car and its occupant. Messages had come through from General Giles in Nashville, and they were not the ones that were desired.

Rebel activity around the capital city of the state had been sporadic, but fierce in its effect on Union operations. Supply lines were cut and just about as quickly restored. Communications had been disrupted, but that had been largely circumvented by couriers. There was no indication that Union forces were anywhere near being overrun or driven out, but extra patrols and sentries were only a palliative measure while the real danger lay in the chance of capture of the leadership and subsequent disruption of the chain of command and authority.

The same was not true in and around the countryside nearer Washington City. The Union forces had prevented any invasion into the nation's capital, and the heart of the Confederacy itself lay exposed and largely undefended.

"Telegrams for you sir," the stationmaster said as he handed the folded pages to Mr. Johnson. "I have them in order that they came in. I will wait for you to read them in case you have any reply."

"Thank you, my good man."

The Yankee from Tennessee, as he had sometimes been called, took the pages from the stationmaster and immediately began to pour over them. First he exhibited a wrinkled brow and then a hint of a smile.

"One wire to General Giles, and the same message to the appropriate eyes in Washington City," the tailor-turned politician replied.

"Yes sir."

"Tell them that I shall do an immediate about face. Do you know where to send each message and how to word it as per the prearranged plan?"

"Yes sir, I do. I have been prepared as directed. I can assure you that all is in order at my station."

"Excellent. Do you have facilities so that I may freshen myself and get a solid breakfast for myself as well my men?"

"Yes, that has already been arranged."

"How did you know to do that?"

"I read the dispatches as they came in, and I took it upon myself to be prepared for just such a measure," the stationmaster answered.

"If your breakfast is as commendable as your efficiency, then I am indeed, in for a treat. I thank you very much, and I appreciate your concern and your efforts on my behalf."

"Thank you sir. But if that is all, I will be about my work."

William and Jubal sat together and ate their fill of eggs and sausage and enjoyed leisure refills of steaming hot coffee from an old stained pot that sat on top of the pot-bellied stove.

"Mr. Johnson been grillin' me over what I aim on doin' once the war be over and I finish my time. He ask me some strange stuff too."

"Like what?" William asked.

"What I do when I go back home and even iffin I want go back there. He ask me what I aim on doin' with myself and my life from now on. He ask me things that I ain't know yet myself. I wonderin' just what it be that he really want me tellin' him. He make me feel like I been addled a bit. I don't understand all his askin's and all that."

"He has questioned me too," William replied.

"He ask ye about me?" Jubal questioned a bit surprised.

"No, not about you, but about myself."

"What he wanna know?"

"More or less the same things that he asked you. He wanted to know if I intended to go back to Ohio and what I would do when I got there. He wanted to know how I planned to make my living and if I thought I could be happy doing that. Just things like that, that's all he wanted to know."

"What ye tell him?" Jubal asked.

"I told him more or less the same things that I have told you about my life and what I believe in and the plans that I have. You recall us talking about those things don't you?"

"Some parts I do. Ye harped on me lots a times about bein' able to see difference twixt night and day, twixt light and dark and all that stuff."

"Well, that is part of what he wants to know about you," William answered as he spooned honey into a new mug of coffee and began to stir it slowly. "He is just trying to find out where you stand on a thing or two. I know what he means, and I think you really know too. You just will not face up to it."

"Are ye fixin' start in on me again?"

"I will if it helps any," William answered.

"Drink yer coffee, it be time we move on someplace else."

"All right, I will not get up on my box now, but just want to tell you one thing before I quit," William shot back.

"What that be?"

"Some time, some place, your entire life is going to flash in front of your eyes. I don't pretend to know when or where, but it will for sure. You need to be sure that what you see stands for something. So many people spend so much life just looking for a way to live that they are old and weary before they learn how to live. They don't know how to enjoy what they are given. You need to realize that we seldom can change the things that we are given, but we sure can change the way we handle those things that we do have. I know you are going to tell me that you don't understand that aren't you?"

"Well ain't you just the smart-arse one?"

"You ever play cards, Jubal?"

"Some. What that got to do with it?"

"We can't change the cards we are dealt, just the manner in which we play the hand. That sums up what I am talking about in words that you ought to see through."

"Sometimes I think ye be the one what don't know how cards is played."

"You miss the whole point," William said, a bit disgusted that his friend had managed to cut him asunder again. "What will it ever take to get you to see?"

"See what?"

"You got to hold to values: work hard, do your very best, speak the truth, put on no airs and trust in your God, have no fears and enjoy the peace that is meant for you."

"Ye got yer wants. I reckon they far off from mine; but they is mine, and I ain't pushed them off on ye. No sir, not one bit. I ain't gonna neither. I just don't understand why ye always be raggin' me about night and day and all that. I reckon I can see just same as ye, and I got a heap better eye fer a long rifle too."

"I will be quiet for now, but I will not pass up one single chance to talk to you. I can see now is not the time, but I wish it could somehow be. Wish it could be this very day. You mean a great deal to me as a friend, as a fellow trooper and as a man. I just want to see that man find and know what I have found."

William got up and went back toward the waiting train. Jubal stood alone on the station platform. He did not hear the clatter of the telegraph key just inside the station house, but did notice the stationmaster head to the train in a hurry with paper in hand. He watched as he climbed aboard and disappeared into the privacy of the gentleman's car. There was discernible movement inside with shadows passing back and forth by the partially shaded windows.

Suddenly, the wisp of smoke from the cars turned to a belching torrid of blackened thick swirling fog laced with the scent of charred white oak. Someone had stoked the old pot-bellied monster and opened the draft. The forward door to the car swung open, and a uniformed Union captain made straight for the engine, climbed aboard and gave instruction to the fireman and the engineer.

Just as quickly, the steam and fire breathing monster awakened and began protest by belching a cloud of acrid black smoke that told of forthcoming clouds of white hot steam. The train and its party were about to move somewhere, and soon. In only a few moments, the steam whistle shrieked. The bell rang incessantly as a summons to assemble and board with haste or get left behind. The station master descended the steps and made haste back to the telegraph and sat down before it. It began its strange but rhythmic language. Jubal wondered who would be listening.

Politics laid aside for the moment. Mr. Johnson assembled his detail and brought them up to date on what he knew and what he wanted to do in the next few hours. The train could make New Bern by nightfall if the tracks remained clear. That would put the whole detail deeper into Confederate territory, but it was a known fact that there was a good measure of Union support and sympathies in that neck of the woods.

"I know that I am asking a great deal from each of you and that there is some risk of hostilities even yet. Those risks exist for me as well as each of you. This is still a voluntary mission, and I will excuse any man who does not feel comfortable by continuing on south. We will increase our risks with each southerly mile until we reach the Nashville area, and I anticipate that we may encounter some resistance. With that in mind, I believe it best that we leave anything and everything behind right here and now that has any indication or connection to the Union. This would include all personal items that could possibly divulge your home town or your home state. For some of you, that would not be an issue." That statement merited a direct eye-to-eye contact with Jubal, but nothing was further said in that respect.

"I would think that New Bern will be near the point of no return. Once there we would need to press on and strive for the information and support that our president dutifully needs and deserves. That is the way I see things this morning. Does anyone have any questions?"

No one had anything to ask.

"Is there anyone who does not wish to continue?"

No one wanted out.

"Excellent," Mr. Johnson said as he sat down at the big oak table in his private accommodations. "We have one half hour before this train comes to life and moves again. In that time you will sort your personal belongings, bag what you wish to leave behind, tag it with your last name only and give it to Mr. Casteel, the stationmaster. We will retrieve it on the return trip. Does anyone have any question or second thoughts now?"

No one spoke.

"Some may be thinking what will come of my things if I do not return? We will not think or reason in those terms. I have reason to know and trust that we will not be in vain. We will return and in good time as well. Things are moving in Northern Virginia in ways that I am not at liberty to discuss with you at this time. I can tell you that I am confident that war will soon cease. And we, as a common people and a nation, will endure the hardships that reconstruction will put to task. It will come by degrees, but it will come sure as the light comes out of the east in the morning. We are still a nation of good-hearted and strong-willed people; and they by the grace of Almighty God will heal themselves and stand up in defense of right and goodness. I believe in this Union, and I support its leadership. Otherwise, I could not ask your efforts on my behalf. I thank you gentlemen, one and all, and I shall stand by that to my very core.

Jubal felt that he now stood just a bit taller and that once he was able to get back into his blue and gold uniform that it would shine in a manner that it had not known before. He was sure that the other young men were just as proud. He even let his mind wander a ways into the future. He could see himself well established in the post war army serving in Washington City as aide to the dignitaries and even possibly as a guard at the congress building somewhere. He would live the good life then, compared to the sweat and toil of a back home dirt farmer.

There seemed to be no choice but to remain in the army, if he ever was to have any of the real pleasures of life. There would be the best of most everything available in the seat of government. He could do something that would mean a great deal to himself and at the same time be appreciated by others. There was much to be gained in the fair city, especially compared to what he had known back in Cane Valley. In his present mind the ties to home had been severed, and he now thought that he had no deep-seated roots. Home would be where the heart was, and right now it was most anywhere besides in the old log home at the head of the hollow.

The train pulled out on schedule and soon trailed streams of thick acrid smoke and diminishing clouds of white steam. Loud creaking and groaning exemplified the strain of iron on iron as the lumbering hissing giant rounded each tangent. The speed was near the point where the flanged wheels could climb the insides of the rails and cause the entire weight and mass of metal and wood to derail and go crashing down some man-made embankment that cradled the roadbed. The speed was ordered by Mr. Johnson; that was what he wanted and that was what it would be.

The fireman worked tirelessly tossing hickory or white oak splits into the firebox. The engineer kept one hand on his throttle and both eyes fixed on what lay ahead. The train crew was experienced and diligent in their task. The conductor knew that the old fireman could coax another ounce or two of speed out of the bellowing machine, and he also knew that the crew would push but not to the point of unneeded risk. Speed was a virtue, but arrival in a safe and secure manner was more virtuous.

The station at New Bern was small, but entirely adequate. The telegraph worked superbly, and the telegrapher was precise in his duties. He had dispatches awaiting the train's arrival and saw to it that they were delivered with haste.

Their recipient poured over them in the order that he received them. There were the usual inquires and reports about positions and times of arrivals or departures. The war reports reinforced the opinions that hostilities would soon cease and that a wounded nation could go about healing itself. Mr. Johnson poured over each communication with his characteristic propensity for detailed attention and thought.

There was a long report about the Battle of Hatcher's Run and what it now indicated as to the strength and capabilities of the Union forces. There were reports still coming in about the back breaking march across Georgia and the devastation it had brought both to the combatants of the South and to the citizens who had been in the path of the sweep.

However, the later of the reports were the ones that commanded the utmost attention of the Vice President Elect. Mr. Lincoln himself had strongly suggested that circumstances in and around Nashville were not nearly as pressing as those now prevalent in Northern Virginia. It would, therefore, be of the best interest to the nation and to the efforts to quickly and efficiently secure a just and lasting end to the hostilities that had so devastated the nation for far too many days now.

The President expressed a strong desire to have his new second in command at his beckon call so that he could be brought in on all the matters concerning the state of the nation. And yes, that included the rebellious states, states that Mr. Lincoln had already indicated. It was in this purpose that Mr. Johnson was called and would return with all expediency available to him. Mr. Lincoln also informed him that all parties involved were to act according to his directives and that preparations for that expedient return were presently in progress. There was no choice. The train would retrace its tracks with haste. Mr. Johnson would not see Nashville on this venture, and Jubal would not see Cane Valley.

The train received high priority on the entire run back to the Washington City area and enjoyed cleared tracks without encumbering delay. Water and wood were provided at each stop and quickly loaded. The lookouts were relaxed just a bit as travel was mainly through Union held territory. The tracks had for the most part, been spared the ravages and destruction of the Rebel forces and where damage had been inflicted, repairs had been completed and control of the road bed reestablished.

It was just breaking light when the belching behemoth crossed the Potomac and glided into the stationhouse near the domed capitol building. A carriage was waiting for Mr. Johnson. But before leaving he instructed the entire detail to remain on standby since he really did not know what Mr. Lincoln might have in store for him. Besides that, the inauguration was just a few short days away and that would call for some new and unusual duties.

Jubal could not see too much need there in the throngs of people and the bustle of the city for a tracker or a sharpshooter. Nevertheless, he had decided that he could be content in the lifestyle that this town had afforded him. He could dine with the best of them, no matter how rough and unrefined he might appear. Did not make a great deal of difference what others thought of him, except Mr. Johnson of course. He knew who he was and what he was all about, or at least that was what he kept telling himself. It was just a bit confusing to him. When he was in the big city that seemed to be the life that he wanted; but yet when he was out in the woods and mountains, he could feel at ease with himself and with all of creation. He returned again and again to the words that Granny Iverson and his Ma had said about peace inside one's self, and it just seemed to haunt him. It would pass for a time but never completely leave. Even William had told him about it, and William most times appeared to have not a worry in the world.

He had never really remembered Mr. Johnson saying much about inside peace, but tarnation, he had a whole country to fret about and see to. One thing sure, there would be no call for politics and public service for this old mountain boy. There just might be something to life in the hills after all.

He thought briefly about schooling like William and some others had. That would be good to have; and he reckoned that it would be worth working for some day, but now did not seem to be the time. Then again, there were those who had taught themselves. Mr. Johnson was a shining example, and he was the smartest thinking man that he had ever been privileged to know. Seemed like he had something in mind for the future as well, but now it was a wait-and-see situation. Wait and see in the big city, that should make for some fun times and merriment. Best get it here while you can, because it ain't to be had back there in Cane Valley.

Once back in Washington City and somewhat settled in, Jubal and his detail had little to do except dress for morning roll call. Usually they would wait around for a bit and then be dismissed for the remainder of the day. Occasionally someone would be needed for charge of quarter's runner or as messenger. William frequently stepped up for that duty because it offered him an opportunity to meet people of distinction and importance, and he enjoyed such. Jubal, on the other hand, shied away from that duty and preferred the solitude of a night watch.

When not on assigned detail, there was little to do in the evenings other than dine at one of the off-street local taverns and engage in revelry as only young troopers can do. They were under strict orders to maintain themselves in a respectable and orderly manner. Having had it impressed upon them that they were subject to call on a moment's notice, they decided that it was in their best interest to conduct themselves accordingly. Promotion or recommendations would be few and far between if there happened to be a record of conduct unbecoming.

That made for some long days and slow evenings, but March did eventually come into being. It came with a torrent of early spring rain, and the streets of the fair city were soon awash with mud and mire. And so it was on the day of inauguration.

Throngs lined the quagmire that bore the name of Pennsylvania Avenue. Jubal and William had been posted as sentries just below the podium where the oaths of office were administered and were privileged to be able to hear Mr. Lincoln's address.

"What did he mean with all that talk about slavery?" Jubal inquired of his friend once they had been dismissed from their post.

"I believe he was not trying to fix a blame on anyone in particular but on the economics and the distribution of the institute of slavery. He acknowledged the divisions that existed between the North and the South and reflected on how both sides had anticipated a swift and determined victory and that none had foreseen such destruction as has been brought to both sides in the conflict."

"It was all done said and over mighty quick," Jubal added.

"You are right, my friend. One will need to read it in depth to really understand all that he said. I plan to do that for myself as soon as I can," William said determined to know more, just for his own satisfaction and enlightenment.

"He said somethin' there on the last about bindin' up our wounds and such. We ain't got no wounds what ain't already healed up."

"He was not talking about those wounds."

"What then?" Jubal asked

"He was talking about the country and healing up all the things that beset us now such as the money issues and the hatred that some people will never be able to let go. There can be and are wounds to the character and trusts that people have for one another and such things as a man's word and his deeds. These are the kinds of things that need healing and mending. There needs to be a national sense of love of our country and for mankind in general. These things will take time. There will be those who will try to take advantage of the vanquished and use them for their own gain. These are the perils that lay ahead for many now, and I think that our President and his new Vice President will work diligently to that end. I believe they share a mutual appreciation for our country and our government, and I believe that both of them equally desire that our nation be at the beginning of a bright and prosperous new age. I believe that Mr. Lincoln will be just and that he really will have malice toward none as he said in his address."

"I reckon that might just be a fact," Jubal added.

"I believe he said that because he really feels it," William added.

News from the Battle of Waynesboro began coming in. Also, favorable news communications from North Carolina served to reinforce the general feelings that the Union had gained the upper hand and were in serious pursuit of Lee and his army.

In early April the Rebel forces attempted to burn the bridge at Little Sailors Creek trying to prevent attacking forces from pursuing them from the opposite side of the Appomattox River. They were somewhat successful in their goal, but the Union forces simply went downstream a short distance and began a pincher move against Lee's forces. The conflict continued on for about a week and culminated in the deciding battle of Appomattox and the subsequent surrender at the like-named courthouse.

Mr. Lincoln had already briefed his Vice President Elect about his reconstruction plans and now informed him that he was ready to start on those measures. He had already directed that the beaten Confederate forces be allowed to keep their arms and simply return home, wherever that might be.

It was unfortunate indeed that the President would not see his plans materialize. He would be cut down by the assassin's bullet at a time that would prove to be most difficult for the nation and for the leaders of the government; a government that had just stood the most brutal of endurances. There would be much to be done in the realms of reconstruction and the wounds indeed would need to be bound up.

Mr. Johnson had been president for only a few days when he summoned his still intact detail to his office. He spoke to them informally as a group and individually.

"Jubal, I recall your home being not too far from my home."

"Yes sir, mine be in Cane Valley."

"Well, I am not real sure that I know where that is, but I understand that is a bit north and east of Greeneville. I had planned, and Mr. Lincoln had wanted me to return there and personally see to some of his instruction and plans. Now, as you are well aware, that cannot happen." President Johnson picked up some papers lying about his writing table and scanned them briefly.

"I see by your papers here that your year of service will soon be up. Have you made any decisions about what you wish to do?"

"Well,...I think," Jubal stammered

"Before you give a definite answer, let me tell you what I have in mind for you."

"Yes sir."

"You have served me well, and your woodsmanship speaks for itself in my opinion. I will be able to use your skills in the coming months and possibly longer than that if I get to do things the way I foresee them right now. However, that would most likely necessitate you agreeing to another full year of service. I am prepared to guarantee you a promotion and possibly an opportunity for some formal schooling. All that, of course, would certainly mean that you would be away from your home and your family for that given time."

"I unnerstand that sir, I rightly do."

"Hold on an minute. I am not finished yet."

"Yes sir."

"I am prepared to offer you the same terms that I have presented to each member of the detail. I think it is fair and equitable."

The offer was explained in detail by one of the President's officer aids. Agreement to another year would guarantee a promotion by mid-summer at the latest. It would also guarantee posting for that year to nowhere other than Washington City itself. Duty would be at the direction of the President himself through his appointed staff and aides. The army would furnish everything that would be needed including a first-line Cavalry horse and gear. Quarters would be provided as well and ample accommodations would be provided anywhere the President should need to travel.

All that lecture about duty and such was near to water off a duck's back to Jubal. The thing that got his attention was that he would be allowed to return home for sixty days and visit with his family. He would then need to present himself back in Washington City and render his decision in writing. He could still decline if that was his choosing.

"What ye gonna do, William?" Jubal quired his friend.

"I thought I wanted to go back home and start teaching, but the offer seems pretty good to me. I could wait a year before taking a schoolmaster's position. A year here in and around government might just teach me more than I could get otherwise. I don't think I want to make a written decision until after the visit home, but I am leaning on staying with the man for another whole year."

"That be how I see it too," Jubal remarked.

Jubal and all in the detail spent the next few days getting outfitted for the two months at home and all the necessary travel. The detail members one and all accepted the President's offer and all were upbeat about their return to Washington City and their assumption of choice duty. Jubal even began to question William seriously about schooling and learning to read and write far better than he had exhibited so far. He needed only to allow his mind a small measure of wandering to see himself down the road as a learned man with influence and position. Here in the seat of national government, he could be a small fish in a huge pond, but back home that situation would largely reverse itself, or at least he envisioned it that way. He thought he had discovered a way to have the good life and all the things that came with it and be able to have his life at home in familiar surroundings, all at the same time. Surely that was what it was all about, and he had just found his way to it.

He and William would travel together part way. Jubal had been given a young grey and black spotted mare named Spirit. She was gentle, but willing. She was strong and sure afoot and could make good time when treated well. Jubal rubbed her down each night and made sure that she had good, clean feed and fresh water. In no time the pair became almost as one, and the trust and understanding between them was strong. Spirit would even nudge Jubal for his attention if she felt that she was being short changed. Jubal never failed to return her attention. He knew that she would carry him well.

Military transport trains were still very busy and one could arrange a ride most anywhere that the tracks had not been destroyed. All arrangements had been made for William and Jubal to take an express train all the way to Cincinnati. There William would mount up and ride the day's journey to his home. He had tried to get Jubal to go home with him, but he wanted to get back to Cane Valley and have as much time there as he could. He had not told anyone, but he had plans of his own to see to.

Jubal was scheduled to travel from Ohio to Knoxville via train, and then he would complete his travels atop Spirit. He had never been to Knoxville, but he knew the way from Cumberland area well enough, he reckoned. He and Wes had made their trek into that neck of the woods not all that long ago. He had a map, and William had marked it for him and explained the landmarks best he could. Jubal knew that if he could find the church and the graveyard that he would be sure of himself all the rest of the way. Spirit could almost jump the mountain and ridges if she needed to.

Jubal had no trouble making his way from Knoxville eastwardly. All he needed do was follow the old wagon road headed to Rutledge community and then look for the easterly running backbone of ridges that end-to-end made a chain reaching all the way up into Pennsylvania. The valley floors were alive with new spring growth, and the thickets and upland timber would soon be thick green with the early May growth of bloom and blossom.

Spirit had an absolute abundance of lush pasture just for the taking at almost any spot. The days grew pleasantly warm by mid-morning, but the chill of night still made its presence known. Jubal had decided that he would ride straight through all the way to the old log home at the head of Cane Creek. He would not push Spirit beyond what she could easily do, but would not tarry unnecessarily either. He had a good stash of hardtack and jerky to sustain him, and he would add to that any time opportunity afforded. Best he could tell by looking at the map and following William's markings, he should soon spot the end of Old Clinch and that would be his first positive landmark. From that point he would look for the gap and cross there, and then he would be in more familiar territory.

It was getting down late in the evening. The light had already begun to fade in the crimson and orange sky, but there it was for sure. It was the west end of the mountain and that meant that the gap was only a few hours' ride on to the east. He had pushed Spirit a bit the last few hours, and she had worked up a right fair sweat. He was a bit tuckered himself as well. A nearby pine grove looked like a good place to bed down for a few hours, and it also offered some hiding from whoever might be passing that way. The war was over. True it was, but there were still those about who held to their former alliances and convictions. It was a good measure not to take any undue risks and to never throw caution to the winds. Jubal would allow Spirit to graze a bit, but would keep her on a loose rein all the while. He would allow himself only a short rest. Then it would be time to be on the move again. He had it figured that he could be home tomorrow night, if all went well.

Jubal awakened just a bit confused. He heard Spirit and realized that he had slept much longer than he intended. The night was well on because he could hear a lone old screech owl off somewhere up in the tall timber. The moon had climbed high into the sky, and its silvery light filtered almost straight down through the dew laden pine boughs. Everything around had taken on the eerie glow that only a full moon could muster up. He got to his feet and headed to Spirit, who easily sensed him and turned to face him. He had not even unsaddled her and now she had probably gorged herself on fresh grasses to the point she would be bloated against the cinch. She was, however, more sensible than he had credited her. She seemed perfectly content and even nuzzled him when he reached her. He took her reins, and they walked out into the open meadow and took stock of their location.

Jubal could easily see the mountain gap in the silver moonlight. He knew where he was now and realized about how far he would be from home once they passed the gap. He looked back to the east and could see no light above the timberline. It would be a while before first light. He thought to himself that he should have been more on watch the past night or so and then he would know how high the moon would ride when daybreak began. He knew now that he would just have to wait for dawn to get some sense of time.

Spirit seemed just about as anxious as he to get on the move. She was in new pastures now and appeared to be anxious to know what lay over the next rise or where was to be found the next stand of sweet grass. Jubal mounted up and headed into the big timber, careful to watch for low-hanging branches or unexpected rock out-croppings. He knew that he would get into rough and rocky ground as they neared the summit. He would dismount and lead Spirit over the unsure footing and down the other side of the steep grades.

He realized that although Spirit had quite well sated herself that he had not eaten anything in several hours. He had a bit of jerky and hardtack left in his saddlebags, but he had his taster set on some of his Ma's biscuits and sausage gravy. That would be several hours off yet, and he had no intention of going without for that long. He thought about the old timer where he and Wes had bought a biscuit. He could not recall exactly where it was, but he could see the ram-shackle old house and the trash all over the yard. He could even see the face of the cranky old man and hear his crusty voice. He felt in his pocket to see if he had any loose coins. He knew there were some gold dollars in his pack, but he had no intention of getting into them now. They would be for when he got home.

He was just a bit put out with himself for not being able to recall all he needed about the trek that he and Wes had made. Just like watching the moon, he should have paid more attention at the time.

He thought about the old barn where they had held up during the rain. He recalled the haul way and the sagging roof. He had a good picture of the old barn and would know it in a heartbeat if he saw it. He just could not remember exactly where it was. A lesson to be learned and remembered. He was not real sure how the new President intended to employ his tracking talents, but he now knew that he must work hard at sharpening those skills and keeping them that way. He was almost sure, at least for now, that he would report back and tell them that he wanted to go another year. That seemed to be the best choice.

He still had a wanderlust that tugged at him. He recalled what he had heard someone in Washington City say about going with the crowd. He remembered hearing that those who go with the crowd will go no more than where the crowd goes, but those who walk alone will go places where no man had been. He cared not so much about going where no other had been, but about reaching places where he had not been.

Jubal and Spirit were down very near the valley floor when the eastern sky began to turn faint shades of grey. Day would be coming soon, and the creatures of the night would grow silent. Jubal knew now for sure that he had slept much longer than he intended. He noted the position of the moon. He would not forget such an important thing again, not tonight nor in a thousand nights. He was unsure of the time it would take to carry him on in home. He had guessed that he could be there by night fall, but now that may have changed a bit. He remembered that he and Wes had reached home from the mountain gap in about a full day, but they had made some stops along the way. He was just not sure of himself and silently blamed himself for being so foolish. It would not happen again.

He rode on into the day, noting the reddened sky as morning grew into the light of day. The signs all said that there would be bad weather in the coming day, but one could hope that light would hold and that the day would be fair. He continued to look for the old barn and the homestead. He never did see it.

Around noon, he spotted the crest of Pine Mountain, and he knew then exactly where he was. He had come too far easterly before crossing the big mountain and, therefore, had missed the house and barn that he sought. There was a good side to that, however, he was now even nearer home than he had thought. He could be at the old log home by mid-afternoon, if he urged Spirit just a bit.

He dug a heel into her belly, and she obediently picked up the pace. A slow but steady trot that made the bends on the old roadbed seem much closer together. He would not let his faithful companion break a heavy sweat, because they were too near the end of their travels to demand anything like that now.

Soon they were abreast the end of Old Pine, and Jubal gently reined Spirit across the narrow meadow and into the edge of the timberline. The sun was to his back now, and he could feel its heat fade as they gained the cover of the trees. It would take only an hour or so to reach the top, then east for a bit until the familiar shaped ridge came into view. Out the top of the ridge, then down the long hollow to the house and home.

The closer they got, the more anxious Spirit seemed to get. Jubal let her have her rein, and he only guided her occasionally. It was getting on down in the afternoon when they reached the long hollow, and Jubal knew that the old log house would come into view in just a few more minutes. He could feel himself growing a bit more anxious.

The sun cast long shadows across the lush green meadows where he and Wes had cut and stacked hay. The tall poplar trees along the ridge slopes made for good shade and good hay ground. Such trees had been cut and hewn years ago to build the house and most of the out buildings, yet there remained an abundance of them just for the taking. The old house had been built around a hundred years ago, but it was still just as sound as ever and offered shelter in all seasons.

Jubal stopped and got off Spirit. He looked all around and noticed that everything seemed to be a bit overgrown and that it was obvious that nothing had grazed in the pastures, probably all spring. There were no stock to be seen anywhere, and the entire place seemed to have an empty silence about it. The only sound he could make out was a lone hawk soaring high above, which let go a shrill call of affection to an unseen but nearby mate. Just a bit early for fledglings, but just about right for setting the nest.

He walked on down the meadow slope until the housetop came into view. Still no sounds, and no gray smoke curling up from either chimney. By now the nights had warmed enough that no fire was needed, and most likely Ma had not made a hot supper.

He walked on and Spirit followed.

There was no sign of life anywhere about the place. No chickens wandered about the barn yard. With Spirit securely tied off to the front porch railing, Jubal opened the door to the living room where he and Julie had talked so many times, where Granny Iverson had read to him, where Ma had poured her heart out to him and where he had spent many sleepless hours before a dying fire trying to think things out for himself. The room was empty! Julie's bed was gone, and the marks on the wide pine boards still bore evidence to where it had stood. The sweeps had been in the chimney so much that the hearth was a heap of soot and creosote flakes. Dust covered everything.

He made his way to the kitchen and cracked open that door. Nothing! The old cook stove was gone, and there was not even the wood box remaining. He could see water stains on the wall around the flu opening. There had been no one here in some time now. He heard Spirit snort as if to be calling him back to untie her and let her have her own reins.

There was nothing left that he could do here. Just to make sure that all was gone, he made his way to the springhouse loft just to check on Wes. Just like everything else, all was gone. The white oak peg where Wes had hung his gourd, well it was empty too. The old barn proved to be the same way. There was a good portion of old hay in the loft, and he reasoned that Spirit might benefit from the dried timothy and fescue heads. She did nuzzle what he threw down to her for a bit, but seemed to not care for much of it. Much better to have the fresh new ones.

There was nothing here for him any longer. He had not heard anything from anyone since he had left the mill yard and started toward the ferry and that had been over a year ago. A lot of things could happen in a year, and a lot of things could change in that time. He had nothing on which to make a judgment. His mind could imagine a whole host of things, most of which he would rather not think about.

He was tired, bone tired. Spirit had to be that way too. The hay loft looked inviting and he knew it would be comfortable. He knew that because he had been there many times before. He climbed back there and threw down some more for Spirit, then went back and unsaddled her. He would eat the last of his jerky and rest until morning. Then they would go to the mill. There had to be news there. Those things would hold for a while. He was asleep just about as soon as the saddle cradled his head, and his body sunk into the soft sweet smelling hay. He had not really thought about how hard he had pushed himself and Spirit. Both would be rested come morning.

Chapter 20

Home

*T*he morning broke gray and overcast. The day seemed to be resentful that awakening time had come. Low hanging black clouds threatened to unleash their fury in the malady of an early summer thunderstorm. No flashes of brilliance darting across the sullen cloud banks so far, but the wind had picked up and carried the scents of fresh rain and a hint of new honeysuckle. The earth had awakened to another day and to the spring rebirth as well. Pastures were green and full of new growth. Hayfields swayed in the wind. The earth was alive, but there was no one around to witness the freshness and the newness that foretold of the bounty that could be there.

The black land dirt had fed its tenders for many a year and rendered a crop as a reward for the toils of those who sought its goodness. The land was good; the labor was hard. It was a living that brought a sense of pride and independence. It fostered a love of the land and a concern for the good of those who worked it. It was a land where a dependence on The Almighty played a large part of living. One was always thankful for the harvest and was always quick to share with those near who had less. It was a hard life. It was a simple life in the minds of some, but it was meaningful and brought a sense of worth to life.

Today must have been a day that the earth needed watering. The rains began just about the same time as Jubal threw the saddle across

Spirit's back. He mounted up and rode out of the old barn haul way only after donning his oilcloth rain gear. Not that it would or was intended to keep him completely dry, but he could keep his side arm and his ammunition pouch away from the elements. A wide-brimmed Cavalry hat would do a fair job of shielding his face. Spirit would not mind. Probably the soft gentle rain would feel good and refreshing to her. She had worked up a right good sweat over the last three or four days, and a good dousing would not hurt a thing.

The road leading down to the mill had obviously not been traveled in some time. The tracks were overgrown in many places. Little rivulets had cut shallow scars into the tracks as they sought to join in with the main branch and make their way on down the hollow. Low hanging branches clamored for the open sunlight of the road bed. No one had bothered to trim them away.

Jubal began to realize that the old log home had been abandoned some time ago. Most likely it had been before the onset of cold winter days, after the harvest was done, whenever that may have been. He realized that he now had no home to go back to. It was the only home that he had ever known, and it was a strange feeling to know that it would never be there for him anymore. The time had come for him to find his own way in this big wide world, and he was of a mind that thanks to President Johnson that he had found that means. Yet he was a bit saddened that his home was now something that he could revisit only as a memory.

He spurred Spirit gently.

"You got to move me Spirit, you have to show me where they are and what I need to do to find them," he spoke aloud as much to himself as to his horse. Spirit would be there for him in any situation and in any need. Spirit would sway him like no other if only he would heed her direction. He did not realize fully what Spirit could mean to him nor what she could do to carry him anywhere in life that he should need. Spirit was good; he just did not know to what measure that was true.

The run to the mill took less time than he had remembered. Of course, he had urged Spirit on a bit ever now and then. He had pulled up for just a bit at the reed patch for a quick look around. Much had happened since the day he hid there.

As he neared the millrace, he could see that the creek was swollen with the rains and the springtime runoff. The mill dam was overflowing the spillway, even with the race opened. He had not yet noted the race when he began to hear the rhythmic swish and splash sounds created as the big overshot wheel groaned to the weight of the restless water cascading down over it. The turning wheel told the boy instantly that there was a task at hand that very moment. Someone was grinding! He hastened his mount even quicker. That someone probably could be Lida! He had not yet admitted to himself how much he had missed her. But now when he reached the mill, he was sure he would run to her and take her in his arms and tell her just how much that she really did mean to him and how much that he wanted her for his very own.

Riding into the mill yard, he could see that the mill door was open and could hear noises from inside. He got down and loosely tied Spirit to the gate post and made his way up the steps and to the door. The gray sky did not give the best of light, but he could see inside well enough to know that the person at their task was not Lida.

"Hello in the mill," he said in a raised voice.

The figure turned to face him and stood, plainly surprised by the unexpected intrusion. It was Ma! She recognized him at once and ran and took him in her full embrace. She buried her face in his chest and sobbed.

"Ma, what be the matter?" he asked a bit taken aback as he placed his hands on her shoulders, pushing her back so that he could see her face. Tears cascaded down her wrinkled and leathery cheeks.

"A whole year and I never knowed iffin ye was alive or been killed. I never heard nary a word and now here ye be. I ain't squallin' cause of nuthin' but happy. It be just like ye was reborned again. Ye done come home and that be what make me tear up so much. I fretted over ye ever day, and I lifted ye up ever day and ask fer ye to be watched over."

Wes came out of a darkened corner of the mill loft and saw who had come as well. He made a beeline to Jubal and threw his arms around him and welcomed him home.

"The prodigal done come home," the old man said as a tear welled up in his eye. "Glad ye come home, son. Glad ye come home."

"Where be ever body else?" Jubal questioned.

"They be a lot to tell ye," Ma said. "Have ye had yer breakfast yet?"

"I had me a jerky piece."

"That ain't a breakfast. Ye get yerself washed up, and I have it tabled up in no time." Ma gathered up her apron and wiped her hands and face with it as she turned without further word and headed for the kitchen.

"Where are the Johnsons? Where be Lida and her mother?" Jubal questioned.

"Like yer Ma say, there be a lot what happened since ye been gone," Wes answered. "There be lots to tell ye. Some of it be yer Ma's place to tell, and some of it be mine to tell ye."

"Then get to tellin' me fer and how because I wants to know," Jubal added a bit demanding.

"Mrs. Johnson had a hard time after losing old C.C. Reckon the grief just got the best of her. Said she couldn't stand it here no more."

"When did that come about?" Jubal asked, now in a more sympathetic tone. "Where did they go?"

"One thing at a time, son," Wes replied. "They left out in late summer after they decided to sell off the mill and everthing else what went with it, house and all. They kept the team and the buckboard and a few pieces of the house furnishings."

Then how come you and Ma is runnin' his mill?"

"We was the ones what bought it off her," Wes answered somewhat confused that Jubal had not seen that so far.

"You bought it?" Jubal parroted in some surprise. "How in tarnation ye ever expect to make enough fer payin' it off?"

"Don't reckon I need fret about that none. It done been paid fer."

"How ye do that? I know it weren't no old woman's mite."

"Ye done lost yer memory, son? Have ye already forgot about the stone crock and us trekin' off to fetch it?

"No, I recollect that."

"Well, that be what been done with most of it. Me and yer Ma needed a place and a livin' where they weren't so much back breakin' work so as how we could make us a good livin' and still not have to kill ourselves all the while with hard times and hard slubbish work."

"I wouldn't never thought it that way," Jubal said.

"Any reason ye think it ought be otherwise?"

"No. No, I reckon not. Ma has worked hard all her life. I reckon she need some let up, and ye ain't able to do that kinda work much more. I reckon it be a gooder thing."

"Besides that, can't nobody say nothin' about her takin' up with a man what ain't her own neither, not since yer blood Pa ain't around no more."

I ain't grieved nary a minute over him since I been gone, and I don't reckon I be commencin' that now," Jubal said. "Is his rotten bones still up yonder where we put him?"

"Yeah, he ain't went nowhere best I know. I ain't been back up there neither."

"Is ye and Ma married now?" Jubal bluntly asked.

"Not yet, but we will be soon as circuit rider come back through here. That be next month, iffin he keep on time."

"How does Julie and the girls and Granny Iverson feel about it?" Jubal asked a bit surprised by the news.

"Ma can tell ye better about that than me. She be the one what needs tell ye all the things that done come to pass since ye been gone. They has been some changes here in the past months. Some is good; some is not so good. Ma tell ye anythin' ye wanna know, I think."

They both heard the clang-clank-clang of the old iron triangle that hung from a rafter end of the kitchen porch. Ma had fresh biscuits out of the cast iron cook stove, and she had already set a jar of blackberry jelly on the table. The signal was for the work hands to come to the house and get ready to eat. In this case it was for the returning son to come and eat his fill. Jubal and Wes both made their way to the kitchen porch without delay. They both knew very well what the sound of the iron meant. Wes had been blessed by the biscuit pan already and certainly would not turn it down again.

Jubal had not really had time in the mill to see it, but now in the full light of the morning sun pouring through the open kitchen door, he could see the change in his Ma. Her face was lighter, and there was an obvious smile on her face. She had lost some of that old broken down and overworked look that hung onto her so much before. Even her shoulders seemed to be not so slumped down. She had on a blue print dress and a white apron and bonnet instead of the dull gray that was once all she had. The kitchen floor was scrubbed and stoned to a shine that any cook would be proud of, and there were lace curtains over the kitchen windows. She now seemed to radiate, and her love of life now bloomed as it had never been allowed to do before.

"Set yerself down here and eat. We got us some catchin' up to do," Ma commanded.

Jubal did as he was told. Wes grabbed up three big biscuits and made for the kitchen door. "I take these back to the mill with me. I needs get back there and tend to my work, and ye two needs time fer talkin' by yerself."

There was little room for talking while Jubal occupied himself trying his best to make biscuits and blackberry jelly go away in as little time as possible. Ma managed to keep herself busy over the stove for the short time he ate.

The fact that he had not eaten anything other than jerky in the last good while made the fresh baked bread seem a royal banquet to him. It made him foolishly think that he should go away and come home more often. Surely Ma would feed her son in a likewise manner time and time again.

"Ma, do you and Wes own this here place now? What done come of Mrs. Johnson and Lida? Where'd they go?"

"Whoa now, one thing at a time."

"Okay, but where be Julie and Granny Iverson?" I ain't seen nothin' of them so far?"

"Let me tell ye about the Johnsons first. That be good with ye?" Ma asked as she took the boy's plate away and wiped the oilcloth in front of him with a clean white dish towel. She could not help likewise clearing away a slight trace of crimson jelly from the corner of his mouth after which, she put a strong right arm around his shoulder and drew him near. He did not react or resist. "Mrs. Johnson just never had it in her to be happy here no more once she lost her C.C. Reckon she just never could get past that terrible day. Said she saw him ever where she looked around here, special anywhere near the mill or any place what had to do with it. Told me that she had to get gone some place else to live."

"Where'd they go?" Jubal asked anxiously.

"Some place a bit east and up the river a ways. Think it be called Long Bend or somethin' like that. Wes knows where it be. Said he been there once or twice before."

"She sold out here and got herself another place?" Jubal questioned.

"Nope, not really like that. Her sister got a big river bottom farm up there some place, and she done moved in there, at least for now."

"Ye had any word from her lately?" Jubal questioned again.

"She sends word ever now and then. It been a bit since we had any news from her. Reckon she be some better up there. She don't say much along them lines none. Kinda keeps to herself in ways, I reckon."

"Well, what about Lida?"

"Lida went with her."

"I see then. I guess I ought make a run up there whilst I be home."

"I think ye owes her that much bein' as how..." Ma hesitated a bit.

"Bein' as how what? What ye mean?"

"She give us her best dress when we had to put Granny Iverson away."

"What happened to Granny Iverson and when that happen?" Jubal asked in somewhat of disbelief. "I never knowed her bein' sickly a day in her life."

"She weren't sick none, son. She just went to bed one night and never woke up, at least not here on this old earth. She got her call and she answered it."

Jubal sat in silence for just a bit. Reality had a hard blow to deal out sometimes, and this was one of those times. Granny Iverson had never really done anything for him in a materialistic way but had always shared and given what she had the most to give. And that was love and affection with a twist of wisdom thrown in for good measure. And now that was all gone, at least as he saw it for the moment. It never came to his mind that all her teachings and all the times that she had set before the firelight and read to him would be a part of him forever. She was a part of him, and he did not even know it.

"When did that all come about?" Jubal asked his Ma in a soft and concerned voice. He did not want to grieve her by asking about things that could hurt so much.

"Little bit after Christmas past."

"Where she be put?"

"We put her in the churchyard a few steps away from where Mrs. Johnson had C.C. put," Ma answered just as softly as she had been spoken to.

"I thought she wanted to go back down on Cloudy Creek where Grandpa Iverson was put."

"Well, me and her talked on that once. She told me that it weren't necessary no more, cause then she would be just dust and dust could be any place. Said home was where family and kinfolks was, and they weren't none of either down there no more."

"How old was she?"

"Don't rightly know. Best we could guess was about ninety-two. Said she could recollect comin' over the mountains when we was knowed as State of Franklin. Ain't positive when that was, but it was before the century turnin' fer sure. She had a good long life and some of it were hard in her early years, but I never recollect her makin' much ado over that."

"I'm sorry fer ye, Ma."

"Ain't no cause bein' sorry over her none, son. She be a heap better place now than we ever be here. Besides, she weren't one who want ye grievin' over her. I know that well as I know my own name, which by the way gonna change some here right soon."

"That what I done hear, and I think it be good too."

"I be pleased ye thinks like that. I got it better right now than I ever had it before. Life be good to me now, and I be thankful more than I knows how to say."

"Ye ain't told me nothin' where Julie be," Jubal remarked. He did not yet really think he had had enough time to think through Ma and Wes getting all married up and such, so he just thought it best not to think on it at all for the time present.

"Julie be doin' right well. She done took her a man now, and they moved out on the old Bray place and took up housekeepin'. Her leg done healed up good. She still be a bit stiff leg and walks with a limp, but she does good, Ma explained.

"Who she marry?" Jubal questioned again. He was beginning to realize just how much had really happened in the time that he had been away.

"She got her a storekeeper man name of Keller, Samuel Keller. They come here down from Exchange place or such. Ain't real sure of the name of their little community, but it be up near next county seat some place. His Pa set him up, and they opened up a store in Widder Bray's old homestead."

"When did that all come about?" Jubal asked.

"Nigh on three months ago, I reckon. She seem like she thinks he hung the old moon and all the stars as well. Never seen a young gal with so much glad in her that it just bubble all over her."

"What about our place? What gonna come with it?"

"Well that be a question I can't answer. It ain't ours no more," Ma told him.

"How that be so?"

"I never knowed it, but yer Pa sold it right out from under us just before he passed on. Sold it to some drummer fer a few bottles and some grubstakes and a old hand gun. Least that what the papers say, what the constable brung us. They was all signed and sealed, and Pa had put his cross mark on it. But that don't matter none to me now, and ye ain't got no cause fer fretin' over that now neither. What been done is in the past, and we can't change none of that. Wouldn't iffin I could. This be our home now, and it be free and clear. Wes got the papers what make it all bindin' and such. I don't never have no hankerin' to go back up there no more. It ain't a good place, and I don't need it no more."

"I reckon I can see that too, Ma. It were a bunch hard on ye there fer a long time."

"That be why I be so grateful fer this here home and all that it means to us all. It far better than we had before, and we done well by it in spite of the war and all. I just hate C.C. had to be took off it the way he was and all."

"That were a bad blow to them, and I can understand how it changed things so much fer them," Jubal answered. "Ye ain't never told me nuthin' how Lida be and all."

"That be a whole different matter, I reckon," Ma said with a complete change of demeanor and expression.

"Tell me, Ma. I think I got cause to know."

"I thinkin' there be cause to know myself," Ma echoed.

"Tell me," Jubal insisted.

"I don't know no other way than to just out with it and let chips fall wherever they wants."

"Just tell me, Ma. I wanna know."

"Well, she be up river with her mother, and she done had herself a boy child. She never said yet whose it be, and she ain't give it no other name yet but her own."

"When it be borned?" Jubal asked timidly.

"Late winter time what I been told."

Jubal thought back on the times that he had known her and knew by all rights that the boy was his. He was not real sure how he felt about having a son, but he reasoned to himself in that moment that he could never not love his son as only a father, a real father could do. He knew in that instant that he had to go and see his son and to thank that son's mother for giving him life. He was not real confident how the mother of this new child would receive him, but he had long since felt that he could have a blessed and happy life with her.

"I will go and see him this very day," Jubal stated with true conviction.

"It be a ways up there," Ma added. "Maybe ye ought go come mornin' and that way ye be there by nightfall."

"Reckon ye can tell me where I needs go, can't ye?" Jubal asked

"I ain't clear on that, but I know Wes can tell ye straight off."

"I go and ask him right now. Reckon ye can poke up them other biscuits fer me?"

"I can, and I will. But I thinkin' ye ought wait a spell," Ma replied truly concerned about her son and his pending trek. She knew enough to know that it would be across the doubles and that was rough territory.

"Wes, how do I go from here to where Johnsons is."

"I can tell ye, but ye gonna need wait a spell first. I done stabled yer horse, and she be nigh done in fer now. Mouth be dry as sand, and she got that moon-eye look about her. She need a rest. How long ye been in saddle with her anyhow?"

"Nigh three days and nights, I reckon," Jubal answered.

"Ye best let her rest up fer a spell, or she ain't gonna take ye very much more fer now. She need about six or eight hours rest and some grain to boot. I was just fixin' to fetch her a oat bag outta the mill. I go and fetch it iffin ye wants rub her down some."

Jubal did as Wes had requested. He did bring Spirit a bag almost full of oats, which she dived into just as soon as the feed bag was slipped in place. Wes then fetched up fresh water from the mill runoff and filled the big white oak tub, being careful not to let her get more water at one time than she could well handle.

Jubal continued to rub her down, and you could almost see her weariness melt away. Spirit was strong, and there was no questioning that. She was soon showing signs of her old self, nudging and encouraging close contact with her companion.

Wes told the boy how he would need to ride past the Cove and on south until he could see the doubles. He would need to head east and take the long ridge that came up the middle of the two high points. He cautioned about the rough rocky trail over the last couple of hundred yards leading to the crest. Once across the top, turn back south and stay that direction till coming to the river. Then he should go back east till he come to the big bend, and then he could find the dwelling houses, and they would know just where to point him. Wes thought he could make that run in about eight hours.

Waiting till morning was not a choice that Jubal could accept. He had talked it out with Ma and Wes and decided that he would leave right before sundown and be there soon after daybreak. There would be a full moon tonight, and the skies had cleared already. There would be plenty of moon to light the way and that would not be a concern. Ma had asked him about stopping in to check on Julie, and he had told her that he would do that on the return trip in a few days. She had accepted that and looked forward to hearing from her daughter.

Ma had fixed Jubal a good supper, and he allowed as how he would not need a thing to take with him. He felt certain that Mrs. Johnson would have no cause not to feed him once he got to her place. Spirit had rebounded and appeared just as eager to get underway as was her rider. Wes had tended to her well.

The ride south was uneventful, and he spotted the doubles with no difficulty at all. They stood as two sentinels to the pass they guarded. An old Indian trail passed between them and had been used by many a settler coming into the river bottom country. The doubles had long been a known landmark all be it that this was unknown territory for Jubal and Spirit.

The climb up the long spine ridge would take a while. The moon was near up now, and the light was enough to be able to see good footing. Jubal let Spirit have her own rein, and she kept a steady unrelenting pace, stepping sure footedly over rocks and roots as they climbed toward the peaks.

The trail snaked back and forth along the ridge back ever ascending, swaying side to side only to miss an occasional boulder that had loosed itself from somewhere above and crashed down to its new resting site some eons ago. The timber was big, but the moonlight still managed to find its way down and play out along the forest floor. The air was warm and heavy with the aftermath of the spring rain, and Spirit soon broke a good sweat. Jubal still let her have her own reins, and she kept herself sure of foot.

Nearer the top, Jubal began to notice the increasing roughness of the trail. Sandstones of all sizes and shapes littered the trail in a haphazard pattern that demanded attention to footing. Spirit began to fret a bit by jerking her head occasionally and taking less care about her footing. Her nostrils flared and her eyes took on a sense of dread or fear. Jubal saw it in her and tried to calm her by talking to her and rubbing her neck. She half-heartedly responded to his touch and his voice. He could excuse her actions because of the rough terrain, but he could not know what she sensed.

Up ahead, a pair of yellow eyes caught a hint of moonlight and reflected it back down the rock strewn trail. The big black momma panther had long since picked up the scent of sweating horse flesh and had positioned herself, waiting motionless and patient. Jubal urged Spirit on, and she responded nervously to his request.

The beast made her leap at the precise best time and bared her claws full out. Her strike was swift and sure. Claws dug into Spirit's neck while powerful jaws locked down around her windpipe.

The terrified animal reared with every ounce of being that she had in her. Forefeet flailed the night air in her own defense in attempts to land a blow to her attacker. She reared and Jubal reached for the pommel, but it was too far gone. He felt himself slide off her flanks. He never really felt the back of his head hit the sandstone, but there was a brilliant flash of light, just for an instant, then darkness. Eternal darkness.

CPSIA information can be obtained at www.ICGtesting.com
Printed in the USA
LVOW12s1042221113

362400LV00002B/574/P